KT-244-666

The Lemon Tree
The Moneylenders of Shahpur
Yes, Mama

Helen Forrester

Diamond Books
an imprint of HarperCollins*Publishers*,
77–85 Fulham Palace Road,
Hammersmith, London W6 8JB

This Diamond Books Omnibus edition first published 1993
9 8 7 6 5 4 3 2 1

The Lemon Tree © Helen Forrester 1990
The Moneylenders of Shahpur © Jamunadevi Bhatia 1987
Yes, Mama © Helen Forrester 1988

ISBN 1 85813 224 X (UK)
ISBN Diamond Books 0 261 66165 5 (international edition)

Photoset in Linotron Times by Rowland Phototypesetting Ltd,
Bury St Edmunds, Suffolk

Printed in France by Maury-Eurolivres

The Author asserts the moral right to be identified as the author of this work

All rights reserved. No part of this publication may be reproduced, stored in a retrieval
system, or transmitted, in any form or by any means, electronic, mechanical,
photocopying, recording or otherwise, without the prior permission of the publishers.

Contents

The Lemon Tree

AUTHOR'S NOTE

The author would like to thank sincerely Mr C. L. Bibby for his encouragement in the writing of this book and for the loan of much useful material, and also Mrs Lydia Hrabi for her descriptions of pioneer life.

The book is a novel, not a history. The Harding homestead, the Lady Lavender Soap Works and the people who lived or worked in them are all imaginary; whatever similarity there may be of name, no reference is made or intended to any person living or dead, except for a few well-known historical figures forming part of the background of the book.

1

'He's a woman,' Mr George Tasker announced lugubriously to Sarah, his wife of thirty years. He pushed the dog off the easy chair by the fire and sat down to take off his boots; they were very wet and were covered with wavy lines of white sediment. He put them neatly in the hearth to dry, as he continued, 'I'm workin' for a *woman*.' His thick Liverpool accent made him sound as if he had a heavy cold in the head.

'George, you know better than to walk on me new coconut matting with your dirty boots,' Sarah scolded. 'And what do you mean – he's a woman?'

'Wallace H. Harding is a woman!'

'Never!'

'He is – that is, *she* is. The Ould Fella's *niece* – not a nephew, like we imagined. She come into our department this morning, large as life, with the lawyer, Mr Benson, and Mr Turner, the chemist.' He stood up and rubbed his cold hands before the glowing fire. 'She stopped and shook hands with me, seeing as I'm the Soap Master,' he added with obvious satisfaction.

Sarah Tasker paused in the act of getting a casserole of tripe and onions out of the oven. She looked up at him through a burst of steam. 'Well, I'm blowed! How queer!'

She turned and laid the casserole on a white-scrubbed deal table. On a wooden board lay a loaf of bread with several slices ready cut; beside it, sat a small dish of butter. She said mechanically, 'Come and have your tea, luv.' She picked up a brown teapot from the hob of the kitchen range and put it on the table, beside two heavy pint mugs and a pitcher of milk. Then, from a built-in shelf, she lifted down the pride of her kitchen, a green glass sugar basin won at a fair. She put it by the teapot.

In anticipation of George's return from his job in the Lady Lavender Soap Works, she had laid his slippers on the fender to warm. George now put them on. He rose and stretched himself, a big, corpulent man, with a ruddy, kindly face boasting three generous chins. He sat himself at the table, surveyed the dish of tripe with approbation, and then said to Sarah, 'Nobody makes tripe better'n you do, luv. I can always savour a bit of tripe.'

He invariably made a similar remark, no matter what she cooked for this main meal of the day, and, equally invariably, she beamed as if she had never heard it before. It was what made George so nice to live with, she reflected. He always appreciated what you did.

'What's she like?' Sarah asked him, as she ladled generous dollops of tripe onto his plate.

Before answering, he considered the question carefully. Then he said, as he stuffed a forkful of tripe into his mouth, 'She's furrin – she's almost yellow. She int a lady like we understand one – and yet she is, if you know what I mean. And she's smart, no doubt about that.'

Sarah did not understand what he meant. She served herself, however, and commenced her meal, despite the flutter of worry in her stomach. This woman, whoever she was, could make or ruin their lives, she considered anxiously. When old Mr James Al-Khoury had died suddenly in November, 1885, they had heard that he had bequeathed the whole soap works, in which George had toiled for nearly twenty-five years, to his brother in the United States. Then Mr Benson, the lawyer, had discovered that the brother had also died, leaving everything he possessed to his wife. It had taken him some time to find out that she had moved to Canada, where she, too, had died, leaving as her sole legatee, Wallace H. Harding.

When George Tasker heard the name, whispered to him by Mr Helliwell, old James Al-Khoury's secretary, he had assumed that the new owner was a nephew of his late employer; Mr Helliwell, priding himself on his secretarial discretion, had not enlightened him further.

And now George was saying that it was a niece!

With a feeling that she was about to choke on her tripe, Sarah realized that this foreign woman from the Colonies, who wasn't a proper lady, would not, of course, be able to run the works, since she was a woman. Presumably she would sell it – and what happened to employees when a firm was sold over their heads, she dreaded to think. Too often, the older men found themselves out on the street. And then what would happen to them, with George out of work at fifty years of age?

George himself was ruminating over the same threat, but it did not deter him from eating his way steadily through his supper. His silent wife leaned forward and filled a mug with tea. She handed it to him. 'Like some more tripe?' she asked mechanically.

George wiped his mouth with the back of his hand and said he would. Then, while Sarah served him, he confirmed her fears by saying heavily, 'Rumour is she'll sell the place 'cos she couldn't run it – being a woman, like.'

'Aye, that's what I were thinkin'.' Then she asked warily, 'Who'd buy it?'

10

'Well, it *has* gone down a bit, since the Ould Fella died,' George acknowledged. 'But there's some as would buy it, I think, though times are bad. There's that Mr Lever what has started up by Crosfield's in Warrington. Soap mad, he is. And there's Crosfield's themselves. They might like it, seeing as it's close to the Brunswick Dock and the Brunswick Goods Station – very handy, it is, for shipping and receiving.' He sipped his tea and moved uneasily in his straight wooden chair.

'Would you keep your job?'

It all depends,' he answered gloomily. 'I'm the Soap Master and they can't make soap without someone like me. But they could buy it and then shut it down – to get rid of a competitor.'

'Well, we'll worry about it when we get to it,' Sarah responded, determined to be brave and not increase her spouse's misgivings.

She wondered how far their savings, hidden under the loose board in the bedroom above them, would stretch if he were unemployed. With jobs so hard to find, he would hardly be likely to get another at his age, even though his mates always said he had a wonderful *feel* for soap.

'What's she like to look at?' Sarah felt very curious about this strange woman who had come all the way from Canada. Since she was the Ould Fella's nearest relative – except for his illegitimate son, Mr Benjamin, who didn't count, poor lad – she must be an Arab, like he had been. George had told her that James Al-Khoury had come from Lebanon, the same Lebanon that she had read about in her Bible. Did that really make him an Arab, she wondered suddenly, and was Miss Harding, therefore, an Arab lady, for all that she had a Western name? She smiled gently. The Ould Fella had been more like a friend than an employer. Many were the times when he had sat in this very kitchen, talking about the soap works. Always talked to George, he did, before making any changes. George and him got on like two o'clock.

With a sigh she pushed her plate of tripe to one side; she would try to eat it later. Arab or not, Mr James Al-Khoury and George had been happy together. Tears welled inside her, but she crushed them back; she must not let George know how worried she was.

While he ruminated over Sarah's question about Miss Harding, George took another slice of bread and spread it thinly with butter.

Eventually, he replied, 'Well, she's tall; same height as me, I should say. Thin as a rake. But when she smiles she's got a lovely face – and great brown eyes like a young heifer. She don't smile much, though. She were talkin' quite sharp to Mr Turner, the chemist. I didn't hear what she said, but I could see Turner didn't like it. He can be a bit uppity, and he wouldn't like being put down by a woman.'

'What was she dressed like?'

'Oh, she were all in black, in mourning, with a black veil thrown back from her face. She'd great rings on her fingers, all gold. No stones. She'd a ring on her marriage finger what looked roughly made; ugly, it was – not much polished. Never seen one like it before.' He picked up his mug of tea and held it between his great hands. 'She int married, though. I heard her correct old Bobsworth, when he called her Mrs Harding. She's got a proud, cold way with her and she said as tart as a lemon to old Bob, "Miss Harding, if you please, Mr Bobsworth."'

Sarah knew Mr Bobsworth quite well and she smiled, despite her forebodings. The strange lady rose in her estimation. Though she would not have hesitated to call Mr and Mrs Bobsworth her friends, they did tend to put on airs, because he was the firm's head bookkeeper and forwarding clerk. 'And her only the daughter of a stevedore,' thought Sarah sourly.

George was speaking again, his heavy, grey brows knitted in puzzlement.

'As I said, Miss Harding shook hands with me, and then with everyone – even Alfie. She asked Alfie if he were born in Liverpool.'

Alfie was the seventeen-year-old mulatto labourer who swept the soap-boiling area. He also fetched and carried for the temperamental soap boilers, who sometimes dared not leave their soap pans, for fear they might miss the moment when the soap must be *proved*, or brine added or the boiling mixture turned off and carefully left to cool. The soap boilers were like housewives producing fine sponge cakes – everything had to be done exactly right. Sarah knew that a few people still regarded Mr Tasker as a magician, because he said he could *feel* how his great cauldrons of soap were getting on. He *knew*, they said. What he knew they did not specify – it appeared to them to be magic.

'She told me she makes her own soap on her farm in Canada,' expanded Mr Tasker. He put down his mug, leaned back from the table and belched. 'She told me as the nearest soap works is hundreds of miles off and there's no proper roads to it. Proper surprised I was, when she said it.' His three chins wobbled, as if to indicate agreement with his remarks.

Sarah omitted to remind him that she never used any soap at all on her face, because she believed that soap spoiled her skin. As a country girl, she had always scrubbed her face with a rag dipped in water from the rain barrel at her father's cottage door, and the present velvety smoothness of her complexion, despite her age, indicated that the natural oils of her skin had never been removed. Her five married daughters thought she was terribly oldfashioned and said that she owed it to her husband to use the soap he made. But she stubbornly refused, and told

12

them that if they followed her example, they would not have to put that new-fangled cold cream on their faces every night. Lucky, they were, she thought, to be married to men with regular jobs, who could afford falderals like an occasional pot of cold cream.

'It's terrible she int a man,' George said with feeling. 'The Ould Fella was a good master, though he never paid out a penny he didn't have to. Young Benji takes after him – pity the lad's illegitimate; he could have followed him very nicely.' He paused to get a bit of bread from between his stained front teeth with his finger. 'Now, if she were a man, she'd be the same – a real firm hand on the tiller, she'd have. Backbone, she's got, by the sound of her. But a woman? What can a woman do? In a soap works?'

He paused, as he contemplated in his mind's eye the woman who now held his future in her slender fingers. Though she was so thin, he thought, she'd a nice waistline – and breasts like it said in the Bible, like pomegranates. Her long black dress fitted so closely, it stirred thoughts in a man, it did, he chided himself ruefully.

'What about Mr Benji?' inquired Sarah, interrupting his contemplation of the new owner's charms.

'Well, I'm sure James Al-Khoury were training him up to take his place when the time came, as a son should. But he only made one Will in his life, according to Mr Helliwell, and that were before Benji were born – and he were born on the wrong side of the blanket, so he int entitled to anything by law, poor lad. His dad could have left him everything in a Will and he would've got it all right. His mam and him and the lawyer has hunted everywhere, looking for another Will; but Mr Benson told Mr Helliwell that he'd have known if there *was* another Will – the Ould Fella would have come to him about it, 'cos Mr Benson used to vet all the firm's legal papers, contracts and such – James Al-Khoury didn't trust 'is own knowledge of English, so anything major he were goin' to sign, he got Mr Benson, his lawyer, to check first.'

'I suppose Mr Al-Khoury thought he'd plenty of time before he'd die.'

'Oh, aye. He weren't yet fifty. He never thought of a heart attack, that I'm sure; it come as an awful shock to all of us. Proper sad it is for Benji and his mam. And him a smart lad, too.'

That night, in many tiny homes round the Brunswick Dock, Wallace Helena Harding was the subject of anxious discussion; times were so bad that the very hint of the loss of a regular job was enough to cause panic. Even Alfie, the mulatto casual labourer, who slept in the back

13

hallway of a nearby warehouse, courtesy of the nightwatchman of the building, and who had endured bitter hardship all his life, viewed with equal terror the possibility of starvation or, the only alternative, the workhouse.

The warehouse watchman was an old seaman with a wooden leg who had known Alfie and his slut of a mother all the young man's short life, but as he sat beside him on the bottom step of the stone stairs of the great warehouse, a candle guttering in a lantern beside them, he could offer the lad little comfort.

'She'll 'ave to sell the soapery,' he said finally. 'It don't mean, though, that the new master won't take you on. Master Tasker'll speak for you, I've no doubt.' He paused to repack his clay pipe and then pulled back the shutter of his lantern to light it from the candle. He puffed thoughtfully for a few minutes. Then he said shrewdly, 'A new master could buy it and then shut it down, to put an end to it. Sometimes happens when shipping companies is sold – every bleedin' seaman that worked for the old company is out on the street – and the company what's done the buying puts its own men in.'

Alfie, who at best was permanently hungry, sat numbly silent, and then nodded agreement. He foresaw a long vista of petty theft to keep himself alive, unless he was prepared to seek out the homosexuals who roamed the streets in search of entertainment; either way, he could land in gaol. He hung his head so that the nightwatchman could not see the despair on his face.

2

Unaware of the stir she had caused in the heart of Mr Tasker, her soap master, or the depth of the fears she had raised in all her employees, the thin, yellow woman from the wilds of Western Canada sat at a cherry-wood desk in the bay window of her bedroom in a house in nearby Hill Street. She was in the process of writing a letter to Joe Black, her partner on her homestead in western Canada.

She stared dismally at the soaking July downpour pattering against the glass. The room smelled damp and was unexpectedly cold. What a grey and black city Liverpool was and, yet, how exciting it was with its glittering gaslamps and heavy traffic. And how alien she felt in it.

This proud Lebanese lady, who carried a man's name and then the name of the patron saint of Beirut, St Helena, and who normally feared nobody, was, for once, feeling intimidated by men. 'If you can call them men,' she muttered. 'Self-complacent barrels of lard.'

She scolded herself that she must not prejudge. 'You're tired with the journey, and the confinement of the ship. And being indoors all day. You must be patient.'

She leaned back and began to tug the hairpins out of her tight bun. 'I don't feel patient,' she informed herself through gritted teeth.

'Come on, now,' encouraged her cooler self. 'If you can make friends with miserable and angry Blackfoot and Crees, and cope with rebellious Metis – not to speak of Oblate Fathers with the power of God behind them – you can cope with an indifferent chemist named Turner, a Benjamin Al-Khoury, head of Sales and Assistant Manager, rude enough not to be here when the new owner of his company arrives – and a lawyer you don't trust too much.' She pressed a tanned fist hard onto the desk, as if to emphasize her thoughts.

Then she absently spread out her fingers to look at her gold, handmade rings. Her eyes gleamed, and she laughed sardonically.

What would these stuffy Englishmen think if they knew that she lived with Joe Black, the son of a freed Ontario black slave and a Cree woman? He would make two of any of them, she thought with quiet pleasure; a big man with a face filled with laughter lines, lines that could harden when he felt insulted, till his jaw looked like a rat trap and his huge black eyes with their back-curling lashes lost their gentleness

15

completely. He rarely struck anybody with his great fists, but when he did it was with the punishing skill of a Cree guard warrior. He had a clear, uncluttered mind, well able to assess a situation, an ability to reason, to negotiate with patience, before he struck.

These latter gifts were invaluable, she reflected, in a country full of wrathful native people; the Hudson's Bay Company had frequently used him as peacemaker between the Indians and themselves – and even missionaries were not past using him as an interpreter.

With one finger, she touched tenderly her gold rings. When Joe had discovered that she valued jewellery, he had panned for gold in the North Saskatchewan River and had fashioned the rings for her. Lots of men had subsequently tried to find the mother lode of the river's gold, but no one had succeeded; it was the rich, black soil which held the real wealth of the Northwest Territories.

She laughed again. 'These pink Englishmen would have a fit,' she told the raindrops on the windowpanes. 'But I'll teach them to patronize a woman,' she promised herself. 'I will decide the future of the Lady Lavender Soap Works!' In which remark, she was a little too optimistic.

As she met the various people in the new world she had entered in Liverpool, she had become slowly aware that she was shabby and out of date, almost a figure of fun – a small snigger from a messenger boy, hastily stifled, a raised eyebrow, a stare in the street. She found the crush of people round her difficult enough, after the emptiness of western Canada, and this added attention had bothered her; it was the first time since she had left Lebanon that she had thought of clothes as anything else but covering against the elements.

She was unaware that, despite her clothes, she had a formidable presence. She moved swiftly with a long effortless stride, and she had responded in cold, clear sentences to the explanations given her by her escorts through the soapery. When, later, she had asked for further explanation, she had surprised them by recalling exactly what had been said.

Most of the men in the soapery wore a head-covering of some kind; but only Mr Tasker, the Soap Master and key man in the whole soapery, had doffed his bowler hat, when she had been introduced to him by Mr Benson, the lawyer. He had answered her questions carefully, his blue eyes twinkling amid rolls of fat as he endeavoured to watch the great vats steaming and heaving, and occasionally said, between his answers to her queries, 'Excuse me, Miss', while he instructed one of his assistants in the delicate task of producing excellent soap.

16

After meeting Mr Tasker and his helpers, Mr Benson had handed her over to Mr Turner, the chemist, who was, in the lawyer's opinion, in the absence of Benjamin Al-Khoury, the most refined of her employees. He should, therefore, know how to treat a lady.

A shy, retiring man, who wanted to get back to his little laboratory, Mr Turner's conversation was strained and desultory and did not particularly impress Wallace Helena. She was interested, however, when he told her that Mr Tasker was probably the best soap man in south Lancashire and could probably have gone to a bigger company.

'You mean they would've paid him more?'

'Yes.'

'I wonder that he did not move.'

'He and Mr James Al-Khoury were great friends. I believe they were together from the first establishment of the soapery. And there's no doubt that he and Mr Benjamin get on very well.'

Wallace Helena murmured approbation.

They went into the Power House together, to meet Mr Ferguson, the Steam Engineer, a middle-aged man with a ruddy face and an air of great self-confidence and dignity. He was dressed in immaculate blue overalls. He was attentive and informative to his lady visitor, well aware that he belonged to a newly emerged class of employee able to cope with the mechanization of industry and was, therefore, a prized servant of the company. He was a trifle defensive with Mr Turner. Wallace Helena noticed this and wondered why. She had yet to discover the subtleties of class in British society; Mr Ferguson was exceedingly proud of his abilities, but he remained a working man; Mr Turner was also a highly trained man – but he was middle-class – a man of privilege as well as ability.

As she walked slowly round the works, she had noted carefully the reactions of her employees to herself and also reactions between them. After watching for years the body language of the Indians who passed over her land, to judge whether they were hostile or friendly, she had learned to observe the slightest shrug, the curve of a lip, the smallest move of hip or hand. She had quickly picked up the general nervousness of the men to whom she was introduced and she had felt sorry for them. In return, she had tried to show herself as a confident, capable person, and she felt that some of them had liked her.

Only Mr Benjamin Al-Khoury had failed to turn up.

According to Mr Bobsworth, the bookkeeper and forwarding clerk, he was in Manchester and would return in a few days' time. 'Life has been very hectic for Mr Benjamin since Mr James passed away, him being Assistant Manager to Mr James, like. Everything fell on him.'

17

Mr Bobsworth heaved a sigh deep enough to make every inch of his five feet quiver.

She had nodded, and remarked that Uncle James's death must have been a shock to everyone.

'Indeed, yes, Miss Harding.' His eyes blinked behind his small, gold-rimmed spectacles, and then he said, 'I should tell you, Ma'am, that Mr Benjamin asked me to convey his regrets to you at not being here today; he's investigating the unexpected refusal of a customer to renew his contract with us – in the cotton trade, they are.'

'I see,' she had replied noncommittally, and Mr Bobsworth had begun to worry that young Benji had offended the lady deeply by his absence.

Now, seated in her stuffy bedroom, she made a face as she recalled the conversation.

If, as she suspected, Mr Benjamin Al-Khoury was her illegitimate cousin, a product of Uncle James's love affair with an English woman, about which she had heard vaguely as a young girl when she was living in Chicago, he was probably suffering from an acute bout of jealousy because she had inherited his father's business.

She was fairly sure that, if he had been a legitimate child, he could have claimed, in law, at least a part of his father's Estate, no matter what his parent's Will had said about leaving all his property to his brother, Charles, her own father. Mr Benson had, however, assured her that there were no other claimants to the Estate, and she presumed that Mr Benson knew his law.

It was possible, of course, that Benjamin Al-Khoury was some very distant relative, whose parents had also managed to survive the massacre of Christians in 1860.

With a wry smile at the foibles of his own youth, Mr Benson had explained to her that, when he was first setting up his law practice and was badly in need of every penny he could earn, her Uncle James had consulted him about the exact meaning of a contract he was about to sign. Afterwards, in pursuit of a small additional fee, he had inquired if Uncle James had a Will and, since he had not, he had been persuaded to make one.

At that time, Uncle James had had no one else to whom to leave his modest possessions, so, at the age of twenty-three, he had left everything to his brother, Charles, in Chicago. And now, as the residual legatee of her father's and her mother's own Wills, Wallace Helena found herself inheriting a well-run soap manufactory.

'Why didn't Uncle James make a more recent Will?' she had asked Mr Benson.

'Dear lady, I do not know. I did mention the matter to him once or twice; but he was a tremendously busy man – and, like all of us, he did not anticipate dying at forty-nine.' He had smiled indulgently at her. 'Do you have a Will, Miss Harding?'

'No, I don't,' she had admitted, a note of surprise in her voice; she had never thought of dying herself, despite the hazards she faced daily in her life as a settler. Mr Benson's question had made her suddenly aware of the problems Joe Black might face if, indeed, she did die. She smiled a little impishly at the lawyer, and then said gravely, 'I'll attend to it.'

She reverted to the matter of her uncle's Will. 'Perhaps Uncle James really didn't have anyone else to leave his money to, except Papa – or me?' In view of her surmises about Benjamin Al-Khoury, the question was a loaded one, and she watched carefully for her lawyer's reaction.

Mr Benson was not to be drawn, however, and he answered her noncommittally, 'Possibly not.' She was left to puzzle about her Uncle James's private life.

Now, as she took up her pen and dipped it into the ink, preparatory to continuing her letter to Joe Black, she decided philosophically that she would deal with Mr Benjamin whenever he decided to turn up.

She wrote in English, a language she had learned in Chicago and from her stepfather, Tom Harding: 'Dear Joe, how I wish you were with me! I need your brains – and I need your love to sustain me.'

Should she tell this man, whom she loved with a passion and depth which sometimes frightened her, how nervous she felt?

No. He would only worry, and worry never solved anything.

With deliberate cheerfulness, she continued, 'Thanks to Messrs Cunard, I arrived safely in Liverpool yesterday morning. At Montreal, Mr Nasrullah, Grandpapa Al-Khoury's friend – a very old man – saw me and my baggage safely transferred to the ship, as we arranged. He was worried that I was travelling steerage, alone; but everyone was very friendly to me, though it was not very comfortable. I gave Mr Nasrullah a hasty note to post to you, and I hope you received it safely. Now that the railway line has reached Calgary, it should make a vast difference to the speed with which we can send and receive letters, even from as far north as Edmonton. (I wonder if Edmonton and St Albert will *ever* be served by a railway line?)

'My dearest, it was good of you to accompany me in the stage all the way down to Calgary, to see me onto the train. I shall never forget the

19

wonderful night we spent in that dreadfully noisy hotel! How I miss you now!

'When the train moved out and your dear figure receded into the distance, I wished I had never set out on such a wild adventure – and yet the English lawyers sounded so eager to sell Uncle's business that I smelled a rat; as I said to you, the works could be more valuable than they would have me know. Could the lawyers make a gain by selling to someone with whom they had made a private agreement?

'Today, I did a fairly thorough inspection of the plant. I have not yet seen the company's books, nor do I know enough to say how well it is doing. I am, however, uneasy that Mr Benjamin Al-Khoury, the Assistant Manager, was not here to greet me; I felt snubbed!

'He was left nothing in Uncle James's Will, and I suspect that he is his *illegitimate* son. No matter which side of the blanket he was born on, however, I am excited at the thought that I may actually have a blood relative. You know how shorn I feel because I have no family – and, without your support, I am sure I would have given up on life long ago – bless you, my dearest one.

'I must bear in mind, though, that this man may be very jealous that I, and not he, now own the Lady Lavender.

'Mr Benson, the lawyer, has found me two rooms near the works, in the house of Mrs Hughes, a widow – the address is at the top of this letter. The rooms are clean and her cooking is good, though I am feeling the sudden change in diet.

'I wish you were with me. The city is very lively. I confess that I doubt if you would enjoy the noise and confusion – or the heavy smoke in the air – near the works, the filth of it is overwhelming.

'The products of the soapery put our home-made efforts to shame. They are sweet-smelling tablets, light brown or blue-grey in colour. To scent them, they use lavender oil, caraway or cinnamon. They have, also, a fuller's earth soap for very delicate skins. They do make plain bars of soap for laundry and for the cotton industry, and these do not smell much better than the ones we make at home!

'The lavender oil is produced by a lady in the south of England. She also makes a perfume of it by diluting it with spirits of wine and bottling it. We act as her northern distributor for these little bottles of scent and they are sold side-by-side with our lavender soap. It is very pleasant to dab a little on my wrist and sniff it.

'The whole operation is so interesting that I am already questioning whether I should sell it. If it is financially sound, I could, perhaps, find a knowledgeable man to run it.'

She stopped writing, and chewed the end of her pen. She knew already what she would like to do, she considered longingly. She had been born and spent her childhood in a city, and she would like to settle in Liverpool, rain and dirty air notwithstanding, and run the business herself. After all, she ruminated, she knew the centre of Liverpool quite well; she and her parents, as refugees, had spent some weeks in it, waiting for an immigrant ship to the United States – and she remembered with pleasure the pool crowded with sailing vessels which had given Liverpool its name.

'With all that Papa taught me, I *could* learn to manage the Lady Lavender – it's obviously got some good employees,' she assured herself. 'I suspect that before I was ten I'd learned more than some of these fat Englishmen know. I don't know the detail of their work, but I can organize people – I can sell. But what on earth would Joe think of it – of coming to a city?'

She considered the question seriously; he wasn't getting any younger; it was possible that he might enjoy the sheer comfort of city life after the remorseless struggle they faced on their homestead.

Wishful thinking! she chided herself, and slowly dipped her pen into the ink.

'If we drew income from the soap works,' she continued, 'we could accumulate more riverside land, as it becomes available, and increase our grain crops – the minute a railway crosses the North Saskatchewan and reaches Edmonton, eastern markets would be opened up to us – and we might even have money to spend!'

She paused in her writing and wondered how many more terrible winters they would have to endure before they made enough to, perhaps, move south to a better climate. And it's not only winter, she considered sadly, it's clouds of merciless mosquitoes, forest fires, unsettled Indians and Metis, floods – and hunger – gnawing hunger – and the endless, endless physical work.

She bit her lips, and continued to write, asking him how the crops were doing. She hoped the cougars were not being a nuisance again this year – that was a huge pair he had shot last year.

Cougars? Bobcats? Wolves? They were a curse when one had livestock. She grinned suddenly at the idea of a cougar sniffing its way comfortably into the yard of the soap works, and then went on to give him a different piece of news.

'Yesterday, in the street, I heard Arabic being spoken, and, frankly, I was surprised that I still understood it – though it is my childhood tongue. Three men definitely from the East, probably seamen, were talking together at a street corner; they had lost their way, but being a stranger myself to this end of the city, I could not help them so I passed on. While I am here, I hope to get some accurate news of the present situation in the Lebanon.'

She put down her pen and slowly stretched herself. It had been good to hear the language of her family. She would give a great deal to walk the ancient streets of Beirut or sit quietly in her parents' courtyard, if it still existed, and listen to cheerful Arab voices.

But there were no familiar voices left, she reminded herself; she would have to sit by herself under the old lemon tree.

She shivered, and a sense of awful aloneness engulfed her, the ghastly loneliness of a sole survivor, with no one else alive to understand completely the horrors she had seen. For a moment she did not hear the horses' hooves in the street outside or the rain on the window or feel the chill of her room; she was lost in a misty ebb of consciousness, through which she heard the roar of a mob out of control and the screams of the dying.

She sat perfectly still in her stiff little chair, her white face covered with perspiration, until the moment passed. Then she got up and stumbled to the washstand, to pick up a damp face flannel and press it to her temples.

3

Feeling a little better after the damp coldness of wiping her face with a flannel, Wallace Helena sat down on the edge of the bed and slowly unlaced her neat black boots. She hauled them off and thankfully flexed her toes. On the homestead she wore soft Indian moccasins and gaiters, for which she traded barley with a Cree woman each year. She kept her precious boots for formal occasions, like visiting Mr Ross's hotel in the settlement by Fort Edmonton. In the hotel, she was sometimes able to contact small groups of travellers in need of supplies, like flour, meat or, perhaps, a horse; they were also occasionally glad to buy well-salted butter or sour cream. The visitors were usually surveyors and miners passing through, but increasingly there were well-to-do British hunters, who had simply come to enjoy a new wilderness and hunt big game. Most of them dealt with the Hudson's Bay Company or one or two other suppliers, who could provide coffee, sugar and salt, tobacco, alcohol and other imports. Wallace Helena, however, kept her prices low and she could usually find someone with little money only too thankful to buy cheaply. They were surprised, and sometimes amused, to be approached by a woman, particularly one who did not fit the usual mould. With her tall, spare figure and her long, mannish stride, her carefully calculated prices and her ability to strike a bargain, she was a well-known local character round Fort Edmonton, particularly disliked by the other suppliers.

Now, she longed to rest on the feather bed, but she felt she must finish her letter to Joe; she had promised to write frequently; and, even with the new railway, a letter would take some time to reach him. She made herself return to the tiny desk in the window.

After the quietness of the bush, it felt strange to be back in the hurly-burly of a city and be immediately plunged into the complexities of a factory, the first modern one that she had ever seen; it was stranger still to realize that, as soon as her uncle's Will had been probated, she would actually own the soap works.

Pen in hand, she stared thoughtfully out of the bedroom window. Already, she had casually remarked to Mr Turner, the chemist, that it might be cheaper for the Lady Lavender to buy seed and themselves press the oil they used, rather than import it.

Mr Turner had replied superciliously that to make it pay, they would probably have to find a market for the residual solids.

It was probably the most sensible remark he had made to her that day, but she had snapped him up promptly. 'The solids can be used for winter food for steers. Don't your farmers know that?'

Mr Turner had gulped and failed to reply immediately; he knew little about farming. What did women know about cattle?

When he had recovered himself, he pointed out that a new venture like that would need capital. 'Presses,' he added vaguely,' and – er – men who understand farming, to sell the residue.'

'Right.' She had stopped to take a small black notebook and pencil out of her reticule, and made a quick note. She might, she thought, cost it out in years to come, when she understood more about the business.

Playing at her father's feet in his large silk warehouse in Beirut or cuddled by her mother's side when the family was gathered together in the evening, she had absorbed a great deal of the discussions going on over her head. Amongst much else, she understood the importance of estimating cost and return – and the ever-present risks of undertaking something new. During her long tour of the soap works, she had felt, at times, as if her father were whispering to her, telling her what to look for, giving her quiet advice.

And then there was the glycerine, which, the chemist had informed her, was left over after the soap was made. He had mentioned that, when properly refined, it was a good base for salves for the skin and for certain medicines; he and Benjamin Al-Khoury were working on a scented lotion for chapped hands, to market alongside the lavender perfume and toilet soaps. At present, he had informed her, the glycerine was sold to explosives manufacturers.

Explosives were used for war, she ruminated, as she enclosed her letter to Joe in an envelope and licked the flap; and she had had enough threat of that round her farm near Fort Edmonton, when the Metis had risen in defence of their land rights. It was only last year that their leader, Louis Riel, had been hanged for rebellion.

Her mind wandered to the problems of her life as a settler. The rebellion had been very frightening; and yet, she considered uneasily, Louis Riel had had a rightful cause. His people were descendants of early European settlers and their Indian wives, and they had been dispossessed of their land further east by the rush of new immigrants from Europe. In despair, they had moved westward to squat on the undeveloped lands of the Hudson's Bay Company. Unlike her stepfather, who had himself been a squatter on the Company's holdings, many of them had not succeeded in establishing their right to remain on the land. She thought smugly that it was thanks to her stepfather's and her own sagacity that she now owned the land she farmed.

A squatter's legal rights were tenuous, she knew; she herself had once not hesitated to try to overset a Metis squatter's right to a riverside homestead which she had coveted.

'But at least I finished up by paying him for it,' she had said defensively to one of the Oblate Fathers from St Albert, when he had dared to criticize her ruthless business methods. 'It cost me all I had at the time,' she had added, hatred in every inch of her. 'I could have hounded him off – like the Hudson's Bay tried to do to my stepfather.'

Her eyes, long, oriental, heavily fringed with thick black lashes, were half-closed and averted from him, as she had continued, 'When I first came to Fort Edmonton, a young innocent girl, that man shouted obscenities after me, because I'm sallow-skinned and he thought I was a Chinese – a man's plaything. And I would prefer not to repeat what he used to call my stockman, Joe Black. Why should I care about him, Father?' She had given a dry little laugh, and had turned and left the discomfited priest standing in the middle of the spring mud of the Fort's yard.

The priest had sighed. He had been warned by an older priest that this wilful, proud, strayed member of the Christian flock, a lone Maronite Christian survivor of the 1860 massacres in Lebanon, had endured a lot of sorrow. She was now in her late thirties, and, in her business affairs, she had the reputation of being as merciless as an Iroquois woman – and when he considered what Iroquois women had done to captured Jesuit priests in earlier times, a faint shudder went through his thin, bent frame, as if the devil had touched him on the shoulder.

Yet, as he trudged along the trail to his Mission in St Albert, he had to admit that during the Metis uprisings she had been one of the few to remain calm. She had prepared to defend her homestead with more common sense than other settlers, many of whom had panicked – even he and his fellow priests, who ministered to the Metis, had been very frightened.

'Nobody has to worry about Wallace Harding or Joe Black,' one of his parishioners in St Albert had assured him. 'They're the best shots in the district and she's got that cabin well defended; the rebels'll go for easier loot.'

Then, of course, there was Joe Black himself, the priest reflected; Joseph Black, the only negro in the district. Joe had a history, too.

According to Father Lacombe, who knew almost everything about everybody, he was the son of a Cree woman and a freed slave who had accompanied John Rowand on his exploration of the Bow River, further south.

He had been brought up in his maternal grandfather's lodge and had then gone to work on one of the early ranches. In consequence, he had a wonderful way with horses – with any animals, if it came to that. Later, he had trapped for a time, following the animals northward, and had finally met up with Tom Harding, an American miner. The young priest had never met Tom Harding, but the story was well known; Tom had been a squatter on undeveloped Hudson's Bay Company land a few miles east of Fort Edmonton.

Disregarding the splutters of rage from the Hudson's Bay Factor at the Fort, who was rapidly becoming less and less able to enforce his company's rights to the immense territory they were supposed to control, Tom Harding and Joe Black had, with sporadic aid from Joe's Cree relatives and a couple of temporarily stranded miners, slowly opened up several square miles, much of it forest. Based on what he had observed in the United States, Tom Harding sowed grass and clover, as well as barley, oats and potatoes. It was backbreaking work and, in addition, they had had the difficult task of protecting their first few animals and hens, not only from predators but also from increasingly hungry parties of Indians.

Despite Joe's abilities as a hunter and trapper, game was scarce and in the early years they were often hungry themselves. Each year, when the ferocious winter descended on them, they would ask themselves why they bothered and would become irritable with each other. But the first sound of water dripping from the snow-covered roof would raise their spirits, and they would begin to plan the coming year. The Hudson's Bay Factor, aware of whispers from eastern Canada and from London about the Hudson's Bay mandate being withdrawn, gave up on them and was thankful, occasionally, to buy or trade for some of their crops, to feed the increasing number of people living in and around the Fort.

The trust between the two men became absolute.

As the early winter cold bit into the priest's own underfed body during his long walk back to the Mission, he secretly envied Joe Black's physical strength. Over six feet tall, Joe was, and built to it, with wiry grey hair, teeth discoloured by tobacco, and big black eyes surrounded by innumerable wrinkles; those eyes, thought the priest, could be cold and watchful, like those of a cougar he had once seen; at other times they could dance with amusement, and his deep rumbling laugh would roll across the room. An old clerk at the Fort had told him that Joe had been a fine, handsome man until he had caught the smallpox. The dreadful disease had left its marks on his cheeks and forehead, the priest reflected with compassion, and probably on his character as well.

To the priest, Joe seemed quieter than his general reputation at the Fort would indicate. Men always said that he and Tom Harding were formidable in a fight, but it did not seem to the young priest that he ever tried to *pick* a quarrel.

He's very astute – and he's older now – perhaps that's why, guessed the priest; he must be at least fifty. But whatever a hard life had done to him, he was alert and quick to grasp a concept; you never had to explain anything twice to the man. And his looks did not seem to bother Miss Harding, Tom's stepdaughter; it was said that she slept with Joe every night.

They were always together, riding their range, branding, setting traps in the autumn, sowing, reaping, or out shooting for the pot – not that there was much left to shoot these days. Sometimes they would be down at the Fort bargaining for sugar, coffee and tobacco, anything they could not grow or get from the Indians, the tall woman with the marks of suffering on her face and Joe with his wide grin like a steel trap.

Wallace and Joe were notorious for never parting with a penny, if they could do a deal any other way, ruminated the priest, though it was said they often gave food from their slender store to hungry Crees and Blackfoot. Tom Harding had owed his life to a Blackfoot; and his half-Cree partner, Joe, fed his own people.

Now, one of the subjects of the priest's idle thoughts undressed slowly in a damp, cold bedroom in faraway Liverpool. She thankfully unlaced the tight corset she had bought in Montreal on the advice of the daughter of Mr Nasrullah, with whom she had stayed whilst waiting for the boat to Britain to arrive. She shivered in the unaccustomed dampness as she slipped on a cotton shift. At the washstand, she poured cold water from a pink, flowered jug into a matching bowl and slowly washed her face and hands with a piece of Lady Lavender toilet soap.

Earlier, her Welsh landlady, Mrs Hughes, had kindly put a stone hot water bottle in the feather bed, and when she climbed into the bed it was still warm. The British summer was abominably chilly, Wallace thought irritably, and she pulled the hot water bottle up from her feet and clasped it against her stomach. It was hard and uncomfortable. Fretfully, she pushed it away from her.

Without thinking, she turned over and opened her arms to the other side of the bed. But there was no one there; and again she felt encompassed by an overwhelming loneliness. What was she doing here? Her life was with Joe, she told herself.

Still shivering slightly under the linen sheets, her mind, nevertheless, wandered to the new world of the soapery and its all-male managers and workers.

From her father she had learned that employees were to be treated like family. You scolded them and kept them in line with threats of unemployment; but you looked after them, and they looked after your interests. In fact, most of her father's employees had been blood relations, distant ones, sometimes – but related all the same.

Were some of the men in the soapery related to her? Or, regardless of that, did they think of themselves as being equivalent to her family? To be protected and cared for by her through good times and bad? It was a formidable thought.

She felt fairly certain that Benjamin Al-Khoury was a blood relation. She remembered vaguely, when her family had been living in Chicago, her father tut-tutting that her Uncle James appeared to be living with an English woman, without benefit of marriage. Such a misalliance would cast a bad name on the Lebanese community, he felt. She believed that he had written to Uncle James, saying that he should marry the lady. Wallace Helena could not recall that her uncle had ever replied to that particular point.

When, after her father's death, Uncle James had offered her mother and herself a home, her mother had explained that he was not married to the lady who lived with him; and this could make life difficult for them, if they joined his household.

Benjamin Al-Khoury was an employee like any other employee. Yet, if he were her cousin, should she treat him differently? If he were highly resentful that she, instead of himself, had inherited his father's Estate, how could she placate him, without losing her status as employer?

As she lay amid the unaccustomed softness of the feather bed, she began to think very carefully about how she could retain her authority and yet convey to him that she understood his probable unhappiness.

To her knowledge, she had no other blood relative and that would make him unique to her, someone very special in her estimation. It would put him on a completely different level from everyone else connected with the soapery.

A tiny thrill of hope went through her. To have a real relation implied a reciprocal obligation. Here might be a person of whom one could ask help and reasonably expect assistance as a duty, as from a brother. One could hope for consideration and affection, given freely. It was a wonderful idea to a woman who had faced as bravely as she could her

28

uprooting from her native soil. And, when she had put down tenuous new roots in alien Chicago, she had been uprooted again, to face a life in Canada so harsh that she had expected to die. But, somehow, she had lived, a lonely refugee, misunderstood and disliked.

'And why I should survive, God only knows,' she thought wearily, with an odd sense of having been left out.

Amid the turmoil of new impressions collected through the day, it did not strike her that she had been thinking of the Lady Lavender Soap Works as an enterprise she would run herself. She had simply been annoyed when her lawyer, Mr Benson, had suggested that she should leave the selling of the works to him; she had brushed the suggestion off as an insult to her as a helpless woman. The fact that the original reason for her visit had simply been to assess the value of the business had been pushed to the back of her mind by the thrilling possibilities she had immediately seen, as she walked soberly round the buildings.

The straggling collection of sheds, which made up her late uncle's factory, suggested to her not only a means of livelihood but also the chance to live in a city again, a place of fine new buildings, and homes full of lively enterprising people – literate people. They might even know where Lebanon is, she considered soberly – even have commercial ties with Beirut; Liverpool ships probably docked in Beirut sometimes.

Could one visit Beirut from Liverpool, she wondered suddenly. By this time the city might have settled down again and be safe for a Christian to visit.

As she lay staring at the moulded ceiling of the bedroom, a tightness from a long, sternly suppressed anguish seemed to grow in her chest. She breathed deeply in an effort to stop it engulfing her, and gradually, like some threatening shadow, it retreated.

She sat up and took a sip of water from a glass on the bedside table. Then she lay down again and curled herself up into a tight, foetal position, as if to protect herself from feelings too painful to be unleashed.

4

She slept uneasily and suffered a familiar nightmare, though some of the hazy, sadistic faces which seemed to peer at her out of the darkness were, this time, reminiscent of the men she had met in the soapery.

She cried out frantically to them, 'I'm not Wallace Harding, I'm not! I'm Helena Al-Khoury – and I hate the Territories. I want to go home to Beirut. Let me go! I want to go home.'

It seemed as if she pulled herself away from restraining hands, and floated easily along a seashore; and then she was in her father's courtyard amid the perfume from the blossom of the lemon tree. Uncle James was picking her up and saying she was as sweet as the flowers on the tree. She laughed in his swarthy, cheerful face, and he was gone. Instead, her mother was there, her blenched face beaded with sweat, as she held Helena's hand and pulled her along. 'Hurry, my darling. Run!'

1860 and she was nearly twelve. As her terrified mother pulled her along behind her father, Charles Al-Khoury, she heard his startled exclamations at the hideous sights which each turn in the narrow streets revealed, the carnage left by a mob gone mad.

Before turning into a narrow alley leading down to the waterfront, they crouched close to the side of the blank wall of a warehouse, to catch their breath, while Charles Al-Khoury peered down the lane to make sure it was clear.

It was already darkened by the long shadows of the evening and the smoke from the ruins of old houses further down, but there was no sound, except for the crackle of fire; the looters had been thorough. The little family flitted silently down it. As they crossed another alley they heard men shouting in the distance, and Charles Al-Khoury increased his pace.

Almost numb with fear, his wife and daughter followed closely after him. Suddenly, he half-tripped over a dark shape lying on the ground. His women bumped into him and clung to him.

They stared down in horror. A woman had had her clothes torn off her. She had been butchered like a dead cow, and the child of her womb lay smashed against a house wall. A horribly mutilated, decapitated man lay near her, and further down the alley were other pitiful bundles, blood-soaked and still.

Leila Al-Khoury vomited, the vomit making her fluttering black head veil cling to her face. Young Helena began to scream in pure terror.

Her father clapped his hand over her mouth. 'Helena!' he whispered forcefully. 'Be quiet.'

She swallowed her fear and nearly choked with the effort.

As they continued to scurry down narrow lanes, leading seaward, her father held her close to him, so that she would see as little as possible of the carnage; dogs were already nosing cautiously at the corpses of the Maronite Christians and being challenged by venturesome birds. One or two dogs had entered little homes through smashed doorways and could be heard growling over the spoils inside.

Wallace Helena, the grown woman, stirred in her bed, and cried out to the only person left to assuage her nightmares. 'Joe, darling! Joe!' But she was not heard and plunged again into her scarifying dreams, her heart beating a frantic tattoo.

Much later on, when they had established themselves in Chicago, she had asked her mother how the massacre had come about. She had been sitting cross-legged on her parents' bed, watching her mother struggle into Western clothes.

Her mother had explained that the Muslim Turkish rulers of Lebanon did not like Christians very much; neither did another sect called Druze.

Egged on by the Turks, the Druze set out to eradicate their ancient enemies, the Maronite Christians, some of whom were enviably richer than they should be. In Beirut, they struck on July 9th, 1860.

'We had heard rumours of unrest amongst the Druze, for some time before,' her mother told her, 'but neither your father nor your grand-father – my father – believed that we should be disturbed.

'Our family had always lived in or near Beirut; it was such a pleasant little place – and you'll remember our visiting our kin nearby. Our courtyard wall was high and strongly built – quite enough, we believed, to protect the house. And we were well-to-do; we could always placate the tax collectors and the servants of the Sultan, Abdul Mejid – may he be eternally accursed!' She sounded vicious, as she lashed out at the hated Turkish ruler. Then she said more calmly, 'You know, it's usually the less powerful, and the poor who can't pay, who are attacked.'

In the hope of obliterating her sickening memories, Helena had screwed up her eyes and covered them with her hands; yet there was a morbid desire to know more.

'Well, why did we run away then?'

'The rabble – Druze and Turks alike – swept right into our neighbour-hood – you heard them and saw them. And your respected father knew then that this uprising was much more serious than usual; he had not

31

believed an earlier warning which his brother had had whispered to him by a kindly Turkish official – he had felt the warning was part of a campaign by the Turks to get the Maronites to move out of their own accord.

'So when the mob came in like a flight of angry bees – they were mad with hashish, I suspect – he knew in a flash that the warning had been a genuine act of kindness. He heard the screams and the gunshots, and he ran upstairs from his office to the roof, to confirm his fears.' She paused, her voice harsh from unshed tears. 'You and I'd been sitting under the lemon tree, by the well – so quiet and peaceful. But from the roof Papa could really see what was happening. Dear Grandpa's house was already a great bonfire and the shrieking crowd was pouring into the square at the bottom of our street; he said the menace of the swords and guns flashing in the evening sun was terrifying.'

Helena said hesitantly from behind her hands, 'I remember Papa leaning over the parapet and yelling to us to come up immediately. I'd never seen Papa really frightened before.'

It was the moment when my whole world fell apart, she thought wretchedly; I simply didn't understand how it could be so.

She watched her mother buttoning her shabby black blouse, getting ready to go to work as a menial in a foreign city, and apparently accepting with fortitude what the Turks had done to her.

Leila continued her story. 'We didn't know it then,' she said, 'but Christians were suffering all over the Turkish Empire.

'When our servants heard the noise, they rushed into the courtyard to ask what was happening. They heard your father shout, and they panicked. Instead of running up to the roof themselves, they followed Cook, who ran to the main gate and opened it! I suppose he thought they would be able to escape before the mob reached us. For a second, I couldn't believe what I was seeing – it was so stupid – our gate was very stout; it might have held.

'As I whipped you indoors, I could hear their screams.'

Helena shuddered. 'I heard them.'

Leila ignored the interjection, as she sat head bowed, her fingers on the top button of her blouse. 'Well, after I'd bundled you into the house, I slammed the front door and turned the beam which locked it. That, and the barred windows, halted the crowd when they rushed into the courtyard, just long enough to allow us to escape.'

Helena sighed deeply. 'I remember the smoke – the yells – men pounding on the door – and the smell of gun-powder – and blood.'

Her mother put her arm around her and held her close.

'We were lucky, child, that we had an indoor staircase, not an outside one like many people have; if it had run straight up from the courtyard, the mob would have come up after us and killed us on the roof.'

'Papa had a piece of rope on the roof, I remember. I was so scared we'd fall, when he lowered first you and then me down into the tiny alley at the back of the house.'

Her mother nodded. 'I think he'd stored the rope up there, in case we needed an escape from fire,' she said absently. Then she added, 'The alleyway saved our lives by giving us an exit to another street.'

'I wonder why we were saved, Mama? Was our neighbour's family at the back saved?'

'Not to my knowledge, dearest. I was told that by the time the Druze and the Turks had finished, the whole area was one big funeral pyre.'

'Why does God allow such terrible things, Mama?' the young girl asked piteously.

Her mother looked shocked. 'We're not here to question God's Will, child.' Her pretty lower lip trembled. 'I didn't ask that even when your brothers died.'

Helena laid her head on her mother's shoulder. 'Of course not, Mama,' she said contritely. 'It was a wrong question to ask.'

Leila looked down at the child cuddled beside her, and she sighed. Her husband had always said that Helena was too clever to be a woman. She hoped he was wrong; women were supposed to accept, not ask questions.

Helena fingered a small pendant embossed with the head of the Virgin Mary that hung on a fine gold chain from her mother's neck. 'Did you bring this from Beirut?' she asked.

'Oh, yes, dear. For months and months that year, Papa insisted that I wear *all* my jewellery all the time. He must've been more nervous about the situation than he allowed us to think.'

'It's important for a lady to have lots of jewellery, isn't it, Mama?'

'Yes, dear – and small gold coins, easily carried. You never know what life has in store for you – life is very precarious. Jewellery is easy to carry – you can trade it anywhere – though at a great loss, of course.'

Helena nodded, and her mother hugged her again.

Leila thought with apprehension of a clouded future; but the child digested the lesson that good jewellery can be an important financial reserve – and that a collection of small gold coins is probably even better.

After a few minutes, Helena lifted her head and said heavily, 'We must've run for ages; I was so puffed.' Her young face was grim, and she swallowed. 'I don't think I'll ever forget the ghastly cruelty – how

33

can men do such dreadful things?' She looked at her mother as if begging for some reasonable explanation of what she had seen.

Leila Al-Khoury had resumed easing herself clumsily into black woollen stockings, while sitting on the end of her bed. Now she turned again to her troubled little daughter and put her arms round her. She wished she had an answer to the child's question.

'My darling, I don't know. Sometimes men seem to go mad.' She stroked Helena's silky black hair. 'In time the memories will go away, my love. And life is not all cruelty. All kinds of nice things will happen to you in your life, you'll see.' She felt Helena give a shuddering sigh, and she added, 'I wish we had foreseen what would happen, so that you could have been spared what you saw. And we might have been able to clear the warehouse and transfer some money – so that we wouldn't be in quite such dire straits. But we lived in a good district; we'd never been disturbed before.'

Helena shut her eyes tightly and wanted to be sick, as she remembered a young boy lying sobbing in the dust, one arm severed, the rest of him terribly cut about as he had tried to protect himself from sword or bayonet. Her mother had paused instinctively, bent on helping him, but her husband caught her arm to propel her forward.

'You can't leave him! He's alive!' she had protested.

He did not answer her. Terrified of what the rampaging rabble would do to his lovely wife and little daughter if they were caught, he dragged her onwards.

The dying boy haunted Wallace Helena's dreams all her life, returning like some eternal ghost to cry out to her in his agony, telling her that even loving fathers could have hearts of stone.

She had clear memories of reaching her father's silk warehouse, as yet untouched by vandals, though deserted by its panic-stricken nightwatchmen, and of meeting a youth of about fifteen when they entered the wicket gate. He was the bookkeeper's son, set to unlock the gate for any members of the family who might not have a key.

In answer to Charles Al-Khoury's inquiry, the boy said that nobody had come, except his own parents and younger brothers and Mr James Al-Khoury.

Charles Al-Khoury told him to continue to keep watch through the grating in the main door and to hurry to the boat if he heard or saw anything suspicious.

The whey-faced boy had nodded assent, and Charles hurried Helena and her mother between bales wrapped in cotton cloth and through the silk carpet section, which smelled of hemp and dust.

They had emerged onto a covered wharf on the seaward side of the building, where a small sailing boat with an Egyptian rig bobbed fretfully on the sunlit water.

Charles's brother, James, was already in the boat. He looked up at the new arrivals and exclaimed fervently, 'Thank God you've come! Nobody came to work this morning – I tried to get back to the house to warn you that something was up; but the whole town seemed to be rioting – and drunk. So I returned here to alert the boatman to be ready. I guessed you'd hear the racket in the town and be warned.' He gestured towards the bookkeeper, and added, 'Then Bachiro, here, brought his family.'

'We got out by a hair's breadth,' Charles responded sombrely, as he took the hand of the Nubian boatman and jumped into the little craft. He turned to help his wife into the boat, and went on, 'I'm afraid Leila's family is lost.'

As James stared unbelievingly up at him, Leila balked and held back, as she cried out in horror, 'Mama and Papa dead? Oh, no! And my sisters – and Auntie and my cousin?'

James said gently, 'We'll wait a while; they may have got out.' He hoped fervently that her women relations were burned in their house rather than thrown to the mob.

Petrified and exhausted, Leila allowed her husband to lift her down into the boat. Uncle James turned to a benumbed Helena. 'Come on, my little lemon blossom, you're safe now.'

Without a word, she sat down on the edge of the wharf and jumped into her uncle's arms. He caught and held her to him for a moment, while the boat bounced unhappily on the water. Then he put her down beside her weeping mother, who snatched her to her. Bachiro's wife began to wail and was hastily hushed by her husband.

'When I went to see him this morning,' Charles muttered to James, 'Leila's father said it wouldn't be the first riot he'd seen, nor would it be the last. I reminded him that I'd had this felucca standing by for a week, in case of emergency, and he as good as told me I was a craven fool.'

His back to Leila, James made a rueful face, while Charles berated himself that he had not transferred money abroad.

'With the Turks watching every move, it would have been almost impossible,' James comforted him.

The wind showed signs of changing, and the boatman said it would be dangerous to linger any longer; the Turks would undoubtedly soon arrive to sack the warehouses along the waterfront. Better to leave while the wind held.

'For Jesus' sake, make him wait,' Leila whispered urgently to her husband. 'Mama – Papa – somebody – may come.'

Charles agreed, and argued heatedly with the stolid black seaman until, encouraged by some silver coins, he agreed to wait until the sun had set.

They waited anxiously through the afterglow, until shouts from the landward side of the warehouse and the sound of heavy thuds on wood brought Bachiro's eldest son speeding to the wharf. 'They're coming,' he shouted breathlessly, as he leapt into the little craft, his eyes starting out of his head with fright.

The felucca slipped seaward, while Leila crouched on a coil of rope and wept unrestrainedly for parents and sisters she would never see again. Charles Al-Khoury stared dumbly landwards and was thankful that his parents had died peacefully some years before.

Seated on the end of her bed in a small apartment in a Chicago slum, putting on her garters over her black stockings, Leila had pointed out in defence of her husband that he had done quite a lot to protect his family. Her deep, vibrant voice shook as she told Helena, 'Papa arranged that a shipment of French silk he was expecting be redirected to our friend, Mr Ghanem, here in Chicago – and he began to wear his special moneybelt with gold coins in it, as did Uncle James. I wore my jewellery all the time.'

Helena sighed, and then she asked wistfully, 'When will we be able to go home, Mama?'

Her mother stood up and shook down her long black skirt. 'Some day, perhaps, dear.' She did not tell her that there was nothing and nobody to go home to. Her courage faltered for a moment, as she said, 'It was a terrible massacre – it'll never be forgotten.'

Helena rubbed her face wearily, and remembered again how they had sailed all night, seasick and then hungry.

As they worked their way from Beirut to Cyprus, there to be sheltered by business friends of her father's, all the certainties of her life had vanished. She had been an ordinary middle-class young girl, happy in a gentle routine of lessons from her mother and social occasions shared with her uncle and grandparents. There had been books to read, festivals to keep, music to listen to and to learn to play, forays into the mountains and walks beside the sea; and, in her father's warehouse, fabulous fabrics and carpets to be admired and carefully caressed, until one could unerringly recognize quality and fine workmanship. And tentatively, beginning to be mentioned in her mother's conversation, was the excitement of deciding who she should marry in a couple of years' time.

36

Instead, she was being shifted nightly from one alien house to another, in an effort to stay hidden from the ruling Turks. Then, when she began to think she would go out of her mind, they sailed one night in a stinking fishing boat to Nice, where they were, at last, safely outside the Turkish Empire. From there, they had travelled by train across France to Hamburg, where a Jewish friend of her father obtained a passage to Liverpool for them.

They had waited several anxious weeks in Liverpool in a boarding house packed with other immigrants, while a passage for America was arranged. Charles and James Al-Khoury, with Helena pattering along behind them, had filled in the time by exploring the city. In the course of their walks, Uncle James had been most enthusiastic about the modern, gaslit city, and despite his elder brother's advice against it, he decided to remain in it. Partly because of the valuable consignment of silk awaiting him in Chicago, which would help him to start a new business there, and the fact that there were already Lebanese refugees in that city, Charles Al-Khoury stuck to his original plan of settling in the United States.

Leila had nearly died during the passage to America in the steerage section of the cramped immigrant ship. Their small funds had dwindled during their journeying and Charles dared not spend any more than he did. Tended by other Christians who had fled the Turkish Empire, Greeks, Cypriots and Armenians, as well as Lebanese, her mother had lain weeping helplessly and muttering with fever. Huddled together in an unventilated hold, on a straw palliasse spread on a shelf-like fixture above another family, Helena was very seasick. She wanted despairingly to die herself, as she watched her father grow more haggard each day, and listened to the horrifying stories of other refugees, of wholesale murder all over the Middle East.

When her nausea eased, her father took her up on deck and they walked together, too exhausted to say much.

After that, there was the incredible noise and smell in the great immigration shed, while the United States Immigration authorities worked their way through the anxious, pressing crowd washed up on their shores. Leila kept a firm hold on Helena's hand, in case, by some awful misfortune, they should become separated, so Helena sat by the listless bundle in black which was her mother and listened to the jabber of a dozen languages round her, amid the maelstrom of noisy, smelly humanity.

The three of them had made an effort to learn a few words of English while in Liverpool. The immigration officials, though harried, were not unkind, and eventually a bewildered Helena was hustled onto the

Chicago train by a father who, for the first time, seemed more relaxed. The bookkeeper had decided to stay in New York with another Lebanese family from the same immigrant ship. They said an impassioned farewell and vanished into the turbulence of the great port.

It was only towards the end of her time in Chicago, when her life was again about to change completely, that Helena realized that, to her parents, Chicago had been yet another nightmare. Being young, she had herself begun to adapt to her new life. As she went to the shops for her mother, and helped her father as he tried to establish a little business in wholesale dress materials, she began to pick up some English.

In contrast, her gently nurtured mother, though educated, was used to being much at home, secure in the knowledge that her parents had married her to a comfortably placed, kindly man. She had rarely been stared at by strangers, never been hungry, never done much except to order her servants and adapt herself to her husband. In Chicago, she was, at first, shattered, unable to make much effort.

Another refugee, arriving after them, confirmed the death of Leila's parents and sisters and, indeed, it seemed of everyone they had known. As she mourned her loss, the fever she had suffered aboard ship returned to her, and Charles Al-Khoury's face grew thinner and grimmer. Helena tried to comfort her mother and not to cry herself. She closed her mind off from any thought of Beirut, feeling that if she allowed herself to contemplate what had happened, she would go mad. In those early weeks in America, the child grew into a stony-faced young woman, physically hardly formed, but mentally aged beyond her years.

Not daring to part with so much as a garnet from his wife's jewellery, unless he was starving, Charles Al-Khoury used the remainder of his little store of gold coins to augment his bales of silk with some dress lengths in other good materials. He found a tiny niche of a store on a main street crowded with immigrants. The door was strong and the windows had good wooden shutters. He paid a week's rent on it to a Greek immigrant, who had been in Chicago rather longer than he had.

Before opening his precious purchases, he bargained for cleaning help from a young negress who lived nearby.

Sally earned her living as a daily cleaning lady, and she came for two successive evenings to give the store a thorough scouring. As Helena said to her, 'You can't sell material for clothes if it's got dusty.'

A quick grin flashed across the black woman's lined face, as she agreed. On her second evening, she brought a toffee apple with her for Helena, and she watched with pleasure when the grim little face lit up at the sight of the gift.

Sally enjoyed working for people who treated her politely. She became interested in the fortunes of the tiny store and continued to clean it, though sometimes Charles Al-Khoury had to defer paying her during bad weeks. She would tease him good-naturedly about his broken English, which he took in good part, being anxious to improve it. She drilled Helena in the English names of everything around her, and Helena became devoted to the strong, graceful woman.

Mr Ghanem, the Lebanese who had kept Charles's bales of silk for him, was very nearly as poor as Charles himself. He had been in the States for a number of years with his own small business as an importer. He had, however, speculated in land and had gone bankrupt. He now had a small fruit and vegetable shop. Because they had been at school together, he had kept in touch with Charles sporadically over the years, and it was his presence in Chicago that had first given Charles the idea of beginning life again in that city.

It was Mr Ghanem who had met them at the station and had taken them in a borrowed horse-drawn delivery van to a room he had obtained for them. When Charles's shop was ready, Mr Ghanem's half-grown sons helped the new immigrant move the consignment of silk from their family's basement onto the shelves of the new store. Mrs Ghanem had done her best to comfort poor Leila Al-Khoury, and she gradually emerged from her prostration, white and thin, but in her right mind.

Much later on, Leila told Helena, 'I thought I'd go mad. There we were, in this strange country; nobodies, lost in a sea of nobodies. God curse the Druze – and may the Turks burn in hell!' The words seemed extraordinary, coming from a beautiful seductive woman, once again restored to health; but Helena understood, and thought burning was too good for Turks.

Leila had continued sadly, 'Outside that tiny room in which we existed, so few spoke Arabic – and nobody seemed to have heard of French! And the noise of screaming women and howling children in the other rooms seemed unending.'

Helena nodded agreement. Watching immigrant children struggle for existence had made her feel that the last thing she wanted in life was to be a mother.

'When Mrs Ghanem suggested that I go to work like she did, I was really shocked,' Leila confided. 'But we needed ready money so badly that finally I agreed. It distressed your father very much.' She giggled suddenly, at the memory of her hard-pressed husband's agitation at the suggestion.

She giggled again, and then added, 'I must've looked a sight. I wore a second-hand black skirt, a black blouse and second-hand boots. I wore a head veil, like I had done in Beirut, and I felt terrible. It seemed to me that every man I passed stared at me.

'The attic we worked in was so badly lit that I could hardly see how to thread my needles. There, Mrs Ghanem and I sat on a piece of sacking for ten hours a day, stitching on buttons and finishing the button-holes on men's suits. I've worked harder since then, but never in such confinement; I had to watch that my tears didn't fall on the fine cloth. What a time!' She threw up her hands helplessly.

Helena put her arms round her mother's neck. 'Poor Mama,' she said.

'Well, I lived,' responded her mother philosophically. 'But I didn't want you to be confined like that, so your dear father took you to help him in the store.'

'And he taught me how to run a business,' Helena had remembered gratefully. 'How to organize it and be neat and methodical. Buy cheap; sell dear. Have the patience of Job. Have a first-class product for the money. Keep two sets of books – one for the tax collector, and one which tells you what's really happening. Make friends – which I haven't done very well. Do favours and collect on them when you need to. Never forget a name – and smile, child, smile.' He would grin at her from under his black moustache. 'And don't trust anybody, unless you have to,' he would reiterate pithily in Arabic.

She would laugh back at him. But she learned, and never quite trusted anyone – except Joe Black.

Afraid to trust a bank, afraid of his wife being attacked in the street if she wore it, Charles hid some of Leila's jewellery in various spots in his tiny shop, a necklace wrapped in a scrap of black silk under a beam in the ceiling, several rings under a floorboard, a pair of hair ornaments in a box stuck to the underside of his long counter. He instructed Helena that, if he were out, she was never to leave anyone alone in the shop for a single second, including Sally.

Leila sewed two gold chains into the waistband of her ugly serge skirt, and her best emerald necklace was carried in a linen moneybelt round her husband's waist. Spread out like this, they agreed, they were less likely to be robbed of all of it; it was capital, partly inherited and partly carefully bought since their marriage; it was not to be used, except in the expansion of the dress material business, if they had some success with it; or, if that failed, to keep them from starvation.

In the store, Helena was in her element. She watched with care how her father set about establishing his new business, learned how to set up the bookkeeping, how to find suppliers and, most important of all, how to find customers. She would sit unobtrusively in the background while he bargained for bankrupt stock from other businesses or cajoled a lady who wanted the price of a dress length reduced, and when his English failed him, she quietly translated – though her own grasp of the language was not very good. When they had a quiet hour, he would reminisce about the family business in Beirut, and, when he found she was interested, would go into detail about its organization, its employees, and its links with distant countries. He was astonished that she knew and understood much of its detailed running already. She laughed at his astonishment and reminded him how he used to take her down to the warehouses to give her a change. 'I used to listen to you talking to people – and when I grew bigger, I used to ask Bachiro to show me the papers that seemed to be like oil flowing to facilitate the movement of everything coming in and going out.'

Her father laughed. 'You did? You nosy little person!'

'I wasn't nosy,' she replied indignantly. 'I was really interested in what you and Uncle James and Grandpa were doing. I kept thinking that if I had been a boy, you would have begun to keep me by your side and teach me everything.'

'Well, you're a great help to me now, little flower. I don't know how I would manage without you.'

Her big eyes shone at the compliment, and he thought that he should get her married as soon as he could, before the harshness of their life in Chicago toughened her too much. Men liked gentle amenable women; a ruthless trader would not appeal to them.

But, without realizing that he was doing it, he had already inculcated in her the basic principles of organization, enterprise, forethought and quick decision-making which were to be her strength in times to come.

5

The two rooms above Charles Al-Khoury's shop in Chicago were occupied by Polish immigrants. When they moved out, he again bargained with his Greek landlord and succeeded in renting the rooms for little more than he was already paying for the shop. Triumphantly, he got Sally to clean the rooms and then he installed his wife and daughter in them.

The tiny store and the flat above it became Helena's world. She carried samples of materials to the houses of well-to-do ladies, when requested; and in the shop she made tea for women who began to discover the fine quality of Charles's stock. They sat by his counter and talked haughtily to him, under the impression that they were bargaining successfully for a better price than others obtained; dressmakers, who also came, always got materials at a better price, but they always received a lower grade silk. As her father warned her, 'Dressmakers are always poor; you can't get more money out of them than they have. Remember that!'

Helena was allowed to handle swatches from the fat bales on the shelves, and she soon learned what constituted a good dress length. Her English rapidly became better than his, so he encouraged her to write his business letters for him and then to keep the accounts. Though she did not write her father's letters in Arabic to Uncle James, she sometimes saw them. It was apparent that her father felt that Uncle James was quite mad; he was boiling soap in his landlady's wash boiler and was selling it door-to-door in Liverpool.

The bales of material were heavy, and Charles lifted them himself. Helena watched with anxiety the sweat pour down his face, as he moved the cotton-swathed rolls from shelf to counter to show them to customers, and, later, lifted them back onto the shelf.

One day, when he had gone with swatches of material to see a particularly high-class dressmaker and Helena was watching the shop for him, Sally remarked to her, 'Your pa's doing too much.' She was polishing the old wooden counter to a fine sheen, as she spoke, and did not appear to expect a reply.

Helena's heart seemed to miss a beat, as the implied threat of illness sank in. From then on, she insisted that she be allowed to help with the tidying-up of the shop, but she was a skinny youngster without much power in her arms; and he would laugh and take the bundles from her to lay them on the shelves.

Apart from his stock, American women found the Lebanese shop-keeper charming and they recommended the store to their friends. The tiny business began to prosper. The Al-Khourys hoarded every cent they could.

At the end of six months, Charles insisted that his wife give up her job with the tailor and stay at home. 'If we are very, very careful, we can manage,' he assured her. 'I don't like you doing menial work.'

Helena took her mother for granted; she did not realize that she possessed unusual beauty, and that, as she learned to dress in Western clothes, her father felt jealous when other men looked at her. He wanted her at home, not veiled like a Muslim woman but decently bundled up like a good Maronite.

Leila Al-Khoury was thankful to be released from the tailor's stuffy attic, but she refused to wear her native dress or veil her hair. She had fallen in love with hats and bought herself a plain black straw which she trimmed with shreds of silk from her husband's shop.

With this imaginative concoction on her head, she pressed herself lovingly against her husband and assured him that he had nothing to worry about. He was partially mollified, though the flowerlike face framed by the hat's brim was, he felt uneasily, very attractive.

Helena had not inherited her mother's beauty. Though she was not ugly, she had her father's strong nose and wide mouth. She was sallower than Leila and there was no hint of pink in her cheeks; and her long oriental eyes with their secretive, sidelong glances were too foreign for Western taste. The tumbling black mass of her hair was restrained in a bun at the back of her head and gave little hint of its richness. Amid the babble of thousands of immigrants, as a skinny young girl she passed unremarked. Until she met Joe Black.

Curled up alone in a feather bed in Liverpool, her dream passed from the nightmares of the Lebanon and Chicago, to Joe.

She smiled in her sleep, as she seemed to hear herself saying to him cryptically, 'You never gave me toffee apples.' And his laughing back at her and saying, 'I never thought of them. Want one?'

Joe had his own ideas of gifts. In her dream, she saw him lounge into their living-room, the original log cabin in which her stepfather had first lived in Canada. Peeking out of his jacket was a tame grey fox, a birthday gift.

One Christmas, he had brought her a muff made from a marten fur he had trapped; his mother had cleaned and tanned the skin and he

43

had then given it to another Cree woman who had fashioned it for him. Sometimes, when he had been south to see his grandfather, he brought her a little opium to smoke, bargained from a lonely Russian farmer who had established his own patch of poppies, or, at other times, a small packet of tobacco from Virginia, passed from hand to hand across a continent, in trade.

The rising sun began to push long fingers between the heavy velvet curtains of her bedroom in Liverpool, and she sleepily stretched out to touch him. But he was six thousand miles away, harvesting a hay crop.

6

Leila Al-Khoury lamented bitterly that it was Mr and Mrs Ghanem who had brought the typhoid into their Chicago home. The infection had, in fact, sneaked through the tumble-down, crowded neighbourhood like a smouldering fire; but Mr Ghanem was the first person to die from it.

The local inhabitants were used to illnesses which ran their course, and the patients were nursed at home. Though guesses were made, no name was put to the sickness. Immigrants had little money, so doctors were rarely called.

Charles Al-Khoury, worked to a shadow of his former self, was in no state to withstand such a virulent infection. The Al-Khourys knew that Mr Ghanem was also ill. His wife told Leila that it was 'Something he's eaten.' It was assumed that in both cases the fever would go away and the diarrhoea would ease, if the patients were kept on a liquid diet. Meanwhile, Helena served in their tiny shop and Leila nursed her husband.

When Mr Ghanem died, leaving a widow with five sons to feed, Leila realized, in a panic, that this was no ordinary illness. She sent for a doctor, only to be scolded by him in English she barely understood for not calling him earlier. Charles died in her arms.

Once more, Leila tore her clothes, and the household rang to shrieks of mourning. Both she and a terrified Helena were devastated, as was Mrs Ghanem in her tiny home. Other neighbours, afraid of being infected themselves, left small gifts of food at the shop door, but refused to come in.

Only Sally walked briskly up the stairs to the Al-Khoury flat, to bring some common sense into their lives. Hiding her own sorrow for a man she secretly adored, she instructed a grief-stricken Helena to get back to the store and mind it. 'I'll look after your ma.'

Helena had obeyed, but she quickly found herself in difficulties. Men delivering cotton and silk her father had ordered through middlemen refused to leave the goods without her father's signature. 'You're too young to sign for it. You can pay cash, if you like,' she was told.

'Could Mother sign for it?' she asked, afraid of parting with the small sum in the secret drawer of the old till.

A man delivering a roll of silk had hesitated at this suggestion, but

45

finally said uneasily that he did not think his company would accept a woman's signature, and went away with the roll still on his shoulder.

Beating down her increasing terror, she served customers from the existing stock with her sweetest smile, as she struggled with the heavy rolls. She knew that, unless she could buy replacement materials, the business was doomed.

Oblivious of the impending end to their sole source of income, Leila sat cross-legged on her bed, allowing Sally and Helena to minister to her. Occasionally, she would fling herself down on the pillows in a fresh burst of weeping.

Between bouts, Helena asked her urgently, 'Couldn't you run the business, Mama? I believe if you took it in hand, the suppliers would accept you – or perhaps we could import some silk direct from China?' She sighed, and got up to pull back the closed curtains to let in the evening sun.

Leila put down the coffee her daughter had brought her, turned her blotched face away from the light, and began to cry again.

Helena went back to her, to sit beside her and put her arms round her. 'Mama, dear, listen to me, please. If you can't help me, we'll have to close the shop – we don't make anything like enough to employ a manager, even supposing we could find an honest one.'

Leila wept on.

As she patted her mother's back in an effort to comfort her, Helena said savagely, 'I know what to do – but nobody will trust me. The salesman from Smithson's chucked me under the chin this morning, as if I were a baby. He actually said, "Pity you're not a boy!"'

'Mama, could we sell something to get money, so that I can pay cash for stock?'

'I don't know anything about business,' her mother sobbed, and continued to moan into the pillows.

In despair, Helena held a big sale and then shut the shop. She made just sufficient to pay their debts, except for one.

'Sally, dear. I don't have any money left to pay you. Instead, I saved these for you.' She proffered a package containing several pretty ends of rolls that she had been unable to sell.

Sally bent and hugged her. She sniffed, and then said, 'You don't have to worry about me, hon. There was many a time when your pa couldn't pay me. You and your ma are welcome to anything I can do.'

Before letting her out of the door, Helena clung to her. 'Thank you, Sally. Thank you.'

Left alone, she searched the little shop to retrieve the remaining bits of jewellery hidden there. 'I'd better take a good look upstairs, as well,' she thought, as she wrapped the pieces up in a scrap of cotton. 'If we don't pay the rent we'll be thrown out fast.'

As she tucked the little parcel well down into her skirt pocket, she cried helplessly. She was nearly fourteen years old, tall for her age and very thin, with eyes that were sadly old for one so young and feet that seemed too big for her stature.

Since her mother was in no state to do it, Helena sat down at their rickety table in their tiny apartment and wrote to her only surviving blood relative, Uncle James in Liverpool, to tell him of his brother's death and the penury of his widow. Tears blotted her shaky unformed Arabic script.

By the time they received a reply six weeks later, the landlord, a kindly man, had grown tired of a tenant who was not paying him rent, even though she was a pretty widow, and told them they had another week in which to start paying again, plus something towards the arrears.

If it had not been for a large bag of rice, which her father had obtained shortly before his death, and the kindness of their neighbours, Helena and her mother would have starved.

In his reply, Uncle James wrote that, if they could manage to pay their fares to England, he would be happy to give both mother and daughter a home. Unfortunately, he was not yet earning enough to send them their fares; he had just leased a small factory building and installed his first soap boiler, and this had drained his reserve and his credit.

He did not know how to express his own grief at the loss of a well-loved brother, so contented himself with the usual polite phrases. Leila's troubles were great enough without his adding to them.

He did not mention that the home he offered would actually be in a house owned by his English mistress, Eleanor. As he wrote, she was sitting on a chair opposite him, nursing their year-old son, Benjamin.

It had taken a great deal of coaxing on his part to persuade this downright little Liverpudlian that he owed shelter to his sister-in-law, Leila, and her daughter, Helena. It was a duty he could not evade, he assured her, and he would have to find another place to live if Eleanor could not help him.

'She's foreign,' Eleanor had protested.

James had looked up from his letter and responded dryly, though with a twinkle in his eye, 'So am I.'

'You're different, luv,' she told him, and smiled at him.

James's eyes were bloodshot from private weeping on top of long hours of work. He looked so drained that she impulsively got up from her chair and leaned over the baby to kiss his cheek. 'Well, never mind. Don't you fret,' she said kindly. 'I suppose I could give 'em the second-floor back room to theirselves. I'd have to give Mr Tomlinson notice, though, so as he can find somewhere else.' Mr Tomlinson was one of her three gentlemen lodgers, other than James Al-Khoury himself. She sighed heavily, as she sat down and rearranged Benjamin on her lap. 'I'd have to ask you for a bit more housekeeping to help out, like, 'cos I'll have two more mouths to feed – and I won't have Mr T's rent.'

'Of course I'll give you more,' he assured her, without any idea of where he was going to get the extra money from. He put down his pen and got up to embrace both mother and child; Eleanor was a wonderful comfort to a lonely man, a real help – and she had given him a son. He prayed to God that his new venture with George Tasker, the Soap Master, would prosper.

Eleanor told herself she would do anything she could for him; she'd never again meet a man like him. Mr T must go; she could not imagine her despair if James left her. She wasn't getting any younger; and now there was little Benji to think about.

In Chicago, a surprised Leila read his kind letter. Puzzled, she looked up from her meagre lunch of boiled rice and weak coffee, and asked Helena, 'Did you write to Uncle James?'

Having seen the English stamp on the letter, Helena was tense with anxiety, as she said eagerly, 'Yes.'

Leila sighed. 'I should have done it.'

'I did ask you, Mama. But you didn't listen.'

In the seven weeks since her husband had died, Leila had grown quieter. Though she did not cry so much, she was very listless. Nothing that Helena could do or say seemed to rouse her to the realization that, unless they did something quickly, they would die of starvation.

Now, seeing the letter, a wild hope surged in Helena. 'May I read Uncle's letter, Mama?' she asked eagerly.

Leila handed it to her without comment.

As the girl read, a tremendous relief made her want to shout with joy, the first sense of wellbeing since her father had died. 'Isn't he good, Mama? And his wife, too. We'll have to sell your jewellery – or some of it, Mama?' A hint of doubt had crept into her voice. Despite their desperate position, Leila had sullenly refused to part with the last of her chains and brooches. Her husband's declaration that he would only sell them *in extremis* had meant, to her, only in the case of death. A Lebanese, longer established than the Al-Khourys, had accepted a gold chain from her and had arranged Charles's funeral. That to her had constituted a time to sell.

48

Leila did not immediately reply to her daughter, she sat fretfully toying with her coffee cup.

'To get the fares to go to England, Mama – we have to get the fares from somewhere.'

Leila felt morosely that fate had dealt her an unbearable blow in the loss of her husband. In these last seven weeks of prostration, she had been waiting for that same fate to compensate her in some way. Her brother-in-law's kindly letter did not appear to do that, and she said capriciously, 'I don't want to go.'

'But, Mama, what else can we do? Uncle James is a dear – you know that.'

'He's kind,' Leila admitted reluctantly. She was quiet for a moment, and then, as if to justify her refusal, she added, 'I simply can't change countries again. It would be too much; I couldn't bear it.' She buried her face in her hands.

Helena swallowed, and replied carefully, 'It wouldn't be much different from America, would it, Mama? I liked Liverpool when we passed through it.'

'It would be quite different,' her mother replied shortly. She rose from the table and, dragging her bare feet on the planks of the floor, she went to Helena's small bed at the back of the room. She lay down on it, her face towards the wall, as if to shut out a life which was a burden to her.

Helena went to sit at the foot of the bed and continue the argument.

Without looking at her, Leila protested, 'Helena, you can't imagine what it would be like to be penniless in Uncle James's house. No matter how kind he is, we would be dependent upon the whims of his – er – wife. She's bound to resent us – or she'd make use of us as servants. It would be insupportable.'

Helena took another tack. 'I always imagined that Uncle James wasn't married?' she queried.

Leila bit her lower lip. She was not sure how to explain Uncle James's domestic affairs. She said cautiously, 'Some men have a woman friend who lives with them. Uncle James's situation could make it harder for us.' She turned slightly, to look at the frightened girl. 'In the West, it's not quite honourable, though I'm sure your uncle has his reasons for not marrying her . . .'

'If she's not his wife, couldn't he send her away? Then we could look after him.'

'I doubt he wants to be rid of her. They've been together a long time.'

49

'I see,' Helena muttered. But all she really understood was that her mother seemed totally incapable of doing anything. It was to be a number of years before she became aware of the profound effect her uncle's lack of a marriage certificate was to have on her own life.

7

Helena continued to sit by her mother on her bed and to beg her to reconsider her uncle's offer. She got no response, except for peevish monosyllables. Hope died in the girl and was replaced by dread.

Finally, in search of comfort, she went out into the street and made her way, through crowds on their way home from work, to Mrs Ghanem's tiny home. Perhaps another widow would be able to help her rouse her mother.

Mrs Ghanem was still at work, her five-year-old told her solemnly. He was helping Mama by looking after his little brother. He pointed to a crawling child behind him.

The children were filthy and the house stank. Poor Mrs Ghanem, thought Helena compassionately; her children and her home had always been immaculate before Mr Ghanem's death.

She promised the child that she would come again another day, and, feeling suddenly very weak, she walked towards home.

As she turned into the familiar narrow street, she caught a glimpse of Sally coming towards her, and her depression lifted a little. She ran towards her.

Sally caught her in a bear hug. 'Where've you been?' she inquired. 'I was just dropping by to see how your ma is.'

'I went to see Mrs Ghanem – but she's still at work.' She turned back towards her home, arm-in-arm with the cleaning lady.

'Uh-ha. So what's new with you, hon?'

Helena hastily told her about her uncle's letter. Then she added uneasily, 'I'm scared, Sally. Mama won't *do* anything. And we haven't paid the rent for weeks – and in a few days there won't be even rice to eat. At least Uncle James would feed us, and perhaps I could find some work in Liverpool; it's a very busy city.'

Sally paused on the ragged doormat at the foot of the stairs leading up to Leila's living quarters. 'Want me to talk to her?' she asked.

'She'd never forgive me for telling you.'

'I guess you're right.'

As they came up the last step, they were both surprised to see that Leila was up. Her hair had been combed and pinned up; she had put on a clean white blouse and her black stockings and boots. She had lifted the nearly empty sack of rice onto the table and had spread some of the grains on a tray in order to pick out any small stones in it.

Helena was astonished. It looked as if Uncle James's letter had had an effect, she decided thankfully.

Sally said to Leila, 'My, you do look pretty! How're you doing?'

The pale, delicate mouth quivered and the eyes were full of pain, but she answered Sally quite firmly, 'I'm better, thank you. Sit down.' She pulled out a chair for her visitor. 'Coffee?'

Sally accepted the proffered chair. Knowing how short they were of everything, she said she did not need coffee. Leila, however, was suddenly aware of neglected social obligations, and she insisted on using the last of their coffee to make a decent cup for her friend.

Helena went quietly to the table and took over the cleaning of the rice. She was afraid that if she said anything she would upset Leila again. Let Sally do the talking.

Sally did talk. She brought in all the polite gambits of the state of the weather, the price of vegetables and the latest news of the war raging further south, while she gravely sipped her coffee and Leila sat with her hands clasped in her lap, barely attending to the rich musical voice.

Finally, Sally told her, with real excitement in her voice, that she had managed to get a full-time job as a waitress in a new coffee shop being opened by Italian immigrants. It was close to the Al-Khourys' old shop.

Leila was genuinely pleased, and congratulated her. Then she sat looking at her hands for a moment, before she went on to say determinedly, 'Tomorrow, Helena and I, we go to tailor to ask for sewing work. Helena sew as good as me.'

'Well, that would keep you going for a bit.' Sally smiled at her, and then said very gently, 'With your looks you could get a healthier job, a clerk in a store, say.'

Leila smiled wanly back. 'Later. Tailor give job now.' She shrugged. 'Nobody give me good job now. English so bad.'

'You're doing just fine,' Sally assured her robustly.

Helena looked up from the rice. She was dumbfounded at her mother's decisiveness. A quick warning glance from Sally told her to be careful what she said.

She deftly picked out a piece of chaff from the rice. 'I'd love to work with you, Mama,' she said softly.

Her mother turned and smiled at her. 'Would you? That's good. We'll manage, darling, won't we?'

Thankfully, Helena got up and went to her. Leila took her warmly in her arms, and Helena wanted to burst into tears with relief.

The Civil War had caused an insatiable demand for uniforms. The tailor was very glad to have two skilled sewers for finishing work, though he bargained the wages down to near-starvation levels, on the grounds that Leila's English was poor and that, at nearly fourteen, Helena was not yet entitled to a woman's wage.

The two clung to each other and managed to continue to exist, two tiny boats bobbing along in a sea of other immigrants, all competing for jobs, cheap rooms and cheap food, in a country where war had caused prices to skyrocket. Their Greek landlord was appeased, and the shop beneath their small nest was re-rented, to a lock-smith and his family, who both worked and slept there. Because they had a side entrance, the two women were not disturbed by them.

Helena had never in her life felt so exhausted. Underfed, she also lacked sunlight, diversions, and exercise. One day, on their return from work, she fainted.

Leila bathed her daughter's pinched, white face, and decided desperately that she would sell her best gold chain. In that way, she could pay the landlord his arrears instead of having to give him extra money each week. They could then spend more on food. She herself felt apathetic and intensely weary, and she thought, with real horror, of what might happen to her daughter if she herself should die.

She took the necklace to a jeweller in a better area of the city, and it was in the jeweller's shop that she met Tom Harding.

Tom was a widowed settler from Fort Edmonton, a Hudson's Bay Company Fort on the banks of the North Saskatchewan River in western Canada, an area as yet barely explored. Though Tom claimed to be a settler, he was, in fact, a squatter on land owned by the great fur-trading Company which had established the Fort. To the Company's annoyance, he also trapped, and, having once been a miner, was apt to dig Company coal out of the banks of the river and to pan small amounts of gold out of the river itself.

His younger brother owned a prosperous grocery shop in Chicago, and their acerbic old mother lived with him. Tom had received an urgent letter from his brother, via the Hudson's Bay Company, saying that the old lady was in very frail health. She had several times expressed a strong desire to see him before she died, and he should hurry.

When he received the letter, Tom thought wryly that his brother had obviously no idea of the distances involved or the difficulties of the journey. He was, however, extremely depressed himself. He had recently lost his Cree Indian wife and his infant son in childbirth. An Indian wife was an enormous asset, besides which he had been quite fond of her and had been looking forward to the child. He wondered if he should return to Chicago and settle there.

After discussing the matter with his friend, Joe Black, who worked with him on his illegally held piece of land, it was decided that Joe could manage to look after the farm, while Tom made the journey. 'And mind you come back!' Joe shouted after him, as he prepared to leave. 'We haven't built this place out of nothing, just to see it go back to forest again. You'll feel a lot better when you've had a change – and I know lots of Cree women who wouldn't mind being Mrs Harding Number Two.'

Tom grinned and saluted him, as he turned his horse onto the trail which led to the Fort, where he expected to join the Company's boats going down the river to Lake Winnipeg. Then another boat down to Fort Garry – about a thousand miles, he believed, and he'd still be in Canada.

As he rode, he chewed one end of his moustache and considered the fragile hold he had on the precious piece of land for which he had struggled so hard. It was certainly Company land, but he reckoned that Joe was far too useful to the Company for them to try to dislodge him from it while he himself was away.

Joe was half Cree, half negro, and he knew the languages of the area. Slow to anger and trusted by both sides, he was frequently used by the Chief Factor at the Fort as a negotiator between the Company and the recalcitrant Blackfoot and Cree Indians. Though he had been known to get involved in fights which occasionally broke out amongst the Company's employees, when all concerned had drunk more than usual, and was consequently sometimes out of favour with Company men ruefully rubbing bruises he had inflicted, he was a godsend to a company which was not always able to keep control in the land over which it was supposed to rule.

In his heart, Tom felt that he himself was tolerated on the Company's land solely because Joe worked for him, that Chief Factor Christie did not have him removed because, if he did, Joe would probably drift back south to rejoin his Indian grand-father, of whom it was said he was very fond; and the Company would lose its best defence against the resentment of the displaced Indians.

Tom did not consider that he, as well as Joe, had built up a friendship with a number of Blackfoot families, because he owed his life to one of them, and that Factor Christie was aware of this useful relationship between a white man and a very proud and angry group of native people.

Tom certainly did not enjoy the hardships of the long voyage in a York boat down the North Saskatchewan to Lake Winnipeg and through the lake to Fort Garry. He was expected to make himself useful on the voyage; and he decided that his own life might be hard, but, being a voyager faced with portages and little but pemmican to eat, he preferred the hardships of a squatter's life.

From Fort Garry, he sailed in a small American trading boat down the Red River, then went by stagecoach to La Crosse and, thankfully, the rest of the journey by train.

Now, he wanted to return home before the winter set in, though his frail ghost of a mother begged him to remain in Chicago. Despite her invalidism, her tongue was as malicious as ever; and she had made him feel a sense of guilt at his decision to desert her once again. To soften the blow of his departure, he had decided to buy her a present.

His finances were limited and, as he pushed open the door of the local jewellery store, he had scant hope of finding what he wanted at a reasonable price.

Instead of a present, he found Leila Al-Khoury bargaining with the jeweller over the sale of a fine gold chain which had originally belonged to her mother-in-law; it had been given to Leila on the birth of her first son, who had died of a fever when he was six. Leila firmly tried to remember the old lady's delight at the child and to forget the gentle woman's terrible death at the hands of the Beirut Muslims. She spoke to the jeweller in the firmest tone she could muster.

Her voice rose and fell, as, in broken English, she refused to reduce the price that she wanted. The jeweller had assayed the gold and knew that the price she asked was not unreasonable, but he was in no hurry, so he let her rattle on.

While Tom loitered behind her, Leila whined and begged and pointed out the flawless workmanship of the Beirut goldsmith, until the jeweller became fed up with her; if he turned her away today, she would probably return tomorrow willing to accept his offer.

Tom shifted his feet uneasily, as he looked idly over a case of brooches. At the slight noise, the lady turned her head to look at him. She wore a plain white summer dress she had made herself and her face was framed by a cheap straw hat. Tom found himself looking into a pair of enormous, sad brown eyes – like a little spaniel's, he thought. A cupid's bow of a mouth trembled, as if tears were near. Under the white dress, a generous bosom heaved slightly.

The whole stringy six feet of Tom Harding shook with desire. What was a woman like that doing on her own? Was she a whore?

As he stared into the eyes of the pretty Lebanese, the argument with the jeweller appeared to have reached an impasse. The jeweller huffily banged the drawers of his counter shut and locked them. Tears glistened

55

on the long black lashes of the lady. The necklace, a handsomely worked heavy chain with several red stones pendant from it, lay on the counter.

The jeweller moved slightly towards Tom. 'Can I help you, Sir?' he inquired politely.

Uncomfortably aware that he was roughly dressed in riding boots, a plaid shirt and a big felt hat, in a city which was quite full of prosperous people more formally attired, Tom looked down at Leila and replied soberly, 'I got plenty of time. Finish with the lady.'

Still looking up at him, Leila scooped up the necklace and put it back into her reticule. 'It finish,' she told him tragically, the words coming out in softly accented English. She bowed her head and began to move slowly and despondently towards the door, her white skirt swaying gently round her.

Tom jerked to attention. Once she was outside that door, he would probably never see her again.

He took off his big felt hat and bowed to her. 'Excuse me, Ma'am.'

She looked doubtfully up at him with a slight frown.

He swallowed. 'I'm in the market for a necklace, Ma'am. Would that necklace be for sale privately?' He paused, waiting for some response, but she had not fully understood what he said and was mentally translating his remarks. He hastened to add, 'It's a mighty smart chain – I believe my mother would like it – if you'll forgive me for being so forward, Ma'am.'

The jeweller threw up his hands and went to tidy a cabinet. He knew when a man was hooked. Nevertheless, a woman should not show a stranger a necklace which was worth twice what he had offered for it; she could be robbed. Then he shrugged. If she were that foolish, it wasn't his business. He took up a feather duster and began to dust the clocks in the cabinet.

At the mention of his mother, Tom was treated to a smile so delicious that he never quite recovered from it. He handed Leila out of the door and down the steps as if she were made of glass and then into a coffee shop two doors down the street.

Between coffee and pieces of pie and regrets that the necklace was too expensive for him to buy, he learned who she was and about her widowhood, her life in Beirut and in Chicago, and that she had a fourteen-year-old daughter. She told him frankly that she and her daughter both worked ten hours a day in a tailor's garret; she had had to beg the afternoon off in order to see the jeweller.

In return, he told her that he had been a miner and had gone west from Chicago, to work in gold mines. Then he had heard a rumour of gold easily panned in the North Saskatchewan River, in Canada. Hoping to stake a claim, he had travelled north with four men also bent on instant wealth.

'We knew that there was at least one Hudson's Bay Fort on the North Saskatchewan, and we reckoned we could make that our jumping-off place. A few other Americans had travelled part of the route before us; they sold liquor to the Injuns for furs.

'The trail wasn't very clear, and it was rough going. We did O.K., though, and we were well north, when we had to make a detour round a huge slough. I was lagging behind because I had to – well, Ma'am, relieve myself.'

There was a hint of impishness in her understanding smile.

Encouraged, he continued, 'And I'd got my eyes to the ground, watching where I trod between the bulrushes on one side and a lot of willows on the other – I guess they were willows. One minute I could hear the others shouting at me – and the next minute I couldn't; and the next thing I know the darned horse got mired, and I called and called to 'em to come help me out. And no answer.

'I couldn't get the animal out – the more it struggled, the deeper it went. Finally, I had to watch it drown.'

'Terrible, terrible,' Leila sympathized.

'I called and called to the other men. I was scared, I can tell you. Finally, I picked my way round the slough, but I'd no idea where I was. I couldn't find a hint of the trail; and I'd nothing – gun, blanket, beans and tools, all went down with the horse. When I couldn't even find the track of the others' horses, I must've gone stark mad. When the Blackfoot found me, I was clean out of my mind.'

'Blackfoot?' queried Leila, wide-eyed, her mouth open.

'Yeah. Injuns. A hunting party. They fed me and put me on a horse. I don't remember much about it – I was too far gone, I guess. Next thing I know truly is I'm in bed in Fort Edmonton, with a Cree woman nursing me better. She told me the Blackfoot simply dumped me at the gate of the Fort and rode away. She was a medicine woman sent for by the Cree wife of one of the Hudson's Bay clerks. I tell you, that old woman had me on my feet and sane very quick. I owe a lot to the Injuns up there – and I never forget it.'

'What happened to your friends?'

'Dunno. When I inquired around the Fort, they'd never arrived. Never heard of one of them from that day to this. Maybe they struck another Fort – or joined up with a group of whisky-runners. Or maybe they got lost, as well – and died.'

Leila nodded her head from side to side in wonderment. 'Terrible,' she repeated, it being the one word she knew in English to describe his experiences.

'We were plumb crazy to go north without a guide. We were miners, not explorers or even trappers.'

'What happen next?'

'Well, to be honest, I was afraid of the bush for a long time. So I stayed put, worked on the farm belonging to the Fort for a while, and got to know the land around so I wouldn't get lost again. Then I found a piece of land upriver, which the Bay seemed to have forgotten they owned. Somebody'd been there before – there was an old cabin there and I reroofed it, made a place to live. And I started clearing the land round it. After a while, I met up with a guy called Joe Black – and we worked together. We've got quite a homestead now – he's looking after it while I'm down here.' He took out a pipe and, without asking whether she minded the smoke, he lit up.

'You find gold?' she asked.

'Nope. I pan a bit out of the river sometimes – but nobody's ever found the mother lode.'

'Mother lode?' she queried in puzzlement, her smooth brow wrinkling slightly.

'The main vein of ore – gold, Ma'am.' He watched her delicately sipping her coffee. What a beauty she was! He wondered if she could endure a wilderness home, and told himself not to be a fool. She must be able to pick and choose the men she would take up with.

He plunged into conversation again. 'I don't make much in cash,' he admitted. 'But one way and another we mostly eat O.K. The worst years are over. We've two other men helping us now – both Crees. And Joe Black's mother came from working at the Fort, to help in the house. She's Cree, too.'

She dimpled, and inquired coyly, 'You're not married?'

'I was, Ma'am. Married a Cree lady – a nice, intelligent woman. But about a year ago, she died giving birth.' He sighed heavily.

'And the baby?'

'Little Wallace? He died a month later; it was a bitter winter and a lot of kids died – and old folk round the Fort.'

Remembering her own dead sons, Leila felt an overwhelming compassion for the man before her. Impulsively, she put out her hand and touched his arm. 'You suffer much.'

'I think you have, too, Ma'am.'

She nodded sad agreement.

He called for more coffee, and then began to describe the country he lived in, its superb beauty, the summers hot and comforting; he

58

omitted to mention the myriads of mosquitoes and blackfly in summer, the problems of getting water into the house during the harsh winter, the vast unexplored territory round the tiny settlement.

She listened in wonderment. It was obvious that the man loved his adopted home. She visualized it as country rather like that she had passed through on the train between New York and Chicago, which had seemed very empty to her in comparison with the Lebanon or even Britain. She watched his face which was leathery with exposure to the weather, and noted the grey in his moustache. He was a fine man, she felt, and her sex-starved body cried out with need, though she was thirty years old – quite old, she told herself.

By the time the fresh coffee had been consumed, Tom was telling himself there was no way he was going to let her go. She could adapt, like other immigrant women to the United States had done. 'She can take one more step in her life,' he assured himself, hope overwhelming his doubts.

He accompanied her home and left her on her doorstep, after agreeing to meet the following evening. Leila went up the stairs in a dream. She slowly took off her hat and laid it on the table. Helena was not yet home from work, so she flung herself on her daughter's bed, spread out her arms as if to embrace the world, and for the first time since she had come to Chicago, she laughed with pure joy.

8

A week later, Leila broke it to her daughter that she was seriously considering remarriage. Since Leila had already mentioned that she had met a very nice man, a Canadian, and had gone out to meet him every evening for the past week, Helena received the confidence without too much surprise. It did, however, sadden her that her own beloved father was to be replaced.

'It hurts, Sally,' she confided to her old friend, as they sat together on the bottom step of the staircase leading to Leila's tiny flat. The weather was thundery and the rooms upstairs stifling. Leila was out with Tom.

Sally took a pull at the cigarette hidden in the palm of her hand and slowly blew out the smoke. 'Your mother is a very beautiful person; it's bound to happen. She must like this guy particularly, though, because I know one or two who've approached her and she's turned them down.'

'Really?'

'Sure. I don't suppose your mother told you, because she wouldn't want to disturb you.' She did not say that the indignant young widow had probably turned the men down because their offers did not include marriage. Mrs Al-Khoury had asked Sally if such offers were customary, and Sally had replied, with a grin, that they were common enough, but you didn't have to accept them. Now Sally put her arm round Helena and reminded her that, when she herself married, Leila would be alone. 'I suppose,' Helena had replied uneasily, and had tried to accept the possible change in her life.

Leila stitched her necklace back into her black skirt. Then she told Helena that she had accepted Tom's offer of marriage, and that they would all be moving to western Canada, probably within the month.

'But, Mama!' Helena gasped. 'You said before you couldn't move to another country! What are you thinking of? Couldn't Tom live here?'

Leila's agitation was immediately apparent. 'He says he can't, dear; he's too much at stake in Canada – and he loves the country.' She lifted her hands in a small helpless gesture and let them sink into her lap.

'Well, you don't have to marry *him*! There're other men in Chicago, surely, Mama? I've got used to Chicago now – and so have you.'

'I don't want to marry anyone else,' Leila replied, almost crossly. 'Marriage is very special, very personal.'

'I know that!' Helena's pinched little face was taut with suppressed fear of the unknown. 'If he wants you, he can stay here,' she said resentfully.

'I've asked him, dear. But he either won't or can't. And I can't let him go.'

'Why not?'

'Because I love him very, very much.'

This silenced Helena. Falling in love was something that occurred in books. It had never occurred to her that it might happen to her mother – or, possibly, to herself. In Lebanon, you accepted gratefully the husband chosen for you by wise parents and then hoped he would be kind to you.

Emboldened by her daughter's sudden quiet, Leila said, 'Consider, my darling, how very poor we are. Where will I get the chance again to meet a really nice man – and he is nice.'

Stifling a desire to cry, Helena nodded dumbly. Their current life was very hard and seemed to lack all hope of change, at least until her mother's command of English improved. She could understand that, to her mother, Tom Harding offered an escape from total penury. But to what?

'Has he told you about where he lives?' she asked dully.

'Yes, he has. And it sounds possible, with a good future for you.'

Three weeks later, a numbed Helena found herself in a Registrar's office, standing behind her mother and acting as her bridesmaid, while next to her was Glenn, a rotund version of Tom Harding, acting as his brother's best man. Behind them stood Sally and Mrs Ghanem and one or two friends of Tom and Glenn. Seated in a chair specially set for her was Tom's scary old mother, anxiously attended by plump, harassed Ada Harding, Glenn's wife.

Old Mrs Harding had already told her besotted son, in front of his new fiancée and her daughter, that he was a fool and always had been one; these women would be no use to him in a pioneer settlement. She had been a pioneer herself and knew what it was like.

Helena had listened to her with growing disillusionment. Leila had been as terrified as if she had been cursed by a witch, and it had taken all Tom's cajolement to assure her that his friend Joe's mother lived on the homestead and would come every day to help her. To beguile her, he said he had a little sleigh which she could learn to drive in winter, and that Helena could go to school, either in St Albert, where there was a Roman Catholic Mission, or in the Fort.

On the eve of the wedding, Helena had sat with her mother in their bare, tiny living-room, while Leila unpacked a beautiful, embroidered head shawl, delivered by Mrs Ghanem's eldest son, with the family's good wishes for the marriage. Helena, seeing the fine Lebanese handiwork of the shawl, had put her head down on the table and wept.

'Couldn't we go home to Beirut, Mama? Please, Mama.' She spoke, as usual when addressing Leila, in Arabic, and the words seemed all the more poignant because of the language used.

'Darling child, you know I've thought of that often, but the times are bad. Even if we weren't murdered by either the Druze or the Turks, a widow woman, with no family to protect her, wouldn't stand a chance.' She put down the shawl and moved round the table, to hold Helena in a warm embrace.

With her head resting on her child's thick black hair, she said frankly, 'I don't know what life holds for us, my love. But I feel Tom is honest and kind; and he has high hopes of giving you a better life. He says there is a great shortage of women round the Fort, so you should be able to make a good marriage when the time comes.' Her voice trailed off, but she continued to hold the girl close to her. She was herself very nervous. She was also desperately in love – and she had no conception of wilderness barely touched by human hands.

Helena did not reply to her mother's assurances. She wept for her father. Through her tears, she looked down at her hands. Her left forefinger was raw from constant pricks from blunted pins and needles at the tailor's workroom, and she remembered the long, dreary days she spent penned up there. If she stayed in Chicago, would that go on forever?

She raised her head. 'How do we know he's even got a farm?' she asked, as she fumbled in her skirt pocket for her handkerchief.

'Well, I've done my best to confirm it. You know that young lawyer on Main Street? He's originally from Lebanon. I asked him if he could inquire for me.'

Surprised at her mother's temerity, Helena glanced up at her. 'What did he find out?'

'Well, he confirmed that Tom's brother has a good reputation – it's been known for years that he had a brother homesteading in Canada. There's nothing to prove it, of course, but a neighbour told him that a few years back Tom asked his mother to join him. She didn't go because her health's so bad. The neighbour also said that the old lady is all against the marriage, because she says I won't be able to work hard enough; I'll be a burden to him.'

A small smile curved Helena's mouth. 'I doubt that, Mama. I think you'll make him very happy.'

Her mother bent and kissed her. 'Thank you, dear.' She paused, and then said, 'The lawyer also advised that Tom should make a Will, to be signed at the end of the wedding ceremony, leaving everything to me, if he should die – which God forbid. Tom's going to do this, so at least we'd have a farm, dearest.'

Though Tom agreed to the Will, he omitted to tell her that he was, as yet, still a squatter and that the Hudson's Bay Company still owned the land; he hoped sincerely that he would gain ownership before he died.

Later on that evening, when Tom came to spend an hour or two with Leila, he tried to reassure the girl.

'The Fathers will teach you school,' he told her. 'And Joe Black or me – we'll teach you how to skate and ride. And you can have a pup if you'd like one.'

She replied heavily, 'I can already read and write in French and Arabic. English is coming. And Papa taught me arithmetic and how to keep accounts – some geography, as well. And how to buy and sell – and judge silk.'

'Then you're a very accomplished young lady,' responded Tom patiently. 'I could use your help, if you'd give it me.'

Though he had caught her interest, Helena looked at him with suspicion. 'Help you?'

'Sure. I can get folks to do all kinds of chores – but Joe and me – neither of us is good at accounts, keeping records and such. And, one of these days I reckon the British Government's going to reach out and take over from the Hudson's Bay Company, which rules us now – and we'll have a pack of Government officials on our backs – and we'll need everything down in pen and ink.'

Helena smiled involuntarily. 'Just like the Turks?' she asked with sudden interest.

Tom did not understand what she was referring to and turned to Leila for enlightenment. Leila told him about the avaricious tax collectors of the Turkish Emperor, and he laughed. 'You've hit it right on,' he told Helena, which made her smile again.

Realizing that much of his and Leila's happiness depended upon Helena being reasonably content, he spent until midnight telling her about the Fort and his homestead. He also told her that he had married a Cree wife, and that the loss of her and of his son had been hard to bear. 'Cree women know how to preserve meat, and how to make clothes out of skins – and how to cure sickness,' he said. 'Joe's Ma is a

63

Cree, and she came to help us when my wife died – and she'll help your Mama, so that it won't be too hard for you.' In the back of his mind, he fretted that two more mouths to feed that winter could be a problem, and he hoped the pig had produced a good litter.

Watching the man as he spoke, Helena felt a sense of pity creep into her. He, also, had lost people he loved, she realized, and she felt a hint of kinship.

He was saying to her, 'I can't make up to you for your pa – I wouldn't presume to. But I'll take care of you as much as I can. You *could* be the only youngster your mama and I'll have.'

The inference that her mother could have more children shocked Helena. She looked up at her mother, who smiled quietly back. It could happen, she realized. She turned to Tom. His expression was quite sad. He said suddenly, 'I'd like to give you an extra name, in memory of my little boy. Then you'd be real special to me. I'd like to call you Wallace Helena.'

She was immediately offended. 'That's a boy's name.'

'It's a boy's or a girl's. We called the baby after my mother – she's Wallace Harding.'

'I don't need another name.' The wide mouth compressed in disapproval.

'Aw, come on, now. Indulge an old man's fancy.'

Helena looked up at her mother again. 'Do I have to, Mama?'

Her mother's mouth began to tremble, as it always did when she was in doubt. Helena saw it and remembered suddenly how close her mother had come to a complete breakdown after her father's death. She considered warily what might happen if she refused Tom's absurd idea. For a moment, she thought that if she raised a tremendous fuss about it, the whole engagement might be broken off, something she had been praying for for the last four weeks.

The silence between the three of them became tense. Helena's hands were clenched, her mother's eyes wide and despairing.

She understood her mother's passion for this man, and that if the couple married she herself would be dependent upon Tom's goodwill – not something she desired at all. But if she succeeded in breaking the liaison, what else was there? A dreadful servitude, unless she herself could marry decently – and she, like her mother, had discovered that in Chicago she ranked as a coloured girl, not suitable for marriage to a white man. She bit her lips as she bitterly considered this fact, and that there were few boys of her age within the Lebanese community and probably none who would want a penniless girl. She was poor and plain and yellow, she told herself, and without any alternative future worth having.

She took a big breath, and said unsmilingly, 'I don't suppose it makes much difference.'

'Well, that's nice of you,' Tom told her, thankful that he had not alienated her; he had regretted his impulsive request the moment he had made it. Leila had, however, been strangely silent when he had casually mentioned the children they would have.

When pressed, she had said, with a faint smile, 'Let's not worry – see what God sends.'

He wanted another son, but it seemed suddenly possible to him that he would not have one. At the thought, he had urgently wanted to perpetuate the memory of the small brown innocent buried with his mother in the black earth of the north pasture. It had occurred to him that he could give the child's name to his stepdaughter and make her Wallace Helena.

When he was leaving, he shook the girl's hand, then held it for a moment, as he looked down at her. 'You won't regret it, honey,' he said warmly.

Wallace Helena smiled up at him wanly. He seemed to her a simple, honest man – but she wanted to cry.

9

Glenn and Ada Harding provided a modest wedding breakfast in their back garden. Since it was a second marriage, only a few neighbours had been invited over to join the party. All of them were curious to see the bride. The men thought she was very pretty and congratulated Tom; the women tended to side with old Mrs Harding in saying that she was not strong enough to be the wife of a homesteader – and they whispered disparagingly that she looked like a Jewess. Acutely embarrassed by their stares, Leila held the soft brim of her summer hat close to her face and stayed very close to Tom.

The bride's daughter sat, almost unnoticed, on a bench under a tree. Sally, who was herself totally ignored by the other guests, saw the forlorn young girl, and came over to join her. She saw tears on Wallace Helena's cheek and she immediately handed her the glass of wine she was carrying. 'Drink it down, hon. You'll feel better.'

As Wallace Helena silently drained the glass, Sally carefully arranged the skirts of her dress; she had made it out of the bits of black silk Wallace Helena had given her. She looked over at the bride, who was also wearing black silk. 'Gee, your mama looks pretty,' she exclaimed, as if she was seeing Leila for the first time.

'Yes,' agreed Wallace Helena, without enthusiasm. Far more astute than her mother, she foresaw problems arising like thunderclouds – and probably considerable hardship in an unexplored country like Canada. Yet, what could she do?

When she had suggested to Sally that perhaps she should remain by herself in Chicago, try to earn enough to keep herself, Sally had been very explicit about what was likely to happen to a fourteen-year-old left alone in a city.

Sally had added sharply, 'You be thankful your ma's found a decent man to take care of you both; I wish I could find someone like him. There isn't nothing to fear about Canada; slaves run away to it, so as to be free.'

'Do they? Could you come with us, Sally? Could you?' Her voice was suddenly wild with hope.

The black woman had laughed down at her. 'That Mr Harding don't need another mouth to feed, baby. And I got my mother to keep. I'm no slave – I'm free.' She had given Wallace Helena a playful shove with her elbow, as she said the last words. 'He's O.K. Be thankful he's willing to take you in.' She hesitated, and then said, 'He'll take care of you; he'll never touch you, I truly believe.'

Wallace Helena did not understand the import of Sally's last words; she was still overwhelmed at having to face another new country.

Old Mrs Harding did one very sensible thing for them. Realizing that she could not talk sense into Tom, as she put it, she persuaded Leila and Wallace Helena to buy a solid pair of flat-heeled boots each and enough veiling to attach to their hats, so that they were protected in some degree from blackfly and mosquitoes – and she ordered Tom to pay the bill.

In the course of their journey, which took weeks, both Leila and Wallace Helena had reason to be thankful to her: mosquitoes and blackfly plagued them most of the way. They went by train to La Crosse, then by stage to the Red River, and, despite the threat of yet another Sioux uprising, by paddle steamer to Fort Garry. There they rested for a couple of days, while Tom made inquiries. They were not very impressed by what they saw of their first Hudson's Bay Fort, and awaited with anxiety Tom's decision as to how they were to proceed. Their landlady, the wife of a miner who ran a small general store, was aghast when told where they were going; as far as she knew, only one white woman had ever travelled that far, and she was the wife of a Hudson's Bay man.

Leila wept, and Wallace Helena begged Tom to take them back to Chicago. Tom laughed, cheered them up and said they would travel by York boat. Several expeditions had gone out recently from Fort Garry to Fort Edmonton by land; but he was not going to chance such a dangerous journey.

The sail up Lake Winnipeg was not unpleasant. But the rest of the journey was done by York boat up the Saskatchewan River, a long dreary drag with little but pemmican to eat, cooped up in a tiny boat, one of a Company brigade returning to Fort Edmonton with stores.

To Leila's horror, the boats were from time to time dragged out of the river, their cargo unloaded and transported on the backs of the voyageurs, to bypass waterfalls or rapids. The boats themselves were hauled along rough tracks, sometimes made of tree trunks and sometimes a well-trodden path. During these portages, Leila and Wallace Helena stumbled along as best they could, following the crew for mile after mile. Despite the heavy veiling protecting their faces and necks, they were badly bitten by mosquitoes and blackfly, which rose like a fog around them at every step; Tom and the other men seemed to have a certain immunity – their bites did not swell so badly. The crew were Metis, short, tanned, muscular men who cursed in fluent French, as they waged their usual battle against the flow of the huge river.

Leila was not a heavy woman, but what fat she had fell off her. She looked so gaunt that both Wallace Helena and Tom began to wonder if she could survive the journey.

Wallace Helena had, at first, thought that she herself would not survive, but the arduous exercise and adequate rations of pemmican actually began to improve her health. She was filthy dirty and nearly insane from the incessant insect bites, and she longed for some privacy, if only to wash herself down in the cold river water. The men did try their best to provide a little privacy, inasmuch as they turned their backs when the women had to relieve themselves, but they had a tight, fixed schedule to follow, and very little time was spent ashore. No special allowance was made for the fact that they had women with them. The party was soaked through by rain and, on one occasion, by sleet. 'Lucky it hasn't hailed,' remarked one man to Wallace Helena. 'Sometimes it hails heavy enough to bruise you.'

When the wind was in the right quarter, sails were rigged to ease the amount of poling which the men had to do; it also temporarily scattered the mosquitoes. Wallace Helena thought that she had never seen men work so hard for a living; yet they remained fairly good-humoured with each other. They were surprised that both women spoke French, admittedly very different from their own patois, but nevertheless enough for both sides to make rueful jokes about their suffering.

Towards the end of the journey, Leila showed signs of having a fever, and Wallace Helena's heart sank. Wrapped in a blanket, she lay shivering beside her daughter, talking sometimes of the old days in Beirut or of her worries about Wallace Helena's future, her mind wandering so that she did not know where she was.

It seemed to Wallace Helena that she had been crammed in the hated boat for months and that the journey would never end. She felt furiously that Tom had embroiled them in an expedition that nobody should be expected to make.

'What if Mother dies?' she asked him desperately.

Dog-tired himself, Tom could not answer her. Although he knew the journey to be gruelling, he had not realized how profoundly different was the strength of his late Indian wife compared with that of city-bred women. He had expected his new wife to complain about the hardship, but he had not thought that it would be unbearable. Wallace Helena had only to see the anguish in his eyes to know that her dread of losing Leila was shared.

Then, when both women had nearly given up hope, it seemed that an air of cheerfulness went from man to man, an excited anticipation. The man in charge of their craft told Wallace Helena, 'Tomorrow, we'll land for a little while – get a chance to wash and stretch ourselves.' He looked at Leila, lying wrapped in a blanket in an acutely uncomfortable position towards the stern of the boat, and added kindly, 'We'll get a fire going when we're ashore, and I'll make a bit of broth for your mother.'

Wallace Helena smiled her gratitude; the man himself looked exhausted. 'Why are we stopping?'

'We have to make ourselves look decent – for when we arrive at the Fort!'

'You mean we're nearly there?' Her filthy face lit up.

'Be there tomorrow night, God willing.'

'Thank God!' Wallace Helena said, and meant it. 'Would you tell my stepfather?' she asked, pointing towards the rowers, where Tom had taken an oar and was rowing with a kind of deadly mechanical rhythm, his eyes half-shut; it was heavy work, and he was almost oblivious of what was going on around him.

He nodded, and she turned round and carefully eased herself closer to the tiny moribund bundle which was her mother, to tell her the good news.

As promised, the voyageur made a soup for Leila. While Tom built a fire, the man cut up some pemmican and put it into an iron pot with water and some bits of chopped-up greenery which he had hastily gathered. A tripod was rigged over the fire and the pot hung on it. When he considered it ready, he added a little rum; and Wallace Helena spooned the resultant soup into her barely coherent mother lying by the fire.

There was much scrubbing of faces and hands in the chilly waters of the river; one or two men sharpened their knives and roughly shaved themselves. Then, fortified with rum, they poled the last few miles. Several canoes came out to greet them, and there was a small crowd waiting for them when they landed at the foot of an escarpment.

The crowd was dumbfounded when Wallace Helena stepped ashore, followed by Tom carrying her mother.

The Factor was furious when he heard that he had two women from Chicago resting for the night in *his* fort; didn't his boatmen know that settlers were not to be encouraged? Tom Harding had been a big enough nuisance, an American carving out a piece of Hudson's Bay land to farm. Now he'd brought a white wife – and her daughter. Other women would follow them; there was already a rumour that a missionary's wife

69

would be arriving in the district one of these days. Settlers would clear the land, ruin the fur trade. What were his men about?

Leila was put to bed in a comfortable cabin by the Indian wife of an acquaintance of Tom's, and, afterwards, she brought Wallace Helena a bucket of hot water in which to wash herself. Tom was sent for immediately to attend the Factor at the Big House.

Tall and silent, an exhausted, worried Tom was harangued in the man's office. Both men were aware, however, that it was largely bombast; the British Government had left the renewal of the Hudson's Bay Company's Charter up in the air, when it had been discussed in 1858; and already Government survey parties were beginning to penetrate the Bay's kingdom; a few people, some American, had begun to settle.

Despite the hardships of his life, Tom loved his land and dreaded being driven off it by the Company; so, when the Factor had finished what he had to say, Tom politely told him that he missed his dead wife and son, and now sought to rebuild his family. He would be transferring his wife to his cabin in the morning – he carefully did not use the word *homestead* which would have implied his ownership of a piece of land claimed by the Company as their own.

The Factor had kept Tom standing and had offered him no hospitality, so Tom felt free to turn on his heel and walk out.

10

Word of the arrival of the brigade was brought to Joe while he was bringing the small herd of cattle he and Tom possessed closer in to the homestead. He had heard a rumour of a party of Blackfoot roaming the area, and he assumed that they had penetrated so far into Cree country because buffalo were getting scarce and they were hungry. He had no desire to have his precious beasts eaten by them.

The boy who brought the message was a Metis, the son of a friend of Joe's working as a cooper in the Fort. While he got his breath after jogging most of the way, he hung on to Joe's stirrup. Then he burst out, 'Mr Harding's with them. Brought a new wife, a white woman, and her daughter. Says to ask your mother to have the place neat and prepare some food. One woman's sick.'

'You're kidding?' exclaimed Joe, well aware of the Crees' sense of humour – and this youngster was half-Cree.

The lad was offended. 'I'm not,' he responded crossly. 'I saw them. They'll be at your place about midday tomorrow.'

Joe sat on his horse and stared down at him. 'I'll be damned!' he muttered.

He roused himself, and drew out a wad of chewing tobacco from his top pocket. He took out his knife and cut a generous piece of it which he handed down to the boy, with his thanks. 'Like to go down to the cabin and have something to eat?' he asked.

'No. Dad wants me back.' The boy let go of the stirrup. 'Mr Harding says not to send horses; he's borrowing two and a cart – from Mr Ermineskin.'

Joe nodded, and handed the boy his water bottle so that he could take a swing. After he had drunk, the young messenger said he would sit under a nearby tree for a few minutes to rest and then go home.

Joe finished the job of persuading his steers into the home pasture, and then rode down to the cabin to break the astonishing news to his mother, Agnes Black. The bachelor home had a very fast tidying up.

Late the following morning, when Joe cantered down the narrow trail towards Edmonton to meet his friend, he could hear the ear-splitting shriek of the ungreased wheels of the Red River cart accompanying Tom, long before he saw him.

The wind was quite brisk and the mosquitoes were few. The breeze was whipping the leaves off the trees, and it was through a sudden storm of them that he caught his first glimpse of Leila, barely visible amid shawls and veils. Tom was riding a heavy, black horse and held her in the crook of his arm in front of him.

Behind him, clutching the reins of a smaller animal, rode a scarecrow of a young girl. She had thrown back the veil of the hat perched on the back of her head, to reveal a sallow face so thin that it seemed to consist of two enormous brown eyes surrounded by masses of newly washed black hair; soft strands of it blew across her hollow cheeks.

For a second, Joe ignored his grinning friend. As Wallace Helena approached and caught sight of him, he saw the desolation in the girl's wonderful eyes suddenly replaced by intense fear. It seemed to him that, on seeing him, she reined in her horse instinctively, and half-glanced back along the trail as if to escape.

Uncertain himself, Joe stopped his own horse and dismounted, to wait until Tom reached him. The infernal shriek of the cart behind slowed and ceased.

'Hullo, there,' said Joe carefully to the party. 'Glad to see you.'

A small hand emerged from the shawls in front of Tom, and Leila smiled shyly at him. Although she looked very wan, Joe understood immediately what had captured Tom. She was a beauty. He turned to look at Tom, whose lined, suntanned visage went suddenly bright red with embarrassment. He managed to say, 'Hi, Joe. Good to see you again.' Then he looked down at Leila and said, 'This is my wife.'

Joe raised his hand in salute to her, and said to Tom, 'Congratulations! Du Pont's son told me the news.'

He turned towards Wallace Helena, who was regarding him cautiously from under her long fringe of lashes. He grinned up at her, and asked Tom, 'And this lady?'

'My stepdaughter, Wallace Helena.'

Joe's eyebrows lifted slightly at the familiar first name. He then raised his hand again to salute her. His eyes twinkled cheerfully, and he was glad to see her relax slightly, as he said, 'Nice to meet you, Miss. Hope you and your ma'll be happy here.'

She nodded, and replied in a shy whisper, 'Thank you.'

Because the path was too narrow to ride abreast, Joe remounted his horse to lead them back to the cabin. The cart resumed its terrible shriek, making any communication impossible. News would have to wait.

Thanks to Jeanette, her hostess of the previous night, a bathed and tidy Leila managed to walk across the threshold of the cabin which was to be her home for the rest of her life.

As she entered on her husband's arm, she paused. The room seemed quite large to her and, except for the hunting and trapping gear hanging on the walls, looked more comfortable than the miserable apartment they had left in Chicago.

During the night just past, her mind had cleared of the fever, and she had come to the conclusion that, whatever awaited her here, it could not be worse than the traumatic journey she had barely survived. Here were four solid walls to protect her from the jungle outside.

With timid determination, she surveyed the cabin's interior. If she could regain her strength, she would make it into a real home for the husband of her choice.

She looked up at Tom and smiled shyly. 'You have a nice home,' she lied.

Very thankfully, he squeezed her arm, as Agnes Black, another shy person, came out of the lean-to summer kitchen. She was a heavily built, short woman, garbed in a full, printed cotton skirt and a black blouse. On her feet, she wore shabby skin slippers. As she waited for Leila to speak to her, she pushed wisps of grey hair away from a face like a raisin. Her black eyes gleamed in the firelight.

Leila had not forgotten old Mrs Harding's remark that she would be no use as a pioneer's wife, and she realized that she would be dependent upon this quiet, foreign woman to show her how to do practically everything. She smiled at her and said slowly to her, in poor English, 'I am glad you here.'

The genuine relief expressed in the words touched the Indian woman. She made a small gesture towards the hearth where a pot of coffee was keeping warm before the fire. 'I've made coffee for you,' she said simply.

Leila nodded and smiled again, and Tom propelled her towards a roughly made wooden chair. She sat down thankfully and closed her eyes; tears of weakness eased out from under the lids.

She wondered how Tom could expose her to such a terrible journey. Yet, when he held a mug of coffee to her lips and she opened her eyes, to see him peering anxiously at her, a warmth coursed through her feeble frame. She drank the coffee slowly, allowing him to continue to hold the mug.

Wallace Helena and Joe Black had followed Leila and Tom into the cabin. Joe took his boots off at the door, so Wallace Helena did the same. Her eyes were wide with apprehension as she looked round her new home. She felt at a loss, almost unable to cope with anything more that was new to her.

Joe's mother poured cups of coffee for them and they sat down, side by side, on a bench to drink it. Most of the attention was focused on Leila, resting in the curve of her husband's arm.

Joe said something in Cree to his mother. She nodded, and asked Tom in the same language if his wife would like to lie down. What was her sickness?

Tom explained about the fever, and Agnes asked if she would like to have a draught which she could concoct; it would help her to sleep and relieve any fever remaining.

Leila was a little reluctant to take a strange medicine, but Tom assured her that Agnes was known for her ability to heal. She was persuaded to lie on his bed to rest, in a tiny, doorless room at one side of the cabin, and after supper she sipped down the bitter mixture which Agnes brought to her. Covered by buffalo robes, she slept for fifteen hours.

Meanwhile, Agnes, apparently unruffled by the addition of two females to the household, showed Wallace Helena the summer kitchen and the clay oven outside, in which she baked rough barley bread.

They inspected an adjacent store house, which had a hole dug into its earthen floor. 'When the river has frozen, Joe cuts out blocks of ice and lines the hole with them – it lengthens the time we can store raw meat,' she explained in halting English. The hut also held smoked fish, pemmican and various boxes and barrels collected over the years to store vegetables in.

Outside the cabin itself, against one wall, was a pile of roughly hewn logs. A middle-aged Indian with long thin plaits on either side of his face was stolidly swinging an axe, as he reduced the trunk of a tree to logs. He paused, put down his axe and leaned on it, as they approached. 'Simon Wounded,' explained Agnes. She spoke in Cree to the man, and he nodded understanding. He did not look directly at Wallace Helena, but lifted his axe again and continued his work.

'He lives with Joe and me over there.' Agnes pointed to a shack on the other side of the muddy yard. She turned and pointed again to a bigger building. 'That's the barn.' They walked over to inspect it and disturbed a flurry of hens.

Agnes showed her the outhouse behind the cabin, and then they returned to the cabin.

While Agnes watched her with some amusement, Wallace Helena walked slowly round it to examine the amazing collection of implements, pieces of harness, lanterns, clothes and wraps on the walls. There were guns on a rack over the fireplace, and shelves at man-height were littered with caps, hats, old boots and shoes, tools, a shaving mug, what looked like folded skins, and a series of beautifully woven round baskets. From the beams hung what Wallace Helena imagined must be traps for small animals, side by side with bunches of herbs, several bunches of onions and two flitches of bacon. Agnes pointed to the latter, and said, 'I finished smoking them a while back. Tomorrow, Tom'll probably find time to make a space in the store house for them.'

Wallace Helena nodded. Despite the clutter, the place had a sense of being a home, long-established and cosy.

As she helped Agnes prepare an evening meal, and Tom went round his domain with Joe, to hear all that had happened in his absence, Wallace Helena began to emerge from the desolation and fear which had gripped her for so long.

She did not like what she saw, but Agnes's quiet competence assured her that there was an organized way of life in the isolated homestead, probably a more dependable one than that they had endured in Chicago.

Sensing the girl's uncertainties, Agnes told her about life inside the Fort, and that there were other forts strung across the country, with which the Company kept in touch. The boats plying the river brought them news from Fort Garry and York House, on Hudson Bay. 'And from London, where they say the Great Queen lives,' she added.

Wallace Helena was impressed and comforted; they were not quite so alone as she had imagined. Good weather also helped her; the autumn skies were a flawless blue and the leaves on the deciduous trees and bushes flaunted their reds and yellows. There was little hint of the bitterness of the winter to come.

Leila stayed in bed for most of the first few days in her new home. Then, as her strength returned, she got up and slowly explored the immediate environs of the cabin. In her soft, poor English, she asked quiet questions of Agnes Black and Simon Wounded about their daily tasks and listened respectfully to their replies. She asked Tom details about what was required to prepare for the winter, which, she had gathered from Agnes, was very severe. Once it was apparent to Wallace Helena that her mother was beginning to take charge of her new domain, she thankfully left her in the stuffy cabin and went out with Joe and Tom. She had ridden once or twice in the mountains behind Beirut but it took her some time to control the pony on which Joe mounted her. With a good deal of laughter, she learned to stay on it and became devoted to it.

Being short of labour because of Tom's absence, they were late in getting in the last of the oats and potatoes, so Wallace Helena fetched and carried for all three men, who worked from dawn to dusk. She also helped Agnes raise water from the well, a long, slow job of lowering a bucket on a rope and hauling it up again. Agnes assured her that it was easier than carrying bucketfuls on a yoke, from the river.

She slept in a bunk in the living-room, so tired that she was not even haunted by her usual nightmare about the little boy she had seen dying in a lane in Beirut.

Though almost overwhelmed by the length and harshness of the journey, Wallace Helena had, throughout, followed Sally's advice with regard to her new stepfather; she had set out to make a friend of him.

A kindly man, worried to death about his new wife's health, Tom Harding thankfully met her half way. It was not an easy adjustment; they sometimes found themselves at loggerheads. Wallace Helena was understandably resentful that she had been replaced by the quiet American as first in her mother's affections.

For his part, Tom remembered his own terror of the empty wilderness, when he had become lost en route to Fort Edmonton. He sympathized with Wallace Helena's obvious fear of the strange, primitive world in which she now found herself. To help her in adjusting, he asked Agnes and Joe Black to be particularly patient with her. Though Wallace Helena was largely unaware of their solicitude, she began to relax with them and to talk to them.

It dawned slowly on Wallace Helena that, though everybody in this untamed land was subject to the vagaries of weather, forest fires, angry Indians and clouds of insects, she was herself much more free than she would have been as the daughter of a Beirut silk merchant. When she considered what her life would have been like had she returned to Lebanon after living in Chicago, she knew she would have found it difficult to endure such a protective environment. Yet, like other immigrants, she often wept, and longed to hear her own language, her own music, have books in Arabic to read, and be able to wear her soft, light native dress. The extraordinary lack of people also bothered her, and she once asked Joe lightly, 'If all the people in all Rupert's Land met together, would they form a decent crowd?'

'Well,' he drawled softly, 'there's plenty of Indians – only they don't build forts or homesteads; they can pack up a camp and move on – and a few months later you wouldn't know they'd been here. You'll see some of them, when they come in to trade at the Fort.'

She asked him what they traded, and so began a long period of learning the background of Indians, Metis and Europeans, now face-to-face in the land which she had, at first, believed to be empty. It was also the beginning of a great friendship with the big, dark man.

11

The outdoor work in pure cool air acted as an anodyne to Wallace Helena's sense of loss, yet again, of her roots. Being young, she had begun to be accustomed to Chicago; faces of fellow immigrants had become familiar to her and she had made a devoted friend in Sally. Her father's little shop had begun to prosper. Within their tiny apartment they ate Lebanese food and spoke Arabic. The day her father died her small hopes had shattered; yet there remained the familiarity of place and neighbours.

Now, she and her mother had to start again. Leila had Tom to console her. Wallace Helena mourned for her father, and wondered if she would ever know again a peaceful life such as they had enjoyed in Beirut until the day of the massacre.

After living in cities, the immensity of the empty land appalled and terrified her; even the mountains of Lebanon did not have the close-packed, silent forests that the Territories had. Her journey by York boat had given her an idea of the hugeness of the country, and, though Agnes had comforted her by telling her of other forts and other settlements further east, she could, for a long time, be suddenly seized by an unreasoning terror of the unknown. When, once or twice, she rode along the old trail following the river bank to the Fort and saw it from a short distance as they came to land that had been cleared, it looked too puny to survive, a tiny anthill liable to be blown out of existence by the merciless gales. Closer to the river, below the Fort, there were usually a few small boats drawn up on the beach, and when she considered the hundreds of miles of river she had seen, they looked like little cockleshells, too small to take her back to civilization, even if she had a place to go to.

The days became sharply colder; the mud of the yard froze to an uneven lumpiness; the breath of men and animals hung like a mist in the air and the snow drifted down on the roofs, first a skiff of it, then short flurries and then the occasional storm. It did not melt but piled high enough for it to be necessary to dig paths to the barn, to the windbreak where the steers huddled against the rough shelter to keep warm, to the privy and to Joe's and Agnes's shack.

Fearing that the roofs might collapse with the weight of the snow,

Joe and Tom several times during the winter climbed up to shovel some of it off. They were watched by both Wallace Helena and Leila with some apprehension for fear they would fall; broken bones could spell disaster for all of them. As the cold increased, their world became the yard and the buildings round it and the steers nearby. Occasionally, Wallace Helena would struggle down the slope to look at the white expanse of the river. Sometimes, there were the marks of a sleigh in the snow covering the ice, and once she saw one and waved to the musher, thankful to greet another person. He raised his whip in salute and she stood and listened to the occasional yap of the dogs as they vanished upriver.

Though she tried to keep a bright face for her mother and Tom and Joe, her courage sometimes failed her. In the privacy of the barn, when she went to feed Peggy, her piebald pony, she would, now and then, lay her head against the animal's blanketed flanks and weep.

Joe found her there, one night, sobbing quietly as she shovelled manure away from the animal, in the light of a lantern flickering on a shelf. He took the shovel away from her and leaned it against the wall. Anxious to stem the passionate tears, he put his arm round her. She put her head against his wolfskin jacket and cried, innocently unaware of the feelings engendered in him, 'It's so lonely, Joe.'

He patted her back as he held her. 'It's not so lonely as you think,' he assured her. 'You've got your ma and Tom and me – and Agnes and Simon.' He rocked her gently from side to side, and his voice was a little thick, as he continued, 'This cold spell will pass and we'll get a chinook wind; that'll send the temperature up.' The sobs began to ease, and he lifted her chin with one hand to look at her face. 'Don't cry, honey. Christmas will soon be here, and if your ma's well enough, we'll get out the sleigh and go to the dancing at the Fort.'

She smiled wanly at him, and said, 'Sally used to call me Honey.'

She felt the great barrel of his chest shudder, as he laughed down at her. 'Did she? Who's she?'

He let her go as she began to tell him. While she spoke, he took up the shovel and finished the job of moving the manure.

'Well,' he said slowly, 'you could write to her, if you know her address. Mail goes in and outta here twice a year at least. Mebbe she'd write back to you.'

'Really? Could I write to Uncle James in Liverpool – in England?'

'I don't see why not. The Bay carries letters for Tom, down into the States.' He hung the shovel on its hook and prepared to help her across the yard.

He had caught her interest. She rubbed the tears out of her eyes, and her expression was suddenly animated.

'I'll ask Tom if he can spare a piece of paper to write on. Mama might like to write as well.'

'Sure. Tom'll spare you a sheet – he keeps some to write his ma.'

He opened the small side door of the barn, and they fought to shut it again after them, while the wind tore at it. The cold hit them, and he put his arm round her to steady her across the yard.

Wallace Helena had been quiet as they battled their way to the cabin door. Now with her hand on the latch, she turned to Joe, and asked him without preamble, 'Joe, could you teach me Cree? Then I could talk to the Indians. When that band came through in the autumn, you and Tom had a good laugh with them. But I couldn't understand a word.' She pulled her scarf up over her mouth against the cold, though they were standing in the lee of the cabin.

Surprised, he said, 'Sure. I'll try.'

'Thanks, Joe.'

The big eyes narrowed in a smile of gratitude, as she lifted the latch. 'Goodnight, Joe.'

He nodded and turned away. Heavy with uneasy thoughts, he went over to his mother's cabin by the barn. Up till then he had enjoyed his bachelorhood; when food had been in better supply, he had gone to parties and special celebrations given by local Crees and had sometimes roistered with young Metis down at the Fort. Though women were a little scarce, there was usually someone happy to lie with a handsome man for a small consideration. When Tom had married for the first time, it had stretched the resources of the fledgling homestead to its limits, and Joe had decided that since there was no one whom he particularly fancied he would stay single for a bit longer.

That evening, as he sat cross-legged making a pair of snowshoes for Wallace Helena, he began to think differently. As he carefully twisted and knotted the gut in the snowshoes, he sighed. He was twenty-seven years old – getting on – to her fourteen; and, though Tom Harding spoke of him as his partner, he knew that Tom regarded the homestead as his, and Joe got his keep and a small share of any cash that came along – as wages. Only the money he earned from his trapline was his own, and furbearing animals got scarcer every winter.

He told himself not to be a fool.

12

A few days later, just before Christmas, Leila asked Tom if he would take her down to the Fort to see Jeanette, who had kindly put her up on the night of her arrival at Fort Edmonton. It seemed warmer outside and the snow was not too deep on the trail, so Tom amiably agreed. Joe had gone to tend his trapline.

Eager for a change, Wallace Helena begged to go with them, so the sleigh was got down from the wall of the barn and, with hot bricks to their feet and blankets and a buffalo robe tucked round them, the women were driven in style down to the Fort. It was a bumpy ride, but they enjoyed it.

Leila was consumed with anxiety about her abysmal lack of knowledge, and while she sat by Jeanette's fire and discussed the duties of a settler's wife, Tom went to have a drink with the blacksmith, and Wallace Helena wandered out into the yard of the Fort, to see what was happening. Both men and women stared at her; she had thrown her shawl back from her head and it gave them a chance to examine Tom Harding's new daughter. Some of the women smiled at her and spoke to her in Cree, but she did not understand. So she smiled back, and passed on. The gate of the Fort was open and a number of Metis were hanging around it, smoking and gossiping. She had to pass close to them to go out of the gate, and one of them said to another in French, 'They're Chinks, all right.' He sounded derogatory and presumably believed that Wallace Helena could not understand French. 'Bit of stuff for a cold night.'

Wallace Helena stopped in her tracks. Slowly she turned to face the speaker. She took a step towards him, and slapped him hard across the face. 'You dirty bastard,' she shouted, and told him in fluent French translation of Arabic phrases who his mother had probably been.

Shocked and then outraged, his face contorted, the man would have gone for her, but he was held back by his friends, whispering anxiously to him, 'Tom Harding will give you hell. Leave her alone.'

Restrained by his friends, he could do nothing but spit at the girl's feet, as she turned and went hastily back to Jeanette's quarters. Terribly shaken, she sat quietly by her mother for the rest of the visit. She never forgot or forgave this first insult and the others which subsequently came her way when the Scottish clerks in the Fort decided loftily that she and her mother were Jewish and that Tom Harding should never have been allowed to bring them into the district; it was doubtful, she thought, if any of them could have found Lebanon on a map.

Leila never went anywhere without Tom, so she was spared direct slurs on her origins. She was willing to go to the dance at the Fort at Christmas, feeling that her daughter would enjoy the gaiety of the season there. The place was packed with men, women and children of all ages, though there were no white women. Leila sat on a bench beside Agnes Black and her sister Theresa, who worked in the kitchen of the Fort. She refused to dance because she thought it was unseemly, but she was polite and charming to those women who spoke to her, speaking French when they understood and her broken English when they did not.

Though both Tom and Joe encouraged Wallace Helena to join them in the mixture of Indian dances, Scottish reels and French folk dances, she was apprehensive and shy and was glad to go back to her mother and stay close to her. The Scots passed her with a scornful look. None of the Metis came near her, having heard the story of how one of their number had been slapped in public by this forward little piece who, if she wasn't Chinese, was indubitably Jewish.

Defiant and insulted, Wallace Helena stonily refused to go down to the Fort again. Since she would not give either Joe or Tom a reason for this, it was some time before the men heard the story and identified the man concerned. Tom was furious and wanted to ride down to the Fort straight away to give him a sound beating. Joe, more cautious, pointed out that the man was a Company employee and that the Factor would probably take his part against a pair of illegal squatters like themselves. It was possible that if they created a fracas, the Factor would make a much greater effort to drive them off the land they occupied. Better to wait and if anybody else insulted either Leila or Wallace Helena to immediately file a complaint with the Company. Meanwhile, one of them should always be close beside them, and not let them out of sight.

A fuming Tom was finally persuaded to agree to this, and Leila continued to visit Jeanette whenever Tom had business at the Fort. Jeanette did not return the visits, mainly because her growing number of small children tied her to her home. It was months before Wallace Helena was persuaded to accompany her mother, and she stayed with Leila in Jeanette's quarters until Tom collected them.

Slowly, the young girl learned Cree from Joe and Agnes. It was learned verbally, because there were no books in Cree, and she often made amusing mistakes, so that the three of them laughed together over them. Tom had a smattering of it, but Leila felt she had enough to learn anyway, without wasting time on another language, and she never learned to speak it, though through constantly hearing it, she often understood what was being said. The language opened the door to communication with friends and relations of Joe's who sometimes arrived in the course of their seasonal migrations. It was another new world to Wallace Helena, and, because she was respectful and a good listener, some of them became fond of her in their undemonstrative way.

As the winter passed and the spring sent the men out on to the land again, Leila discussed with Agnes the tremendous list that Jeanette had given her of the duties of a homestead wife. Neither spoke English very well, but Agnes understood quickly enough Leila's doubts that she would be able to fulfil them all.

Agnes said comfortably that there were two of them, which cheered up Leila a little. The Lebanese proved to be a good organizer; she had been used to supervising servants in her Beirut home. She could cook, and learned from Agnes how to make the most of what food was available to them. Between the two of them, they looked after the all-important vegetable patch and the precious hens, milked the cows, scrubbed clothes and sewed garments for all of them, either out of trade cloth, bought from the Hudson's Bay Company, or from skins that Agnes cleaned and tanned.

Prompted by Jeanette, Leila discussed quantities with Tom and Joe. How much wood, how much meat, how much grain should be ground for the winter? How many hens should they kill in the autumn? How many pigs – how much bacon? They soon learned to be thankful for her forethought.

As her health was restored to her, she used her own experience in Lebanon and made better use of the milk they had by preserving it for a few days as yoghurt, then making butter of it. She got Joe to make a small churn to her design and, later, a rough copy of a cheese press that she had seen in Chicago, so that she could make cheese.

The men got used to her shrill voice scolding Simon Wounded or Joe, reminding Agnes, calling in Wallace Helena to do something. Her daughter grinned, as she heard the familiar tones of an Eastern lady asserting herself in her domestic sphere. Leila was, however, generous with praise, as if, at times, everyone was a miracle worker, and she would croon tenderly over those who suffered the inevitable knocks, cuts and burns of their hard life, learning from Agnes something of local cures and sedatives.

Agnes, Simon and Joe often laughed at her privately, and occasionally cursed at her insistence on jobs being finished when she said they were to be. She treated them, however, absolutely as friends and equals and she often took their proffered advice. When she found their friends hanging round her door, she would always find something in her store-room to feed them with.

Not everything went perfectly. In the first years, there were often domestic disasters, like the awful day when Leila clapped her hands at a skunk when it came into the summer kitchen and the skunk sprayed everything. Leila would cry passionately on Tom's shoulder, venting her frustration for all to hear. Yet he never regretted his marriage.

Under the weight of work in a harsh climate, her beauty soon faded. They became dear friends and often laughed at secret jokes, which sometimes made Wallace Helena feel left out.

Wallace Helena not only inherited Tom Harding's son's name, she also learned to do the work that he would have done, had he lived. It was as well that, though not large-boned, she was lithe and, as she grew older, she acquired considerable physical strength.

Joe Black reluctantly decided that he was much too old for her and continued his bachelor ways, visiting the obliging women who lived in a shack not far from the Fort when he felt the need for feminine company. As they worked together, however, he did shyly share with her his profound knowledge of the wildlife round them and of the sorely distressed aboriginal people who were beginning to feel the pressure of the white settlements in the east. She learned to speak enough Cree to enjoy a joke with them, and one young man asked Tom for her in marriage. She turned him down.

Though so hard-worked that she had little time to think of herself as a person with needs of her own, she was not unaware of the stirring of desires in her that, as far as she could see, could not be met. She nursed a terrible resentment of the men in the Fort and it became a latent bitterness as she grew older.

She thought of Joe as being of the same generation as her stepfather, though in fact he was much younger, and considered him the equivalent of an uncle.

Often dressed in an Indian woman's moccasins and gaiters, she would ride alongside him and became nearly as adept as him in caring for the livestock. She left the slaughter of pigs and steers to him, but she soon got used to cutting the throats of chickens, snaring and skinning rabbits and catching fish and gutting them.

Leila was, at first, shaken at what her daughter was doing, but Agnes Black laughed and told Leila she was lucky not to have to do the butchering herself. Leila cheerfully cooked whatever the others brought in, learning from Agnes the art of reducing a beaver, a lynx or, once, a bear, to edible stews. The skins of the wild game were carefully cleaned by Agnes or Tom and were sold into the fur trade, providing either much-needed cash, or credit at the Hudson's Bay trading post.

As Wallace Helena grew into a tough independent young woman, rejecting the people in the Fort as ignorant and uncivilized, Agnes Black, quiet and observant, worried a little about her son. Sometimes, after shutting the yard gate after them, she would stand and watch Joe and Wallace Helena race out along the rough lane which strung Tom's and Joe's holdings together, the girl nearly as skittish as the mare under her.

Joe should have got married years ago to some decent Cree girl, she thought. But she had never persuaded him to do anything he did not want to do; and his grandfather was too distant to exert his influence. Now, she sensed Wallace Helena's attraction for him; she saw it in the careful way he always dealt with her, keeping just sufficient distance between them to discourage intimacy.

On summer evenings, before they all went to bed, they would sometimes sit outside to catch the evening breeze, Leila and herself on the cabin step, Tom, Joe and Wallace Helena on the nearby fence. The men and Wallace Helena would smoke. Joe had taught the girl how to use a little Indian pipe or roll a cigarette for herself if papers were available. When she first arrived, she had been so on edge that Joe had feared she would be ill, and he had suggested that she learn to smoke, to calm her. Now, she could not imagine being without tobacco, and she looked forward to this quiet half hour when sometimes they talked and at other times were glad simply to relax under the wide, darkening sky.

Once the afterglow had faded, Leila would call them in, because, ever since the brush with the skunk and a later encounter with a porcupine, she had been afraid of wild animals straying in after dark. Wallace Helena never demurred and went in with her mother, and Agnes saw her son's eyes follow her.

'If he wants her,' she thought fretfully sometimes, 'why doesn't he ask her?' And she answered herself by saying that Tom would not tolerate it.

13

Though Leila sustained a friendship with Jeanette, she never became close to anyone else. The Harding homestead was less than five miles from the little Fort, but it was too far for frequent contact, particularly when the narrow trail along the river was often very muddy or, in winter, choked with snow. Except for the Indians and a few trappers, most of the activity of the Fort was with its connections downriver; what small traffic there was went that way and did not pass the Harding place. Even with Jeanette, both Leila and Wallace Helena sometimes found themselves at a loss, because they had had some education – Jeanette could not even read – and, further, they had had the experience of living in two other countries. On Jeanette's part, she could not understand Leila's disinterest in children – or her lack of them.

When Tom first married his pretty Lebanese, he had hoped for another son, but when he saw Leila collapse during her journey to Fort Edmonton, he realized that, as his mother had warned him, she had not the strength a pioneer life required. He began to fear that he might lose her in childbirth, as he had done his first wife. So, as the months went by and his new wife did not become pregnant, he was relieved. He soon tumbled to the fact that the few days each month during which she refused to make love, on the grounds of religious observances, had a twenty-eight-day cycle, and probably had something to do with the avoidance of pregnancy. Haunted by the fate of his first wife, he humoured her and settled down to being cosseted by a wife trained, since the day she took her first tottering steps, to please a man.

He appreciated the tremendous effort she made to do her part in running the homestead as well as a Metis woman would have done, except that she did not give much help in the fields or garden. He knew he was fortunate in having three women on the place who got along very well together; they rarely quarrelled and soon made up again; and, as he said one day to Joe, 'Between the three of them, they shift a hell of a lot of work.'

Joe grinned. From the hill that sloped upwards behind the cabin, he could see how far they had extended their cleared land since the advent of Leila and Wallace Helena. 'Yeah,' he agreed, 'and you and I've shifted a lot, as a result of being freed up a bit by them!'

Tom nodded agreement. 'We'll fence this section before the fall,' he said.

'The Company's not going to like it – it's still their land.'

'The Company won't last forever. They can't hold the land, as it is. If they could, they would've tipped out every Metis who's built himself a cabin and dug a vegetable garden, not to speak of running me out of town.'

'Well, mebbe you'll have a son who'll own it.'

'Humph.' Tom flicked the reins of his horse and started it down towards the cabin. He had been married three years, and Joe must be wondering why he had no more family. Well, he could keep on wondering.

Wallace Helena was seventeen. She had fully expected that by this time she would have some small brothers and sisters, and one day after visiting Jeanette and her brood, she asked her mother why none had arrived.

Her mother smiled secretively, and said, 'I'll explain it next time the boys are out and Agnes has gone to visit her sister at the Fort.' It was time, she felt, that Wallace Helena should understand these things.

Seated by the fire, one cool autumn evening, some mending in her lap, she said frankly to her daughter that, once she had seen the lonely little Fort and the still more lonely cabin, she had decided that she did not want to bear infants in such a deserted place only to see them die.

'An awful lot of them do die round the Fort, I know,' Wallace Helena agreed, holding up the sock she was knitting to see how she was getting on.

'I lost both your little brothers and that was enough. Thank goodness I have you, my darling, and that you are strong and healthy. And I have dear Tom, bless him.'

'I would hate to see my babies die,' Wallace Helena said. 'I felt awful when the boys died.'

'I know, dear.' She looked suddenly old, as she sat with needle poised over the patch she was sewing and stared into the fire, to visualize the world from which she had come, the warmth, the vivacity, the sophistication of it – and the two small graves.

She shook her head and forced herself to attend to what she wanted to say. Smiling gently, she said, 'One day, perhaps some nice Lebanese will find his way here – and he'll marry you and take you away to a more civilized place. Then you can give me some grandchildren.'

Wallace Helena smiled back at her mother, but said nothing; Mama was entitled to her little flights of fancy.

Bored with knitting, she got pen, ink and paper down from a shelf, to write a thank-you letter to Uncle James for the small box of Arabic books he had sent them. The wonderful present had taken nearly a year upon its journey, and Leila had cried when she had lifted out the works of her favourite poet.

After the letter was written, Wallace Helena went over to the fireside, to pick up her knitting again. Tom and Joe were in the barn dealing with a mare which was having difficulty in dropping its foal.

'Mama, how is it that you can avoid having children? Agnes says children simply come, whether you like it or not.'

Her mother was mending a rent in one of Tom's jackets. She broke the thread with her teeth, as she considered the question. 'It is a delicate matter. You have to watch the moon and your monthly show of blood – and you have to find an acceptable excuse to give your husband for not lying with him on certain days.'

Wallace Helena picked out another ball of the coarsely spun knitting wool with which she was making socks. 'The moon, Mama?' she asked, a little incredulously, a suspicion of laughter in her voice.

'Yes. The moon. I'm not teasing you. It's a system usually used to help women conceive – if they've had no luck in becoming pregnant. But it can be used in reverse, to avoid children.' And she went on to share with Wallace Helena the observations of generations of women, that there appeared to be certain days in the monthly cycle when a child might be conceived – and that these days were limited. By watching the moon's twenty-eight-day cycle or by consulting a calendar, one could relate a *woman's* twenty-eight-day cycle to it – and thus know that at the rising of the moon, say, one should try for a child – or avoid those days if you did not want one.

Wallace Helena sat spellbound. 'What do you tell Tom, to avoid him on the wrong days?'

'I tell him I have certain religious days when I must make special prayers each month,' she replied placidly. 'And he humours me.'

Wallace Helena had always understood the relationship between man and wife; there was little privacy in the crowded busy homes of Beirut, and women talked and complained endlessly about their menfolk. Now, however, finding the young woman was interested, Leila began to instruct her in how to please a man. 'When you are older, you will marry,' she said, 'and you'll keep a man faithful, if you give him pleasure.'

'Do women get pleasure?'

'Certainly, my dear. But sometimes men are stupid and ignorant – and then you have to teach them what pleases you.'

'Humph.' Wallace Helena found it impossible to relate what her mother said directly to Tom; it was as if the faded, knowledgeable woman was a teacher, not her mother, and the man about whom she spoke was not Tom, but some abstract man conjured up to use as an example.

When Leila fell silent, Wallace Helena did not know what to say. Her mother had opened up a weird world which she had always known existed but had never really considered; it made her feel very uneasy.

Finally, she said lightly, 'It's easier to make moccasins than to knit this awful wool.' She flung down her needles irritably.

Leila agreed, and no more was said about the art of sex. Wallace Helena began to look at men with new eyes, however. Black, white or brown, were they all the same? She began to speculate whether women were as powerless as they often appeared; her mother seemed to believe that men could, through sex, be easily manipulated.

She got up briskly from her chair, and said, 'I'll go over to the barn.' Then she paused, and asked idly, 'Mama, do you feel it has been worthwhile – leaving Chicago, I mean?'

The unexpected question startled Leila. She looked puzzled for a moment, and then said slowly, 'I don't think about it very much. When I first came I thought I was going to die, and I wished I had sent you, at least, to your Uncle James.'

Wallace Helena bent to kiss her mother lightly on the top of her head. 'I'd never leave you, Mama.'

'Bless you, child,' Leila responded absently, and then reverted to Wallace Helena's question. 'Once I was here, I was sure I could never face the return journey – or any similar journey – so I have made the best of it. And Tom is very dear to me,' she added defensively. 'I didn't make any mistake about him. He works like a devil for our sake.'

'Yes, he does,' admitted Wallace Helena. She sighed. 'We all work very hard.'

Her mother spread her hands on her knees and looked at the broken nails, the ingrained soot and their redness. 'Yes, dear,' she agreed, and then her usual optimism reasserted itself, and she said, 'Tom's saving to get us a proper iron cooking stove.'

'Good heavens! Where would he get that from?'

'He's trying to find out – and see if he can get one sent overland, now the trail is better.' She got up from her chair and shook out the jacket she had been mending. 'Up to now, he's had to collect farm implements – tools of every kind. Now it's my turn to have something, he says.'

'Great,' responded Wallace Helena, with enthusiasm. 'A stove will

88

be a godsend.' She took her shawl from a hook and wrapped it round herself. 'I'll go over to see if the foal's born yet.'

Ice crunched under her moccasins as she walked across the yard to the barn. Her mother had not really answered her question regarding her inner feelings about living in such a primitive place. Did she find the small world of the homestead and its six inhabitants satisfying? Was the battle to survive each year perhaps a challenge that she enjoyed meeting? Yet, she had cried when she saw the tattered anthology of Arab poems which Uncle James had sent.

She stood in the yard for a moment, looking up at a peerless night sky where every star seemed to twinkle with the clarity of a view of them from a desert. It was uncannily quiet, except for the muffled sound of the men's voices in the barn. The wind was chilly and she began to shiver as she gazed at the cold silver of the rising moon. Living in the Territories was as lonely as living on the moon, she thought. There was nothing comfortable in the thousands of miles of unexplored forest and prairie that surrounded her. The untouched land sat there like a mountain lion waiting for prey – and it could spring nasty surprises on you just as quickly, she thought bitterly. And no matter what happened, there was no extended family to call on for help; no community. Nothing. Just nothing. Did Adam and Eve feel like she did, when they were cast out of Eden to face just such a world?

She began to shake with helpless fear, just as she had when she first arrived. Perspiration rolled down her face, and she wanted to turn and run. But there was nowhere to run, except into the very land which scared her so much.

The side door of the barn opened and Joe was silhouetted against the light of the lantern inside. He was wiping his hands and arms with some straw. He did not see her at first, but when he did, he asked, in surprise, 'Hi, hon, what are you doing out there?'

She turned. Her blanched face gleamed in the lantern light. She looked at Joe for a moment as if she did not recognize him. Her mouth tightened and she seemed much older than her seventeen years, as she sought to control her terror. She said shakily, 'I came to see if the foal was born.'

Joe threw away the dirty straw, and grinned. 'Sure. He's fine. And Queen'll be all right.'

She tried to smile, but there was no rejoicing in her; Uncle James's little lemon flower felt as bitter as a lemon fruit.

14

Leila was not the only one marked by the remorseless round of work on a homestead: Agnes Black was feeling her years. After talking the matter over with Joe and Simon Wounded, she suggested to Tom and Leila that they might take in an orphan girl from amongst those cared for by the Grey Nuns in St Albert, a small Metis and Cree community founded by an Oblate priest, Father Lacombe, about ten miles away.

'The girl could help in the house – and I'd teach her,' she promised. 'We wouldn't have to pay her anything for a while.'

They debated the problem of another mouth to feed, but, though the harvest that year had been good, the men were uneasy; some years they felt as if they had their backs to the wall. Another person was another responsibility. Leila, however, jumped at the idea, particularly since the girl would not be coming straight from her tribe, but would have been taught by the famous Grey Nuns. She had never met the nuns; they tended to stay close to their work in St Albert, but she had heard from Jeanette that they were white and were educated, and might even know what a Lebanese Maronite was.

So, speechless and terrified, Emily, aged ten, was added to the motley family. She clung to Agnes like a small brown ghost.

At first, Wallace Helena did not take much notice of her. She herself worked with the men outside; Emily would work with Leila. Then she noticed casually that the child never smiled and did not seem to grow much, though she ate with the family and consumed a fair amount of food. When spoken to, the girl slid behind Agnes, who often answered for her. This bothered Wallace Helena and she mentioned it to Joe, while they sat on the fence having their usual evening smoke.

Joe carefully crumbed up some tobacco in the pink palm of his hand, before he answered. 'Maybe she don't understand anything but Cree,' he suggested. 'What do you talk to her in?'

'English. She must know English. I tried French one day, but she just looked at me as if I were insane. I took it for granted that being with the nuns all her life, she didn't know Cree.'

'Try Cree – slowly.'

Wallace Helena followed his advice, though her own Cree often made a gleam of amusement rise in the eyes of Indian visitors. And slowly she began to unravel the small, grubby, miserable person that was Emily.

She was startled to find a mirror image of herself, when she first came to Fort Edmonton, a child uprooted, its origins and forebears either ignored or disparaged. In addition, she was parentless. Agnes Black, though not unkind, was often short with her because, as Emily told Wallace Helena, 'I'm slow, because I don't know anything. And Mrs Harding – I can't understand what she says. So she gets cross.' She did not cry; she avoided looking directly at her questioner, her face expressionless.

Wallace Helena nodded, her own face suddenly grim. Poor Mama had declared that knowing three languages was enough – she was not about to start on Cree; she spoke English to Agnes.

Emily slept in the bunk in the living-room where Wallace Helena had herself wept through her first weeks in the homestead; Tom and Joe had since built on a little room for her which backed on to the living-room fire-place and was warmed by it. She sighed, and looked again at the child before her. It was late, and Agnes, Joe and Simon had long since gone to their shack. There was a faint murmur of voices from her parents' room, as they, too, prepared for bed. With a sudden surge of pity, Wallace Helena took both the youngster's hands in hers. 'I think I understand how you feel,' she said. 'It happened to me once, when I couldn't speak any English.'

Emily's eyes opened wide and, for the first time, she stared directly at Wallace Helena.

Wallace Helena continued. 'I'll explain to Mrs Harding, and she will ask Agnes to translate for you. And you can speak Cree to Joe, Mr Harding and Simon Wounded.'

At the men's names the girl looked frightened.

'What's the matter?' asked Wallace Helena.

'The Reverend Mother said we must never, ever, speak to men; it's dangerous for us.'

Wallace Helena leaned back in the old wooden chair and laughed. Emily looked totally discomfited at her sudden mirth.

'I don't think any of the men here will hurt you; they are more likely to protect you from other men. If any one of them does touch you in a way you don't like,, tell me immediately. I'll take care of you.'

The girl squirmed, and then smiled slightly. Wallace Helena got up and suggested cheerfully, 'Let's have some hot milk before we go to bed. And tomorrow I'll teach you how to milk a cow.'

* * *

The next morning, she rode out with Joe to look for a missing steer; their herd was small and any absence was noted almost immediately. Unlike further south, where cattle ranged on the hills, Tom kept his in fenced pasture land, which he had taken a lot of trouble to improve.

Joe's handsome, high-cheekboned face creased up with laughter when she told him of little Emily's woes and mentioned the Reverend Mother's warning. His black eyes flashed, as he rose in his saddle to squint across the country in search of the lost animal.

'Tell your ma about her; she'll spoil her to death, once she understands what's the matter.'

His assumption was correct, and Emily became another little daughter to train, always a quiet shadow in the house, but devoted to Wallace Helena and Leila.

They found enough remains of the steer to indicate that someone had slaughtered it and taken almost all of it away with them.

'Must've been a party of 'em, blast them,' he muttered. 'I sometimes think we were crazy to bring cattle up here. Nobody else did for a while. I guess we lost this one to Indians last night – but if it isn't them, it's cougars – or they go eat something they shouldn't and make themselves sick; they haven't got the brains of mice. I'll never forget the time I had bringing the first three up from Fort Benton.' He bridled as he continued, 'I got them here, though – a bull and two cows, as scrawny as they could be and still stand on their feet.' He chuckled again. 'The fellows down at the Fort laughed their heads off and said it was a lot cheaper to hunt; but we nursed 'em along and we got calves and had meat when they didn't.'

As they went back to the cabin, laughing and making jokes about the chickens he had also bought, on another occasion, from American settlers further south, Agnes Black looked up from the barrel in which she was doing some washing, outside the door, and she sighed. Again, that night, she suggested cautiously to Joe that he should take a Cree wife.

He told her dryly that he and Tom had enough mouths to feed, without his adding to them. 'Tom looked as black as Old Nick when I told him about the steer this morning,' he added, as if to confirm the difficulty of feeding everyone.

15

Over the years, Tom and Joe struggled on, through good harvests and bad ones. They increased their holding and the cattle on it by not asking anyone's permission to clear land; they felled trees and then ploughed, and argued afterwards with the Hudson's Bay Company. The Company's Chief Factor finally gave up and decided to ignore them.

Then, in 1879, came the smallpox, sweeping through the west like the Black Death once swept through Europe.

Tom was the first to catch the disease, probably from a family of Crees he had met casually on the trail, who were subsequently wiped out by it. Leila and Agnes Black nursed the stricken man and both of them became infected; regardless of contagion, Leila held her husband in her arms when his pain was greatest, whispering to him to hold on and that he would soon be better. Inwardly, she was torn with anguish, as she watched his well-loved features almost obliterated by the huge pustules the disease produced; they blocked his nasal passages and his mouth so that he could not swallow the sedatives that Agnes brought. He died in a wild delirium, held down by both women, so that he would not roll off the bed.

As his poor racked body relaxed in death, the elderly Indian woman and the suddenly bereft wife stared blankly at each other across the bed as if stupefied. Then Leila screamed and flung herself across Tom, beating his pillow with her fists.

Agnes hastened round the bed to lift her away, calling at the same time for Joe to come to help her. He heard her and came immediately from the yard. Together, they half-carried the frantic woman into the living-room. She fought them off, continuing to scream and then to tear her clothes in mourning.

'Stay with her,' Agnes ordered. 'I'll get Wallace Helena – and something to soothe her.'

Not attempting to stop her rending her garments, Joe spoke softly to her and gradually persuaded her to sit down. Wallace Helena came running from the vegetable garden, where she had gone for a few minutes to get vegetables to make a soup for the invalid, a soup he would not now need. She knelt by her mother and wept with her. Then she persuaded Leila to sip the cordial Agnes brought for her and this helped to calm her.

When symptoms suggested that Leila herself had caught the disease, she shuddered inwardly and quailed at the thought of the suffering she must undergo. Secure in the belief that Tom would be waiting for her, she was not afraid of dying; without her husband, she felt she had no reason to live. While her mind was clear, however, she gathered up her courage; Wallace Helena was a woman now, but she needed to be able to continue on the land that sustained them. She sent Joe post-haste to bring a priest to her.

Two Oblate Fathers came from a nearby Cree encampment, where they had been tending the sick as best they could. They were surprised to find a woman who did not want to confess or receive extreme unction; she wanted them to write a Will for her and witness her signature.

'I may die, Father. I want to make sure that everything that belongs to me – including anything my beloved husband has left me . . .' Her voice broke as she struggled through her increasing pain to convey her sense of urgency to the priests. 'He wrote a Will when we were married – I haven't had the heart to look at it yet – but it's probably in his cash box.' She stopped, to gather what strength she had, and then continued, 'Everything to go to my darling daughter, Helena – Wallace Helena.'

It was arranged before the disease engulfed her completely. The priests did not stay; they returned hurriedly to the stricken encampment, only to die of the same disease themselves a short time later.

As Wallace Helena tended her mother, she wept openly for her well-loved stepfather, and she faced, with terror, the prospect of losing Leila as well.

Joe dug Tom's grave, near that of his old friend's first wife, and himself carried the body wrapped in a blanket down to it, and laid him in it. After throwing the rich, black earth back over him, he stood alone in the starlight, grieving for his boon companion of so many years, while in the cabin his mother and Wallace Helena strove to alleviate the death pangs of Tom's second wife.

The following day, Joe's mother showed signs of having the disease and took to her bed in their little shack, to be nursed by Joe. He had to order a terrified Simon Wounded to dig a grave for Leila, though, to save Simon from being infected, he left his mother for a few minutes while he took Leila gently from the arms of a shocked Wallace Helena and laid her in her last resting place.

He would not allow Wallace Helena near Agnes; the girl had, as yet, shown no sign of illness, and he hoped to save her from it. So Wallace Helena, wide-eyed and unweeping, cooked and brought food to the door of the shack, while Emily, whimpering like a lost kitten with nowhere safe to run, fed horses and hens, milked the cows, and, somehow, kept things together.

The night before Agnes Black died, it was obvious to Joe that he had become the next victim. He shouted to Wallace Helena that she was not to come near him, just bring water to the door.

She shouted back, 'Don't be a bloody fool; we'll live or die together.'

She marched into the little cabin, clean sheets over her arm, and helped the almost incoherent man out of his clothes in the hope of easing the pain when it came. She bullied a quivering Simon Wounded into helping her move Agnes's body outside, and sent him off to dig yet another grave. She shouted to Emily to take the bedding off her mother's bed and burn it outside. She was to remake the bed with clean bedding. Then she was to wash herself and boil her own clothes.

Simon Wounded did not have to be asked to take Agnes Black to her grave; pale and shaken, he silently did it, and took himself off to bed in the hayloft over the barn, to mourn alone.

The next morning, he helped Wallace Helena move Joe into the main cabin. The man was burning with fever and understood little of what was being done. Between them they nursed him through it. Emily was not allowed near him, but she kept the four of them fed, and, with unexpected stoicism, faced the fact that she might get the disease.

Wallace Helena, Emily and Simon worked to the point of exhaustion to prepare for the winter, none of them wishing to suffer near-starvation during it.

It was a shadow of Joe who survived, and it was months before he was able to handle his chores.

When, one night, he thanked Simon and Emily for not deserting them, Simon responded dryly, 'There was nowhere to go – everybody'd got it, except the Fort – and they weren't going to let anybody in from a homestead that had had it!' And he exchanged a toothless grin with Emily.

The family had been fortunate in being able to bury their dead. Amongst the terrified Indians, whole groups had died, their bodies torn apart and eaten by wild animals, their only monument a teepee centre pole bent by the uncaring wind.

Nobody really knew why Wallace Helena, Simon and Emily had not caught the disease. Simon said he had been through a plague of smallpox before on the prairies, and perhaps he and Emily had gained some immunity from it. Wallace Helena remembered a number of unnamed fevers she had survived as a child in Beirut, where small-pox also existed, and wondered if she had had some milder form of the disease which gave her immunity.

Wallace Helena burned Agnes's and Joe's hut, and as soon as they could get some help to do it, a new one was built with room for three helpers on the homestead. Joe stayed with Wallace in the main cabin, their devotion to each other, as yet, not verbally acknowledged. Joe had seen his face in the mirror and was shocked by the sight. Wallace Helena, with so much unexpressed grief penned up within her, hardly knew how to continue; she blundered on from day to day, simply trying to keep the farmstead going.

When Joe was fit to sit on a bench outside the cabin door, she said dully, one early spring day, 'I'm almost out of fodder; it's more than time I put the cows out to pasture. If we don't get any more snow, they should be all right. I'll do it tomorrow – Simon must plough.'

'I'll come with you,' Joe said suddenly.

'You're too weak yet; you couldn't even mount.'

'I could – and I will. I'll never get right sitting here.'

The next morning, he got Simon to give him a heft onto his horse and he rode out with her, to move their small, lowing herd through the mud in the yard and into a fenced pasture, beyond the field that Simon was ploughing. They would move them further out on their land when the possibility of spring snowstorms lessened.

They were silent as they rode. Wallace Helena's tired brain was filled with lists of neglected tasks, and Joe was concentrating on staying on his horse.

Though they were not out for long, the fresh spring breeze did them good. Wallace Helena began to unwind a little and talk desultorily. As they approached the yard again, however, her conversational efforts petered out, and she suddenly burst into violent tears.

'What's up?' Joe forgot his own weakness in the shock of seeing her acute distress.

Wallace Helena made a small hopeless gesture towards the cabin. 'Mama – Tom – they're not there,' she wailed, bending over her saddle, as great sobs racked her.

Joe leaned over and took her horse's reins in his hands, as they entered the yard. 'Emily,' he shouted urgently, 'Emily!'

The young woman flung open the door almost immediately and peered out, quivering like a rabbit scenting danger.

'Come here and help Wallace Helena – and help get me off this damned horse – and shut the gate behind us.'

Wallace Helena sat her horse, her head bent, and cried as if her heart would break, while a shaken Emily steadied Joe as he laboriously descended.

She held his horse, while he moved to take hold of Wallace Helena's mount's bridle; he wondered how long he could stay on his feet.

'Come on! Down you come, girl,' he ordered her as firmly as he could.

Though her grief seemed beyond control, Wallace Helena dismounted obediently and Joe put his arm round her, as much to steady himself as to comfort her. He said to Emily, 'Hitch the horses and then shut the gate. And go make some coffee.'

'I'm in the middle of making the bread,' Emily protested.

'To hell with the bread. Do as I say.'

He took the distraught young woman into the cabin and sat her down in a chair. She wept on. He pulled up another chair facing her, and sat in it, while he unlaced her boots and took them off. She made no move to stop him. He untied the scarf she was wearing round her head, and he realized, with a pang, how thin her face was, the sallow skin etched with new lines.

'You're tired out,' he told her very gently. 'Come and lie down.'

Still moaning, she allowed herself to be led to her room and onto her bed, a bed which Joe had hastily constructed for her soon after her arrival at Fort Edmonton. It had a bearskin over it, from an animal he had shot during an unexpected confrontation on their trapline. She lay down on it, her face to the wall.

Joe pulled a stool close to the bedside, and thankfully sat down on it. He understood very well her need to cry. In the privacy of the night, he had wept himself, at his own weakness, at the loss of his friends and, not the least, for the loss of his mother. He was surprised that she had not expressed her grief at her mother's death long before.

Emily brought in two mugs of coffee and hovered beside him, looking down at the tightly curled-up figure on the bed. 'Put the coffee on the floor by me, and give me that shawl off the hook over there. And get out!'

Shocked by his snarl, Emily did as she was bidden; and, over the bread dough, she burst into tears herself. Joe had never been so sharp with her before, and added to that was the fear engendered by Wallace Helena's sudden collapse. In a burst of self-pity, she felt, quite rightly, that nobody had considered what *she* had gone through during the smallpox epidemic.

Joe laid the shawl over Wallace Helena and sat, for a while, watching her, while he quickly drank one of the coffees which Emily had brought in. Then as the passionate sobs did not seem to be decreasing, he leaned over and tentatively put his hand on her heaving shoulder. To his surprise, one of her hands emerged from under the shawl and clasped his tightly.

A surging need to weep himself hit him. Still holding her hand, he eased himself off the stool and onto the bed. He lay down on his side and folded himself round the curve of her back, his face half-buried in the mass of her hair. She felt the comforting warmth of another human being and sensed his own despair. The sobs faltered as she turned over to face him.

'Oh, Joe, darling Joe,' she wept. 'It's been pure hell, hasn't it?'

He nodded, and folded her into his arms.

They lay together for a long time, two exhausted people who loved each other with the deep devotion of years, made humble by a load of trouble they could not bear alone.

When, finally, Wallace Helena ceased her crying, she said, 'I'm sorry to inflict this on you.'

He managed to grin at her. 'I'm not in much better shape myself,' he confessed.

There was silence between them for a while, and then Wallace Helena said, 'You know, Joe, I don't understand why some are taken and some are spared. Do you? Mama came through that terrible time in Beirut – and it was no fun in Chicago either – simply to die out here – in nowhere. Why her? Why not you and me?'

'That's the way life is.'

'It doesn't make sense.'

They heard Simon Wounded clump into the cabin and ask Emily where everybody was. Joe hastily swung off the bed and sat a little dizzily on the stool. 'We're here, Simon,' he shouted. 'Wallace Helena isn't too well. I'll be right out.' He got up.

'Now, you stay here. I'll get Emily to bring you some supper.' He bent down and kissed her. 'You'll be better tomorrow.'

'Somebody's got to milk the cows.'

'We'll manage.'

He left her, closing the door softly after him. The cabin smelled of the bread Emily had taken out of the oven. He said to her, 'She'll be all right now. She was crying for her mother.'

Seated in his favourite corner by the fire, Simon Wounded packed his pipe and nodded agreement. Emily gave a heavy sigh. She had been through weeks of fear of the smallpox and day upon day of overwork. She said, 'I cried when *my* mother died; I thought Wallace Helena never would. She's never shed a tear that I know of, before this.'

'She'd everything to see to – including me,' he snapped. 'Tell me when supper's ready.' He staggered in to Tom and Leila's old room, where Simon and Wallace Helena had nursed him, and threw himself onto his bed. He thought about the woman on the bed in the next room, and wondered what he had started.

Much later, when Emily was snoring comfortably in her bunk in the corner of the living-room, behind a curtain made of sacking, and Simon had gone over to his cabin, Wallace Helena got out of bed. She was garbed in the old petticoat she used as a nightgown and, as she picked up her candle and went out of the room, she shivered slightly.

She slipped into Tom's room and eased herself quietly under the bedclothes beside the sleeping man. She never afterwards slept anywhere else and, once he had regained his strength, he saw that she never regretted it.

The few white women in Edmonton gossiped about misalliances. But Joe knew that he and Wallace Helena were like two halves of the same coin; they belonged completely to each other.

16

When it seemed that the smallpox had run its course, Joe's aunt, Theresa Black, who had for years worked in the kitchens of the Fort, came to Joe and Helena's cabin to take her sister Agnes's place; they were very glad to welcome her into their devastated home.

The Fort she left slowly spawned a hamlet, and the first small signs of federal government replacing the old Hudson's Bay Company rule became apparent. A few stores, a hotel, a telegraph office and a postal system of sorts made their appearance. The Roman Catholic priests of St Albert, who had served the early inhabitants of the Fort, were joined by Methodists and Anglicans. Government surveyors arrived to subdivide the Territories into districts. Instead of bartering, the inhabitants were tending to use money. Land ownership had to be registered.

When the Hudson's Bay Company finally handed over jurisdiction to the government in Ottawa, Wallace Helena claimed the land which she and Joe had continued to farm. Tom had left everything to Leila and Leila to Wallace Helena. Joe was still technically an employee.

Thanks to a first-class lawyer, her claim to have been resident on it since 1862 and her stepfather for many years before that, and that between them they had cleared and developed it, was accepted.

Once she was assured that even though she was a woman, the land had been truly registered in her name, she ordered the lawyer to re-register it in the joint names of Joe Black and herself, as being a married couple according to the customs of the country. If one of them died, the other automatically inherited the whole.

Wallace Helena met the lawyer when she rode over to St Albert to return some books to the Oblate Fathers. They had brought him in to help them establish the claims of Metis to land along the Sturgeon River, and Joe often laughed at the dislike she had expressed at their having to part with every cent of the cash they had hoarded in her mother's old trunk, in order to pay the man's bill. But it was the best bargain they had ever made.

He had been surprised and touched when she told him that she had arranged to share the ownership with him.

*   *   *

Now she had undertaken this tremendously long journey to the place where her Uncle James had lived, and Joe was missing her badly.

Back home after the 200-mile ride to Edmonton, after seeing her onto the train at Calgary, he had slept the clock round, and now he crawled out of bed in a cabin already overly hot. He peered out of the small, glazed window to look at the yard. Emily was already plodding across the well-trodden bareness of it, towards the barn. She was carrying two milk pails.

Good harvesting weather, he thought. Hope it holds.

He shaved himself with a cut-throat razor, in front of a small hanging mirror, much prized by Wallace Helena because it had been her mother's. The mug of hot water which Aunt Theresa had brought in to him a few minutes earlier was already cool and the home-made soap was not lathering very well. He succeeded in nicking himself with the razor. Cursing softly, he pressed a finger on the bleeding cut, and unexpectedly chuckled; the scar would hardly be noticed amid the pits left on his face by the smallpox. In the sixteen years since he had had the disease, the dreadful scars had not improved. He remembered clearly the moment when he was better and had wanted to shave, and Wallace Helena reluctantly handed him a mirror, as he sat up in bed. The appalling shock had been no joke, he considered more soberly; and still, people who didn't know you stared at you as if you might still be a source of contagion. 'It sure didn't improve your looks, Joe Black,' he said.

He was only one of many in the district who carried the marks of the dreaded disease, and all of them would have been thankful for a salve to remove the ugly scars.

He made a face at himself in the mirror. A lot of Indians looked worse than he did. Funny how few men in the Fort had caught it. Wallace Helena and Simon Wounded had nursed him through it, and neither of them had caught it. He remembered how they had tied his arms to his sides so that he could not scratch the horrible pustules on his face.

He leaned forward to peer at his teeth. Though he still had a full set, they were stained by tobacco and coffee. He made another wry face at himself. Then he poured water from a jug into a tin bowl to rinse his face and splash the water up over his grey, tightly curling hair. If there were time, he might go down to the river, later on, for a quick swim. He had a sudden memory of Wallace Helena's slim, pale body flashing through the water beside him on other occasions, and his spirits fell a little. God, how he missed her lively presence.

101

As he dried his face, he shouted, 'Hey, Aunt Theresa, what about some coffee?'

'Comin',' responded a muffled, cracked voice from the direction of the lean-to which still served as a summer kitchen, though Joe had recently added a third bedroom for Emily and Aunt Theresa.

His aunt shuffled slowly into the bedroom, carrying a coffee mug in one hand and a piece of bread in the other. Her face was as wrinkled as an apple held too long in store, and she grumbled that tomorrow he could come to the kitchen and get his coffee himself; she and young Emily had more things to do than wait on him. She said this to him most mornings.

The corners of his mouth twitched, as she put the mug down on the chest of drawers beside his razor. He knew very well that she would be put out by any alteration in this morning routine, so he didn't reply. He picked up a wide-toothed comb which he had carved for himself and ran it quickly through his bushy hair, while she retreated to the kitchen. He'd better hurry, he considered. Simon Wounded and the jinglers would be in for breakfast soon.

Later on, that hot summer morning, he rode over to survey the barley crop. As the merciless sun beat down on him, he wished heartily that he could find a couple of reliable labourers to help him. Now that the railway had reached Calgary, some Metis from Manitoba and a few white families had felt it worthwhile to come the two hundred miles further north by wagon to Fort Edmonton to take up land for themselves; there were few who would work for someone else for long. Over the years, he had seen a lot of miners pass through on their way to search for gold. One or two of them would have been good employees, he thought; but the lure of gold was too great, and they passed on west or north, or, in a few cases, preferred to pan for gold in the nearby river, or to mine the coal in the valley.

There were the Indians, of course. Some of them would sometimes work a season with him to oblige a friend, or if they were hungry enough. They were, however, still largely nomadic; they did not take kindly to settling in one place. Further, their numbers had been pitifully depleted by the smallpox. Many of their usual lodges were overgrown by bush; there was no one left to use them. Other white men's diseases, like measles and diphtheria, picked off their children. The buffalo herds on which they had depended had been wiped out by over-hunting, leaving them famished and destitute, with all the apathy that hunger brings in its train.

Thank goodness for old Simon Wounded, thought Joe; he, at least, seemed to be happy to stay put. In addition to him, they were currently employing two drifters, who lived with Simon in the bunkhouse. They had come up from the States, single men who had tried mining, whisky-running and being cowhands on a ranch south of Calgary. Wallace Helena was not very satisfied with them and said sarcastically that they were probably wanted by various sheriffs south of the border. She would not have them in the house, and they cooked for themselves; it was obvious that they were not happy sharing the bunkhouse with an Indian and resented Simon's privileged position in the household. Joe hoped they would last until Wallace Helena returned.

Emily was scared of them and, at first, they teased her. Joe noticed, and told them that if they touched her, he'd see that they were not much use to a woman after it. Because he was bigger and tougher than they were, they sulkily heeded him; they also bore in mind that behind Joe stood a woman like a ruthless witch, noted in the district for her almost superhuman abilities to get her own way and to pay back an insult.

'She'll take her time,' a labourer in the village had told them, 'but sooner or later, if you cross her, you'll find yourself run out of the place on some excuse – if you're not struck dead.'

Though they laughed at the old man, they bore the information in mind.

Wallace Helena had never killed a person in her life. But, once, she had had such a fearsome row with a Metis, who had tried to settle on a corner of her land, that the man had had a stroke and had subsequently died. The incident had been more frightening to the British inhabitants, in that the row had taken place in fluent French on the main trail through the settlement. Finally, she had poked him in the chest with a long forefinger and had sworn at him in *Arabic*. He had stormed back at her, and then he had suddenly clutched his throat and fallen to the ground.

Burning with rage, Wallace Helena had remounted Peggy and had ridden away, leaving him lying in the dust of the trail.

Though the more educated people understood what had happened, many did not. They knew that Wallace Helena came from some strange Middle Eastern country, and nestled in the back of their minds there remained the idea that she might have mysterious powers on which she could call; such powers could account for Joe's and her success as mixed farmers.

Joe and Wallace Helena grinned at each other, when the latter rumour reached them. They both knew that their thriving farm was due largely to Joe's and Simon's profound knowledge of the country, of its weather, its animals and the customs of the Crees. To help them further,

Uncle James had sent them a steady succession of books on animal husbandry and grain farming, particularly in cold climates, like Russia. Tom had loved his land and had broken the sod; Wallace Helena and Joe were devoted to making it blossom, come drought, come bitter winter.

Though Wallace Helena was a proud, fierce and tetchy woman, she had not been so proud that she could not face picking the brains of the Manager of the Hudson's Bay Company's own farm, in order to avoid repeating any mistakes they had made. She also talked to the Oblate Fathers, when they came south from Lac St Anne or St Albert. None of them liked her very much; she did not belong to their flock and she lived in sin with Joe Black. She had the advantage, though, that she spoke fluent, educated French, and in their work of settling the Metis, they were just as interested as she was in good farming; so they exchanged ideas with her like scientists, regardless of their personal feelings, and, with a similar sense of rivalry, watched each other's experiments.

After breakfast, Joe Black went out into the yard to inspect a sapling he had brought up from Calgary, after seeing Wallace Helena onto the train. He had been told that it was almost impossible to grow apples so far north – the cold spring wind blew the blossoms off before they had set; he had expected that the tree would die during the several days he had taken to ride the two hundred miles home from Calgary, with it tied to the back of a packhorse, beside a couple of new pickaxes. The tree, however, was looking quite healthy; it had retained its leaves, and its branches were stretching upwards. In the hope that rabbits would not be able to get at it, he had fenced it round with a precious piece of chicken wire.

He smiled grimly to himself. Wallace Helena never wanted anything to be planted that could not be either eaten or traded. He had noticed that some of the white women now settling round Edmonton had planted little flowerbeds near their cabins or clapboard houses. He had asked Wallace Helena if she would like him to bring in some wild flower seeds, to start such a garden.

She had looked up at him from her account book, and had asked in a bemused voice, 'Why?'

'Well, the white women seem to plant them. Would you like some?'

She had caught his great hand and squeezed it, while she laughed up at him. 'I'm not white – any Metis would be happy to tell you that I'm yellow.' Her lips met in a thin line. 'I'm Lebanese. Flowers might seed amongst the vegetables – and we've got enough weeds already.'

'O.K.' He turned to leave her, but she still held his hand firmly. She said suddenly and very wistfully, 'I wish I could get a lemon tree.'

He had never heard of or seen a lemon, so he asked, 'What's that?'

She shrugged her shoulders, and laughed. 'It's a fruit tree – the blossoms have a heavenly perfume. We used to have one in my father's courtyard, at home.'

As Joe digested this, he looked down at her. She rarely mentioned Lebanon and he had tended to forget that she came from anywhere else but Chicago. He wondered where he could possibly obtain such a tree.

She laughed, and pulled his hand playfully. 'The fruit's awfully sharp. But its flavour is delicious in drinks – and in cooking.' She sighed, and then smiled up at him. 'But it couldn't live in this harsh climate.' She tugged his hand again, and ordered, 'Bend over, so that I can reach you.'

Clumsily, he bent his head towards her, and she kissed him soundly on the lips. He had gone away laughing, wondering for the umpteenth time exactly where Lebanon was. Some time, he must ask the priest who taught school in the village to show him on a map. It was further away than England, Wallace Helena had assured him of that.

After he had gone, Wallace Helena had sat staring at the rough logs of the old cabin's wall, her face drawn and infinitely sad. She saw, in her mind's eye, a country of beautiful mountains and rushing rivers, and, tucked along the coast and on the plateaus, orchards, flowering orchards, of oranges, lemons and apricots with a perfume so sweet that it hurt to think about it.

Well, he'd done his best, Joe considered. He had brought her a Macintosh apple tree.

With a half-peeled potato in her hand, Aunt Theresa had come out to view the tree when it had been planted. She had assumed he was planting it for shade.

'What kind of tree is it?' she had asked.

'It's a fruit tree – an apple tree.'

Aunt Theresa had never seen an apple, and she fingered one of the leaves with interest. Then she said circumspectly, 'It has always seemed to me that trees – and plants – need others exactly like them round about, before they'll propagate.'

'I never thought of it.' He looked glumly at the little sapling. 'Will it flower?'

'If it lives, it probably will.' Then, to cheer him up, she added, 'You could watch out for a chance to get another one or two. Then you might get some fruit.'

'God knows where I'd find them. This one came on the train from the east, in a pot.'

'Trains bring lots of settlers. They bring plants they like with them,' prophesied Aunt Theresa shrewdly.

Next time he was in the little village outside the Fort, he dropped in on a member of the Agricultural Society, and explained his first effort at planting a tree. 'Usually, I'm felling them, to get them out of the way or because I need timber. I never thought of planting one before.'

Pleased to be asked for advice, the man confirmed Aunt Theresa's information.

Joe's face fell, so the man kindly went on to suggest how the sapling might be kept alive through the winter, until Joe had the chance to buy some more. 'I doubt you'll get many apples,' he finished up. 'Our winter's so cold, and the wind'll strip the blossom off in no time.'

Joe shrugged, and thanked his adviser. 'I'll nurse it along,' he said. And as he got on his horse and rode away, he thought of the young girl he had nursed along through her early years at Fort Edmonton. She'd turned out strong enough, God knows. Maybe the tree would, too.

17

Wallace Helena ate without comment the third English breakfast provided for her by her landlady, Mrs Hughes. The breakfast consisted of oatmeal porridge followed by two boiled eggs served with thick slices of toast. Though she enjoyed the luxury of wheaten bread, she found she lacked her usual appetite, and she realized that she did not need so much food. After days of train travel and the confines of an immigrant ship returning to Liverpool, she was now penned up in the odiferous soapery all day. She politely refused Mrs Hughes's offer of more toast with some home-made marmalade.

Mrs Hughes was uncertain whether or not she approved of Wallace Helena. In repose, the visitor's face was almost forbidding, though she was gracious enough in a foreign kind of way. While the Lebanese ate her breakfast, the puzzled Liverpool lady fluttered round the dark, high-ceilinged dining-room, straightening ornaments and pictures and commenting on the raininess of the day. She hoped to overcome Wallace Helena's uncompromising reserve and learn a little more about her.

Mrs Hughes considered that, despite her stuck-up looks, Wallace Helena was no lady. In justification of this observation, she had already told her next-door neighbour that Wallace Helena licked the butter off her fingers after eating her toast. 'Mr Benson told me,' she added, 'that she's a colonial from Canada – but she looks *real* foreign to me.'

In an absent-minded way, Wallace Helena was aware of her landlady's reflections, though she did not know that, from being much outdoors, her skin was dark enough, and the sweep of her black eyebrows and eyelashes was great enough, to make Mrs Hughes wonder if she were harbouring an East Indian, like the lascars she sometimes saw in the city.

Wallace Helena was used to being disliked – because of her dubious origins, as one Scottish clerk at the Fort had once put it – and also because, around Edmonton, few people got the better of her when bargaining. She had become stiffly proud, and particularly quick to take offence if anyone cast a slur on Joe Black. She accepted that the pair of them were outcasts, and, in consequence, they owed no special loyalty to anyone except each other and those who shared their home. They took tender care of each other, and minded their own business.

As she drained her last cup of tea, her thoughts strayed for a moment to Joe. Despite her fascination with the new world into which she had plunged, she would have given a lot, today, to skip going to the soap works and, instead, to ride out with him under hot sunshine to the boundaries of their land, to check that the fencing was still in place; they could do with another hand to give most of his attention to fencing, she felt, and she wondered if the Liverpool business could provide her with enough money to invest some of it in the homestead. If a railway finally came as far as Edmonton, she might be able to sell grain to Europe – or even steers; amid the turmoil of coping with a Liverpool soap works, it was a cheering thought.

Stiff from lack of exercise and fretful from weeks of sleeping alone, she rose awkwardly from the breakfast table, aware of her heavy black skirt and petticoats dragging at her. She longed for the soft, worked skins of her old Indian tunic and leggings. Even her boots, newly cleaned by Mrs Hughes's maid-of-all-work, hurt feet normally encased in moccasins. Ordinarily, she wore formal clothes only when going down to Edmonton or to visit the priests in St Albert.

'I'll walk down to the Brunswick Dock, Mrs Hughes,' she announced. 'I need the exercise. Would you kindly tell Mr Benson, when he arrives with his carriage, that I have gone on ahead. I'll meet him by the dock gates – I presume the dock will have a gate?'

'Yes, there's a gate, Miss. But it's no district for you to walk by yourself, Miss. I wouldn't advise it.'

Wallace Helena laughed shortly. 'Don't worry. I'm used to being alone in wild country. Mr Benson says that *he* has to take me into the dock, because otherwise they won't let a woman in. Ridiculous, isn't it?'

Mrs Hughes ran her tongue round her teeth before replying. Then she said carefully, 'I appreciate your comin' from Canada and being used to all kinds of strange things, Miss, but Mr Benson's right to escort you. You could get accosted, like. We got worse 'n Red Indians round them docks, believe me. It's no place for a lady by herself.'

'Mr Benson will probably catch up with me in his carriage long before I reach the dock.'

'Well, if you get there first, you tell the Customs Officer or the policeman at the gate who you are, and you stay close to him till Mr Benson comes.'

Wallace Helena promised, and went upstairs to put on the black straw gable-brimmed hat which she had bought in Montreal; it suited her much better than the beaded bonnet she had bought in Mr Johnstone Walker's newly opened store in Edmonton. She reflected with amusement that Mr Walker had not thought much of a woman who tried to beat down the price of his millinery, so painfully freighted up by ox-cart from the railway at Calgary.

Since it had been raining and the air felt clammy, she put a black woollen shawl round her shoulders, and, when she went downstairs again, she accepted the loan of a long black umbrella from Mrs Hughes.

Mrs Hughes followed her uncertainly towards the front door. 'Now, you be careful of yourself, Miss Turn left at the bottom of the hill and keep walking. You can't miss it.'

'Thank you, Mrs Hughes. I do know the way. Mr Benson drove me past it yesterday.'

Thankful to be out in the air, temporarily washed clean by the early morning rain, Wallace Helena ran down the wide stone steps of the house. Sunlight was creeping through the lifting clouds and the damp pavement shone in its rays. Two little girls were skipping towards her. She smiled at them and they smiled shyly back at her. She passed a number of women dressed in black, carrying shopping baskets on their arms. They stared at her as she strode past them, her unfashionable gathered skirt swinging round her a couple of inches above her ankles. Even to a city accustomed to immigrants of all kinds passing through, Wallace Helena seemed eccentric; her rapid, masculine walk, her almost scornful expression and an aura of great energy, barely suppressed, aroused casual interest.

As she walked, Wallace Helena concentrated on the day before her. Though she had made a list and it was safely tucked into her reticule, she went over all that she had learned from the Canadian lawyer who had secured her homestead for her, all she knew from her father about contracts, bookkeeping and running a business in Beirut, and her own limited experience, as first Tom's Will had been laboriously proven and then her darling mother's. Lastly, she thought of all that her father had done to re-establish himself in Chicago. Surely, she considered, between the lot of it, together with running the farm, I have enough experience to cope with the Lady Lavender Soap Works; it's not that big, really.

She felt a nervous excitement at the challenge she had been presented with. She had come to check what was being done by Mr Benson, the Executor of her Uncle James's Will, to make sure that selling the business was in her best interests and that she was going to get the right price for it. Now, already in the back of her mind, she itched to get her hands on it, to run it herself. She had not yet faced all the implications of this sudden desire.

Though its owner had died, the works seemed to be functioning fairly well under the care of Mr Bobsworth, the bookkeeper, and Mr George

Tasker, the Soap Master, who had been with the company almost from its inception. Despite their devotion to their duties, however, she had noticed in some sections a lackadaisical air, a lack of good housekeeping which she would not, for one moment, have tolerated on her homestead; she sensed that the general discipline of the place had slipped a little.

Even when she, as the new owner, walked in, there had not been that quick shuffle to appear busy, which she would have expected. 'Perhaps they reckon I'm not going to be their new employer, since I'm a woman,' she thought with a wry grin. Then she muttered to herself, 'Little do you realize what is going to descend on you, my boys.'

If Joe Black could have watched her during that brief walk, he would have grinned lazily and would have sat back and watched the carnage she would subsequently wreak amongst the slothful. And then, had he been there when, drained and hungry, she had returned home, he would have encouraged her to eat plenty and afterwards spread herself before a good log fire, while he rolled a cigarette for her and listened to the successes and failures of her day. In their intimate enjoyment of each other, they would have found much to laugh at in the soap works.

The tightly packed rows of town houses, each with its shining brass doorknob and letterbox, past which Wallace Helena strode, seemed to shut her in, enclose her like some long narrow box. They soon gave way to humbler, even more closely packed homes, and then to small works and warehouses.

Over the stone setts of the street, huge horses pulled drays loaded with bales, barrels, boxes, and sacks of coal, all the needs of a great industrial country. The horses' big hooves splashed through puddles left by the early morning rain, spattering the passersby. Sometimes, they stood patiently slavering by the pavement while being loaded or unloaded; and clog-shod men in flat caps and sackcloth aprons shouted upwards to others peering down at them from behind blocks and tackle used for hoisting goods to the upper floors of the warehouses.

Suddenly, a black shadow passed over Wallace Helena. She looked up quickly.

'Mind yourself, Queen!' a man shouted urgently and pushed her roughly aside. Uncomfortably close to her, a sacking-covered bale was lowered swiftly onto a stationary dray at the kerb. 'Aye, Missus, watch yourself. You could've bin killed.'

Though a little alarmed by the unexpected danger, she managed to smile at the labourer and thank him.

Before she continued on her way, she edged past the great flanks of the horses, to stand well in front of them, so that they could see her, despite the blinkers that they wore. They were chomping at their bits as they waited. Another labourer stood idly by them.

'Are you the carter?' she inquired.

The man touched his cap. 'Yes, Missus.' Though he was respectful, there was nothing humble about him. His interest was aroused by her foreign accent, and he turned a brown, foxlike face towards her. 'You visitin' here, Missus?'

'Yes.' Her eyes were on the Percherons before her. 'May I pet them?' she asked.

'For sure, Missus. They're real gentle.'

She spoke softly to the nearest animal and, after a moment, it stretched forward to nuzzle her. She stroked its nose and neck.

The carter warned her. 'Be a bit careful, Missus. Bobby, here, could be a bit jealous.' He need not have worried; Wallace Helena had already transferred her attention to the other horse. Then she stepped back. 'I've got horses at home – but nothing as good as these; I could use a pair of them, especially in winter.'

'Where are you from, Missus?'

'Canada.' She turned to look him in the face and smiled her wide, generous smile. To the man, it changed her from an austere, strange lady into a warm human being. Emboldened, he asked what Canada was like.

'Very cold – and very hot,' she told him, and then added thoughtfully, 'It's big – the distances are enormous.'

She remembered suddenly the lawyer she was supposed to meet, so she smiled again and turned away.

At the bottom of Hill Street, when she was about to cross the road, her eye was caught by a flutter of brown sail in a gap between black buildings. She stopped to get a better look.

Between the Coburg Dock and the Brunswick Dock lay a small quay. It was being approached by a fishing smack floating lightly on the silver river. A man was reefing sail. Near the quay was a muddle of low domestic buildings, half surrounding a cobbled square, in which fishing nets had been spread to dry. Ivy nearly smothered a particularly pleasant-looking cottage at one corner; in its clean, curtained window sat a canary in a cage. Two men in rough blue jerseys came out of the cottage and went down to the quay to watch the smack tie up. At their approach a cloud of gulls glided into the air and circled the boat. One of the men leisurely lit a clay pipe. Despite the threat of rain, nobody seemed in a hurry; it was a peaceful vignette, next to the maelstrom of activity in the main road.

Wallace Helena thought a little wistfully how pleasant it would be to

111

walk into the quiet square. She had a feeling that its inhabitants might greet her in a friendly country way, as she had been greeted as a little girl when her family had gone up into the mountains to avoid the damp heat of Beirut's summer.

For a minute, she stood entranced, poised on the corner of Hill Street, the soapery forgotten. 'That's how Liverpool must have been long ago,' she guessed. Then she roused herself and crossed the road. She was accompanied by a band of small ragamuffins; they ran in and out of the traffic, followed by the scolding voices of the draymen, who were afraid the scurrying mob would make their horses rear.

Before crossing Sefton Street, she paused again. Further along, in another side street parallel to Hill Street, lay the soap works. Across the road before her lay the Brunswick Dock. She watched carefully, as at the dock gate the driver of a cart paused to speak to a uniformed man at the gate and was then allowed to drive in. She presumed that everything that came into the Brunswick Dock for the Lady Lavender Soap Works would have to be off-loaded onto just such a cart and be taken the very short distance to the works to be unloaded. She had the previous day overheard a brief conversation between Mr Bobsworth, the bookkeeper, and one of his underlings from which she had understood that goods left long in the dock warehouse were subject to high demurrage charges; everything must be removed quickly to its own warehouse or yard. She was as yet unaware that the soapery had its own spur railway line, along which its goods could be rolled straight from the dock to its yard. She retreated to a niche in a wall, while she fished out a small black notebook and pencil to make a note to remind herself to ask Mr Bobsworth more details of the movement of ingredients and finished goods; the notebook was already nearly full of observations and questions in her small, cramped handwriting. Accustomed to the acute shortage of good farm workers in and around Edmonton, she had been shocked at the mass of labourers involved with the soap works, and many of her queries were in connection with the cost of this; she had as yet little idea of the cheapness of labour in Liverpool.

As she returned the notebook to her reticule, she wondered where on earth she could get something to smoke. She had smoked her last cheroot aboard ship and she was feeling the acute lack of nicotine.

She saw an elegant, dark green carriage drawing up at the dock entrance and, recognizing it as that of Mr Benson, her uncle's lawyer, she hastened towards it. She was nearly struck by a bicycle as she stepped off the pavement. The black-suited rider swerved to a stop, surprised to see a lady in such a place. He assumed that she must have come down to the docks to distribute temperance pamphlets to dockers.

As he regained his balance and cautiously circled behind her, Mr Benson saw her and sprang forward from the pavement.

'My dear Miss Harding,' he expostulated, as he took her elbow and guided her solicitously towards the gate. 'Really, you should have waited for me. Anything could happen to you down here.' In the back of his mind, he was appalled to think of the awful problem of probably having to trace yet another legatee, if she managed to get herself killed by a cyclist. The very idea made him nervous.

'Nothing happened to me,' Wallace Helena stiffly responded. 'It was a most interesting walk, I assure you.'

Several men were leaning against the dock wall, enjoying the weak sunshine, while they laughed and joked with each other. They were dressed in flat caps, stained trousers and striped shirts without collars; one wore a leather waistcoat and carried a curious metal hook. They stopped their conversation to watch the peculiar-looking woman passing by, and, for a moment, Wallace Helena hesitated and stared back with cold, brown eyes. Mr Benson's hand under her elbow compelled her forward again, as she asked, 'Who are those men, Mr Benson?'

'Those? Just casual labourers – dockers – they come down here twice a day in the hope of getting work.' His tone was uninterested.

'Humph. I wish I had three or four of them on my farm.'

Mr Benson raised his eyebrows slightly, but made no comment. Idle men were two a penny on the dock road.

After stating their business, they were allowed into the dock, and Mr Benson led her over to the Dock Master who was standing at the far end of the wharf on the west side. Mr Benson had met him once before in the course of his duties as Executor of James Al-Khoury's Will, and he now introduced him to Wallace Helena.

The heavy, bearded Dock Master received her courteously, though he wondered why she should trouble to come to see the Lady Lavender's raw materials coming in. He assumed that Mr Benson was simply entertaining her; it did not occur to him that he faced a woman intensely interested in following all the processes of the soap works from beginning to end.

Holding on to her hat against the capricious wind, Wallace Helena turned to survey the scene before her.

On the other side of the dock, two sailing vessels were being unloaded, derricks bent over them like pecking vultures. The shouts of the dockers attending them came clearly across the water. Nearer at hand, two men stood by an iron capstan, presumably waiting for a pair of barges being slowly towed through the dock entrance. Another group of men, shirt sleeves rolled up, red kerchiefs round their necks and

113

blackened leather waistcoats protecting their humped backs, seemed also to be waiting for the same vessels. The sun glinted on the hooks they carried and on the fair hair covering their reddened arms. Wallace Helena stared at them unabashed. Used to dark Metis or Indians or to men so wrapped up against the cold that it was hard to discover what colour they were, the red and gold colouring of the English dockers was a rarity to her; she wondered idly if the rest of their bodies were equally red and gold.

Her thoughts were interrupted by Mr Benson saying, 'Mr Bobsworth informed me that a shipment of carbonate ash was expected this morning from the manufacturers – and a cargo of salt – the salt's shipped by canal from the Cheshire salt mines.'

Wallace Helena nodded her head in acknowledgment of this information; she presumed that the carbonate ash was similar to that used by Aunt Theresa and herself when, each spring, they boiled soap in the yard.

Anxious to show that he understood something of his late client's industry, Mr Benson went on to explain, 'I understand they make it liquid and caustic by putting it into vats with lime and water.'

'In other words, they make lye out of it?' suggested Wallace Helena.

'Yes,' responded the lawyer, a trifle surprised that a woman would be aware of such chemistry.

Between watching the progress of the barges, the Dock Master had been eyeing his female visitor with some interest. He now mentioned to her that the shipping agent's representative was at that moment in the dock office ready to attend to the paperwork in connection with the expected cargoes.

He was a little disconcerted to have a number of relevant questions shot at him. Who did the actual unloading? How many men did it take? How were the goods transferred to the Lady Lavender warehouse? How long did it take?

He hastily swallowed his amusement as his replies were entered in Wallace Helena's notebook. As she wrote, he examined with curiosity the woman's firm mouth with faint lines down either side, the long nose which added further strength to a face which gave a feeling of anything but womanliness. She snapped her notebook closed and looked up at him, her brown eyes twinkling as if she knew exactly what he was thinking. Embarrassed, he dropped his own bloodshot blue eyes. He was further surprised, when they went into the dock office to meet the shipping agent's representative, to find that she understood much of the paperwork connected with the movement of goods, both within a country and when importing.

114

The enthusiastic young shipping agent ventured to congratulate her on her grasp of the matter, and she told him honestly, 'My father dealt in silk for export and I was often with him. When we were in Chicago, I was frequently his interpreter and his clerk. I grew up amid imports and exports.'

This was news to Mr Benson, too. James Al-Khoury had never mentioned to him what his brother had done for a living, and that his niece should understand something of the world of business seemed very odd; he had always believed that oriental women lived in strict seclusion. Even English women did not concern themselves with the outside world; the home and family were their sphere.

When Wallace Helena moved to go outside again to see the actual unloading, the Dock Master asked her kindly, 'Would you like to stay in the office and watch through the window? It's chilly out there – and the dockers' language is sometimes not fit for a lady's ears.'

Wallace Helena laughed. 'I have one or two male employees – I am quite used to being among men. And I love the fresh air.'

After stuffy offices, the wind was a joy and though it whipped at her skirt and shawl and she had to hold on to her hat, despite its huge hatpins, she leaned happily against it while she watched the dockers do their work. Mr Benson resignedly shrugged himself deeper into his Melton overcoat, and consoled himself with the thought that the Al-Khoury Estate would have to pay him well for these hours with its heiress.

Once she had the general idea of what was happening, she turned to him, ready to continue her morning in the Lady Lavender Soap Works itself. Looking over his shoulder, she pointed suddenly towards a young man entering the dock gates. 'Isn't that a boy from our works? I think he does messages for Mr Tasker.'

Mr Benson did not know the lad, but the Dock Master asked, 'The coloured boy? He often comes over from the Lady Lavender for one reason or another. Name of Alfie.'

Carrying a white envelope, the youth jog-trotted into the office.

'I'd like to speak to Alfie,' Wallace Helena said, as the messenger reappeared and moved with them towards the gate. Mr Benson immediately called him over.

Alfie whipped off his cap to expose a head of brownish, tightly curly hair. He smiled nervously at Wallace Helena and ran his cap through long, brown fingers. 'Yes, Sir?' he inquired of Mr Benson.

'Miss Harding wishes to speak to you.'

Alfie turned fully towards her, a wary expression on his face. 'Miss?'

115

'Alfie, you smoke, don't you? I saw you outside the works yesterday, smoking something.'

The youngster's thick lips parted in surprise and she saw his body tense, as if he might take flight. He replied uneasily, 'Well, yes, Ma'am.' He fully expected a lecture on the evils of smoking.

'Can you buy tobacco and papers – or ready rolled cigarettes round here?'

The astonishment on Alfie's face caused Wallace Helena's grim mouth to relax slightly. 'Yes, Ma'am.'

'Well, get me some. How much will it cost?'

He shrugged slightly and told her. Then, realizing that she was serious in her request, he added, 'You can get cigarettes ready rolled, Ma'am, if you like.'

'I would prefer to roll my own,' she replied, as she opened her change purse.

'Allow me, Miss Harding.' Mr Benson took out a net purse from his inner pocket and loosened a ring at one end in order to get at a silver coin.

She looked at him, shocked. 'Oh, no,' she replied firmly. 'I mustn't put you to expense.' She handed Alfie a shilling and asked him to leave the purchase with her late uncle's secretary, Mr Helliwell. She said that he could keep the change.

Disconcerted, Mr Benson restored his purse to his pocket. Mrs Benson had instructed him to ask Miss Harding to dinner the following evening. What would she say if Miss Harding lit a cigarette in her drawing-room?

Wallace Helena again faced the wind, as she glanced back once more towards the gaily painted barges. Bright red, yellow and blue flower designs ran riot all over them, and a metal ewer standing on a ledge at the front of the first barge had the same colourful patterns on it. She had been surprised that the person throwing the rope ashore from the first barge had been a well-built, middle-aged woman. Now the woman was sitting on the edge of the dock, her legs dangling over the water. She had a baby at her breast.

Mr Benson saw Wallace Helena's bemused expression at the sight, and he explained as they approached the dock gate that whole families lived permanently on the canal barges. 'There are probably more children inside,' he told her.

Outside the gate, Mr Benson instructed his groom to pick him up from the Lady Lavender Soap Works in one hour's time. Then he and his client did a quick tour of the Brunswick goods station from which another railway spur line sunk into the street ran into the soap works.

Pointing to the spur line, Mr Benson told her, 'That'll be the way in which your company's goods travel from the Dispatch Department to the railway.'

She nodded. Mr Bobsworth, the bookkeeper and dispatch clerk, had already told her that the lavender oil to perfume their toilet soap was shipped in by rail from Kent and that tallow and oil from seed processors was sometimes similarly shipped. He had said, 'Though it's quicker by rail, it is more expensive, so much of our raw material comes in by barge. We distribute our finished goods by rail – or by delivery van.'

Wallace Helena was very thoughtful as they walked over to the soap works. The general pattern of manufacture and distribution was clarifying in her mind. This afternoon she would look over the books with Mr Bobsworth and see exactly how their finances stood. 'Do you know if the Lady Lavender makes anything else other than soap?' she asked casually of Mr Benson as they walked through the soapery's yard.

Mr Benson cleared his throat. 'Well, Mrs Benson uses a very delightful scent which they sell. You'll have to ask Mr Benjamin Al-Khoury about anything else.'

'I will,' she replied gravely, 'when he returns from his trip to Manchester.' Then she said, 'I think it is always better to deal in more than one commodity. At home, I produce barley and oats for the Government – and to feed ourselves. But some years the crop gets lost to hail or is simply poor. Then I'm thankful to have steers and a hay crop to feed them – and a vegetable garden. Or I can cut wood. I keep hens, too, mostly for our own eating and for eggs, of course; but nowadays there is even a market for these sometimes.'

'We have mixed farms in Britain.'

'Do you? My partner also runs a trapline for furs, though we do have a constant battle with the Hudson's Bay Company over it; they seem to think they still run the Territories and are entitled to buy anything they fancy.'

'So your farm isn't being neglected while you are over here?'

She smiled. 'Far from it. Joe Black is a very capable man – he used to be my stepfather's stockman.'

'Indeed?' The lawyer was already beginning to wonder if she would sell the soapery. Her general understanding and quick grasp of detail made him sense that she might attempt to run it herself, especially if her farm had someone in charge of it. He was sure she would face a lot of prejudice; neither the firm's employees nor the business community were likely to accept a woman very willingly.

As he handed her over to anxious, obsequious Mr Bobsworth,

117

he wondered what Benjamin Al-Khoury would feel about her; James Al-Khoury's son had been cruelly cut off from his anticipated inheritance by his father's unexpectedly early death and he was hardly likely to welcome his cousin.

18

When Wallace Helena arrived at the soapery, she found Mr Bobsworth very busy in the Shipping and Forwarding Department. He was in his shirt sleeves, and in his hand he held a brush dripping with black paint. He was in the midst of carefully marking boxes of soap with identifying numbers and with the addresses to which they were to be delivered.

Embarrassed at being found in his shirt sleeves by a lady, he hastily put down his brush and wiped his hand on a cloth exuding a strong smell of solvent. He then groped behind him for his jacket, while apologizing to Wallace Helena for his disarray.

'So sorry, Miss Harding. I've always supervised Shipping and Forwarding myself; it avoids errors and delays in delivery, you understand.' He shepherded her gently into his little office. 'The smell of paint must be overwhelming to you,' he suggested, as he pulled out a chair and his assistant, Mr Le Fleur, sprang respectfully to his feet. He turned to Le Fleur, and ordered him to go and finish marking the crates. The young man went reluctantly; he had no desire to get drips of paint on himself, and old Bobsworth had a great streak of it across his chin.

As diplomatically as she could, Wallace Helena informed the accountant of the streak. This sent him flying to a mottled mirror hanging over a tiny office sink in the corner, where he rubbed it ineffectually with his handkerchief. 'So sorry, Miss Harding,' he breathed anxiously.

'Don't worry, Mr Bobsworth. I think it's time I looked at the company's books and inventory; I think I would first like to see what we owe and what is owed to us – and what orders and commitments we presently have.'

Poor Mr Bobsworth hastily stuffed his hanky back into his trouser pocket and felt around in his waistcoat for the key to his wooden book cupboard. He looked quite flustered, as he took out several account books and his ledger. 'I'm sure you'll find everything in order, Miss Harding. Mr Benson has, more or less, left the accounts to me while we are waiting for Probate, though his auditor has popped in from time to time to see that all is well. Would you like to sit at the table here?'

'I'm sure everything will be just fine, Mr Bobsworth. No doubt Mr Benson has informed you that you may show the books to me?'

Though he assented, the remark sent him into another flutter; he hoped she would find his handwriting easily readable.

In dire need of a smoke, Wallace Helena rose from the table clutching the heavy books to her and announced that she would work in her uncle's office.

Mr Bobsworth took the books from her and escorted her.

Mr Helliwell, her uncle's private secretary, received her with the calm assurance of a man who had always enjoyed his master's total confidence. He had studied Mr James Al-Khoury with the greatest attention and had understood his whims and foibles. As he often said to his wife, his lips were sealed. 'Not even to you, dear heart, would I say anything about Mr Al-Khoury's affairs.'

He was a pleasant, slightly pompous man around thirty years old. Wallace Helena thought him rather stupid, but Mr Benson had told her that, like Mr Bobsworth, he was as faithful as a bulldog. She did not hesitate to ask him if the tobacco had arrived and if he had any matches.

He nodded and pulled out the desk chair for her. She sat down mechanically in front of the books and absently tore open the packet of cigarette tobacco handed to her by the secretary. While he watched the quick deft movements of her fingers as she rolled a cigarette and licked the paper to seal it, she said to him, 'Mr Helliwell, we use olive oil and other kinds of oil in our soap, don't we?'

'Yes, Miss Harding.'

'Do you know if anyone has discovered an oil which will heal smallpox scars?'

Though the question was unexpected, Mr Helliwell answered immediately in the negative. 'I believe I would know if there were such an oil. My wife's eldest sister is badly scarred – we still get smallpox here, sometimes – and I'm sure that if such an oil existed, we would have tried to obtain it for her.' He leaned forward, struck a sulphur match and lit Wallace Helena's cigarette. She thankfully inhaled.

'Poor woman,' she said with feeling. She half closed her eyes, sickened by the sudden memory of her stepfather's and her mother's last hours. It appeared that Joe would be terribly marked for the rest of his life, and she sighed. Then she smiled faintly. He was still her irrepressible Joe, always optimistic that the next harvest would be better, the next winter milder or that the trapline would unexpectedly yield a wondrous collection of valuable furs.

As she took another puff at her cigarette, she said to Mr Helliwell, 'Mother and my stepfather both died of smallpox.' The heavy lids of her eyes were, for once, lifted towards him and he saw and understood some of the tragedy of her life reflected in them. 'It took a third of our population,' she went on a little heavily, 'and the living are scarred to this day – that's why I asked.'

Mr Helliwell blinked. 'Dear Miss Harding,' he exclaimed with genuine feeling, 'how very sad for you. I wish I could suggest something for those who are pocked . . . you might ask a doctor, while you are here. Just in case something has recently been discovered – one never knows what science may divulge.'

'Very true. I must ask.' She looked up at him and said a little stiffly, as though she regretted the confidence, 'I'm sure you must have work to do. I'll ring if I need you.'

Dismissed, Mr Helliwell went back to his own small cubbyhole. Poor lady! She must also have gone through the same travail in Beirut that Mr James had; he knew about that because, once a year, on its anniversary, the old man had taken a holiday. He had explained to Mr Helliwell that on that particular day he wanted to be by himself to remember his friends killed in Beirut. As far as Mr Helliwell knew, he simply spent the day walking in the country. And, on top of that massacre, this poor woman had gone through a smallpox epidemic. He wondered how she had herself survived the latter unscathed, and decided that it was pure luck; God chose those He would take.

Now, she had lost her uncle, as well as her parents. He decided that she needed his complete support as much as he needed to keep his job.

Mr Helliwell's perception of her was in contrast to that of nervous Mr Bobsworth, who became more and more defensive, as, for several days, she waded through his beautifully kept account books and pried into all his other responsibilities. He was a portly little man, with the colourless face of someone who has little time in the fresh air. There was a permanent deep frown line between his thin eyebrows; and his old-fashioned side whiskers stuck up over his winged collar in an equally permanent, untidy bristle. As he trotted importantly through the works, his pen parked comfortably behind one ear, Wallace was often beside him. When he sat in his tiny office, amid a sea of invoices and bills, receiving constant interruptions from boys or men in big aprons, who came for instructions, Wallace Helena was often there, too, perched on a stool to watch what went on. As the days went by, he began to regard her as a female busybody, an interloper in a life already made difficult enough by the death of his old friend, James Al-Khoury.

'Mr Tasker and me – we've bin here almost from the day Mr Al-Khoury started up. We all worked together to get the business going. You really don't have to worry.' He took off his gold-rimmed glasses and polished them on a spotless pocket handkerchief with quick impatient

121

movements. 'And Mr Benjamin Al-Khoury – he's been keeping tabs on everything as much as he could, ever since Mr James died.'

'I'm sure you have all done very well,' she soothed. 'My uncle's passing must have been a personal loss to you, as well?'

Surprised, he glanced quickly at her. 'Indeed, Miss Harding, it was,' he replied a little huskily. 'We were very good friends, if I may presume to say so.'

She was kind, he admitted to Mr Tasker. But she was a pest. 'Forever at my shoulder, as if I can't be trusted,' he complained. He was further annoyed that Mr Tasker seemed to be entranced by her – and at his age he should know better. Why didn't she get on with the sale of the place, so at least they would all know the worst, he asked Mr Tasker.

'She's not got no Probate yet,' responded Mr Tasker. 'She can't do nothing till she gets that.'

19

Though, as a refugee, Wallace Helena had passed through Liverpool on her way to an immigrant ship to take her to the United States, she had not mixed with its inhabitants. Now, in the Lady Lavender soapery, she had come face to face with a society very different from anything else she had previously encountered. Unlike Chicago, the city had a long history and well-established customs. Her new employees were touchy about any suggestion of change. Dealing with them was stretching her quick intelligence to the utmost.

While she was going through the books, Wallace Helena sat late in her uncle's office long after everyone else, except the nightwatchman, had gone home. She felt she needed uninterrupted quietness while she considered the ramifications of what she was looking at. Twice, on following mornings, she had ordered a spot check of a particular stock, which caused a lot of grumbling amongst employees in the particular department; they could not think why she bothered, since she was not likely to remain at the soapery; anyway, Mr Benjamin always did stocktaking.

Undeterred, she confirmed the accuracy of the records, and learned the exact duties of each employee.

She thought irritably that she could have acquired an overall view of the business much more quickly if Benjamin Al-Khoury had seen fit to be at the Lady Lavender when she arrived. As assistant manager, he could have told her much that she had had to deduce herself. On further consideration, she concluded that, as she did not know anything about him, a personal check of the books was not a bad idea. Mr Bobsworth had been quite helpful.

Like Mr Tasker and everybody else, Mr Bobsworth seemed to have all kinds of duties.

'With Mr James Al-Khoury no longer with us and Mr Benjamin on a special visit to Manchester, I'm hardpressed,' he told her, hoping she would leave him alone to get on with his work.

Though her respect for the busy accountant grew daily, Wallace Helena had no intention of going away until she was certain that the two key employees in the business were absolutely trustworthy. Young Mr Benjamin was apparently assistant manager, but she felt that

Bobsworth and Tasker were the two who set the standard for the other employees.

'Some of our customers seem to have very long credit,' she remarked one morning; she could almost hear her father advising to collect from debtors as fast as possible and pay one's own bills only at the last possible moment – it gave a firm a better flow of money for temporary use elsewhere. She picked up three files from the desk. 'These firms seem to be particularly favoured.'

Mr Bobsworth answered her patiently, though his head ached abominably. 'They're our biggest and best customers in the Manchester-Warrington area, Miss Harding. We can't do less for them than our competitors would. We're having a real fight with a Mr Lever, who is marketing a soap he calls *Sunlight* – a washing soap.'

This was the first time that Wallace Helena heard the name of this formidable man, who was in the process of revolutionizing the soap industry. It was his aggressive selling practices which had sent Benjamin Al-Khoury on a special visit to the firms with whom Lady Lavender dealt in Manchester, in the hope of persuading them that his company's soap was far superior to anything Mr Lever could produce.

Wallace Helena had already learned from Mr Tasker that the soap industry was very competitive, and she now said, 'Somebody mentioned that we advertise our soap and that, unlike many soap companies, we mention the name Lady Lavender, so that housewives ask for it by name.'

Mr Bobsworth's side whiskers seemed to bristle more than usual, as he responded to the mention of advertising. He did not believe that newspaper advertising could improve sales; he thought it was a waste of money. *Women* bought soap, and how many working-class women could read? he was liable to ask.

He answered Wallace Helena primly, 'Lines of credit were always negotiated by Mr James – Mr Benjamin does it at present. As for advertising, that is something Mr Benjamin introduced. You'll have to ask him about it.'

Wallace Helena nodded. 'I have not, of course, met Mr Benjamin,' she said, and paused. Then she added slyly, to see what Mr Bobsworth's reaction would be, 'He must be a relation?'

Mr Bobsworth flushed. He slowly put down on her desk the purchase ledger which he had been holding. He was tired and wished Wallace Helena would invite him to be seated. Coming from a rough, frontier society, Wallace Helena had wrongly assumed that if he wanted to sit down he would do so.

His reply was careful. 'Well, Mr James brought him into the business when he was about fifteen – and he knows the trade very well. He keeps an eye on Mr Turner in the laboratory, and he's in charge of all sales.' He stopped, and ran his finger round the inside of his stiff, winged collar as if it were too tight. 'As to his being a relation, you would have to ask him.' He hastened on to explain, in the hope of diverting her attention, that the firm distributed a lot of unperfumed toilet and washing soap through middlemen, and washing soap directly to cotton mills. 'We've also got three representatives, working on commission. They travel all the time in their own districts, to sell our best line, Lady Lavender scented toilet soaps, to chemists' shops and hairdressers, even a little to haberdashers; likewise, our line of Lady Lavender perfume – Mr Benjamin wants to extend our scent sales – scent is quite a profitable sideline in some places.'

The rough gold rings on Wallace Helena's fingers caught the sunlight, as she slowly drew on a cigarello which Alfie had brought her as a possible alternative to cigarettes. Mr Bobsworth carefully kept his eyes averted; his head enveloped in smoke, he was afraid that his expression might betray his disapproval of a female smoker, particularly in a works full of oils and fats where *No Smoking* signs were prominently displayed.

Wallace Helena let the subject of Mr Benjamin rest, and said, 'Mr Turner mentioned, when I spoke to him in his laboratory, that a residue of soap manufacture is glycerine. He said he is experimenting with a view to producing a line of emollients for ladies' skins? Another idea was a cream to clean delicate skins instead of soap?'

Mr Bobsworth drooped; it looked as if this interview would go on into the evening. He pulled out a chair and defiantly sat on it; he *had* to sit down.

Wallace Helena made no comment. If he wanted to sit, he was welcome. She had come to the conclusion during the last few days that Englishmen must enjoy standing, since none of them sat in her presence.

'Is glycerine really good for skins?' she asked.

'I believe it can be, Miss Harding. Mr James Al-Khoury was beginning to feel that there is a market for modestly priced products to enhance women's skins. City life seems to ruin complexions.' He paused, to clear his throat, and then went on. 'The aristocracy has always used beauty aids, but he had in mind the lower classes, that he would pack creams in small tins to cost a few pence. I warned him – and I have since warned Mr Benjamin – that we have a lot of Nonconformists in Lancashire who would decry the use of emollients as vanity – some of them are against baths for the same reason. The market may not exist here, in the North.'

Wallace Helena remembered the ladies of Beirut and their proclivity for using scented unguents and she grinned. She saw in her mind Leila

125

rubbing a mixture of flour and lard into her reddened hands, in a prairie land where everybody's hands were work-worn. Vanity? How extraordinary.

She was suddenly very tired herself. She had had to keep up a firm façade before the men in the works; they seemed to consider that they were indulging her in permitting her to inspect her own property – her own except for the technicality of Probate.

'Damn them,' she muttered, as she rose slowly from her chair and began to walk stiffly up and down the dark, narrow room, to loosen her muscles.

'You said something, Miss Harding?'

'No.' She blew out a cloud of smoke, and then said, 'I believe you mentioned that Mr Benjamin will be back tomorrow morning. I'd like to see him at two o'clock.'

'I'll ask Mr Helliwell to put a note on Mr Benjamin's desk to that effect, Miss Harding.' Let Helliwell do something for his living, he thought crossly.

Wallace Helena stretched herself, and then she leaned over the desk to butt out her cigarello in an ashtray. 'Mrs Hughes will be expecting me for supper.'

Mr Bobsworth rose, his lips even tighter. Stretching herself in front of a man! Really, the woman had no manners. He said politely, 'I'll escort you home, Ma'am.'

'No need,' she responded lightly, as she pinned on her hat. 'I can walk up the hill by myself.' She took up her shawl and wrapped it round her shoulders.

'It's not safe, Miss Harding.'

'I am used to lonely country, Mr Bobsworth. There are no cougars or bears on Hill Street!'

Mr Bobsworth argued politely that there were other, unspecified dangers. She countered that she had kept him so late that she now wanted him to go straight home.

The man was tired to the bone, so he suggested that Alfie might still be cleaning out the stables. 'He usually does this job after hours, to earn a bit more. He's very reliable. He'd take care of you.'

Resigned to the inevitable, Wallace Helena agreed to Alfie, if he could be found. She sat down again in her chair, while Mr Bobsworth went to collect his top hat and cane and then find the youngster.

Wallace Helena was interested in the patient mulatto, who bought tobacco and cigarellos for her from sailors' shops in the Goree Piazzas. If she had had a child, she considered, he would probably look very like Alfie – though not so crushed.

A very bewildered Alfie, cap in hand and smelling distinctly of horse manure, knocked at the office door.

Wallace Helena rose and picked up her reticule. 'Come in, Alfie,' she said gently.

20

The following morning, Wallace Helena sent for a hansom cab and went to see her uncle's lawyer, Mr Benson, at his office. She was immediately seated in a leather chair by the window of his room. Mr Benson was holding a weighty tome on the laws of succession and this he placed on his desk, as he sat down before it. He assumed that she had come to see how the matter of Probate was proceeding. This had not been her intention, but she let him talk about it.

'The Court will not be long now,' he assured her. He thoughtfully twirled the end of his neat moustache, and then continued, 'I felt, as Executor, that such an excellent little business should not be wound up or sold, until you were consulted, though I always presume that you will put it up for sale.'

Wallace Helena ignored the question of selling, and asked a little absently, 'What exactly is Probate, Mr Benson? I am not at all clear. When Mama and her husband died of smallpox, I was fortunate in finding a lawyer who had come west to work with the Oblate Fathers in St Albert, on the subject of Metis land claims. Father Lacombe recommended him to me. I was so upset, as you can imagine, that I left everything to the lawyer, and I'm not sure what he did. But he worked so well that I ended up with thirty-six square miles of good farm land and timber.' She smiled at the lawyer, and added, 'I thought I would never manage to pay his bill – cash is in short supply out west!'

At the disclosure of the size of her land holding, Mr Benson looked surprised. She must already be a well-to-do woman, despite her remark about a lack of cash.

In reply to her question regarding Probate, he said, 'The Court has to be assured that the Will is genuine and that it is the last Will made by the deceased. They then have to ensure that the Estate is handed over to the right person.'

'Was it difficult in my uncle's case?'

'It has not been simple, but, despite a lengthy search and much advertising, no other Will has come to light – in any case, it was likely that Mr Al-Khoury would have asked me, as his lawyer, to make it for him. I held only the Will made when he was a young man.'

'Then you had to find me?'

'That wasn't difficult. Mr Helliwell had your address; he said he had posted boxes of books to you from Mr James Al-Khoury. The problem was to prove that your dear mother was Mr *Charles* Al-Khoury's sole legatee; secondly, that her Will leaving everything to you was in order, and, thirdly, that you were indeed Helena Al-Khoury, and not, perhaps, a daughter of Mr Harding by an earlier marriage.'

He was surprised to see Wallace Helena's firm mouth trembling; she looked as if she might burst into tears. He went on hastily, 'You were able to provide me with all the necessary addresses, and, though you had not birth certificate, there were several people still in the Hudson's Bay trading post who were able to confirm that you had arrived with your mother, and that Mr Harding had no known daughters. We found other confirmation in letters from you and your mother, written at Fort Edmonton, amongst Mr James's correspondence.'

'Good,' Wallace Helena muttered, and blew her nose hard. Mama, Mama, her heart cried, why did you have to suffer so much?

'I must tell you that I did mention, once or twice, to Mr James that he should update his Will,' the lawyer added. 'But he always seemed in good health and said he would do it some time; we none of us expect to be taken suddenly in middle life.'

He realized that she was no longer listening and he coughed to draw her attention. She turned to him, her eyes so full of pain that he was shocked. Like Mr Helliwell, he began to realize that this rather irritating, forward woman had undergone some very harrowing experiences in her life, experiences still in the forefront of her mind. She looked haunted. He wondered if she had known *any* happiness in her life; frontier life, such as she now led, was not, presumably, very easy.

In the hope of amusing her a little, he began to talk of her uncle's early days in Liverpool. 'Mr James was a very enterprising man, as you may know. He began boiling soap in his landlady's cellar wash boiler. What gave him the idea, I have no notion, except that the use of soap was becoming common. He peddled the soap from door to door. Then he found a tumble-down cottage with a similar boiler. He rented this, and was able to keep his store of fat and so on in it – I imagine much to his landlady's relief!' He smiled at his client and the haunted look began to fade from the enormous brown eyes. 'Then he met Mr Tasker, a real Liverpool character. Together, they found a large shed which is now a part of the present soapery, and it was at that point that he came to me, because he wanted to understand exactly the terms of the leasing of the property – and his English was not too good – and, for some time, I vetted every agreement he signed.'

129

Wallace Helena forced herself to pay attention. 'Is Mr Tasker a partner, then?'

'No, he has always been an employee – a very trusted one, I may say.' The lawyer smiled again at her, as he saw the sorrow fade from her face. 'I'll always remember Mr James and Mr Tasker as being so exuberant and cheerful. Mr Al-Khoury always said, however, that family were the most important people in a man's life; without family a man was lost. In the early days, he spoke several times of his hope that your father, Mr Charles, would join him, and he was greatly distressed when Mr Charles died – and even more so when he discovered that your mother had married again and had taken you to live in a part of Canada almost unexplored. He couldn't believe it.'

'Why didn't he get married himself?' inquired Wallace Helena, trying to turn the conversation towards her original reason for calling.

'I'm not sure. He mentioned once a desire to return to Lebanon, when it became more peaceful – he always said it was the most beautiful country in the world – and he missed the perfume of the fruit trees.'

'That's strange. I do, too. I sit and dream of the smell of lemon tree flowers, sometimes.'

'Do you really? He may have thought that an English wife would not want to live there – and there are few prospective Lebanese wives in this city.' He stopped abruptly, as if he had intended to say more and had then thought better of it.

'I don't suppose there are any Lebanese here, male or female,' Wallace Helena suggested.

Feeling that it was time to terminate the interview, Mr Benson got up from his desk and returned the book on succession to its shelf. Across his stout stomach, the seals on his watch chain tinkled. Then he considered that he should ask her precisely what her intentions were concerning the Lady Lavender, so he sat down again and put the question to her.

Wallace Helena's long eyes narrowed. 'I've not yet made a decision,' she replied cautiously.

Mr Benson nodded understandingly, but did not reply. He sensed that she had more to say.

She stared out of the window at the tiny cobblestone court and watched expressionlessly as a man relieved himself in a quiet corner of it. Then she said, 'It would be nice to live in a lively city, like Liverpool – to be able to buy books and listen to music – and wear pretty clothes.' She smiled ruefully at her feminine desire expressed in the last words. Then she said, 'And you cannot imagine how wonderful a water tap is, particularly one which produces *hot* water! We have a well, which is better than having to haul water up from the river – but it's still very inconvenient, particularly in our climate.'

'Indeed,' he agreed, and waited.

As if she had made up her mind to trust him, she went on, 'I believe I could run the Lady Lavender, with the aid of Mr Bobsworth and Mr Tasker. I have, however, a homestead – a large one – and obligations in the Territories. So I must consider carefully what I am to do.' She gave him a bright, artificial little smile.

She seemed to have finished her confidences, so he said diplomatically, 'Well, it is not essential that you make a decision until Probate is received. I think it would be wise to be ready to decide immediately after that. Businesses do not thrive on indecision.'

'Indeed, they do not,' she agreed.

He went on to warn her about taxes that would have to be paid in connection with the transfer of the company to her. 'You'll need cash,' he warned. 'Mr Al-Khoury did have a small personal bank account, and, as you know, the Lady Lavender account has funds in it – but these will be needed for the day-to-day workings.'

Wallace Helena mentally saw the last really fine necklace that her mother had left her vanishing into the hands of moneylenders or a purchasing jeweller to cover taxes, but she answered smartly. 'Perhaps the company would be allowed to pay in instalments?' she suggested.

'Possibly,' he agreed.

A sudden thought struck Wallace, and it brought her to the real point of her visit. 'Who paid Uncle's funeral expenses?'

Mr Benson hesitated. 'They were initially paid by one of Mr Al-Khoury's friends.' He shifted uneasily in his chair. 'I've since refunded the money from his Estate.'

Now, she thought, I can broach the subject of Benjamin Al-Khoury – at last. She took a cigarello out of her reticule, together with a box of matches, and lit up, while she looked shrewdly at her embarrassed lawyer.

She leaned back and blew a cloud of smoke into the air. 'A lady friend?' she asked finally.

Mr Benson rubbed his neat grey beard, and blinked as the smoke got in his eyes. A most peculiar young woman, he considered, before he answered, 'Yes. It was a friendship of long standing.'

'She's not mentioned in his Will. I would have thought he would have left her at least some small remembrance?'

'Well, his Will was old. He was a young man when he made it . . .'

'Father Lacombe's lawyer wanted me to make a Will, but I couldn't

131

afford any more on his bill!' She laughed, and looked round for an ashtray. Mr Benson hastily offered her his. She smiled her thanks.

Mr Benson bent his head slightly in response and wondered who her beneficiary would have been. 'Very wise to make a Will, Miss Harding. Very wise.'

Wallace Helena drew on her cigarello and her mind wandered for a moment. 'If I die,' she thought, 'will Joe get all I possess? If the new railway brings in a lot of immigrants and there is a real demand for land, he could be a very rich man.

'He wouldn't really care about that,' she considered dispiritedly. 'He's happy. As long as he has familiar people around him, a good horse under him and something to eat, he'd be content.' In this she under-estimated Joe Black; he appreciated the power of money, but he wanted it to ease the life of his treasured Wallace Helena.

As her lawyer watched the play of expressions across her face, it suddenly lit up with a mischievous smile, as she imagined what he would do if he suddenly found himself with a soap works.

'What? Me?' he would splutter. '*Women* make soap!'

Mr Benson saw the smile fade. Again she looked tired and grim. He had heard from an irate Mr Bobsworth how hard she was working. 'She ignored Sunday!' he had complained. 'I never got to Mass at all and the wife was furious.'

Wallace Helena realized with a jolt that there had been silence in the book-lined room for at least a minute. She remembered the question she wished to ask.

As if preparing to get up and leave, she picked up her gloves with studied leisureliness, and then inquired casually, 'Has Benjamin Al-Khoury anything to do with Uncle's lady friend? When I tried to ask Mr Bobsworth where he fitted in, he evaded the question. I need to know, because he's coming to see me this afternoon.'

Mr Benson suddenly saw the reason for the protracted interview. It had taken her a long time to get down to the real reason for it. 'He's her son,' he replied uncomfortably.

'I see. And she is known, perhaps, as Mrs Al-Khoury?'

Mr Benson's face went suddenly pink above his beard, as he answered her frankly, 'Yes, Miss Harding.'

'But she's not Mrs Al-Khoury?'

'No.' He hesitated, and then explained, 'I went to see her to confirm it, because if she was married to Mr James, she would have certain dower rights – and Mr Benjamin, also, could have claims against the Estate.'

At Mr Benson's obvious discomfiture over such a delicate subject,

Wallace Helena repressed a smile, and inquired gravely, 'So like a good Lebanese, he saw that her son had a decent job?'

'Yes, Miss Harding. I understand that he was sent to a good grammar school – and when he was fifteen Mr Al-Khoury took him into the business. Mr Tasker and Mr Bobsworth think very highly of him. I've met him, and he is a pleasant young man. Business associates – and the employees – fully expected that he would inherit the Lady Lavender.' He looked down at his hand lying on his desk and then tapped his fingers gently along the wooden edge. 'Be patient with him, Miss Harding. Not only has he lost his father, but he has been sadly humiliated publicly.'

'Because he is illegitimate?' she asked baldly.

'Yes. He could only inherit if his father had specifically willed the business to him.'

'I see.' She rose to leave. 'I'm glad you have been frank with me; it has confirmed what I believed before I left Canada. But I had to be sure.' She pulled on her gloves and held out her hand to the lawyer. 'Leave the matter with me. I will be careful with him. I naturally want to meet my only blood relative.'

Mr Benson had not considered that she might welcome a relation, and he shook her hand warmly with relief. Her attitude might at least mitigate a clash between their very strong characters.

21

Wallace Helena had expected to be away from home not more than two months. But July inched into August and she had still not mentioned a possible date of return. In August, a depressed and overworked Joe Black asked her in his letters to name a date. But he finally got a letter explaining that she was held up by some nonsense called Probate. The fact that their letters crossed constantly added a note of confusion to their communication with each other.

In one letter which Joe received in mid-August, she inquired, 'How would you feel about living in Liverpool? It's such a marvellous city – it has everything. I believe I could manage the soapery and that it would provide a good living.'

The very idea of being penned up in a white man's city made Joe shudder. Born in the Bow Valley when first it was explored, and brought up within his grandfather's usual hunting grounds, he had never been further than Fort Benton in Montana, to the south, or St Albert in the north. He had never seen a city. He had heard about the human swarms in such places and he had no desire to become a human ant. He told his beloved to come home.

In another letter, she mentioned that the previous night she had dreamed of Lebanon. 'For once it wasn't a nightmare,' she wrote. 'I was gazing up at the mountains, and I saw the anemones shedding their red petals in the wind – my nurse once told me they were drops of blood shed by a beautiful god called Adonis, who was killed in a fit of jealousy. Then I found myself floating along the narrow seashore and I listened to the singing of the water. It felt very strange.

'I am told that a number of refugees have returned to the country. It reminded me that between the mountains of Lebanon and those of the Anti-Lebanon lies the Buka'a Valley, good farm land watered by two rivers – the air there is as pure as that of the prairies. If we could buy such land, darling . . . but it would mean that you would have to learn yet another language as well as accept another culture.'

Joe began to worry, and told her again to come home as soon as she could. They were beginning to do fine in Edmonton. Why go anywhere else?

Twice a week, he rode the five miles down to the post office in

Edmonton village. Though the post office had not been established very long, collecting the mail from it had become a bi-weekly social event for the whole district; it was a chance to meet neighbours one did not otherwise see. Everybody stood patiently gossiping in the queue, while they waited for the mail to be sorted by the slow meticulous man behind the counter at the far end of the long narrow room.

For the most part, Joe would lean silently against the office wall, his empty pipe cradled in his hand, unlit out of courtesy to the few women present. He did not invite conversation and did not get beyond a remark about the weather or the state of the harvest. He was, as ever, regarded with respect by those who knew him well, because of his knowledge of livestock breeding and also for his ability to talk sense into angry, despairing Crees and Blackfoot; as settlers slowly increased, face-to-face confrontations were more common with Indians, who did not think much of their limited treaty rights. Being half-Cree himself, Joe was often furious at the treatment of his relations by both Government and settlers. But he knew that on the homestead he had to live with whites around him who disliked a negro owning land, so he was extremely wary in what he said. Friendly overtures had always been treated by both Wallace Helena and himself with reserve; and he never forgot that Wallace Helena faced prejudice because of her race and was solidly hated for the contemptuous arrogance with which she had countered it from the day of her arrival.

As he waited for his letters, Joe sometimes thought how strange it was that both he and Wallace Helena had learned to love Tom Harding, an American of almost silvery fairness. There was nothing saintly about Tom, he ruminated with a grin, but the man had always played fair; if he promised something, he did his best to keep that promise. And he never seemed to see what colour a man was. He looked straight *into* you, as if judging what you were really like, and, if he liked what he found, he was generous and open. Joe missed him like he missed his Cree grandfather; both men had had in common an inner wisdom sadly lacking in others. The only time Tom had seemed unwise was when he had fallen in love with Leila and had brought the poor woman to the Fort. She had made him happy, though, and Joe hoped suddenly that she had known a little happiness. If she had not come, he would never have known the bundle of vitality that was her daughter.

Now, he was beginning to sweat with anxiety that he had lost Wallace Helena to a damned soap works.

He shifted his feet and wished the post office clerk would hurry up with his sorting.

If Wallace Helena could not be dissuaded from leaving Edmonton,

Joe worried, he would be as lonely as he was when his grandfather died. Without her, he felt, the struggle to keep the farm going would be pointless; almost everything he did was for her sake.

It had been different when he and Tom first set out to establish the place. He had been young and adventurous and it had been a great joke to cock a snook at the heavy-handed Hudson's Bay Company.

At a New Year's Day party, he had found himself drinking with Tom Harding, and the white man had inquired if the negro had come up from the States. Joe had replied tartly that he was no American slave; he had been born free in Canada.

They had gone on to an amicable, though drunken, exchange of reminiscences, Tom about his not very successful trapline and his desire to put in a vegetable patch and, if possible, plant a crop of barley. Joe confided that he hated working on the Hudson's Bay's farm a few miles north. He said his father had also been a Company employee under Factor John Rowand.

It was the beginning of a lifelong friendship and a long, not uninteresting, vendetta with the Hudson's Bay Company, the latter ending only when Wallace Helena got title to the land.

The two men might both have died the first winter they lived together in the old cabin, had it not been for Joe's mother and his Aunt Theresa, both of whom were working in the kitchens of the Chief Factor's house. They stole barley and oats for them, to eke out the rabbits the men snared and the fish they got by fishing through a hole in the ice of the river. Tom had the dream of owning his own farm to sustain him, and Joe found it a welcome relief to be treated as a friend and equal.

Joe brought his own small mare with him to the cabin, and, later, he stole two horses that appeared to have got loose from a Blackfoot encampment some distance away. He hoped that by leading them through the shallows of the river, the Blackfoot would not be able to track them down, and they never did.

'Our need's greater than theirs,' Joe affirmed stolidly. It was true that the partners were quite as thin as the hungry Indians. The horses, very unwillingly, pulled the plough they had persuaded a friendly blacksmith in the Fort to make for them.

When times got better, Tom acquired his first wife, a plain, amiable Cree, and discovered that she was a gem of a helpmate. When she died in childbirth, both men mourned her.

Two years later, Tom had brought home Leila and her daughter. They belonged to neither the white nor Metis world of the Fort, nor were they Indians. They were, like Joe, outsiders.

The Scots in the Fort publicly called them Chinks or Jews, as they jeered at them if Tom was not with them. Both women looked down at them with silent contempt. Tom had not expected such reciprocal dislike. He became truculent and defensive of his womenfolk, fearing that they might be raped by men who obviously regarded them with such odium. He knew he could not hope for protection for them from his long-standing antagonist, the Chief Factor.

Leila regarded the Fort's inhabitants as clodhoppers, peasants, men without origins or history. She loved her fair-haired American husband and respected Joe Black for his courtesy and knowledge. The ill-assorted little family turned in upon itself; they were like bison anticipating an attack, forming a tight, protective knot.

When, many years later, Wallace Helena successfully acquired title to a piece of land much larger than others, and had then made Joe her equal partner, the locals again began to call her a bloody Chink. Their jealousy was very great. It did not help her to make friends.

Joe loved her with an intensity which sometimes scared him; it was the only part of his life over which he was not in complete control. 'Prickly as a porcupine,' he would warn himself – and then he would laugh.

When the postmaster finally handed him several letters from her, he grinned his thanks and stuffed them inside his old wolfskin jacket.

Without a further word to anyone, he pushed his way through the small group still waiting. His horse was hitched to a post outside. He absently undid it and mounted. With the stiff envelopes crackling against his chest, he rode the old trail along the river escarpment, splashing through a couple of creeks, regardless of the fact that by then part of the track ran over lots owned by others. Alder and scrub oaks brushed him, as he passed, and flies buzzed crossly round him, but it was the easiest route home and he wanted to read his letters. If Wallace Helena was right in her predictions and if the railway came to Edmonton, there would soon be roads criss-crossing the whole district. There would be hordes of people glad of land and space, and they would form a ready market for everything a mixed farm could produce. But then, she had always been a bit of a dreamer, he considered wryly. He hoped that she was wrong; there were too many white folk and Metis around already.

Aunt Theresa stood expectantly at the cabin door and Emily ran out to open the yard gate for him as he rode in. Simon Wounded, out in the fields, saw him from a distance and came running to hear any news of Wallace Helena. They crowded round the scrubbed table in the old cabin, regardless of the fact that it was August and there was an immense amount of work to do.

Joe had been taught to read by an Oblate priest, and he read the letters slowly and accurately, translating into Cree some phrases which were difficult for his listeners to understand. He omitted paragraphs that were personal to him. Some parts of the letters were almost incomprehensible to them; they were too far removed from city life.

As he put down the last page, he felt a little forlorn himself. As if she understood, Emily brought him a hot cup of coffee from the kitchen lean-to. He nodded, and then sent them back to their work. 'Barley'll be ready for cutting,' Simon warned him.

Joe nodded again. 'We'll start tonight – it'll be cooler. And start again at sun-up. I'll be out to have a look at it soon.' He picked up the letters again and turned them over. Simon sighed and went to look at the pigs. He felt suddenly very old and was not looking forward to the long, arduous days of harvest without Wallace Helena's help.

Joe read parts of the letters again while he drank his coffee. Wallace Helena sounded too damnably comfortable amongst her lawyers, soap masters and accountants. Unlike the men in Edmonton, these men seemed to be treating her with some respect, though she had admitted flatly that being a woman was a disadvantage to her. He felt a strong twinge of jealousy.

He leaned back in his chair and lit his pipe. Until he had begun to receive letters from her in Liverpool, he had never felt himself to be less than she was; he had his own wide areas of knowledge and experience – she had hers. He knew how to foretell the weather with some accuracy and he decided when they should sow and when they should reap. He could hunt and trap as well as his grandfather had. Ahead of the other settlers, he knew the movements of the dispossessed Cree and Blackfoot, understood the desperate frustration of the Metis – hadn't he foretold the Riel rebellion long before it happened and prepared himself for it as far as he could?

Mr Tasker in Liverpool might have a *feel* for soap, but I have a *feel* about this land, he argued. Wallace Helena may do the bargaining with agents buying food for the railway gangs building further south or for the Indians, poor devils; it's me – me – who delivers steers and grain safely to their camps – and that's no mean feat, lady, in a country riddled with rivers and creeks and bogs to be crossed.

Frustrated by distance, by the strangeness of the world she described in her letters, he was vexed and confused. She wrote with affection and consideration for him – but she appeared far too happy!

Feeling sullen and resentful, he went to join Simon Wounded in the fields.

That night, he wrote asking her to come home as soon as possible; he needed her. He gave her no news of the harvest or the excellent contact he had made with a railway surveyor nosing round Edmonton and in need of provisions. He continued to reply to her letters, giving no news but simply asking when she expected to return.

The replies he finally received in answer to his campaign of near silence were positively acerbic. He chuckled with satisfaction. The epistles were full of inquiries about the homestead and himself; not one of them mentioned soap. Had he arranged for the threshing crew? Was he reading the *Edmonton Bulletin* and keeping in touch with its editor, Frank Oliver? Mr Oliver was a ready source of news of surveying or other parties passing through, who might need to be victualled. And he should keep up his contacts with Mr Taylor, the telegraph operator, who was in a better position than anyone else to have early news which would help them sell the crop or the animals they did not want to winter over. How was the vegetable garden doing?

He felt better, and was able to write to her that he and Simon had got the barley crop into the barn, one day before a heavy rainstorm carrying hail in it had destroyed neighbours' fields. Yet, when he thought of Wallace Helena's new world, the sense of inadequacy resurfaced. Against the comforts of a city, he had little to offer her, except himself, and the continuation of a harsh, uncertain life in a climate which would test anybody's fortitude.

22

After her visit to Mr Benson, Wallace Helena asked the cabbie to put her down at the gates of the Lady Lavender. She walked slowly through the wicket gate. To her left was the carpenter's shop, and she glanced through its open doorway. The boxes in which the soap was transported were made here, and at one end a young wheelwright repaired the delivery vans and their wheels. Heaps of wood shavings and sawdust lay in every corner of the shed, and, seeing them, she realized what a fire hazard they represented.

Without hesitation, she walked in and told the elderly carpenter to sweep them up and dispose of them. 'They could cause a fire,' she said sharply.

The man had taken off his cap when she entered, and now he scratched his head, while he gaped at her. 'Never in me life have I bin told by a woman what to do in me own shop,' he told his wife that night. 'Who's she to tell me what to do?'

Wallace Helena scouted round the rest of the shop. The young, dark-haired wheelwright ignored her and gave earnest attention to a wheel he was refitting to a light van; he didn't want any trouble.

As it became apparent that she knew the names of most of the tools lying around the shop and what they were for, the carpenter began to recover himself, and when she returned to his side to remind him again to sweep up, he stammered, 'Mr Al-Khoury were goin' to get me an apprentice, Ma'am. Me last one's gone to be a journeyman in another place; done well for himself, he has. An apprentice'd clean up for me, like. I gotta lot of work here.'

'Which Mr Al-Khoury?'

'The ould fella – Mr James, Ma'am.'

'I see. I'll see what can be done. Meanwhile, perhaps Mr Tasker could spare his labourer, Alfie, to sweep up for you. I'll speak to him.'

He heard the note of authority in her voice and muttered, 'Yes, Ma'am.'

The stable was next door, and she realized that she had not yet visited it, though from the wage sheets she knew the names of the employees working there. The stableman was eating his lunchtime bread and cheese, while he leaned against the open doorway. A heavy, red-faced man, he straightened up as she swept in. Lifting up her skirts, she walked the length of the building and returned to storm at him. How could he expect the horses to be healthy with weeks of manure underfoot? It was enough to make employees ill, as well. She ordered an immediate clean-up and the establishment of a manure heap in a corner of the yard which did not seem to be used. Horse manure was valuable to farms; she would find a market for it and have it collected weekly. 'It's a wonder that the city has not complained at such a conglomeration,' she raged. 'How do you dispose of it at present – when it gets up to your knees?' she asked with heavy sarcasm.

The man hung his head sullenly and did not reply. In fact, he periodically sold it himself; he considered it a perk which went with his job. But he wasn't going to tell a bloody bitch like her.

There had been a solitary horse in the stable and Wallace Helena had taken a good look at it. Now, finding that the man was not going to reply to her, she said, 'And give that animal a hot bran mash. I'll take another look at him in the morning.'

The man lifted his head and looked her angrily in the eye. 'I done it,' he replied.

Wallace Helena pursed her lips into a thin line. 'Right. I'll come in the morning.'

'Sour as a bloody lemon, she is,' this man told *his* wife, and then added thoughtfully, 'Seems she knows somethin' about horses, though.'

Outside the stable, Wallace Helena paused to scrape some of the muck of the stable off her boots. She sighed, as she rubbed the sides of her boots against cobblestones which she noticed were heavy with grease, presumably from the barrels of fat and oil stored on the far side of the yard. Here was another fire hazard, she considered uneasily.

Before moving, she pulled the hatpins from her hat and took it off, to let the light breeze cool a face flushed with anger. Not only did she feel hot, she felt nauseated from the reek of the stable. She thought she might vomit, and she turned to the office intending to run over to the latrine behind it.

She almost knocked down a stocky, well-built young man in a black suit and bowler hat. Off balance, he stumbled and dropped the carpet bag he was carrying. He was saved from a fall by the vicelike grip of Wallace Helena's long fingers on his arm. As he steadied himself, she took a large breath in an effort to quell her nausea.

Though the collision was not his fault, the man apologized for bumping into her, as he mechanically bent down to pick up his bag again. She nodded acknowledgment, and hurried away to the privy. He was left with the vague impression of a very thin, plain woman with a sickly, sallow face, dressed in shabby black and carrying a small hat; he assumed that she was the wife of one of the workmen, bringing in his midday meal.

Only when Benjamin Al-Khoury was discussing a minor complaint with Mr Tasker, and Miss Harding's name came up, did the likely identity of the woman in the yard occur to him.

The bitterness that had haunted him since his father's death welled up once again. His father had failed both him and his mother; and he wondered for the hundredth time why his parents had never married. They were obviously devoted to each other and the home was a happy one. His own illegitimacy had been well known in the neighbourhood and he had suffered the usual snide remarks flung at such children; presumably his mother also had had her share of opprobrium. It didn't make sense.

And now this wretched woman had been dug up by the lawyers as the legal residual legatee of his father's Estate; his patrimony was going to a cousin he had never heard of, because she was the only legitimate descendant of the two brothers. And, to add to his sense of a world turned upside down, she was presumably his employer – unless she sold the business, as expected, in which case he could lose his job as the new owner moved in his own choice of men. It was not a pleasant prospect.

He left Mr Tasker amid his bubbling cauldrons and went to see Mr Bobsworth, with whom he intended to have lunch. He was met by the information that Miss Harding would see him at two o'clock.

'Blow her,' he muttered, though he realized he could not put off meeting her much longer.

As if reading his thoughts, Mr Bobsworth said, 'Better to get it over with, lad.'

'What's she like?'

'A Tartar,' replied Mr Bobsworth gloomily. 'Thinks she owns the place.'

'She does, old man. Let's go and eat. I'll leave the orders I've got with Le Fleur – he can send them to be made up.'

'I'll check them as soon as we return,' Mr Bobsworth promised. 'I always label everything myself, you know that. Want a job doing well? Do it yourself.'

It was old Bobsworth's usual remark, so Benjamin let it pass.

In the shabby dockside café, crowded with seamen, Customs men and men from the warehouses nearby, though no dockers – they had their own, even smaller, eating houses, where the stench of the cargoes they handled was more acceptable – Mr Bobsworth found his usual quiet corner table. They hung up their bowlers, undid their jackets and sat down. Unasked, a florid woman in a coloured apron put a pint of bitter in front of each of them. 'Like to order?' she asked, a stub of pencil poised over a grubby notebook.

They both ordered steak and kidney pudding, and, while they were waiting, Benjamin brought up the problem of the rabid competition in the Manchester area, where the cotton mills consumed a massive amount of soap.

'This man Lever's started to wrap his *bar* soap in bright yellow paper with *Sunlight* printed all over it. Even his delivery vans are plastered with sunrays and the same word. And he's advertising "Don't just ask for soap – ask for *Sunlight*." He's making a hole in our market, I can tell you.'

'We make better soap,' responded Mr Bobsworth uncompromisingly. 'Tasker makes better soap than anybody.'

'Yes, but we're not telling everybody that – and women seem to love having their washing soap wrapped.'

'We wrap our toilet soap.'

'In mouldy grey paper – beige for the cinnamon and fuller's earth! Anyway, it's plain bar soap that everything gets scrubbed with – it's our bread and butter. I'm sure Dad would have done something about it.'

'Your father had in mind to branch out into lotions and scents for working-class women. He'd even thought of a kind of paste to tint the skin – cream colour for pale skins, pink for rosy youth – packed in chemists' little bottles and boxes. Vanity! Nothing but vanity, that's what I say.'

'Girls in the mills have a bit of money to spend, a few pence here and there. Dad would've been selling them something better than gin.'

'He had a job persuading their mams to let them have a bath with scented soap – and get the mams themselves to put a bit of lavender on their Sunday handkerchiefs.' Mr Bobsworth was a Roman Catholic and did not think much of Methodist austerity. On the other hand, he did not like to think of his wife and daughters painting their faces like actresses or worse; so he was quick to condemn cosmetics.

Plates of steak and kidney pudding were thrust under their noses. Though the pudding looked as flaccid as chicken waiting to be cooked, the aroma was delicious, and both men were hungry. They were silent as they ate their way through the steaming mass.

Afterwards, Benjamin stretched himself over the back of his chair, and sighed. Reverting to the subject of their business, he said dejectedly, 'It's not much use our discussing what we should do about Lever.

It's out of our hands. Whoever buys us out will have to decide. And we'll be lucky if we have jobs.'

Over his beer mug, Mr Bobsworth made a glum face, and Benjamin went on, 'I don't know why she bothered to come over. It'd have been a lot quicker if Benson had sent her all the papers and arranged the sale for her. Wish I could afford to buy it – I'd make something of it.' Mr Bobsworth put down his mug. 'She's a rum type,' he said. 'She's queer enough to think she could run the place herself. She's bin lookin' over everything.'

'A woman? What a hope!'

'Well, she's not like any other woman I ever met. She's smart at figures, I can tell you. Tasker says she's got a huge farm in Canada and runs it. I'd say the question is, does she want to live here?'

'Maybe somebody'll marry her – and take over the works as well,' Benjamin offered. He drained his mug and stood up, while he felt in his pocket for a tip for the waitress. He tucked two copper coins under his empty plate.

Mr Bobsworth rose, too. He wondered suddenly if Benjamin had the idea of marrying Miss Harding, and so gain control of the soapery. Perhaps he should remind the boy that, only a few years back, a law had been passed to protect the property of married women; it wasn't so easy nowadays to take over their assets. In any case, he hoped that Benji would fancy one of his own daughters.

He said soberly, 'Frankly, Benji, she'll be lucky if she finds anybody who wants to marry her. She's as thin as a flagpole – no comfortable pillow for a man's head! And she can come over the acid like some spinster headmistress of a girls' seminary.'

'Well, I've got to see her this afternoon, so we'd better hurry.' His usually lively expression drooped; he was suddenly aware that he had not shaved well that morning, and he supposed that his usual blue-black bristle was already visible. If he wanted to make a good impression, he should have gone home first, to shave and change his suit, creased with a week's travelling. Then he decided that it did not really matter; the person to worry about and smarten up for was the man who would buy the soapery.

23

Before he had set out on his trip to Manchester, Benji's mother, Eleanor Al-Khoury, had told him that, during the night, she had remembered his father saying that Charles Al-Khoury had a *daughter*. She looked exhausted from much weeping, and she added, as she wiped her eyes with a sodden handkerchief, 'When your uncle died in Chicago, your dad wanted to bring his wife and child over here, to live with us. I was that upset about – about your dad's passing, that I forgot. Funny to think you could've bin brought up together, in this house.' Her nose was running and she sniffed.

He had looked down at her rather helplessly. 'It doesn't make any difference, Mum. It was my recollection, too. But I was put off by the name *Wallace*; I thought I'd been mistaken. Now, don't you cry any more. I'll look after you, you know that.' He hugged her, and in hope of comforting her a little, he went on, 'When I get back, we'll go and find a real nice memorial for Dad's grave.'

She rubbed the tears off her fair lashes, and said as bravely as she could, 'Oh, aye. We'll do that, luv.'

'I'll ask Mrs Tasker to step in, as I go down the street,' he promised, as he kissed her goodbye. 'I don't want you to be too lonely.'

'I'll be all right,' she told him, her face so sad he could have wept himself. She shut the door quietly after him and began to weep some more.

A few minutes later, a concerned Mrs Tasker arrived. She had a seed cake, freshly baked, balanced on her ungloved hand, and she trotted straight into the big kitchen and proceeded to provide tea and kindly sympathy, while the bereaved woman sat by the fire and sang the praises of her Jamie. Mrs Tasker had heard it all several times in the previous few weeks, but she felt that the more Eleanor wept the quicker she would recover. She made the tea very strong.

Mr Tasker had said that the Will held, no matter whether Eleanor was married to James Al-Khoury or not. But Eleanor knew that a wedding cancelled out earlier Wills; if she'd been married and there had been no other Will, Benji would have inherited; and she mentally belaboured herself for accepting the status quo for so long. She wept not only for James Al-Khoury but also for her sadly humiliated son.

While she sipped the tea made by her friend, she recounted to her the story of how the handsome, cheery young James Al-Khoury, who spoke English in a proper funny fashion, had come to her front door in search of a room to rent. 'He hadn't even the money to pay for a week in advance,' she said with a dim smile. 'But he looked that handsome, I took a chance on 'im. Put 'im in me best room – front ground floor. And, aye, he were lovely.'

Ten months later, little Benji had been born, as Mrs Tasker knew, though it was before she had come to live in the same street. Eleanor must've endured a fair amount of backhanded whispering over that, Mrs Tasker meditated, as Eleanor droned on. Why hadn't the stupid woman insisted on marriage if she loved the man so much? And he was lovable, there was no doubt. She wondered suddenly if James had left a wife in Lebanon, to whom he had intended to return in due course.

'He charmed the hearts of the women round about,' Eleanor reminisced tenderly, 'and they bought his soap, what he made in me cellar, without hesitation.' She stopped and then smiled at her friend, who had joined her by the kitchen fire. 'Then he met your George – and we never looked back, did we? And just when it seemed nothing could stop him, he goes and gets a heart attack.' Her face became ugly with grief and again the tears trickled down her lined face. 'You take care of your Georgie, Sarah. He int gettin' any younger.'

'Oh, aye. He's all right,' she replied with more certainty than she felt. George worked very hard and was on his feet all day.

'Our Benji's got his dad's charm. Not so fine looking, but a nice lad,' Eleanor said after drinking her tea down to the dregs. She put her cup down in the saucer, as a memory struck her of Benji coming home from school with a bruised cheek and an oozing nose. He must've been about nine, she thought, and a couple of bullies had called him an Arab and a bastard. Lucky for Benji, he was a heavily built boy and he had fought back. After that, Jamie had shown him a few ways to defend himself which must have been shudderingly painful to the recipient of the blows. Gradually, the boys left him alone – too alone. His best friend had been George Tasker's eldest, Albert, who'd gone away to be a soldier. In India, now, he was.

Mrs Tasker was fond of Benji and agreed with his mother that he was a nice lad. She laughed unexpectedly, and added, 'Maybe he could charm Miss Harding into marrying him; then he'd get the soap works right into his hand.'

Eleanor forgot her grief for a moment. 'You're right. But you never can tell with young people, and I'm told she's quite old.' She put down

146

her cup into the hearth and stood up. 'I must start tea for me gentlemen. They all like a hot tea.'

'How many have you got?'

'Three of 'em. All very respectable.'

Mrs Tasker sighed. Lodgers would be a lot of work for Eleanor and she nearly fifty years old. 'Lucky for you, you own the house,' she said. 'Though I'm sure Benji'll take care of you.'

'For sure he will,' Eleanor agreed. 'But me dad thought I'd be alone all me life, so he made sure I had the house. He left it in good order, too, just like his auntie left it to him. We always had lodgers; it kept him in his old age.' She began to take out her mixing bowl, rolling pin and wooden spoons. 'And he had a water closet put in the back yard,' she added proudly. 'I started looking for good lodgers the minute our Jamie was buried, in case Benji loses his job. Gives us a bit of independence, it does.' She took out her scales and began to weigh flour for pastry. Through the dust rising from the shaken-out flour, Sarah Tasker watched her friend's face. It was pitifully woebegone.

To cheer her up, Sarah said, 'Well, let's hope Miss Wallace Helena falls for Benji. Then you could live like a lady, like Jamie managed for you these last few years.'

24

Wallace Helena leaned back in her office chair and stretched herself. In front of her was the correspondence which had accumulated for Benjamin Al-Khoury's attention during his absence. She had already read it. Her mouth twisted in a grim little smile, as she congratulated herself on having hit on such a simple method of keeping track of much that was going on in the soapery.

There was a quiet tap on the door. Mr Helliwell entered to announce Benjamin's arrival with Mr Bobsworth. She told him to show them in, and pushed the correspondence to one side.

As they entered, she stared at the handsome, untidy man who followed Mr Bobsworth in. He's quite young, she thought in surprise, younger than Helliwell, and, despite his western dress, he looks like an Arab. He seemed more relaxed than an Englishman, though he had the same self-confident air as Mr Benson. Although he was stocky, she gained an impression of physical fitness – and mental alertness. Very much his father's son.

Her stare was merciless and it embarrassed Benjamin, who was already very irate at the news that she had taken the week's correspondence to read. Beneath his black moustache, his mouth was clamped as tightly as hers.

The woman had eyes like stones, he thought as he greeted her with the courtesy of an experienced sales representative. She leaned over the desk to shake his proffered hand, smiling slightly, her eyes expressionless.

'A bloody Mona Lisa,' Benjamin added to his first impression, as she indicated the visitor's chair and he sat down.

Wallace Helena turned her attention to Mr Bobsworth standing primly behind Benjamin.

'Thank you for bringing Mr Al-Khoury in, Mr Bobsworth. I mustn't keep you from your work any longer.'

Mr Bobsworth reluctantly retreated with Mr Helliwell. It was improper for a lady to receive a man alone in an office. He himself was nearly old enough to be her father, so he felt it did not matter if he were alone with her. But it was different when young Benji or even Mr

Helliwell were closeted with her; things could happen. A woman who smoked was not quite what she should be – Benji should watch out.

As Benji loosed Wallace Helena's long cool hand, his heart sank. He had had, in the back of his mind, the same vague hope that his mother had, that *things* might, indeed, happen. What he had not inherited because of his illegitimacy, he could perhaps gain control of by marriage, despite the new law.

But the long, almond-shaped light brown eyes, so like his own, were as cold as rain-washed pebbles on a November morning. The firm, wide mouth seemed infinitely unkissable, and the thin, pliant body, which had stirred Mr Tasker to unseemly thoughts, appeared sticklike to a younger man used to the plumper women of his own generation. Had Joe Black been present and able to read Benjamin's thoughts, he would have cuffed him like an angry bear for being so uncomplimentary about such a fine woman.

Wallace Helena understood men well enough to be subtly aware that she had not aroused any admiration in him; she did not feel the instant rapport that she had felt when meeting George Tasker.

She could see the family likeness between herself and him; he was indeed his father's son. She had at one point, when thinking about him, wondered if he was a child conceived in an earlier liaison of his mother's and foisted upon her uncle. The man before her had, however, the broad, muscular build of a Maronite from the mountains, the deep chest of peoples used to high altitudes, and muscles adapted to hard physical work, though in Benji's case town life had made them tend towards fleshiness. His nose was not as prominent as her own and had a slight upward tilt at the end. His glossy black hair waved back from his face and his skin was a weather-beaten olive. There was nothing about him to indicate that he had an English mother.

She broke the silence between them by saying, 'I'm very glad to meet you – at last. I understand you were in Manchester when I arrived?'

He took this as an implied reproof for his absence, and, pulling himself together, replied quickly, 'Yes. I must apologize for not meeting you off the ship, but we suddenly lost a good contract to a new company setting up in Warrington. The Manchester market is so valuable that I thought I must go to see the customer myself.' He did not say that he had spun out his absence, by going to pay courtesy calls on other customers, because he did not feel that he could face her until he had gained command of the anger and frustration he felt. He had wanted to beat his breast and tear his clothes, get away from his rightly distraught mother.

149

'What had happened in Manchester?' Her voice was cool and she sounded very alert.

'Lever offered them a better price – and supporting advertising.' He went on to explain that Lever had begun to wrap his common washing soap in gaily coloured paper, and to scent it with citronella to drown its normally unpleasant odour.

'Humph.' She shifted in her chair. 'We'll have a meeting with Mr Tasker and Mr Bobsworth – and perhaps Mr Turner – that's the name of the chemist, isn't it? We'll go into the matter thoroughly, so that the minute I have Probate we can take some action. How did you leave the matter?'

'I asked them to let us tender next time the contract came up – they're middlemen and buy in bulk.'

She nodded agreement, and then banged the bell on her desk. As soon as Mr Helliwell materialized in response to it she ordered tea. While it was being made, she began to ask Benji a little about himself and the position of Assistant Manager, which he held.

Tight-lipped Mr Helliwell brewed tea in a pot, paid for out of Petty Cash with much grumbling from Mr Bobsworth. He was glad he had a gas ring in his office and did not have to go down to put the kettle on the watchman's coke brazier, which was not always alight on summer days. It would be humiliating to let the yard know that he made tea like a parlour maid. Mr James had always asked young Le Fleur to make it.

Benji had learned from his father the gentle art of making a customer feel comfortable – and tea or coffee had always been one of his father's ploys, whether the visitor drank it or not. He had also passed to his son, brought up in an alien culture, something of his own quick-wittedness and business acumen passed down to him through generations of traders in Lebanon and Syria. This began to surface in the son as he explained his duties in the company to Wallace Helena. In the back of his mind he wondered why she bothered, if the business was to be sold.

He mentioned that the idea of selling a scented soap for the skin had been his. 'There's plenty of competition,' he told Wallace Helena. 'But we make our tablets small and hard, wrap them and sell them as cheaply as possible. It's been my opinion, for a long time, that there's more *cash* in working families nowadays and they can afford small luxuries. My mother says that, in the old days, the women hardly spent anything on themselves; it was a matter of survival only. Now, I sell them not only a bit of scented soap but a little bottle of scent as well, despite the old diehards who say it's vanity – of course, old people often think having a bath is vanity!'

Wallace Helena laughed. 'Good heavens!' she exclaimed.

Emboldened by her spontaneous laugh, he went on, 'Another thing I think I could sell is a cream for hands. All the cleaning they do – with soap – takes the oil out of their skins, and immediately the cold weather comes they chap and the skin splits very painfully. In the country, on the farms, there's always a bit of lard or goose grease they can rub into the sore spots, but it's very sticky – and women in cotton mills and suchlike can't afford to have sticky hands. We've glycerine left over after the soap-making; Turner's working on the refining of it, to use as a base for a cream. We know how to do it, but we want something very, very cheap that will have a small mark-up and a big turnover – I've been pricing small ointment tins and glass jars to pack it in.'

'That's another thing to talk about after Probate,' Wallace Helena replied. 'We've got to decide what we'll make in future, particularly since competition seems to be getting more intense. I can see that Mr Turner may be invaluable.'

He was heartened that she said *we*, as if taking for granted that, whatever was to happen to the company, he was, as far as she was concerned, to be included in the decision-making. He wondered if Bobsworth's idea that she wanted to run the firm herself was correct.

He nodded agreement with her remark about the chemist. Then he said, with an amused expression on his face, 'Mr Al-Khoury used to watch and listen for news of towns putting in waterworks; he'd go personally to any such place and sell our soap to every grocer or hardware store he could find. "Once a woman has a water tap in the house, she wants soap," he would say. "So we get ours in first."'

Benji's description of her uncle's impetuosity was so apt that it made her smile. She mentally saw him bursting into the office of the silk warehouse in Beirut, eager to suggest something new to his elder brother; or, in the house, snatching her up from her play to whiz round with her and tell her she was his little lemon flower.

Benji watched the passing expressions on her face and wondered what she was thinking of. He was surprised by her next question.

'Aren't there any rich ladies in England?' she inquired. 'You speak all the time of women who do their own work. I thought everybody in England had servants?'

'Well, not everybody has servants. We're going after working-class women, because they're a comparatively new market. Rich women have bought quite expensive soap from their hairdressers, for years. The competition in that kind of soap is *very* keen.' He chuckled a little

151

ruefully. 'For a long time in the new cities, like the cotton towns, working people didn't have access to much water – they had to endure the filth around them. Now, many of them have a decent water supply, so Fath . . . Mr Al-Khoury set out to sell them cheap soap. A small mark-up, but, on the other hand, a huge market.'

He was beginning to feel more at home with Wallace Helena, and he leaned back in his chair and shoved his hands in his pockets. 'But now we're faced with a very innovative competitor, in the shape of Mr Lever, trying for the same market. We often undercut the older firms, because our overheads are low – but Lever is another kettle of fish. He's causing ripples throughout the industry.'

'We'll try to give him a run for his money,' Wallace Helena promised, intrigued at the chance to outwit a smart man.

'Well, I was trying to persuade Mr Al-Khoury to improve the presentation of our toilet soap, at least – a brighter wrapper, or something. But he passed away before we got down to it – and now we're in limbo.' The last words came out with a sigh.

Wallace Helena observed his change of expression, the sudden woodenness of his rugged face. She began to realize his personal uncertainty – in limbo, he was, personally, and he also shared the uncertainty of the other employees. She knew she must soon make up her mind whether she would stay in England to guide the company – or sell it. It was not fair to the employees to dither. But there was Joe to consider. Could she persuade him to settle in a city, and if she did, what would he do? It would be like caging a tiger.

She thought bitterly that, if Joe didn't exist, she would never return to the hardship of her life in Canada – she would stay in Liverpool, and even, perhaps, take a look at making a second move back to Lebanon. And what would you do there, without a family or at least a man to protect you? she asked herself. She suddenly hated her kind, generous uncle for facing her with such a dilemma.

In an effort to clarify Benji's position, she said, 'I remember Uncle James writing to Father and mentioning that he had a little boy. Was that you?'

'Yes, Miss Harding.' He fidgeted uncomfortably, taking his hands out of his pockets and then clasping them in front of him on the side of her desk. He said abruptly, 'I didn't know you existed – I never saw your father's letters, of course. Mr Benson told me about you.'

'My father was the eldest and he used to worry about Uncle James. I'm sure he must have often scolded him when he wrote to him. That'll be why you never saw the letters!' There was a hint of humour in her voice, but it did not raise his spirits. 'Probably you were too small to be able to read, anyway.'

'Yes, Miss Harding.'

'Stop *Miss Harding* me. I'm your cousin – that's almost like a sister. Call me Wallace Helena, like a relation, can't you?' She got up from her chair and began to pace up and down impatiently. Then she stopped in front of him, and said contritely, when he didn't answer, 'You must miss your father dreadfully, and I'm truly sorry you've lost him.'

'Thank you. I do miss him.' He suddenly looked very exhausted, and she said gently, 'I understand why you did not get any of Uncle's Estate – and I'm sure it was not Uncle's intention that I get it. But I'm stuck with it – and it's causing me considerable heartache, believe it or not.'

'Is it?' He was surprised out of his depression. 'Father simply didn't expect to die, so he didn't prepare for it. Which of us ever does?'

'Not many,' Wallace Helena admitted glumly. Her full skirt swished, as she returned to her chair. She opened a heavy box on her desk. 'Like a smoke?' she asked.

'No, thanks. I smoke a pipe.'

'Well, get it out and smoke it,' she suggested, as she put a cigarello between her lips, and struck a match to light it.

There was a strict *No Smoking* rule in the works, but he did not think this was an appropriate moment to mention it, so he took out his pipe and tobacco pouch and proceeded to pack the pipe. She threw the box of matches to him across the desk. 'Your official designation is Assistant Manager, isn't it?'

'Yes.' He struck a match and lit his pipe.

'Well, you continue what you're doing for the moment, though I'll consult you all along the way. We can't make any changes until Probate is granted; but I'll do my best to make up my mind quickly. If I sell, I'll make sure you get a decent contract with the new owner, if you want it. How would that be?'

'It'd help,' he admitted, and pulled on his pipe. He had never before broken the *No Smoking* rule, for fear of fire. 'Supposing you don't sell?'

'I'll manage it myself,' she replied, without hesitation. 'I'll work very closely with the senior employees, as Uncle did.'

'As a woman, you'll have particular difficulties.'

'So I'm told,' she responded dryly. 'We shall see.'

He warned her further. 'You should be aware that a lot of changes are taking place in the industry. Mechanization on a big scale – it's already very advanced in the bigger firms. Some employ German scientists – they've brought in some profound changes.'

Wallace Helena whistled between her teeth, while she considered this. 'That means money, doesn't it?'

'Yes, capital.'

She grinned at him suddenly. 'We live in interesting times, don't we? I imagine that if we have our wits about us, we can cope as well as anybody?'

His mood lightened. It felt good to be included in the battles to come. She was obviously willing to face a challenge. But he agreed cautiously, 'Well, yes. Minnows can swim along quite well beneath bigger fish – and not all of 'em get eaten!'

She laughed, and he continued, 'Tasker, Bobsworth, Ferguson – the Steam Engineer – and Turner. We've got good, informed employees. They used to meet in our sitting-room in the evenings. They'd spend hours bickering with each other, working out how to run the place, while Mother dished out cake and beer.'

'Like family?'

'Exactly.' He drew on his pipe and settled back in his chair more comfortably. 'Frankly, Turner's a bit of an expense for a small firm like ours. But he'll be useful if we go into emollients. And Frank Ferguson – well, he's like all engineers, nowadays, he's a king. He can name his own price anywhere. He was fond of my father, though, and I think he'll stay with us, if we treat him properly. He's always at war with old Bobsworth over costs.'

Wallace Helena's eyes glinted with amusement. 'I know. When we were going over the books, Mr Bobsworth must've said a dozen times, "Mr Ferguson doesn't appreciate that we can't go rushing out to buy every bit of equipment that comes on the market. When we started we managed it much more cheaply without anything fancy."'

She had mimicked Mr Bobsworth's petulant complaint exactly. They looked at each other and began to chuckle like a pair of disrespectful youngsters.

He was agreeably surprised at what laughter did to her. She suddenly became human, approachable. And she was obviously perceptive – she'd got old Bobsworth down to a T.

She was looking at him with kinder eyes now, though there was still a twinkle of amusement in them. She said, 'Don't worry too much. I shall be very careful in what I do.' She picked up the sheaf of letters and handed them to him. 'Meanwhile, there must be a lot of work which has accumulated in your absence – I guess you'd better get on with it.'

He put the letters down on the desk, while he dowsed his pipe by fitting a small tin cover over the bowl. Then he got up slowly, nodding acknowledgment of her remark about his work as he did so. Having talked to her, he felt easier in his mind, but he wished his father were still sitting in the chair she occupied.

'Thank you, Miss Harding.' He bowed and quietly left the room.

She wanted to get up and go after the young man to comfort him. He was cousin-brother to her and had been bereaved. But she felt that if she was to maintain her authority, she must keep her distance. It was a lonely feeling.

25

The next morning, when Benji arrived at the plant, he found the day's correspondence neatly piled on his desk. When asked, Mr Helliwell said that he had, as usual, opened the envelopes and, at Miss Harding's request, handed the letters to her to read. He saw Benji's lips tighten at this information, and hastened to add, 'She said it was the quickest way to find out what was happening in the works. She said you'd deal with everything.'

'Humph,' Benji grunted, as he shuffled quickly through the pile. Wallace Helena had scribbled her suggestions on one or two of the letters and he made a face when he saw her notes. He said to Helliwell, 'I'll give you some dictation to be going on with, and we'll do the rest when I've done my round of the works.' He supposed he ought to be thankful that she had left any decisions regarding the matters raised in the letters to him. At least it showed a little trust.

He met his cousin coming out of the small laboratory presided over by Mr Turner, a lanky man in his thirties. Wallace Helena's set face told Benji immediately that she had not got along very well with the chemist. He looked past her at Turner and raised an eyebrow in query.

Turner blinked back at him through his gold-rimmed spectacles and shrugged almost imperceptibly. She had asked him to show her round his small laboratory and he had politely obliged, though tending to talk down to her as if she were a small girl to whom he was explaining profound mysteries. He had been taken aback when she made it clear that she knew the principles of soap-making; she made her own every spring, she had informed him tartly.

When she saw Benji, she managed to smile and greet him. Without stopping to thank Mr Turner, she fell into step beside him and accompanied him through the works, as he went to see Mr Tasker about one or two matters and then to Mr Bobsworth about some points raised in customers' letters. 'Going to see the various mandarins?' she remarked to him. He grinned at her, sensing that they would often share small jokes, treating each other like cousins, not employer and employee.

They talked about the overheads of the works, how much they must sell to cover the basic costs of keeping the soapery open.

As they left Mr Bobsworth's office, she said, 'I imagine that having a fox terrier like Mr Bobsworth barking at the heels of our mandarins saves a lot of waste?'

'It does,' he responded, though he did not sound very happy about it. 'It's also frustrating, because only Mr Benson can authorize any real change in expenditure. He's the Executor – and he tends to execute.' He waited for her to appreciate his pun, but she did not understand it, so he said, 'I think he simply wants the soapery to tick over until Probate is received.'

Or until I make up my mind, ruminated Wallace Helena fretfully. But what could a black man do in Liverpool? I've only to look at Alfie – the bottom of the pecking order here – to sense the prejudice. And I doubt if I could live in Liverpool without Joe.

Benji found it irritating to have her often at his heels; he was young enough to feel that she might criticize the orders he gave to the various employees, and it was certain that the men tended to stare at her when he was speaking, rather than attending to his instructions. He underestimated the enormous curiosity about her amongst them.

A couple of days after his first interview with her, he mentioned impatiently that old Bobsworth was, as usual, complaining because he, Benji, was about to run an advertisement for their toilet soaps in a number of local Lancashire newspapers. 'He says our female customers can't read, so what's the good of an advertisement? Let them tell each other how good our toilet soap is, he says. It's nonsense! A lot of women can spell out a newspaper. A sketch of a pretty woman and the words, "Your daughters need a perfect complexion. Use Lady Lavender toilet soaps" will draw their attention.'

Wallace Helena could not resist a small giggle. Then she suggested shrewdly, 'To keep the cost down, why not put it in two newspapers for several consecutive issues – you should be able to squeeze a better rate out of them for several advertisements. And see if sales improve in those particular districts. If they do, you could possibly persuade Mr *Benson* to agree to a wider series of advertisements, despite Mr Bobsworth's opposition. You're in charge of sales.'

'I know – but I'm only Assistant Manager. If Father were here, he'd tell him to stick to his bookkeeping. But with Father gone, Bobsworth tends to throw his weight around – though he means well.'

Wallace Helena gave one of her little whistles between her teeth. Then she said, 'Well, I'm not supposed to make any decisions until Mr Benson has finished probating the Will, but I'd back you, if you want to ask him to O.K. the expense of the advertisements. Make sure you've plenty of soap in the towns you choose, though.'

157

'Thanks. Advertising doesn't always have any sudden effect; it simply reminds customers of the name.'

Well, I leave you to decide,' she said, and then brought up another subject. 'If I'm to sell soap and emollients, I should like to know more about English women. I really haven't met any since I've been here, except Mrs Hughes, my landlady.'

He turned to glance at her sallow, haggard face. Her remark brought home to him that she was not only struggling to understand his father's business, but a whole society which was alien to her. He put down the layout of his proposed advertisement, to give his full attention to her.

'Yes, of course. You don't know anybody, do you? Father had a lot of business friends and acquaintances. I doubt if he ever met their wives – who might have called on you. Mother's best friend is Sarah Tasker; they both know every woman living round them, but they're not the kind to make formal calls, any of them – though I think they'd make themselves known, if you were living in the same street.'

'Hmm. I've met Mrs Benson – but strictly between you and me, I thought her dreadfully ignorant and stupid. And Mrs Hughes, who pries.'

He surveyed her carefully, a small twinkle in his eyes. 'I think you'd find most middle-class women total bores. I do.'

She looked relieved. 'It's nice of you to say that; probably I'm boring to them.'

'You're streets ahead of 'em,' he assured her firmly. 'Too much for them; they don't know how to cope with a woman as experienced as you are.'

Though he had, in his irritation at her constant presence, been rather short with her that day, she warmed to him. Her long lashes flickered, as she glanced obliquely at him.

He asked, 'Would you like to meet Mother?' His voice was uncertain, because, though she understood his mother's relationship to her uncle, she might strongly disapprove of it.

'Good God,' she exclaimed, and sat down suddenly on her chair. 'What have I been about?'

He was shaken by her unexpected response, and he said defensively, 'You don't have to, if you don't want to.'

She smiled at him. 'No. No. Of course I want to meet her. I'm so cross with myself that I did not consider her more. She must be feeling dreadful. Her loss is the greatest. And I've never thought about it.' She banged her closed fist on the desk and her rings flashed in the morning light. 'Mr Benson mentioned her in connection with the Will, but, if I thought of her at all, it was as a lady who would resent me so much that she would not *want* to meet me. Do you really think she would want to meet me?'

'Well, she's very curious about you, now she's got over the first shock of Father's death.' He sighed.

'Should I go to see her?'

He made a little face. 'I think it's usual for the resident lady to call on a newcomer.'

'Humph. Well, tell her I'd enjoy meeting her and ask her to let me know when it would be convenient for her to call. How's that?'

He grinned. 'I'll ask her,' he promised. It would be a much-needed diversion for his mother, even if the two women hated each other on sight.

26

Benji evidently went home to lunch that day, because in the afternoon he brought a pink envelope to her office.

As he waited expectantly while she ripped open the envelope, she smiled at him. Behind the smile, she was rather regretting the impetuosity of her behaviour that morning. Supposing the woman turned out to be a servile sycophant, bent on manipulating favours out of her for her son? And just how much could she trust Benji himself?

On pink notepaper decorated round the edges with improbable-looking small flowers, Eleanor Al-Khoury wrote in a large, irregular hand that she would be pleased to call at half past six that evening, after tea, and please to tell our Benjamin if that would be all right.

Feeling that she was already committed, she agreed to the visit, though she said, 'I've got a bad cold – I hope she doesn't mind.'

'We've all got them,' Benji reassured her, and, indeed, his own voice suggested a thick catarrh.

As he was about to leave the office, she asked him, 'Have you any brothers or sisters?' It had not occurred to her before that there might be a number of young Al-Khourys.

He shrugged. 'No. I don't think I've got any relations. Mother hasn't any – except she told me once that there were some cousins of hers in Wales; but I don't think she ever kept in touch with them. She was an only child, and her father left her the house we live in. And Father had no living relations, except your family.' He paused thoughtfully, and then said, 'So she must feel very lonely now – though I do my best for her.'

'I'm sure you do. You must've had a lonely childhood?'

'Well, I always had a few good friends. George Tasker's eldest son, for one – till he went into the army.' He fell silent, as he remembered the bullying of the local boys. They'd given him hell and called him Blackie, until he and Tom Tasker had grown big enough and ruthless enough to fight back to good effect.

Watching him, Wallace Helena guessed that the young man's passage had not been easy. She had been much despised herself, because she was thought, in her early days at Fort Edmonton, to be part Chinese and, when this was discounted, to be Jewish and, therefore, not someone anybody white wanted to know. Thank God for Joe and his Cree relations, she considered grimly. Without them, she would have been very lonely, too.

He was speaking again, asking a personal question suggested by her remark about his loneliness. 'Do you have help on your farm – someone you can leave it with? Bobsworth told me you had a big farm.'

She gazed at him thoughtfully, the long narrow eyes weighing him up once again. 'I've a partner,' she admitted cautiously.

'What will you do, if you want to stay here with us?'

'I don't know yet whether my partner would wish to continue managing it or would want to sell up. I'm awaiting his reactions to some suggestions I have made by letter.'

That accounted for her dilatoriness in making up her mind. He was relieved that there was a sensible reason for her slowness.

But in her heart Wallace Helena knew that if she was not in Edmonton and he did not want to come to England, Joe would take his horses and drift back to the south, perhaps into the United States, to peddle his expertise in warmer climates; he did not have Tom Harding's passionate love of the land; he loved only her.

And how could she desert him? Yet she was tired of the un-equal struggle in the Territories, the hardship; her body had begun to crave the comfort of a civilized city. 'Tush, I must be getting old,' she muttered. 'Wait and see what Joe has to say. And, meantime, get on with the job here.'

Benji was turning to leave the office. She took a handkerchief from her sleeve and blew her nose hard, her goodbye somewhat muffled.

27

Living in the same district, Mrs Hughes was well aware of the social standing of the self-styled Mrs Al-Khoury, and, when the unfortunate lady presented herself on Mrs Hughes's snow-white doorstep, she treated her with supercilious disregard, as if she had never seen her before.

Eleanor Al-Khoury was in full mourning. The opaque black veil of her widow's bonnet had been thrown forward, to shield her face from the gaze of the vulgar. In one black-gloved hand she held a black-edged handkerchief and in the other a worn black change purse. She told the landlady in a low voice that Miss Harding was expecting her.

Mrs Hughes kept the visitor standing in the hall, while she went to inquire of Wallace Helena whether she was at home this evening.

Rather startled, Wallace Helena replied in tones muffled by her cold that, as far as she knew, she was right here. Why?

'A woman wishes to see you.'

'Mrs Al-Khoury?'

'I believe she goes by that name.'

'Why didn't you bring her right in?' Wallace Helena demanded irritably, as she rose from her fireside chair. Mrs Hughes sniffed and, full of offended dignity, re-opened the sitting-room door, and snapped, 'You can come in.'

Holding her handkerchief to her streaming nose with one hand, Wallace Helena held out her other hand to Eleanor and drew her towards the fire. 'Come in, Mrs Al-Khoury, close to the fire. You must be quite chilled – it is so damp outside.' She pushed her handkerchief into her waistband, and saw the visitor comfortably seated opposite to her own chair.

Immediately a little relieved by the fact that Wallace Helena had called her Mrs Al-Khoury, an indication, she felt, of acceptance as a member of the family, Mrs Al-Khoury sat down.

'Do take off your bonnet and gloves,' Wallace Helena urged, anxious to make the bereaved woman feel at home. 'Let me take them from you.'

At such kindness and condescension, Eleanor Al-Khoury felt she wanted to cry again. She carefully lifted the ugly bonnet off, and handed it to Wallace Helena.

A round, pleasant face was revealed, framed by puffs of light brown hair streaked with white. Deepset blue eyes looked red from weeping and lack of sleep. Though the round cheeks were a deep pink, the lines of the face spoke of exhaustion. When Eleanor peeled off her black cotton gloves, Wallace Helena noted that her hands had the same work-worn look as did her own, except that Eleanor's were bright red from frequent immersion in hot water and soda.

The visitor sat bolt upright in her chair, as a lady should. When Wallace Helena, smiling, sat down again, she returned her hostess's inquiring gaze without faltering. Then suddenly she bent her head and burst into tears.

In a moment, Wallace Helena was on her knees beside her. She put her arm round the bent shoulders and pleaded, 'Please don't cry. There's nothing to be afraid of.'

'I'm not afraid of you, luv,' the woman snuffled through her tears. 'It's 'cos everything's gone topsy-turvy, like – and I miss'' im so much.' She sobbed for a moment, while Wallace Helena held her and tried to soothe her. 'And it hurts so much that he never thought to leave me even a bit to live on.' Her voice rose to a wail.

'It was an accident, Mrs Al-Khoury; he simply did not expect to die for a long time yet. I'm told he appeared to be a very stalwart man.'

The straightforward use of the word *die* instead of a euphemism caused another paroxysm of grief, which Wallace Helena did her best to stem by suggesting a nice, hot cup of tea. She had been much amused by Mrs Hughes's prescribing tea for every ill; colds, aches, lack of appetite, headaches, all yielded to a nice cup of tea, according to the landlady. Nothing like it.

While Mrs Al-Khoury sobbed her thanks, Wallace Helena pulled the bell to call Violet May, Mrs Hughes's maid-of-all-work.

By the time Violet May had arrived and had been asked for tea and cake or biscuits, Eleanor Al-Khoury had begun to gain control of herself. To divert her, Wallace Helena asked her if she lived nearby.

'Oh, aye. I'm only a little ways away, round the corner. Me pa left me the house, and it's a godsend, it's bin. It's old-fashioned, but Jamie liked it 'cos it's close to the soap works.'

Wallace Helena asked how she had met Uncle James, and Eleanor told her the story of how, as a young immigrant, he had knocked on her door and asked if she had a room to let. 'And we went on from there,' she said more cheerfully. 'He were always so good to me – that's why I can't understand . . .' Her face crumpled again and she took out her handkerchief to hold it to her quivering mouth.

'He was good to me as well. When Mama and my stepfather died and I decided to go on farming, I asked if he could get me some books about agriculture in a cold climate. He sent me several very helpful books. He must have had to send for some of them from other countries – one was in French and two on botany were in Arabic.'

Eleanor stopped weeping and looked at Wallace Helena in great surprise. 'I didn't know that,' she said.

'I gathered from the lawyer that Mr Helliwell did the dispatching.'

'Oh, aye. He'd have all the boxes and wrapping paper he needed by him in the office. That'd be it.'

Wallace Helena nodded. She recalled with amusement that he had never mentioned either Eleanor or Benji in his covering letters to her. He had, however, given her the name of a friend of her grandfather, long established in Montreal. She had written to him to ask if he knew of any research being done on farming in Canada, and he, too, had been very kind. He had sent her two papers on sowing pasture and one on the problems of raising wheat in a short growing season.

As Eleanor droned on with the story of her life with Uncle James, Wallace Helena berated herself for not keeping in closer touch with her uncle. But the distance had been so immense that she was always amazed when a letter or a box actually did arrive from him. And often the daily life of herself and Joe had been so hard that it had left little time to think of anything except the next task to be done. But the books had been a wonderful help, especially one he had obtained on Russian farming.

Eleanor was saying, 'Me next-door neighbour told me I were mad to take in a foreigner what could hardly speak any English. But he sounded loovely.' She stopped, and then added with a shy smile, 'And he were loovely to look at, with the same nice smile our Benji has.' She clutched her handkerchief in her hand, and wondered how she could explain to this woman from the Colonies the particular, magical attraction of James Al-Khoury as a young man of twenty-two.

The stranger would have understood perfectly. Had she not fallen in love at the age of eighteen with a fine, six-foot-tall, black cowpuncher and horse-breaker, whose voice still held traces of the deep vibrance of his Zulu forefathers?

Without apology, Wallace Helena blew her reddened nose hard; she wondered if she had a temperature.

The tea was brought by Mrs Hughes herself. Though annoyed at having to provide it, she was not averse to intruding on the visit. It was disappointing that, apart from Wallace Helena's murmured thanks, the two women remained silent while the tray was arranged on a low tea table. Eleanor did not smile at Mrs Hughes, though she managed a stiff inclination of the head. Mrs Hughes acknowledged it with a slight nod, as she left the room disappointed at not being drawn into the conversation.

As Wallace Helena poured the tea and proffered biscuits, Eleanor continued her tale. 'Though 'is English never were that good, he could speak French and Arabic – and our Benji grew up with three languages. They'd talk away for hours in one lingo or the other, till I says, "Let's have a bit of English, so I can be included in."' She smiled at this reminiscence, and then sighed. 'Clever, he was – and so's our Benji. He insisted on bringing me buckets of coal up from the cellar, and it was there he saw me wash boiler, and got the idea of making soap – came to 'im out of the blue, it did. So I managed to keep 'im fed, while he got started.'

'So you really gave him his start?'

'I suppose. I haven't never thought of it. He were welcome.'

As Eleanor became more relaxed over her cups of tea, Wallace Helena listened and watched her carefully. She had learned in the hard world of Chicago, and had it confirmed in the Territories, that behind the most innocent face could lurk a convoluted mind capable of all kinds of perfidy. She wondered if mother and son had any plan to undermine her ownership of the Lady Lavender. She could not immediately think what benefit the Al-Khourys might get out of a scheme to unseat her, but she did not underestimate the power of angry, overlooked relatives.

Finally, Eleanor Al-Khoury became quiet. Then she broached a fresh subject.

'Our Benji says as how you would like to know how an English lady lives – bearing in mind soap, like?'

Wallace Helena nodded. 'I would indeed,' she responded. 'Canada is so very different.' She sighed, but did not elaborate. She dabbed her reddened nose, which was feeling very tender. 'I've been to Mr Benson's house – it was, of course, a formal visit. I didn't like to ask about their private use of soap!'

Eleanor laughed suddenly, her face crinkling up to show the merry person she usually was. 'Well, I don't mind showing you, as long as you'll take me as you find me. If you don't mind clouds of steam, you come along on Monday morning – I do me wash then. I'll have me boiler goin' long before you arrive, and we can sit a few minutes and have a cuppa tea before I start to scrub.' She paused to ruminate over this statement, and then went on, 'That's where most of the soap gets used. I use some of the soapy water, afterwards, to scrub the floors and the steps.'

'In summer we do *our* washing in the creek,' Wallace Helena confided, feeling on safer ground. 'We pound it on a smooth rock. In the winter, the creek's frozen over, so we have to do our best in a wash tub in the cabin – it gets put outside to dry, though, spread over the bushes. It freezes solid and yet it gets almost dry. Then we finish it off over a line inside.'

'It must be proper hard for you livin' out there amongst the savages,' responded Eleanor sympathetically, though, despite her liaison with James Al-Khoury, her own life had been a hard one.

Feeling that she had stayed long enough, she rose to take her leave. She smiled down at Wallace Helena, and said, 'You've been proper kind to me tonight, and you so poorly with a cold. Would you like to come on Monday?'

'I would.' She rose slowly from her chair, as her visitor went over to the centre table to pick up her bonnet and then came back to the fireside to arrange it in front of the mirror over the mantelpiece. 'It's been very nice meeting you,' the Lebanese told her, remembering her manners, as she shepherded the visitor towards the door of the room.

In the hallway, before lowering her black veil over her face, Eleanor surprised Wallace Helena by standing on tiptoes and gently kissing her on her cheek, despite the likelihood of catching her cold. At the same time, she squeezed her hand tightly.

Then she turned and let down her veil, while Wallace Helena, smiling, opened the front door for her.

'See you Monday,' Eleanor said with false brightness.

'I'll look forward to it,' Wallace Helena promised, hiding her general unease.

After Eleanor had gone down the spotless front steps, the hem of her skirt making a soft plop on each step as she descended, Wallace Helena slowly shut the front door and, as quietly as possible, turned the key; she had no wish to bring Mrs Hughes from her back sitting-room to begin a speculative conversation in the chilly hall.

Back in her own sitting-room, she sat for a long time before the dying fire, reflecting on Benjamin and his mother. Would they, in their bitterness, become her most dangerous opponents? Eleanor was, according to Benjamin, a close friend of Mrs Tasker and Mrs Bobsworth, who could, in turn, influence their husbands. The two men and Benji could make it impossible for her to keep discipline in the works, though they probably would not go so far as to ruin the business – all three earned a living out of it.

She remembered, with a sardonic smile, that in Edmonton, nowadays, men were distantly civil to her, but when it came to business transactions, there were no holds barred. She wished Joe Black could have a look at the mother and son; like a dog, he would sense whether they were to be trusted or not.

Dear Joe. I want this soap works and I want you; *and* I need Benjamin Al-Khoury's managerial know-how. And I'm not too sure how to secure any of them permanently.

28

Lying in bed that night, unable to sleep because of her cold, Wallace Helena began to feel once more the sense of desolation that had, from time to time, haunted her ever since her mother's death. It was born of the knowledge that, after Mama had gone, there was nobody left who understood what the massacre in Beirut had done to her, that her whole life had been ripped apart, her roots destroyed, all the kindly people that she had known in her childhood cruelly murdered, simply because they were a minority, a fairly prosperous Christian minority. She knew she should be thankful that she had escaped, not only the massacre but subsequent death from small-pox; yet, at moments like this, when other problems impinged and seemed insoluble, a sense of being punished for surviving hit her. Was she to be a foreigner, a strange one forever, like the Wandering Jew who had to live until Christ returned to earth, alone, unliked, distrustful of everybody and everything?

Usually, Joe could comfort her a little when such morbid fancies sent her to bed to lie shivering helplessly in a kind of Hades. Tonight, Joe was six thousand miles away, and she felt bereft of courage, deserted, left behind.

Towards the end of the night, she must have slept, because, when Violet May knocked on her door to say breakfast would be ready in half an hour, for a second she could not recollect where she was.

She answered the girl. Then she slowly dragged herself out of bed to bring in the ewer of hot water left outside the door for her by the servant. She ached all over, and her nose and throat seemed half-choked with the cold.

After washing in hot water, she felt better, and, scolding herself for being so self-pitying, she went down to breakfast.

When Mrs Hughes brought her meal in and saw her, she said immediately that Wallace Helena should on no account go out that day; the milkman had forecast more rain, and he was always right.

Feeling that she could not endure sitting all day in the gloomy, over-furnished house, Wallace Helena insisted on going to the Lady Lavender. She asked her landlady if, when she went shopping, she would buy her a couple of dozen more handkerchiefs, and she agreed to do this.

Then, with unexpected solicitude, she ran upstairs to fetch four of her late husband's big handkerchiefs to use in the meantime.

Although she did not like Mrs Hughes much, Wallace Helena had to admit that she was being very kind, and she accepted the proffered hankies with gratitude. Though she was just as capable of blowing her nose through her fingers as the labourers in the soapery did, she had quickly learned, when she did it once in their presence and heard their subsequent amused remarks, that English women did not do this. She wondered how such women felt when faced with a lonely homestead, where every scrap of material was precious; she herself used her few handkerchiefs only when visiting Edmonton village.

That evening, she returned pallid and obviously worn out, her clothes soaked by a summer rainstorm which had swept up the river.

As Mrs Hughes relieved her of a dripping umbrella lent her by Mr Helliwell, she protested, 'Miss Harding, you *must* take care of yourself. You'll get tuberculosis, if you don't watch.' She took the umbrella from her and put it to drip in the basin in an adjoining wash room. Then she returned to help her lodger remove her sopping wet shawl. 'I'll dry it for you in front of the kitchen fire,' she promised. 'And you give me your wet boots as well.'

'Thank you, Mrs Hughes. I'll be all right. I'm used to rough weather.'

She was not all right; she felt dispirited and very tired. Though she was used to extremes of heat and cold, she was not accustomed to damp, the penetrating dampness of the gentle rains of Lancashire. In her bedroom, she took out her hairpins and rubbed her hair dry; her hat, also, was wet, and she cursed, because she did not know how to hold an umbrella to best protect herself. She longed for hot sun and clear skies, and wondered if the sun ever shone properly in Liverpool.

When Mrs Hughes came up to assure her that the fire in her sitting-room was lit and blazing well, she asked her landlady if Liverpool ever had any fine days.

'Of course we do,' Mrs Hughes assured her. 'It's just not such a good summer this year.'

'Humph. My bad luck?'

Mrs Hughes looked amused, and said that if Wallace Helena liked to change her dress, she would get Violet May to press her present one dry. Although she was inquisitive and very snobbish, Mrs Hughes was not unkind, and she did not want her lodger to become seriously ill.

The younger woman hastily unhooked herself and handed the garment to her.

'You'd better change your petticoat as well,' the landlady advised, as she noticed the wet mud along its hem.

Dressed in a white blouse and a black skirt, Wallace Helena went down to her sitting-room and was grateful for the warmth of the fire in the wrought-iron fireplace.

Violet May knocked at the door and brought in a tea tray. 'The mistress says to have a cuppa, while you're waiting on dinner,' she announced, as she put it on a table by Wallace Helena's chair. She wiped her big red hands on her apron, and asked, 'Will I pour it for you, Miss?'

'Thank you, Violet May.'

Wallace Helena felt inside her placket pocket and brought out a packet of Turkish cigarettes. Alfie had brought them to her that morning, after she had complained that, with such a cold, she could not taste the cigarellos she had formed the habit of smoking. 'You might like to try 'em, Missus,' he said. 'They got a real, strong scent.'

Violet May watched, pop-eyed, as Wallace Helena put a cigarette in her mouth, took a spill from a brass container in the hearth and lit it from the fire. She put the light to the cigarette, then leaned back in her chair and exhaled a stream of smoke.

Suddenly remembering her duties, Violet May drained the contents of the teapot into the flowered cup. As she leaned over to put the tea closer to Wallace Helena, she whispered conspiratorially, 'The Missus isn't goin' to like the smell of smoke, Miss; the Master always smoked 'is pipe in the back room. She sniffed around the other day, when she come in here. We thought as a heavy-smoking man might've called on yez from the works, and the smell of smoke on 'is clothes 'ad spread into the room. But I really knowed it was you, Miss, 'cos your clothes always smells of smoke when I irons them.'

With an amused glint in her eye, Wallace Helena turned to look at the girl. 'I never thought of it troubling Mrs Hughes, Violet May; I'm so used to smoking.' She looked careworn as she added, 'I simply have to have a cigarette tonight – I'm so tired. What shall I do, Violet May? She won't want me smoking upstairs in the bedroom.'

As Violet May handed Wallace Helena the sugar bowl, she swallowed uncomfortably. She knew the mistress needed the money from her lodger; she'd been proper hard up since the old man died. She rubbed her hands on her grubby white apron, and said hopefully, 'What if I open the window by you and then one of the bay windows? That'll make a cross-draught and clear some of it.' She looked anxiously round the room, and then added with a mischievous grin, 'I can shake up the bowl of potpourri on the table – real nice, it smells – it'd help to drown the smoke a bit.'

Wallace Helena laughed, and agreed. So she sat in the cool draught and enjoyed her cigarette with her tea.

'There's a letter for you,' Violet May told her, as she was going out of the door. 'It's on the hall stand. Will I bring it to yez?'

The weary woman in the chair sat up straight, flicked ash into the fire, and replied with alacrity, 'Please do.'

In his scrawling handwriting, the despair of the priest who had taught him, Joe reported the flattening of the oats in a brief hailstorm just before harvesting. The crop would be good only for animal feed. He had also lost a sheep, he thought to a cougar; there were certainly cougar tracks near the fold. He had been trying to track it down. The sheep were more trouble than they were worth and, if she wanted to raise a big flock, she'd better bring a shepherd from Britain – and a trained dog. 'It's another mouth to feed,' he noted sourly. 'You should think about that.'

Though he signed the letter with love, the tone of it was unusually testy. She put this down to the loss of the oat crop; it did not occur to her that her letters to him had been full of the men she had met, the charms of the city, the money that might be made out of the soapery. Joe was feeling more than a twinge of jealousy and had already begun to worry that she might not return.

With the idea of raising money for more modern farm implements to take back to Canada, she had brought with her the last of her mother's necklaces and three rings to sell. She thought it highly likely that she could get a much better price for them in a sophisticated city, where they might be regarded as exquisite workmanship rather than so many ounces of gold and a number of stones.

Now, she began to fret that she and Joe might need any money she got for the jewellery, to supplement their living expenses the following winter; even if they agreed to sell the homestead, it would take time, and they would have to live through the winter.

The cost of her trip to England, with its concomitant need for respectable clothing, had drained the cash she had saved in her mother's trunk. Mr Benson had lent her funds against the Estate to cover her current living expenses. It was worrying, however, to draw money from the Estate, when the soapery would obviously need further investment in modern equipment, if the various staff she had talked to were to be believed.

Should she sell the Lady Lavender to help sustain the farm? Or persuade Joe that they should sell up in order to get investment funds for the soapery?

But would Joe even consider coming to England? She had asked him in a letter to which she had not yet had a reply.

The thought of Joe in a business suit and a top hat made her giggle. Yet you never knew with people. He sometimes complained that he was sick of winters; he might seriously consider her suggestion, particularly if they could buy some land near Liverpool – he might enjoy that. And she could run the soap works.

Round and round in her head went her longing to live in a civilized place – and have Joe, too. Alfie's sad face floated before her. Would Liverpool crush Joe like that? She thought not; Joe was much, much tougher – but it could be a fight.

She had another bad night.

29

In comparison with Mr Benson's elegant home in Falkner Square, Eleanor Al-Khoury's house seemed small and dark. Dark green linoleum polished to a high gloss covered the narrow entrance, the hall and the stairs. Near the front door stood a branched wooden hatstand on which Eleanor hung Wallace Helena's shawl and hat.

Eleanor's sleeves were rolled up, to expose plump mottled arms, and she wore over her dress a large white bibbed pinafore. Over the pinafore was wrapped a thick striped cotton apron.

'Come in. Come in,' she cried hospitably to Wallace Helena. 'How's your cold?'

As she was ushered down the hall to the back of the house, Wallace Helena replied that the cold was not much better. 'It'll go away soon, no doubt.' In fact, her chest felt badly congested and she had coughed steadily during the night.

'This is me kitchen-living-room,' Eleanor told her, as they entered a pleasant, cosy room with a big window facing a back yard. Under the window was a yellow sink with two shining brass taps, and beside it a wooden drain board. A large iron stove took up most of one wall; it had two ovens at one side and the fire was big enough to hold two iron kettles side by side. From the ovens came a distinct odour of mutton being stewed. A steel fender protected the hearth.

Against another wall was a table covered by a dark red chenille cloth which reached to the floor. A vase filled with dried flowers stood in the middle of it. Three dining chairs were tucked round the sides of the table, and much of the rest of the room was taken up by two easy chairs on either side of the fireplace. Over the mantelpiece hung two large amateur watercolours in mahogany frames, which Wallace Helena supposed were portraits of Eleanor's parents. Two small photographs in metal frames stood on the mantelpiece and immediately drew Wallace Helena's attention. 'Why, that's Uncle James!' she exclaimed, touching the unsmiling face with her finger. 'And this must be Benji when he was a little boy – in a sailor suit!'

Eleanor came to stand by her. 'Oh, aye,' she agreed. 'I got a nicer one of Jamie in me bedroom. Took about four years ago. I told him I wanted one of him smiling for me birthday – 'cos it were natural to 'im

173

to smile and laugh a lot. I must've had a feelin' he wouldn't be with me that long.' She gave a long sobbing sigh, and turned away without saying anything about Benji's picture. 'Come and sit down, luv.' She gestured to one of the easy chairs, and Wallace Helena obediently sank into the collection of patchwork cushions which nearly filled it. 'I were just goin' to slice me soap for the boiler when you come. If you don't mind, I'll finish it afore we have a cuppa.'

Wallace Helena said she should go ahead exactly as she usually would. She remarked that she thought the picture of Benji was delightful. They talked desultorily about the peccadilloes of little boys, while Eleanor spread a piece of newspaper on the table and proceeded to shred up a bar of soap.

'What are you going to do with that?' Wallace Helena asked.

'I'll put 'em in the hot water in me boiler downstairs, and they'll melt. Then I'll put the clothes in and boil 'em. Then I'll scrub the clothes on me washboard and rinse 'em. I'm hoping it won't rain today, so as I can hang 'em in the yard to dry.'

'A lot of work,' Wallace Helena said.

'Oh, aye. Me gentlemen keep me busy. I got three, and then there's Benji. It makes a lot of shirts and sheets. I'm ironin' most of Tuesday.'

'Gentlemen?' queried Wallace Helena.

'Yes. I do for three gents. One has a bedroom and the front parlour, and the other two is younger and they have a bed-sitter each. I make a bit on them to keep the house goin', like. Our Benji's real good. Ever since his dad died he give me housekeeping in addition to the bit he always gave me for his own food. But letting the rooms makes it easier to manage.'

'Do you cook for them?'

'Oh, yes. Bed, board and laundry is what they get.' She smiled suddenly. 'I look for decent young fellas, and they often stay with me till they get married. Of course, I gave up for a good many years, 'cos Jamie were doing well and there were no need. But I've bin real thankful these last few months that I had the house and could go back to takin' gentlemen.'

'I'm sure you have.' Wallace Helena's voice was sympathetic; looking at the worn face and roughened hands of the woman at the table, she felt a sense of guilt.

The sliced-up soap smelt awful, and Wallace Helena was reminded that Mr Lever was putting citronella into his bar soap to drown its natural odour. Two can play at that game, she considered grimly. Perhaps they should put a splash of lavender into the soap she was responsible for. She made a mental note to talk to Benji about it.

174

'Do you get free soap from the Lady Lavender, since Benji works for us?' she asked. It was a loaded question.

Eleanor answered innocently, 'Well, you know, there's lots of bars as don't get cut quite neat; or they get dropped on the floor, so they look dirty. But it's still decent soap. So the men take it home to their wives. Benji brings me a bit regular.'

'I see.' Wallace Helena sounded so noncommittal that Eleanor paused in her slicing to look up at her. 'It goes with the job,' she said a little defensively.

'I understand.' Wallace Helena made another mental note; this time to check on theft, which she had felt from her quick checks on the inventories might be more widespread than was tolerable. She would have to walk lightly, because she saw the common sense of allowing the men to have stuff which was definitely unsaleable. It was possible that the Cutting and Stamping Room was being deliberately careless. In slums even faulty soap could be sold; all kinds of goods had been available in the back streets of Chicago, she remembered grimly.

Eleanor was again giving her attention to the soap. She hoped uneasily that she had not told Wallace Helena something that Benji would have preferred to keep from her. 'There,' she said, and put down her knife while she carefully gathered up the soap chips into the newspaper. 'The water in the boiler downstairs must be hot now. Would you like to come down with me?'

Wallace Helena smiled and followed her hostess down the worn stone steps to the cellar. It had been stiflingly hot in the living-room and she hoped that the cellar would be cooler.

She found herself in a dank, windowless room lit by a kerosene lamp hanging on the wall. It was half divided by a partial wall; the furthest section held coal which gleamed faintly in the light. Nearer them, in one corner in a whitewashed area, was a steaming copper built of brick and clay; under it lay an iron grate protected by a perforated iron door; through the perforations, Wallace Helena caught a glimpse of glowing coals. The copper itself had a loose wooden lid over it. Nearby were two rough wooden tables, obviously well scrubbed. On one table were several heaps of damp, wrung-out dirty clothes; through the steam Wallace Helena could smell the odour of men from them.

Eleanor took the lid off the copper and sprinkled her soap chips into the heaving water. 'I always add a bit of soda,' she said, as she picked up an old earthenware marmalade jar and poured a little of its contents into the water. She then stirred the water with a pair of wooden tongs. She picked up a pile of white shirts and dropped them in, stirring them around and lifting them up with the tongs until they were thoroughly wet.

'There, now,' she said cheerfully, 'we can leave that for a bit, and go and have a cup of tea.'

'Will they come out nice and white?' asked Wallace Helena, in an effort to make conversation.

'By the time I've finished, they will,' Eleanor assured her. 'I'll put bleach in the second rinse. Then I rinse 'em again with blueing. And finally I rinse that out. With me sheets and tablecloths, I don't scrub 'em; I put them in this tin bath and I dolly 'em, after I've boiled 'em. Give 'em a couple of rinses, dollying them again, and that's it. I put everything through the mangle in the yard, before I hang it out – gets rid of any dirty water in it, better'n handwringing.'

Since Wallace Helena had never seen a dolly or a mangle, she was gravely introduced to the dolly in the corner of the cellar. It looked to her like a three-legged stool attached to a spade handle, and Eleanor showed her how she lifted it up and down and half twisted it to pound dirt out of a bath of clothes. The mangle standing in the yard seemed quite new. It had two heavy wooden rollers, but the rest of it was iron and was beginning to rust. 'Benji keeps the wheels oiled for me, but I've got to watch I don't get the grease on me clothes. He sometimes turns the mangle for me, if he can get home for lunch on Mondays, 'cos it's heavy work – though not so hard as hand-wringing sheets.'

Wallace Helena thought of the fast, perfunctory wash done on her farm, and asked, 'Is it necessary to work so hard?'

Eleanor looked at her as if she had queried the existence of God. 'Oh, aye,' she affirmed without hesitation. 'The clothes get filthy in the town, and my gentlemen work in offices or shops, so they have to be well turned out. Mr Jenkins wot has the ground-floor front changes 'is collar twice a day – not that I do 'is collars – I send 'em out to a woman wot does nothin' else.'

'It must take you all day to do so much.'

Eleanor sighed, and then said with a wry grin, 'It does. I put everything to soak the night before, and I were up at half past five this mornin' to get the boiler lit and the first load in afore I started breakfast for me gentlemen. And afore I go to bed tonight I'll get Benji to help me pull and fold me sheets and tablecloths ready for ironing. And I'll use the nice soapy water from the copper to scrub the kitchen and the bathroom floors.'

Wallace Helena glanced down at the kitchen-living-room floor; it was made of stone flags and had rag rugs under the table and near the fireplace. She decided she preferred to have to work outside, despite bitter winters or broiling sun. Her respect for Eleanor grew, as she realized the appalling amount of work the woman did.

She was grateful for a strong cup of tea and a piece of pound cake before she left. 'I do me cakes and pies on Fridays,' Eleanor confided. 'I used to bake me own bread when Jamie was alive, but lately I haven't had the heart, so I buy it.'

As the two women were going down the passage to the front door, and Wallace Helena reached for her hat, Eleanor said, 'You should take a mangle and dolly back to Canada with you, when you go. They'd save you a lot of work.'

Wallace Helena nodded. It was possible that by now she could obtain such worksavers in western Canada; the railway had suddenly made everything possible. She answered Eleanor circumspectly, though with a smile. 'I haven't yet decided whether to go back to Canada or not. I may stay here.' She was anxious that any idea that she *must* sell the soapery be dispelled; such gossip would not improve the price she would get if she did have to part with it.

Eleanor looked taken aback. 'What you goin' to do with it? You couldn't run it yourself.'

'I believe I could.'

'But you're a woman!'

'Women can do anything they set their minds to.'

'Well, I nevaire!' Then Eleanor's eyes twinkled. 'Good thing your uncle can't hear you.' Then she looked sad. 'He didn't like women going to work.'

'I wonder if he believed they didn't work at home? You work crushingly hard.'

'I don't know, luv.' She picked up Wallace Helena's shawl and wrapped it round her shoulders. 'Now, you take care of yourself, luv, with that cold. You've coughed quite a bit this morning; you should stay home today.'

'Thank you very much, Eleanor,' Wallace Helena said with feeling. 'You take care of yourself.'

'I'm all right, for sure. Now I must go and start me coloureds and me woollens. I haven't done nothing about them yet.'

30

Wallace Helena went back to Mrs Hughes's house for lunch, but, after Eleanor's pound cake, she only picked at the sausage, mashed potatoes and peas, followed by cold apple pie, which Mrs Hughes regarded as a light lunch.

As she drank a pot of tea, she reviewed carefully many of the things that Eleanor had mentioned. Cheap soap, she had said, had filler in it – fuller's earth or sand – and it was not much good if you wanted a clean wash. She had also told her that she kept her supply of soap on a shelf for weeks to harden it, because it then didn't melt so quickly and she got a better lather. Was the latter true? If so, how long did the Lady Lavender keep its soap in store? Did Mr Lever store his soap for long?

It seemed clear that the Lady Lavender would have to sell on quality and low price, to stay in business. She wondered if the patronizing Mr Turner had ever tried to deduce exactly what was in their various competitors' soap – it could be interesting to know. Mr Turner seemed a bit of a luxury for such a small firm, despite what Benji had said about him; she would put him to work.

That afternoon she discussed some of her ideas with Benji, and particularly asked him straightforwardly about theft.

He confirmed his mother's remark that the men were allowed to take soap that was, in some way, not fit for their customers. She suggested that the system be tightened up and that the handling of the finished soap should be more carefully supervised, so that it was not deliberately made unsaleable.

He chewed the end of a pencil, while he considered this, and then he said, 'I don't think it's out of hand yet. But it could be happening, if you say the inventories are not too accurate. The business has grown so much in the last three years that we need to look at the organization of the staff and the chain of responsibility. I haven't had time to do a thorough inventory for eighteen months.' He put his pencil into his top pocket and took out a handkerchief to mop the perspiration off his face. Though the stiff office window had been prized open by Mr Helliwell, on Wallace Helena's instructions, the room was still uncomfortably

178

warm, and the smell of the fats and the oils and the boiling, together with that of manure, drifted unpleasantly round them.

Wallace Helena closed her eyes. Her head felt heavy and her chest hurt every time she coughed; for once, she was not smoking.

She said slowly, 'As soon as we get Probate – Mr Benson says it will be a few weeks yet – and we're free to really manage, we'll look at the whole staff situation in the light of what we intend to produce – and we'll look at the long term – new machinery, and so on.'

'So you'll stay here? Have you heard from Canada?'

'Not yet. But I intend that if we have to put this place up for sale, we get the best possible price for it – and the best arrangement we can for the employees. And we can only do that if it looks like an excellent purchase.'

'Of course.' She was talking sense, but he wished the uncertainty was over. He was tired of being asked persistently by worried men if he knew what was to happen.

She was feeling exactly the same. The tug-of-war between what she wanted to do and what was possible was getting her down; and now she was so full of cold that she felt downright ill.

As the days moved into weeks, Wallace Helena got impatient at the length of time Probate was taking. Mr Benson assured her that it always did take time; she was not to worry. During August, she began, bit by bit, to take control, regardless of the fact that she did not yet own the firm. Mr Benson seemed to be glad not to be bothered with day-to-day problems, and arranged that Mr Bobsworth and Benji could jointly sign cheques under a certain value. She was careful to consult Benji or Mr Bobsworth as she took her first steps in management; and the company began to function better.

The bad cold which she had had left her with a hacking cough, which was not improved by her smoking. She ignored it. She was feeling the change in her lifestyle very keenly. As the summer wore on, the damp heat and the polluted air seemed stifling. If she opened the office window, her desk and papers were rapidly covered with black dust, and the collar on her dress was grey before evening came. After the dryness of the Territories, the humidity of the Lancashire climate made clothing and bedding feel damp to her. To her surprise, she began to appreciate the pristine blue skies and the strong sunshine of her faraway homestead.

She also found the food unsatisfying. After years of eating her own beef and pork or wild ducks and moose brought in by Joe, she thought it tasteless. Even a plate of Aunt Theresa's beaver tails would have been welcome.

Yet both the city and the soapery fascinated her. Encouraged by a friendly Eleanor, Benji introduced her to the pleasures of the music hall and the theatre. Eleanor would not go herself; she said it was too soon after her husband's death to consider it. Anxious to foster the relationship between her son and Wallace Helena, she did, one Sunday, accompany them on the ferry boat, to New Brighton, where they walked along the shore and ate a picnic lunch; it was a relief to Wallace Helena to find brisk, clean breezes and an open space to walk.

Another time, Benji took her to a concert in St George's Hall and for the first time saw her overawed. 'It's so beautiful,' she cried, and she sat spellbound as the mighty organ was played by the City Organist, Mr W. T. Best. Nothing would please her until he took her again, and she wrote ecstatically to Joe about it.

'I've never heard such music,' she told Eleanor, her face alight.

In Benji's eyes, Wallace Helena improved on acquaintance. He reckoned she must be close to forty, but she could be so light-hearted and enthusiastic that you'd never know it, and it was street lore that an older woman was more interested in you, because she was grateful for a sex life. He began to think seriously of marrying her. He was aware that under a fairly recent law about married women's property the soap works would not automatically become his on marriage; nevertheless, he took it for granted that, in practice, he would be in charge of Lady Lavender if he married the owner – women always deferred to men.

His own sex life had been somewhat limited. His father kept a close hold on him, because he wanted him to marry a Lebanese. He had, however, met young women at church social events, and had been out on the town with young Tasker a sufficient number of times to be acquainted with the ladies of Lime Street.

On her part, Wallace Helena was amused by him. Though she was ignorant of English marriage laws, she knew it was not simply cousinly solicitude which had sparked so much attention, and she awaited events with detached interest. She was also very lonely in Liverpool. Not only did she miss Joe as her lover; she missed him as a close companion with whom she could freely discuss anything. Despite her growing trust of Benji, he was a poor substitute; he was too young, though indubitably very capable. She wondered idly what he would be like in bed; she had never slept with anyone but Joe. She decided the boy would probably be charming, like his father had apparently been, and she then dismissed the matter. She was not going to mix business with pleasure.

One close bond the couple had: after Eleanor's remark that he spoke both Arabic and French, Wallace Helena spoke to him daily in Arabic, and was delighted to find that he understood the subtlety of it, although he was not acquainted with any of its poets – or with Middle Eastern music. Wallace Helena's English, though adequate, was not nearly as good as her native tongue, and the bond of a common language grew between them.

When she was alone in the evening and the day was fine, she occasionally walked in the park or in the centre of the city. At other times, she sat in her high-ceilinged, gloomy sitting-room and read books culled from her uncle's office shelves on various aspects of soap-making, and one or two on factory planning and management. Without chemistry and without personal knowledge of other great industries in the north of England, she sometimes had difficulty in understanding what she had read. At such times, she would either consult Benji or seek out Mr Turner or Mr Tasker and ask them to clarify the text for her.

Mr Tasker was, by far, her favourite. 'Without a good product to sell, you can't do nothing,' he once said, mopping the perspiration from his face with a large, red-spotted handkerchief. 'And good soap begins with good ingredients. And that's me first task – to check on the incomings.'

'What about Mr Turner, the chemist?'

'Oh, aye. Mr Turner can analyse and tell you what he reckons is in a barrel of tallow. But he don't allow for fiddles.'

'Fiddles?'

'Aye. Like when there's a bit o' summat inferior at the bottom, and such. Pass something like that and you've clarified it before you know it int up to snuff. Meself, I go and stand over an open barrel and I smell it – careful, like. I can tell you right off, when they're tryin' to fob us off with somethin' inferior.'

He did not explain who *they* were and she presumed they were the butchers and farmers who sold their surplus fat to soap makers. She was amused when he finished his remarks by a long slow sniff, as if to demonstrate the power of his nose.

She also felt a sense of trust growing between her and dapper Mr Helliwell, who was already betting to himself that she would be his new employer, after Probate. She knew that he had been aware, before her arrival, that Wallace H. Harding was a woman. He knew, because he had packed up and posted the books sent to her by Uncle James. Yet, since Mr Benson had not seen fit to mention her sex, even to Benji, while he was checking that he had tracked down the right legatee, Mr Helliwell had apparently maintained absolute silence on the subject. As he had once said to her, Mr James's business was confidential; if anybody knew about it, Mr James had told them himself. 'And you, Miss Harding, may be sure of the same confidentiality.'

181

Wallace Helena intrigued him. Seeing her each day at her uncle's desk, sometimes at bad moments coping with the many problems which inevitably arose in a small business, he felt that she would deal fairly with him and the rest of the staff, possibly better than a man would. And, like old Mr James, she was interesting.

Like Mr James, she swore and bullied, and he was fairly certain that anybody wanting a rise in pay would have to ask for it more than once; she obviously knew the value of every penny. Again, like her uncle, she showed signs of being quite human. He had, each year, treated the whole works to a picnic on New Brighton beach, and he had made himself pleasant to their wives and children. When Mr Helliwell had ventured to inform her that, owing to Mr James's untimely death, the picnic had been cancelled, she had sat thoughtfully, her chin cupped in her hand, and then suggested, 'Perhaps we could clear enough space in the factory, somewhere, and have a Christmas party – with dancing – instead.'

Mr Helliwell assured her that it was a splendid idea. She had, however, asked him not to mention it to the staff until a firm decision had been made about the future of the Lady Lavender, and he had bowed and again assured her of his complete discretion. He did, however, assure the wheelwright, when he wanted a day off to attend his father's funeral, that she was a very human lady, and the man should go into the office and ask her.

When the request was immediately granted with a few words of kindly sympathy, Mr Helliwell was secretly triumphant that his belief that she belonged to the human race had been confirmed.

When she dictated a note to Mr Bobsworth, carbon copy to Mr Benjamin, saying that the man's wages for the day of absence were to be paid, he ventured to remark that it was just what Mr James would have done. 'Mr Al-Khoury very rarely had any trouble with labour, Miss Harding. Like you, he was compassionate towards the men's genuine problems. Once a man had a tally from the company, he did his best to keep him in work – even when we weren't doing very well. He knew everybody he employed by name – more than many employers do.'

'What's a tally?' It was the first time she had heard the word.

'Oh, hasn't Mr Benjamin mentioned them? Perhaps the need for giving one out has not arisen since you arrived. It's a tin tag that a man can produce to show that he's worked for us before. A decent, sober man, once he's taken on, we like to keep him. If business is so slack that we have to lay him off, he'd be the first to be taken on again – before any stranger.'

Wallace Helena nodded. Her father's firm in Beirut had treated casual labour in the same way, most particularly in connection with those, however humble, who could be considered related to the family. She wondered irrelevantly, as she looked up at her hovering secretary, whether any had survived the massacre. From stories she had heard from one or two other refugees who had followed them to Chicago, it would seem unlikely; the massacre had been horrifyingly thorough.

She said, 'I noticed that most of the men had a small metal disc pinned to their jackets or overalls. Is that the tally?'

'Yes, Miss Harding. It's a quick way for the supervisors to spot an intruder. If he's not wearing a tally, he's immediately stopped and asked what his business is with the company.'

'Do you know if the men are worried about what is going to happen to them in the present situation?'

'Well, naturally they will be. Unemployment is rife in Liverpool.'

She stubbed out the cigarello she had been smoking and rose, preparatory to going back to her lodgings for lunch. 'Perhaps I should talk to them,' she said.

'They might appreciate it, Miss Harding.'

'Hmm. I'll speak to Mr Benjamin about it.'

31

Bidden to an informal meeting with their new mistress, the foremen and department heads crowded towards the door of Wallace Helena's office. One or two of them made sly jokes about now owning a mistress, until Mr Tasker overheard them. Incensed, he reminded them that she owned them, because their jobs depended upon what she decided to do. Immediately sobered, they slid through the door of the office, to find the lady sitting at their old master's desk, enveloped in a cloud of tobacco smoke. At their entry, she quickly stubbed out her cigarello and rose to face them, looking tall, angular and forbidding in her high-necked black dress.

As the men came in, they took off their caps, and when they were all assembled, she surveyed them carefully. Most of them looked middle-aged or over, some of them almost purple from years of exposure to rough weather; others were pasty-faced from too long hours indoors. Many of them shuffled uneasily, and only Mr Tasker and the Steam Engineer looked self-assured, probably because of their highly marketable skills. At the last moment, Mr Bobsworth entered and shut the door behind him. He felt a little resentful that he had not been asked to stand by Wallace Helena at the meeting. Young Benji was there, just behind her. Why not himself?

She began to speak, reminding them that she had already met most of them when she first arrived, and that she had realized that the sad passing of Mr James Al-Khoury had caused a crisis in all their lives – and in her own. They must be worrying about their future.

The word *crisis* caught their attention and her understanding of their own uneasiness about their jobs impressed them favourably. She went on to explain the matter of Probate which was holding up a final decision on the future of the works. The Executor of the Will could have sold the soapery immediately, but he had consulted her and she had decided not to sell at the moment. She would use the time before the Court granted Probate to learn all she could about it and then make a decision when the Lady Lavender became her absolute property. Not all of them understood what Probate was, but they had seen Mr Benson about the place and knew he was a lawyer, so they assumed it had something to do with him. At least they now knew why there was such a lack of

184

information about their future. The woman had not yet made up her mind; women never did know what they wanted.

Until then, not even Mr Bobsworth or Mr Tasker had been given an explanation as to why the Lady Lavender had not been sold; their questions to Benji and to Mr Benson had not been answered. Her lack of decision did not give them peace of mind, but at least they now knew that, once Probate was granted, a decision would be made.

Wallace Helena was continuing. She said, 'In the meantime, I want the soapery to proceed with its usual efficiency. There are a few matters which we can currently address, the main one being the neatness and cleanliness of the plant and the yards.'

The face of the Transport Manager darkened. The stables came under his jurisdiction and he had been reprimanded for the laziness of his staff. Alerted by Wallace Helena, Benji had delivered a very stiff lecture. The stables were now mucked out daily.

Wallace Helena went on to say that each of them was to look at his own area and see where the labourers had failed to clean up. 'Get rid of rubbish,' she ordered. 'I myself slipped and nearly fell in the tallow yard, for example. It is to be scraped and sanded and spills mopped up as they occur. You know very well that some of the materials we use are hazardous, lye, for instance; and grease can cause a disastrous fire if we get slack, which will put you all out of work.' She paused, and looked again at the faces before her; some appeared sullen.

She resumed her speech, her tone a little lighter. 'I cannot alter the circumstances under which you work until the legal process is complete and we can look at the final balance sheet. But I understand that you have no proper place to brew tea or eat your noon meal. If I decide to undertake the management, this is one of the first things I wish to provide: a clean, decent room where you can eat and make tea. I suspect, also, that there is need for better immediate care for any of you who have an accident here.

'I see from correspondence that Mr Al-Khoury had in mind to begin some form of contributory pension for his people. I hope that we shall, in future, have regular meetings together to discuss such matters. Meanwhile, it is important not only that the Lady Lavender continue to do business successfully, but it should *look* successful, and a works that is as neat as a pin gives a good impression. After all, we're selling cleanliness! I want it clean! If I have to sell it, a smart-looking outfit is less likely to be closed down by a competitor buying it out.'

Some of the men grinned at her little joke about selling cleanliness, but the yard foreman lifted his hand and said sulkily that he was short

185

of a labourer and did not know who to ask about it. 'Mr Benjamin not always being here, like.'

Wallace Helena looked up at a silent Benji. He certainly was away from time to time, since he was supervising sales. She turned back to the foreman, and ordered him to call in a man holding a company's tally as a temporary labourer and to give his name to Mr Bobsworth for the wage sheet. 'I'll discuss with Mr Benjamin whether the position will be made permanent. Meantime, pay him the casual labourer's rate.'

Mr Ferguson, the Steam Engineer, ventured to ask if she expected to actually run the works herself, if she did not sell it.

'For the moment, Mr Benjamin will deal with the day-to-day problems, as usual. If he is away, come to me. In the longer term, you will be the first people to be told my final decision. Our lawyer tells me that Probate should be granted within a matter of weeks now.'

With a dawning feeling of confidence in her, as she stood in front of them with as much presence as any man, most of her employees smiled slightly. Nobody else ventured a remark, however, so she dismissed them politely, after reminding them to take their problems to Mr Benjamin as they arose.

As she sank into her chair again and reached for her cigarello, Mr Tasker lingered behind.

She looked up at him. 'Yes, Mr Tasker?'

'I wanted to say, Ma'am, that it's not surprising that the men get a bit confused. Mr Al-Khoury was his own Plant Manager, Mr Benjamin having his own areas of command, like. Since Mr James passed away, Mr Bobsworth, Mr Ferguson and even Mr Turner've got into the way of giving orders outside their departments, and the foremen don't know for sure that that is what you want or who they should obey – especially if the orders is conflicting.'

'Blast!' She drummed her fingers on the desk, and turned to Benji. 'I'll make it clear that you make the decisions and report to me later. On the days when you have to go somewhere, the men are to come to me and I will tell them who to go to or what to do. I presume that all the men who were here today know what decisions they can make themselves within their normal departmental duties?'

George Tasker answered immediately. 'I think so, Ma'am.'

'Then I'll talk to Mr Bobsworth, Mr Turner and Mr Ferguson. I'm sure they've simply been worried and tried to fill in for the late Mr Al-Khoury during the present hiatus. We'll soon get straightened out.'

Mr Tasker smiled down at her, touched his forelock and went back to work. Real chip off the old block, she was. And he was glad she was bringing forward young Benji. Could be worse things happen. He began to whistle.

32

When Mr Tasker had gone, Wallace Helena turned and grinned at Benji. 'Come and sit down,' she invited. 'We must do something about keeping Bobsworth, Ferguson and Turner in line – stop them interfering in other departments. Any ideas?'

Benji shrugged and sat down. 'It depends on how much Benson is agreeable to our doing. He's still the Executor.'

'Well, he's been in once or twice to see how I'm getting on. He seems content to leave me to it, now he knows me better. He's warned me not to be extravagant in anything I do personally or in connection with the Lady Lavender – there are taxes and legal fees yet to be paid which could be quite a burden, if I want to keep the soapery.'

Benji laughed. 'Old Bobsworth was moaning that you are almost too careful. I think you've been a revelation to him. You didn't even pass all my Manchester expenses without query!'

'Sorry.' She bit her lower lip and smiled roguishly at him. Then she said, 'The problem is that you're away some of the time, looking after sales, and I'm still feeling my way – besides which I don't want to be bothered by day-to-day decisions, as I am beginning to be.' She picked up a coffee cup from her desk, saw that it was empty and rang for Mr Helliwell to bring two fresh cups. While he went to get them, she continued, 'My feeling is that you should be here all the time and that we should try to find a top, full-time salesman to take your place, somebody we could also consult about wrappers and advertising, someone who knows the soap trade.'

'Even on commission, such a man could be expensive. I think you're right, though.'

'Would it suit you? Or do you want to be a representative full time?'

'I hate selling. Father gave it to me to gain experience, so that I would have some knowledge of every department. Now we've got to face much more intense competition, we need a first-class man like you suggest. I'd be much better in the office; I can keep a tight hand on the organiz-ation of the staff and the buying, and so forth.'

With fresh coffee in front of them, they went on to hammer out exactly how to proceed. They concluded that Benji should cost out roughly what a full-time sales manager could expect, with the idea of recruiting such a man as soon as Probate had been received and taxes paid.

'He could cost a fortune,' Wallace Helena said nervously. Then, more bravely, she admitted that the challenge of Mr Lever had to be met.

To bring the old employees into line and stop them giving orders where they had no business to give them, Wallace Helena said she would send out a memo to all supervisory staff confirming Benji in his position as Assistant Manager responsible for day-to-day management and that, in his absence, she herself was to be consulted. 'If Bobsworth and the others don't take note of the memo, I'm not past firing them,' she said fiercely. 'Only Mr Tasker is absolutely irreplaceable at present, as far as I can see.'

'It won't come to that,' he assured her. 'The foremen will tend to come to me.' He got up and strode to the end of the room and back, then he added frankly, 'They expected me to take over immediately Father died – and I didn't. Backed by your memo, it'll seem natural to them to come to me.'

Wallace Helena suddenly had what Benji called her Mona Lisa look. Watchful eyes and a tight small smile made him regret his frankness. Looking at her seated in his father's chair, resentment flared in him once again. Because of a narrow, old-fashioned quirk of law, she was queening it in an office which should have been his.

As he stood up and collected his papers, preparatory to going back to his own small niche of a room, he raged inwardly. He was not suffering because he had quarrelled with his father or because his father thought him incapable. On the contrary, everything pointed to the fact that he was being trained to take his father's place when the older man had had enough. He cursed his father's blithe belief in his own immortality.

She had not responded to his last remark. She simply sat waiting for him to go, her long, weather-beaten hands, with their heavy, ugly rings, spread out before her on the battered desk.

Before turning towards the door, he nodded farewell, and she looked up. 'Cheer up,' she told him, her mouth softening a little. 'We'll both do well out of the Lady Lavender before we've finished. It's a tight little ship, as Mr Bobsworth says.'

Startled, he stopped in mid-stride to the door. Was the damned woman a thought reader, as well?

She chuckled, but did not say anything more.

His face like a thundercloud, he did not answer. It took all his self-control not to slam the door after himself. She could laugh, if she wanted; he could not.

33

As a result of the meeting which Wallace Helena had called in her office, it now became public knowledge that their new, female employer smoked in the works, as Alfie, the labourer, had said she did. The graffiti on the enclosure round the rough earthen lavatories in the corner of the yard consisted largely of pictures, since most of the men could not write; the drawings now featured a bosomy female with a cigar in her mouth.

Because of the acute danger of fire amid fatty substances, an employee found smoking had traditionally been immediately dismissed. Now, the men began to resent the rule; if the Mistress could smoke, so could they.

While waiting for a delivery van to be loaded or unloaded, the carters began to light up their clay pipes. The yard foreman demanded that they knock them out, and, when they became impudent about it, he threatened them with dismissal. This had the desired result; they grouchily put them away.

The threat had no effect on a grizzled old labourer, Georgie Grant, who had been steadily employed by the company since its inception.

'Herself is smokin', int she?' he inquired loftily of the foreman. 'Why can't I?'

'You should know – because of fire, you stupid old bugger.'

Georgie lifted his chin, thick with snowy stubble. 'Don't you go callin' me names. If the Mistress can smoke here, I can,' he responded stubbornly, and heaved a wooden box into a waiting van, his pipe firmly between his few remaining teeth.

The foreman controlled his seething temper. 'Now look here, Georgie. I don't want to fire yez. You put that pipe out for now, and I'll ask Master Benji if the rule is the same as always.'

Georgie took his pipe from his mouth and turned to look at his superior. He grinned. 'Not the Mistress?'

The foreman wanted to hit him. 'Mr Benji'll do the talkin' to her,' he replied through clenched teeth.

Georgie looked down his bulbous red nose at the foreman. Then very slowly he took a tin lid from the pocket of his fustian trousers and held it over the bowl of his pipe to dowse it. A mere woman was not going

190

to tell him when he could or could not smoke, unless she obeyed the rule, too. 'Aye, you ask him,' he said with patent satisfaction.

Feeling that the threat of dismissal would probably quench Georgie's thirst for equality, the foreman did nothing. Whiffs of tobacco continued to be easily detectable in the yard and the stables.

Caught between an old, respected employee and a new, untried employer, the foreman gave up and went to see Benji. Ould James's bastard *ought* to have been the new master; he'd give sound advice.

Benji was seated at a crowded, high desk in his office, a tiny room next to the laboratory. The office was walled with clear panes of glass through which he could supervise much that went on in the works. He was in the midst of dictating letters to Mr Helliwell, when the foreman knocked and came in, doffing his cap as Benji lifted his head from his work. Seeing the worry on the man's long, hatchet face, he asked, 'What's up, Will?'

The foreman explained the recalcitrance of Georgie Grant. He ignored the silent Mr Helliwell.

'You don't want to dismiss him, do you?'

'Georgie? 'Course not, Sir. He's makin' a point. First, he don't like workin' for a woman and, second, if there's a rule it's for everybody, includin' Miss Harding. He don't approve of a woman smokin', anyways.'

Benji badly wanted to grin. He could visualize the monkey face of the old labourer, who had been born and brought up on the Earl of Sefton's Estate and would not have been afraid to tell a belted earl what was acceptable in an earl's behaviour. A soap mistress would be small fry in comparison.

'I doubt if Miss Harding has realized the danger of fire. I'll talk to her about it. Tell Georgie from me that there'll be no more smoking in the yard. If he disobeys send him up here.'

'Yes, Sir. Thank you, Sir.'

Benji slowly took off the paper cuffs he used to protect his shirt wrist bands and put on his jacket, to go to see Wallace Helena. Fire was too serious a matter to delay action.

'She's down in the Crutching Department,' Mr Helliwell told him, as he resignedly closed his notebook.

'Blast!' exclaimed Benji, and Mr Helliwell looked at him with closely pursed lips.

He finally ran her to earth as she watched the stamping of Lady Lavender soap tablets with the company's name on one side and what was meant to depict a bunch of lavender on the other side. Behind her, two boys of about sixteen were busy wrapping the tablets in a rough,

191

greyish paper which they closed with a bright, painted sticker showing a reasonable facsimile on it of a sprig of lavender surrounded by the name of the company.

She did not think much of the imprint on the soap, and, when Benji approached, looking rumpled and a trifle harassed, she addressed him before he could open his mouth.

'The soap looks messy,' she said, petulantly tossing a tablet up and down in one hand. 'I think we put too much colouring in it – and couldn't we make it look shinier? And the paper it's wrapped in is so dull. No wonder Mr Lever used bright yellow.'

Normally Benji would have agreed with her; new packaging and finish had been under discussion just before his father's death. Today, however, he resented her criticism, particularly when he had a much more basic problem, that of fire, to discuss with her.

'Leave this,' he ordered. 'I need to speak to you in the office.'

The young man in a white apron who was doing the stamping looked up and raised one eyebrow suggestively towards the other lads placidly wrapping tablets not far away. Ears pricked, they waited for the Mistress's response.

She looked coolly at her cousin. He had no right to speak to her like that in front of junior employees; it could destroy her authority. She replied with asperity, 'I'm busy. I want to see the next few bars go through the stamping machine – Dick, here, has just adjusted the machine slightly, to see if we get a clearer stamp. I'll see you in the office in about half an hour.'

Benji's face darkened. He was equally sensitive to a slight to his authority, and it was his job to see that the finished product was marketable. He said angrily, in Arabic, 'Let it wait. I'll check it later. This is a matter of safety, and we must act quickly on it – before the place goes up in smoke!'

'Smoke?' she queried in the same language.

'Yes. Fire!' he snapped back.

'Very well.' She turned and said, with a smile, to the three young men concerned, 'We'll look at it again, later. For the moment, continue as before.'

Head held high, she swept out of the department and towards her office, a fuming Benji having difficulty in keeping up with her. Mr Helliwell in his tiny office scampered from his wooden filing cabinet to open the door of her office. She went through without so much as a nod of acknowledgment and Benji, like a rolling thundercloud, straight after her. Very thoughtfully, Mr Helliwell went back to his filing, and listened to the rising voices in the inner sanctum. He wished they would speak English.

The fear of fire temporarily forgotten, Benji was raging. 'If I'm the Assistant Manager in charge of day-to-day matters, why can't you leave me to manage? I know we need new stamping machines – we're going to need new everything before long!' He hammered on her desk with his fist, while she stood waiting for him to finish. He straightened up and shouted, 'And it's your job to plan what we're going to do in future. Where we're going to raise money. How we're going to meet competition – rabid competition in a slumping market, in case you don't remember it!'

The moment he stopped for breath, her reply came out in a menacing hiss. 'I have not forgotten anything,' she said. 'But you seem to have forgotten that I own this soapery – or will in a week or two. And, therefore, I will decide what I need to know before I begin to plan. And who will manage!' The last words came out in a threatening snarl.

He was immediately sobered, feeling that his livelihood was in jeopardy, though suppressed mortification made him tremble. He stepped back from the desk and stared across it at her. He'd get another job as soon as he could, he promised himself.

She glared back at him. Then cold common sense flooded back into her, as she realized his humiliation. She had gone too far. She needed this man; it would not be easy to replace him, because it seemed likely that her large competitors would be able to offer more to such an employee.

Unhesitatingly, she apologized. 'I'm sorry, Benji.' Then she smiled. 'We must learn never to be angry with each other in front of the men. My partner and I always fight it out privately.'

He was still hurt to the quick. She walked round the desk and laced her hand into his. He did not grasp her fingers, but he did not withdraw his hand either. She bent towards him and gently kissed his cheek. 'Come on, Benji. I'm cousin-sister, remember. We can say things honestly to each other – privately. Sit down and tell me what it was you wanted to see me about. You said something about fire? Have we had one?' She was still holding his hand and sensed that he had relaxed slightly. 'We need each other.'

He remained a picture of wounded dignity, though he sat down.

She was suddenly smitten with a spasm of coughing, convulsed with it, unable to get her breath. She leaned against the desk to steady herself, clutching her chest as if to ease a pain. Benji leaned forward and poured a glass of water from the carafe on the corner of the desk, but she could not steady herself sufficiently to take it from him.

193

Concerned, he got up and put his arm round her back and held the glass to her lips. She took a tiny sip, swallowed it and then another, which made her splutter. She got her breath and made a big effort to swallow more. Gradually the spasm reduced and he led her to her chair. She sat there silently, breathing deeply, until she was a little recovered. Meanwhile, Benji pressed the bell for Mr Helliwell and told him to bring a hot cup of tea with plenty of sugar in it.

Mr Helliwell had heard the frantic coughing and needed no explanation. He hurried out to his gas ring.

Benji remained standing by her. 'You must stop smoking until that cough's gone,' he told her. 'Mother said you coughed a lot last time you visited her – she thought you ought to see a doctor.'

'Mrs Hughes was lecturing me about seeing a doctor, but I'm moving from her house tomorrow to a more airy place. I hope it may settle the cough. The wind blows straight off the river and there should be less smuts to irritate my throat.'

'Where are you going?'

'It's called The Cockle Hole – it's like a village by the water, next to the Coburg Dock.'

'Oh, I know it. Do you need any help?'

'I'll give Alfie a tip to carry my bags down; I don't have much.'

He nodded. Her need for help while she coughed had deflected his thoughts from his own distress; it had put him momentarily in command and he felt better.

Mr Helliwell brought in a steaming mug of tea and smilingly put it in front of her. She thanked him and dismissed him.

While she slowly sipped the sickeningly sweet brew, Benji sat down opposite her and explained about Georgie Grant.

'I think you must, for safety's sake, stop smoking in the plant. And let it be known that you have. I don't want to fire people like Georgie. He's as honest as anyone I'll ever find. Besides, he's been here all my life, very nearly.'

She did not miss the point that he considered that he had the right to hire and fire men in her soapery, but she felt it unwise to say anything so soon after their bitter row.

She said wearily, 'I've smoked for years. Joe brought me the kind of tobacco the Indian women smoke – and it's different from this stuff.' She pointed to the wooden box in which her cigarellos lay.

'Whatever you smoke is going to cause trouble,' Benji said. 'I enjoy a pipe – but I never smoke here.'

Her hands clasped round the mug of tea, she considered his remarks and saw the wisdom of them. She smiled ruefully, and said, 'I'm not

194

sure how I'm going to survive. I was aware of the fire hazard – you heard me demanding that the works be cleaned up, largely because grease and straw can catch so easily. And I've fought prairie fires in my time. I imagined the office was far enough away from everything – that it would be safe to smoke.'

Benji made a face. 'It probably is, but the men would resent you having the privilege.'

'Hmm. I'm their Mistress!'

There she was again, emphasizing that she had the last say. He was no longer angry with her; he felt instead a terrible sadness, a sense that his father had discarded him, leaving him at the mercy of an eccentric woman.

He made an effort to appear conciliatory. 'If you continued to smoke and the men could not, they might try to get back at you. Liverpool men can be very pig-headed when they're angry; they've got their own ideas of what's fair. Though times are hard and they wouldn't want to lose their jobs, they could be obstructive. You've no idea how stuff could be inexplicably lost; they can forget to deliver verbal messages; horses would cast a shoe in the middle of a busy morning; a spoke fall out of a wheel. Once or twice when Father fell foul of them, all this happened. They can send management nearly out of its mind!'

'Really?' She began to laugh, until her cough recommenced and she hastily stifled her amusement.

He smiled. 'You ask any ship's officer,' he said. 'They'll tell you.'

'All right,' she said. 'You can tell Georgie that I have stopped smoking – in the soapery.' At the same time, she wondered if Benjamin considered himself a Liverpool man and was warning her that he could bring down the soapery if he wanted to.

34

With Alfie's help, Wallace Helena moved to The Cockle Hole. Later that evening, encouraged by Eleanor Al-Khoury, Benji called on her to see if she was comfortable.

The door was answered by a young woman in the late stages of pregnancy. There was none of the formality of Mrs Hughes. The woman wiped her hands on her apron and said, 'Come in, Sir.' She opened a door to his right and called, 'You've got a visitor, Miss.'

When Benji entered, he found his cousin standing by an open window looking onto the river. White curtains billowed in the breeze.

'Would you like a fire made, Miss? John'd do it in a tick,' the woman asked Wallace Helena.

'No, I'm warm enough, thank you, Elsie.' She turned to Benji and said, 'This is Mrs Fitzpatrick. She cooked me a beautiful fish dinner.'

Benji bowed to the blushing young woman, who smiled, and said, 'It were nothing.' She closed the door softly, as she went out.

Benji looked round the austere little room. Its white-washed walls and bare, scrubbed floor gave a sense of coolness and space. A rag rug by the empty fireplace and cretonne-covered cushions on a pair of rocking chairs gave a touch of colour. A plain wooden table and two chairs stood under the open casement window, through which he had a view of the river. Another table with a single chair tucked under it held Wallace Helena's books and papers, not yet put in order, and an unlit oil lamp. Additional light was promised by two big brass candle-sticks sitting on the mantelpiece, each with a large, fresh candle in it.

Wallace Helena sat down in one of the rocking chairs and invited Benji to take the other one. As he sat down, he told her that his mother was very tired after a day's baking, and that he had persuaded her to go to bed early. She would come to see her on Sunday afternoon.

'I'm sure she needs the rest; she works very hard.' She wondered if Benji had told her about the row they had had, and whether she had sent him to mend his fences. She told him she would be delighted to see his mother, anytime, and then said, 'Elsie was going to bring me a tray of tea, so she'll probably bring an extra cup.'

He nodded. Because of the fight they had had, he was not sure what to talk about. Yet, for his own and his mother's sake, a truce must be declared. She had offered him the chance last time they had spoken, and on the surface they had parted amicably. Inwardly, he had still been boiling with rage, and he guessed that she had realized it.

Finally, he cleared his throat and, for want of anything better to say, inquired how many rooms she had.

'I've two. I've the bedroom above this room. It looks out on the river, and there's a window-seat to sit on to watch the ships going to and fro. It's got a washstand – and Elsie has promised me as much hot water as I want. There is a water closet in the yard. It's all very simple, but I like it – and it is very quiet.'

He nodded. It certainly was peaceful and the air was fresh.

'I think I shall enjoy Elsie and her husband, John. They're unpretentious – unlike Mrs Hughes.'

He did not know Mrs Hughes, but her address was enough to suggest the type of woman, and he could understand that Wallace Helena might find the atmosphere in her old rooms oppressive.

He had had an argument with Eleanor over the need for this visit. He simply did not want to face his cousin for a little while. His mother had said, however, that one of them should go down to The Cockle Hole to inquire if she were comfortably settled. In her anxiety to keep on good terms, she had said desperately and almost in tears because her feet were so swollen from long hours of standing, 'Well, if you won't go, I must.'

Because he knew how very tired she was and could see her feet bulging along the edges of her shoes, he had given in. She had said he ought to take some flowers; but the only flower shop was closed, so she had pressed upon him a bottle of lavender from the soap works, wrapped in crumpled tissue paper. He now presented the little parcel to his cousin with apologies for the lack of flowers.

She was pleased. She had handled the sample bottles in the soap works, but had not thought of taking one for herself. Now she unscrewed the bottle and shook a little of the scent onto her wrist. Immediately the small room was flooded with perfume.

She inhaled luxuriously. 'It smells sharp and sweet at the same time – like citrus fruit.' She glanced up from sniffing her wrist, and her voice became wistful. 'You know, I miss the smell of the orchards in Lebanon. Oranges, lemons, apricots – they all smelled so lovely.'

'I've never seen them, of course,' Benji replied a little stiffly. 'Mother's got a mock orange blossom in the back yard. It's got a nice smell. When girls we know get married, they beg bits of it to make wreaths to hold their wedding veils.'

197

'What a charming idea.' She put the stopper back into the scent bottle. 'You've never thought of getting married, Benji?'

She had rarely asked a personal question of him, and this one made him more uneasy than ever.

'No,' he said, and then, feeling that he should give some explanation of the single state of a man of twenty-five, he said, 'Father wanted to find a Lebanese girl for me, and I wasn't too keen.'

'He'd have a long search in England, I imagine?'

'There are a few, I suppose.'

The advent of Elsie with the tea tray saved him from further questioning; she had brought a dish of hot, buttered scones to eat with the tea.

Wallace Helena busied herself with serving him, and then sat down again herself. She began to cough, and hastily put her teacup down in the hearth, in case she spilled some of its contents. It was not such a violent spasm as the one she had suffered in the office. When it lessened, she dabbed her lips with her handkerchief and picked up her cup again.

Her mind had obviously continued to run on the subject of marriage, because she said chattily, 'I've never married myself, though once a Cree Indian asked my stepfather for me. Tom had to be very diplomatic about turning him down – because we live outside the Fort we could be attacked very easily by anyone feeling disgruntled! I have quite a number of Cree friends now.' She went on to tell him of the sufferings of the Indians round her. 'My partner is half-Cree, and his relations come to call from time to time.'

'Must be an interesting man,' responded Benji, feeling an unaccountable pang of jealousy, despite his resentment at Wallace Helena's treatment of him.

'He is,' replied Wallace Helena. Then she said thoughtfully, 'I've written to ask him what he feels about my taking over the Lady Lavender; whether he would like to buy my share of the homestead.' She was lying because she felt suddenly embarrassed at having brought up Joe in a conversation about marriage; she had, after all, only asked Joe whether he would like to come to Liverpool. If he came, then it would be possible to sell their holding and he could invest his share in an English farm, if he felt like it. She fumbled for her handkerchief.

'I don't think, really, that he would want to run the farm by himself – there is too much work. But it's cleared and yielding well most years, so we could probably sell it to an immigrant – a few of them have money to invest.' She stopped to dab her nose, which was threatening to run, and Benji tried to visualize her life in Canada and what kind of a man her partner was.

She tucked her hankie back into her waistband, and then said she thought that Joe might like to consider moving to England and buying a farm, because the winters would be much less severe.

She leaned back in her chair and closed her eyes. The letters she had written to Joe suggesting that he should move had been difficult to compose, and she was sure Joe would think she was quite mad.

Benji said thoughtfully, 'Good farm land is costly in Britain – in spite of the depression.'

'Well, Joe was with my stepfather when he first squatted on Hudson's Bay land, so I mentioned it as another option he could consider.' She did not say that she had not mentioned the option of her return to the Territories; she wanted to live in a decent city or near one – with Joe by her side. In truth, there was little hope of his deciding to leave Canada; but she clung to that slender thread – he just might like to try something new.

Apprehensively, Benji asked if her partner would ever consider working in the soapery. He was relieved when she answered, 'Not him. He's an outdoors man, through and through.'

'Do you really like Liverpool?' Benji inquired.

Her face lit up. 'Yes, I do. I understand the kind of problems we face in the Lady Lavender – but, believe me, doing business here seems less trouble than in the Territories – despite Mr Lever!' She had opened her eyes, and she saw his astonishment at this remark.

She grinned, and then told him what a bitter struggle it had often been to stay alive and provide for themselves on Tom's land. Now that they had surpluses to dispose of, they constantly pursued Government contracts to feed the Indian tribes round about. 'We watch, like lynxes, for news of surveyors and other travellers passing through – they need supplies to continue north or west. I try to find out who is expected at the hotel or the Fort; I even made the acquaintance of the man who runs the telegraph office, because he often gets news first!'

For the first time in his visit, Benji relaxed a little and laughed. He could well imagine her striding in where other women would fear to tread. She had the same drive as his father and himself.

Wallace Helena picked up her teacup and drained it. 'You know, when I set out from Canada, I never expected to find you here. I knew Uncle had fathered a child – but since he never mentioned you or your mother in his letters to me, I assumed your mother had left him and taken her baby with her; I'm told it's common enough. I imagined him living alone, except for some kind of housekeeper.' She paused to reflect for a moment, and then said, 'Mr Benson didn't mention you either.'

'In the circumstances, I don't suppose they would.' He fidgeted uncomfortably.

'You mean because Uncle didn't marry your mama?'

'Yes.' There was a world of bitterness in the single word.

'Tush! People cohabit for all kinds of reasons,' she responded briskly, suddenly acutely aware of her position with regard to Joe. They'd never even discussed marriage. Isolated, and with no intention of having children, they had not thought it mattered.

Benjamin looked down at the painted wooden floor, his expression grim and disillusioned. His situation certainly mattered to him, Wallace Helena realized. She examined him curiously in the light of the setting sun glowing through the window.

His eyelids were darker than those of English people she had met, the eyebrows heavier and smoother. His newly clipped hair was like a black satin cap on his big head. His hands, loosely clasped between his spread knees, were wide and stubby-fingered, the hands of a heavy, powerful man. When she had seen him walking about the soapery, he had given every indication of self-assurance and incisive confidence. Only when she asked stupid questions, she told herself, did he show the hurt man beneath.

He did not reply to her last remark, and, when the silence began to be painful, he lifted his eyes to look at her. Though his face was more youthful than hers, she had, once more, a feeling of looking in a mirror and seeing herself slightly distorted; they both bore lines of suffering and had the same air of cynicism and disillusionment.

'You've had a rough time, haven't you?' she asked gently, as if trying to reach out to him. 'Was it because your parents weren't married?'

'Of course. Marriage is very important here,' he replied with sarcasm.

'I suppose it is,' she agreed reluctantly. She got up from her chair and went to the side table to get herself a cigarello. As she lit it, she turned and inquired, 'Have you ever asked Mrs Al-Khoury *why* she didn't marry Uncle James?'

He was shocked. 'You can't ask a parent a thing like that! You don't mention such things – at least, not in this society, you don't.' He spoke in English and, as a Liverpudlian, he muddled up his negatives in his confusion. 'Actually, I thought Father must have a wife in Lebanon, perhaps an arranged marriage when he was very young?'

'No. He was not married in Lebanon. But I don't see why you could not ask your mother. You're obviously very fond of each other, and you're grown up. I could ask Mama anything.'

Benji gathered up his scattered wits, and said diplomatically, 'You must have been unusually close, being a daughter.'

'We were very close. We went through a lot of terrible things together, she and I. She was wonderful under the most appalling circumstances.'

She took another puff at her cigarello, and said absently, 'I miss her very much.'

Benji's father had said to him once that his sister-in-law was one of the most charming women he had ever seen. He said, 'Father was upset when he heard how she had died – smallpox! Poor lady! A terrible death!'

Wallace Helena felt her eyes prickle, as if she were about to cry. She swallowed hard and tried to control herself.

Noting her struggle, Benji said with compassion, 'I'm sorry.'

A tear ran down his cousin's sallow cheek. She nodded her head as if in disbelief, as she told him, 'It was horrifying. Afterwards, I stopped believing in God! The God for whom we had endured persecution had abandoned us. Mama and my stepfather – and Joe – suffered such agony – and each of them had already endured so much hardship in their lives.' She sounded savage, as she went on, 'If God exists, He is infinitely cruel.'

Benji had never thought very much about a deity. As a child, his mother had taken him to an Anglican church which they still attended fairly regularly, though she had once let slip that she had been born a Catholic. Early in his life, he had noticed that she never took Communion and, later on, he learned that she could not, because, as a neighbour's son told him scornfully, 'She lives in sin, she does; and me mam says you're a bastard.'

He sighed. It had not occurred to him, until Wallace Helena had mentioned it, that his father had been hounded out of Lebanon solely because he was a Christian. God had not been very kind to him either. Perhaps that was why he had never been known to attend a place of worship; he had always occupied his Sunday mornings by checking the Lady Lavender account books and entering any profits in his private book, which he kept at home.

Wallace Helena had seated herself again in her rocking chair, her head leaned back against the cretonne cushion. Her cigarello dangled in a listless hand as a second tear slowly ran down her cheek.

Benji watched it. She looked very different from the assertive woman who had offended him so badly that morning. Whether he could bring himself to marry her was doubtful. But she was his cousin-sister and they had both let down their guards tonight, as if they were, indeed, siblings who could talk frankly to each other. He got up clumsily and went to bend over her and put his hand on her shoulder. 'Would you like to walk a little in the fresh air?' he asked, not sure what to do to comfort her. 'You might feel better outside.'

She put up her hand to touch his. 'Yes,' she said.

35

As Wallace Helena and Benji paced slowly round the cobbled square outside the Fitzpatricks' cottage, they discussed frankly the future of the Lady Lavender. It was as if during their slow conversation in the cottage, in which they had said very little, they had succeeded in communicating a great deal on a different level.

Benji had not forgotten the arrogance she had displayed during their hectic day, but he knew now that he could offer her something more than good management of the soapery. He could offer her an understanding and tolerance of her aggressiveness and arrogance; her tears had brought home to him forcibly the overwhelming hurt of the loss of her homeland and the subsequent loss of her father and mother, who had, in the alien world of North America, given her some tie to the country of her birth. Her description of the hardships of the first years in Canada had secretly appalled him, and even now it did not seem too easy; no wonder she was enjoying Liverpool, despite the rainy summer they had had. He was glad, for her sake, that September had brought more sunshine.

He had, as he grew more aware of his father's origins, caught glimpses in the man of the same terrible sense of isolation that being a refugee engendered; he knew there had been days when even his patient, cheerful mother could not console him. When his father found himself at loggerheads with a businessman born and bred in Lancashire and, therefore, having a different approach to whatever they were trying to negotiate between them, he would go out and walk for miles in the streets of Liverpool. When his frustration eased, he would return, sometimes late at night, tired, but himself. Eleanor and Benji would not comment on his absence but would cosset him with warmed slippers and the particular coffee, thick as creosote, which he liked.

It was late and the moon rose, but still they walked together, and Wallace Helena was grateful for the gentleness in his voice and the warmth of his presence; it was different from the comfort that Joe gave her because it was less easily defined. It had something to do with the soft Arabic phrases that he used and with an occasional gesture he made which was evocative of his father, when she had known him as a young man.

He did not attempt to court her in any way, for which she was grateful. He stuck firmly to the subject of the business in which they were both involved.

'I've been stewing over what we should do,' he told her. 'I'd like to suggest that, once we're up and running again after Probate, we should concentrate, first, on retaining and extending our market for soap. It's our bread and butter. Keep up our quality and speed of delivery – and go for a narrow margin of profit.' He put his hand under her arm and guided her down the slipway until the water nearly lapped their feet. The moon laid a pathway across the river and anchored ships looked like dark hulks on either side of it. Then he said, 'This assumes you're not going to sell.'

'Yes?' she queried, sensing he had not finished.

'Turner reckons that he now knows exactly how George Tasker gets such good soap. The next job – a bit further down the road – would be to reproduce it mechanically with consistent quality. Not that we'd ever want to get rid of George. No matter how good machinery is, there's no substitute for a good soap master watching it.'

She looked up at him thoughtfully. 'Are you afraid he's getting old?' she asked.

'Yes. He's older than Father was, and we'd be in deep trouble if he were ever ill – or, worse still, passed on.'

She saw the danger immediately. 'Aren't the men under him any good?'

'They know their jobs. But it's George who has a feel for soap. Without him, they'd be lost. Lever has two of the best soap masters in the business, but I'm sure they wouldn't want to leave him; I'm told they rule the roost there. Crosfield's have some good ones – they're right next door to him.'

'Really next door?'

'Yes. That's why he can't expand where he is; there's no space. Mr Benson said someone representing him was sniffing round our place, to see what room there was for expansion if they offered for the Lady Lavender.'

'Is there room to expand, if we wanted to?'

'Not really. I'd like to keep the operation small; maybe make better use of the floor space, but not try to become very big. It's not easy to raise capital in these depressed times, and we're debt-free at the moment. The way we run the Lady Lavender, our overheads are low, and we can go for a lower priced market, if we're not too extravagant when getting a sales representative.'

'Could we choose a new employee to follow Mr Tasker – say, let him choose somebody himself?' Wallace Helena asked, shaken by the idea that they could lose their most important employee.

'He wanted his son to follow him, but he went into the army instead. We've never tried for an apprentice since then.'

They forgot their inner sadnesses, as they tossed ideas backwards and forwards in rapid Arabic, with an occasional English sentence to express a technicality. Three fishermen sitting cross-legged near the slipway mending nets shrugged and laughed surreptitiously at the strange couple; middle-class people were not often seen in The Cockle Hole.

Wallace Helena saw the point of Benji's caution in not launching any new products for the moment, though her suggestion was that, when they did, they should offer emollients, based on glycerine, as the beginning of a line of very cheap cosmetics. 'So many women work, in Lancashire,' she argued, 'and you yourself said there's more money in working-class households nowadays. If they've got a little money to spend, the young ones will want to make themselves pretty, like the ladies in the shows you've taken me to.'

'They'd be afraid of censure if they used paint; their fathers would probably beat them if they did!'

'I realize that. That's why I said we should begin with creams to soften or heal the skin.'

'In time, in time,' Benji assured her.

She coughed, holding her hand to her chest to ease the pain. Then, when it passed, she managed to chuckle. 'It's good that you're here to restrain me; Joe always says that I want to do everything at once. He's suffering with my efforts to raise sheep at present – my latest idea.'

'When do you expect to get an answer from him about what he wants to do?'

'Soon,' she replied. She did not say anything more. Once his reply was in her hand she would have to make a choice, and the thought made her heavy-hearted.

The fishermen spread their nets over an upturned rowing boat, and stood around lighting their pipes in the cool moonlight. Though Wallace Helena seemed to have retreated into herself, Benji had in the quietness become aware, from the warmth of her beside him, that he had a woman on his arm, a woman still young enough to be desirable. He turned to her, lifted her chin with his free hand and kissed her on the mouth. It was a longing kiss, his tongue searching to open her mouth.

She broke away from him, immediately alert and teasing. 'Benji, you scoundrel! That was not a cousinly kiss!'

Behind them, the fishermen laughed. A little mortified, Benji did not attempt to follow it up, and she caught his hand, and said, to his utter surprise, 'I'm spoken for. You go find yourself some pretty young thing. Now walk me to the door.'

Dumbfounded, he did so and answered her cheerful goodnight with a bewildered 'See you tomorrow.'

36

While she waited for a reply from Joe, Wallace Helena continued to probe into the soapery. She was careful not to spoil her newfound freedom with Benji by failing to consult him. Though intrigued by her as a woman, he made no further sexual approach, being cautious about touching her in any way. He reluctantly assumed that she was committed to her Canadian partner.

She again visited Eleanor, and was taken to a local stonemason's yard, to see the marble cross which was being carved as a memorial to be put on her uncle's grave. Eleanor wept over it, and Wallace Helena tried to comfort her.

She had a long conversation with Mr Turner, who, this time, was less patronizing. She asked him particularly to describe to her any new technical advances in the soap industry of which he was aware. He confirmed the need for an experienced soap master, no matter what machinery was eventually installed. He was flattered when, after listening to him for an hour, she asked him to sit in on a meeting with Mr Tasker that she and Benji proposed to have, where, amongst other matters, they would discuss the need to train an understudy for the soap master.

He looked at her curiously. She appeared to have understood his explanations of the approaching changes in methods of manufacture, and, since he was, like everyone else, a little apprehensive about his position, he asked shyly, 'Do you propose to stay with us, Miss Harding, or will you sell out?'

She answered him as she had done when at the meeting of the staff in her office. 'I'm not sure yet, but you will be one of the first to know my decision. It should not be more than a few weeks at most.' She smiled, as she picked up her notebook. 'Be patient a little longer. If I sold, I would do so on condition that all my senior employees are accommodated with the new company.'

His anxiety somewhat relieved by her last words, he bowed her out of his laboratory. He had no real desire to be absorbed into a larger company, where he would probably be outshone by more brilliant German chemists, and he hoped the Lady Lavender would continue. He smiled as he put on his white laboratory jacket. No lady would ever run a company, so Benjamin Al-Khoury would run it – a capable, forward-looking man of his own generation with whom he got on well.

Wallace Helena had, quite early in her visit to the soapery, felt that a full-time chemist was rather a luxury in such a small soapery, and had wondered why Uncle James had recruited him. It did not occur to her that her uncle might have been a little dazzled by other soap merchants employing well-known German chemists. Not being able to afford such exotic creatures himself, he had found an intelligent man with a modest B.Sc., who, in a depressed economy, was thankful for a respectable job testing the ingredients and the end products of the Lady Lavender.

Though Turner was not a Ph.D., and was, therefore, not a true research man, he was quick to understand the research of others and he read everything he could find on soap technology. He liked and respected Mr Tasker and listened patiently to his explanations of the need for a sense of smell and the delicate interpretation of exactly what was happening in his great cauldrons, when the well-sniffed-over ingredients were put together. In between his routine duties and his experiments with glycerine, he had sketched a design for a mechanized line for soap production. A good working chemist, Turner felt, should be able to reduce Mr Tasker's magic *feel* for soap to an exact recipe. Quite soon, machinery would make possible a constant flow of evenly mixed and formed bars of soap; and he discussed these possibilities with Mr Ferguson, whose alert and inventive engineer's mind sometimes ranged much further than his precious boilers and steam pipes. Mr Ferguson had done his apprenticeship in Manchester and was still a member of a Mechanics' Institute there. As he often said, he knew what was going on, because he had friends with whom he kept in touch, remarks which would have gravely disturbed other soap-makers, who were doing their best to hide any of their advances in technology from their competitors.

The Steam Engineer always made himself a can of tea to drink with his sandwich lunch, which he ate at an old desk in a corner of the shed which housed his boilers. Sometimes, Mr Turner would drop in to share a mug of tea with him. Mr Ferguson always set great store by the visits.

When Mr Turner mentioned Wallace Helena's talk with him, Mr Ferguson said earnestly, 'Other soap companies are on to mechanization like you'd nevaire believe. If there's anything left of the Lady Lavender by the time the lawyers and Miss Harding are finished with it, you and I should get together with Mr Benji right away.'

Unaware that she had been mentally dismissed by two of her more important employees as a minor aberration in the life of the Lady Lavender, Wallace Helena walked along busy Sefton Street to her lodgings in The Cockle Hole, for lunch.

She felt tired, and her chest hurt when she coughed. As she walked, she wondered idly if Mr Turner could, some time in the future, make anything of her mother's beauty recipes. Her mother had had her own little mixtures for enhancing her looks, though, once she was married to Tom and had moved to Fort Edmonton, she had not had much time to use them. In Canada, she had used lamp black as kohl for her eyelids, instead of antimony. It had certainly made her eyes look enormous and had enhanced their glitter.

Wallace Helena wondered if she could ever sell kohl to Lancashire women, and decided regretfully that, from what she had been told about them, she probably could not.

Better to do as Benji advised, and stick to making soap. But not forever, she promised herself. Fashions could change; women were already converted to using soap. Why not cosmetics?

Her mother's recipes did not have expensive ingredients. Packaged in small enough quantities, they could be sold cheaply and yet make an excellent profit. 'Buy cheap and sell expensive,' her father had told her, and she grinned. She might do better to buy very cheaply and sell inexpensively.

As she washed her hands before lunch with a sliver of washing soap put in the soap dish for her by Elsie, she realized that Mr Lever's idea of scenting his soap with lemon was a good one. The piece of soap smelled very badly, and yet surrounded by the reek of stable and cowshed, of unwashed, sweating men and strong tobacco, she had, at home, never noticed that the soap she made did not smell good. She made a wry face at the discovery; she wondered if the smell bothered Eleanor – or Elsie – surrounded with Monday washing, boilers and dolly tubs.

When she went down to her sitting-room, she was surprised to find her meal served to her by a stranger, a flustered elderly woman, who carefully set a dish of scouse before her and ladled the mixture of lamb, onions and thin slices of potato onto her plate.

'I'm Mrs Barnes from next door,' she introduced herself. 'Elsie's beginnin' to feel 'er pains. It's too early yet to get the midwife, if you know what I mean. But it's her first, like, and she's nervous, so I come in to be with her for a while – and I'll be lookin' after yez while she's confined.'

Wallace Helena nodded and asked if she could be of help. 'I've never delivered a human baby, but I've helped cows calve and horses in foal – and I even managed a sheep that was in trouble last spring.'

'Really, Miss? Well I never.' She smiled down at the soap mistress, and said confidentially, 'I've helped a few into the world meself in me time, but I don't like doin' first births – sometimes they're difficult. Anyways, John Fitzpatrick's in regular work and he insisted Elsie have the midwife.'

'I hope she'll be all right,' Wallace Helena said, as she picked up her knife and fork.

Mrs Barnes heaved a sigh, 'Oh, aye, we all go through it – and she's a strong girl.' She went over to the mantelpiece and took down a letter which she handed to Wallace Helena. 'A Mrs Hughes sent this down for you by her maid.' It was from Joe, and Wallace Helena tore it open eagerly.

It was a month old and was full of the small problems of a homesteading family looking towards the threat of winter. His short sentences made his letter sound petulant. She tossed the letter down on the table and picked up her fork again to eat a meal that she did not want.

She decided irritably that he had probably already dealt successfully with most of his troubles; surely he could manage without her for a few months. Then she chided herself that she was being unreasonable; he was carrying her work as well as doing his own, and harvest time stretched the capacity of all of them. Joe would ensure that all the outside work would be done, she thought uneasily; but it was she who drove Aunt Theresa and Emily to bottle enough fruits and vegetables, bury carrots in sand, make sauerkraut and pickles, even do another boiling of soap, so that the six people she had to feed during the winter kept well. And there were always hungry Indians passing along the trail – they had to be found a meal, somehow. She must remind Joe to chase Simon Wounded to urge him along to build up the woodpile ready for the cold weather; they had now cleared so much of their land that he had to log trees towards the edge of their holdings. Soon she would have to buy coal from the miners who dug the dirty stuff out of the river valley – and that meant they must pay out cash, an idea which made her feel even more irritable.

Tush! Here she was thinking as if it were certain that she would return to the Territories, and she did not want to. She rose, and put down her napkin on the table. The letter she slipped into her pocket. Hurry up, Joe, she muttered, and tell me you'll take a chance on a new country and come here.

The sudden movement of getting up set her coughing again. Mrs Barnes came in with a kettle of hot water to fill up her teapot, and said, 'Aye, Miss, that's a nasty cough you got. I can hear you wheezin' from here.' She whipped the tea cosy off the teapot and poured a little water into the pot. 'I'll give yez some tea to sip.'

The paroxysm was so intense that Wallace Helena could not protest and found the teacup held to her lips. She tried to control herself sufficiently to drink a little and slowly her throat cleared, and she sank down onto the chair again.

Mrs Barnes put down the teacup and, hands on hips, surveyed the younger woman. 'You should see a doctor, Miss. You could get T.B.'

'Yes.' That was what Mrs Hughes had said. She asked, 'Is tuberculosis common here?'

'Oh, yes, Miss. Me little sister died of it – only eleven, she was.'

Wallace Helena sighed. 'I am so sorry,' she said.

'You could buy yourself some honey and lemons and mix 'em with hot water. It might ease it.'

Wallace Helena smiled and nodded. The coughing had tired her more than she liked to admit, so she promised to try Mrs Barnes's remedy. She inquired after Elsie and was surprised to learn that Mrs Barnes had sent her outside to walk up and down in front of the house. 'It'll help her later,' she informed Wallace Helena.

As Wallace left the house to return to work, she paused for a moment to wish Elsie a safe delivery.

Joe had mentioned in his letter that two families had come west on the train to Calgary and then felt it worth-while to trek north to take up land only a couple of miles from their boundary. 'Fort Edmonton's going to be a town one of these days,' he wrote. Wallace Helena smiled to herself. Joe was not fond of new immigrants; every white family in the district put further pressure on the dispossessed Crees. The plight of his mother's people troubled him and he often shared his own expertise as a farmer with them, in the hope that it would make their reserves more productive.

On her arrival in her office, she found on her desk a slender volume of verses by Mr William Wordsworth, which she had asked Mr Helliwell to buy for her.

Apart from conversations directly concerning the soap works, she had sensed in the bustling city a great pride in a newly acquired literacy. Even Mr Tasker read the papers; and he could quote an appropriate biblical text in almost any answer he gave her. Mr Helliwell, a man in his thirties, was very fond of larding his discourse with poetical quotations, and she had even come across a Latin tag in one of Mr Bobsworth's letters to a debtor.

She had been brought up as a child amongst talented, cultivated people, and she found her employees' carefully inserted quotations endearing, and had asked Mr Helliwell to buy a few poetry books for her. She promised herself that that evening she would read Mr

210

Wordsworth's book instead of one on oils and fats lent her by Turner. The more she saw of Liverpool, the more she realized what was lacking in her life in the Territories; there was more to existence than a battle for survival. There were other places, besides Beirut, where people had time for pleasure.

She slipped William Wordsworth into her reticule, and leaned over her desk to study a sheet of paper which was spread out on it. The scrawls on it looked like an untidy family tree descending from herself. Her name was written at the head of the paper and was joined by a line to that of Benjamin written immediately below. From him, lines arched out to the names of the senior employees. Beneath them, were the names of the men who reported to them. At the very bottom, were listed people like Alfie and the recalcitrant Georgie. By each name, in brackets, were a few words describing the man's duties.

She wanted now to ask Benji at what points in the structure she had depicted they could, perhaps, provide simple machinery to speed up their lines and their delivery process.

She rang for Mr Helliwell. He was busy making her two card indices, one of the name and address of every supplier from whom they had bought and another of every company who had ever made a purchase from the Lady Lavender. When she had first asked him if a proper record existed, he had replied simply, 'Mr James knew the names of everyone; he didn't need any more record than Mr Bobsworth's account books, occasionally.'

She now asked him to find Benji and see if he could spare her a few minutes. He bowed slightly and, with huge dignity, sailed into the works to find the man.

During the last week, as a result of Wallace Helena's memos, Benji's position as Assistant Manager had been clarified, and the men thankfully turned to him for their orders. Most of them would have agreed that a *woman* couldn't even run a kitchen properly, never mind a soap works.

When Benji entered, she said, 'Come and see what I've done.'

He went to stand close to her, while, with one beringed finger, she pointed out various employees' names and checked that she had correctly described their duties. As they talked to each other, he again began to be aware of her as a desirable woman. He flushed with embarrassment and tried to concentrate on what she was saying, but she was so close that he wanted to put his arm round the thin waist and forget about diagrams for a while. Perhaps his mother was right; she would make a good wife.

He carefully put his arm round her waist to see what would happen.

Nothing did; she simply went on talking, her finger squarely on one man's name, waiting for his reply. She did not even look at him.

She was in fact acutely aware of him – Benji would not be a difficult man to fall in love with. The more she saw of him, the more she liked him.

But there was Joe. If he were here, she would not even think of anyone else.

Benji was disappointed. When she began to cough, he let his arm drop, as she moved to take her handkerchief out of her waistband.

They sat down and she began a discussion to explore whether their present staff and equipment were utilized in the best way. At first he answered her in monosyllables, but he soon became engrossed in what she was saying and began to put forward his own ideas.

She mentioned her first visit to his home to learn exactly how an English woman used soap. 'I saw your mother slice up the soap to put it in her boiler. Could we produce a ready-sliced soap?'

'I've a recollection that someone tried it, but that it did not catch on too well.'

'Perhaps it was too expensive? Or was it not sliced thin enough? Your mother said it must be sliced very thin, so that it melts and doesn't cling to the clothes.'

They were in the midst of a lively argument as to whether a line like she had suggested was a possibility for the Lady Lavender, when Mr Helliwell knocked at the door and brought in a written message for Miss Harding.

Mr Benson presented his compliments and would be obliged if Miss Harding could call upon him that afternoon. Probate had been received and he needed her signature on a number of papers. He apologized for not calling on her, but he felt it advisable that she should come to his office, so that if she required clarification on any point of law or needed advice about how to proceed as the new owner, she could have the benefit not only of his counselling but that of his partner as well.

Wallace Helena raised her eyebrows at the formal missive and passed it to Benji, while she scribbled a note for the lawyer's office boy to take back to him, saying that she would be with him at half past three.

Benji read the letter. This was it, he thought bleakly. From this afternoon she would hold his future in her hand. He must now decide whether he should stay to serve her, whether he should try to court her or whether he should apply to other soaperies for a position. He looked round his father's office as if seeking an answer. He had, all his life, taken it for granted that from this little room he would preside over an expanding Lady Lavender, whenever it suited his father to step down. For that, he was sure he had been carefully groomed. And now the whole dream was gone, gone because of a crazy quirk of the law.

37

After Mr Helliwell and the lawyer's messenger had gone from the room, Benji and Wallace Helena continued their discussion a little longer.

Benji said, 'Talking about new lines, I don't know the extent of father's Estate, but I do know that he was saving like mad to finance an expansion. He believed in ploughing money back into the business.' He glanced at Wallace Helena out of the corner of his eyes, and continued ruefully, 'You've probably realized that we lived very modestly – he didn't keep any kind of carriage, for instance.'

Wallace Helena nodded. She had realized, when seeing Eleanor's house with its shabby furniture, that either the soapery did not make very much or the family were very careful spenders. His remark about savings confirmed Mr Bobsworth's records that the soapery, after the first few anxious years, had produced a healthy profit – even the current quarter had showed a gain, despite the intrusion into the market of the redoubtable Mr Lever.

In the back of her mind, she had wondered what Uncle James had done with his money. Now she thought, with a flash of humour, that he probably stashed it into an old trunk, exactly as she did. She hoped Mr Benson had the trunk and that it had been sealed before witnesses. And there must be a private account book, somewhere, if he were anything like Father, she considered.

She said, in response to Benji's remark about their standard of living, 'I have every faith in Uncle James's business acumen. I'll know this afternoon exactly what the position is.' She did not want to appear too mercenary by expressing her inward relief that there might be some hard cash forthcoming, apart from the firm's working capital in the bank.

As she folded up the diagram she had made of the staff's positions, she asked her cousin if he would instruct Mr Helliwell to order a cab to take her down to Mr Benson's office.

He had had a faint hope that she would ask him to escort her. He would have liked to know the exact value of the Estate and what taxes would be levied; the sums could make all the difference between having to sell the works or not. In any case, the levy would be a burden for them to carry, at a time when they needed further investment.

Unfortunately, in her excitement, Wallace Helena had not considered the wisdom of including Benji in the interview, so he went off a little huffily to order the carriage.

While waiting for the hackney to arrive, Wallace Helena tried to rest by sitting in her chair, her gloved hands holding her reticule in her lap. She wished she dared to smoke; it was so comforting to smoke, and she supposed that was why a compassionate Joe Black had taught her to smoke like a Cree woman. It had certainly helped; or had it been the presence of Joe himself, a self-assured man showing her that there was nothing to be unduly afraid of, and saying, 'You've got to respect living things, but you've got to take enough to stay alive yourself – and this is how the Indians've always done it.'

She smiled wryly. By the time the Indians had discovered that their old ways would hardly keep them alive, in the face of the white invasion of their territory, Tom and Joe were managing to raise crops and a few precious animals. Smoking had helped her through the long and excruciatingly cold winters, when food became short and tempers even shorter.

And now, a surly old man called Georgie Grant made it impossible for her to smoke while working at her desk. He had done what even her mother had been unable to do – banished the cloud of smoke usually wreathed around her head. The thought made her want to giggle; the giggle became a laugh. When Benji came, she was in a high good humour and she surprised him by giving him a friendly peck on the cheek, as she stepped into the vehicle.

The kiss was noted by the men moving about in the yard, and they smirked at each other; Mr Benji seemed to be doing well for himself.

Because she and her parents had had to wait in Liverpool for an immigrant ship to take them to America, she knew the layout of the centre of the city, except where new construction had altered it. The family had taken lodgings in a hostel run for European emigrants. It had been crowded and dirty, so her father and her uncle had taken her for walks in the town, to try to distract the young girl from the hard facts of what had happened to them. Now as she looked through the window of the vehicle, she saw in her mind's eye the two brothers flapping along in clothes that made the local inhabitants stare, as they made jokes to keep her amused. They had tried so hard, she ruminated, to repair the ruin of their lives, and both had died comparatively young. Now, only she was left to carry the scars of their dreadful, shared experience. Once again, she wondered why she should have been spared.

215

It was a very sad, dignified lady who was led into Mr Benson's private office by an elderly solicitor's clerk.

Mr Benson had ready for her a number of papers requiring her signature, and he waited patiently while she read them through carefully. Sometimes she did not understand a sentence and had to ask him for an explanation.

She was shocked at the amount of tax, but Mr Benson assured her that he had arranged for it to be paid by instalments, rather than see the Estate drained to such an extent that the Lady Lavender would have to be sold.

The cost of Mr Benson's administration was not small, but he had paid himself, from time to time, so that most of it had already been met.

'If you decide to sell the soap works, the total tax assessed would be immediately payable,' he warned her. Then he explained that, as of that moment, he could no longer sign cheques on behalf of the Estate, and that she should see the firm's bankers immediately, to arrange for her signature to be honoured by them. She promised to visit the bank in the morning.

After the work had been done, she accepted a glass of sherry and they drank the health of the company together.

She leaned back in her chair, twisting her glass in her fingers. She felt more overwhelmed than she had expected, almost afraid. All the problems of the soapery were now hers. All its employees would turn to her for sustenance; and behind them were their families depending upon her to feed them, as surely as if they were impecunious blood relations. Though she did not doubt her ability to steer the little soapery quite competently, she was well aware that, as in Canada, a woman was regarded as an inferior being, put on earth to serve her masculine betters. She would have to compete with men in a system devised by them.

The sheer load of responsibility appeared very great, and she whistled softly under her breath, while her lawyer, a male, watched her with interest. 'It can't be worse than the Territories,' she said aloud.

'Pardon?'

She laughed, and made a deprecatory gesture with one hand. 'I meant to say that I don't think running the Lady Lavender will be any worse than running my farm in the Territories.'

'So you will manage it yourself?'

'Probably. I have written to consult my partner in Canada, because any decision I make will affect him – he owns half shares in the property. I expect to hear from him in a week or two. There are many ramifications in a move to England – and I've been giving them considerable thought over the last few weeks.'

'I'm sure. Please don't hesitate to consult me if I can be of help. Company law is quite complex, especially for a lady, who may not have come in contact with it before. I presume Mr Benjamin will be staying with the company?'

'Yes, indeed,' she answered automatically, and then hastily amended her statement, as she suddenly remembered the closed-off look on Benji's face when Mr Benson's note had been delivered. 'At least, I hope he'll stay,' she said a little anxiously.

Suddenly, the fear that he would not stay swept over her. Already very weary, her face went white, her glass fell from her fingers and she fainted.

Mr Benson half-rose from his chair. 'Miss Harding!' he exclaimed, and banged his bell frantically. When his clerk flew in, he demanded that his typewriting lady be sent to help his client.

In a few seconds, after a timid knock, a plain, small mouse of a woman, smelling salts in hand, slipped in.

'Oh, dear, dear,' she whispered, viewing Wallace Helena slumped in her chair. Blinking nervously behind her glasses, she put down the bottle of salts and very carefully removed Wallace Helena's hat. She put her arm round the unconscious woman's neck to raise her head a little, picked up the little bottle of *sal volatile* and waved it under her nose.

Wallace Helena did not stir. The typist turned a frightened face to her employer. 'Could we lie her down, Sir? I ought to loosen her lace collar – and, if you'll forgive me mentioning them – her stays – she probably laced them a bit tight.'

Mr Benson's expression had the slightly hunted look of a man suddenly enmeshed in a situation he wanted to get out of at all costs. He rang his bell again and sent for reinforcements. Two young clerks were instructed to lift the lady onto a straight-backed sofa on the other side of the room, a sofa usually sat upon by submissive wives, not directly included in a client's consultations with the lawyer.

Wallace Helena was rather tall for such a stiff narrow piece of furniture, but they tucked her feet up onto a chair hastily pushed close to it. The three men then stared uncertainly down at her, while the typist tried again to revive her with the smelling salts.

Fortunately, she began to stir, so the two clerks were dismissed, and Mr Benson went to his desk to find the bottle of brandy he kept there, for emergencies; sometimes, information he had to impart to clients was so shocking that they needed something to stiffen their resolve. It was the first time that a lady had actually fainted in his office, however, and he wondered, as he poured a little of the spirit into a sherry glass from the same cupboard, exactly what had caused Wallace Helena to lose consciousness. Al-Khoury had left her a good business and a reasonable bank account on which to draw for immediate needs, not to speak of a strong box holding a very nice sum in good golden sovereigns. What would make her faint?

He was not more puzzled than Wallace Helena. As she came round and was persuaded to drink the brandy, she was ashamed at her weakness.

'I've never fainted before, except once from hunger – one spring when we were down to porridge and very little of that.' She shrugged, as she handed her glass back to the typist and thanked her. 'It's probably the immense change from being out-of-doors all the time to spending most of my time at a desk.' She smiled up at her lawyer. 'I wonder if you could order a carriage for me?'

'Indeed, I will, and Miss Williams shall go with you.'

Mr Benson refused to accept Wallace Helena's protestations that she would be quite all right alone, and Miss Williams, armed with her return fare to the office by the clerk, was very happy to escape, though tomorrow she would have to finish the work left undone.

Though sapped of strength, Wallace Helena was still alert enough to notice a hoarding that they passed at the side of the dock road. It exhibited a large poster advertising Pear's Soap. 'Right on my doorstep!' she exclaimed to Miss Williams, with mock indignation. She immediately drew out her notebook and scribbled a reminder in it, to talk to Benji about a poster of their own.

Benji! He was the core of the whole ambitious enterprise she had in mind. And at a moment of intense pressure, the thought that he might leave the Lady Lavender, leave her stranded when she most needed him, had been the last straw. Already run down by the chill she could not shake off, she had fainted. Joe would never believe it!

38

Joe never opened his letters at the post office, as many people did in their excitement; he waited until he reached the least travelled part of the track home. Then he would dismount, take the letters out of his shirt pocket and, leaning comfortably against his patient horse, would read them uninterrupted by Aunt Theresa or Simon Wounded who, at home, would clamour for news of her. Today, when he read her letter, he was glad of the solitude of the old pathway.

She had mentioned Benji a couple of times before and the reasons for his not inheriting his father's Estate. Now, she repeated how kind Benji and his mother had been to her, in spite of their disappointment at being left out of the Will; and a nagging fear in Joe's heart became a torrent of jealousy. He sensed that Benji was courting his precious lover. She had been away nearly three months, an extremely passionate woman, disdainful of church or state or custom, who had expressed that passion with him. He and Wallace Helena had established their own customs, he considered grimly.

But now she had this cousin, of whom she wrote with affection. A young man who spoke her own language! Who would probably enjoy bedding such a beautiful woman! He could barely read the whole missive.

He closed his eyes against the long slant of the late summer sunshine and to keep out the vision of Wallace Helena's slender legs curled round another man. He wanted to throw something, smash something, weep.

His horse turned to nuzzle him, as if she understood he was upset, and he leaned against her neck for comfort, until he had curbed his wild fury. Then he mounted her and rode slowly home, her reins loose in his hand and her hooves rustling sadly through the crisp, frozen leaves of autumn.

He unsaddled the horse and let it loose in the paddock, and then strode into the cabin. He flung his saddle into a corner, and shouted, 'Hey, Auntie! Got any coffee? Emily?' He pulled off his battered wolf-skin jacket and flung it after the saddle, kicked off his boots, and went to stand by the small log fire that his aunt had made to cook a stew. 'Damn her! Damn her!' he swore under his breath.

'Shut the door,' shouted Aunt Theresa from the kitchen. 'It's getting chilly – I can feel the draught out here.'

Continuing to swear under his breath, he went to the heavy door and kicked it shut. Then he turned the beam across it to lock it; the beam thudded into its socket with a squeak of complaint.

Aunt Theresa shuffled in with a mug of coffee from the blue-enamelled pot on the back of her iron stove, where she had been preserving berries. Her soft moccasins made little noise.

She took one look at Joe's darkly flushed face, and asked in Cree, 'What's up? Did you get in a fight?'

'No.' He took the coffee from her and drank half the mugful, while she watched him, her anxiety hidden behind her blank, seamed face. She sensed a boiling distress which she had not seen since his mother had died of smallpox. 'A bit more, and he'll burst into tears,' she thought.

She moved round him and pushed a chair behind him.

'Sit down and tell me,' she ordered, as she lifted another chair close to him and sat down herself.

Joe ignored her, and continued to stand staring into the fire, his great fist clenched around the coffee mug, until the heaving of his chest under his check shirt became more normal.

Without taking his eyes from the fire, he sat down suddenly, as if the strength had gone out of him.

The old Cree sat patiently waiting.

At last he said slowly, his voice constricted, 'It doesn't seem as if Wallace Helena will ever come home.'

'Why not? Of course she will. You're here, aren't you? Who else has she got?'

In the flickering light of the fire, Joe's face had the frightening fixity of an African mask. Then, as if the information were being dragged out of him, he said, 'Remember she said in one of her letters she'd met a cousin, a white man, who works in the soap place?'

Almost imperceptibly, Aunt Theresa stiffened, like an old brown fox that suddenly smells something in the wind. She nodded.

'He keeps taking her out – walking with her – and, she says, planning with her.' He turned his eyes on his aunt, and said with anguish, 'I'm fifty-one, and my face is pocked – like the face of the moon. She's found this younger man – a city man – like she is.' He nodded his head helplessly. 'I've never seen a city. I don't know anything compared to her – I'm the son of a slave.'

Aunt Theresa thought this tirade over carefully, her face showing only her usual expression of resignation. She said quietly, 'I knew your father; he was a clever man. Don't put him down. He couldn't help it

220

if he was taken as a slave. Mr Rowand who owned him thought a lot of him. And my father, Two Tailfeathers – your grandfather – taught you well. And you can read and write. You're as smart a man as she'd ever find in the Territories.'

'Yeah! In the Territories,' he repeated, with heavy sarcasm. He banged one fist on his knee and shifted himself angrily on his chair.

After a moment or two, Aunt Theresa went on, as if she had not heard the interjection.

'If it was looks that Wallace Helena wanted, you'd have been sent packing long ago!' She smiled faintly. 'She could have married Gagnon who used to hang around her, when she went down to the Fort. He was really handsome – and French-speaking.'

'A handsome fool!' retorted Joe.

'Right. And she knew it.' She chewed the end of one of her wispy white plaits. 'And you stop thinking wrong of her; she's clung to you like a burr ever since she was a girl, and she's been good to all of us – like her mother.'

Aunt Theresa rarely spoke her mind. When she did she was straightforward and without censure. Joe rubbed his eyes and his face, as if attempting to dispel his seething anger.

Aunt Theresa watched the play of emotion across his scarred face. She felt a great compassion for her big nephew, and had shared his mother's worries for him when they were young. He stood astride two nations, Cree and wherever his negro father had originally sprung from, and both peoples had suffered from white intrusion – were still suffering, she considered with a shiver, as she thought of the tattered, starving Crees, who occasionally knocked on their door to beg a little oatmeal or a bit of meat. Joe had been very lucky to have work with the Company and then to have made a good friend of Tom Harding, a simple man, she remembered, generous and outward-looking, who had taken a Cree as his first wife. After his death she had been glad to come to try to knit the shattered household together again; and seeing the affection between her nephew and Wallace Helena blossom had made her glad for both of them. Of course, the priest, who sometimes made the round of outlying homesteads, always said they should marry, but to Aunt Theresa it had not seemed a very important issue – until now.

At the moment, she thought that the added tie of marriage might have made Joe more confident that he would not be deserted, and would have eased the uncertainty within him. Privately, she could not imagine Wallace Helena being satisfied with some bleached-looking white man.

As she looked at Joe's bent head with its tight grey curls, she said firmly, 'Come on, boy. You must trust her. Read her letter to me,

221

before Emily and Simon return – looks as if they're trying to lift all the turnips tonight. Where's the letter?'

Reluctantly he drew the offending missive from his pocket and, translating into Cree as he went along, tried to render it accurately. His jealousy lay within him like a dark, forbidding pool.

His aunt gestured helplessly with her hands. 'I don't know why you're making such a fuss,' she said. 'She's asking you to go to her. It's not you who've any worry. It's Simon and Emily and me who should be worried! What would we do, if you both moved?'

'I'm not moving. What would I do in a town?'

'She says what about a little farm? And she wouldn't be asking you to join her if she was thinking of marrying her cousin.'

He saw the sense in her remarks, but he was not comforted. He had many a time listened to Wallace Helena's longing for Beirut, heard her rail against the bitter winter, the lack of books, music, sometimes the lack of the basics of life when times had been bad. He judged rightly that, though Liverpool was probably different from Beirut, it might be a good substitute for her own city. And she had a relation to help her to settle there. He sat staring at the pot of stew plopping softly on the fire, folding and unfolding the letter with his long, splayed fingers, as he considered a future which seemed more hostile than the worst winter, the worst prairie fire, the worst invasion of grasshoppers.

He had believed that the soap works would yield some useful money with which she could buy good agricultural machinery, that she would be back home by this time. Instead it was creating a nightmare for him. Who, in the name of Jesus, wanted to live in a country other than his own?

Feeling that some of the tempest had passed over, Aunt Theresa heaved herself out of her chair and shook out her black skirt. 'You think carefully, boy, before you write back to her. She wants to stay there, I've no doubt. If you want her back here, you've got to tempt her, like you would a mare that's got loose and is running with a wild herd. Remind her of her warm stable and her bag of oats.' She allowed herself a small grin, and added, 'And the stallion in the paddock.' She unhooked a ladle hanging from the mantelshelf and bent down to stir the stew.

39

Though Wallace Helena had noticed, when visiting Mr Benson on other occasions, that he had a typewriting lady at work in a corner of the general office, she had never spoken to her. When they were ensconced in the hackney together, however, she asked the woman how long she had been working for Mr Benson, and then leaned her head in a corner to rest, while she listened to the whispered flow of Miss Williams's confidences. She gathered from them that Miss Williams found herself the target of a great deal of hostility and misunderstanding, because she worked amongst men. 'But I felt that the shift-key typewriter was the coming thing, Miss Harding, and I have to keep my dear mother, so . . .'

Wallace Helena roused herself sufficiently to respond that she fully understood Miss Williams's difficulties, because she herself was aware of similar attitudes to her ownership of the soap works. 'We shall have to teach men that we are to be respected, shall we not?'

Miss Williams agreed unhappily that they would have to be teachers. When they arrived at The Cockle Hole she refused an invitation to take tea, saying that she would like to go home to her mother as quickly as she could. 'Mother is an invalid, and she gets very lonely at times.'

Wallace Helena shook her hand and thanked her for her kindness, before descending carefully onto the cobblestones. She felt unusually weak.

She was surprised to find Elsie's front door open. To get out of the way of the hackney driver turning his horse around, she stepped quickly inside and found the house in turmoil. Sharp, short cries came from upstairs, as Mrs Barnes emerged from the kitchen-living-room at the end of the narrow entrance passage. Her hair hung in wisps from her bun and she seemed agitated. Two small boys were fighting over marbles in the hall, and a strange young woman was running up the stairs.

As Mrs Barnes saw Wallace Helena, she bent to slap one of the little boys and told him to be quiet or he'd have to play in the square. 'Our Elsie's in labour,' she told the Lebanese. 'I've got your tea ready, though.' She opened the door of Wallace Helena's living-room and bade her enter.

Wallace Helena went in and sat down thankfully. She took off her hat and laid it on another chair. Seeing her face, Mrs Barnes inquired kindly, 'Are you all right, Miss?'

Wallace Helena made a face. 'I fainted in my lawyer's office.'

'You're not well, Miss, I can see that. Elsie was sayin' as you've been coughing somethin' awful. You might like to walk up to see Dr Biggs, after you've had your tea. He has an evening surgery at seven o'clock. He's just round the corner, like. No distance, and he's proper kind. He'll see you all right – you might have to wait a bit.'

Wallace Helena nodded, and inquired how Elsie was.

'She'll be a while yet. It's her first and she's scared.'

'May I go up and visit her after I've had tea? It might take her mind off her pains.'

'For sure, Miss. The midwife's gone to have her tea – she reckons she'll have a long night of it. She'll be back in an hour. Don't make yourself too late, if you want to see the doctor, though. He shuts his door at nine o'clock.'

Aware that she had not eaten much lunch, Wallace Helena asked that her tea be brought in. She hoped that food might make her feel a little more energetic, though she felt more like taking to her bed than anything else.

Tea proved to be a filleted kipper on toast, followed by bread and butter and jam and a plain cake. It was tasty without being very fatty, and Wallace Helena ate all the kipper and then some bread and butter. She drank several cups of tea from the shiny brown pot. Feeling stronger, she found herself a cigarello and sat at the table smoking it with her last cup of tea. The smoke made her cough once or twice but she had no violent spasm.

She ground out the stub in a pottery ashtray liberally decorated with gold paint, and then went upstairs to wash her face and see Elsie.

When she knocked at Elsie's door, she was bidden to come in by her landlady, in a gasping, hoarse voice.

Elsie lay on the bed, her fair face flushed and perspiring. She was covered by a sheet and blanket, which had become tangled, as she heaved herself round in an effort to make herself more comfortable. Like the rest of the bare room, the bedding was spotless. On a table, the midwife had put a bowl, a pile of newspapers and some neatly folded clean rags. An empty bucket stood under the table and a flower-wreathed chamber pot was visible under the bed. A small fire had been laid in the fireplace; it had not yet been lit. A wooden chair stood by the bed.

Elsie smiled at her visitor and half rose, only to wince and fall back on her pillow. 'I'm sorry,' she gasped. 'Did Mrs B. give you your tea all right?'

'Oh, yes. Don't worry your head about things like that.' Wallace Helena approached the bed and sat down on the chair. 'I just came to sit with you for a few minutes, if you feel able to have a visitor. I believe the midwife will be back in a little while?'

Elsie agreed that she would, and added, 'Our John'll be home from work soon – and he'll sit with me a while later on. He's bin real good, helpin' me and having a real midwife and all.' She arched her back suddenly and cried out.

'Let me rub your back for you?' suggested Wallace Helena.

'Oh, I couldn't let you, Miss.'

'Why not? It's very comforting.'

''Cos you're a Miss, Miss.'

'Don't let that worry you,' Wallace Helena said with a laugh. 'I've helped many a cow calve. Turn on your side and we'll tuck the blanket under your stomach to support it. Now, then.'

Wide-eyed and doubtful, Elsie did as she was told, and long capable hands smoothed and soothed. After a minute or two, the girl was persuaded to sit up and Wallace Helena hitched her nightgown higher and eased and kneaded round the waist and down again. Elsie began to relax, and breathe more easily.

Wallace Helena kept it up until she herself was seized with a fit of coughing, and had to stop. It was her turn to say, 'I'm sorry,' as she fumbled for her handkerchief. 'Mrs Barnes says there's a doctor near here. I think I'll go up and see if he can give me a cordial to ease this stupid cough.'

Elsie caught her lower lip between her teeth, as she lay back again on her pillows and pain shot round her waist. When it had passed, she confirmed that Wallace Helena should see the doctor. 'We're all afraid of coughs round here,' she said, ''cos of T. B.'

Mrs Barnes could be heard slowly climbing the stairs, so Wallace Helena took Elsie's hand and said goodbye. From Mrs Barnes she obtained exact directions to the doctor's house, and, with a quick smile to Elsie, she went to put on her hat and shawl.

As she was about to descend the stairs, she had a sudden thought, and she put her head round Elsie's door to ask, 'Can I get your mother or your mother-in-law for you – take a message to one of them?'

Elsie smiled sadly from the bed. 'Me ma lives in Dublin and she hasn't got the money to come – she sent me that lovely shawl hanging on the hook there – knitted from wool she got from the walls and hedgerows, where the sheep rub themselves; spun it, she did, and then knitted it. And our John's mam's crippled with the rheumatism – you should see her hands. She's comin' to live with us, once the baby's born.'

'My, you're going to be busy,' Wallace Helena said with a smile, as she pulled on her black cotton gloves.

'Oh, aye, but she's a real nice woman.' She winced, and Mrs Barnes leaned over to hold her hand.

Wallace Helena went slowly down the stairs, thinking soberly that wherever women lived, their lives were not easy.

The doctor's wife let her into the house and ushered her into what looked like a dining-room. A huge, polished oak table took up the centre of the room and matching chairs with seats covered in black oilcloth were ranged round the walls. At the door of the room, she said, 'He's nearly through. You won't have long to wait.'

'That's O.K.,' Wallace Helena responded.

The American phrase aroused the woman's attention. She had realized that Wallace Helena was a foreigner, and now she inquired, quite politely, if she was from the United States.

Wallace Helena glanced at the pallid, lined face turned up towards her. 'No,' she replied, 'I'm from Canada.'

Two other people in the dining-room looked up, as Mrs Biggs said with forced cheerfulness, 'Well, now! Then you won't have been here before? It's as well you'll be his last – he likes to get the medical history of new patients, and he'll have time to do it without keeping anyone else waiting.' She smiled absently at the two other patients and softly closed the door behind Wallace Helena.

The room was made gloomy by heavy, dusty red curtains draped over lace ones. The dim light caught the mahogany features of a middle-aged working man in rough clothes and a battered bowler hat. He stared unsmilingly at the new arrival.

Wallace Helena sat down next to a heavy woman wrapped in a shawl. Her greasy black hair was caught up in a tight knot on the top of her head. Her hands were folded under her shawl. Her face was ashen and her lips compressed.

Despite her obvious pain, the woman looked sideways at Wallace Helena. Though Mrs Hughes might think Wallace Helena dowdy and old-fashioned, to residents close to the docks she seemed much better dressed than most of Dr Biggs's patients. As an opening gambit, the woman said to Wallace Helena, 'Doctor won't be long now; you're best off comin' late I always says.' She sighed.

'Yes?'

'Oh, aye. He's goin' to have to take 'is time on me finger. I got a whitlow, and he's goin' to have to cut into it, to get the pus out.'

'That sounds very painful.'

'Aye, it is, luv. Have you never had one?'

'No.'

'Well, they come if you get a splinter under your nail. Wood floors is the divil! I were scrubbin' the floor a couple o' weeks back and one went right under me nail. Proper mess it is. I won't show it to yez; you'd throw up if I did.'

Wallace Helena felt that she had dealt with enough sickness and injuries not to vomit. 'I hope it won't be as painful as you expect,' she said gently.

'Well, me hubby give me the money to come to Dr Biggs, rather than go down to the Infirmary or the Dispensary. Dr Biggs is proper kind. Does "is best not to hurt you. He cares, he does." Then she said, "You're furrin, aren't you?"

For the second time, Wallace Helena said she was from Canada.

This caused an outpouring of information about the woman's nephew, who, she said, was working as a carpenter in Winnipeg. As she spoke, a distant bell rang and the man left the room. Distracted from thoughts of her painful finger, the woman seemed to gain a little colour, so Wallace Helena told her that she had actually been to Winnipeg, and this kept the conversation going.

When the bell rang again, the woman rose, bobbed gracefully to Wallace Helena, and said, 'It's bin a pleasure talkin' to you, Missus. I'll try not to be long.'

It was, however, almost ten o'clock by the black marble clock on the mantelpiece and the room was dark, before the little bell rang again.

Wallace Helena got up and went uncertainly into the hall. She paused, and then saw that the door opposite was marked *Surgery*. She knocked and a male voice told her to come in.

When she entered, she faced an unexpectedly long room. At the far end, between two long windows covered by the same type of dusty curtains she had seen in the waiting-room, a man sat facing her, at a desk. He was obviously elderly, and two sharp eyes peered at her over small, metal-rimmed spectacles, as she slowly crossed the room towards him. He gestured towards the chair set opposite to him, and said in a soft, melodious voice, 'Please sit down. We haven't met before, have we?'

She mechanically drew off her gloves, as she sat down. The doctor's shabby black suit and his bald head both shone in the light of lamps set on either side of his desk. He had a generous white moustache which

227

emphasized a firm, but kindly, mouth. He continued to look at her, while he waited for her to reply.

Wallace Helena subjected the doctor to a slow, shrewd stare. Then, deciding that she liked what she saw, she told him about the cold and her subsequent coughing, and, a trifle reluctantly, that she had, that day, fainted in her lawyer's office.

In view of the fact that most of his patients hardly raised their eyes to him, he was rather amused at the weighing up of him that she had obviously done. He put her down as a lady coming to a slum doctor to whom she was unknown and where she was unlikely to meet an acquaintance, a lady who had something to hide.

'Well, well,' he said. 'Let us start from the beginning.' He went on to ask her name and address and what illnesses she had had in her life. Was she married or single?

She said she had enjoyed excellent health all her life, despite the harsh climate in which she had lived. He seemed interested, so she told him a little about her life as a homesteader and that she was now the new owner of the Lady Lavender Soap Works. She said she wanted to run the firm herself, and, therefore, particularly did not want to be ill at this moment.

He caught in her words the mispronunciation of the letter p and one or two other small slips amid her American accent, and he asked if she had been born in Canada.

'No, I was born in Beirut, in the Lebanon,' she told him with a hint of pride.

His wife brought in a glass of hot milk and put it silently on his desk for him. He accepted it with an absent nod; he was very tired. But the woman in front of him was most unusually interesting, so he carefully drew out of her the story of the massacre, of which he made a special note, of the flight to the United States, the awful journey to western Canada, and the subsequent loss of her mother and her stepfather.

'You have had a most eventful life, Miss Harding. And now you expect to begin yet another life in England?'

'All being well, I do.'

'May I ask whether your lawyer had something stressful to impart to you, that you should faint?'

'On the contrary, it was all good news. But I am very tired, as you can imagine, with such a long journey and profound change in life; in fact, I feel it may have precipitated the change of life in me.'

'What made you think the latter?'

'Well – er – my flowers have not come these past three months.'

'I see. And you are thirty-eight years old?'

'Yes.'

'It is possible.' He considered her for a moment, and then he said, 'I would like to listen to your chest and look down your throat, to see what is causing the cough. And, if you are agreeable, I would like to check you generally. Sometimes a cough is only a symptom of a deeper disorder.'

'Certainly. I am anxious not to be ill.'

'Well, well. We'll ask Mrs Biggs to come in.' He got up slowly and shuffled to a side door to call, 'Sarah, my dear. Could you spare a minute?'

Mrs Biggs put down her knitting and rose from her favourite basket chair. As she came into the surgery, she looked towards Wallace Helena, and inquired, 'Yes dear?' of her husband.

Dr Biggs explained the examination he wanted to do, and Mrs Biggs turned briskly towards Wallace Helena, to help her remove her bodice. She was surprised to find that Wallace Helena wore no stays under it; only a chemise and a camisole. Wallace Helena unbuttoned the fronts of both garments and slipped them down to her waist, to reveal a creamy body and firm small breasts with dark nipples. The doctor knocked with his knuckles, first down her back and then her front. When he had finished, he continued to look at her breasts through tired eyes, half-closed. Then, as she lifted her camisole to cover herself a little, he asked, 'Have you noticed any other symptom of ill-health – a change in your normal weight, for example – during the last few months?'

'Not really. The change to city life, after being outdoors all the time, has been quite profound. I don't seem to be quite as energetic as I usually am. I've not lost weight; I've gained – probably because I'm confined – not out on horseback all day!'

He lifted one of the small lamps from his desk and handed it to his wife to hold, while he depressed Wallace Helena's tongue and looked down her throat. 'A little sore,' he told her, 'probably from coughing. It's not putrid in any way.' He stepped back and put down the spoon. He smiled gently down at his patient, and then said, 'Miss Harding, I would like to examine you thoroughly all over, if you wouldn't mind, to satisfy myself that all is well. I would not like you to walk out of here without help if you need it.'

Fear of the unknown shot into Wallace Helena's eyes. 'Are you looking for tuberculosis?'

'I doubt if you have such an infection.' He laughed quietly, and added, 'There are, however, so many woes that afflict the human race that I would like to make sure while you are here that everything is all right.'

Wallace Helena shrugged. 'O.K.,' she agreed reluctantly.

229

While the doctor went back to his desk and added some notes to his record of her, Mrs Biggs took her behind a screen where she divested herself of the remainder of her clothes. The doctor's wife wrapped a sheet round her, and then told her to lie on her back on a narrow, high bed against the wall. 'Nothing to be afraid of. Doctor is being thorough, that's all.'

Mrs Biggs hovered in the background, as the old physician went slowly and carefully down her body, uncovering only that part of her which he was immediately examining. He prodded round her stomach, turned her over and ran his fingers down her straight backbone, noting the firmness of her muscles. Then he turned her on her back again, and said, 'Spread your legs, please. This will feel a little odd to you, but it won't hurt.' He checked that she was not a virgin; then she felt his fingers probing carefully within. She lay perfectly still, gripped with fear. That was where cancers sometimes grew; she had heard about them. He said gravely, 'You may dress now,' and went to a washstand on the other side of the room, to wash his hands.

Mrs Biggs helped her off the bed and handed her garments to her, one by one. When she was dressed, she escorted her back to the chair in front of her husband's desk. Then, smiling sweetly, she slipped out of the room.

Dr Biggs did not look at her. He sat chewing his bone pen while he read his notes.

Then he looked up, and sighed, sharp eyes again peering at her over his glasses. Fiddling with his pen, he said, 'The cough is caused by a trickle of catarrh down your throat, made worse by the cold you have had. Such catarrh is common here and difficult to eradicate. I see from the stains on your fingers and teeth that you smoke, and this is making the catarrh worse. My first advice is to stop smoking. And I'll give you something to help to clear the catarrh.'

Wallace Helena smiled wryly. 'I'm not sure that I *can* stop smoking.'

'It's difficult, I know.' He paused, and then added, as if the words were being dragged out of him, 'I recommend that you stop for another reason.'

A fresh twinge of fear went through Wallace Helena. 'Why?' she almost snapped.

'Well, you must be aware that you are *enceinte*; it's not good for the child.'

'I'm what?'

'With child.' The doctor was obviously embarrassed, but he went on firmly, 'You have already mentioned that you've observed a cessation of your menses – discharges. During the last three or four months?'

Wallace Helena looked at him, speechless, as the colour ebbed from her face. Finally, she exclaimed, 'But I'm thirty-eight! I'm too old! It's surely the change of life?' She nodded her head unbelievingly. 'I've never been pregnant before – it's impossible.'

'I think you know that it is quite possible, Miss Harding.' The old man's voice seemed suddenly frigid.

Wallace Helena breathed slowly and shallowly, as the inference sank in. It seemed to her that all her hopes and dreams lay shattered round her feet. A spinster soap mistress, pregnant, facing her employees? Proud, scornful Wallace Harding riding down the main street of Edmonton, round with child? And Joe? What would he think, after all these years of never fathering a child? She shuddered to imagine it.

The doctor was saying, 'I'm quite sure, Miss Harding; I suspected it when you walked in.'

Wallace Helena licked her lips and stared at him dumbly, while with some bitterness, he added, 'Women sometimes consult a poor slum doctor, who does not know them, in the hope that he can abort a child for them. Otherwise, I do not often see middle-class women in my waiting-room. So I watched your walk – and looked at your skin – your complexion, as you came in.'

Wallace Helena was amazed. 'Is it that obvious?'

'Probably not – if you do not expect to observe it. People see what they expect to see.'

'I had no idea. I merely came about the cough and the fainting spell I had. With regard to – to my flowers, I simply thought I was getting old.'

'Can you expect that the father will marry you, Miss Harding?'

'He's in Canada – way out west. It would take months to arrange.'

'And you mentioned that you want to stay here to look after the Lady Lavender Soap Works?'

'Yes.'

'I see.' He sat considering the implications of all she had told him, and finally said, 'There's a nursing home in North Wales, an expensive but very discreet one – they could arrange matters for you, if you don't want to bear the child. It's a risky procedure – and time is running out for you; you should make up your mind immediately.'

Wallace Helena made an enormous effort to get a grip on herself again. She bit her white lips and clenched her hands in her lap. Joe's child. And Joe himself?

No words came to her.

40

In the distance the marble clock in the waiting-room chimed eleven. It reminded Dr Biggs that he had had a very long day and he might well be called out to a patient during the night. He got slowly up from his chair, and came round the desk to assist the frightened woman who had consulted him.

Realizing that she had kept him very late, Wallace Helena rose and thanked him stiffly. She promised to pick up tomorrow the cough medicine which he would make up for her.

He realized that his diagnosis had shocked her to the core, and his manner towards her softened; it was clear that she had not suspected that a pregnancy was the basis of her fatigue, and, in the back of his mind, he wondered why she had discounted this obvious result of coitus. At her age, surely she knew where babies came from!

She said, 'I will think about what you have told me, and I will come to see you again, if necessary.'

'Well, you're in good health,' he assured her. 'But remember that at your age you should have a doctor, preferably a specialist, in attendance when the child is born.'

Wallace Helena laughed shakily. 'If I go home to have it, there's only one doctor in the whole of the Territories and I doubt if he would want to come specially to Edmonton for the sake of a normal pregnancy.'

They were walking towards the door, and Dr Biggs suggested, 'Have the child here, and then go home.'

'I have yet to decide to have it,' she reminded him, her eyes large and sad.

He looked at her with pity, and said kindly, 'Well, come and see me again, if you need any further advice.'

Her pride in the dust, she walked slowly through the dark streets, empty except for a couple of cats growling at each other. She felt numb, unable to think clearly.

Though it was so late, the lights of the Fitzpatrick house still gleamed softly through the white curtains. She saw a woman's shadow flit across the window of the small upstairs hall. It jolted her. She had forgotten about Elsie's struggle to bring her baby into the world.

The panting cries of a mother giving birth and the mumble of other women's voices hit her ears the moment she opened the door. From the kitchen came the rumble of men's voices, and she presumed that John had a friend sitting with him to sustain him through the birth. He heard her entry and came out to meet her. Behind him she caught a glimpse of one of the older fishermen who also lived in The Cockle Hole.

Whether it was because he had company or had been drinking fender ale, John looked fairly cheerful as he greeted her.

'Elsie said as you was to have a fresh cup o' tea when you come in. Would you like one, Miss? It'd be no trouble – I'm up for the night, anyways.'

She stared at him, as if she had not taken in what he had said. She looked so desolate that he wondered if Ould Biggs had indeed found her tubercular – Elsie had told him where she had gone. She swallowed and responded with an effort, 'I would, John. I'd be most grateful.' She hesitated, and then inquired, 'Do you happen to have any rum? If you do, could I buy a thimbleful from you?'

'I don't, Miss. But I bet Ben here has. He can usually find a bit of brandy or rum for any as wants it.'

Even in her misery, Wallace Helena felt a quirk of humour, as she undertook to buy a small bottle of top-quality Jamaica rum from a smuggler. But she needed something to ease her sense of helpless shock. A few minutes of complete abandon had cost her her future. Even if she went home, would Joe believe the child to be his? She had not lain with anyone else, so it was his, conceived during a mad night in a noisy hotel in Calgary, while they waited for the train to take her to Montreal. For the first time, she had ignored the careful count she had always kept of the natural cycle of her menstruation. Like her mother, she had had no desire to bring children into her hard, relentless world. And no amount of importuning had made her break that rigid rule; not until she had been faced with parting from Joe for the first time since she was twelve, she thought. And she sensed again his anxiety at the long journey she was undertaking. Even then he had been afraid that she would not return, she remembered.

And she had promised that she would come back, that all she wanted to do in England was to see that she was not being cheated over the sale of the soap works.

Because of the slowness in obtaining Probate, she had remained in England much longer than she had intended, long enough to realize the comfort that life in Liverpool offered, long enough to make her want Joe to join her there. What a stupid hope! Every letter that Joe wrote asked her when she was coming back; and his jealousy, when she mentioned the men she had met, was clear in every word. He had ignored the letter in which she had first slyly mentioned the possibility of his coming to England; neither had she received a reply to her direct question in a later letter.

And now she feared she was caught in a trap. Would Joe believe the child was his?

As John pushed the door of her sitting-room with his foot, bringing in a tea tray which included a modest-sized bottle of rum, a gasping scream rent the air. John stopped, then hastened to put down the tray. He listened intently. Perhaps the child had come. It had not. Loud moans followed, and the twittering voices of women comforting.

'Who's up there?' asked Wallace Helena, pulling a chair to the table to sit down and pour the tea.

'Mrs Murphy, the midwife, and Mrs Barnes is helpin' her.' He gave a little laugh. 'Mrs Murphy says as all's well and not to worry – but you can't help being wishful that she didn't have to go through this so that we can have a family.'

John looked quite shaken, so Wallace Helena assured him that, once she had the baby, she would forget about the pain. It was a trite remark, but it seemed to comfort him.

'Yes, Miss. Thank you, Miss.' He withdrew, his expression still apprehensive. The baby could be safely born; yet, all too often, the mother could die of childbed fever within a week. He hoped he had been right in putting his faith in Mrs Murphy, the midwife.

Wallace Helena splashed rum into her tea and thought dejectedly that she would have to go through the same ordeal as Elsie, if she kept the child. Alternatively, an abortion often led to a painful death for the woman.

But, above all, she dreaded the calumny she would face, whether in Liverpool or in Edmonton, if she carried the child to fruition and Joe refused to marry her. And the child itself would suffer, like Benji had suffered.

Better to abort it, she decided grimly, as she poured another cup of tea and added rum to it.

41

Wallace Helena did not hear Elsie's triumphant shriek as John Patrick Fitzpatrick entered the world, nor the happy running up and down of the women attending to mother and child. She was sound asleep on top of the coverlet of her bed, still in her camisole and petticoat; the rum had done its work.

She slept until nine in the morning. Then Mrs Barnes knocked on her door, to inquire rather anxiously if she would like her breakfast. 'I've brought you a can of hot water,' she called through the door.

Dragged back from the dark oblivion in which she had spent the night, Wallace Helena responded sleepily. Then as consciousness returned, she swore. Oh, my God! The soapery! The bank! The child!

She stumbled out of bed and shouted that she would be down in a quarter of an hour. Her natural liking for Elsie asserted itself, so she opened the door and hissed down the stairs after Mrs Barnes, 'How's Elsie?'

Mrs Barnes turned her cumbersome body to slowly look up at her, her careworn face beatific. She whispered back, 'She's fine. She's slee-pin' now, thanks be. It's a boy – and he's loovely. You must see 'im later on.'

Wallace Helena had to smile at the woman's pleasure. 'I will,' she promised, and shut her door.

Once she was washed and her hair brushed and neatly knotted at the nape of her neck, Wallace Helena's mind cleared and she went down to breakfast with some of her usual energy. The rum must have been excellent quality, she thought, as she tackled her breakfast bacon; she had not slept so well for weeks. She quelled the sense of panic that began to rise in her, at the thought of the decisions she must make, and told herself that other women must have faced some of the same problems. Last night she had had a terrible shock; today, she would try to keep calm and deal with it.

No matter how she tried to gather up her courage, she still felt an appalling aloneness amid her difficulties. She longed to have her mother to talk to. She feared Joe's reactions, and, in any case, he was so far away; she must make a decision within a few days, at most.

Before she left for the office, she told Mrs Barnes not to bother to make lunch for her; she would eat at work. That, she thought, would ease the pressure in Elsie's house. She took a last pull at her after-breakfast cigarello and regretfully stubbed it out. She doubted if she could ever stop smoking.

It was easy to say to herself that she would analyse coldly the difficulties she was in; it was much harder to do it. The minute she allowed her thoughts to rest on any aspect of her predicament, such a turmoil of emotion rose in her that common sense was blotted out. Common sense said, 'Go quietly to North Wales for a holiday and be rid of the intolerable burden within you. You have enough problems already.' Sentiment whispered, 'It's Joe's child, an unexpected expression of years of devotion to each other. Remember, you may not be able to have another one. Remember!'

'If the pregnancy is aborted and you can live without Joe, you can stay in Liverpool – and never have to face a Canadian winter again. You can live a civilized, refined life – with every comfort.'

'And without Joe, it would be as empty as the food cupboard before the harvest,' prompted sentiment. 'He's all the family you've got – except for Benji, who in his deprivation of the Estate is another problem of family, blast him.'

Family? What is a child, if not the perpetuation of a family?

In the course of the morning, she and Mr Bobsworth discussed the satisfactory financial standing of the Lady Lavender with two greybeards at the bank. Specimens of their signatures were then put on file, so that cheques could be honoured by the bankers.

Wallace Helena gave only half her attention to these formalities. She kept thinking about her mother delightedly nursing a little grandson; Leila had nearly gone mad when her brothers had died as children in Beirut, Wallace Helena remembered; and here she was, ready to consign her own child to perdition. As one of the bankers tenderly blotted her signature, she wanted to cry.

Though respectful to her, the bank staff persistently addressed Mr Bobsworth and not herself, assuming that he would be in charge of the company's finances, and that Mr Al-Khoury, whose signature they would collect later, would be running it.

With a picture of her mother's grandchild dancing before her, Wallace Helena smartly disabused them of this idea with a polite snub. Responsibility for the soapery was not going to slip away from her like that; it would be passed down the family by her.

It was curious that the unthinking machismo of two old men in a bank should infuriate her so much that it drove her to an immediate decision. But it did. Sparked by bitter resentment, a mother instinct began to rise in a woman who had never wanted to be a parent, feeling that the world was too cruel a place into which to bring a child. Somehow, she swore, she and Benji would nurse the soapery along. It offered a way out from the slavery of a homestead, if not for her, for the baby. And her half share in the homestead might grow more valuable – might even now have a market value, since the railway had come to Calgary and opened it up to Europe.

As she and Mr Bobsworth, looking gravely important, sat quietly in a hackney carriage weaving its way slowly back to the Lady Lavender, she hoped that soon there would be a letter from Joe. She had given him the alternatives; he might feel old enough and tired enough to come to a more clement country and marry her – but there was so little time. She began to panic that some sharp-eyed employee, like old Georgie Grant, used to so many *enceinte* women in the packed streets in which he must live, would spot what Dr Biggs had – and make her name mud in the Lady Lavender. Pride made her clamp her lips together, till her face looked as if it had been hewn from rock. When, a little later, she sent Mr Helliwell out to get some lunch for her from a nearby café, he wondered anxiously what had happened to the charming lady who had asked him to buy a copy of William Wordsworth's work for her. She had given her orders to him as testily as her uncle would have done on a bad day. When he set a pile of beef sandwiches in front of her on her desk, however, she did say, 'Thank you,' and a few minutes later, when he brought a pot of tea for her that he had made himself, she was immersed in reading Mr Wordsworth's 'The Solitary Reaper'. Must've been hungry, he comforted himself, and thankfully went to have his own lunch.

Wallace Helena was unexpectedly very hungry, and she ate all the sandwiches; she did not have the same success in absorbing 'The Solitary Reaper'. No matter how hard she tried, the charming words danced in front of her eyes and made no sense. Eventually, she put the volume down. Crossly muttering, 'Damn Georgie Grant,' she took out a cigarello and smoked it.

It calmed her fretted nerves, but by the end of an afternoon spent in setting down her ideas for the immediate future of the Lady Lavender, for discussion, first with Benji and later with Mr Tasker and Mr Bobsworth, she was coughing badly.

She put down her pen, wiped her face with her handkerchief and looked at the somewhat disjointed jottings before her. It seemed suddenly pointless. If she kept the baby she would be out of circulation for some months, no matter what she planned.

She had gathered from one or two conversations with Elsie that most women did not go out more than was necessary, when they were breeding. Elsie said that middle-class ladies were penned up like chickens. 'If they go out in the street, they sometimes get jeered at,' she had added.

Wallace Helena mentally recoiled, both from the idea of being confined and of being humiliated in public. Her hands clenched in her lap, she stared out of the grubby office window at a sky promising perfect harvest weather. Frustration made her furious to the point of tears.

If the bloody Turks had had an ounce of compassion for their Christian subjects, she considered bitterly, she would probably now be living contentedly in Beirut, with full-grown sons, and summer holidays in Beit-Meri to look forward to; not a real worry in the world. Once one's roots were gone, the normal values by which one lived shattered, it was easy to trip up and be plunged into situations which would never have occurred, had the even tenor of one's life been left undisturbed.

She felt sickened, as she considered the attitude of the men round the Fort, if she had an obviously illegitimate child. She would be open to propositions as if she were a prostitute. They might call after a vinegary woman they believed to be a despised Jewess, but they would not touch her; with a bastard in her arms, it would be far, far worse. Unless Joe married her.

She closed her eyes. Her head throbbed, and she cursed that she had not realized, earlier, what the stopping of her menses spelled out. 'What you don't expect, you don't see,' she fumed helplessly.

She longed for Joe's slow, rich voice patiently sorting out the chaos in her mind for her, pointing out the options she had and the probable outcome of each of them. Between the two of them, they had always found ways out of situations that had left their neighbours decimated; snowstorms, grasshoppers, drought, Indian uprisings, epidemics – they had crawled through all of them to better days. But there was a real joker in the pack this time – a baby, which she was not prepared to plan away.

There was a knock at her office door, and she roused herself. Benji put his head round the door. 'All right if I come in?' he queried cheerfully.

She smiled as best she could and told him to enter. She had not seen him all day, because he had been across the river to Birkenhead, to see a middleman who distributed their products in Cheshire. Now, as he came in, he asked if all had gone well at the bank.

'Quite well,' she told him. She poured herself some water from a carafe on her desk and drank a little.

He stood looking down at her, hands in pockets, and she went on,

'I've arranged for you to see them tomorrow, to give them a new specimen signature. They've now got Bobsworth's and mine, and they'll honour cheques signed by any two of us.'

'Good,' he responded, and then, as she began to cough, he said, 'You *must* see a doctor.'

She was startled by the remark and glanced quickly up at him, her eyes wide, as if suddenly frightened. Then she looked down again at the sheaf of papers on her desk, and replied, 'I saw one last night – and I must remember to pick up the prescription he's making up for me, on my way home tonight.'

The last words came out slowly, as if her mind were elsewhere, and to Benji she looked extremely dejected. He wondered if the sudden absolute responsibility of the soapery was weighing on her. He had expected her to be bubbling with ideas and plans; dejection was not something he normally associated with her.

He had been on his feet all day, so he slowly pulled forward a chair and sat down beside her.

By degrees, he was realizing that the Lady Lavender had always been part of his life and that he did not want to leave it. This meant that he must resign himself to working with Wallace Helena, provided she stayed in England; and, though he often found her maddening, he liked her. She was family, and he felt a surprising warmth at having someone to whom he could speak frankly, without fear of serious censure. She barked and snapped like an irate terrier, but she rarely bit.

Wallace Helena put her elbows on her desk and rubbed her eyes with her fingers. Make up your mind, she ordered herself. You've either got to tell Benji everything and go on from there, or you have to say that you're tired and are going to take a week's holiday in North Wales.

Since she did not seem inclined to start a conversation, he told her about a successful arrangement he had made with the Birkenhead middleman to distribute posters with their washing soap; and he'd cut the wholesale price by a halfpenny to encourage him.

Though she nodded acquiescence to this agreement, she showed no enthusiasm; it was as if a light had gone out.

'What's to do?' he asked himself. Something was wrong. Had the company's finances proved to be in a worse state than anticipated? She had not yet told him the details of her visit to Benson.

'What's the matter?' he asked softly in Arabic.

The sound of her own language always drew her closer to him; it was the language of her childhood filled with nuances of love and respect. His concern was obvious, and she put out her hand towards him in a

239

hopeless gesture. She said with a break in her voice, 'I don't know how to tell you, Benji. How to explain. What to do.'

He went rigid. 'Is it to do with the Lady Lavender?' he asked tensely.

She made a wry mouth. 'Yes – insofar as what happens to me affects it.'

Oh, Lord! Something must have really blown up; she certainly looked a wreck. He swallowed and, filled with foreboding, said, 'You'd better tell me.'

'I'm going to have a baby.'

He looked at her in complete astonishment, and then burst out laughing. 'Well, I'm blessed! Congratulations! You always insisted that you were single and I accepted it. But I suppose you felt it would be better in business to be known as *Miss* Harding?'

'I am single; that's the trouble.'

His grin vanished. 'Are you engaged – or courting?' he asked.

'No.'

He looked at her in wonderment. This stick of a woman casually bedded? She wasn't the type. He couldn't believe it. Benson? Helliwell? Don't be funny, he told himself.

'You weren't attacked – in the street – or down in The Cockle Hole?'

'Raped? Far from it.'

Feeling he was sinking in deep water, he inquired, 'Will the father marry you?'

'I'm not sure. You see, the father is in the Territories, at Edmonton. If I write to him, it'll take months to get a reply – and my condition will be obvious pretty soon. And I'm not too sure that he'll believe it's his – because of the dates.' She gazed at the astonished man before her, the frank despair in her eyes communicating her distress to him.

This is how my mother must have looked, he realized uneasily, when first she knew I was coming. Pity welled up in him.

Wallace Helena was telling him about the obliging nursing home in North Wales, and he instinctively revolted against the idea. To his knowledge, he had not fathered any children himself, so this was the first of a new generation. 'You can't do that,' he protested, 'you could die yourself.'

'Oh, I don't want to lose it. I want it,' she said forcibly, as if to confirm her earlier decision at the bank. 'It's simply that I also want to stay here and see the soapery flourish – and Liverpool is such a beautiful place in which to live.' At the last words, her voice dropped wistfully.

She pursued a slightly different line of thought suddenly, and said, in the hope of conveying to him something of what she had been through, 'I'm so alone – not physically – but I am mentally. There's nobody left who knew me in Beirut, nobody who understands – or has, perhaps, a duty to try to understand, what it's like to be torn up by the roots and be tossed into an absolute wilderness.' She stopped, and he waited, feeling that there was more to come. Then she said, 'At least my own child is part of me, flesh of my flesh, as I was to my mother. It's probably the last chance I'll have to recreate a lost family.' She smiled a little grimly. 'At least I can teach it Arabic!'

Her cousin echoed her smile. He remembered how carefully his father had taught him Arabic; he must have felt like Wallace Helena.

'Would the father agree to settle in Liverpool?' he asked. Who was the man anyway? Her partner?

She sighed. 'I honestly don't know. I doubt if he would be happy here. But I have asked him.'

It must be her partner, Benji decided. His mind began to race. She had said once that the man might like to farm here. He hoped to high heaven that he would not want to poke his nose into the affairs of the soapery; if she didn't have a special marriage contract, the man might well manage to take over the Lady Lavender under some pretext or other.

Wallace Helena was looking at her hands tightly clasped on the desk. She loved Joe, would always love him – and it was his child; she had been completely faithful to him. It was all very well to say that the babe was flesh of her flesh; it was his, too. He was, however, clearly jealous of the people she had met in England, and this sudden pregnancy, after so many years with him without children, would look highly suspicious. She had been a fool, she thought bitterly, to break an iron rule in Calgary. Her mother had always warned her that it took only one mis-count and one could be pregnant. But her fear of the long journey, of doing everything alone, had been overwhelming, and she had given herself to her lover with the despairing feeling that, even on a train, the journey was so long and dangerous that she might not survive. A last fling, she considered wryly.

She laid her face on her clasped hands and closed her eyes. While she smiled at the memory, she cursed herself for being so stupid.

When he saw the gesture, Benji thought she was going to cry, and he leaned forward as if to touch her, but she turned her face towards him and said, 'How can I face the staff here, looking as round as a full moon? I can't. If I go home, what am I to do about the soapery? It takes time to sell anything at a decent price. I'd be as fat as butter before I could make a deal – I've already put on some weight.' She patted her waistline. 'And I don't want to sell,' she finished savagely.

'You could marry me,' Benji said softly. 'We'd get on all right.' And very practically added to himself, 'And you'd bring one hell of a dowry.'

He had the decency to feel a little ashamed at himself for considering that, as her husband, he, too, would indubitably try to gain complete control of the firm; against that, if her lover took it over, it could go out of the family as surely as if she'd sold it.

She straightened herself up, and smiled very sweetly at him. 'Bless you, my dear,' she said gently. 'I can't let you do that.'

He asked quite cheerfully, 'Why not?' He shrugged. 'I know there's a difference in age, but I don't mind – and I wouldn't mind betting that you could produce another little one a year after this one. Two's a nice family.'

She drew out her handkerchief and blew her nose hard. 'Benji, you're sweet. But it's more complicated than that. It would be obvious that the child isn't yours.'

'Who's to know?'

'Everybody who sees it will know. It'll be black – or at least as dark as Alfie at the works!'

42

She saw Benji recoil in shock – and distaste. She hated him for it, and it immediately told her something about the unborn child.

Benji had had a father from the Middle East, but he had been moulded in the streets of Liverpool, a city built on the backs of slaves traded to the New World. To be black in such a city was to be a nobody – and she thought of Alfie, thin, sad, at the bottom of the pile. Not for my child, she thought proudly.

Benji had once or twice mentioned bullying he had endured as a child, not only because he was of mixed blood but because he was also illegitimate. How much worse would it be for a thoroughly brown boy who was illegitimate? How could Benji sit there looking so disgusted, when he had gone through so much himself?

In this she did Benji an injustice; it was precisely because he knew what Wallace Helena's baby would face in the back streets of Liverpool that he was so shaken. He didn't want to be a party to its happening. Better by far that she go back to Edmonton, where presumably there were lots of Red Indians who would look much the same.

Benji simply did not know what to say. Poor little bastard, he thought with compassion. To fill in the silence, he asked her to tell him about the child's father. 'Do you want to marry him?' he asked.

The answer was straightforward. 'Yes, I love him very much.' She lifted her head and stretched herself. 'You ask what he is? He's simply one of the finest men I've ever met.' She went on to tell him of Joe's origins, and he listened fascinated.

At the end, she said, 'He's like a bridge between the Crees and the Metis and white people. He grieves at what has happened to his mother's people. Like his Cree grandfather, he knows that the Crees don't stand a chance against the whites, now the buffalo herds are gone – the herds were a source of food. So he's spent his life trying to smooth out things where he could, trying to ease those he knows into farming. But these people have been cheated by the Government at every turn. So, when he had the chance he joined my stepfather, Tom Harding, in clearing a homestead – and trapping.'

She sighed. 'He and Tom went through some terrible times together – but they were great friends. Now the farm usually provides a surplus of one grain or another – and some meat. Up to now, it's been difficult to sell a surplus – but once the railway reaches us, we'll be able to sell it abroad. There's real hope now – for us – but the Crees, as a whole, are still in sorry straits.'

Her mind wandered from her own difficulties; and Benji saw the absolute fatigue and sorrow on her face, as she saw in her mind's eye the hungry people who often knocked at her door.

Benji roused himself. 'So your little one won't go hungry, if you take him back to Canada?'

'Not while I'm alive,' she replied with grim determination.

'What do you want to do?'

'I really don't know. My very first thought is to go to town and buy one or two nicely draped dresses to hide my condition in the next month or two – it's not really obvious yet, but it will be very soon. I'd noticed that my waistbands were tight, but I thought I was putting on weight from lack of exercise! Do you think a dress shop could help me in this?'

'I'm sure they could. Try Frisby, Dyke's on Lord Street.'

'Thanks. It may buy me a month or so, to get a reply from Joe – and think how best to keep the Lady Lavender going.'

'Well, I can manage it – as you know. So don't worry about it for a bit.'

'I know you can do it, Benji.' She smiled at him. 'And I must remember in all this that I have to take care of you and your dear mother.'

'What about talking to Mother about the baby?'

She considered this suggestion, and then said, 'I don't think I will, for the moment. Perhaps later. What I need is a couple of days, to collect my scattered wits. Then I'll find my way. At the moment I feel like a drunken seaman in a storm.'

She had spoken the last two sentences in English, and he laughed. 'You sound like an American seaman,' he told her.

'Not surprising – I learned my awful English in Chicago, remember – in a slum.'

He nodded. God, she'd been through it, he thought, as he rose. He went round to the back of her chair, and pulled it out for her. She turned, her face close to his. Very carefully, she kissed him on the cheek. 'Thanks, Benji,' she said.

'If all else fails,' he told her, with a quick grin, 'my offer of matrimony still holds. I'd protect the baby – and you – as best I could.'

'I really believe you would. Thank you, my dear.'

43

Prejudice? The spectre raised its ugly head, in Wallace Helena's mind, as she walked swiftly up to Dr Biggs's house to collect her prescription.

Mrs Biggs opened the door to her and invited her into the hallway. A bottle of bright pink liquid, neatly labelled with her name, was waiting for her on a little table. Mrs Biggs handed it to her with a tiny slip of paper which proved to be her bill. She paid this by putting the coins down on the table, sensing that it might be rude to put the money straight into the hands of the doctor's wife.

Mrs Biggs thanked her and told her not to hesitate to return if the cough continued beyond another ten days. Wallace Helena smiled agreement, and wondered if Mrs Biggs knew she was pregnant. She wondered sardonically what the lady would think if she knew the child was coloured.

After the door closed on her, she hesitated on the pavement, and then she turned and walked up to Park Road, in the hope of finding a small shop that sold baby clothes. John Patrick Fitzpatrick had to have a present.

'Would it be for a boy or a girl, Ma'am?' the stout female behind the counter inquired.

'A boy.'

'Ah, then. It's blue you'll be wantin'?' She added coyly, 'Blue for boys; pink for girls.'

This was news to Wallace Helena, who had, for most of her life, seen only little papooses tucked into wood backed bags on their mothers' backs. She accepted the word of the shopkeeper, however, and bought a blue knitted jacket. Then, feeling this was not enough, she bought a crocheted baby blanket, as well. Armed with these offerings, she went down to The Cockle Hole to have her dinner.

When she lifted the latch of the front door and entered, the house looked far from pristine; it did not even smell the same. An untidy woman met her in the hall. She had a bucket full of nappies in one hand.

'I'm Mrs Kelly,' she told Wallace Helena. 'I'm doin' a spell while Chrissie Barnes 'as gone to see to her hubby. I thought I'd do a fry-up for yez. It don't take long.'

'That sounds fine,' Wallace told her, though she was not certain what would arrive on her plate. 'May I go up to see Elsie?'

'For sure. She's learnin' the baby to suck, but she won't mind.'

The bedroom was stuffy and smelled of dried blood and another distinctive odour, which was, Wallace Helena supposed, a damp or dirty baby. The young mother was propped up in the muddled bed. She had opened her nightgown to expose perfect swelling breasts, and she was patiently trying to persuade the baby to accept her nipple.

At Wallace Helena's hesitant entrance, she hastily pulled the sheet up over the baby and her breasts, and greeted her with pleasure and apologies that her tea would be late.

Wallace Helena said it did not matter and sat down on the chair by the bed. 'How are you?' she asked, 'And how's the baby?'

Tenderly, Elsie slipped back the sheet, so that her lodger could admire the crumpled red face of her first-born. Large, blank eyes stared back at her between folds of fat, and tiny lips moved uncertainly. 'Would you like to hold 'im?' Elsie asked, and she lifted the tiny bundle and held it out to Wallace Helena.

Wallace Helena braced herself to take the weight without dropping the child – and was startled to find that it seemed to weigh almost nothing. She cradled the baby instinctively and looked down at the child's fuzzy head. In less than six months, she thought with wonderment, I'll be holding my own baby. And then a real fear that she would not know how to care for it struck her; she suddenly longed to ask Elsie to help her, show her what to do, prepare her for the advent of the child. And, if it's born in the Territories, it'll still be winter. What shall I do in that remorseless cold?

Elsie's voice broken in on her reverie. 'Shall I take 'im back, Miss? He might spoil yer frock.'

Wallace Helena forced a smile and handed the child back. She then proffered the parcels she had brought, and with one hand Elsie shook the presents out of their tissue paper. 'They're lovely, Miss. Proper kind of you – but you shouldn't have . . . you didn't have to.'

Wallace Helena told her it was a pleasure, and she was delighted to see mother and child so well. 'Oh, aye,' responded Elsie cheerfully, 'I'll be up and around a bit tomorrer, and the place won't be in such a mess.'

'Don't put yourself out for my sake. Mrs Barnes has been most kind, and I'm sure from the nice smell coming up the stairs that Mrs Kelly is making something good.'

'Oh, aye. I've wonderful neighbours. Most of them was in, some time

246

or other, today; and they all brought a bite of food to help out – and some of their men's out of work, an' all.'

'I'm glad they're so kind.' Wallace Helena made her farewells, and went downstairs, wondering who would come to her aid when her child was born.

A perspiring Mrs Kelly was just coming out of the kitchen carrying a plateful of food, and Wallace Helena sat down to a dish of bacon and eggs, fried bread and fried cabbage, with a pile of bread on the side. Wallace Helena said it looked wonderful and ate the lot, while her brain searched for the best way to deal with her own child.

Dr Biggs had said she should have a specialist available, because she was older. This meant, though, that she would have to be delivered in England. On the other hand, if she went home, Joe would probably marry her – or would he? And there would be only Aunt Theresa to help the baby into the world – unless Aunt Theresa knew someone at the Fort who was knowledgeable and would come.

She had a bad night, and by morning she was still no further ahead. A crying baby did not help.

She rose early and washed herself in cold water from the ewer in her room. When she went downstairs, John Fitzpatrick opened the kitchen door and looked a little alarmed. She put her finger to her lips and then said quietly, 'I'm going for a little walk. Don't worry about me.'

John looked relieved. 'Thank you, Miss. I'm away to work in a minute, but Mrs Barnes'll come to make your breakfast and help Elsie.'

'Rough night?'

A grin spread over his face. 'A noisy one, Miss. I hope you weren't bothered.'

'Not at all,' she smiled.

She walked down to the slipway. Mist was clearing from the river and in places the sun dappled the water. People were already astir in the cottages, and a canary sang sweetly by an open window.

She wondered what these fisherfolk would think if a black man came to live amongst them – or a black child.

She was not certain of the answer, so she posed the question the other way. What would Joe feel like, hemmed in by cottages, docks, warehouses and manufactories? She knew the answer immediately.

Unless he saw possibilities in it which she could not envisage, it would be like trying to cage an eagle from the Rocky Mountains; he would wilt and die. The baby as it grew up might make some sort of a place for itself. But not Joe.

She realized that he was too old to change much. And why should he? Apart from being part-owner of a fairly successful homestead, he

247

was well regarded in and around the Fort and among his Indian relations; his knowledge of Indian languages and his negotiating abilities were prized by both sides. Apart from that, he and Wallace Helena herself had lived in the district far longer than most of the inhabitants and had acquired a degree of wisdom in handling both livestock and crops in such an inclement climate; Joe was often asked for his advice.

On the whole, she thought, Joe did not suffer too much from being black. She knew from the taunts she had received that it was his association with herself, a yellow woman, which put him at a disadvantage. Moreover, both she and her mother, being educated, considered themselves superior to ordinary folk; they weren't humble like the Chinese labourers who worked on building the railway, she thought sarcastically.

But, if she went home, what was she to do about the soapery? To sell it, she must somehow gain some time. And then she remembered Frisby, Dyke's – the shop which Benji had mentioned.

With sudden determination, she turned back towards her lodgings. Outside the house next door, two little girls had marked out the pavement ready for a game of hopscotch. She stopped, and asked if their mother would let them take a note to the Lady Lavender. Fingers in mouths, they said they didn't know – they would ask her.

A thin harridan in a dirty apron came out and said she didn't want the girls straying. Her son would take it on his way to work, if that would suit the lady. Wallace Helena took her notebook out of her pocket and hastily scribbled a note to Mr Helliwell to say that she would not be in until ten-thirty. She tore out the page and addressed it. She gave it to the woman, together with a threepenny piece for the boy.

After breakfast, she tidied herself and walked up to Park Road, where she caught a horse tram to town.

She found Messrs Frisby, Dyke and Company at 58 Lord Street. She had never been inside such a large shop, and she paused before entering to look at a pretty display of dress materials in the window. Then, summoning up her courage, she approached the door. It was courteously opened for her from the inside by a white-whiskered shopwalker in a stiff white collar and a morning coat. He bent slightly towards her and asked if he could help her. She told him that she needed at least two dresses, and would like to be served by an older assistant.

'Yes, indeed, Madam. Gowns and Mantles, Madam. Come this way.'

It was early and the shop was not very busy. She noticed that all the young women dusting or arranging their displays wore skirts like she did, but the older ones looked quite fashionable in garments with fitted waists, modified bustles and an apronlike drapery at the front; such dresses were not going to offer much disguise for her present condition, she decided with some trepidation. They passed through a department selling scarves and handkerchiefs, and she was suddenly charmed by a tree of hankies being created by a young woman standing on a stepladder. She shook out each hanky and poked it into a metal frame. To Wallace Helena, the result was like a pine tree of white and pastel colours, and her tight lips curved in a little smile.

Haberdashery was the only department that was so busy that the assistants could obviously hardly deal with the rush. All the customers were very young women, with swatches of material clutched in their hands. The shopwalker had paused, to make a way for her through the throng. 'Who are these young women?' Wallace Helena whispered.

The old man smiled. 'Dressmakers' apprentices, Ma'am. Not well-mannered at all, Ma'am. They're matching cottons and buttons and bindings for their employers.' Faced with the back of a struggling girl, he said, 'Now, Miss, make way,' and with a scared look on her pale face, the girl stepped back, and Wallace Helena swept after her escort.

He handed her over to a middle-aged lady neatly gowned in rusty black and with a velvet pincushion shiny with pins buttoned to her left wrist.

Since Wallace Helena was not known to the shop she stated frankly that she was expecting and wanted some dresses to disguise the fact for as long as possible.

The woman bowed slightly. 'Of course, Madam. Madam will not wish to remain indoors longer than necessary. May I ask your name, Madam?'

'M – Mrs Harding.'

'Ah, yes.' She wrote the name down on a pad hanging with its attendant pencil from her waistband. To her, Wallace Helena did not look very prosperous, so she said, 'We have a number of dresses made up, or partially made up – requiring only fitting and finishing. Our dressmaker can adjust anything to suit you. Or we can arrange for any pattern to be made up for you, in any material you desire?'

Amused by the formality, but feeling pressed for time, Wallace Helena said she would try on some of the ready-made ones. 'Suitable for everyday wear and for walking out,' she added, fearing suddenly the arrival of dinner gowns.

The woman was a genius, Wallace Helena thankfully decided. After measuring her customer, she found her a plain grey wool dress with a softly defined waistline. It had a loose overjacket with long grey velvet lapels that closed with a single button below the waist. A white fichu tumbled in frills to fill the neckline of the jacket. Though it made the expectant mother look stouter than she was, it would disguise an expanding waistline for a little while. It was the nicest frock Wallace Helena had ever owned.

She also bought a black cashmere costume, with a loose, fringed wrap and two different black bodices; the latter, though cut out, had to be made up. 'We cut them quite generously,' the shop assistant assured her; she had been temporarily joined by an elderly cutter and fitter, attended by a shrimp of an apprentice who gazed popeyed at Wallace Helena. The two new arrivals circled round their customer with a polite, 'Pardon me, Madam,' as the apprentice passed pieces to the cutter and that lady draped them on Wallace Helena and stuck pins in strategic places.

Once the fitting was completed, the shop assistant stepped forward again, and said, 'You will be surprised how well it will look, Madam, and it will certainly hide your little secret for a few months longer.'

The small apprentice had been picking up dropped pins. At the assistant's remark, she glanced up in surprise. The fitter saw the glance, as she was taking the pinned bodice off Wallace Helena, and she scowled at the girl and told her to get back to the workroom; apprentices should not stare at a customer – it might disconcert a lady.

Wallace Helena smiled at the shop assistant, and before she knew where she was, she had also been sold a grey silk dress, which had obviously been designed for the portly older woman. It had a drape of silk from one shoulder which swirled gently across her small chest and then round her waist. The result was a suggestion of the apronlike drapery which many women seemed to be wearing, but without a tight waistline. 'For best occasions,' the shop assistant said firmly, and the cutter murmured that Madam looked charming.

Feeling greatly cheered up and quite pleased with herself, Wallace Helena asked when the bodices would be ready.

'In two days' time, Madam. We can send them up to your house. The other slight adjustments can be done in twenty-four hours.'

Wallace Helena was alarmed. She said hastily, 'I'll come in – I enjoy coming to town. And you can see them on me – and make sure that everything is just so.'

Pleased by the implied compliment, the assistant agreed to this, and then asked cautiously, 'Madam has an account here?'

'No. I'm a visitor. I'll pay for the dresses now, and for the costume when I come for the clothes.'

As the assistant wrote out the bill, she inquired politely, 'Madam is from America?'

Wallace Helena froze slightly. She did not want to be identified. After a second, she said, 'Yes. From Chicago.'

'I trust Madam is enjoying her visit?' The assistant pushed Wallace Helena's sovereigns into a little brass tube, screwed it into a container hanging above her head, pulled a handle and, to Wallace Helena's delight, the whole contraption shot across the store, to be fielded by a prim gentleman seated in a tiny glass-enclosed office. Her change came back the same way.

It had been a most entertaining hour and she felt much better; the dresses should buy her a couple of extra months.

In the workroom, the small apprentice, Lena Grant, was bursting to tell her friend, Bettina, who sat next to her, that a lady whom she knew to be a Miss had a *little secret*, and she had just bought three dresses to cover it up. She dared not open her mouth, however, while the dressmakers were sitting nearby and constantly calling for cotton or tapes or bindings or even their heavy dress forms.

She worked until seven-thirty that night and forgot about her piece of gossip until she got home.

Her grandfather, Georgie Grant, had preceded her and was eating his tea at the bare wooden table in the tiny living-room. Her widowed mother was sitting opposite him, her youngest son in her lap. Lena had passed her other two brothers, who had been playing in the street.

"lo, Mam. 'lo, Grandpa,' she greeted them, as she took off her hat and hung it on the back of the door. 'Guess what I saw today. Your Miss Hardin', Grandpa.'

'You did?' He stuffed some more bread into his mouth and pushed his cup across to her mother to have it refilled.

The girl pulled out a stool and sat down at the table. She snatched up a piece of bread from the wooden board in the centre of the table, and began to eat. 'Oh, aye, and you know something, Mam? She's expectin'.'

Georgie Grant swallowed and then put down his piece of bread and the spoon with which he had been eating stew. He looked at his granddaughter in stunned amazement. Then he warned, 'Be careful what you say, you stupid judy. You probably got the wrong woman. You don't know Miss Hardin'.'

Lena tossed her head, and said, 'Everybody round here knows her. We see her walkin' over to the works from The Cockle Hole – that's where she lives, int it?'

Seeing fury slowly mount in Georgie's reddening face, her mother said anxiously, 'Now, Dad!'

Georgie half-rose from his seat. He shook his spoon in his granddaughter's face and roared at her. 'You mind your own business, you busy lizzie! What the gentry does int none of your business. You keep

251

your bleedin' mouth shut or you'll soon be out of a job – and I'm not goin' to feed you, if you go on like that.'

Lena cringed away from the old man. 'I didn't mean nothin', Grandpa.'

He leaned forward and hit her with his tin spoon. She yelped with the pain, and he shouted, 'That's nothin' to what I'll give yez if you so much as open your mouth again about Miss Hardin'. First, it's a bleedin' lie and, second, if it int, all the more reason to keep your gob shut.'

He plunked himself back in his seat and his daughter handed him his refilled cup. Lena began to whimper and then leaned towards her mother. 'I didn't mean nothin', Mam!' she howled miserably.

'Jaysus Mary!' the old man swore and got up from the table. 'Shut up, will yez.' He picked up his cap from the mantelpiece and slammed it onto his head. 'I'm goin' for a jar,' he said, and swung out of the tiny house.

As he walked angrily down to his favourite pub, he muttered to himself, 'Our Mr Benji's jumped the gun, I suppose. The stupid bugger! Couldn't wait to ring the bell. The kid must've heard her say *somethin'* – Lena don't lie.'

44

Back in her dusty office, Wallace Helena found that Mr Helliwell had opened the mail and put it on her desk.

'I gave two complaints direct to Mr Benjamin, Miss Harding – and an order to Mr Bobsworth. I believed you'd wish them attended to immediately.'

'Very sensible, Mr Helliwell. I forgot last night to ask Mr Al-Khoury to give me some time today. There are all the papers handed to me by Mr Benson yesterday to go through. See if he could arrange to spend the afternoon with me.'

Mr Helliwell bowed and was about to leave the room, when she called after him, 'And ask Alfie to get me something to smoke. Here's a florin.' She slapped a silver coin onto the end of her desk.

Rather shaken, Mr Helliwell turned quickly round, his mouth open as if to say something. He was forestalled by Wallace Helena who assured him with a twinkle in her eye that she was not going to smoke in the office.

He ventured to smile back at her and went off quite jauntily to find Benji. The old girl was much more herself this morning, thank goodness.

Wallace Helena skimmed quickly through the pile of letters on her desk and then knocked them into a neat pile again ready for Benji. She got up from her chair and unhooked her reticule from the coat-stand near the door. She opened it to take out Dr Biggs's medicine and a spoon. Then she took the prescribed dose, and made a face as she went over to the tiny sink in the corner of the office to rinse the spoon. In the excitement of going to Frisby, Dyke's, she had forgotten to take the medicine after breakfast and had snatched up the bottle as she left the house.

As she dried her hands on a small towel, she began to pace up and down the narrow room, methodically sorting out in her mind, first, where the child was to be born and, second, whether to put the Lady Lavender on the market. She kept coming back to what Joe would think about the child.

Then she began to worry about her employees. She did not want to sell the company only to see it almost immediately closed down. It was small in comparison with other companies making soap; yet it had the potential for growth. A bigger company might very well buy it to get rid of the competition.

Into this rumination intruded the idea that she could leave Benji to manage the firm for a few months, until the child was born; then, perhaps, keep the baby outside the city with a wet nurse.

It would not solve the matter, she decided almost immediately. The baby would still be as illegitimate as Benji, and that, added to its colour, would leave it terribly disadvantaged, no matter how well she endeavoured to educate it and provide for it.

And could she really desert Joe, for the sake of a comfortable life? She stopped dead in the middle of the dull brown linoleum of her uncle's office, as she faced the question squarely.

Through the open window, she heard the yard foreman shouting at his labourers, and the thud of boxes being loaded on a cart. A horse neighed and jingled its harness. Beyond these noises, it was as if she heard a door slowly close, as she answered, 'No.'

With no one watching her, her face saddened and, if Joe had been there, he would have recognized the resigned despair which he had seen on the scratched face of a fourteen-year-old girl riding towards him on a borrowed horse, so many years ago.

She must go back to Fort Edmonton; and trust that, when Joe saw the child, he would be convinced it was his.

She heaved a great sigh, and wanted suddenly to go home soon, to get it over with, to pick up the threads of her settler's life before the winter really set in, and plan with Aunt Theresa how best to deliver the baby. She smiled wryly. It wouldn't be the first child to be received into a fresh rabbit skin, instead of a blue crocheted blanket.

Perhaps the sedation of the cough medicine had lowered her resistance a little, because she sat down suddenly, and began to cry slow, hot tears, not because of her current predicament, but for all the intense effort she had made since the terrible day when her father had lowered her from the roof of her home, while fire from other homes made a thick haze round them. She had stayed alive, she told herself, as she took out her handkerchief, but it seemed as if she was never to be allowed to crawl onto a plateau where she could rest – and *enjoy* life.

When Benji came in to say that he had asked Helliwell to get both of them some lunch, so that they could gain more time that afternoon, he found her sitting quietly, her head bent, her handkerchief clutched tightly in her hand.

She looked up at him and he saw the empty hopelessness in her wet eyes. She seemed to have aged suddenly. She nodded agreement to working and lunching with him at the same time. Then, she grinned at him unexpectedly, and ordered, 'Tell Helliwell to bring a pot of hot, very strong tea. I need it.'

He was relieved to see her smile, and he asked, 'Would you like a bottle of wine? He's not yet gone to get the lunch – he could bring one in.'

'Yes,' she agreed slowly. 'I'm not sure what it does to babies, but I would like a glass.'

Benji laughed. 'I'm sure the little tyke can stand a glass or two. I'll tell Helliwell.'

As she sipped a rather raw Italian wine from a teacup, Benji was thankful to see some animation return to her.

She proposed a toast to the longevity of the Lady Lavender, and they drank it with gusto; it cheered him up. After hearing that she was in the family way, he had worried about his own future. Now, at least she seemed to think the firm would survive; otherwise, why had she toasted it?

She brought out the papers she had received from Mr Benson. They went through the various financial statements, so that it was clear to him that the firm was in a sound position. Then she told him about the box of gold sovereigns. 'It was in the bank strong-room – a dead weight – and three locks.'

He whistled. 'No wonder he wouldn't part with a halfpenny if he could help it.'

'I'm sure he intended to plough the money into the company, as he seems to have done before, at times.'

'Yes, he did. I can remember a couple of times when he went on a spree of buying for the firm.'

'It seems to me, Benji, that he intended to bring the firm right into the 1880s; and I think his first moves were to recruit Mr Turner and Mr Ferguson.'

'I wouldn't be surprised.'

'Well, I'm having the sovereigns transferred to a special Capital Account, so that if all goes well it can be used to mechanize production, or start a new line – when we're ready. I shall keep it in such a way that, if I have to sell, that account remains with me.'

Benji sighed, and she said to him robustly, 'Now stop worrying. I have an idea in mind, but I want first to see Mr Benson and possibly talk to the bank people again. All you have to do is to keep the place going for me, and in a couple of days or so it should all be sorted out.'

'Have you heard from your partner, then?'

'Not yet.'

He waited for her to say more, but she seemed satisfied that they had

255

completed what she wanted to do, so he took out his pocket watch, and said, 'It's still quite early, so I'll get back to my desk.'

She nodded agreement, and he unfolded his big, rumpled body from his chair and tucked his pencil into his breast pocket. He took up the notes he had been making and folded them into a neat square. 'See you later,' he said, and moved towards the door.

'And Benji,' she called to him, as he was about to turn the handle.

'Yes?'

'You're a sweetheart.'

He grinned in sheepish surprise, and left her.

She put her head down on the desk and burst into weary tears. Now, she had the difficult job of convincing Mr Benson about what she had decided to do, without telling him that she was pregnant.

45

Mr Benson was unable to see her for two days, so in the meantime she collected her new dresses from Frisby, Dyke's. The enterprising shop assistant led her over to the Millinery Department and persuaded her to buy a new autumn hat which went with both the daytime dresses. She failed to sell her a pretty little veiled straw hat with a bunch of white feathers at the side to wear with the grey silk, for tea parties. 'Enough is enough,' said Wallace Helena grimly. The shop assistant wondered suddenly, when she saw Wallace Helena's forbidding expression, who her client really was; her rather shabby old-fashioned clothes had suggested someone of neither wealth nor eminence. Now, when Wallace Helena was shown out of the store by the shopwalker, she was not so sure.

That morning, Wallace Helena had received a letter from Joe, in response to one of hers in which she had first hinted at the idea of his coming to Liverpool and making a new life with her in the city. In four lines, he told her to hurry up with selling the soapery and come home. Did she realize she had already been away two months?

And now it's over three months, Wallace Helena considered irritably; Dr Biggs had made her acutely aware of the calendar.

The following morning, she walked through the soap works dressed in her new black skirt, bodice and carefully draped shawl. She looked round the stables and commended the stableman on their cleanliness, peeped into the carpentry and wheelwright's area and nodded good morning; she noticed that it was well swept – Benji had obviously followed up on her complaint about the plant's housekeeping. As she crossed the yard, she noted that it had been washed down and sanded. She spent a friendly half hour with Mr Tasker and suggested that they try again to get an apprentice or two for his department. He sucked his teeth over this, while he watched one of his men check the contents of a boiler and, at the same time, considered her suggestion.

Satisfied, he stepped down again and apologized for interrupting her. 'What with the silicate of soda and the boilin' of the soap, the framin', the crutchin', and checkin' of supplies, I've got me hands full. There's no end to it all.' He rubbed his hands down his thighs, and moved a little away from his assistants, to say quietly to her, 'I need a real bright youngster to train. These lads are all right, but they'll never be soap masters.'

Wallace Helena smiled, though she took his remarks very seriously. She assured him that she and Mr Al-Khoury were discussing a better organization of the work throughout the plant and he would certainly be consulted. Meantime, he should consider a good apprentice, or even a journeyman who had already some experience in soap-making; perhaps there was someone he knew who would like the job.

Within herself, she was saying goodbye to all her employees. With their tremendous humour, their eccentricities and their obvious interest in the Lady Lavender as an entity, they had enriched her life; and she wondered how she was going to bear her isolation when she returned home.

As she was crossing the yard to the Power House, she saw Georgie Grant. He was waiting to unload a wagon of barrels of fat. The carter was backing the horse to manoeuvre the wagon into a more convenient position.

'Good morning, Mr Grant.'

George straightened his bent shoulders a little, his wickedly shrewd blue eyes staring as he took in the obviously new dress; he could smell the newness of the material. So young Lena had not made a mistake.

'Mornin', Miss,' he said, smiling kindly, his few ugly teeth well displayed. 'Nice mornin'.'

'It is indeed, Mr Grant,' she replied, and passed on.

He watched her as she went up the steps of the Power House, and weighed her up carefully. Then he turned back to the wagon to unhitch the tailgate. He suspected that Lena had been right about there being a bun in the oven. Mr Benji had better get a move on and get the banns called.

Being received by Mr Ferguson was a bit like being received by a prince in his palace, Wallace Helena thought with amusement. Mr Ferguson belonged to the new wave of skilled mechanics, and he knew it.

After a few pleasantries, she asked him if there was any spare capacity in his installations – if she wanted to put new machinery into the plant which would need additional power.

'For sure, Miss. Much of what you see is fairly new; the Ould – I mean, Mr James Al-Khoury, had in mind to expand – and when he engaged me and the present power plant was built, we made plenty of provision.' He hooked his thumbs into the braces that held up the bib of his overalls, and continued, 'I told 'im to allow for expansion – and he done it.' While she digested this information, he took off his peaked cap, which he regarded as a badge of status, and scratched his balding head. Then he said, 'I reckon he were dead set on expansion, Miss. And put a lot of what he made back in the business. And very good he was at driving a bargain.' He grinned at her, his ruddy face shining in a shaft of sunlight. 'And so is Mr Benji; he learned 'im!'

She surprised him by holding her hand out to him when she was leaving. He took it shyly and shook it. 'Thank you, Mr Ferguson, for being so helpful,' she said, as she withdrew her hand, and he saw that, though she stood as straight as a guardsman and that her lips smiled, the expression of her eyes and the lines of her face were those of someone who had endured considerable grief. He wondered how old she was. Younger than he was, he reckoned. He longed to ask her if she was going to manage the company, but felt he had been forward enough; no doubt Mr Benji would tell him soon.

Her lips trembling, Wallace Helena made her way back to her office. A few minutes later, Mr Helliwell brought in her mid-morning cup of tea, and found her leaning back in her chair, her eyes half-closed, the lustrous lashes failing to disguise the fact that she had been crying.

At his entry, she straightened up quickly and he mentally kicked himself for having forgotten to knock at the door before entering.

She thanked him, and he asked, with some anxiety, if there was anything more he could do.

'No, thank you,' she replied. 'Mr Al-Khoury can deal with the letters. You know I have an appointment with Mr Benson for this afternoon. Perhaps you had better order a hackney for me for a quarter to two.' She made no effort to wipe her face.

Though he remained as calm as a good butler, Mr Helliwell was shocked. Something was definitely wrong; she had not really been herself for several days, though her cough seemed to have diminished, thank heavens.

He promised to order the carriage, and withdrew to his own small cubbyhole next door. He prided himself on being aware of everything that went on in the works, but he could not think of anything which would reduce Miss Harding to tears. Rage, yes; but not tears.

Benji breezed in, with a list of items he wished to discuss with Wallace Helena. 'Is she free?' he inquired, nodding his head towards his cousin's door.

Mr Helliwell replied in an uneasy whisper. 'She is – but she seems very upset about something. Perhaps you should leave her for a few minutes.'

'In a temper?' Benji had known Mr Helliwell since the man had first started work with them at the age of thirteen, as an office boy; there was real affection between them.

259

Mr Helliwell screwed up his lips. 'Far from it,' he responded, again in a whisper. 'She's upset – like a woman.'

Benji restrained a grin. Apparently Helliwell did not think that, normally, Wallace Helena belonged to the feminine gender. 'I'll chance it,' he said, and went to knock on her door. An unexpectedly firm voice bade him come in.

He stood over her, big and clumsy-looking, his list in his hand. He saw immediately that she had been crying; she had the wide-eyed, heavy, exhausted look his mother sometimes had after a spate of tears.

'What's up?' he asked, without preamble. He himself was feeling good. The fact that she was, indeed, leaving the general management of the soap works to him had restored some of his customary optimism. To add to it, his mother had remarked, only a few evenings back, that if she was a Lebanese as good as his father she would never do anything to harm him – he was all the family she had.

Until now, he thought suddenly, and felt a twinge of jealousy about the coming child.

In answer to his question, she replied, 'Have a seat. Nothing's really happened. I got a letter from Joe in response to one of mine some time back. He wants me home, as I thought he would. I'd hinted that he should consider coming here, but he's ignored it. I've written since, of course, telling him about the baby, but it'll be weeks before I get a reply – and, frankly, I don't think it's worth waiting for one.'

'Don't cry,' he comforted. 'Things'll work out.' He wondered if he should again ask her to marry him. Not yet, he told himself. Let Joe Black make a move.

He went on, 'You know, you shouldn't have to bear all this alone; you should tell Mother; she can be as silent as a tomb – but she could be a comfort to you.'

Wallace Helena nodded. Eleanor was indeed very kind. 'Will she be home tonight?'

'Yes,' he replied, with relief.

'I'll come about eight, if that's all right. Now, what've you got on that list?'

46

When Wallace Helena called on Eleanor Al-Khoury that evening, she found her alone.

'Our Benji hasn't come home yet. He said he'd be late – he sent me a little note by that coloured lad what works in the Lady Lavvie, so as I'd know you was coming. How are you, love? You're lookin' a bit peaky.' She took Wallace Helena's hat and shawl from her, and ushered her into the front parlour. 'All me gents are out tonight, so we can have a nice little get-together in here. Haven't seen you in ages.'

Wallace Helena kissed her and asked how *she* was.

Eleanor heaved a deep sigh. 'I'm not so bad, all things considered.' She moved towards the fireplace in which a small blaze gave cheerfulness to the room. As she bent down to put a black kettle on a hob and turn it over the fire to heat, she said, 'Sit down by the fire, love. Aren't the nights drawin' in? I made a fire 'cos it seems to be a bit chilly.'

Wallace Helena obeyed, and asked, 'What's making Benji late?'

'Well, he said the other day you gave him all the files in his dad's private drawer to read – so he thought he'd do it when he wouldn't be interrupted. I've saved him a bit of dinner for when he comes.'

Wallace Helena nodded. She decided Benji was probably making the reading of the files an excuse to give her time alone with his mother. Aloud, she said, 'I felt that, as Manager, he'd better know everything about the company – his father's private negotiations with suppliers, anything there was about the staff. I've read them, and they do contain good background information.' She bent towards the fire and rubbed her hands to warm them; she had not bothered to put gloves on.

They chatted desultorily about the weather, and agreed that they had both enjoyed an organ concert to which Benji had taken them about three weeks earlier. 'Aye. Mr Best's a lovely organist – there somethin' about organ music, int there?'

Wallace Helena agreed there was, and wondered how to bring up the question of her pregnancy. She helped Eleanor to lift a small tea table closer to the fire and, while Eleanor poured boiling water into the brown teapot, she mentioned that her landlady, Elsie Fitzpatrick, had had a lovely baby boy, and that her mother lived in Dublin and could not come to her.

'I expect the neighbours came in,' Eleanor responded placidly. 'Everybody loves a baby.' She stirred the pot vigorously, and put a teacosy over it while the tea mashed.

'I suppose,' Wallace Helena replied. She stared into the dancing flames of the fire, and then she said, 'Eleanor, Benji suggested I should come to see you tonight – because, quite flatly, you're the only woman who might care about me or mine!'

Eleanor had just lifted the milk jug in order to pour milk into the teacups – her best ones. Now she put it slowly back on the tray.

'What's to do, love?'

'I'm in the family way myself, Eleanor.'

'And it's our Benji's?'

Wallace Helena laughed suddenly. 'No, no. I'm much too old for Benji – though, when I told him about it, he did offer to marry me – to protect me, so to speak. Bless him.'

'You mean you're not married?'

'Right.'

'Well I never.' She was quiet, while she poured out two cups of tea. Then she said gently, 'Not to worry, love. If our Benji wants to marry you, and don't mind being a papa to your baby, you haven't got nothin' to worry about. There's a few people at the Lady Lavvie as would be thankful if you was married to each other.' She smiled warmly at Wallace Helena, and continued, 'And I can think of lots worse to have as a daughter-in-law. I know you're older, but you don't act like it. Benji'd be fine with you.'

'You're very kind, Eleanor,' Wallace Helena replied, with genuine gratitude. She went on to explain that, even if she loved Benji to distraction, she would not dream of marrying him, because the child would not match up. 'Literally, it won't,' she assured a puzzled Eleanor. 'It'll be too dark.'

'Too dark? Well, who is its dad? Will he marry you?'

'Its father's my partner in Canada. He's half-Cree, half-negro, so his baby's going to be dark. He's a fine person, and I'd be happy to marry him. But, Eleanor, I'm in a terrible jam.' She stopped, and Eleanor waited, wondering what on earth was to come. 'You see, Eleanor, I must've conceived in the last day or two of my time in the Territories. He might not believe it's his. I'm terribly afraid, Eleanor.' The last words came out in a rush.

The other woman took a moment to assess this, then she said, with a laugh, 'He'll believe it when he sees it. There int many Blackies rou nd these parts – and you'd never meet any, anyways.' She put some more

262

sugar in her tea and then stirred it. She added, with dry humour, 'Rub the kid over with boot polish, to make sure!'

Despite the strain she was under, Wallace Helena began to gurgle with laughter. It set Eleanor laughing, and soon they were rolling in their chairs with mirth. It finished when Wallace Helena had a fit of coughing.

'Really, Eleanor! You're dreadful.'

When they had sobered a little and had mopped up the tea they had spilled, Eleanor asked, 'Will you be going home?'

'I'll have to. For a while, I had a hope that I might persuade Joe to settle here – the last few winters have bothered him; we get such bad ones. But thinking it over, I know he'd never be happy here. So I'll go home. I want the baby to have a father.'

'Oh, aye. That's important.' Eleanor's face was suddenly very sad, and Wallace Helena ventured to ask, 'Why didn't you and Uncle get married?'

'Me hubby's still alive,' answered Eleanor, her voice dull and hopeless.

Wallace Helena's mouth dropped open in complete surprise. 'I didn't dream you'd been married. I don't think Benji knows, does he?'

Eleanor looked at her suspiciously, wondering how much Benji had talked about her with his cousin. She sighed, and said, 'I don't think nobody knows by now. It were a long time ago.'

'Couldn't you have divorced him?'

'I couldn't – being Catholic, like. Anyways, what for? He's mental, you see.'

'You poor woman!' Wallace Helena forgot her own problems. 'How did it happen?'

Eleanor swallowed, and looked round her rather helplessly. 'It were really me dad's fault,' she said. ''Cos I were so young – and proper innocent; with no brothers or sisters so I could see the difference between boys and girls – or guess where they come from. I didn't know what marrying was all about.' She twisted her arms into her apron, as if to protect herself from something, and then she went on, 'You know me dad left me this house?'

'Yes.'

'Well, he and me mam run a boot and shoe shop for years. Me dad were much older 'n me mam; but she were killed in a fall from the stepladder in the shop, when I were ten. And me dad couldn't stand the shop after she were gone, so he sold it when his auntie died and left him this house; and we started doing bed and breakfasts. We had some as was waiting for a boat and some as come on holiday to see relatives, or somethin', and not a few commercial travellin' gentlemen on their rounds.' She sighed gustily. 'I used to make the breakfasts and see to the washin' and all.'

'That's a lot for a ten-year-old.'

'Me dad helped with the cleaning and that, and he'd carry some of the trays. And it were better'n working twelve hours a day in a shop or being in service.'

'So, how did you meet your husband?'

'Well, when I were about sixteen, he come here with his mam and dad. He must've been about eighteen. They'd come from Cardiff on a visit, they said, and they was ever so friendly. They stayed about ten days, going out and about all over the place. We supposed they was on a holiday, but it come out afterwards they come to show the boy, Hughie, to a specialist.'

'Did he look mad?'

'No. Just a bit stupid, like some youths do. He didn't talk much, and he did whatever his dad told him – and I realized afterwards that him or his mam told him every step of the way. He weren't too bad-looking – dark hair and blue eyes, like a smiling china doll. I was never alone with him for a minute – his mam or dad saw to that. Dad watched out for me pretty well, too, seeing as men were always coming and going in the house; but mostly much older men – being sales reps, like.'

She sniffed, as if to dismiss salesmen as not being worthy of much notice. 'Anyways, his parents made up to me dad like anything, and, two months later, they come back for another stay. They said as Hughie's uncle had got him a job, here in the docks. He were a big, heavy boy, so it sounded likely. And it seemed no time at all before his pa was saying to Dad what about a match between us.'

'Didn't your father see that he wasn't all there?'

'No. If you weren't expecting it, it weren't too obvious. When his mam said to kiss me, he wouldn't, and she said he were a proper shy lad. When he was alone with me, he'd be a lion, she said – and I remember her laughing.'

'Doesn't sound as if there was much to laugh about,' Wallace Helena said. 'What happened then?'

'Well, me dad hadn't been well for some time, and I think he were worried about me being left alone; and here were a decent family with a son with a job, a quiet enough boy who didn't drink – none of the family did. So he said it would be all right. And I were sixteen and thought, like most young girls do, that married life would be less work than being single; and me dad was going to buy me a new dress. I felt that important!

'So Mr Jones goes with Hughie to get a special licence – 'cos they've got to get back to their business in Cardiff. No time for calling guests or anything, and the next thing I know I'm in church being married, and Hughie being whispered to by his dad as to what he's to do and what fun it will be.' She paused reflectively. 'And that frightened me. We got back to the house, and I'd baked a cake and decorated it, so we had tea and cake. And Hughie was laughin' like an ape and eating half the cake. Then Mr Jones brought down their luggage, when a hackney come for 'em. He says goodbye, Hughie. They canter down them front steps as if the devil was after them, and away they go, leaving Hughie standing gaping in the hall. Me dad shuts the front door, and Hughie nearly goes berserk. He smashes the glass in the inner door, and out he goes, with his hand bleeding, screaming, 'Mam!' after the carriage.

'Me dad went down the steps after him, wondering what had bitten him. Hughie turns round and hits me dad to the ground and comes back up the steps. I ran upstairs, I was so frightened. And I could hear him smashing the tea things on the table and then a big crash as he threw something through the sitting-room window here. He was a big lad and he made such a noise, a neighbour come out. Dad shouted to him to call the constable. Dad come in and couldn't see me; only Hughie tearing everything apart in an absolute little-boy paddywack, kicking and screamin'.

'I called Dad from upstairs, and he shouted back to stay where I was. It took the constable and me dad and the neighbour to arrest him.'

'How awful!'

Eleanor nodded. 'I were that scared, I thought I'd never come round,' she admitted.

'Whatever did you do?' asked Wallace Helena.

'Well, both me dad and me was terribly upset, as you can imagine. When Hughie were brought before the Magistrate, Dad went down to the Court. He told them he thought the man was mad, and told how he come into our house. The Magistrate agreed with him and the poor constable did, too. So they sent him to a hospital to be examined, and then they put him in a loony-bin.'

'And is he still there?'

'Not in that one. They finally traced 'is parents – they'd given us a wrong address, 'cos what they was doing was dumping him on us – getting rid of him, never wanting to see him again, like. He were like a little kid in his mind, and he acted like one when he realized his mam was leaving him with strangers.

'Me dad was heartbroken that he'd been had like that. All he wanted was a respectable fella to live in the house with me and bring a bit in. He died himself not too long after.'

'But it was considered a legal marriage?'

'Well, a long time after I heard that the Church could annul it. You see, being Catholic, as I said, I couldn't divorce him. It's a big job to get an annulment – and it costs. And the priests ask you such terrible private questions. And I were still young – I hardly knew what normally happened after the church service – working in the house all the time. I didn't have a close girl friend to talk to, like other girls have.'

'Did you talk to your priest?'

'I went once,' she said sulkily, 'and he read me a penny lecture about having to stay married even if your husband was sick. In them days, I was scared of God and the priests, so I took their word for it. I wasn't going to get married again, anyway – not after that basinful.'

Wallace Helena leaned forward and caught her hand. 'You poor girl,' she said.

Eleanor smiled dimly at the kindly gesture, and said, 'Then, years and years later, your Uncle Jamie come along.' A slow tear ran down her cheek.

'Did Uncle James know what had happened to you?'

'He did later. After Benji were coming, he wanted to marry me. But, you know, I couldn't apply for an annulment without the whole neighbourhood knowing. And as long as I kept quiet I doubt there was anyone around who knew the marriage had taken place, except the priest. Our next-door neighbour took it for granted that Dad had just had a spot of bother with a lodger.' She leaned towards Wallace Helena confidentially. 'And if I let it be known – or the Church did – that I'd been married to a loony, they could likely think that I were without me wits, too. And that would be proper awful for me – and for Benji. It'd only need a bit of a rumour.'

'Would they really be that stupid?'

'Oh, aye. They're more afraid of lunacy than anything else round here. Once they feel it's in a family – goodbye!'

'So you and Uncle James stayed quietly together?'

'Yes. It were a bit rough on Benji, but better than it going round that, maybe, he were me husband's kid and, therefore, tainted.' She sighed again, 'And I believed Jamie when he said he'd never leave me. Nor he never did. He were took, poor dear.'

She bowed her head and wept.

Wallace Helena hastily left her chair and eased her way round the tea table to comfort her. With her head against Wallace Helena's skirt Eleanor cried heartily.

'And now,' she sobbed, 'you got to go home, so the Lady Lavvie'll have to be sold – and what are we goin' to do, I'd like to know?'

'You've nothing to worry about there,' Wallace Helena assured her, as she took out her own grubby hanky to wipe Eleanor's face. 'Everything's going to work out just fine – as long as Benji agrees.'

There was the sound of a key in the front door lock.

'That'll be Benji,' his mother said, and hastily wiped her eyes with her hands. 'What was you sayin'?'

'I said everything's going to be all right. Just wait till Benji's here, and I'll tell you.'

As a very tired Benji came into the room, she straightened up and forced herself to smile. Behind it, she felt as weary as he looked. She had had to give comfort, when she had hoped to receive it.

47

That afternoon, Wallace Helena had spent over two hours with Mr Benson.

As soon as she was seated in his private office, she had gone straight to the point.

She said, 'You will be pleased to hear that I have reached a decision about the Lady Lavender.'

Mr Benson nodded, and drew a notepad towards him. 'What are you going to do?' he asked, with real interest.

'I'm going back to Canada,' she told him. 'But I don't want to sell the Lady Lavender.'

'Oh, really?' he queried, in some surprise.

'Yes, really. I want you to draw up an agreement between Mr Benjamin Al-Khoury and myself, which will make him a full partner in the enterprise. So that we share the company half-and-half. He'd run it – he'd have full responsibility for it.'

The lawyer looked at her in some perplexity. 'That would be very generous, Miss Harding. You do realize that you'll be sacrificing a considerable capital sum – which you'd get if you sold the property?'

'I know,' she replied, a little irritated because she was tired. 'But I believe I'll get a steady income out of my share of it for many years – and Benji – Mr Al-Khoury – has to be considered.'

'Does he know about this plan?'

He was surprised when she answered in the negative. He had imagined that young Benji had sold her the idea. She said, 'I'm buying his expertise with a partnership. If I leave him as Manager, he could be easily tempted to go to another soap company for higher pay – and I would not trust a new man. Then I would *have* to sell.'

'I see.' He sat quietly for a minute, while he thought the matter over, and she wondered if she could possibly explain to him the closeness which had grown up between her and her cousin. Would a lawyer understand such closeness? Or did he, as a family solicitor, have to negotiate, too often, between factions warring over Wills?

Finally, she said, 'As far as we know, Benjamin and I are the sole survivors of our family; we have no roots, except what lie in each other. Because of this and because I think he's an extraordinarily capable young man, I'm going to give him the chance of making a good living. He can draw a salary as Manager, and then whatever we make we share. Simple as that!'

'You have thought this over – and you're certain this is what you want to do?'

'Yes.'

'Well, frankly, I'm delighted for Mr Al-Khoury's sake. I've felt a great pity for him, ever since his father died. Mr James Al-Khoury always said that he could not have a better son.'

'He couldn't have had a more capable one,' Wallace Helena said.

They hammered out the details of the agreement, and Mr Benson promised to have a draft ready for her and for Benji to consider within a week. She reluctantly agreed to this. She wanted to be gone. The winter was coming.

It was the content of this interview that she unveiled to Benji and his mother, as they sat round the kitchen table while he ate his warmed-up dinner.

When she said flatly that she was arranging with Mr Benson that he should have a full partnership with her, he leaned back, fork and knife still in hand, and stared at her dumbfoundedly, and his mother, who was not quite certain what the partnership implied, looked anxiously at her son.

Then as it sank in, he swallowed hard. 'I don't know what to say!' he blurted out.

'Don't you like the idea?'

'Wallace Helena, it's wonderful! I never dreamed of such a thing.'

Wallace Helena heard Eleanor let out her breath as she relaxed. She leaned across the table to pat her hand absently, as she watched Benji. He put down his knife and fork, pushed himself away from the table and came round to her. He put his arm round her shoulder, and said, his voice thick, 'I won't fail you. It's going to be tough, but I believe I can make something out of the Lady Lavender.'

'What do you mean? Tough?'

'The competition's very keen.'

'Tush! We're tougher. As I once said, "We live in interesting times!"'

He squeezed her shoulder and went back to his dinner. 'When do I start?' he asked, an eager light in his eyes.

'In about two weeks' time.'

Eleanor had seen the same expression on his father's face, the face of a man accepting a challenge. There's a lot of Jamie in our Benji, she thought happily.

'Are you ready for your puddin', luv?' she asked.

48

Joe had fumed and fretted for weeks over Wallace Helena's prolonged visit to Britain. Admittedly, she wrote regularly to him, keeping him informed of what she was doing. He did not reply to all she wrote; he was hardpressed in her absence, first with the harvests of barley, hay and vegetables – and what little was left of the oats after a hailstorm, and then with the preparations for winter.

He had sometimes used Emily to help him and Simon Wounded, because the two hired hands were not very reliable and they had a fair herd of cattle to watch this year. Aunt Theresa complained when Emily was borrowed from her; she wanted her in the kitchen, to help to make pemmican and preserve vegetables.

As long as she did not have to go near the hired men, Emily never complained; she was easily frightened by any strange male, and she clung to Aunt Theresa as if she were still a child clinging to the nuns. It was as if she had suffered so much as a little girl that her mind and her normal responses to other human beings had been frozen. Joe did not think of her very much; she was simply another person to be fed and clothed in return for her work. Emily's real love, however, was for the hens that she fed and kept clean; they roosted in the barn and would come fluttering down from the beams, when she called them to be fed in winter. In summer, they fended for themselves and she clipped their wing feathers, so that they could not stray very far. During Wallace Helena's absence, she had set two clutches of eggs under broody hens, and she now had a goodly number of pullets scratching round the yard. She was anxious to show Wallace Helena how the flock had increased, before some of her feathered friends had to have their throats slit; the flock was thinned severely every year, once the weather became bad, because they could rarely spare enough grain to feed a large number of birds until spring. She ventured to ask Joe one night over supper when he thought Wallace Helena would be home.

Joe had become more and more taciturn as the summer passed. He fought a growing fear that she would never return. He sensed that she had been seduced by the city – she was originally a city girl, wasn't she? He hoped that one of the fancy men around her had not also seduced her. Aunt Theresa had told him not to worry; but if Wallace Helena, without him, felt anything like he did without her, the temptation to seek consolation would be very great.

In answer to Emily's question, he grunted, 'Dunno.'

'Maybe there'll be a letter when you go down tomorrow,' Aunt Theresa suggested, as she ladled beans onto his tin plate. She spoke in Cree.

It took precious time to fetch the mail from the village which was growing up round the Fort; yet he knew he would go, because his longing for something of her was so great.

There was a letter. As was his custom, he slipped it into his jacket pocket; he would read it while on the trail riding home. Though a few more people now used the trail, it was still no more than a muddy lane, and ice from an early frost crackled under his boots as he dismounted to open the letter.

He was stunned by its content. A baby? How did he feel about becoming a proud father at his age? At her age? At first he grinned sheepishly. Then the idea hit him that it wasn't his – she said it was due in March.

It was as if he had been unexpectedly struck by a friend. The hurt in him felt worse than the pain he had suffered when he had caught the smallpox. Here she was, making smart little jokes that he would have to go out and shoot a rabbit so that there would be a warm skin to wrap it in – and yet how could it be his child?

By mutual agreement, they had always followed her mother's regime, so that they would have no children in such a harsh environment; he himself was easy about it because the tribe from which his mother came was either dead or scattered; his children would not have any particular group to belong to, and Wallace Helena had nobody, except her new-found cousin in Liverpool.

His attention had been so completely caught by her news of the baby that he hardly took in the information that she had divided the soap works between herself and her cousin; and that, given ordinary luck, there would be a remittance each year from her share, some of which could be used to help them out at the homestead.

His face was grey as he remounted and rode towards home.

As the sun sank lower, a cold wind arose in the north. It freshened him, and he tried to order his chaotic thinking and decide how he would deal with the situation.

She had said in her letter that she would probably be sailing across the Atlantic before the letter reached him; that meant she could be in Calgary within a week or two. What should he do?

When he rode into the yard and dismounted, he still felt so distraught that he thought he would vomit. Emily had just shooed the last of the

271

hens into the barn for the night, and he asked her if she would stable the horse and rub it down for him. She took one look at his stony face, and nodded. She patted the animal and it went with her. His hunting dog, Bessie, heavy with puppies almost ready to drop, trotted over to him and nuzzled his hand. He ignored her, and she slunk away.

As he opened the heavy, wooden door into the cabin, Aunt Theresa looked up from the hearth; she was making bannock for supper. The cabin was still redolent with the smell of the dried meat, fat and berries of the pemmican she had made earlier in the month. Most of the work had been done outside, but she had finished the pounding of it indoors, because, she said, the wind had been so keen that it had made her old bones ache. Now, the smell was mixed with that of bannock, and to Joe it felt welcoming and homely.

He pulled out a chair and thankfully sat down. Aunt Theresa noticed, as he took off his felt hat and laid it on the table, that he was shivering slightly. He put his hand into his shirt pocket, took out Wallace Helena's letter and flipped it onto the table beside the hat.

Aunt Theresa got up slowly from her squatting position and, in the silence, Joe heard her knees crack as she straightened them. The door also creaked, and he looked up. He had forgotten to shut it properly, and Bessie, his dog, nosed her way in. Half looking at Aunt Theresa, she slid almost on her stomach towards the fire. Aunt Theresa did not like dogs in the house, but Emily had accidentally shut her out of the barn, where she had found a warm corner in which to deliver her pups, and she knew her time was very near.

Aunt Theresa ignored her. She was far too concerned about her nephew. 'You ill?' she asked. She looked down at the letter and feared, suddenly, what it might contain. At no point had she thoroughly understood why Wallace Helena had had to go to Liverpool, the concepts involved were too far removed from her own experience.

Joe sighed. 'No, I'm not ill,' he said.

Aunt Theresa bent down and expertly turned over the bannock cooking on the hot stone in the hearth. 'What does she say?' she asked suspiciously, pointing to the letter.

'She's coming home – home within the month, I'd think.'

'You don't sound too happy about it.'

'She's going to have a baby.'

Aunt Theresa's normally immobile face broke into a suggestion of a smile. 'Well, that'll be good – we're all getting too stuck in our ways; there *should* be youngsters around.'

'How do I know it's my kid? We never had any before,' he snarled.

Aunt Theresa had turned back to her cooking. Now she froze where she stood. She was outraged.

When she found her voice, she was almost snarling herself. 'Joe Black! You've no reason to doubt her. She's never been flighty; if she had been, she'd have found a way to do it long since.'

'If it's not mine, I don't want it.'

'This is her home – and yours. If she wants to have it here, she'll have it here.'

'It don't mean I've got to stay here. I can go anywhere and make a living.'

Aunt Theresa clenched her teeth. She bent and took the last bannock to cook off the stone and wrapped it with the others in a cloth. Then she came round the table, to face her nephew. She had no children of her own, and he was the nearest thing to a son to her.

She said softly to him, 'We've all been together in this cabin for a long time; we know each other – and we've learned to trust each other. She's always shared what she had with us, good times and bad times. And she saved your life, when you had the smallpox, remember? If the child is yours, it's great to have a kid, especially if it's a boy; if it's not yours, then she'll need all our help very badly – she wouldn't be coming home if that weren't true.'

He did not respond. After she had waited for a moment, she touched the crouching dog's flank with her moccasined toe. 'You're not turning Bessie out because she's come home with a belly full of pups; are you going to turn away from Wallace Helena when she needs a place for her baby?'

He swallowed, and said, 'It'd be hard to be father to another man's brat.'

'Bah! It wouldn't be the first time a man's found a good kid by taking in a foundling. Anyway, she'd tell you straight if it wasn't yours – she's not afraid of anyone.' She put a comforting hand on his shoulder. The wrinkles on her face rippled as if, suddenly, she was trying to control a smile, and then she asked him, 'Are all Englishmen white?'

He looked sharply up at her in surprise. 'Sure,' he said. 'I've never seen a black one.'

'Well,' responded Aunt Theresa, with a flicker of triumph in her expression, 'where's she going to get a brown baby from in England? Any kid of yours she has is going to be easily recognizable.'

He stared blankly at her for a moment, and then he began to laugh, almost hysterically.

She did not let him see the triumph in her eyes. She merely said, in her usual gentle way, 'Now you get your stuff off the table so that we

can have supper. Simon and Emily'll be in soon – starving, as usual.'
She busied herself round the fire, and then remarked, 'I know I'll be
thankful when Wallace Helena's back – there's too much work without
her. And if we're going to have a little kid round the place, I'll enjoy
it, I know that.'

Joe nodded, and slowly took off his boots and jacket. He went to the
water barrel and took out a pannikin of water to wash his hands. Aunt
Theresa spread tin plates round the bare table.

'You know, Joe,' she said to him, 'lately I've wondered who would
look after you and Wallace Helena when you grow old. Our tribe's
scattered, your uncles and cousins are dead, except for one – and he's
in gaol in Montana. There are no young men to take a lead in bringing
the tribe together again. I reckon you need a kid more than you need
anything in the world.' She slapped spoons down by the plates. 'It'd be
someone to continue here, after all the work you and Tom have put
into this place – and Wallace Helena.'

He bit his lower lip and did not answer her while he wiped his face
with a bit of towelling. She had brought up a subject which he had
never before considered. He and Wallace Helena had always been smart
enough to plan ahead for the homestead; but he himself had rarely
thought about his old age. When he had thought of death it had always
been because of an immediate threat – epidemics like scarlet fever,
diphtheria, tuberculosis, a dozen scourges to which prairie dwellers had
been subject. He remembered his terror the day he had been cut off
by a forest fire – that would have been fast but painful death. And out
on the trapline, alone, a small accident could incapacitate a man
and leave him to freeze to death. There had been for years the
hovering fear of starvation. That he and Wallace Helena might
grow old and weak, in need of the help of others, had never occurred
to him.

As he sat down at the table, he shuddered at the idea of being dependent upon others; but that was why his old grandfather had had a
number of wives – to breed sons to protect the tribe and their hunting
grounds when he was too old to do it, the best man amongst them to
take his place when he died.

He never said a word throughout supper. Afterwards, he went over
to the hired men's bunkhouse to have a word with Simon Wounded
about the work for the next day. Then, though the temperature was
dropping fast, he sat on the fence and again thought about becoming
old.

Amongst the surviving Cree and Blackfoot, he had a number of
friends and even distant relatives; he also considered some of the Metis

who had settled round the Fort to be his friends, though Wallace Helena would have little to do with them; she had, in her youth, been too often insulted by them. Some of them already looked older than he himself did!

Partly because he had left his grandfather's lodge so young and partly because of the decimation of normal Indian life by the intrusion of white people – even the first settlements thousands of miles away in the east had had a ripple effect across the country – he had considered himself a loner, perfectly capable of looking after himself. He had never considered that he might need care from someone else.

Even as a young man, he had realized that the traditional Indian way of life was coming to an end, and he had seen the wisdom of joining up with friendly, easy-going Tom Harding in an endeavour to wrest a living from the land. That decision had been a wise one, which had brought Wallace Helena into his life as a wonderful, additional gift.

He was lucky, he reflected, as he struck a match to light another cheroot, that he had a large homestead – half a large one, he corrected himself – which was flourishing very well. And now Aunt Theresa had suddenly knocked his feet from under him, by telling him he needed a child because he was going to grow as old as some of the toothless gaffers sitting on the bench outside Ross's Hotel on a warm summer day. And who do they live with? he asked himself suddenly. The reply came equally fast – with their sons or daughters!

So, for his own sake, Aunt Theresa had advised him to welcome Wallace Helena's baby, foundling or not.

He did not like the way his thoughts had led, and he jumped off the fence, to walk up and down the frozen yard. He was getting stiff with cold, he realized.

He was reminded of Wallace Helena sitting with him on the fence, evening after evening, and it was with deep longing that he considered her imminent return. Suppose Aunt Theresa was right and that the yellow bastard who was her cousin had not touched her; that by some fluke the child was his own? How did he feel about that?

Could the kid have been conceived in Calgary? That had been quite a wild night. He had always trusted her to tell him when they should not make love – he never bothered to count; his days were always so busy he was lucky if he knew whether it was Monday or Friday.

She'd been afraid that night, afraid of the long journey and of meeting a whole bunch of strangers, the first time he had seen her really nervous for years. He had tried to comfort her and she had cuddled into him, maybe thinking she'd get away with it, for once. Maybe she hadn't.

275

He slowly began to grin. He stopped walking to look at the moon shining through slowly falling ice crystals. He took a quick pull on his cheroot, dropped the butt and ground it under his heel. That, he decided, would be something else.

49

Wallace Helena sat silent and withdrawn beside the driver of a Red River cart, as it bumped its way along the familiar trail from Fort Edmonton to her home. The path was already covered by a light fall of snow and the trees that lined it were leafless; only a few spruce amongst them stood straight and proud, their evergreen branches holding a sprinkling of snow. Except for the piercing shriek of the ungreased wheels of the cart, there seemed to be no other noise. She had forgotten how still the countryside could be in winter; her ears had become attuned to the constant rumble of heavy horse-drawn traffic on city streets.

The five-day journey by stagecoach from Calgary had drained her strength to such a degree that she wondered if she would manage this last five miles without fainting; bearing a child certainly took all one's stamina, she decided ruefully, her hands clasped across the base of her stomach to ease the jolting of the cart.

In view of her condition, Benji had insisted that she should travel second class on the boat, rather than steerage, which to save money she had been prepared to do.

'You're not that poor,' he had told her with a laugh. 'In any case, I won't hear of it; somebody's got to take care of you – and you'll have more care second class.'

Parting from Benji had been much harder than she had expected. Once he knew about the baby and then about the partnership, he had cared for her as if she was something infinitely precious. He showered affection on her, as did his mother. Once again, he offered to marry her, saying he would do his utmost to help the baby.

It would have been so easy, she meditated, to be cosseted at home and be the soap mistress in public. And Benji loved her, she felt, even if he were not in love. Young and vigorous, he would have given her another child inside twelve months.

And yet, she could not imagine life without Joe. It was no good. Without him she felt she barely existed. And it was his child. So here she was going back to the day-in-day-out battle of being a settler.

'You're as crazy as a coot,' she told herself, but she grinned with anticipation of the end of the journey.

It was as well that Benji had insisted on a more comfortable sea journey, because she had been so seasick that she had feared she would miscarry. The steward had finally suggested that she would be better up on deck in the fresh air, and she had dressed and crawled up, to sit in a deck chair. The man had brought her a few precious apples to eat.

He had been right, and on the third day the seasickness had abated. Wrapped in a heavy winter shawl, a farewell gift from Eleanor, she was soon walking unsteadily round the deck.

In the fresh sea breeze, she felt suddenly happy to be going home. Her longings for Lebanon had slowly declined in the friendly atmosphere of Liverpool. When she had been tired or depressed, it had been to Joe that her thoughts had turned, or sometimes simply to the sunlit, snow-covered landscape and the keen, clean winds of Alberta. Lebanon, with its lovely scents, orchards, wines and silks, its wondrous mountains and tumbling rivers, its cosmopolitan, sophisticated people, had receded, had become an unattainable Garden of Eden, to which there was no return.

Perhaps, by the time her baby was grown, Lebanon would have thrown off the Turkish yoke and be at peace, and he could visit it, to see from what great beauty his mother had sprung. A sweetness from it would remain with her always, like the delicious after-taste of a good lemon sherbet; but she sensed that she would never see it again.

In her womb, feeling very uncomfortable with the bumping of the cart, lay a child whose roots lay in the history of the Northwest Territories. She smiled a little ironically when she thought about it. Its father would teach it to farm and trap, and she would teach it all the languages she knew, especially Arabic. Perhaps, by the time it was old enough, it could journey east to Upper or Lower Canada to have better schooling than the nuns and the priests in the Territories could give it.

When she and Joe were gone, it would own the biggest farm in the immediate neighbourhood and half of a soap factory in Liverpool; with luck, it would have friendly cousins in that city whom it could visit. It would have its niche in the world.

She began to think about the farm. After much debate with retailers, she had not brought any agricultural implements with her; instead, she had brought a number of catalogues from them for Joe to see.

When staying in the house of her grandfather's frail old friend, Mr Nasrullah, for one night after landing from the boat at Montreal, she had again mentioned to him her continuing interest in new farming practices. He had assured her that one of his sons, who lived with him, had already been asked to obtain any papers or magazines he could from eastern Canadian sources, for her. 'He knows everybody worth

278

knowing,' the old man assured her, his dark eyes twinkling. 'He says there's a lot of research being done in Upper Canada, and with the postal system so improved because of the railway, he'll put you in touch with the right people.'

She had been very comforted at realizing that there was at least one more family in Canada which spoke Arabic, though the old man complained that his grandsons spoke only French, and to be assured that the Northwest Territories were not nearly so isolated as they had been. It was with a certain amount of hope that she sat in the train for over two days and watched the hundreds of miles of forest and silent lakes past which the train chugged. It disturbed huge flocks of birds, but very few other living things, except for an occasional tiny settlement. Winnipeg had been a turmoil of people, mostly men; other than that there was little to suggest that human life existed.

She had been bitterly disappointed that Joe had not been at Calgary to meet her, though it was probable that he had not yet received her letter giving the likely time of arrival.

Because the weekly stagecoach up to Edmonton would not leave until the following day, she stayed the night at the same hotel in which she and Joe had stopped on her outward journey. The public rooms seemed full of male rowdies, so she prevailed on a hurrying young man in a white apron to bring her up a plate of dinner, and to obtain for her a basket of bread and cheese to sustain her on her journey north. The following morning, the same youngster helped her down with her luggage and onto the stagecoach.

She and a sturdy-looking Scottish youth were the only travellers; the driver said he thought some people had been deterred by the threat of snow.

In an accent which was difficult for Wallace Helena to follow, the boy confided that his name was Alex McLeod and that he had come from Glasgow to be a clerk with the Hudson's Bay Company. He was most impressed when she told him that she had farmed near the Fort since 1862, and he was further impressed when she slipped effortlessly into French to speak to the Metis driver.

Her attitude to the young Scot was very different from that which she would have exhibited had she met him before her visit to England. Though in Britain men had sometimes patronized her unmercifully, she had met with a lot of friendliness in Liverpool, and she had responded to it. Added to this had come the realization that, though she and Joe had lived their lives in comparative isolation, her baby would need friends. Her instinct to protect the child and smooth its path had become

279

intense, and the lonely, rather scared young clerk was the first to experience her change of heart.

The driver knew who she was and her reputation for arrogance; he was surprised that she bothered to speak French to him and was pleased at her straightforward friendliness. They became quite a merry party.

The journey was bitterly cold, as if the wind was coming through snow. They were grateful for the four stops they made en route, where they could rest for a while, the horses were changed and the calls of nature dealt with. By the time they left Red Deer Crossing and were on their way to Battle River, Wallace Helena had become so fatigued she wondered if she would survive the remaining hundred miles. She was fortunate that snow did not hit them until they were on the last part from Peace Hills to Edmonton; it came down in short, sharp flurries, which made it difficult for the driver to follow the trail. It also seeped through the inadequate canvas roofing of the stagecoach and accumulated in a caked mass on the robes covering the passengers.

When they finally drove down the hill to John Walter's ferry and could see the Fort on the other side of the river, Wallace Helena was truly thankful; and young McLeod, though forewarned what to expect, wondered what on earth he had come to. They descended while the coach was loaded onto the ferry and they crossed the river, and they finally parted at Mr Ross's Hotel, McLeod to report to the Fort, Wallace Helena to seek rest and a meal in the hotel.

She felt better once she was thoroughly warmed and fed, and she was able to arrange for a carrier with a Red River cart to take her out to the homestead.

Now, as she was driven along the home trail, on top of her fatigue was the anxiety regarding the reception she would get from Joe. Perhaps he had not come down to Calgary to meet her because he was furious with her? Did not believe the child was his?

It was Aunt Theresa's sharp ears that first heard the squeak of the Red River cart and then the creak of the yard gate opening; it was Emily who ran out to hug her as she descended. Old Simon Wounded came limping out of the barn which he had been mucking out; he reeked of manure, but, with tears in her eyes at how he had aged in her absence, Wallace Helena flung her arms round him. He simpered shyly. Aunt Theresa met her at the cabin door to welcome her with her familiar gentle smile.

She stumbled into her home and sat down immediately on the nearest chair. Slowly she looked round her.

It was very untidy, she noted with a faint grimace, and it needed cleaning; but it had the same homely simplicity as Elsie's house down by the Mersey River; everything in it was there for a purpose.

While Aunt Theresa invited the driver in to have something to eat before he returned, Wallace Helena unpinned her hat. Emily promptly took it from her to examine it. She had never seen such an interesting bit of headgear before, and she giggled at it.

Wallace Helena closed her eyes; she was swaying on her chair with a fatigue deeper than she had felt for many years. Yet it felt so good to be home. Until she had arrived at Edmonton, she had not realized how well she understood her surroundings in Canada; everything was perfectly familiar to her. It was a harsh world that had helped to make her what she was and she knew how to cope with it. Except for Joe. At the moment, she was not too sure how to cope with him.

'Where's Joe?' she asked carefully.

Simon Wounded answered her. 'He's up checking the windbreaks – for the steers. We both reckon heavy snow is coming in. I thought he'd have heard you coming.'

'Wind's in the wrong direction,' Aunt Theresa told him absently as she brought out her coffee mugs.

'I'll go up and get him,' Simon Wounded offered.

'No. Don't bother him. Let him come when he's finished. I won't have coffee, thanks, Aunt Theresa. I need to lie down for a while. It's been a long journey. Could you bring my luggage in, Simon, when you've finished your coffee?'

She got up and lurched to her bedroom. The bed was a tumble of feather-filled covers, which had replaced the buffalo robes of long ago. She took off her boots, coat, skirt and bodice and, in her petticoats, lay thankfully down and pulled a quilt over her and slept.

She was still dead-asleep when, in the late afternoon, Joe came into the room. He stood looking down at her, and then he grinned. He was in his stockinged feet and now he threw off his jacket and very quietly crawled in beside her. She stirred and murmured, 'Joe, you old devil,' and took him in her arms.

*   *   *

Three weeks later, Joseph Black, bachelor, and Wallace Helena Al-Khoury Harding, spinster, were married in the little wooden church of St Joachim, in the hamlet of Edmonton. It was a small gathering attended by only a few Roman Catholic Crees, a few Metis friends of the bridegroom and their wives and children, and a young Scottish lad, Alex McLeod, recently come to serve the Company.

Leila Helena Black was born on 10th March, 1887, to astonished,

281

adoring parents. She was helped into the world by wise old Aunt Theresa and another knowledgeable old Cree lady friend.

'A girl!' Joe exclaimed. He began to laugh. Already besotted, he touched the tiny scrap of humanity's dark cheek with a tenderness surprising in so big a man. 'I can't teach a girl to trap, or – or castrate a bull!'

Wallace Helena turned her head on the pillow. 'Why not?' she demanded. 'Women can do absolutely anything, if they set their minds to it!'

He bent to kiss her, and said, with mock resignation, 'I guess if they're your kids they probably can.'

SELECT BIBLIOGRAPHY

Anonymous Liverpool and Slavery. A. Bowker and Son. Liverpool, 1884

Bibby, John P. *The Bibbys of Conder Mill and Their Descendants*. J. P. Bibby. Liverpool, 1979

Bibby, J. B. and C. L. *A Miller's Tale*. J. Bibby and Sons. Liverpool, 1978

Becker, Horst J. *Gateway Guide to Jordan, Lebanon, Syria*. Methuen. London, 1967

Cotton, E. J. *Buffalo Bud*. Hancock House Publishers. North Vancouver, 1981

Dempsey, Hugh A. *Big Bear – The End of Freedom*. Douglas and McIntyre. Vancouver, 1984

Dempsey, Hugh A. *Indian Tribes of Alberta*. Glenbow Museum. Calgary, 1988

Fawcett, Raymond, Ed. *Soap – Where Does It Come From?* Gawthorn. London, 1949

Gell, Robert. *Liverpool's Railway Stations 1830–1985*. Heyday. Crosby, 1985

Hitti, Philip K. *The Near East in History*. D. Van Nostrand Co., Inc. Princeton, 1961

Horne, J. B., and Maund, T. B. *Liverpool Transport Vol. 1*. The Light Railway Transport League. London, 1985.

Jackel, Susan. *A Flannel Shirt and Liberty*. University of British Columbia Press. Vancouver, 1982.

Jarvis, Anthea. *Liverpool Fashion, The Dressmaking Trade in Liverpool, 1830–1940*. Merseyside County Museums. Liverpool, 1981.

Leonard, David. *Richard Secord*. Richard Secord. Edmonton, 1981

Loren, W. *Black People Who Made the Old West*. Thos. Y. Crowell. New York, 1977.

Macdonald, George Heath. *Edmonton – Fort – House – Factory*. Douglas Print Co. Edmonton, 1959

MacGregor, James G. *A History of Alberta*. Hurtig. Edmonton, 1972

MacGregor, James G. *Edmonton, A History*. Hurtig. Edmonton, 1967

Metcalfe, V. *Journey Fantastic*. McGraw-Hill Ryerson. Toronto, 1970

Mohr, Merilyn. *The Art of Soapmaking*. Camden House Publishing, Ltd. Camden East, 1979

Nevitt, R. B. *A Winter at Fort McLeod*. McClelland and Stewart. Toronto, 1974

Pears, A. and F., Ltd. *The Story of Pears' Transparent Soap*. Pears. London, undated

Scott, Dixon. *Liverpool*. Adam and Charles Black. London, 1907

Thubron, Colin. *The Hills of Adonis*. William Heinemann, Ltd. London, 1968

Williams, Edmund. *The Story of Sunlight*. Unilever PLC. London, 1984

Wright, T. W. *Overlanders 1858 – Gold*. Western Producer Prairie Books. Saskatoon, 1985

The Moneylenders of Shahpur

This is a novel. Its situations and characters
are imaginary. No reference is made or
intended to any person living or dead.

Extracts from *The Panchatantra*
translated by Arthur W. Ryder.
Copyright © 1956 Mary E. Ryder and Winifred Ryder.
Published by the University of Chicago Press.
All rights reserved.

To Dianne, with Love

You are worried when you hear that she is born;
Picking husbands makes you anxious and forlorn;
When she marries, will her husband be a churl?
It is tough to be the father of a girl.

At her birth she steals away her mother's heart;
Loving friends, when she is older, fall apart;
Even married she is apt to bring a stain:
Having daughters is a business full of pain.

The Panchatantra,
trans. by Arthur W. Ryder from the
Kashmiri version 1199 AD.

PROLOGUE

'They'll think I'm mad,' muttered Dr John Bennett to himself, as he waited for the station porter to load his luggage into a tonga. 'To come back to India, when so many Indians are trying to settle in the West. It won't make sense to them, even though I was born and brought up here.' He smiled wryly to himself. 'Mad dogs and Englishmen . . .'

For over a year now, he had been thinking seriously of returning to India. He was bored by his job as lecturer in Asian Studies. He was tired of Liverpool, its cold, its dampness, its depression; he longed for sunshine. Suddenly, he could stand it no longer. He had his Air Force pension and some savings; he had no family. At the end of the 1949/50 university year, he packed up his books and joyfully took a boat out to India.

Now he stood unsteadily at the top of the imposing steps of Shahpur station, a thirty-four-year-old Englishman, whose war wounds in his legs ached abominably, and wondered if he would still be welcome; India had, after all, fought very hard to rid itself of the British, and it had had its freedom for only two years.

People pushed and shoved past, their luggage perilously poised on the heads of porters. Where once there would have been a number of white faces amongst them, now there was none. Amid the crowds of Hindus and Muslims, a fair sprinkling of Jains stood out, distinguished by their plain white clothes and their more sedate movements.

Looking across the railway lines, he could see the Chemical Works which his father had managed until his death. He observed from the neon sign that its name had been altered to the Star of Asia Chemical Company, and a large addition had been built. The smell of sulphur and other chemicals from it far outweighed the more traditional odours of horse manure and open drains.

He shifted his weight off his wounded legs and on to the two sticks with which he supported himself. God, how the heat made his wounds throb – but at least here he would not have to stand on them while he lectured, he consoled himself. He would try to find his old friend, Dr Ferozeshah, and get him to prescribe a pain reliever for him.

A dignified, elderly Jain came slowly up the steps, his quiet, saintly face lit by a smile, the palms of his hands held together in greeting.

'John, I am pleased to see you. I'm sorry I'm late. Your letter arrived only an hour ago.'

He paused for breath, and then looked aghast at John's sticks. 'You've not been cured?' he asked, a quaver in his voice.

John was sharply reminded that Jains regard physical disability as a punishment for misdemeanours in previous lives, and his heart sank a little.

'No,' he replied, as he watched his father's old friend trying to overcome his repugnance. 'But I can manage quite well with my sticks – and on a bicycle.'

The older man recovered some of his composure.

'I am very relieved to hear that,' he said, looking again uneasily at the offending legs, then averting his gaze to look round the station yard. 'We must get a tonga.'

'I have one,' said John, as he slipped a coin into the eager palm of the hovering porter.

They moved slowly to the little carriage, which was weighed down with a trunk, a bedding roll and three suitcases.

'Thank you for coming to meet me, Dr Mehta.'

'I was most happy to come,' replied Dr Mehta with conviction. 'Since the death of your dear father and mother in that dreadful aeroplane accident, I have felt as a parent to you – and I hope you will regard me as such.'

John warmed to the kindly old man, and he felt sad that someone so gentle should have aged so much. The once upright figure was bent and thin, the face fine drawn. The voice which he remembered so well from many a lecture on English literature had lost its richness and was faded.

'You are very good,' he said.

He struggled into the carriage after Dr Mehta, using a firm grip on either side of the door at the back to swing his awkward legs up and over the difficult steps. He cursed under his breath as he hit his knee.

'And how is little Anasuyabehn?' he inquired, as Dr Mehta and he settled themselves on the side seats. 'She was about to be married last time you mentioned her in your letters.'

Dr Mehta arranged his white dhoti neatly round his legs before he answered. His ascetic-looking face registered an uneasy frown. Finally, he said, 'Her betrothed died, so she is not yet married – being motherless makes life a little more difficult for her than it should be – but I shall arrange another marriage for her soon. She must have time to recover.' He did not mention a grave shortage of suitable young men in his caste or that he had left his child's marriage rather late, because he found it hard to part with her.

John nodded politely.

'She's getting into touch with your father's old servant, Ranjit. We felt sure you would like to have him to serve you. He went back to his village after your father died.'

John was delighted. 'I'd like to have him very much,' he said. Ranjit was a Hindu, and he remembered the happy hours he had spent nestled against the strong, kindly peasant, listening to his harsh country dialect as he told him tales of the great Arjun, and of Ram and his faithful Sita. He also remembered suddenly his gentle, easy-going ayah who had taken him with her to pray in Jain temples; he could almost feel again his offering of flowers clutched in his hand.

The carriage jogged along the narrow streets. Women were standing in queues to draw water from street taps, to carry up to their families who lived over the open-fronted shops. From behind white saris or red veils they peeked shyly at the strange Englishman.

In the Moneylenders' Quarter, the sweepers were busy brushing the pavements with small rush brooms. They worked their way phlegmatically in and out amongst the beggars, who sat on their heels with their backs against the high compound walls surrounding the moneylenders' communal family homes.

The carriage swept through the ancient Red Gate and John caught a glimpse of the temple to which his ayah used to take him when he was a little boy. It had a double row of lepers lining its imposing steps from top to bottom. Then, within a few minutes, they were engulfed by the overwhelming perfume of the Hindu flower bazaar.

The bazaar marked the end of the city. Dr Mehta raised his hand to point towards a group of fine, modern buildings, fronted by well-kept flower gardens.

'Our new Government University,' he announced with pride. 'You can just see our original college – which you'll remember – through the trees.'

Indeed, John assured him, he did remember – he had been happy when he had attended it. Many of his fellow scholars had been the sons of merchants and moneylenders from the Jain community, sent to the college to obtain a good command of English.

He had always been interested in Jains. They were so determined not to kill anything, not even an insect or one of the souls they believed inhabited the air or crowded into root vegetables and unripe fruit. Their desire not to commit violence meant that they could not use any implement, be it plough or typewriter; so they were usually moneylenders or merchants, though there were many monks and nuns amongst them and a fair number of scholars like Dr Mehta.

291

'My bungalow is one of those facing the campus, along that lane over there,' said Dr Mehta. He clutched the side of the carriage as it bumped suddenly off the gravel road and into the rutted lane he had just indicated. Then as it began to trundle more safely along, he asked, 'I'm not sure, my dear John, what your plans are . . . ?'

John's voice was a little defensive, as he replied, 'My *History of India* is selling so well in the States, and in Britain and India, that I thought I might follow it with a history of the Gujerat – approaching it, perhaps, through the story of the Marwari Gate temple here in Shahpur.'

Dr Mehta nodded, and directed the driver to his bungalow.

'An old bachelor like me doesn't need a great deal,' John said. He did not know how to explain to Dr Mehta his desperate need to rest and be quiet. England had been as alien to him as to any other immigrant; his upbringing in India had not prepared him for the difference in its way of life. The struggle to earn a living when crippled had also been exhausting.

After the war, he had expected to marry the girl to whom he had become engaged before being taken prisoner, but she had looked with undisguised distaste at his torn legs and viewed with horror his tentative proposal that they should live in India. She had left him sitting in a wheelchair in a military hospital and, a month later, had married someone else. This unhappy experience had tended to make him brusque and defensive with women and he had never proposed to anyone else. He never considered that in spite of his damaged legs he was still a fine-looking man, with his brush of black hair lightly touched with grey, and blue eyes which normally twinkled cheerfully from under straight, bushy eyebrows; he had never really examined himself in a mirror for years.

As they descended from the carriage, Dr Mehta murmured gentle agreement with John's plans. The driver began to unload the luggage and dump it into the sand.

The compound gate was opened by an excited boy servant. Behind him, fidgeting nervously, was Dr Mehta's sister, who kept house for him, an old lady in white widow's garb, her cunning face creased with anxiety about her English visitor, whom she remembered as a precocious, ever curious young man.

Anasuyabehn, small, plump and passive, stood half behind her aunt, peeking at John through thick fluttering eyelashes.

John whistled under his breath. It always defeated him how Jain women could look, at the same time, so prim and so seductive. No one looking at a Jain, he thought, could guess at the passions raging beneath their placid exteriors.

Smiling, both women advanced timidly, putting the palms of their hands together in salute.

As John bowed and said how pleased he was to see them again, he was thinking that if he were Dr Mehta, with a twenty-four-year-old daughter like Anasuyabehn, he would marry her off fast, before she got entangled with someone unscrupulous.

1

The office of the Vice-Chancellor of Shahpur University was extremely hot. It seemed as if the white walls of the Arts and Science Building had, that September morning, absorbed all the heat of the surrounding desert, and it had then become concentrated in the Vice-Chancellor's usually pleasant room overlooking the carefully cultivated gardens in front of the building.

The Vice-Chancellor, Dr Yashvant Prasad, drummed his fingers irritably on his desk and tried to concentrate his attention on the papers before him, but the fan kept fluttering them and finally he closed the file and handed it to the Dean, Dr Mehta, who was standing by the desk.

The Dean's gnarled brown hands shook a little as he took the file from his superior. Today was a fast day and he felt suddenly very weak and weary and thought wistfully of his retirement, still twelve months away.

He flicked over the pages of the file, which was neatly labelled *Dr Tilak, Zoology*, and said, 'Dr Tilak should arrive this afternoon. I'm giving him two rooms in the students' hostel for the present.'

'That will do very well,' agreed the Vice-Chancellor.

'There's a small room next to the Botany Museum which has water laid on, and I have arranged for him to have it as a laboratory.' The Dean paled a little. He had long considered the requirements of Dr Tilak, the first staff member to be recruited for the new Department of Zoology. Would he, for instance, pin dead insects on to boards, as they had done in the Bombay Museum? Would he dissect animals? Perhaps, knowing how sacred life was in the Gujerat, he would teach with the aid of pictures and diagrams. Dean Mehta fervently hoped so, as he continued, 'I – er am not sure what his research involves, but doubtless a little money will be forthcoming for equipment for him?'

'I doubt it,' said the Vice-Chancellor glumly. 'It was difficult enough to squeeze his salary out of the provincial government.' He chewed his lower lip thoughtfully. 'I'll try again,' he promised.

Several flies were buzzing round the office, so the Vice-Chancellor banged the bell on his desk and called to the peon outside the door to shut the window.

The peon, a thin wraith of a man clad in crumpled khaki, slipped down from his stool and trailed languidly across to the window, skilfully palming his small brown cigarette as he passed the Vice-Chancellor's desk. He banged the window shut and returned to his stool.

The Vice-Chancellor leaned back in his wooden revolving chair and fretfully pulled at his long straight nose. He thought longingly of his native Delhi and wondered why he had ever agreed to come to the Gujerat to head this struggling university at Shahpur. He had, he thought despondently, only two fellow mathematicians on the staff – poor company for a Harvard man like himself.

The peon brought him a cup of lukewarm, oversweet tea, and, momentarily forgetting the Dean's presence, the Vice-Chancellor viciously swatted a fly about to descend upon it. Flies all winter, roasting heat all summer; then the humidity before the rains, then the rains themselves with their following of cholera, typhoid and typhus. When the rains stopped there were clouds of mosquitoes carrying malaria to contend with. Really, Shahpur was only fit to live in for about two months of the year.

The Dean tucked the file on Dr Tilak under his arm and said anxiously, 'I hope that a Maratha like Dr Tilak will fit comfortably into our Gujerati ways.'

'I am from Delhi and I am managing to do so,' responded the Vice-Chancellor tartly.

'Ah, yes, indeed, my dear sir,' said the Dean, realizing his slip immediately. 'You are, however, *so* understanding.'

The Vice-Chancellor bridled and said jokingly, 'Well, well, at least the British left us a common language, so that it makes no difference that Dr Tilak's native tongue is Marathi, yours is Gujerati and mine is Hindi.'

'Oh, yes,' agreed Dr Mehta hastily. But his mind revolted at the idea that an alien tongue united his beloved Gujerat with the cocksure southerners and the stupid northerners. His thoughts began to wander.

Although he was a professor of English, knew the plays of Shakespeare nearly by heart and had bookshelves crammed with the latest works in English, his heart lay in his little glass-fronted bookcase amongst his sacred Jain writings, laboriously collected over the years, some of them manuscripts written in Gujerati or Prakrit or Magadhi. Before this bookcase he would sometimes put a little offering of rice; and he would carefully take the writings out and dust them at the appropriate festival.

Vice-Chancellor Prasad glanced up at the Dean's thin, lined face, clean-shaven except for a moustache, with its drooping eyelids and calm, firm mouth. The Dean saw the glance and came back to earth immediately. He pulled his watch out of his trouser pocket; it was a fine gold one which had belonged to his father, and he flicked the lid open carefully.

'Dr Bennett is coming to see me for a few minutes at about twelve o'clock. He wants to go over the Marwari Gate temple; so if you will excuse me I'll go now.'

'Certainly. I should like to see Dr Tilak as soon as he arrives – I'm particularly anxious that our new Department should start off properly.'

'I, too,' replied the Dean with more fervour than he felt. He had advised against a Department of Zoology and he had an uneasy feeling that Dr Tilak could find himself on a collision course with Jain members of the staff.

That same morning, a very bored Anasuyabehn Mehta had been to the library to change her books. Domesticated and obedient as she was, she trusted implicitly her father's promise to arrange another marriage for her. But in the meantime, she seemed to be living in an empty limbo, too old to associate with other single girls, yet without the advantages of matrimony.

Her aunt frowned at her as she entered and put the library books down in a corner. 'Go and wash yourself, child, before entering the kitchen,' she instructed. Then she turned to chide the boy servant for putting too much charcoal on the fire. 'Savitri is waiting on the roof,' she shouted, as Anasuyabehn trailed off to the bathroom.

Her friend, Savitri, knew her well enough to wait a little longer, thought Anasuyabehn, as she filled the bath bucket. Before commencing to wash herself, however, she went to the bottom of the stairs and called to Savitri that she would be up in a few minutes.

Savitri, comfortable in the shade of a tree taller than the bungalow, shouted that she had not to be back at work for an hour.

Anasuyabehn quickly bathed, washed her hair and changed her petticoat, blouse and sari. Then, taking a towel and rubbing her hair as she went, she climbed the stairs to the roof, promising herself that she would go down to help Aunt in the kitchen after a few minutes' gossip with her friend.

Savitri lived such a full and interesting life, she thought enviously. She actually earned her living as a chemist. She herself had never been able to persuade her father to allow her to work.

'Have you had lunch?' she asked Savitri. Her voice was solicitous and deferential. It rejuvenated the other girl's self-esteem, which always sank when she saw Anasuyabehn.

She turned her thin, heavily bespectacled face towards her friend and said she had eaten. She thought mournfully that she had a university degree and competed successfully in the world's hardest labour market; but when she and Anasuyabehn walked together in the evening it was at Anasuyabehn that young men cast longing glances. Savitri's needle-sharp wit might enliven a party, but it was to Anasuyabehn's shy acquies-cing answers that men really listened – negative, obedient Anasuyabehn – so obedient, thought Savitri grimly, that it was just as well that she had few opportunities to meet young men alone. Savitri herself had haughtily repelled her father's offers to find her a husband and yet she craved for a man of her own.

She sighed, and watched without interest as a tonga loaded with luggage rumbled down the lane beneath her.

A thin, sharp shriek of 'Niece!' up the stairs broke into their conver-sation and reminded them suddenly that a caustic-tongued old lady awaited Anasuyabehn's ministrations.

The girls grimaced at each other.

'I wish I were married,' they said in chorus and then dissolved into laughter. They were still laughing and joking when two gentlemen walked down the lane.

2

John Bennett had found the peace he sought in a high-ceiilinged, stone-floored room in the house of a retired teacher, a few doors away from Dr Mehta's home. The room was light and airy and austerely furnished with a wooden couch for sitting and sleeping, a big desk and a chair, and a table from which to eat; there was also a large cupboard for his books and other possessions. On a veranda behind the room, Ranjit camped contentedly among the cooking pots; and on another veranda, to the front of the room, were comfortable basket chairs.

Since his arrival, John had immersed himself in his new history and was almost happy. Though he could not trace any of his former English friends, he had met some Indian ones again and found that none of them held any rancour against him for being English. He had visited his old friend, Dr Ferozeshah, at his surgery, where he was introduced to his head nurse, an English lady of quiet, professional demeanour, Miss Armstrong; Ferozeshah told him that she had previously served in a medical mission north of Shahpur.

As time went by, he was able to discard one of his walking sticks, though his legs still caused him pain occasionally.

While Savitri and Anasuyabehn chatted on the roof of Dean Mehta's bungalow, John took the record of Beethoven's Fifth Symphony off his record player and dusted it carefully.

He opened the cupboard and laid the record on the top shelf, put the record player on a lower shelf, and closed and locked the door.

'Ranjit,' he called, as he began to unbutton his shirt preparatory to changing.

'Ji?' responded his servant. He put down the tray of wheat he had been cleaning and creaked slowly to his feet. Though elderly, he was a powerful-looking peasant. He had come to Shahpur from United Provinces forty years before, when only a boy. Except when the Bennett family was on leave in England, he had never left them. He had made a close study of Shahpur and was well known for his profound knowledge of exactly where to place a bribe to hurry officialdom or obtain a favour.

'Put those papers into my briefcase, while I change my shirt. I've an appointment with Dean Mehta.'

Ranjit wiped his seamed face with the dish towel draped over his shoulder and, with surprisingly deft movements, he packed the briefcase. He turned a toothless smile upon John. 'Will you be in for lunch?' he asked.

John buckled his belt, and, balancing himself by holding on to various pieces of furniture, he went to the bathroom in search of a comb.

'Yes,' he decided, as he combed vigorously at his hair, which never would lie down properly. 'I won't go to look at the temple until tomorrow.'

When he was ready to leave, Ranjit preceded him through the shady compound, in order to open the gate for him.

'Sahib, there's a tonga here.'

John presumed that the occupants of the carriage had come to visit his landlord. He viewed with interest, however, the tall, slim man who sprang down into the dusty lane. An elderly woman and a thin young girl still in the carriage peeped at him from behind their veiling saris.

'Excuse me,' said the man in good English. 'Can you tell me where to find Dr Mehta, the Dean?'

'Certainly. His house is the eighth one from here, down that way,' replied John, indicating the way the tonga had come.

'I'm really looking for his office.'

John looked thoughtfully at the man. Definitely not a student, he decided.

'I'm going to his office now,' he said. 'Would you like to come with me?'

The young man glanced up at the two ladies, who were whispering to each other, and seemed undecided. The tongawallah, on his high perch, started to fidget and began to mutter about people who made him wait forever and lose business. It was apparent that, at any moment, he would demand an increase in the agreed fare.

'I don't know what arrangements have been made for us. Mother is tired after our long journey.'

John's perplexity must have shown on his face, because he added, 'I'm Tilak from Bombay. I'm to teach Zoology here. In which department do you teach?'

'I'm not a member of the University staff,' John replied. 'But Dr Mehta mentioned that you were coming. I hope you'll like it here.' He extended his hand to the newcomer.

Though Tilak's fingers looked slim and delicate, his grip on John's hand was firm. 'Thanks,' he said.

'Perhaps the ladies would like to rest in my room,' John suggested. 'My servant would look after them, while we go to see the Dean.'

The offer was accepted with alacrity. With Ranjit's help and with much puffing and blowing, Mrs Tilak and her daughter were installed in John's room. John left to Ranjit the task of offering refreshments to the ladies. He had no idea of their caste or orthodoxy. If they were very orthodox, they would refuse all refreshment, in spite of the fact that Ranjit was himself a Brahmin.

Dr Tilak and he walked down the line of flat-roofed houses and bungalows before turning into the path which led to the Arts and Science Building. Tilak looked about him in a brisk, almost military manner which proclaimed his Maratha forebears, in marked contrast to the stolid, slower movements of Gujeratis. He seemed excitable and full of life, and remarked enthusiastically upon the green lawns and little flowerbeds which had been conjured up out of near desert.

Tilak had the beauty of face and form, thought John, which had made Indians famous for their looks, though he was gaunt and very dark-skinned. Though he did not know who John was, he was respectful to him, and he soon drew from him some details of his writings, in particular, about his new book on the history of the Marwari Gate temple and the surrounding district.

But Tilak's expression lost some of its exuberance, as they chatted. Finally, he said, 'I wonder what these Jains will think of my subject?'

'Why? I expect there is a demand for Zoology courses here. Otherwise, it would not have occurred to the University to appoint you.'

'There's a demand – probably from Hindus. However, it may not have occurred to anyone that I'll require small mammals to dissect for the benefit of my students – and fish to dissect for my own research.' He turned to John, his face very earnest, 'One can never be sure with Jains.'

John smiled at the ominous tone in which he pronounced his last sentence. His eyes twinkled, as he replied, 'The Vice-Chancellor is a graduate of Harvard – I'm sure he'll understand the requirements of modern research. We have some old diehards here. A few staff fought against the establishment of a Science Faculty. Dean Mehta is, himself, quite orthodox in his personal life – but I've never noticed his trying to impose his views on anyone else.'

Tilak relaxed a little and was about to make some further remark, when his attention was caught by a flutter of pink on the roof of the Dean's bungalow, which they were approaching.

John, also, had noticed Anasuyabehn on the roof, her pink sari almost obscured by her long, black hair which she was drying in the sunlight. She was generally a very retiring girl and, presumably, imagined that she could not be seen from below or she would undoubtedly have dried her hair indoors; her Western education had failed to rob her of her modesty or dignity. Now, she stood, in all innocence, shaking out her wonderful tresses, and laughing and chattering with her friend, Savitri, who was seated on the low parapet which guarded the edge of the roof.

John thought what a contrast the two women made. Anasuyabehn had an inborn winsomeness, and, as she raised her arms to rub her hair, her fine figure was readily apparent; yet her laughing face and cheerful voice had all the ingenuousness of the carefully protected woman. She was no beauty; but he knew that when she felt at ease with people, she could be quite charming.

Savitri – well, Savitri was Savitri. Thin as a camel after a desert journey, hair cut short and permanently waved last time she had been in Bombay, large, horn-rimmed spectacles; an assertive woman, whose violent efforts to be modern sometimes had results which left her acquaintances gasping. Yet she and Anasuyabehn were old friends, products of the same school and the same college – but different parents, thought John. Though Savitri's parents were Hindus, their home was almost completely European, while in Dean Mehta's house, despite his study of English, many of the old Jain ways still lingered.

As he and Tilak came level with the bungalow, Anasuyabehn approached the parapet, and, parting her waterfall of hair with her hands, she looked out across the compound straight at Tilak.

Tilak stopped in his tracks, fascinated by the gentle, fair face, made stronger looking by sweeping black brows, and by the marvellous hair rippling down past the girl's knees. In that unguarded moment she did, indeed, look very different from her usual modest self. Behind her, the leaves of an overhanging tree rustled and cast a dappled shade over her, guarding her from the searching rays of the sun.

She stood for a moment, as if captivated, and then, suddenly realizing her dishevelled state and the impropriety of staring at a man, she whipped away across the roof to the staircase.

Tilak continued to stare at the spot where she had stood, as if the shabby, white parapet had mesmerized him.

'Heavens,' he breathed in English, and then blinked and turned his face away, as he realized that he was being insolently scrutinized by Savitri, who was still seated on the low wall.

Embarrassed by this merciless examination, he turned to John and said in his stilted English, 'What were you saying about the Vice-Chancellor and the Dean?'

John was also acquainted with Savitri. He gravely lifted his stick in salute to her. She smiled acknowledgment and he turned his attention again to Tilak.

Though Tilak had reopened the conversation, it was obvious that he was not really listening to John's reply. His face was rapt as they walked along, the eyelids narrowed, the lips parted, and John felt uncomfortably that this lean, attractive newcomer was probably far too emotional to slip quietly into the life of the University. An intense man, thought John, with a difficult subject to teach, in a district where the life of every crawling bug is sacred.

In the middle of a story being told to him by John of how local villagers refused to spray a locust invasion, because of their beliefs, Tilak asked suddenly, 'Whose was the bungalow where the two girls were up on the roof?'

As they climbed the steps of the Arts and Science Building, he looked up at John, impatient for his answer.

A quizzical gleam in his eye, John glanced back at Tilak. 'It was Dean Mehta's bungalow. Why?'

Tilak flushed at the query and did not reply at once. Then, with a burst of inspiration, he said, 'It is helpful to know exactly where various members of the University staff live, and so on.'

In the hall, he saw the name of the Dean on a door facing him, and he promptly changed the subject, a slight grimness in his voice. 'Well, here I go. Now we shall see what effect Zoology creates in a Jain world!'

But Dr Tilak was received with quiet courtesy by Dean Mehta and his fears were allayed. The Head Peon was instructed to help him remove his mother and sister and luggage from John's room and he left to do this, while John arranged with the Dean to visit the Marwari Gate temple with him the following morning.

3

The Marwari Gate temple had been built by an emperor as a sacrifice for the sins of his teeth. John had visited it on a number of occasions, but this time he wanted to arrange to see some of its sacred manuscripts.

The next morning, with clean handkerchiefs held politely over their noses, he and Dr Mehta followed their amiable guide, a monk, through the courtyard and into the halls and sanctuary. He marvelled again at the lacelike carving of canopies, roofs and figures of Tirthankaras, all in white marble.

It was explained to him that some of the manuscripts he wished to see were kept in the Treasure House and no stranger could be admitted to that. He was allowed, however, to examine the outside of the Treasure House. It was covered with finely engraved silver. The engravings told the story of the fourteen dreams of Trisala, the mother of Mahavira who was the founder of Jainism. John asked if he might make sketches of these.

The monk was reluctant to agree to this, and called several others to consult them. John remembered again that a limp is considered punishment for past sins, and, from the conversation, he thought he would be turned down because of this.

They finally agreed, however, and John arranged to visit them again in a few days' time.

Dean Mehta wished to remain at the temple with his religious teacher, so John wandered off by himself.

A few minutes' walk brought him to the flower bazaar and to the big, frowsy cinemas; the latter were tawdry with electric lights and hand-painted posters showing languid, suffering film heroines.

Near one of the cinemas, he stopped to buy some hot sweetmeats from a man clad only in a loincloth, who had a tiny stall tucked into the angle of a wall.

While he slowly ate his sticky sweets out of the palm leaf in which they had been wrapped, he watched an artist in the cinema entrance painting a poster to advertise the next film. Crowds of people pushed impatiently around him. A beggar woman, clutching a naked, swollen-bellied child, squatted at his feet and whined hopefully. He put a coin into the child's hand and the woman blessed him, while the starving child stared unseeingly over its mother's shoulder, giving no sign of life, except to clutch the coin firmly in its mouselike hand.

Although such sights were familiar to him from childhood, a sudden wave of pity swept over him as the woman crept away. With an irritable gesture, he threw away the dripping palm leaf, and made to move out into the crowd.

'Bennett Sahib!' exclaimed a cheerful, feminine and very English voice. 'How could you?'

Startled, he looked round.

Diana Armstrong, Dr Ferozeshah's head nurse, was standing half behind him. Down her rumpled khaki skirt was a spreading splash of sugar syrup, where the palm leaf had struck her. Her freckled face, brick-red with heat, was crinkled up with laughter. Her red hair was plastered down against her head by perspiration and her khaki shirt was equally soaked and clung to her slim figure.

John's first thought was that he had never seen a more bedraggled-looking Englishwoman. Then he hastily collected his wits. She was, after all, his doctor's head nurse.

'Miss Armstrong!' he exclaimed. 'I am so sorry.'

He looked around him helplessly.

'Can I get you a tonga in which to return home? Or perhaps the restaurant across the road would find us something to wipe it with.'

'The restaurant, I think,' replied Miss Armstrong. Her voice had suddenly lost its laughter and was rather quavery. 'I think I'd be grateful for a cup of tea as well.'

John looked at her sharply. The flush was ebbing from her face and he saw the blue smudges of fatigue under the clear green eyes. Poor woman, he thought. Why on earth does she work as she does, for an Indian doctor who probably pays her in annas?

He put his free hand under one of her elbows and, marshalling his stick, he guided her firmly across the street to the restaurant and into the gloom of a family cubicle at the back of it. He took her little black nurse's bag from her and sat down. He knew her quite well as Dr Ferozeshah's efficient shadow, but had never wished to know anything more of her, except to wonder idly how she came to work for Ferozeshah; and he was now quite surprised at his own temerity. She was, however, English like himself and obviously not feeling too well. He would not admit to himself that he wanted to speak English to somebody English.

'Tea,' he told the white-shirted, barefoot waiter, who was goggling at the rare sight of an English couple in his humble café. 'English tea with sugar and milk separate – boiling water for the tea. And a clean cloth to wipe the Memsahib's dress.' He pointed to the sugar stain.

'Would you like something to eat?' he asked. 'They make nice kabobs here.'

She smiled, showing uneven, very white teeth. 'No, thank you,' she said. 'Just tea.' She leaned back and closed her eyes for a moment, looking, in her exhaustion, soft and vulnerable.

The waiter departed, not too sure how to make English tea, but hoping the cook would know. He brought a cloth to sponge the skirt, and Miss Armstrong removed the worst of the stickiness.

'It doesn't matter,' she said. 'I'm a wreck anyway.'

John was inclined to agree with her but had sufficient diplomacy to stop himself saying so. He just twiddled his cold pipe which he had taken out of his pocket, and wondered what to talk about.

Miss Armstrong leaned her head against the wall of the cubicle and hoped she would not faint. She had certainly walked too far and too fast that morning. This John Bennett, though he was something of an oddity, was very kind and she was overwhelmed with gratitude at his bringing her into the restaurant and his concern at her spoiled skirt. She wished suddenly that she was beautiful, charming and amusing so that she could really entertain him with witty conversation. The ceiling gave a sudden swoop and was obliterated by a cloud of darkness for a second.

'I think you had better sip some water.' His voice came from far away, though he was bending over her and holding a glass, clinking with ice, to her lips.

She sipped gratefully and the faintness receded. John's lined, red face, topped by its unruly brush of dark hair, came into focus.

'Thank you,' she said with a wobbly smile, 'I am all right now.'

'Perhaps you're working too hard,' ventured John. 'Surely Ferozeshah doesn't expect you to work all the hours God sends?'

'Oh, no. He's very reasonable – though he works like a machine himself.'

She leaned forward and put her elbows on the stained, battered table, and ran her fingers across her eyes. Her shirt was open at the neck. John found himself a little flustered by a glimpse of lace barely masking full, incredibly white breasts. It had been a long time, he thought depressedly.

Unconscious of the stir she had caused in her companion, Miss Armstrong relaxed in the welcome gloom of the restaurant. The dark, varnished wood partitions and the smoke-blackened ceiling gave it an air of shabby, homely comfort.

305

'There's so much to do here – for a nurse,' she said, a note of compassion in her voice.

John sought uneasily for a further source of conversation. Finally, to bridge the growing gap of silence, he asked abruptly, 'Were you visiting someone sick, just now?'

'No – this is my spare time. I don't have to be in the operating room until eleven, today. However, some of the big Jains here are trying to do a real survey of the city. They want to find out how many people live in each district, what water supplies they have, what parks or playgrounds for children. It's an awfully difficult job. I've been counting refugees from Pakistan camped out on the pavements round here.'

John's bushy eyebrows shot up in surprise.

'That's a departure – for Jains. They've always believed that suffering is brought upon oneself. I didn't realize they cared how the other half lived. What's the idea?'

'To raise funds to provide some amenities in the worst slums.'

Miss Armstrong rubbed absent-mindedly at a water ring on the table. She looked up at John's strong, calm face.

'Humph,' grunted John. 'Times they are a-changing!' His wide, thin mouth broke into a grin. 'Jains are usually more interested in protecting animals than humans – charity is simply giving to monks and beggars.'

'I know,' replied his companion. 'That's why I want to help them.'

She removed her elbows from the table, so that the waiter could put down the tea tray. When he had gone, she seized the teapot in a small, strong hand and poured out the tea.

John took the proffered cup and himself added sugar and milk, while Miss Armstrong sipped eagerly at the black brew in her own cup. She sighed. 'That's better. Mind if I smoke?'

'Not at all. Do you mind if I smoke a pipe?'

Miss Armstrong dug a packet of Capstan out of her shirt pocket. After he had given her a light, she began to look a little less flushed and her skin took on its more normal appearance.

'Cream velvet powdered with freckles,' reflected John in some surprise. 'She can't be much over thirty.'

He told himself hastily to stop thinking like a naive youth, and he dragged his mind back to the prosaic subject of the proposed map. 'I know Shahpur quite well,' he told her. 'I was actually born here, and I think I could draw a map of most of it. I'm sure that a proper one doesn't exist, particularly since the influx of refugees – they've built all kinds of shanties – I've watched them go up.' He laughed a little grimly. 'I bet the postmen are the only ones who really know Shahpur.'

'You're right.'

'It would save a lot of time, if you had a map – and, believe me, I could fill in a great deal of detail – mosques, temples, ruins, fountains – what few gardens there are . . .'

'Would you *really* draw one?' Miss Armstrong asked eagerly. Her face was alight, the mouth a trifle open to show the tip of a tongue as narrow as a cat's. 'Could I tell Lallubhai – he's the Chairman – about your offer?'

'Certainly,' replied John, and wondered what possessed him to undertake such a monumental piece of work. 'Do you want a wall-sized map – or sections?'

She looked doubtful and then quickly glanced at her watch. 'I'm not sure. Look, I've got to be in the operating room by eleven.' She picked up her bag. 'Could we meet somewhere to talk about it?'

John was immediately appalled at this complication. There was not a single European restaurant in the city. He could not very well ask her to his room. A vision of Ranjit's horrified face floated before him – an English Memsahib in his room would probably ruin her reputation. He had no idea where she lived or with whom. What a fool he was to get involved.

He fumbled with his pipe, matches and stick, at the same time trying to open the swing door of the cubicle for her. She waited patiently while he sorted himself out and thought of an answer to her question.

'Perhaps you should first talk to your Chairman, Mr Lallubhai,' he temporized, as he finally managed to push the door open with his elbow. 'If a student or artist would volunteer, I'd be glad of a little help. Any map I draw is not going to be technically perfect, but it'll save your Committee a lot of work.' He paused outside the cubicle, and then asked, 'I wonder if Mr Lallubhai has thought of asking the City Engineer for a look at his maps. He'll have some showing drains, waterpipes . . .'

Miss Armstrong's little white teeth flashed in a quick smile. 'I'm sure none of the Committee has thought of it. I'll suggest it. I'll write to you – your address is in Dr Ferozeshah's file.'

As they moved through the crowded restaurant, customers paused in their conversation to watch them pass. At the bottom of the narrow entrance steps, they were besieged by beggars. Miss Armstrong ignored them. She looked up at John, and said, 'You're a brick to offer to help – it's a big job – are you sure you want to do it?'

She looked anxiously at him, and he could not say to her that he wished he had not volunteered, and said instead, 'I shall enjoy it – it will be a change for me. Now, can I get you a tonga?'

She was dismissed and, in spite of his affirmative reply, felt unaccountably a little hurt.

307

'No, thank you,' she muttered, 'I'll walk. Goodbye – and thank you.'

She turned stiffly on her heavy, flat-heeled shoes, and in a moment was lost in the jostling crowd.

John waved at a passing tonga, and the driver drew into the pavement.

'University Road,' said John, 'How much?'

'Eight annas, Sahib,' said the driver outrageously.

'Four annas and not a pice more.'

'Sahib,' the voice was full of reproach.

'Four annas.'

'Six annas,' said the driver, 'and not a pice less,' and he lifted his whip to start his horse, to indicate that he would rather go without a fare than reduce his price further.

'All right,' said John, and clambered in through the door at the back of the carriage. A little boy, who had been sitting by the driver, scrambled down, ran round the tonga and locked the door after John.

John smiled at the boy and gave him an anna. But behind the smile he felt cross. In two days two new people had entered his life, if one counted that Miss Armstrong had previously been only a pair of hands passing papers to Dr Ferozeshah. They both seemed to be people who would disrupt the peace of his life; Dr Tilak appeared likely to seek his advice quite often and Diana had momentarily disturbed his usual composure.

Since his dismissal by his fiancée, he had tried to avoid women, swearing that he would never let himself be hurt again. Almost every time he walked, he was reminded of the repugance in his fiancée's eyes, when she saw how crippled he was; and then he would damn all women.

He told himself not to be ridiculous. Nevertheless, by the time he was deposited at his compound gate, he had worked himself into a thoroughly bad temper. When Ranjit saw him, he scampered out to his own veranda, from which he did not stir until he had listened to the typewriter pounding steadily for more than half an hour.

Later, when he crept into the room to ask the Sahib what he would like for dinner, he was surprised to find him leaning his head disconsolately against the typewriter, looking as miserable as he had when first he returned to Shahpur.

'Sahib?' queried Ranjit, his wizened face full of concern. 'Are you well?'

The Sahib did not raise his head from its hard resting place, but he smiled up at Ranjit out of the corners of his eyes, and with a jolt Ranjit was reminded of the small boy John had once been who wept and raged his frustrations out of himself.

'I am all right now, Ranjit. Sometimes I get fed up because I don't walk very well.'

Ranjit scratched his jaw, and wondered if that was the only trouble. He decided, however, that this was not the time to probe further, and said, 'Your legs improve daily, Sahib. Don't get depressed.' Then in a cheerful managing voice, he asked, 'What would you like for dinner? I have some good lady's fingers, succulent and green.'

'I'd rather have them smooth and white,' said John with sudden spirit, while Ranjit looked at him aghast.

4

It was about three weeks later that John was again reminded of an uneasy sense of unwanted change in his life.

Ranjit came in to tidy his room and, seeing that he was not working, sat down on the floor to gossip.

He regaled John with a detailed description of the contents of Tilak's baggage, Mrs Tilak's disgruntlement at the poor lodgings provided for her son by the University, Dr Tilak's hot temper and, by comparison, the quiet character of his sister, Damyanti. Mrs Tilak was a widow, he said, and she and her daughter normally lived with her elder brother-in-law in Bombay.

John lay resting on his wooden couch and laughed at Ranjit. He lay on his back, with one muscular arm curled round his head, and Ranjit, as he watched him, thought that he must be much taller than he seemed when standing. When on his feet, he tended to stoop and put a lot of weight on his stick. A strong man, however, and very virtuous, though, in Ranjit's opinion, he was too young to live in quite the sagelike manner that he did.

'It defeats me, Ranjit,' remarked John, 'how you manage to find out all these things.'

'Sahib,' replied Ranjit primly, 'I do but listen to the conversation of others. Ramji told me himself that Mrs Tilak upbraided him personally because, she said, the lavatories were filthy, and, you know, Sahib, that he does his best to clean them.'

John thought of Ramji's apathetic efforts at cleaning, and snorted.

'And anyway, Sahib, what else does one expect a lavatory to be except very dirty?'

'Ours is clean,' said John, yawning and stretching like a cat.

'You clean it yourself, Sahib,' said Ranjit disapprovingly.

'If I left it to you and Ramjit it never would be clean.'

He rolled over to face Ranjit and his eyes were suddenly a little flinty.

'Why should one not clean one's lavatory, may I ask? Gandhiji set everyone a good example by taking a sweeper's broom and doing a sweeper's work.'

'I am a Brahmin, Sahib, and well versed in the scriptures.'

'You cook for me.'

'True, Sahib – but times are changing and I must change with them,' said Ranjit huffily, fingering the little shikka on his head. His grey hair was thinning rapidly, but he cultivated carefully this precious tuft of hair by which God, in due course, would pull him up to Heaven.

John abandoned what he knew to be a useless argument and swung his legs down to the floor.

'Let's look at the account book,' he said. 'It's time we did.'

Ranjit heaved a sigh and produced from his shirt pocket a much thumbed notebook, in which were entered in Gujerati characters the various expenditures of their small household. John ran an experienced eye down the list, to make sure that not overmuch of any one item was being used; occasionally, Ranjit's hospitality to his family extended to gifts of tea or sugar out of John's store, as well as free meals.

Meanwhile, Ranjit took out of his shirt pocket a dirty screw of newspaper and from this extracted three rupee notes and a handful of small change, which he carefully counted out on to the floor in front of the couch. John checked the amount with the book and found it balanced. Satisfied, he returned the housekeeping book to Ranjit, heaved himself up and unlocked the almira, took out his cash box and went back to the couch.

Without thinking, he sat down cross-legged and was surprised that he could arrange himself in that position without pain. Ranjit held out an incredibly wrinkled brown hand and John counted his wages into it. He then gave him money for a week's supply of food and fuel.

The servant folded the notes up carefully and stowed them away in a grubby handkerchief, after which he sat looking rather gloomily at a small line of ants marching across the floor, until John asked him, 'What's the matter, Ranjit?'

'Sahib, you have thousands of rupees in the bank and yet you live like a monk. It is not fitting, Sahib, for an Englishman to live so. You should have a pukka bungalow with a compound – and a mali to cultivate the garden – and a kitchen boy to help me.'

'Ranjit,' said John with a sigh, 'you should be in the Secret Service. Do you by any chance know the exact amount of my bank balance?'

Ranjit flushed under the implied reproof, though he answered steadily, 'Yes, Sahib. Rs. 40,581, As. 3.' He cleared his throat, and went on, 'Further, Sahib, you will soon get another letter from Wayne Sahib, your book man in America, with more money; and you have two wealthy students to coach here – more money!'

John leaned back against the wall and roared with laughter.

'You know more about my finances than I do,' he said.

311

'The Statement from the bank lies on your desk,' replied Ranjit blandly.

The idea of launching out on to a sea of housekeeping appalled John; he liked his present existence. It was comparatively uncomplicated, he had plenty of learned men for company, and for a change he could take an occasional trip to Abu or Delhi or Bombay, without having to worry about the cost of it. Already Tilak and Miss Armstrong had stirred in him a faint premonition of unwanted change, and here was Ranjit lecturing him about rearranging his life. A sharp reproof rose to his lips, but he stifled it hastily – Ranjit cared more about his wellbeing than anyone else.

'I'll think about it,' he told Ranjit gravely, and dismissed him.

He sat down at his desk and commenced reading the notes he had made on the Marwari Gate temple.

The evening was approaching and there was a comfortable clatter of saucepans from Ranjit on the veranda. Behind it John could hear the wind whining among the bungalows and University buildings. He rose and stretched. Balancing himself by holding on to the furniture, he went to the door and opened it. The sky was flushed with sunset, the pinkness dulled by the threat of storm in it.

His landlord's grandchildren were playing, as usual, in the compound, and the smallest child was in the act of unlatching the compound gate. As he watched, it managed to heave the gate open and peep through it, and then ventured outside. John called to it to come back but it did not, so he got his stick and walked as quickly as he could to the gate.

The toddler was sitting in the middle of the lane cooing to itself, while a small black carriage, drawn by a single horse, bowled smartly towards it.

As he went to retrieve the child, he shouted a warning to the driver. He pulled the youngster to its feet and, with a pat on its behind, sent it back through the gate. He paused himself, because the awkward bending had hurt his legs. The mangy horse drew up by him, and its owner leaned down from beside the driver.

Mahadev Desai smiled and bowed. 'Good evening, John. Can I give you a lift anywhere? Nice to see you.'

John surveyed the plump speaker through the dust engendered by the carriage. He had known Mahadev casually for most of his life. He was the son of a powerful moneylender and jeweller; but today he wore, like any fairly prosperous businessman, a plain white cotton shirt, jacket and trousers. A white Gandhi cap surmounted a moonlike, though not unhandsome, face. Shrewd eyes stared unblinkingly, while he awaited John's answer. Behind him, sat his younger brother and sister-in-law, who murmured 'Namuste' in greeting.

'No, thanks,' replied John. 'I called to you, because I wasn't sure if your driver had seen my landlord's grandchild – the little tike had strayed into the lane.'

'I saw him, Sahib,' the driver interjected hastily, lest he be blamed for carelessness.

John nodded, and inquired after Mahadev and his family. The cadences of the man's voice, he thought, had not changed over the years. He knew the nervous respect with which Mahadev was treated in the city. The Desai Society in which he lived was nearly in the centre of the old town, and from it, financial tentacles stretched out into the mills and homes of half the city, even as far as Delhi and out to Europe, it was said. Nobody held more mortgages and family jewellery in pledge. Nobody could put pressure on a hapless debtor faster than the Desais, or produce a bigger bribe when needed. Their knowledge of invective, that priceless asset of any Indian moneylender, had not been lost as their business became enormously expanded. John had heard Mahadev himself, before he had taken charge of their business in France, screaming in the bazaar at some unfortunate businessman, while a crowd gathered to see the fun, and the police vanished.

Desai was speaking to him.

'I am going to catch the Delhi Mail, after calling on Dean Mehta,' he confided in a slightly pompous whisper.

'Indeed,' said John absent-mindedly, his thoughts already wandering back to his book. 'A pleasant journey.'

'Thank you,' replied Desai graciously. 'A-jo.'

'Goodbye,' said John, stepping back as the driver, in response to a gesture from Desai, whipped up the horse.

John went slowly back into the bungalow. The children had gone in for their evening meal. The wind still whined its threat of a dust storm.

He went back to his desk and looked again at his sketches of the Dreams of Trisala, so often meditated upon by Jain women. He saw instead the ivory-coloured face of Mahadev.

The wife of one of his father's old friends on campus had told him that the well-known moneylender was considering remarriage; as one of the richer men in Shaphur he was of interest. His first wife, she said, had died in childbirth and, soon after her death, he had been sent by his father to Paris, presumably in connection with their business in fine jewellery. Rumour had it that he had opened an elegant jewellery shop

313

there, where they sold silver filigree and other Indian-designed ornaments. By all accounts, this venture had thrived well.

Now Mahadev was home again and, perhaps because of his hairstyle, looked rather Westernized. He was not so influenced, however, that he had lost the ancient instinct of a moneylender to hide his wealth; he was still dressed quite humbly and drove a half-starved horse.

John smiled to himself, as he remembered Ranjit's description of why Mahadev Desai was being encouraged to look for another wife.

'It is well known, Sahib,' Ranjit had said, 'that the older Desais fear greatly that Mahadev may take a French woman to wife – France is next to England, isn't it, Sahib? And there has already been enough trouble in the Desai Society.

'The Society was quite happy when ruled by Mahadev's mother and father, and his little daughter blossomed in spite of the lack of a mother. But when the old lady died and that shrew of a younger sister-in-law became the eldest lady, then, Sahib, trouble seemed to spread from house to house inside their compound. The cousin brothers went away because their wives would no longer stand the ceaseless nagging. Then the wretched woman complained to all the neighbours that she was worked to death, because there was no other woman in the house – though they do have a number of servants, Sahib.'

Ranjit had stopped to blow his nose into a corner of his handkerchief which was not knotted round the housekeeping money, and had then gone on disparagingly, 'Trust them to think of the most economical thing to do – they are persuading Mahadev that he must marry again.'

5

As Mahadev continued on his way to visit Dean Mehta, he mused on the charms of his possible future wife.

He wished to marry for reasons other than economy. He had discovered, to his cost, that a well-to-do Indian jeweller, alone in Paris, could be quite popular amongst women; and their bare legs and tight dresses had been a constant temptation, to which he had, too often, succumbed.

He thought that an educated Indian wife might keep him out of further mischief; he could take her on his travels. He also passionately desired a son. He was fond of his little daughter, but, all too soon, she would grow to marriageable age and leave him, whereas a son would be a joy to him all his life.

For different reasons, the older Desais were of the same mind. Mahadev had hardly distributed the gifts he had brought from France several weeks before, when, with sly hints, the matter was broached. Girls of suitable caste and orthodoxy were suggested; Mahadev found fault with all of them.

'It looks as if our French investment will flourish,' he reminded his father, 'so it is important that I should have a wife able to mix with French ladies.'

'French women!' exclaimed his father. 'She'll live in this house. She doesn't have to go with you to Paris.'

Mahadev felt the perspiration trickling down his back. He did not know how to explain to his father the witchery of the women he had seen in France. The amount of sin he had accumulated during his visit appalled him; somewhere, sometime, it would have to be expiated.

'It's the custom in France to travel with one's wife,' he lied in desperation. 'It's expected of one.'

His father digested this information in silence. He was aware of the pitfalls of travel. There was the temptation to eat meat, for example.

As if reading his thoughts, Mahadev said, with a burst of inspiration, 'It's extremely difficult to eat properly without someone to cook for me.'

'Ah,' exclaimed his father, satisfied at last. 'Most of the girls whom

315

your uncles mentioned can read and write. They'd be docile enough and do whatever you asked.'

Mahadev mentally dismissed the whole solemn, dull collection of them. He had seen a woman walking, with her boy servant, near the University. He had known her for years by sight. He remembered her long plait of hair swinging softly over pretty, rounded shoulders, her delicate ivory skin, her demurely lowered eyelids. Swallowing hard, he inquired of his father, 'Did Dean Mehta's daughter ever get married? Her father's with the University – you may remember him.'

Old Desai looked at him. 'She's not one of our people.'

'I know,' replied his son, rather crestfallen. 'But she *is* a Jain.'

Desai Senior pursed his thin lips, and considered the merits of the match. Finally, he said uneasily, 'She's not a lucky woman – she's been bereaved even before being married – and her horoscope may not be correct.'

Mahadev dared not show the irritation that he felt, neither could he describe the subtle seductiveness of Anasuyabehn or say that he had thought her beautiful long ago, when he was a young man and she was a quiet school girl travelling to and from her lessons. He had never questioned his father's choice of his first wife, who had been a good, obedient girl, but now Mahadev was no longer young – he was a rich, experienced man who hungered for a woman of his own choosing. He wanted Anasuyabehn, the sight of whom made him tremble. And of what use was being rich if one could not buy what one wanted?

The elder Desai listed a multitude of reasons regarding Anasuya-behn's unsuitability as a wife, but they only hardened Mahadev's determination to wed her.

'Perhaps eldest aunt from Baroda could inquire discreetly about the horoscope,' he said, trying to keep his face impassive.

His father looked at him penetratingly. Mahadev seemed set upon this woman, and he himself was very anxious to see him safely married. Mahadev was his favourite son; in comparison, his younger son was a dunderhead – and the boy's wife was an avaricious shrew. He wondered what kind of a temperament Anasuyabehn had; something about her evidently pleased his son.

'Have you spoken to this girl?'

'No, father.'

'Have you seen her?'

'Yes, father. Many times since childhood. She used to go to a school near the Red Gate and I would see her getting off the bus at the flower bazaar with the other girls.'

'Hm,' murmured his father, thinking that young men did not change much from generation to generation. 'I'll consult your uncles.'

The elder man waved his hand in dismissal, and Mahadev knew intuitively that he had won. He got up from the mattress on which he had been sitting, bowed and made for the door.

'Wait,' said his father, and Mahadev turned apprehensively.

'You realize that a man in your position can choose almost any girl in our caste – parents would happily approve of you.' He paused, and then went on, 'You should consider this carefully, for I do not know whether the Mehtas will be so happy. Dean Mehta presumably has had other offers for his daughter.'

Mahadev, secure in his family's financial empire, had never thought of being snubbed by Dean Mehta and he was nonplussed for a moment, and then said, 'Would Baroda aunt cause inquiry to be made on this point first?'

He is quite determined, thought his father fretfully. I should be firmer about it – and yet the other boy is very unhappy with his witch of a wife.

'Very well,' he said grudgingly. 'Here, take these photographs and have another look at them – you might change your mind about one of them – Baroda aunt's young sister-in-law looks quite nice.'

Mahadev reluctantly took from him the half dozen or so studio portraits of prospective wives, promised to consider them and made his escape.

A man of thirty-four, who had seen the world, he fumed, should surely be allowed to choose a wife; and yet, beneath his resentment at his marriage being arranged for him, lay the knowledge that his father was being extremely patient.

He wandered into the compound, round which were ranged dwellings dating back a hundred years or more. How crowded and dirty it looked! Its smoke-blackened stone verandas with their steps hollowed out by generations of feet, its rotting woodwork, its lack of paint, depressed him. Later on – he would not admit to himself that he meant when his father and his Partner Uncle died – he would build a new Society in a more salubrious neighbourhood, and leave this compound to his brother.

Now that India had settled down after the horrors of 1947, others, less rich than he was, had moved out; he would, too. He sighed, and looked at his watch. Time to go into the office and relieve his brother.

In the gloomy, dusty office, his brother was haggling superbly with a rather cowed local landowner about a loan against his next crop. Mahadev went to stand quietly by him.

His father might consider Younger Brother dull and commonplace, but Mahadev was fond of him and felt he would make an excellent junior partner, completely reliable in all matters, and, as far as the family was concerned, painstakingly honest. It was a pity that his father was so hard on him.

Gradually, Mahadev was drawn into the argument, and in a very short time he was engrossed in squeezing a higher interest rate out of their client.

The would-be brides soon had an account book banged down upon their neatly photographed features – and were forgotten.

6

Anasuyabehn's widowed aunt had made her home with her brother and his daughter because she had no sons and disliked the idea of living with one of her brothers-in-law. She had constantly berated the old scholar about his neglect of his daughter in respect of finding a husband for her. The only reply she had been able to obtain from him had been, 'We should wait a full two years from the time of her betrothed's death – it is not judicious to hurry the girl.'

As a result of this, Aunt had almost given up hope of ever seeing her niece married, since the older a girl became the harder it was to marry her off. Aunt felt that her own abilities as a matchmaker were simply withering away. She had, therefore, been delighted when, by devious routes, it was made known to her that the Desais would make an offer for Anasuyabehn, if they could be sure of not being snubbed. This was an opportunity which could not be ignored, a real test of her match-making skills, which would benefit dear Anasuyabehn immeasurably. She consulted nobody, but assured the lady from whom this indication had come that such an offer would be well received. She was over-whelmed by the idea of being the instrument by which such a wealthy alliance could be brought about; it would crown all her previous success-ful efforts on behalf of other relations. After this, all her female relations with children to marry off would crowd about her, begging her favours on behalf of their offspring. Her thin, hooked nose quivered at the anticipation of her future importance in the family.

She conveniently forgot the difference in caste. She thought only of the Desai bank balance and willingly became the mediator between the two fathers. Two other offers for Anasuyabehn from the parents of poverty-stricken scholars were left to die from neglect on her part.

When she first broached the subject, Dean Mehta looked up from his book, said flatly, 'No,' and returned to his studies.

Undeterred, she continued to sit in front of him, chewing her thumb. He again glanced up, and added, 'I'll advertise for a husband for her in early spring.'

'The girl is already twenty-four years old.'

'I know, I know,' said the Dean testily, 'but Desai is not a Mehta.'

'He's near enough,' said his sister, 'and he's rich, healthy and in love with her. What more could we want in these changed times?'

'Does Anasuyabehn know Mahadev?' asked the Dean suspiciously. It would, he thought, be quite easy for her to carry on an intrigue without his knowledge – after all, she occasionally went shopping or to visit a friend by herself.

'No,' said Aunt decisively. 'Someone would have seen her and told me, if she had ever spoken to him.'

The Dean sat silently at his desk for a few minutes, staring out of the heavily-barred window and idly twiddling his fountain pen. He reviewed carefully all he knew of the recent history of the Desais, the hints he had heard of their holdings in many new enterprises, their influence amongst Government officials, Mahadev's travels. At last he said, 'Discuss the Desais with Anasuyabehn. She's old enough to be consulted.'

His sister hid her satisfaction at this reply, and merely said, 'All right.'

Her bare feet made a soft brushing sound on the stone floor as she shuffled off to the kitchen, ostensibly to consult Anasuyabehn.

The Dean continued to think about the Desais. Except on grounds of caste, there could be no reasonable objection to the match, and for years he had been preaching that Jainism had originally been a revolt of the Kshatriya military caste against their overbearing Brahmin priests; there was no caste among the original Jains. Young Desai was reasonably educated, had a good, though old, house and was certainly rich; his trips to Europe would have broadened his outlook and, indeed, these days, the family seemed to be financiers and jewellers rather than orthodox moneylenders.

It was said that Mahadev's father was ailing and his uncle was very old, so it would not be long before Mahadev became the head of his communal family. Further, in less than twelve months Dean Mehta would himself retire, and he dearly wished to give himself to a life of contemplation – to become a monk; he had for some years been quietly directing his life towards this goal by study, fasting, confession and the taking of those vows permitted to a layman. To have Anasuyabehn settled now might mean that he would see a grandchild before he severed all earthly relationships by taking his final vows.

He re-opened his book and composed his mind again for work.

'We'll see what Anasuyabehn has to say,' he decided.

Aunt, meanwhile, had sat in a corner of the kitchen and helped to prepare vegetables, while she considered what to say to Anasuyabehn.

The kitchen was quite modern. It had a water tap and beneath it, on the floor, had been built a low, stone enclosure to confine the splashes from it and guide spilled water down the open drain. The walls were whitewashed and, on a built-in shelf, glittered the brass cooking utensils. A watercooler reposed on a stand in a corner near the casement window, and huge double doors, which led on to a veranda, stood open to let in the morning freshness before the real heat of the day began.

'Take the new box of charcoal outside,' Anasuyabehn said to her little servant, 'and brush it.'

The boy picked up a small handbrush and the box and obediently went out into the compound, where he could be heard happily talking to a squirrel, as he gently went over each piece of charcoal with the brush to make sure that no insect was accidentally burned when the fire was lit.

Aunt seized the opportunity to say, 'I saw Mahadev Desai this morning.'

'He's been away a long time,' said Anasuyabehn. 'I don't suppose many people will be glad to see him. He drives even harder bargains than his elders, I'm told.'

She was sitting idly on her kitchen stool waiting for the boy to come in with the charcoal. A neat pile of prepared vegetables, flanked by a tin of cooking fat and her spice box lay on the well-scrubbed floor beside her. The empty charcoal stove was out on the veranda and soon the servant would light a cooking fire in it and bring it to her, carrying it gingerly with long pincers so that he did not get burned.

'Tut,' said Aunt. 'You listen to too much gossip.'

Who's talking? thought Anasuyabehn grimly.

'He's concerned mainly with the jewellery side now – opened a shop in a place near England.' As she snipped away at the vegetables, she tried to think of aspects of Mahadev which might appeal to a young woman, and added, 'He had a Western suit on this morning. I saw him driving through the cantonment, when I was on the bus – on my way to Mrs Patel's.'

'Did he?' murmured Anasuyabehn politely, and thought absently that she must buy some more glass bracelets next time a bracelet seller came round.

Aunt had no intention of discussing matrimony with Anasuyabehn, but she did want to obtain from her some words of approbation in respect of the Desais, which she could carefully misinterpret as assent to a proposal. Mistress of domestic intrigue, dedicated matchmaker, she had no intention of giving Anasuyabehn the opportunity of refusal, and she was certain that a man with the taint of moneylending about him would be refused. She, therefore, said no more that day, but during the weeks that followed Anasuyabehn was regaled with quite a number of stories of the nobility and kindness of Mahadev Desai.

Anasuyabehn should undoubtedly have realized what was in her aunt's mind, but she was entirely absorbed by ideas of marriage elsewhere. The memory of the beautiful, intense features of Dr Tilak staring up at her, as he walked past her home with Dr Bennett, had occupied her thoughts recently, and she only half listened to her aunt's chatter.

Aunt, meanwhile, luxuriated in the thought of bringing off such a superb alliance in spite of the difficulties of Anasuyabehn's advanced age and partly Christian education. If only her sons had lived, she thought sadly, how much more interesting life would have been to someone as skilled in matchmaking as herself; there would have been grandsons and granddaughters to marry off. Why the cholera should strike at her sons and leave her daughters was beyond her; and what trying daughters she had – always complaining because they had been married off to brothers who lived in Bombay, so far away from Shahpur. They were lucky, she thought bitterly – at least they ate twice a day, which was more than she had done in the first days of her marriage.

How good her brother had been, she reflected, to give her a home. Anasuyabehn, too, was a charming, respectful girl; Aunt would enjoy taking an interest in her children, though, of course, she would not see very much of them – once a girl was married she belonged to her husband's family, not to her father's family.

First, however, Anasuyabehn must have a husband.

If I can get my brother so enmeshed in marriage arrangements that it would be difficult for him to retreat with dignity, he also will press Anasuyabehn towards the marriage. And I must prepare Anasuyabehn, so that at least she does not immediately object when the offer comes.

Lucky women went to and fro between the parents' houses, and it was curious how, every time a visitor was expected at the Mehta house, Aunt thought of something which was required from town, and Anasuyabehn and her boy servant were dispatched to purchase it, whilst the horoscopes of the proposed bride and groom were discussed and compared.

Anasuyabehn was not a gossip; she had no reason to suspect anything. Even Savitri, her best friend, who might have told her, knew no one else amongst the Jain community and, busy with her work as a chemist in a cotton mill, heard nothing.

Skilfully the old lady spun threads of praise and flattery between the unsuspecting fathers – the wily old moneylender, who was busy trying to rid his family of most of the taint of moneylending and to gain instead a reputation as a jeweller and financier of integrity, and the absent-minded scholar, who, having inspected and spoken to Mahadev, liked him very much. There were times, not so long since, thought Dean Mehta ironically, when neither of them would have dreamed of speaking to the other, but many things were permissible nowadays – the walls between the castes were crumbling down, and Dean Mehta was quite prepared to give them a helping push.

Once Dean Mehta asked his sister, 'Is Anasuyabehn content about this marriage?'

'Oh, she has all the foolish ideas of a young girl – but she will appreciate a good man. She agrees that the family in this generation is becoming a most worthy one – and she has been most interested in my stories of Mahadev.'

'Ah,' said her brother, a little relieved. 'I'm content, as long as she has no antipathy to the match.'

'None at all, none at all,' said Aunt, with considerably more conviction than she really had. She hoped fervently that all her propaganda directed towards her unsuspecting niece was having sufficient effect to ensure an affirmative answer when the time came.

As she became further committed, the horrid thought of how other women of the family would snigger behind their hands at her, if she failed, began to haunt her – they might even suggest that she was, with advancing years, losing her skill, and that would be hard to bear. She put these thoughts firmly behind her; dear Anasuyabehn should have a wonderful marriage – and all through her aunt's sagacity.

7

The day on which Mahadev would make a formal visit to his prospective bride's family drew near. Unfortunately, his aunt had to return to Baroda to nurse a sick son, so it was understood that Mahadev would be accompanied by his brother and sister-in-law.

That morning, Anasuyabehn's aunt hinted to her that her father had a well-to-do and charming suitor in mind for her. Anasuyabehn, who had done little else but dream about the new, unmarried Professor of Zoology, ever since she had seen him from the roof of her father's bungalow, asked with interest, 'Who is he?'

'Ah-ha,' responded Aunt, all cheerful coyness. 'Your father will tell you in due course.'

Anasuyabehn could not think of any particularly eligible man who had swung into their orbit recently, other than Tilak, and she smiled happily.

Aunt had informed her brother that all was now arranged. The first gifts had been exchanged, and Aunt explained, 'I locked them in the almira, so that they will be a nice surprise for Anasuyabehn, when you tell her that the final arrangements have been made.'

The Dean smiled. He liked the idea of giving his daughter a pleasant surprise. He had been extremely busy, because the enrolment in his Faculty had increased markedly that term, and he had hardly exchanged a word with his daughter for weeks. He felt that he really must now talk to her about her marriage, though his sister, he was sure, would already have discussed everything with her.

He opened his study door, and called, 'Daughter, come here.'

'Well,' he greeted her, as she entered a little apprehensively. 'This is a happy day for us, isn't it?'

'Yes, father,' she answered submissively, masking a tumult of anxiety in her heart.

Aunt shuffled in behind her and sank on to the couch.

Dean Mehta sat down in his desk chair and took his daughter's hand. 'Well, now, are we quite happy at the idea of leaving our old father and going to a fine, young husband?'

Anasuyabehn did not know how to reply, and raised her heavily kohled eyes to her father.

Finally she said, 'I don't want to leave you, father – but I know it *is* time I was married.'

'Good, good. You won't be going far from me, anyway.'

He contemplated his daughter benignly. A placid, obedient girl, educated and yet without the flighty ideas of some of the women students on the campus. He beamed at her with satisfaction, while she waited with as much patience as she could muster. Then she said, in reply to his remark, 'That will be nice, father.' After all, Tilak would probably remain for years at this university.

Dean Mehta dug his key chain out of his pocket and selected a key, which he handed to his sister, while he nodded his bald head in amiable agreement.

'Get the parcels out of the cupboard,' he instructed her, and Aunt creaked to her feet to do so. Anasuyabehn watched her with pleasant anticipation, willing to go along with their desire to tease her gently.

'The Desais have sent some beautiful gifts,' said her father, as he watched his sister bring out a number of bundles.

'The Desais?' Anasuyabehn looked at him with blank incomprehension.

Dean Mehta glanced quickly at her, startled by the surprise in her voice. She was looking at him as if she had suddenly discovered a corpse.

'Yes – Mahadev,' he said.

Anasuyabehn sank into the visitor's chair by her father's desk, dazed by the shock. Far away, she could hear her father's voice, but the only word she really heard was Mahadev. She was so aghast that it seemed to her that she never would take breath again; however, her aunt evidently turned the fan towards her, because she felt the breeze on her face. Gradually, the world took shape again. Out of the mist loomed her father's face, full of anxiety, and his voice boomed into her ears.

'Dear child,' he said, full of self-reproach. 'I kept you standing too long on this hot day. Let Aunt give you some water.'

Aunt had already poured a glassful from his carafe, and she held it to the girl's lips. For once, the old woman could not think of anything to say.

Anasuyabehn sipped obediently, and life flooded furiously back into her. All her aunt's gossip of the previous few weeks came back to her and fell neatly into place.

'Marry a moneylender?' she gasped scornfully. 'Oh, no, father. No!' The last word came out in a wail.

Dean Mehta looked at her in some astonishment.

'He's hardly a moneylender, child. He's a big financier. Desai Sahib and his associates put up no less than half the money for the new chemical works at Baroda. Anyway, I thought you wanted to marry Mahadev.'

'Why should I think of marrying him?' Anasuyabehn asked, through angry tears.

'Your aunt assured me that you wanted to.'

'When I spoke of him,' interposed her aunt hastily, 'you agreed what a nice family they were. You made no criticism whatever.'

'I never thought of marrying one of them,' retorted the girl. She dabbed her eyes with the end of her sari.

Dean Mehta looked at his sister, and demanded sharply, 'What've you been doing? Didn't you ask her?' He seemed suddenly fierce.

Aunt looked uncomfortable. Her mouth opened and shut, as she searched for a reply. She had not expected serious opposition from Anasuyabehn, once her father was committed to the match. She thought the girl would accept fairly contentedly the prospect of such a fine, rich bridegroom.

Anasuyabehn's faintness had passed and she glared at the old woman, whose white widow's sari served only to remind her of the troubles of early widowhood, the likely result if one married a man much older than oneself. Only a lifetime of training stopped her from screaming with rage at her aunt.

Aunt mustered her forces. She said indignantly, 'I've talked of little else for weeks. I told her all about the family and about the return of their eldest son. I was sure she understood.'

'Marriage never occurred to me,' Anasuyabehn defended herself, through gritted teeth. 'They're not the same caste. I just thought you were telling me the news – gossiping!' The last word came out loaded with rage.

'Sister!' Dean Mehta's voice was full of reproach. 'Now we are committed. You stupid woman!' Mentally he reviled himself for leaving so important a matter to her.

'It's a good match,' said Aunt defensively. 'Mahadev could marry anyone he chooses round these parts – and he chose Anasuyabehn.'

'*Chose* me?' exclaimed Anasuyabehn. Since she had never even spoken to Mahadev she had assumed that his father was arranging the marriage.

'Yes,' replied Aunt quickly. 'He's admired you for years. However, you were betrothed. But now he finds you are free, and dearly wants to marry you.'

'Oh,' said Anasuyabehn, surprise for a moment overcoming her anger.

The Dean, thoroughly exasperated by his sister, nevertheless saw his chance, and said to his bewildered daughter, who was agitatedly running her fingers through her hair, 'My daughter, your aunt is right. It is a good match in these troubled times.' He pursed his lips, and then went on, 'Certainly she should have talked it over thoroughly with you – I regret not asking you myself, but I've had so much on my mind lately – however, here we are committed to it, and before we do anything more, I want you to consider it carefully.'

Anasuyabehn looked at him helplessly. She felt, as her father pressed Mahadev's suit, that her last Court of Appeal was being closed to her, and she sat like a silent ghost while her father extolled Mahadev's virtues. When he produced an exquisite sari which had been brought, as a token of the engagement, by one of the ladies concerned in the negotiations, she sat with it half opened in her lap, and hardly heard his voice.

'Child, it was sad that your betrothed should die – I know you liked him. And, unfortunately, it made you look a little unlucky in the eyes of parents . . .' He tailed off.

'Mahadev is a handsome man,' put in the old woman, her voice almost wistful, only to be crushed by an icy look from Anasuyabehn.

'And a generous and thoughtful one,' added her father, cheering up a little, as he picked up a small box from his desk.

Mahadev had often been impressed by Anasuyabehn's quiet and dignified demeanour when he had watched her in the streets; she walked with the perfect foot placement and timing of an elephant, he had many times told himself. Older and wiser than most bridegrooms, he greatly desired to win the favour of his wife-to-be. He had, therefore, insisted that the traditional bags of white and brown sugar be sent to her home, burying in them, instead of the usual two rupees, a small silver box with which to surprise her. It was this box which her father now handed to her.

Though she was very dejected, Anasuyabehn's curiosity was aroused by the unexpected token. She took the box from her father and opened it.

On a fluffy bed of cotton reposed a small nose ring consisting of a single diamond set in gold. Exquisitely cut, it flashed in the sunlight with a delicate blue radiance, a beautiful ornament which spoke, with fabulously expensive eloquence, of its donor's wealth, and of his interest in her as a person. With an odd quirk of humour, Anasuyabehn saw the mental agony with which a close-fisted, traditional moneylender must have parted with such a valuable gem. He must be in love to the point of insanity, she thought grimly.

Fascinated, she lifted the ornament out and laid it on the palm of her

327

hand, a hand that began to tremble with a deep fear of the unknown. Here was proof positive that her suitor would not take a negative answer easily. The gift was really valuable and quite unnecessary at such a time.

Until her father had handed her the little box, she had taken it for granted that, somehow, she would be able to escape from the marriage agreement. But now fear seemed to creep out from the blue stone and wind itself round her heart. A man who loved passionately was not going to be fobbed off so easily – nor was his powerful family, who seemed to be bent on rising socially as a caste. She knew what it was to be in love, she admitted, in love with a strange Maratha from Bombay, and, as she met Tilak on various social occasions, she had begun to feel the white heat of it. What might a powerful man like Mahadev do, if he felt the same?

And deep down inside her was a little worm of added fear, nesting in her Gujerati respect for money, that, because of Mahadev's undisputed wealth, she might be tempted to be unfaithful to the new unnourished love which possessed her – though Tilak was not a bad match; a professor had everyone's respect and a steady, if not large, income.

She could feel fresh grief rising in her, in belated mourning for her original betrothed. If he had lived, she would have had a family by now and would never have lifted her eyes to Tilak – and Mahadev would have looked elsewhere for a wife. She had not cried at the time of her fiancé's death – one rarely does about someone seen only once; but now she wished deeply that his thin, tuberculosis-ridden body lay between her and the fires of passion and fear now consuming her.

I'll object, she thought, and her inward sense of weakness made her outwardly more belligerent. She gritted her teeth and glared furiously through her tears at her aunt.

Her father took her silence for reluctant acceptance, and said quite cheerfully, before her defiance could be expressed verbally, 'Well, daughter, now you can see how highly Mahadev thinks of you. I think well of him myself and I believe you would learn to, too. Come, let us make him happy and give him a marriage date.'

Toothless and shrivelled as a dry orange skin, her aunt squatted on the floor, nodding her head and smiling amiably.

'An astrologer should arrange it,' she said, taking out her betal box and scraping round in it for a suitable piece of nut to chew. 'Though first there should be some parties, so that my niece may meet her future husband.'

'I don't want to be married,' said Anasuyabehn in a small tight voice.

'Tut, tut,' said her aunt, grinning as she chewed.

'I'd rather be a nun.'

328

'You'll change your tune when you have a small son in your arms,' said the old lady, waving one scrawny arm to hitch her sari further over her shoulder.

'Father,' implored Anasuyabehn, tears pouring down her face. 'Must I?'

The Dean scratched his head in embarrassed silence. Finally, he said, 'Daughter, I have loved you too well and kept you by me too long. It will not be easy to find anyone else as well-to-do, so healthy or so influential.'

'I don't like him, Papa. I don't care about him being rich.' She sniffed back her tears. 'He's not the only man in the world.'

'Come, come, daughter,' he said. 'You have not yet even *met* your future husband. We'll have all the tea parties, as if you were just a young girl, and you may speak with him. Don't cry, child. I am sure you'll be a patient and dutiful wife and will be amply rewarded.'

Her aunt sniffed and looked at the ceiling; her own rewards in marriage had been few. It was unnatural, however, for a woman not to be married; and this is what came of leaving girls single too long – they became stubborn.

Anasuyabehn covered her face with her sari and, under its comforting darkness, she saw for a moment a dark, thin face looking up at her as if enchanted. The new Zoology man was a fine man to look upon. She gave a little, shivering sigh.

'Father, could you try for somebody else?'

'Who?'

'Perhaps someone in the University.'

'They're all married.'

Anasuyabehn tried to bring herself to the point of saying that the Professor of Zoology was not, but her courage failed her and she whispered, 'Not *all* of them.'

'Who isn't?' asked the Dean, his ire against his sister again beginning to rise.

Aunt cackled. 'I know,' she said. 'I've seen you with the other girls, making sheep's eyes.'

'Well, who?' queried the Dean again.

'The Zoology Professor!' laughed Aunt.

The Dean digested this information slowly. He had honestly not considered this young man, but the suggestion did not meet with much approval. Marathas were not popular in the Gujerat; thin, taut, warrior-descended, mentally agile, they were the very antithesis of Gujeratis; and this particular Maratha, with his demands for journals, for more

329

lecture time, for a greater water supply, for a laboratory assistant, was already proving a bane to the worthy, but slow-moving Dean.

Meanwhile, Anasuyabehn stared unbelievingly at her aunt, marvelling at her powers of observation; she tended to think of her as part of the furniture, a necessary encumbrance, without life in herself.

Her fears redoubled.

Very quickly, Aunt loosed the deadliest shaft she possessed.

'A man who kills and cuts up animals,' she said.

Dean Mehta stared at her, horrified, his worst fears realized.

'No!' he exclaimed.

'Oh, yes. The mother of one of his students told me.'

'I must see him about it,' he muttered.

Making a great effort to be calm and firm, he turned to Anasuyabehn. 'A young man about whom we know so little would not be suitable, child. I would prefer you to marry a Gujerati, at least.'

Anasuyabehn nearly burst with rage at her aunt, and was about to explode verbally, when her little servant boy slid into the room.

'The young Desai Sahib is here,' he said to Dean Mehta. 'He's sitting on the front veranda.'

Anasuyabehn's rage gave way to panic; she sprang to her feet as if to fly.

Her father and aunt got up immediately, and her father said kindly, 'Don't be afraid, child. Would you like to see him?'

'No!' said Anasuyabehn fervently, while her aunt exploded, 'Tush, what are things coming to?'

'All right,' said the Dean a little testily, and, turning to the servant, he told him to bring Mahadev into the living-room.

Anasuyabehn fled to the kitchen veranda, picked up a basket tray full of millet which she had been cleaning earlier, and began feverishly to pick the small bits of stone and the insects out of it. When she was sure all the insects were out and carefully deposited over the side of the veranda, she tossed the grain up and down on the tray to bring to the edge any other impurities. She picked these out and then emptied the millet into a shopping bag.

'Bhai,' she called to the servant, 'take this to the miller.' Her voice still shook, but she had gained some comfort from her domestic task.

The boy shouted that he was making tea for the Sahib, and she waited quietly until he had finished and had taken the tea to the study.

He came slowly back to her, his bare feet dragging, and took the bag from her. He did not leave her at once. He stood first on one foot and then on the other, his grubby face as woebegone as Anasuyabehn's. In the moment or two he had been in the study his world had crumbled;

330

from the conversation he knew that Anasuyabehn, whom he loved as much as his mother, far away in his native village, was going to marry the terrifying Mahadev Desai. He was only ten, and he could not visualize life in a house which held only a tart, old lady and an absent-minded old gentleman.

'Well?' asked Anasuyabehn.

'Bahin, are you really going to be married?'

Anasuyabehn nearly choked, as sobs rose in her and were hastily crushed down.

The boy looked frightened, and she took his hand and pulled him to her. 'I'm not sure,' she said. 'But you mustn't worry. Your work will be here just the same.'

He was not satisfied; a child's instinct to sense trouble was with him, and he feared change.

'Can I come with you to serve in Desai Sahib's house?'

'I don't know, boy. I will ask. Do you want to come?'

The boy fell to his knees and touched her feet. He would have lifted her foot and touched his head with it, but she restrained him. Such devotion from so small a person hurt her. 'My cup is full,' her heart cried. 'My cup is full.'

'There,' she said comfortingly. 'If the marriage is finally arranged, I'll ask the Sahib. Go and get the clean shopping bag, to put the flour in – and remember to feel the flour as it comes out of the chute. Last time you brought back half of someone else's rubbish which was already in the machine. The miller is a rogue.'

Her gay tone made the boy laugh. He crammed his round, black cap on to his head and was soon on his way.

Anasuyabehn sat stonily on the veranda. The first panic had ebbed from her and she felt tired and exhausted. Furthermore, she had no idea what to do. She was no fool; she knew that by worldly standards an alliance with the Desais was desirable; the difference in caste troubled her not at all – she had gone to school with many different castes – but the possible Bania orthodoxy of the Desais' home life did. It was an orthodoxy which forbade more than a minimum of communion between husband and wife, judged success in life by the amount of money buried in the floors of the house and regarded its acquisition as a religious duty.

Then there was Tilak, whose burning, narrowed eyes sought her out from among the other women at the tea parties and badminton parties given by the University staff, so that she blushed and had to put her sari up over her head to hide her confusion.

In angry revolt against her father's wishes, her tired mind sought

331

frantically for a solution. She could become a nun, she considered desperately, and gain universal respect thereby – but the Jain religion offers little of true comfort for a woman.

She could run away – to what?

There is no place in India for a woman by herself, she thought bitterly, no honourable means of earning a living alone.

She remembered mournfully those brave Jains who sought release from the cycle of rebirth by starving themselves to death. She thought of her soft, round body tortured by hunger, reduced to an ugly bundle of suffering.

'I couldn't do it,' she acknowledged miserably. 'I want to live – life could be so sweet.'

She thought of Tilak and the weight of disapproval that would descend upon him, as a result of her aunt's remark about his dissecting. What an old troublemaker she was. She wept.

As her weariness gained on her, fear receded. Eventually, half asleep, she began to dream of a real lover, someone who thought her beautiful in mind and body, someone who would give her a son like himself, tall, slender, dynamic, and a little girl to dress in frilly, Western dresses. But the fact that Desai obviously thought of her as a very desirable woman was forgotten.

Desai had stayed half an hour, listening politely to his would-be father-in-law and hoping to catch a glimpse of his betrothed. At last, reluctantly he took his leave, and it was arranged that he would call again more formally, bringing his relations with him to meet Anasuyabehn. The Dean gave no hint that his daughter might repudiate the agreement, because he heartily hoped she would not. Orthodox he was in much that concerned himself alone, but he was intelligent enough to know that his grandchildren were going to live in an entirely different world, and he felt that that world, as far as India was concerned, was going to belong to those with capital and initiative. The Desais had both. He knew that many might criticize his choice of a husband for his daughter; yet his instincts told him that he was right. Moreover, he liked Mahadev personally; the man was neither ignorant nor stupid and he heartily respected his future father-in-law's learning.

John had heard all these things from devious quarters. It provided him with considerable quiet amusement to listen to the sweeper, to Ranjit, to the milkman, the vegetableman, the washerman, all the horde of people who daily came up his veranda steps and took a tremendous interest in those they served. It was John's opinion that it was impossible to eat something different for dinner without all the neighbours being informed by their servants of the details of it. To John, it was like a play which he watched as an audience. His own life was so plain, so austere, that he cared nothing if his neighbours knew all about it he gathered from Ranjit that it met with their approval, even if Ranjit himself felt that his lifestyle should be a little more suited to his station.

As John sorted out his sketches of the Dreams of Trisala and prepared to write captions for them, for his book, he wondered idly how Mahadev would get on at the formal family meeting in Dean Mehta's house; and whether Tilak was aware that his name was being coupled with that of Anasuyabehn. Did Anasuyabehn herself realize the fact?

8

John soon dismissed Mahadev Desai from his mind. After finishing the captions for his sketches, he began to draft a description of the enclosing cloisters of the Marwari Gate temple, with their fifty-two small shrines, each of which seemed to be the work of a separate person.

He did not hear the students shouting goodbye to each other as they left the badminton courts and the cricket pitch, nor Ranjit gossiping with the milkman when he brought the evening milk.

When Ranjit brought his tea on a small, brass tray, he forgot to drink it; and Ranjit took one look at the dark head bent over the manuscript and at the scuttling fountain pen, and turned on the desk light. Then he retired to the kitchen veranda and took a nap, knowing well that on such a day dinner would not be required until late.

A sharp rap on the outside door, however, forced John to lay down his pen and call, 'Come in.' He fumed inwardly at the interruption.

His irritation quickly turned to pleasure when he saw who the caller was.

'Why, Tilak!' he exclaimed. 'Come in.' He waved a friendly hand towards the couch. 'Sit down. How are you?'

It was odd, he reflected, that this excitable, tense man had found his way into his affections so quickly. Perhaps it was because his ability to be one minute exalted and the next minute cast down was almost child-like and one automatically consoled him as if he were still a youngster.

As Tilak took the proffered seat, he looked unsmilingly at John. Then the door was flung open again by the wind, and a swish of sand flew across the stone floor. With a muttered exclamation, he jumped up to shut it. 'Sand storm coming,' he said, as he shot the great, brass bolt with unexpected force, as if to keep at bay something more than the whirling wind.

He plonked himself down again on the couch and sat there silently, pounding one clenched fist into the palm of the other. It was obvious that he was in a dreadful temper; his face was as grim as an idol of an avenging god.

John hastily abandoned all thought of his work, and asked, 'Anything the matter?'

'Everything,' said Tilak.

'Like to tell me about it?'

'Yes, indeed. I came to you . . .' he started and then stopped, realizing that he really did not know this monklike Englishman very well. The man was famous in the city and in the University, he told himself. Everybody spoke of him with admiration, and one of the first questions any member of the staff asked him was whether he had yet met him. Surely, he would understand. He looked at the face before him; a typical lantern-jawed English face, the skin made red and leathery by much exposure to the Indian sun, lines of pain etched deeply into it, yet with a long thin mouth as sensitive as his own and narrow, blue eyes, bloodshot with study, observing him sympathetically. Compared to Marathas, the English were not a handsome race, he ruminated with sudden pride. He sensed, however, that this eccentric Englishman had an integrity, a trustworthiness, which was rare enough anywhere, and he badly needed to talk to somebody outside the University.

John always seemed willing to give him time, time and a considered opinion when asked for it, so Tilak made a real effort to control his rage; but the words he wanted would not at first come to him in English.

John turned his chair so that he faced Tilak, took his pipe out of his pocket and resigned himself to listening. Quite often he found himself consulted by irate members of the University staff deeply provoked by the petty politics of the campus – as if I were some antiquated guru, he thought ruefully, guaranteed to give impartial advice. He knew that all he had to do was to listen for an hour and then suggest a little moderation on both sides, and the men concerned went away comforted. Most of the squabbles were incredibly petty and he got some amusement out of watching them resolve themselves.

John offered Tilak a cigarette from the little wooden box which lay on his desk, and it was accepted eagerly. He struck a match for his guest, and watched him puff like a steam engine until he was wreathed in a cloud of smoke.

Since Tilak did not seem to be able to get started, John eventually asked, 'Well, how are things?'

'Things are very well, thank you,' said Tilak, grinding his teeth, 'except that it seems that I am not to do the work which I came here to do.'

'Really?' exclaimed John, rather puzzled by the intensity of rage in Tilak's voice.

Tilak scowled, his fine face distorted with anger, and ground the end of his much abused cigarette into an ashtray.

'These fools! These lunatics,' he muttered. 'These religious maniacs!'

John surveyed the bent and shaking shoulders. He was almost afraid

335

of such intensity of rage – it appeared unnecessary and unseemly to him. But when Tilak buried his face in his hands, and muttered that he might as well be dead as in Shahpur, John got up and went to sit beside him, not even noticing that he had managed several steps without the aid of his stick. He put a kindly hand on Tilak's shoulder.

The friendly gesture calmed Tilak. He began to speak more coherently.

'After weeks of dealing with new students,' he said, 'preparing lectures, attending endless tea parties, fighting for the supply of a few magazines – at last, I tell you – at last it seemed that I might have a few hours for my own research; I'm doing some work on the gills of fish. So, off I went to the Muslim fish bazaar, and arranged for a small supply of the particular fish I wanted – you'll know that fish are shipped up here from Bombay in salt-water tanks, live.'

'Well?'

'Well,' responded Tilak. 'I took some fish back to my laboratory. They were dead but fresh, so I began work. I had three fish on a slab beside me, ready to put into formaldehyde, and one dissected. Then there was a knock at the door and the Dean came in.

'"Ah, good day, Dr Tilak," he greeted me, all charm.'

'He is a very pleasant man,' said John, a little on the defensive immediately.

Tilak snorted.

'Humph,' he said. 'He came close to the table and peered at what I was doing.

'"Whatever is this?" he quavered.

'"A fish," I said. "In fact, altogether four fishes."

'He went quite white and looked at me horror-stricken.

'"But, my dear sir, we cannot have this kind of thing in our University," he said.

'I didn't know what to say. I was not quite sure what part of my operations was disturbing him. He looked very shaken.

'"This is Jain community, Dr Tilak, a Jain seat of learning. We cannot have life taken haphazardly right on our campus."

'I was so dismayed that I could only say stupidly, "They were dead by the time I got them here."

'He made a great effort to control himself, "I know that the sciences must be taught, but surely it can be done without taking life? Do you make a habit of this?"

'"I dissected a frog this morning for Zoology I," I said. Whereupon he was immediately violently sick all over my fish.'

John suppressed a desire to burst out laughing.

'What did you do?' he asked.

'I assisted him outside, and sent a servant across to his bungalow to get him clean garments. Anasuyabehn brought them herself. He did not address me further, and refused my help while changing in my office.

'After he was cleaned up, he went home, leaning on Anasuyabehn, while I walked behind him carrying his briefcase and the bundle of dirty clothes. I felt a complete fool.'

He got up and walked with three swift strides to the end of the room, turned and, with eloquent gestures of his hands, went on, 'When we got to the gate of his compound, he turned round and said, "I'll see the Vice-Chancellor tomorrow. In the meantime, please arrange to use only diagrams during your lectures."'

'What did you reply to that?' asked John, a twinkle showing in his eyes, despite Tilak's fury.

'I just said, "All right" and left them and went home. What could I say? While Anasuyabehn was there I couldn't quarrel with her father – such women as she are rare and I would not wish to trouble – and furthermore, he *is* the Dean, and I have only been here a few weeks.'

Tilak's rage was fizzling out and he looked haggard.

'When I went back to the lab. this afternoon, there was a different padlock on it – and that seemed the final insult. I couldn't even get into my own laboratory. I'm tired, Bennett Sahib. No Hindu will take life wantonly – but the situation here is absurd.'

He sank his head again into his hands and groaned, the drama of which was lost, as the veranda door burst open, admitting three of Ranjit's grandchildren, who must have been visiting him. John knew them well. They liked to peep around the door and examine the white Sahib, unbeknown to him, they imagined.

Ranjit shouted to them from amongst his cooking pots to come back, but John held them with a smile.

'Tilak,' he said, 'stay and have your evening meal with me. We can send a message to your mother by the children, and we can talk about the Dean.'

Tilak looked relieved.

'Dean, Dean,' shouted the children like parrots.

John laughed, and explained to them what he wanted. Tilak wrote a note for them to carry to Mrs Tilak and gave them an anna each. They hitched up their ragged little pants and were away through the front door and were scudding through the gloom of the dusty lane, before an irate Ranjit was aware they had gone.

9

Anasuyabehn had been very frightened by the message from Tilak, asking for a clean set of clothes for her father. As she flew to the almira to get out the garments, she questioned the peon.

The man knew only that the Dean had vomited. A cold fear nagged at her that he might be seriously ill – he fasted so much.

She decided that she would herself take the clean clothes to the small corner of the University building in which the Zoology Department had been lodged.

Two silent, embarrassed men awaited her. The peon carried the clean clothes into Tilak's office, so that the Dean could change in privacy, and then sat down cross-legged outside the door, to wait. Except for him, she was alone with Tilak for the first time.

Although she had already met him at several parties, she felt very shy, and her eyes uneasily examined her toes peeping out of her sandals.

Tilak cleared his throat, and after two false starts managed to say, 'It's nothing very serious. Dr Mehta was a little upset.'

Anasuyabehn raised her eyes as far as Tilak's middle shirt button, became painfully aware of the fine, muscular body showing through the sweat-soaked shirt, and despairingly raised her eyes to the thin, black face at least a foot above her own.

'What upset him?' she asked.

The shy scrutiny to which he was being subjected was too much for poor Tilak. Unused to having many women about him, he was acutely aware of every detail of the small, plump person before him. He could not think how to reply; he was aware only of the turmoil caused in him by a pair of rather deepset eyes, carefully rimmed with kohl, looking anxiously at him. He had a frightening desire to touch her softly rounded cheek and tell her that all was well.

He turned abruptly and took a couple of steps away from her.

'I dissected a fish and a frog,' he said.

Anasuyabehn was shaken out of her shyness by this admission, and she asked with a faint trace of awe in her voice, 'Did you kill them?'

'Yes,' said Tilak defiantly. 'It's part of my work – it doesn't hurt them.'

'Oh,' said Anasuyabehn. 'I didn't attend the science courses at the convent – I don't know much about these things.'

She lifted her sari over her head, so that her long hair, now carefully plaited, was hidden. She held the sari a little over her face, so that neither the peon nor Tilak could see her trembling lips. She again examined her toes, while the peon smoked a cigarette hidden in his palm.

A shaken Dean emerged from the office. He accepted the support of his daughter's arm, and they walked slowly homeward, followed by Tilak carrying the neatly bundled dirty clothes.

She prevailed upon the Dean to rest in the big swing which hung on the veranda and brought him water and a bowl in which to cleanse his mouth, face and hands; she was grieved to see that his hands shook, as he washed himself.

She set her little servant to preparing rotis and herself completed the making of a light lentil soup, which task she had had to leave unfinished when called to the University.

The need to hurry with her household tasks steadied her; her heavy lower lip ceased to tremble. With quick, experienced hands, she relit the charcoal fire, selected spices and pounded them, and took out the shining brass talis ready for serving the meal, as if nothing had impinged on her quiet life with her father.

Only after the meal was over and her father had gone to lie down for a little while, could she retire to her own room and acknowledge the tumult within her. Her aunt had spent the last few days extolling the virtues of the Desais to her. She was sick of it and was thankful to lean her tired head against the cool stone wall by her bed. The old lady had, that morning, gone to visit another elderly gossip nearby, so presumably, by now, the whole neighbourhood would know that she, Anasuyabehn, was to marry a Desai. Anasuyabehn cursed softly and fluently, as only suppressed, orthodox women the world over can curse.

She allowed her mind to wander back over the past few weeks. Her lips curved tenderly. Her pulses pounded, as she remembered the boring tea parties through which she had sat patiently with the other women in the kitchen, in the hope of glimpsing a certain tall, soldierly figure.

The advent of a new, high-caste bachelor on the campus had, of course, caused quite a lot of interest among the few unmarried girls in the families of the staff. They all agreed that, if he had not been so dark, he would be handsome – and he was so *Western*, that magical word vaguely associated with delicious licence and peculiar freedoms.

And the wonder of today. To stand alone, quite close to him, and actually speak to him. One by one, as if they were gold, she went over the words of their little conversation. He kills animals, she reminded herself, and was shocked to discover that she did not care whether he did or not. She, who had once hotly defended a scorpion against the thwacks of a University gardener's spade, found suddenly that anything done by Dr Tilak must be right, regardless of what the scriptures propounded.

Her aunt returned from her visit and crawled on to the end of her niece's bed, to sit cross-legged and reflective for a moment. Out of courtesy to the older woman, Anasuyabehn moved to get up, but with a slight gesture of one gnarled hand, she was told to remain where she was. Rheumy eyes regarded her kindly.

'Your future husband is calling again in the late afternoon,' she informed Anasuyabehn. 'Put on your best sari – he wants to see you.'

Cold commonsense flooded back. Who was she to dream?

'Yes, Aunt,' she replied sadly, doing her best to hide the burning resentment she felt. She knew she had no right to complain. Parents decided who one married.

Aunt watched her, as she changed into a blouse to match her best sari. 'In my young days,' she said, 'things were much more formal. But, then, this is a late marriage.' She shifted the piece of betelnut in her mouth, and then added, 'I am glad you're seeing sense at last.'

She wiped her lined face with the end of her white sari, while Anasuyabehn, feeling very helpless, got her best sari out of the cupboard and unwrapped it. The bright orange silk spoke to her of many a wedding attended in it, and her depression increased.

'I ordered a basket of ladus,' said her aunt conversationally. 'Dadabhai will make and deliver them himself. One never knows how many people will come on these occasions, and one should have plenty to eat in the house. I bought extra vegetables last evening for pecawlis, and I was looking for the boy to prepare them. Where is he?'

'At the grain shop. He won't be long. I'll prepare some of the vegetables now, and put on my sari later.'

The habit of obedience to her elders was so strongly ingrained in her that her acquiescence and her offer to help to prepare the tea for her unwelcome suitor were automatic. Only much later did it occur to her that she could have refused to have anything to do with the visit.

She was still tying her sari when she heard the carriage draw up at the compound gate. There was the sound of strange voices mingled with those of her father and her servant. She hastily brought the end of her sari forward over her bosom and tucked it into her waistband; the soft folds failed to disguise completely the generous curves of her figure, and she wished heartily that she was fat to the point of ugliness.

She felt so afraid of the interview before her that she was tempted to shut herself in her room and refuse to come out, but Aunt came to inspect her and quickly swept her out towards the front veranda.

'You look very well,' she said approvingly. 'That dark green blouse shows off your pale complexion. Hurry up, now. Your future husband has to catch the Delhi Mail.'

'Oh,' said Anasuyabehn, 'I wondered why the visit was so late.'

To her nervous fears was added more resentment. So she was being sandwiched in between business, was she? Her lips closed tightly, and it was a very distressed young woman who followed her aunt out on to the shadowed veranda.

A woman was seated on the swing; she was very thin and her expensive, flowered sari drooped on her. Huge eyes looked insolently out at Anasuyabehn from a heavily-boned face. Her lips smiled, however, and she put the palms of her hands together in salutation.

A small fat man in spotless white, who was seated in a basket chair near her, sprang anxiously to his feet and also saluted her. The lady immediately frowned at him and he subsided obediently back into his chair.

Another man who had been observing her quietly from the shadows now rose and made his salute.

Anasuyabehn was terribly afraid and looked down at the floor as she put her palms together in greeting. Except for a crow squawking in a tree in the compound, there was complete silence; all eyes regarded her, and she knew what it must be like to be a slave on sale in a market.

The stillness was broken by a shrill giggle from the visiting lady.

Anasuyabehn bit her lips and slowly gained enough courage to look up at Mahadev.

Her first thought was that he was much bigger than she had envisioned him to be. In spite of his plumpness, he had a commanding presence. Though she had no knowledge of the business world, she understood suddenly why he might be successful in his work. There was a dignity about him which spoke of a man who would not tolerate any nonsense, and his bright, intelligent eyes gave indication of the quick wits which were essential to his caste. Today, however, he had put aside his business for an hour and was looking down at her with benign approval.

So great was her respect for male authority and her desire for male approbation, that she held down her fears and treated the moneylender like any other visitor.

Mahadev himself was very nervous. He was anxious to make a good impression, and that bitch of a sister-in-law with her arrogant laugh was too much altogether. He scowled at her, and she retired behind her veiling sari to sulk.

341

He turned back to his wife-to-be, and the scowl cleared from his face. From a distance, he had watched Anasuyabehn many times in the bazaars and on the campus, but seeing her closely he was enchanted. She had a skin like ivory and the innocent expression of a child. All sorts of ideas shot into his head. That piece of land they owned down by the river – he could build a house upon it – a house for his father, himself, his daughter and Anasuyabehn; a quiet haven by the water. And she should wear emeralds – he had some perfect stones which only needed cutting.

Behind his impassive expression, his quick brain was already circumventing for this charming little woman the ills which she must most fear, particularly the one now sitting on the swing. After his experiences in France, he felt restless and anxious to shrug off the collar and lead of custom and try himself in the new world evolving in free India.

Anasuyabehn looked down at the floor again, and he was disappointed. He felt that the lid of a box had closed just as he was about to discover the contents.

'Let's all sit down,' said Mahadev, and Anasuyabehn and her aunt obediently sat down on basket chairs a little way from the Desais.

A painful silence ensued, which was providentially broken by the arrival of another carriage. Everyone, except Anasuyabehn, whose head was swimming with fresh fears that she might not be strong enough to fight the match, got up and went to the veranda rail, while the servant danced excitedly to the gate to let the new visitors in. They proved to be a stout, middle-aged couple accompanied by two wide-eyed schoolchildren.

'My respected father's cousin-brother,' announced Mahadev. 'Father and Uncle were unable to come owing to business. Father mentioned it to you last time you saw him, Doctor Sahib,' he said to Dr Mehta.

The Dean nodded, and room was made for extra chairs brought by the servant. Everyone again sat down and stared at Anasuyabehn.

Aunt ordered the servant to make tea, and the children cuddled close to their mother, who turned an amiable, lined face to Aunt.

'It's so hot still,' she said. 'It should have cooled a little by now.'

She accepted a glass of water brought by the servant, who carried a tray as big as himself from one visitor to another until all were served, and then vanished into the kitchen.

Aunt smiled at her, and inquired the names of the children. This launched the fond parent on the history of her offspring, their misdoings and shortcomings.

Anasuyabehn excused herself and went to help in the kitchen.

Mahadev watched her go with regret; he would have dearly liked to talk to her.

Dean Mehta was, however, talking about making a visit to Abu during the summer and he had, perforce, to give his attention to him, while in the kitchen Anasuyabehn deep fried savouries for him and wished he would kindly fall in love with someone else.

She was very bewildered. Her first fierce hatred of her suitor had died on seeing him; he did not strike her as the kind of man she could hate, nor did she despise him or his power. She felt like a mouse in a Gujerati cage trap; her thoughts rushed round and round and saw no way of escape. It is harder to fight an enemy one does not hate, she thought. Curse Aunt and all her machinations. 'Oh, Tilak Sahib,' she muttered, 'could you not make a move to save me?'

Why should he? asked commonsense; he doesn't know what you feel for him.

'I'll stall as long as I can,' thought Anasuyabehn, and then winced as the boiling fat she was using spat and burned her wrist. 'Time might offer some escape.'

She handed a dish of savouries to the servant to take out to the visitors, and then put a saucepan of water and milk on to the roaring Primus, for more tea.

She was sitting on her little stool, watching the mixture, when Aunt brought the two lady visitors into the kitchen. Though she stood up respectfully, she looked surly; then the heavy eyelids were again lowered.

The cousin-brother's wife was startled by the resentment apparent in Anasuyabehn's quick glance; it was unexpected, since the family had been assured that Anasuyabehn felt very honoured at the match. She sighed softly. She hoped that this new addition to the family would not cause more trouble; the thin stick of malice standing by her was a big enough trial. Mahadev should have looked in his own caste for a wife – this girl was too well educated for comfort. Mahadev's father had, however, agreed, so the good lady extended an invitation to the sullen girl to make a formal visit to the Desai household, in company with her father and aunt.

Anasuyabehn did not reply, so her aunt spoke for her. They would come in a week's time. She shot a reproving look at her niece, who ignored it. They could arrange her life for her – let them get on with it. She saw no reason to give them much help. She needed time – time to draw Tilak's attention to her. But how?

The gentlemen could be heard pushing back their chairs to leave, so the ladies put their hands together in farewell and an unsmiling Anasuyabehn did likewise.

The Dean saw his guests to the gate and afterwards walked slowly up and down the compound. A good, respectable family, he thought. And to think that Anasuyabehn had allowed her thoughts to stray towards that bloodthirsty horror, Tilak. The Dean shuddered as he remembered the murdered fish.

'Tomorrow, I'll talk to Dr Jain of Mathematics,' he considered, 'and together we can see the Vice-Chancellor. By this time even he must have heard about it.'

Indeed, by dinner-time most of the staff was debating the matter, the story having been spread by the peon who had overheard Anasuyabehn's and Tilak's conversation while they waited for the Dean to change his clothes. The story had lost nothing in the telling. The younger members of the staff laughed gleefully at the Dean's predicament. Despite persistent propaganda from the Central Government in Delhi that locusts, vermin and invading armies might be dispatched without sin, the older staff held strongly to the view that all life was sacred.

10

That evening the heat was still so great in John's room that he and Tilak decided to sit on the veranda, despite the occasional gusts of wind carrying sand. John propped his front door open in hope of cooling the room a little.

As he settled himself carefully in his basket chair, he tried to assure Tilak that he should not take Dean Mehta's fussing over his fish and frog too seriously. 'It may take a little time, but there are other, more worldly people on campus who'll prevail – don't forget that they want a medical school here one of these days.'

Tilak thought this over and then said, 'It isn't the Dean's being sick that troubles me – anybody unaccustomed to seeing meat or corpses might react in the same way. It's his assumption that everybody thinks the same way that he does – he's supposed to be Western educated and is a university man – he should have room for other people's ideas.'

'I know, but ahimsa is pretty well embedded anywhere in India, and especially so in the Gujerat.'

'If it were village people who had complained, I could understand it,' said Tilak, twisting himself round in his creaking basket chair. 'The village people here are Gandhiji's own people, and their belief in ahimsa – non-killing – was reinforced by him. It would be very hard to persuade them to kill anything, under any circumstances.'

'I think that's correct,' replied John. He remembered, again, the story Ranjit had told him about Government officials who had, a couple of years previously, tried in vain to get the local farmers to spray the locusts in their fields. They had faced starvation before they gave in, too late to save that year's crop.

'You know, Tilak, the Gujerat furnished both money and brains for Gandhiji's cause.'

'We all did,' sniffed Tilak.

'Kana,' shrieked Ranjit from the kitchen veranda, much to John's relief. He realized that they were both getting irritable from hunger, and he got up immediately and ushered his friend into his room.

A cloud of moths was dancing round the lamp and in the circle of light reflected on the ceiling, so he told Ranjit to move the table into a corner where they would not be bothered by falling bodies.

When they were seated, Ranjit went to the kitchen and returned with a bowl, a jug of water and a towel, so that they could wash their hands. Then, with a clatter of brassware, he brought in two talis laden with food, and the two friends ate ravenously in spite of the heat. Lentil soup, vegetables, fresh Indian rotis and curd vanished remarkably quickly, and Tilak looked considerably better when he finally accepted a cardamom from a carved box proffered him by John.

John took a clove from the same box, and they tipped back their chairs and grinned quite cheerfully at each other.

'I didn't eat much lunch,' said Tilak, almost apologetically.

'You would hardly feel like it.' John lit his pipe. 'Would you like a cigarette?'

Tilak accepted a cigarette, lit it and drew slowly on it.

'To someone like myself,' John remarked reflectively, 'Mehta is typical of all India – keeps his own customs, but is tolerant of other people's – except when it is a matter of killing something.'

'He's far too reactionary to be typical.'

'Not in everything,' John protested. 'He doesn't seem even to press his daughter to comply – she actually finished her education at a Christian convent school – and then her engagement – that's not a bit orthodox.'

'I heard that the boy died,' Tilak replied idly, as he blew a smoke ring.

'Yes, but I wasn't thinking of him. I was thinking of her new fiancé.'

'Her new one?' Tilak was shocked. His thin hands gripped the arms of his chair.

'Yes, she's going to marry the Desais' elder son – you know, the family which seems to have a financial finger in any pie round here. They're really moneylenders, but on a big scale these days.'

Tilak asked in a breathless voice, 'When is she going to be married?'

'In a month or two, I suppose.' John glanced quickly at Tilak. The Maratha's face was immobile, the lips compressed, the black eyes staring into the darkness, as if he saw, unexpectedly, something frightening. 'Why?'

'Because I want to marry her myself,' Tilak almost snarled between his clenched teeth.

'Well, don't bite me, old chap,' said John humorously. 'I didn't know you were interested – seriously.'

Tilak stood up and went to the veranda rail. 'I am most interested,' he said sadly.

'I'm sorry,' John said sympathetically, and wished suddenly that he, too, could feel as strongly about a woman. Now, however, he looked

346

at Tilak with some concern. The man had seated himself on the veranda rail and was feverishly cracking his finger joints, pulling first one finger and then the other as if he would dismember himself.

'I've no father to advise me, and my uncle would not understand,' he said. 'Bennett, what can I do?'

John shifted about in his chair.

'Do you *really* want to marry her?'

'Of course I do. It's time I married and I want to marry her.'

'She's a different caste and religion.'

'Don't be old-fashioned, Bennett Sahib. Plenty of people are marrying out of caste now.'

'Surely your family would object?'

'Uncle will – and so will mother, at first – but mother I can persuade.' He spoke with all the certainty of a spoiled younger son. 'It's Dean Mehta who is the stumbling block.'

'And the girl? What does she think?'

Tilak looked startled for a moment, and then said, 'I haven't asked her.'

'Well, perhaps you should find an opportunity to know her better, and then ask her. You'll have to be quick, though.'

Tilak gave up cracking his finger joints and gnawed one instead. 'I feel that it is all right with her – I've seen her a number of times.'

'Have you spoken to her?'

'Twice. The last time was when she brought clean clothes for her father this morning.'

John marvelled at the speed with which Tilak had made up his mind. Yet was it so very different among English people? One saw a girl and sought to know more of her and, after a while, one realized one was in love; yet probably that love was present from the first moment, unacknowledged.

'Look,' John said, 'I can't see, really, how you can forestall the marriage arranged for her, without a concerted effort on her part. Even then, I can't imagine how you're going to persuade the Dean to let her marry you – you're simply not popular with him, at present.'

'I'll do it, somehow.'

John whistled under his breath. 'Be careful, Tilak,' he warned him. 'It's not worth ruining your career.'

Tilak agreed, and then laughed sardonically. 'To have a wife and no food for her would be a disaster.'

'I saw Desai and some of his relations going to visit them, earlier this evening,' John told him, as he relit his pipe.

Tilak started to pace up and down, and John pushed his chair back, to give him more room. 'Don't do anything rash, old man.'

'Humph.' Tilak swung back to John's chair. 'I'll go home, Bennett Sahib. Come to visit me one day.'

'I will,' John promised, and escorted his friend down to the compound gate. 'Take care,' he said.

Tilak hardly heard him. He was already swinging swiftly down the dark lane, towards the hostel.

After he had vanished into the gloom, John stood for a moment holding the heavy compound gate ajar. It was not a pleasant night. A small crying wind was whipping up little whirls of dust. Families, who would usually be strolling up and down at this time, had obviously stayed at home because of the threat of a storm. Even the pariah dogs, who could ordinarily be heard rustling in the bushes or snarling at each other, seemed to have taken refuge. In spite of the puffs of wind, the heat was intolerably oppressive, and John took out his handkerchief to mop his forehead.

As he tucked the hanky back into his shirt pocket, he heard the sound of galloping horses approaching up the lane. Fools, he thought, to ride so fast in the darkness.

They were passing him almost before he could see them; four turbanned figures, their turban ends wrapped across their faces to protect them against the dust, naked feet thrust into high stirrups. He wondered who they were; there were few riding horses in the district, camels and oxen being the working animals. Horses were used for carriages.

Strangers, he guessed. Visitors of some kind, following the lane through until they would, eventually, strike the new road that had been built to connect more distant villages with Shahpur. It was a road which ran parallel with the railway and would, one day, be driven right through to Delhi.

Encumbered by a stick, it was not easy for him to shut the gate and shoot its great iron bolt. He felt tired and was thankful to reach his couch again, to lie down under the slowly turning ceiling fan.

11

John rose early the next morning, with the intention of working steadily through the day. He felt restless, however, and found himself doodling idly in the dust deposited on his desk by the dust storm the previous night.

The storm had begun soon after Tilak had left. The wind had howled round the small bungalow, like a lonely ghost. It had stirred up a dust so thick that windows and doors had had to be shut tightly, to avoid near suffocation. This morning, every leaf on the trees in the compound had a thick coating of dust balanced precariously on it. Inside the building, a fine powder lay on every floor and ledge; food tasted gritty and hair and skin felt dry and uncomfortable.

'Ranjit!' John shouted. 'Come and clean this room – it's not fit for a dog. Get the chattya wetted, to cool the place.'

'Ji,' came a resigned response from the back veranda. Brass dishes clattered against the stone floor, as Ranjit stopped doing the washing up and found his duster. Then John heard him shriek across the compound to Ramji, the sweeper, to bring his broom; Ranjit himself would not touch a broom – he was high-caste.

Ranjit appeared at the veranda door and surveyed his fretful master. 'Sahib, do your legs hurt?' he inquired solicitously. 'When I go to the bazaar, shall I ask the Doctor Sahib to come?'

'It's not my legs this time, Ranjit; my brain won't work.' He pressed his hands over his eyes. 'I can walk fairly well now with only one stick. In fact, I think I'll go for a walk.'

Ranjit grunted agreement. So that he could dust, he piled all the books and papers on the desk into one tottering tower. Ramji came in silently and began to sweep, shuffling across the floor in a squatting position, the soft fronds of his broom making a sighing sound on the stone flags.

As Ranjit removed the cover from the typewriter and shook the dust off it, he remarked, 'That murder on the Mail train was a bad business.'

John was halfway into a clean shirt and his voice came muffled through the cotton cloth. 'What murder?'

Ranjit ran his duster along the window sill, and Ramji clucked as the dust fell where he had already swept.

349

'You haven't heard, Sahib?'

'I haven't been out today. How will I know if you haven't told me?' A flushed face emerged through the neck of the shirt. 'Who's been murdered?'

Ranjit paused in his work and twisted his moustache thoughtfully before he answered, 'An English lady travelling on the Delhi Mail.'

'Not Miss Armstrong?'

Surprised at the sharp concern in his master's voice, Ranjit hastened to reassure him. 'No, no, Sahib. That was not the name. She was going up from Bombay in the First Class – a stupid place to travel, Sahib. It's where thieves will go first – she should have gone in the Ladies' Compartment.'

John smiled, as he buttoned up his shirt. It was true that when trains were held up, the Ladies' Compartment, full of screaming women, all of whom would have sent their valuable jewellery ahead by post, was not usually tackled by thieves.

'Where did this happen?' he asked.

'About four miles up the line, Sahib. You know where the train curves into that cutting? – I think it's called Ambawadi.'

'A good spot,' said John.

'Yes,' said Ranjit, 'Harichandra says there were many of them, some on horseback, some travelling on the train, and they –'

'On horseback? I saw four men on horses pass, when I was seeing Dr Tilak out of the gate last night.'

Ranjit stopped dusting, and Ramji looked up and gaped at John.

'Did you, Sahib? It could have been some of the Sindhi refugees – some of them brought horses when they came, and have made a little business trading in them – but horses are not very commonly ridden here, Sahib, are they? They are mostly for pulling carriages.'

'Yes,' said John. 'Perhaps it was just some Sindhis taking horses to a customer.'

He ran his fingers through his hair to straighten it. 'Make something with puris for lunch,' he instructed. 'I'll go for a walk round the campus and maybe call on Dr Tilak.'

'Ji, hun,' agreed Ranjit. 'The campus will be the only place free of police today.'

'Do you think they'll scour round this district as well?'

'They will come bothering and badgering, no doubt, Sahib. Locusts!'

'Tut, Ranjit. They have to work fast, or the dacoits will be out of the province before they can say Jack Robinson.'

Ranjit opened the door and Ramji continued his sweeping across the front veranda. He grunted. 'Police – work?'

John laughed, and went out into the merciless sunshine. Although it was hot, the air smelled sweet after the storm, and he began to whistle cheerfully, as he wandered along the lane. From inside the houses he passed he could hear the lively chatter of women's voices and the thud-thud of spices being pounded. The dhobi, bent nearly double by the great bundle of washing on his back, saluted him. Children stopped their play to listen to his whistle, fascinated at the strange, sweet sound, and he called a cheerful 'Hullo' to those he knew. It was a pleasant morning and his spirits rose.

He found Tilak emerging from a lecture room, followed by a crowd of students who drifted down the corridor, their shirt tails wafting gently behind them. They were all talking at once, their voices as shrill as cockatoos'.

Tilak drew John into the welcome quiet of his small laboratory which, he informed him, he had found unlocked that morning. He bade him sit down on a stool, while he washed the chalk from his hands.

'My frog and fish seem to have sparked a great debate,' he remarked, as he dried his hands on an old duster. 'The families of some of the students are really orthodox, and their relations are making a fuss. They don't want their children to take such Courses.'

'O, Lord,' groaned John sympathetically.

Tilak flung the duster into a corner.

'The old folk want the impossible,' he said. 'They want their young men to get enough training to put them into the better paid Government jobs, without their usual way of life being upset. It's the same everywhere.'

'Surely, it's only amongst the Jains that you would find it. And you have to remember that they are really a very cultured people. Seeking work outside their traditional occupations is new to them.'

'A pack of village moneylenders,' snorted Tilak.

John laughed. 'Come, Tilak,' he said. 'It's not so bad. They'll get used to you. After all, you must have had a battle with your family to get permission to take up research.'

'No. Father went to Cambridge,' replied Tilak tartly. 'He did physics.'

John felt snubbed, but he managed to say, 'That must have made your path much easier.'

Tilak caught the slight sarcasm in his friend's voice, and repented his sharpness.

'It didn't,' he said with a rueful laugh. 'He was insisting all the time that I take physics.'

John relaxed and laughed, too. 'Do you want to do some work now?' he inquired. 'If so, I'll leave you.'

'I prepare my lectures at home. Like to walk over with me? I can offer you some coffee.'

John assented, and they went out together and walked through the flower gardens in front of the building.

On the lawns, water-sprinklers slowly revolved, with an opulence which always made passing villagers stop to gape, because they themselves were so short of water. Blackbirds hopped in and out of the gentle downpour and the flowers glittered with tiny droplets; their perfume in the desert air seemed strange and exotic to John.

Tilak interrupted his thoughts by saying, 'Mother and Damyanti went home to Bombay this morning. They caught the nine o'clock train.'

'Really?' exclaimed John.

'Yes. They missed the gaiety of Bombay – and the heat here was hard on mother. I suppose I must get myself a servant.'

'I can imagine their being homesick.'

'Can you? Is it that you are homesick for England?'

'No. When I was in prison, I used to be homesick for Shahpur!'

Tilak laughed, disbelievingly. 'That is not possible. I wish I had never seen the place. You were in prison?'

'I was a prisoner of war.'

'Ah,' said Tilak, highly interested. 'I once did three months for participation in a riot.'

'All the best people in India have been in jail.'

'True,' replied Tilak. 'How else would we have got Independence?'

They came on to the road which bordered the campus. Students were standing about in sullen groups, all apparently engrossed in shrill argument. On the verge, a group of villagers was squatting in a circle, resting for a while from their long walk to town. As they leaned towards each other and gave respectful attention to an old man haranguing them, their big, ruby-red turbans looked like great raspberries ripening in the sun. Their red-clad womenfolk sat placidly behind the men, gossiping amongst themselves, while their half-naked children, oblivious of the heat, darted about like minnows in a stream.

John paused and regarded the scene lovingly. So colourful, so sane.

'Arree!' shouted Tilak suddenly. He stumbled and clutched at one shoulder.

John jumped, and turned to him in astonishment. 'What happened?'

Tilak picked up a half brick. 'This,' he said grimly. 'It was thrown at me.'

John's eyebrows shot up. 'Good heavens!' He turned swiftly to look back along the road.

The groups of students were melting rapidly away; those who had bicycles had already mounted them and were pedalling hard into the distance.

The villagers had shot to their feet and were staring aghast at the two men. Except for squawking crows, there was a profound silence.

'Did you see who threw that brick?' John called to the nearest villager, a middle-aged man.

'No, Sahib.' His face looked like a dried raisin, and he fluttered work-roughened hands. John could well imagine the panicky fears of accusation going through the man's head; fears of arrest, of beatings, of a fine levied against his village. He would never open his mouth.

John turned back to Tilak, who stood looking down at the brick in his hand. With the other hand, he ruefully rubbed his back.

'Are you much hurt?' John asked, in some anxiety. 'Turn round. Let me see your back.'

'I'm only bruised, I believe,' Tilak answered, as he turned. 'My frog is avenged, I think.' He dropped the brick in the dusty road.

There was some blood on Tilak's shirt, so John said, 'Let's get back to your room, so that you can take off your shirt and I can see better what the damage is. Are you steady enough to walk?' He put his hand under Tilak's elbow, and they continued slowly towards the hostel. 'I don't think a villager threw that brick – they would not dare to,' John continued. 'It was a student, all right. We'll get the Dean to institute an inquiry – he'll find the young devil.'

'The Dean?' exploded Tilak. 'No, John. I'm grateful to the brick-thrower – he's made up my mind for me.' He stopped and faced John. 'I'd like to be alone,' he said, his expression sad and disillusioned. 'I'm not badly hurt.'

'Of course, if you wish it.' John bit his lower lip. 'Are you sure you'll be all right? Don't do anything rash, will you?'

'My friend, sometimes one must grasp life by its shirt tail. Otherwise, it flashes past before you realize it.' He raised his hand in salute and left John to ruminate over this cryptic remark, while he strode away towards the students' hostel and his empty rooms.

12

When John approached the gate of his compound he was surprised to see Ranjit squatting outside it, when it was reasonable to suppose that he would be on the back veranda preparing lunch. John quickened his step, and, as he approached Ranjit, he observed an unusually tense, tight-lipped look about him.

'What's up?' he asked in Gujerati.

Ranjit stood up, and his clean, white loincloth gleamed in the sun, as he set his legs belligerently apart.

'A Memsahib has called and is waiting in your room,' said Ranjit, rank disapproval apparent in every line of him. Never, in all the time he had served the Sahib, had a Memsahib called. Why, the Sahib hardly ever visited English people himself.

'A Memsahib! Who is it?'

'Armstrong Memsahib.' Ranjit had an excellent knowledge of English names.

'Oh,' said John. 'She's come about the map, I suppose.'

'Map, Sahib?'

'Yes, Ranjit, I'm going to help her and Lallubhai Sahib prepare a special map of the city – showing drains and playgrounds and parks.'

'I see,' grunted Ranjit, relaxing a little. One never knew, however, what happened when a Memsahib was made free of a gentleman's home – Ranjit could not imagine a worse disaster.

John knew fairly precisely what was running through Ranjit's head and the gossip which would sweep through the campus, and yet, as he hurried across the compound, he was full of pleasurable anticipation. He forgot Tilak and his frog and thought only about talking to someone English; he found it hard to admit this need but knew it to be true.

He paused at the top of the veranda steps to rest his legs, then approached the door more slowly.

She was seated nervously on the edge of the chair by his desk, her face turned expectantly towards the door. He smiled as he approached her and shook her hand. Behind the smile there was great surprise.

He had previously seen her only in her nurse's uniform and again on the occasion of meeting her in the bazaar, when she had been garbed in grubby khaki. Today, her red hair shone with washing as it fluttered in the breeze of the fan, and, though her green eyes still had rings of fatigue round them, they were oddly appealing in a face no longer brick-red from exertion. Like many English women in hot climates, she wore little makeup, and the natural gold of her eyelashes and the delicate pink of her mouth reminded him of one of his mother's beautiful china figurines.

The same artist's eye which could note and transfer to sketch book the incredible detail of Jain sculpture saw and realized the implications of her plain white dress, obviously made at home from the cheapest mill cloth, and the plastic chuppells on her feet. Propped against her chair was a black umbrella, the cheapest way to protect herself against the ruthless sun.

God, thought John, Ferozeshah must pay her in annas. Yet, in spite of her obvious poverty, she made a pleasant picture, sitting in his working chair.

She explained shyly that Lallubhai and his Committee had come to the conclusion that the housing needs of the refugees were very urgent, so the previous evening they had asked her to convey their thanks to John and to discuss with him the map and the data already collected by the Committee. As she handed him a file of papers, she added her apologies for descending upon him so abruptly, but she had only one day a week free, and this happened to be it. 'I didn't want to delay it another week,' she went on. 'We have only four months before the rainy season and we hope that the maps will show up small open spaces, which we can begin to beg from landlords in order to put huts on them.'

John smiled and soon made her feel at ease, and she continued by saying that they had enlisted the help of the reluctant, overworked City Engineer, who had agreed to let them have access to his records, inasfar as they touched on the mapping of the city. The Mayor was already on the Committee, so civic co-operation was assured, as long as it did not get bogged down in the usual inertia of Indian officialdom.

John listened with pleasure to the rather deep voice, slightly tinged with a Gloucestershire accent, as she made each point clear. Occasionally, he asked a question. They had no hope, she said, of compiling a properly surveyed map, but, using John's and the City Engineer's maps as a base, they hoped to fill in most of the blanks sufficiently well to discover the more pressing needs of the population.

John considered all this for a minute or two. Then he said, 'They'll have to watch that the funds don't get misappropriated somewhere along the line.'

'Lallubhai is incorrupt,' said Miss Armstrong, 'and so are some of the others.'

'Yes. It's a very good Committee. Jains are like the little girl with a curl in the middle of her forehead. When they're good, they're very, very good, and when they're bad they're horrid.'

Miss Armstrong laughed.

'Could you stay to lunch?' asked John, and he was amused to see her go faintly pink as she answered that it was her free day, and all she had to do was to visit an old woman in Pandipura later in the day.

John went to confer with Ranjit, who was grinding spices on a flat stone, with a stone rolling pin. He still looked as sour as old milk but agreed that he could feed the lady, if she could take the north Indian food he usually prepared. John said that he was sure that she could eat it, provided he did not put too many chillies in it.

John returned to his guest and explained the situation to her, and she confirmed that she enjoyed Indian food.

'I eat a good many meals with the Ferozeshahs,' she said. 'Mrs Ferozeshah is a friend of mine – she was trained in Edinburgh as a nurse.'

'Ah, I wondered how you coped in a purely Indian hospital.'

Miss Armstrong blushed at the implications of the remark.

'Oh, I've never had any trouble,' she said. 'Dr Ferozeshah and his hospital have an excellent reputation, and he's always treated me very well. He's an FRCS, you know.'

'I know. He's lucky, though, to have a State Registered Nurse to help him.'

She beamed at him, and fingered the tiny brooch pinned to her dress; its enamel and gilt indicated her nurse's status.

'I find the work very worthwhile. Doctor does a lot of work in the City Hospital – and a good deal in the villages round about. You should see his doorstep at Divali – people come from miles around to bring him thankofferings of flower necklaces or fruit – he won't take anything else from poorer people.'

John was enjoying this feminine company more than he cared to admit, and wanted badly to know more about her. He chanced a direct question.

'Have you been with Ferozeshah long?'

'About two and a half years – I was with the Mission of Holiness before.'

John had never heard of such an institution, and said so.

'They have a tiny Mission about twenty miles north of here – almost in the desert. There were two American nurses, besides myself, and an elderly doctor.' She hesitated, and then said, 'They do excellent medical work . . .'

'A bit "holier than thou"?'

Miss Armstrong grinned mischievously.

'Very,' she said. 'I couldn't stand it any more, and yet I liked India and was in no hurry to go home. One day, when I'd come to Shahpur to buy shoes, I met Mrs Ferozeshah also trying on footwear. She saw my nurse's brooch and spoke to me, and ended up asking me to have tea at her house. She used to help her husband in his work, but now she has children she has not much time; and after another visit, when I met Dr Ferozeshah, I was offered my present post. The salary isn't much – a little more than he would pay an Indian nurse – but I can manage, and both of them are wonderfully kind to me, and I love their children, too.'

'You could nurse in England – and you must have friends there, also.'

'Yes, but the need there isn't so desperate. Maybe when I'm older and can't stand the heat so well, I'll go back home. My father would like to have me at home with him – he is a minister, a widower – and would like me to settle down at the parsonage and keep house for him.' She looked shyly out of the corners of her eyes at John. 'I simply couldn't face it,' she said with feeling. 'At least I'm alive here.'

'It can't be very entertaining for you, here, though. So few English people around.'

'On the contrary, I find I have quite a social life. The Ferozeshahs have introduced me to a number of their friends, and I get invitations to tennis parties and tea parties from all kinds of people. I feel very content. Nobody drives me in any way – I am free.' She unclasped her hands, which she had previously held tightly in her lap, and made a little opening gesture as if to show how her character had expanded in the wide latitude of Indian life.

John deliberated over this, and then said, 'You're right – I have the same feeling of freedom from social pressure. People aren't pressed so tightly into moulds here, are they?'

'No, they're certainly not.' She gave another of her low soft laughs. 'Is that why you stay here?' she asked.

'Me? I – er – well, after the war I just came back to the place I knew best.' Her question had confused him. He could feel an old depression creeping over him. 'To be honest, I felt after the war that we should be blown to hell pretty soon and, since there was not much I could do about it, I wanted to enjoy what time was left doing the work I like best. So I came home to Shahpur. After all, I was born here,' he finished up a little defensively.

The laughter went from Miss Armstrong's face and she stared unseeingly out of the window. His reminder of the menacing atomic shadow over the world brought back to her her reasons for taking up nursing.

A desire to repair, to build in some small way in a destructive world, had become a dedication so that she had soon lost herself in her work. Now, she never thought further than a day or two ahead, and that mostly when she was arranging Dr Ferozeshah's tight schedule of visits, operating, and so on.

She glanced quickly at John. He had absent-mindedly taken out his pipe and was packing tobacco into it, and at the sight of this male refuge being prepared, she smiled.

'I'm told that your coming here has been very fruitful. I've read your book about the conquest of the Gujerat in the thirteenth century, and, frankly, I found it so gripping that I read it at a sitting.'

She wanted badly to cheer him up and see him laugh. Today they were alive and there was time enough to worry about other days when they arrived. She was delighted to have such a cultivated Englishman to whom to talk and wanted desperately to please him.

He was grateful to her for turning the conversation, and replied, quite cheerfully, 'Ala-ud-din the Bloody in 1297. He was nearly as thorough as present day conquerors.' And once launched, he kept her spellbound, while he told her tales of ancient Shahpur.

The door to the back veranda swung open. A frigid Ranjit, in clean shirt and dhoti, announced that lunch was ready.

Miss Armstrong ate neatly with her fingers, using pieces of bread as a spoon where necessary, as did John. Afterwards, he persuaded her to wait a little, in the hope that the heat would decrease, before she set out to see her patient in Pandipura; but it was still very hot when she announced that she must go, and firmly picked up her small, black bag. He looked at her uneasily.

'Would you like Ranjit to accompany you?' he asked. 'The police are supposed to be looking for the train robbers in this district.'

'I heard about it,' she said. 'But I shall be all right, thank you very much. The police know me and most of the villagers do, too.' She went to the door and opened the umbrella. 'Mr Lallubhai has promised to invite you to the next Committee meeting. I do hope you can come.'

'Certainly,' said John. 'Only too happy to help.'

He was rewarded by a quick smile from beneath the ugly umbrella, and he felt reluctant to let her go. The Indian countryside was not a place for a woman to walk alone, particularly when it was believed dacoits were in the district. He told himself that his disquietude was unwarranted, that she was obviously accustomed to going about by herself and that the robbers had probably made all haste back to Saurastra, their usual stronghold.

He saw her out of the gate and received again her thanks, then closed the gate and shot the bolt.

Back in his room, he surveyed with distaste its cell-like bareness; only the desk with its untidy piles of paper spoke of life and work. He sat down on his chair and thumbed idly through his notes, which represented months of research. Determinedly, he picked up his pen and began to write.

13

Tilak went slowly up the long, stone staircase which led to his rooms. His back hurt more than he had admitted to John, and his spirits had suffered an equal blow. He could still hardly believe that a student had stoned him.

He dropped his briefcase on to the cement floor of his living-room, shut the door quietly and locked it. His second room led off the first and had been used by his mother and Damyanti.

He peeled off his shirt and vest to examine the backs of them. They both had a little blood on them, so he took down the cracked piece of mirror which served him when shaving, to have a look at the wound.

By holding the mirror at an angle and peering over his shoulder he was able to see the nasty weal, raw in places, which the brick had caused. He put the mirror down on his work table, on which the remains of a hasty breakfast still lay.

Deeply depressed, unsure of what to do, he crawled on to his unmade bed and lay there through the long, hot afternoon until darkness fell, his thoughts wandering miserably backwards and forwards over the events of the previous few days.

Footsteps in the passageway stopped at his door, and a white envelope shot under it and across the floor. He sat up quickly, winced when his back hurt him, and went to retrieve the missive.

In a polite note, Professor Jain regretted that a tea party, to which Tilak had been invited, had been cancelled, owing to unforeseen circumstances. 'Arree,' grunted Tilak. 'Poor frog – you are now called *unforeseen circumstances*.' Irritably he screwed up the note and flung it into a corner.

This letter reminded him of another, and he went to his briefcase and took it out. Delicately, he unfolded the two precious sheets of paper, and went back to his bed to sit down and read them again. The first page said:

Dear Dr Tilak, I am requested by the Committee of the Thomas Jones Foundation to inform you that they have considered your recent application and are pleased to grant you a Thomas Jones Fellowship, tenable at our laboratories in London from October 1st, 1951, for two years, after which consideration may be given to extension of this period by a further year. The scholarship consists of a grant of £700 per annum plus travelling expenses to and from England, and a small sum to cover visits to universities during your stay here. Kindly let me know when you expect to be able to take up the Fellowship.

Yours sincerely, Ian MacAngus, Secretary.

The second sheet was an informal and kindly epistle from Mr MacAngus, congratulating him and offering advice regarding travel and accommodation.

Tilak caressed the letters gently with his fingertips. The Head of the Foundation was Sir Andrew Diamond, a specialist in Tilak's field; and Tilak knew that, working under such a great man, he would expand his own knowledge and could hope for international recognition of his research.

Could he marry Anasuyabehn in a civil ceremony, get her a passport and whisk her out of the country, before her father could catch them? An elopement, that was the English word for it. The problem was that the Fellowship was not available until October and as yet it was only March; the Desai marriage was probably planned for sometime in the next two months.

'What the hell shall I do?' he fumed. 'What *can* I do?'

Would his uncle offer for her? No point in that; he would almost certainly be turned down politely, on the grounds that she was already betrothed. Alternatively, if he approached the Dean himself and begged a reconsideration of her present commitment, he would court an immediate rebuff. His dead frog would be enough to put the Dean off, never mind the problem of untangling himself from an agreed marriage. To add to the problem, there was always the argument that they were of different religions and different language groups.

While he stewed over the problem, he lit his Primus stove and made a cup of coffee. He took it over to the open window and sat down on the sill.

From the floor below rose the din of brass on brass as seven Brahmin students were served their dinner by the Brahmin servant they jointly employed to cook for them, and Tilak realized fretfully that the vegetable seller had not called on him that evening. This worthy, being the brother of the nightwatchman, was able to go through the hostel hawking vegetables, and he had never missed calling on Tilak before.

Perplexed, Tilak put down his cup and went out into the passage, in case he had failed to hear his knock and the man had left some vegetables outside his door. There was nothing. Three doors down, a

361

wilting green leaf testified to his passing. Tilak's eyes hardened and he went quickly back into his room and banged the door shut.

The vegetable seller was a Muslim and it meant nothing to him that Tilak chopped up animals or fish for his research. It did, however, mean a great deal to him if some of the larger Jain families or groups of Jain students, who lived in or around the students' hostel, indicated that they would take their business elsewhere, if he continued to serve Dr Tilak on the second floor. Undoubtedly, the vegetable seller's memory would slip conveniently, and Dr Tilak would be forgotten. Tilak wondered if the milkman would also forget.

He surveyed the grain bins in the corner of his room and wondered if he should cook himself some rice and lentils. He decided that it was too much trouble. Instead, he took down a round brass tin from the shelf and extracted half a small loaf of bread from it. Dipping pieces of it into another cup of coffee, he wandered round the room eating it. Though the bread was very dry, the austere meal revived him and improved his ragged temper.

Tilak could hear the nightwatchman doing his first round, stumping his staff on the ground to warn thieves, snakes and scorpions of his coming. He went back to sit on the windowsill. The chatter of students returning from their evening walks subsided, and a later wave, returning from the cinemas, was also swallowed up by the great hostel, and still Tilak sat grappling with his problem – Anasuyabehn.

The parade to the communal bathrooms could be heard shuffling up and down the corridors and slowly sleep crept through the building. In that time, Tilak finally made up his mind.

14

While Tilak dozed the afternoon away and John worked, Diana Armstrong trudged through the blinding heat to Pandipura village. She wished she could have afforded a tonga, but she had already spent eight annas on one to John's house, and that was the limit if she were to be sure of eating for the rest of the month.

'You don't *have* to see this old girl at Pandipura,' she told herself, as she paused to wipe the sweat from her eyelids with her handkerchief. She had, however, volunteered to keep a watch on her, so, after a moment, she went on again.

The operation on the scrawny body had been a success, and it seemed as if the woman's excellent constitution would lead to her early recovery. They had not counted, however, on the stark fear of being cut open, nor on the fact that she had expected that such a cut would fester and that she would die.

Dr Ferozeshah had found her by the roadside near his house when taking his usual early morning walk. She and her niece had been on their way to the market with a basket of vegetables when the pain which had been bothering her for some days had suddenly flared up. The young girl was seated with the woman's head in her lap trying to soothe her. Though the old woman was doubled up with pain, it had taken the united efforts of the watchman's wife and Diana, hastily called by the doctor, to persuade her to come into the consulting room to be examined. Nothing would persuade her to remove her cotton skirts, so the doctor had to feel through them to find the source of the pain.

He diagnosed appendicitis and advised an immediate operation, which was enough to send the old woman nearly into hysterics. She tried to get off the examination table. Dr Ferozeshah, and the sharp agony within, persuaded her to lie down again, while he sent the watchman's son out to Pandipura to get her brother-in-law.

Once over her first panic, she gasped to Diana that she had been a widow for years and that her brother-in-law, with whom she lived, disliked her very much. It was better that she should die.

Diana suggested that this would be tantamount to suicide, since the doctor had the power to cure her. She took a cloth and wiped the sweat off the sick woman's face, and added,

'There may be work for you to do yet, respected mother. Grandsons or grandnephews to guide. Motherless children to look after.'

A gaggle of relations had come running, babbling with fear of the unknown. They had blenched when the doctor had explained what needed to be done. The brother-in-law, his small, bright eyes shifting uneasily from the doctor's feet to his face, had said, 'I remember, Sahib, that when the cholera raged, you and the city Doctor Sahib came to our village and put needles in us to save us. I do not forget this, Sahib – but a cut like that would fester and mean certain death. Why bother? A little opium may help her to get over the pain and recover.' He shrugged, as if to suggest that the woman's life was of little importance.

His sister-in-law had all this time been lying on the examination table, breathing heavily and trying not to moan. Suddenly she had spoken up.

'There is no particular reason why I should live,' she gasped, 'but let the Doctor Sahib assuage the pain in any way he can. If I don't recover, who will mourn me?' She turned her head and glared malevolently at her brother-in-law.

The brother-in-law spluttered about the cost.

'I shall not charge,' Dr Ferozeshah assured him, and before anybody could say anything more, he called the bearer to wheel the woman into the next room and told Diana to scrub up.

A cry of real fear burst from the forlorn little group behind the brother-in-law, but the doctor turned and said authoritatively, 'One of you stay here to cook for her. There is a veranda where you may sleep and cook, and a well in the yard. Bring in a little food to which she is accustomed.'

With much going to and fro and grumbling and fussing, it had all been arranged. After a few days, the invalid had been carried home on a stretcher borne by her nephews. She was cheerful and had undoubtedly enjoyed being made a fuss of and the unaccustomed rest in a real bed with a cotton mattress. Not so many of her caste practices had been flouted, and she hoped that prayer and suitable ablutions, when she was well, would appease her caste brethren.

Diana reached the village and stood for a minute in the shade of a tree by the well, to recuperate from the heat.

How very quiet everything was. Though it was long past the hour of afternoon naps, there was none of the usual shouting back and forth between housewives across the lanes, no sound of scolding mothers, no sound of goatherds playing their flutes – or a cloud of dust on the horizon to herald the return of the buffaloes to be milked. A few men sat on string beds outside their houses. They were talking quietly, heads close together, not arguing loudly with lots of gesturing, as they usually

364

did. When a woman with a small child on her hip came out of one house, crossed the lane and went into another house, Diana relaxed. It must be the heat, she decided. She walked briskly down the main lane and then turned into another, in which her patient lived.

The woman's brother-in-law and his sons rose from their string bed outside the hut door and greeted her politely. Two women came out and led her inside to the old woman. They watched quietly, as Diana checked and changed the dressing, and took the woman's temperature and blood pressure. It was obvious to her that her patient was far from well; yet the wound appeared clean and healing. The silence of the waiting relatives oppressed her – Indians were not a silent people. Diana slowly put her thermometer back into its case. She wondered if something had happened to the village as a whole; had a fine been levied collectively for some misdemeanour? Or were they afraid of some infectious disease? Or had they lost a crop?

The hut in which she stood was clean, she noted, its earthen floor smooth and shining from a recent application of cow dung; the talis and other eating utensils twinkled on a shelf cut out of the earthen walls; the womenfolk's spare skirts and a couple of clean, unwound turbans hung neatly over a rope stretched across the hut, so as to divide it and give a little privacy; a figurine of the Elephant God, Ganesh, shone softly in a corner, a small offering of rice before it. Everything was as it should be, and yet she sensed that something was wrong.

The woman opened her eyes, knew her and tried to smile. Again, Diana took her wrist to check the faltering pulse. In slow, clear Gujerati, she teased the old lady that she would soon be up and making flower offerings in the temple in thanks for her recovery. Now she was going to give her a pill, something like opium, which would give her a good, long sleep, after which she should feel very much stronger.

'Radhabahin,' murmured the sick woman. 'Sister of God.' She trustingly swallowed the pill.

As Diana went outside to speak to the three men and the two older women who followed her, she was worried. She reiterated to the relations that the woman would live, if the family would help her. Perhaps the little niece could be delegated to sit with her, hold her hand, fan her, make her feel she was needed and respected.

'She's not easy to live with,' the brother-in-law said frankly.

Diana laughed, and responded, 'We all grow old and impatient, in time.'

The response was an absent-minded smile, instead of the light joke which she had expected. She snapped her little black bag closed and said she would return on the following day.

It's as if all their cheerful gossip has been turned off, by order, she thought crossly.

Across the way, she was almost relieved to see Miss Prasad, a volunteer who came each week to teach women to read. She was asking Jivraj, a member of the village council, if he could send a donkey to fetch her servant, who was sitting by the side of the track leading to the village, unable to walk because she had a thorn deeply embedded in her foot. After the lesson, Miss Prasad would like to retain the animal to take her servant home. She would see that it was returned the following day.

Jivraj was looking most uncomfortable. He was an old man and he walked with the support of a grandson, a quiet, wide-eyed boy, round whose shoulders he draped one arm. In his right hand he held a staff for further support. His short, frilly jacket hung loosely on him and his dhoti flapped against sticklike legs. Jivraj had faced many famines, many disasters, and Diana thought that life could hardly present him with a problem he could not solve; and, yet, the polite request for a donkey from a most respected lady had obviously put him out.

'All the donkeys are at work, Miss,' he was telling her. He dug his stick into the sand and looked around him doubtfully. 'They will be busy for several days.' Then relief dawned on the lined, tired face. 'My grandson can go and help her,' he said.

Miss Prasad's earnest face still showed some anxiety, but she agreed to this. His grandson helped the old man back to his seat on the string bed outside his house, and then skipped away to find the servant.

'Good afternoon,' Diana called as cheerfully as she could to Miss Prasad.

'Namuste,' responded Miss Prasad briskly, as she gestured to a growing group of women and children to follow her to the shade of a nearby neem tree. She set up a tiny blackboard, and, as Diana made her farewells to her patient's family, the women sat down cross-legged and began to chant the letters of the alphabet, as she wrote them on the board. Diana had seen her do this in many villages, and usually the women made a social event of the occasion and there was much laughter. Today, they kept their veils across their faces and sometimes their excellent memories slipped.

'I can't imagine what's up,' Diana thought irritably, as she waved to them in passing. 'But something is.'

15

Tilak waited patiently until the students' hostel had been perfectly quiet for over an hour. Then he moved swiftly.

He dug out a clean shirt and cotton trousers from his untidy cupboard. Taking a towel and a sliver of soap, he walked with his usual, quick, masterful stride down to the indescribably filthy bathrooms. He found a shower cabinet less disgusting than the others and made a hasty toilet. Back in his room, he put on his clean clothes and his chuppells and slipped his torch into his pocket.

Very quietly he opened the door of his room.

The passage was empty, except that at the far end a servant lay sleeping on a mat outside a door.

Tilak glided across the passage and down the ill-lit main stairs. Behind the last flight of stairs he found a narrow door, made originally for the entry of Untouchable cleaners. It creaked when he opened it and he waited for a second or two to make sure that the nightwatchman, sitting on his stool towards the front of the building, had not heard him. Then he slid silently through it and left it a trifle ajar for his return.

The moon had risen and cast a great shadow of the building. Tilak made full use of it. The ground was rough, undeveloped land, criss-crossed by tiny paths made by many student feet. He found one of these paths leading to the lane bordering the campus, and followed it. Once out of the shadow, he might be seen by a watchman, but he would be far enough away not to be recognized.

He began to breathe more easily. There was no curfew to prevent his taking a walk at night, but anyone observing him would undoubtedly gossip speculatively about his being out at such a late hour.

On the other side of the lane bordering the campus, grazing land stretched for at least a mile, and he could hear heavy beasts moving about and snuffling at the herbage. The herdsmen must be somewhere near, he thought, and he walked lightly, using the shadows of a few mango trees to mask his presence as much as possible.

He saw them before they saw him. They were crouched in a tight circle, their woollen blankets clutched around them against the night chill. When they heard him, they sprang to their feet and raised their

367

staffs ready. Tilak lifted his hand in salute and passed on quickly; he did not know whether he was recognized or not.

He reached the row of bungalows in which many of the senior professors lived. Here he paused, beside a small Jain temple which lay a little to the rear of them. His head throbbed and his throat was dry. He had walked so fast that his breath came in short gasps.

He wanted the eighth bungalow from where he stood. He forced himself to think carefully. The Dean, he reasoned, would at this time of year probably be sleeping in the courtyard, the boy servant nearby; Anasuyabehn, with her sharp-eyed aunt, would be either on the inner veranda or on the roof. The problem was to get close enough to the girl to talk to her without waking her family. Would he have to get on to the roof? And thence, possibly down to the veranda? That, he decided, would be madness.

He began to move, rather uncertainly, down the field path that ran at the back of the bungalows. His heart sank when he realized that a bungalow emitting a great deal of light from its back window was that of the Dean.

'I'm crazy,' he muttered, and wondered if he should look for an opportunity to speak to Anasuyabehn when she went out to the bazaar or the library. 'But it could take days,' he told himself, 'and then she might have the servant with her.'

The lighted window was open and the thin curtains flapped sporadically in the night breeze. Was a late-working Dean behind the curtains? Or a sleepless old lady? Or Anasuyabehn?

The curtains solved the problem for him by suddenly billowing inward. Before they subsided, he caught a glimpse of Anasuyabehn sitting on an iron bed, reading. His mercurial spirits rose. What luck!

He crept forward to stand at the side of the window, so that he would not be silhouetted against the light. He had to find out if she were alone. When, eventually, the curtains obliged by flipping inward again, he could observe no one else, so he chanced anyone being in the corner outside his line of vision, and called softly, 'Bahin!'

The quiet voice calling 'Sister' through the window shocked Anasuyabehn. She dropped her book and jumped off the bed to slam the window shut before the impudent student or would-be thief had time for action, but again the voice came, 'Anasuyabehn!'

'Ramji!' she exclaimed, and gripped a window bar for support. With the other hand, she parted the curtains slightly. The shadow of a neem tree dappled the side of the house and she could see no one. 'Doctor Sahib,' she whispered.

'Put the light out,' whispered the disembodied voice hoarsely.

In her agitation she vacillated.

'Don't be frightened,' urged Tilak, his usual irritability apparent in his tone. 'There are excellent window bars between us.'

Shakily, she went across the room and switched the light off. Then she wrapped her sari closer round herself and returned. A small plump hand timidly drew one of the curtains back. 'Bhai,' she whispered. 'What are you doing here? Go home before you're caught.' Here was romance straight out of a Western novel, but it was too scary.

There was no reply to her question, so she gripped the window bars to peer out, and gave a frightened squeak as a masculine hand closed over one of hers. 'Brother,' she gasped again imploringly, as she tried to free her hand.

Tilak was entranced and held her firmly. He could just see her face glimmering in the moonlight, despite the tracery of the tree shadow, and behind her was the immense shadow of her loosed hair. Though the folds of her cotton sari covered her completely, she was blouseless and petticoatless. He could feel the heat of her body and smell her perfume. He nearly choked with desire and leaned close to the unyielding bars.

As he put his arm through the bars and then round her shoulders, she sobbed, 'Bhai, please, please go home. You'll be caught – and I've enough grief to bear without any more.' She burst into tears. Without thinking, she laid her wet face on the arm which gripped her, and Tilak came to his senses.

'Don't cry,' he said softly. 'I'm sorry I frightened you.'

He had come to find out if his feelings were in any way reciprocated. Now he knew by the trustful way in which she wept in his arms that love was there. All the ancient love stories seemed suddenly to be true. He was going to fight for this woman.

The words came tumbling from him. 'Rani,' he said. 'All I want to do is to marry you and take you to England and make you happy. I'm going to England to study – I can take you with me . . .'

'I'm to be married to Mahadev Desai,' she interposed, her voice lifeless. 'Tomorrow some relations will arrive – the first guests – and Aunt has already sent for the astrologer to name the day. Desais have already sent the last gifts before the marriage. I am inundated with silken saris and jewellery.'

The jackals howled at the moon and the insects sang, while Tilak silently digested this information. In the distance, the nightwatchman called to his relief man to take over.

'I have to be quick,' he told her. 'When is the marriage likely to be?'

He slipped his hand under her hair and ran his fingers along her neck. She shivered, and said, 'Two or three weeks, probably.'

'You must prevaricate – bribe the astrologer. Pretend to be ill. Defer it somehow while I make arrangements.' She was trembling under his touch, but she did not draw back, and he thought that few would let him come so near, bars or no bars. She loves me, he rejoiced.

Her deepset eyes searched the gloom to see his dark face. 'Father is so upset by you. He'd never give permission.'

'Nothing's hopeless,' he assured her passionately. 'We're old enough to decide for ourselves. Would you like to marry me?'

Her teeth flashed, as she smiled up at him, and the heavens rang with pure joy for him, before she even breathed out, 'Oh, yes, of course.'

With a curious prescience, Tilak felt that this was the happiest moment of his life, and he savoured it.

The fresh watchman's staff was plunking down the front lane. 'I must go,' he said. 'Meet me tomorrow. Where?'

She sighed helplessly. Then she said, 'I'll try to be at the Marwari Gate temple about nine o'clock. But how shall we manage everything?'

'Never fear. I'll arrange it all.' He stepped back reluctantly and bent to kiss the hand holding one of the bars, and then he was gone.

16

The following morning, preparatory to going to the Marwari Gate temple, Tilak wrote a note on the blackboard of his lecture room, telling the students that the lectures for that day were cancelled.

He had spent most of the night going over his financial position, a record of which he kept in a battered account book. He had some savings and a little money in Government Bonds left him by his father, but it was not enough. He wondered which of his relations could be prevailed upon to lend him some more.

He was certain that his uncle would be pleased about his Fellowship and would stand surety with the passport people, so that he would not have to find the considerable deposit which would, otherwise, be demanded of him.

Suddenly, he stopped writing. How was he to get a passport for Anasuyabehn?

His uncle would certainly not connive with him in the abduction of a young woman. He had planned to marry her and then take her straight on to the boat or plane for England. This would not give time to have her name included on his own passport; and to obtain a separate passport would take even longer. Speed was of the essence if they were to avoid her family's wrath breaking over their heads, not to speak of the anger of the mighty Desai clan.

He was standing staring with glazed eyes at the blackboard, when Dr Yashvant Prasad, walking along the corridor, spotted him.

'Ah, Tilak,' he called. 'I was about to send my clerk to find you. Will you come into my office for a few minutes.'

Tilak turned sharply, trying vainly to think of an excuse to evade the interview.

'Ji hun,' he assented, and followed the Vice-Chancellor with lagging feet. 'My murdered frog,' he thought glumly and correctly.

As Tilak sat opposite him, Dr Prasad's pleasant voice meandered on. Tilak said, 'Yes, sir,' and 'No, sir', wherever it seemed appropriate, and thought of Anasuyabehn loitering alone by the temple. He prayed that she had sought seclusion inside the building.

'I propose,' said the Vice-Chancellor, putting his fingertips together,

371

'to speak personally to each Jain member of the staff and urge tolerance.'

'Thank you, sir,' responded Tilak, seething with worry under his polite exterior.

'I also propose to call on the more influential and forward-looking Jains in the city, to seek their help. I hope through them to reach the more orthodox groups with whom we do not so frequently come into touch. There is a very powerful family of Desais here, for example – if one could get people like that . . .'

'Desai?' queried Tilak, jerked back from thoughts of the Marwari Gate temple.

'Yes. Big financiers – they live in the centre of the city.'

'I've heard of them,' responded Tilak. It dawned on him that it was probably one of these Desais who was to marry Anasuyabehn. He thought bitterly that it would be too ironical to lose Anasuyabehn to a family which might be able to influence favourably his own position in the community.

The Vice-Chancellor was continuing.

'It will be slow work, I fear. In the meantime, Tilak, lock the laboratory door while doing your researches.' He smiled conspiratorially.

Tilak felt despairingly that if the Vice-Chancellor went on much longer, all his anger at the Dean, all his worry regarding Anasuyabehn and his frustration in respect of his work would explode out of him. He took a large breath, however, and then managed to reply, 'Certainly, sir.' Now was not the time to precipitate his resignation.

Desperate in his general agitation, Tilak half rose, hoping that Dr Prasad had finished.

'Before you go, I would like to ask your opinion about establishing a postgraduate course,' Dr Prasad went on remorselessly. Tilak sat down in his chair again and commended Anasuyabehn to any gods who happened to live in the temple.

He emerged at lunchtime at a loss to know how to communicate with her. He strode across the campus through the broiling heat of the sun. Suddenly his legs faltered and he had to stop in the shade of a tree. He watched the tree ants make a detour round his fingers and continue their endless running up and down the tree trunk, while the trembling in his legs eased. As the faintness passed, he remembered that he had not eaten a proper meal for over a day, and he wondered how to get one without travelling into town; he had only a little rice and lentils in his room.

He remembered John, ever kind and sympathetic.

'Perhaps he'd be kind enough to give me lunch,' he thought, 'and maybe Ranjit could find me a boy as temporary servant.'

A very exhausted Tilak again presented himself at John's door and was fed by a resigned Ranjit and comforted by John, who assumed that his friend's shaken appearance was due, largely, to lack of food and the long session with Dr Prasad about the murdered frog and fish.

17

'I thought I might be able to pick up a little Delhi rice,' Anasuyabehn told her aunt that morning, in the hope of justifying a visit to the Marwari Gate bazaar in which the temple lay. They had both been busy, getting ready for the expected arrival of their relations, and Anasuyabehn would, ordinarily, have gone to the nearest bazaar for the day's vegetables. She watched the indecision in her aunt's face. She knew the old woman loved the long delicate grains of Delhi rice, so hard to obtain in Shahpur, even on the black market.

'Well,' the older woman said finally, 'perhaps I could spare the boy for an hour to go with you.'

'I'll be all right alone, respected Aunt,' Anasuyabehn assured her quickly.

'Very well, then. Be a modest, circumspect girl and keep your sari over your head. I hope no Desais see you.'

Anasuyabehn obediently hitched her sari over her head, seized her cotton shopping bag, checked that sufficient money was tied safely in a tucked-in corner of her sari, and fled before Aunt could change her mind.

The bazaar was packed with people. After she had made her purchases, including a seer of Delhi rice from under a stall, she paused apprehensively to scan the crowd for Tilak. A young man on a bicycle eyed her insolently and, as he approached her, began to slow down. She moved hastily closer to the stalls, only to be jostled by a group of millhands going off shift. They touched her obscenely and shouted ribald remarks, as, impeded by the heavy shopping bag, she tried to shrink from them. In a moment, they were past her and clambering into a bus, leaving her nearly weeping with humiliation.

A countrywoman shouted a stream of abuse at them and then called to Anasuyabehn to come closer to her. Anasuyabehn stumbled towards her, wiping her face with her sari and trying not to be sick, while a policeman, rifle on back, leaned against a door jamb and laughed at her.

The woman nodded her head towards the pavement beside her. 'They won't bother you if you don't stray on to the street. Stay here, near us.'

Anasuyabehn nodded and made her way quickly into the temple

behind them. She went only as far as the outer cloisters, feeling that Tilak would be sure to find her there.

The building was cool and shadowy. Morning prayers were long since over. The cloisters, with their fifty-two small shrines, were almost deserted. Only at one end a man and a young boy sat together, cotton masks over their mouths, and told their beads. The boy looked up as she entered, but a reproving glance from his companion made him hastily bow his head and continue his prayers.

Anasuyabehn stood leaning against the wall and drank in the peace of the place after the heat and hurly-burly of the bazaar outside. The minutes ticked by and her pounding temples and nausea eased.

Where was Tilak? He should have been there fifteen minutes ago. She went to the top of the entrance steps and looked out over the crowd. No sign of him. She retraced her steps inside and continued to wait.

When her watch told her she had been waiting half an hour, she turned reluctantly and sadly once more to the entrance. Perhaps he had regretted his impetuosity of the previous night and decided that his suit was hopeless.

Head bowed to hide her tears, she did not see, until she nearly trod on him, the monk who had been silently watching her from behind.

Tall, naked except for a tattered cloth covering his genitals, it seemed as if he had no flesh, that the skin was drawn straight over his skeleton. His body was ingrained with dirt and his bald head was covered with sores, where the hair had been painfully plucked out by hand. In one emaciated hand he held a peacock feather and in the other a begging bowl. For a moment, until he drew hastily back from her, her face was within a foot of his.

Her father's guru, his religious teacher, Anasuyabehn realized, with a sense of shock.

As if to pierce her soul, penetrating, bloodshot eyes had looked deep into her own, and made her shiver.

She recoiled from him, feeling as if her mind lay naked to the man and that he had divined her reason for being alone in the temple. She cringed with sudden fear of his super-natural power. Then she bowed low, to touch the horny bare feet.

He knew her. Mehta's daughter, a modern miss with no real respect for her religion. He had warned her father once that he had left her too long unmarried. For his own spiritual good a man must see his children married before he dies. Marry her into an orthodox family, he had counselled. He had heard, however, that he was marrying her, instead, into a monied one.

375

And now, what was she doing in the temple? She was obviously not there for worship; her clothes were not fresh and she had shopping with her.

He knew that he should not care, that he should turn away from her; but perhaps the child had, of her own accord, sought to return to her religious observances and was not sure how to accomplish this.

Perplexed, he surveyed her ashy face as she rose from her obeisance. She could not go out through the gate until he moved, and he had been so long cut off from any consideration of time, that he was unaware that he had kept her standing there, head bowed, for several minutes.

Anasuyabehn was frozen with fear, as she suffered an intense examination by serene, intelligent eyes, that had spent years looking for the Ultimate Truth, and seemed now to be able to look through her and past her.

She was suddenly acutely aware of her own pettiness compared to men like this. Though she might assure herself that she had discarded her religion, she knew in those scarifying minutes, that it could not be shrugged off like a Kashmir shawl; it was part of the warp and weft of her life, hopelessly woven into her thoughts and actions, and now showing its strength, by making her stand, so frightened, before this uncanny, withdrawn monk.

At last the monk spoke. His voice was soft, so as not to disturb the souls in the air. 'You were looking for me?'

'No.' The answer came in a whisper.

It was an essential part of a monk's creed that he feel no personal interest in anyone. It was laudable, however, and would gain him merit, to hear confession or to instruct in the scriptures. Furthermore, try as he might to conquer it, he was curious to know what had caused her to visit the temple and why she was so obviously terrified.

If he stares at me much longer, thought Anasuyabehn, I shall die at his feet.

The man saw her sway. A bad conscience, he diagnosed.

'You wish to make confession?'

'No.'

'I am here each day. Go home and examine your conscience. You may ask your father to bring you to see me, if you wish, and I will hear you.'

After this pronouncement, he seemed to forget about her, and he turned along the side of the cloister, slowly sweeping the floor in front of him with his peacock feather, so that he would not kill an insect by treading on it. Anasuyabehn tottered out into the blazing sunlight, to the shrieks of the bazaar radios and the vendors' voices.

The bustling crowd around her did little to dispel the mesmeric effect of the monk's frightful godliness. For, to her, godly he undoubtedly was, with a personality purged of all human desire. She felt he did not need to hear her confession to know all that was in her mind.

Hypnotized by the mystic, she forgot to look again in the bazaar for Tilak and the bus was well along the road to home before she remembered him.

18

Mahadev Desai's father sat on the worn stone steps of one of the verandas that faced the courtyard of his home. Though the morning sun shone warmly upon him, he was shaking as if with cold. The hands that held the telegram, which his servant had just handed to him, trembled so much that he could hardly reread it, to assure himself that he had understood it.

'Send my brother and my son to me,' he snapped finally, his wizened face looking more than usually owlish as he tightened his lips under his large, hooked nose.

The scared servant flew to obey, while, with quivering fingers, old Desai smoothed the crumpled edges of the telegram.

His second son, his usually blank face full of apprehension, rolled across the courtyard like a billiard ball slowly into a pocket. His uncle followed him, still tucking in his flapping dhoti as he came.

They each read the telegram and, as its full implications sank into their minds, utter consternation made them both burst into speech. Yet the message was such an innocent one. It merely informed them that Mahadev had not arrived on the Delhi Mail and asked on which train he would be travelling.

'The diamonds,' wailed Uncle, his hawklike face blenched.

'The rubies!' exclaimed his nephew, a mass of dithering fat.

'My son,' gasped old Desai. 'My only intelligent son,' and he glared at his second son, who shrank visibly at the insult.

The smell of trouble had by this time brought others to the scene. A knot of servants and hangers-on had gathered at a little distance and were watching the conference speculatively. The daughter-in-law of the wicked tongue could be heard approaching, scolding Mahadev's daughter as she came. The child trotted in front of her, silent and sullen. Automatically, her grandfather hid his fears and called her to him and she thankfully nestled down by him on the step. She stuck her tongue out at her aunt, who mercifully did not see the impudent gesture.

'What's the matter?' the daughter-in-law asked in respectful tones.

'It does not concern you,' replied old Desai coolly. 'I must, however, go out on business.' He turned to his younger son. 'Have the carriage brought out.' His voice sounded as brittle as his frail limbs looked, beneath their thin cotton covering.

The man went obediently, doing his best to crush the rancour he felt at his father's unkind remark. 'It's unjust,' he muttered under his breath. 'I work so hard.'

Old Desai's waspish daughter-in-law hung on to every word, in the hope of obtaining a clue as to what was wrong.

'Daughter,' he addressed her. 'Get out a clean set of khadi and put it in my room. I must change. Your husband will accompany me and will need the same.' He motioned her away impatiently with his walking stick.

The woman's face fell. Her temper flashed out as she called to a servant to get the clothes requested.

'Brother, you must stay here. Several important people are coming in this morning. I'll go to see the Chief of Police immediately.' He sighed deeply, and then exclaimed in apprehension, 'Heaven help us! I hope Mahadev is all right.'

His brother nodded his bald head. 'I was afraid for him when we heard of the robbery,' he said.

'I thought he would be all right,' said the older man. 'He's so quick-witted. I should have sent him by plane – it would have been much safer – though very expensive,' he sighed.

'I've never known dacoits in this district take someone right off a train – usually they rob and murder on the train – or just by – in which case the Railway Police would have found him, and his death would have been reported at the same time as the white woman's.'

'Someone here must have betrayed him, either deliberately or by gossip,' said old Desai suspiciously.

'The dacoits must have been primarily concerned with the registered mail, as usual,' reassured his brother. 'They could, of course, have stumbled on Mahadev by accident.'

Mahadev's father rubbed his chin thoughtfully. 'I doubt if they could have done,' he said at last. 'There was nothing to distinguish him from fifty other Banias who must have been travelling on the train – the boy was himself so sure that he would not be picked out in such an event as this – that is why he carried the stones with him, rather than entrusting them to the registered mail – as you know, some of the stones are particularly good. Our honoured customer, the Maharaja inherited some excellent ones – and they were a good partial surety for the loan to start his factory. Now he's ready to pay his debt – and we have lost them – and our boy.'

He got up wearily.

'Brother, you had better arm me with some money – and a gift – a good ring, perhaps. Some presents are indicated to speed investigating feet. Arree! Shall I ever see my son again?'

His brother touched his arm comfortingly, and assured him, with more confidence than he felt, that Mahadev was probably safe. The much maligned police were not really so inefficient. There would certainly be a dreadful row about the murder of the English lady and that would galvanize them into action.

The little granddaughter, still as a scared mouse, had all this time been sitting, forgotten, on the step beside them. Her father was a magical person to her, who was often away from home. But when he returned his suitcase was full of presents for her and he had wonderful stories to tell. She opened her mouth suddenly and howled.

Her grandfather and great-uncle jumped guiltily, and, until a servant came to say that the clothing was ready, they kept assuring the little girl that Papa would be all right. She must, however, say nothing about him until Grandpa came home again – and maybe he would bring her a gift from the bazaar when he returned.

'I'll keep her with me,' promised Great-Uncle, and swung her cheerfully up into the air, and carried her off towards the counting house. He stopped suddenly, and turned back to his brother. 'Shall I inform Dean Mehta?' he asked.

'Tell nobody,' replied old Desai. 'Let's first try to find out what's happened.'

Old Desai climbed into the little black carriage, and told his second son to drive fast. No servant went with them. This business had to be kept as quiet as possible, he reflected, if only because he did not wish the Income Tax collector to read in the newspaper anything of their rapidly expanding operations. There was safety in a fair display of poverty. Where riches are splashed about, there come the thieves, the spongers, the hangers-on, the tax collector. Better to hide behind the ancient walls of one's Society, deep in the older part of town. A story of valuable rubies and diamonds lost would alert every robber to the possibility of large quantities of valuables hidden in the floors of the Desai Society, he thought dismally, however poverty-stricken it looked. They would not realize that nowadays money was invested in ships, planes, factories and machinery, instead of being buried as gold.

The traffic was held up by the Red Gate, which was too narrow to allow the vehicles to flow through fast. Old Desai shouted to a toy seller on the pavement, and the man fought his way through the stalled vehicles to the middle of the road. Old Desai solemnly bargained for and then purchased a monkey-on-a-stick.

'Father's reached his dotage,' thought his second son gloomily, as he whipped up the horse again.

19

Although the Income Tax authorities might not yet be aware of the extent of Mr Desai's fortune, the police knew of the plainly dressed old man. Doors were immediately opened to him, and it was not long before he was ensconced in a chair in the office of a police chief of gratifying eminence, a small, calm Bengali who had come down from Delhi, armed with instructions to solve the robbery mystery at all costs, before there was a diplomatic row over the death of Mrs Belmont-Smythe.

He sat quietly and listened, while Desai told him of his son's non-arrival at Delhi and his fears for the young man's life. Desai minimized somewhat the value of the jewels he was carrying, but indicated that it was sufficient to tempt a professional thief.

Desai had spoken in Gujerati, his knowledge of English being limited to being able to read it, and his son translated as he went along. There was a pause at the end of the recital during which time the Delhi detective removed his shoes and socks thoughtfully, so that he could sit comfortably cross-legged on his chair. At last he said, 'No body, other than that of the English woman, has yet been found; and these dacoits, as you know, rarely hold anyone for ransom. Perhaps he missed the train.'

These remarks did little to console Desai. 'No. My head book-keeper saw him on to it. Perhaps some of the other passengers saw what happened to him?'

The detective made a wry face and shifted the papers about on his desk.

'We still have in custody a few suspicious characters who were on the train, and we have, of course, the names and addresses of a number of passengers. The majority are untraceable.' His voice rose with decision. 'I'll cause further inquiries to be made, and will have the railway embankments searched again.'

Desai had already decided to obtain the help of his caste brethren in a private search round the scene of the robbery, so he took his departure.

He was conducted to the door, with painstaking respect, by a local inspector, who promised that he would himself again question the railway police who were aboard the train. 'They were overwhelmed by the force of the attack,' he said almost apologetically.

'They always are,' replied Desai dryly, and climbed wearily into his carriage.

As his younger son drove him deeper and deeper into the heart of the city, the old man's spirits sank lower. Why did one scheme and amass money, if it were not for one's sons and their sons? The boy must be dead, dead without leaving a son to tend his funeral pyre, he thought bitterly. The nincompoop beside him had two sons, satanic images of their mother, for whom he felt no affection. It had been Mahadev's sons he had wanted to see before he died himself.

'If he lives, I'll hasten his marriage,' he promised himself.

Hearing his father's mutter, his younger son turned to him. 'Ji?' he queried respectfully.

'Nothing, nothing,' replied Desai testily.

He had told neither Mahadev nor his brother about the opposition of older members of the family to the marriage to Anasuyabehn. The elders had argued that a wealthy girl in the Desai community could be found, a girl strategically placed to increase the power of the caste. Intercaste marriages, they said, dissipated wealth and weakened authority.

Desai had been tempted to agree. When he read the *Financial Times*, however, and when men of other castes planning big enterprises asked his financial help, he felt that to become a power in the new, free India, it was wiser not to emphasize caste.

No one, not even his trusted brother, had ever seen Desai's small private ledger with a swastika drawn, for luck, on its first page. In this, the final results of all his business were entered. He planned that most of what that ledger represented should pass to Mahadev, just as his own father had chosen him to head the business when he had retired. It was, therefore, a good idea that Mahadev have a modern wife, but a wife without bossy caste relations.

The carriage jerked to a stop in front of the plain wooden door behind which lay the Desai Society. Old Desai was helped down from his perch by his son, who handed the horse and carriage over to the care of a servant squatting on the step.

Old Desai went immediately to the counting-house. Partner Uncle was immersed in work, his little grand-niece playing contentedly at his feet with a piece of paper and the office's entire collection of rubber stamps. She received the monkey-on-a-stick with great glee.

'The police,' said old Desai, 'are doing their best, I'm convinced. However, so much is at stake – our reputation for reliability – and poor

Mahadev – I'm worried to death about him – that I think we should attempt a search ourselves.'

'I suppose we could,' said Partner Uncle doubtfully.

'Of course, we could,' snapped old Desai. 'We can send for Brother-in-law from Baroda to help organize it, and we have plenty of servants and clerks to help.'

'What about the business?'

'The business can wait,' snorted old Desai, to which unheard of heresy his brother had no reply.

20

Diana and Dr Ferozeshah's sweeper wearily tidied up the operating room. Dr Ferozeshah, his legs shaking with fatigue, washed his hands and wished he could afford air conditioning. Perhaps next year, he thought. His reverie was broken by Diana's voice.

'. . . and so I promised to go over again today. Would that be convenient to you?'

He turned round, his hands dripping.

Diana was struggling out of her white gown.

'Go where?'

'To that old body in Pandipura. She doesn't seem to be doing very well.'

Dr Ferozeshah surveyed his employee. In spite of her lack of weight, she was plum-coloured with heat and exertion. Too thin, he decided; she needed more rest.

'She'll be all right for a couple of days,' he said, 'and you should rest for a while – we've had a busy morning.'

'I am tired,' admitted Diana, 'but I feel uneasy about her. If you don't want me this afternoon, I could go up on the bus.'

Dr Ferozeshah's perfectly modelled face broke into a mischievous grin. 'All right. Go to see this illustrious patient – and then take the evening off.' He picked up a towel to dry his hands. 'Mirabai can do the evening rounds with me – you've taught her very well.'

A whole evening off was a rare luxury. It sounded as if Ferozeshah was at last satisfied that Mirabai, the new nurse, and a new Sindhi dispenser were competent to undertake some of her work, and she heaved a sigh of relief.

She thanked the doctor, took her handbag from a locked cupboard, and went slowly through the waiting-room for high-caste clients and down the steps to the tree-lined road. She had a room in the house of a widow further down the road, and, as she strolled towards it, she looked back over the previous thirty months. She smiled a little as she remembered how the small private hospital had helped to fight epidemics, patched broken limbs after riots, done operations that in England would have been left to specialists, delivered babies and consoled the bereaved. Though the doctor was making money, much of it was

385

spent on precious pieces of equipment – the X-ray machine, for example, what a help that had been – and the big sterilizer.

When she knocked, her landlady, Mrs Jha, unbolted the front door to let her in. She was a stringy-looking woman, garbed in a plain white sari, her grey hair clipped close to her head to indicate her widowhood. Though she was quite orthodox in her way of life, her grandson, Dr Ferozeshah's lawyer, had persuaded her to take in Diana.

The two women had become good friends and, quite often, Mrs Jha would cook some vegetarian delicacy for the girl and bring it to her. As a caste Hindu, however, she would not eat with her. The line was drawn there.

In return, Diana respected her caste rules and tried not to infringe on her privacy. She never entered her landlady's part of the house lest she defile it. With the aid of a tin bath in her room, she washed herself and her clothes. The sweeper came twice daily through a special sweeper's door into the cupboardlike bathroom, to clean her commode and remove her garbage. Mrs Jha's own servant, for a small tip, drew water from the well in the compound and filled her water-pots on the veranda, both morning and evening. It worked quite well.

Now Mrs Jha was full of news. Mr Lallubhai had sent his peon to ask Diana to attend a meeting at his house the following evening. The man had also brought more news of the train robbery. 'He said,' she commenced in a hissing whisper in case the dacoits might hear, 'that in the bazaar they are saying that this is no ordinary train robbery, and that they must have had local help.' She pursed her lips and glanced over her shoulder, as if expecting to see someone listening to her. 'They think it was not Saurashtrian dacoits who did it – and that makes sense, when you think of it. They wouldn't be foolish enough to kill an English Memsahib.'

She pushed her key ring more securely into the waist of her petticoat, as if to guard it carefully, and looked expectantly at Diana.

Diana, however, knew the value of bazaar rumours, and replied quite cheerfully, 'Except for the murder, the newspaper this morning didn't seem to think there was anything special about it. Just that they were after the registered mail.'

Mrs Jha refused to relinquish one scrap of her morbid excitement, and wagged her head slowly in negative fashion.

'We must be prudent,' she said earnestly. 'When my nephew comes home from work, I shall ask him to clean the gun. And he and his sister can escort you whenever you want to go out.'

Diana restrained the gurgle of laughter which rose in her throat. Mrs Jha's nephew was a huge, flabby, amiable youth and in a crisis, Diana was sure, his only thought would be to find a cupboard big enough to hide in. His shy young sister was hardly necessary to act as chaperon.

She thanked Mrs Jha and retreated to her room.

It was an airy, comfortable room, though, by Western standards, rather bare.

A divan, covered with a homespun bedspread, lay along a white-washed wall, a few gaily coloured cushions piled upon it. Above this hung a carefully arranged group of family photographs in plain, black frames. There was a small bookcase, crammed with novels, a few travel books, the Bible, a Gita, English translations of the Upanishads and the Light of Truth; on top of it, by a brass vase of wilted wild flowers and grasses, lay some library books, including one of John Bennett's histories. Her few dresses hung on a rail set across a corner of the room, with her shoes in a neat row beneath them. A trunk, its careworn appearance disguised by a frilled cover, held her underwear and a pre-cious tennis racket. On top of the trunk there was a workbasket in which lay balls of wool and knitting needles.

There was little else in the room, except for a small wooden table with its accompanying chair, and a locked cupboard for her modest stores of food, linen, clothing and other oddments.

Diana hurried to her veranda, where she kept her cooking tools and Primus stove. She quickly put together a pan of khicharhi and, while it was cooking, she washed herself and changed into a khaki blouse and skirt, relics of her Mission of Holiness days.

To eat her meal, she sat in a basket chair and looked out over the little courtyard, with its well in one corner and a drooping neem tree in another. Near the well, tiny flowers bloomed between the paving stones, watered by splashes from the water-bucket. A sacred, well-tended tulsi tree flourished in a stone pot in the centre of the courtyard.

Diana never trespassed into the courtyard, and now she thought how nice it would be to do so. 'I'd like a home like this,' she pondered a little wistfully.

'You could have it, if you took a nursing post with a European com-pany here,' she told herself.

'And get caught up in the empty world of club life? Ugh!'

Marriage would also have brought her a home, but she always shrugged when she thought of it. 'I'm past it,' she would say quite philosophically. During her probationer days in Edinburgh she had dated other students, but her shyness made her boring. She had turned to her studies and had become a reliable, cheerful surgical nurse, losing her individuality behind her starched uniform.

It would not have been difficult for her to obtain a well-to-do Indian husband; her ordinary English prettiness was a thing of unusual beauty in Shahpur. She knew, however, that the adjustment to such a life would be too difficult for her.

Her mind wandered. 'What about your new friend, John Bennett?'

Tears stung her eyes. In a moment of honesty, she realized that John had ceased to be only a patient to her and had become a special person, unlike anyone she had met before; a man of integrity, considerable physical strength and high intellect, she reflected wistfully.

She stirred her food around a little, to cool it. Perhaps, she thought rather pitifully, there was good reason for a quiet, older woman like herself to keep away from him, if she wanted to avoid being hurt. Absorbed in his work, he would hardly think about her.

He had an enviable war record and, amongst the University people, he was famous for his kindness – and his celibacy. No hint of gossip ever seemed to touch him, she had observed, not even the assumption, common enough in regard to a man who lived like he did, that he was a homosexual.

She pushed away her half empty dish, and wiped her lips on her handkerchief. 'It doesn't matter, anyway,' she told herself. 'Just because a man is courteous and thoughtful of you, doesn't mean much.'

She pushed back her chair, took a glass and went to a water-jar. She drank a glass of water and also filled a small water-bottle, which she put into her black, nurse's bag.

She picked up her black umbrella and went out to catch the bus.

21

In comfortable solitude, Diana swung along the meandering field path which led from the end of the bus route to Pandipura village. After the smell of the city, the air seemed sweet and heavy with the odour of drying foliage. Even the occasional goat she met stood comatose, the tiny goatherd usually fast asleep in the nearest patch of shade. She became aware, however, of an irritating hubbub further along the path. Loud cackles of laughter and birdlike shrieks smote her ears, increasing rapidly as she approached. When she rounded a bend an unlovely, though familiar, sight met her gaze.

The remains of a dead donkey, by now almost reduced to a skeleton, lay across the path, and though not much was left, four or five vultures still argued and jostled each other over the spoils. One bird had found a particularly succulent morsel and had it clasped in its beak, its bald head and neck bobbing as, with ungainly hops, it tried to find an opportunity to swallow its prize, while the others pushed and shoved around it in an endeavour to rob their companion.

'Blast,' muttered Diana, and drew back hastily.

The vultures ignored her, if they had noticed her at all; they are no animal's prey. They were big birds and Diana teetered uncertainly at the edge of the path, wondering how long it would take them to finish their revolting work and fly away. Finally, she decided to strike into the bush and make a circle round them. She had on heavy shoes and there was little danger from snakes in such heat – most of them would be hibernating. She followed a goat track in and out of the thorny bushes, taking her direction from a distant mango tree which she could see growing further along the path.

Except for an occasional glance at the mango tree, she watched the ground she covered, in case of scorpions. Because of this, she observed a scrap of clean paper clinging to the base of a cactus. Newspaper was not uncommon in the countryside, but any other type of paper was. This was not newspaper. It was linen-backed, with threads still attached to where it had been torn. At one point a light blue line ran across it. Small, unimportant, a piece of rubbish – but out of place.

Her curiosity aroused, Diana stooped to pick it up, and, as she proceeded on her way, she turned it over and over in her hand. Guessing at its origin provided an amusing little puzzle to ease the monotony of her walk.

She reached the mango tree and rejoined the path to the village. The tree gave welcome shade, so she paused to wipe her face free of dust and sweat.

'Namuste, Memsahib,' said a thin, cracked voice behind her.

Diana jumped, and turned towards the voice.

A very old man, who had been sitting in the shade further round the trunk of the tree, was struggling to his feet.

Diana knew him, and sighed with relief. She shoved her handkerchief and the piece of paper into her shirt pocket and picked up her bag and umbrella.

'Namuste,' she greeted the village bone-setter.

He grinned at her, his white-stubbled face dissolving into a mass of wrinkles, and, as she made to continue on her way, he accompanied her. His staff dragged in the sand as he described to her a boy's arm which he had just set. She had once admired an ankle he had set and she had, in consequence, added to his local prestige. He now regarded her as a medical colleague, much to her amusement, though she had to admit that he was surprisingly competent for one who had learned his art only from his father in the traditional way.

'Are you going to Vichand's house?' he inquired, naming the brother-in-law of Diana's patient.

'Yes.'

The bone-setter stumped along for a few yards, and then gave his opinion. 'She'll live, Memsahib. She has been worrying about things which are no concern of hers. Sick people shouldn't worry – it makes them sicker.'

'It does,' agreed Diana.

'The Panchyat will worry about the village – it's *their* job.' His tone was vicious. He would dearly have liked to be a member of the village council himself, but saw no hope of it.

'What's the trouble in the village? I thought there was something wrong when I was there yesterday. Have they been fined for something?'

'Not yet,' replied the bone-setter. He looked up at her from under his grubby white turban, clamped his pinched mouth tightly shut, and refused to say anything more until they reached the village. Still wordless, he saluted her and left her outside Virchand's house.

Her patient was awake and tried to sit up as Diana entered. She made her lie down again, while she took her temperature, which proved to be normal. The deathly look of the previous day had also gone, though she was not very cheerful. The scar of the operation was knitting well.

She sat down on a mat by the bed and advised Virchand's wife how to get the old lady on to her feet again, while the patient herself occasionally put in a word. The young niece brought into the hut a shy mother with a little boy who had a boil, and asked advice. Tea was offered her. Everything was as usual.

Whatever was bothering them must have passed over, Diana decided. She had seen before how a caste group or a family would shut up like clams while they dealt with a domestic scandal or even a murder. Distrusting both police and lower courts, they tried their best not to seek help from anybody in authority.

Diana sighed. They were brave and resourceful, but, because of their poverty, they were open to all kinds of bullying. She hoped, however, that her elderly patient was now safely on her way to recovery and that her brother-in-law would not aggravate her in any way for the next week or two.

The wind was rising, making the sand fly unpleasantly, so she said her farewells. 'If the patient does not seem to be improving, please send a message immediately to Dr Ferozeshah,' she instructed Virchand, sitting in his usual spot on the string bed outside the door.

'Ji, hun,' he agreed, and rose and saluted her.

As soon as she was clear of the village, she stopped to drink the bottle of water she had brought with her. Without water, she would assuredly get sunstroke, and she dared not eat or drink anything in the village for fear of dysentery.

The vultures had departed, leaving the small skeleton to the jackals; a rustle in the undergrowth hinted at their presence. The shadows were lengthening, so she stepped round the skeleton and increased her pace. In the distance she could hear the herdsmen shouting as they rounded up their charges, preparatory to driving them home.

Two red-clad milkmaids, with their big brass vessels of milk, were squatting at the bus terminus. There she hesitated. John Bennett lived not far from the following stop. If she picked up the bus there, she could call in to tell him of the meeting at Lallubhai's house, in case Lallubhai had forgotten to inform him.

She persuaded herself that Lallubhai could indeed be so inefficient, despite his pleasure at John's offer, and walked on. She was followed by the stares and giggles of the milkmaids; her flushed face and short skirts always caused amusement to village women who did not know her.

The compound gate was unbolted, and she pushed it open and went in. John's light was already switched on and she could clearly see, through the open windows, that he already had a visitor.

391

As she stood uncertainly on the path, shyness over-whelming her, the gate swung slowly shut behind her.

John heard the gate click and turned in his chair to look out of the window. When he saw her, he waved, and a few moments later, he opened the door to her.

He was leaning on his stick, as she entered and stopped just over the threshold. Rather primly, she delivered her message.

'Of course, I'll come,' he assured her. He turned to Tilak, who had risen at Diana's entrance, and introduced him to her.

Tilak put his hands together in salute. What a weird-looking woman – her face was as red as burning charcoal.

She sat down in the basket chair indicated to her, and John sank on to the divan. The divan was low, and he winced; for the thousandth time, he cursed his inability to move properly.

The wince had gone unnoticed by his guests. He turned his attention determinedly to them and they were soon talking quite easily to each other. The story of the dead frog was told once more, and Diana was quick to sympathize. In return, she told them about some of the bigotry she had observed in the Mission of Holiness.

As her shyness receded, her face became more animated and her green eyes twinkled. She accepted a cigarette and smoked it slowly, enjoying the rare luxury of it. John apologized for Ranjit's absence and his own inability to manage the Primus stove to make tea for her. Ranjit had gone, he explained, to find a boy servant he thought would suit Dr Tilak.

The mention of tea brought back her former diffidence. She said hastily that she had not intended to stay, and looked at her watch. 'I think I should catch the next bus,' she said.

Tilak surveyed her gloomily from under lowered brows. He had discussed with John the fine opportunity of the English Fellowship, and had been about to consult him regarding taking Anasuyabehn with him, when they had been interrupted by Diana's knock. Now the moment was gone, taken by this fool of a woman with her maps and her nursing. As he chewed his nails and tried to enter politely into the conversation, the insoluble problem of the passport whirled in his mind.

Diana was picking up her bag and umbrella and John was saying that he should see her on to the bus. But his legs were hurting savagely and his voice did not carry conviction.

Diana sensed his reluctance, though she did not realize the cause. She said stiffly, 'I shall be quite all right alone.'

Tilak had come to the door, too. He felt that John's interest had transferred itself to the woman, and that he would not give his full attention to Tilak's own problems. 'I must go, too,' he said sulkily. 'I have lectures to prepare. Ask Ranjit to let me know about the boy.'

'Certainly,' replied John absently. He looked at Diana a little coldly, feeling that she was, in some way, distancing herself from him. He hesitated, holding the door half open. 'I don't think you should go alone in the dark,' he said to Diana.

Tilak felt he would never escape and he suddenly wanted to get out of the hot little room. 'I'll take Miss Armstrong to the bus,' he offered.

Diana accepted the offer gracefully.

So Tilak found himself escorting an English lady down the sandy lane, past the Dean's bungalow. From the roof, Aunt observed him with astonishment.

At the bus stop, a group of children was playing Horses and Riders. The smaller boys were riding piggyback on the bigger boys, and they pushed and shoved in an effort to unhorse the riders. The fun they were having was infectious, and Diana laughed when one of the riders, with a deft push, caught another one off balance, and, to shouts of acclamation, horse and rider went down into the dust.

The bus arrived in a flurry of sand. Diana hastily thanked Tilak and eased her way into the crowded vehicle.

The little unhorsed rider rolled, puffing and laughing, to Tilak's feet, while, from a nearby house, a shrill voice shouted to the children to come in at once. Three children fled, leaving the fallen one sitting rubbing his back. He looked up at Tilak and grinned beguilingly. Tilak knew him, and his pulses jumped at his good luck.

'You're Mehta Sahib's servant?' he asked.

The boy scrambled to his feet, picked up his black pillbox hat and crammed it back on his head. 'Ji,' he replied respectfully.

'I want you to take a note to Miss Anasuyabehn,' he told the child. 'It is about a special secret with which she will surprise Mehta Sahib, so you mustn't show the note to anybody. Do you understand?'

'Ji.'

Tilak took out his notebook, tore out a page and scribbled a few words on it with his fountain pen. He fished a four-anna piece out of his trouser pocket and handed it, with the note, to the servant.

The boy put the note into his shirt pocket and the coin into the pocket of his ragged pants. He grinned at Tilak and ran happily across the road towards the Dean's house.

Meanwhile, Aunt stumped thoughtfully down the stairs from the roof, where she had enjoyed a short nap. She had just risen from the mat on which she had been lying, when she had observed, over the parapet, Diana and Tilak going to the bus stop.

Still feeling physically and mentally drained after her confrontation with the guru in the temple, Anasuyabehn was seated on the kitchen floor preparing dinner for the visitors. Two chattering female cousins were helping her. The parents were seated on the veranda, sipping lemon water.

The servant had been sent to the house of a neighbour with a full water-pot, the neighbour's tap having ceased to function, and Anasuyabehn said, as her aunt entered, 'I wonder where the boy is? He's been gone quite a long time.'

'Playing with the children down the road,' replied Aunt sourly. 'Saw him just now.' She sat down by a small charcoal fire, which one of the cousins had been tending. She took up a rolling pin and uncovered a pan of dough, which had been put ready for her by Anasuyabehn. The cousin put a pan of oil on to the fire to heat. As the older woman began skilfully to roll out puris on a small pastry board, she said, 'I saw something else, while I was on the roof.' She dropped a puri into the fat and pressed it under with a spatula, while the three girls looked up expectantly. 'That troublesome Dr Tilak was walking down the lane with an English lady – the one who visited Dr Bennett the other day!'

The Dean had put his head round the kitchen door to see how the dinner was coming along. The meal was late, and it troubled him to have to eat after nightfall – no Jain liked to do that. 'Indeed,' he exclaimed. 'You must have been mistaken.'

'My sight isn't that bad,' snapped Aunt. 'Perhaps,' she added cunningly, 'he asked Dr Bennett to introduce him.' That, she surmised, might damn him in Anasuyabehn's eyes. She glanced quickly at her niece, never ceasing the quick rolling of the bread she was making.

The girl sat as if turned to stone, her eyes wide, a lid in her hand poised over a saucepan of vegetables. Suddenly, within her, raged jealousy so raw that she could have spat like a fighting cat.

So that was why he had not come to the temple. Given the chance of an English girl in marriage, he had dumped her like a coolie dumping a bag of sugar.

Aunt smiled contentedly down at her frying puri.

'He would never allow himself to be seen walking with her unless he intended to marry her.' She flicked her sari back from her face and looked up at her brother. 'What do you think?'

The Dean lifted a hand in a dismissive gesture. 'I don't know,' he replied. 'It doesn't matter, anyway.'

Matter? Anasuyabehn nearly screamed aloud at him. It matters terribly, and I don't know how I can bear it.

22

The boy servant slipped silently into the kitchen. No one noticed him, except Aunt, who hissed out of the corner of her mouth, 'And where have you been, Maharaj?'

The sarcasm of the appellation made him cringe. He shrank into a corner, scared by the thought of the money in his pocket.

Consternation grew in him; supposing she found the four-anna piece? Its weight burned against his thigh, its delicious promise of sweets lost in overwhelming fright. If she found the coin, the old owl would shriek and nag at him until she discovered how he came by it; and, dimly, the little boy understood that this would cause not only trouble to himself but, possibly, to his dear Anasuyabehn as well. The fact that the note might be more incriminating than the coin did not occur to him – he regarded it merely as a piece of paper.

In a funk, the child moved to the charcoal bin. As if to make up the fire, he took a piece out and at the same time dropped the coin into the box. It fell with a soft plonk into the slack at the bottom.

At the sound, Aunt turned round. 'Don't make up the fire now,' she snorted.

His fear receded. She had not seen. Obediently, he put back the piece of charcoal and stood waiting for the family to finish their dinner, so that he could have his.

The Dean suggested a walk in the Riverside Gardens. Everyone agreed, and, with a swish of saris, the ladies rose and went to the bathroom to wash their mouths.

Aunt turned to the servant. 'Next time you're sent on a message,' she growled, 'come back at once, do you hear me? At once. Otherwise, I'll take an anna off your wages for every five minutes you're late.'

The boy skulked in a corner and hung his head.

'No dinner, tonight,' added the indefatigable crone. 'Now, clear up the dishes.'

The hungry boy hardly heard her. If they all went for a walk, he would be alone in this terrifyingly big bungalow, where the spirits in the air went *shush-shush* as they flew round the compound; and they rattled at the door bolts and made the curtains flutter at the windows.

As he stared at the discarded brass talis on the floor, they seemed to grow bigger, like staring eyes, too big for a little boy to scour. The littered kitchen floor stretched out before him like the desert of Rajasthan, miles of it to be swept and washed before he might curl up on his mat and lose his misery in sleep. He sat down on the floor and wept loudly.

Anasuyabehn heard the noise and came swiftly back to the kitchen. 'What's up?' she asked her aunt.

'I've told this naughty boy that he can't have any dinner,' replied Aunt.

The sobs redoubled.

Anasuyabehn tried to look stern. 'You're right, of course,' she said, and then paused. 'Perhaps, tonight he could have his dinner, and, if he ever dawdles again, he could go without?'

Aunt got up to follow the others to the bathroom. Over her shoulder, she snapped, 'You spoil him.'

'I'm sure he's very sorry.'

The boy stopped crying, wiped his nose with the back of his hand and nodded vigorously.

'All right, if you wish,' replied Aunt and swept out of the kitchen, all injured dignity. The servant ran to Anasuyabehn and touched her feet.

'Eat quickly,' she told him. 'Wash the talis and clean the floor. You can do the saucepans in the morning.'

'Ji, hun,' he assented, still sniffing, while his eyes made an anxious inventory of the amount of food left in the saucepans. Obsessed by the need to eat, the note lay unremembered in his pocket.

Long ago, in the days of the East India Company, an Englishman had built himself a miniature palace by the river and, round it, had laid out a fine park with a wide promenade along the river bank, the whole surrounded by a high wall. His grandson, an irascible bachelor appalled by the overcrowding of Shahpur, had willed it to the city, to be a park forever, open to all castes and classes to walk and play in.

The people thronged into it, happy to be free of traffic and dust. Admittedly, the grass had worn a bit thin in places, and, at one point, the surrounding wall had broken down, yet it was still a blissful retreat on a hot evening. The palace was now a boys' school, sadly lacking in paint though high in reputation. Like the park, it was open to Untouchables, as long as they could pay their fees.

Beggars were kept outside the gate by an officious chowkidar. They gathered as near to the gate as they could get, however, exhibiting a horrible collection of deformities and lifting distorted hands to the passersby. Like some dreadful opera chorus, they chanted hopefully, 'Ram, Ram, Ram.'

Through this ghastly crew floated like petals on the wind girls and women in pastel coloured saris. They were closely escorted by their white-clad menfolk and were accompanied by a bevy of grave-eyed children. Amongst them, Anasuyabehn walked demurely behind her father and her uncle, a giggling cousin on either side of her, while the two aunts brought up the rear.

Though it was getting late, the park was far from gloomy; each path had its line of electric lights. The evening breeze blew coolly off the river, and the party walked the length of the promenade.

Anasuyabehn found it difficult to maintain her outward composure. Great gusts of fury kept sweeping over her. That Tilak should one day make protestations of love to her, and the next night be seen walking with an English lady was incredible. In this provincial town, nobody would walk alone with an English woman unless he had designs upon her. She forgot that Tilak was from Bombay.

'You're really so dull and depressing about your marriage,' complained one of her cousins. 'I'd give my eyes to be engaged to such a wealthy man – a man who sent me diamonds.' Her voice rose in sharp envy. 'And he looks so handsome in his photo.'

The reminder of Mahadev's generosity struck Anasuyabehn forcibly. She lifted her head proudly and her lips curled in a hard smile. At least her fiancé wanted her badly.

They came to the end of the promenade, and the older ladies sat down to rest for a few minutes on a stone bench, upon which they arranged themselves so that there was no room for anyone else. The two gentlemen walked slowly up and down the path in front of them, while the cousins stood patiently nearby. A lamp illuminated the bench, though it served only to deepen the shadows cast by a huge, drooping tree behind it. Faintly from the burning ghats on the other side of the river came the smell of burning wood, a sad warning of man's mortality.

The cousins grew tired of Anasuyabehn's long silences and ran across the walk to the balustrade, which divided the river shore from the park. Thankful to be alone, Anasuyabehn paced up and down on the grass behind her aunts. Under the shadow of the tree, her green sari made her almost invisible.

A husband and wife, who knew her family, stopped by the bench to pay their respects to the aunts, and Anasuyabehn stepped deeper into the shadow, rather than face another barrage of good-natured jokes about the joys of matrimony. Though very exhausted, she was still simmering with anger.

When she heard the very softest whisper behind her, she was shocked. Stifling a shriek, she turned. 'Go away,' she whispered back to Tilak. 'How dare you come near me? And how did you find me?'

Tilak's black jacket made him invisible against the tree's great trunk, as he breathed, 'Followed you from home. Now, listen. Quickly. Have you a passport?'

Indignation welled up. 'How dare you? How dare you?' she upbraided him.

'I'm sorry, I couldn't get away.'

'No? I imagine you were very pleasantly occupied.'

Puzzled at her attitude, he said irritably, 'Tell me, Rani. Your passport. I have to make plans for us.'

Anasuyabehn peered at him through the gloom. He was so close to her that she could feel his warmth. In the midst of her rage, her physical desire for this handsome man tore through her. One touch from his hand would have diverted the flood of jealousy into channels of self-recrimination and explanation.

'Sister, sister, where are you?' called one of her cousins, running back across the walk.

She whipped round, and, then, forcing herself to advance casually into the light, she called back, 'Here I am.'

Bewildered and frustrated, Tilak slunk into the darkness.

23

Old Desai sat on his wooden divan in his dismal counting house, his portable desk beside him. Sitting near him was his sister's husband, hastily summoned by telegram from Baroda. With him had come his sister's sons, aged fifteen and eighteen respectively.

Leaning against a battered filing cabinet and staring vacantly at the visitors was Mahadev's brother, his face showing none of the sense of panic within him. Mahadev and the Maharajah's jewels were missing and unusual decisions had to be made. He would probably have to go out to help with inquiries amongst dull Hindu clods in the villages, and he was not looking forward to it.

Why didn't his father leave the job to the police?

He knew the answer only too well. His father loved Mahadev above everyone; he would literally leave no stone unturned in order to find him.

The stout, plain man in his round black cap gave a small quivering sigh, and tried not to think of his wife's bitter tirade that morning. She had said she hoped that Mahadev would be found, since there had to be one brain in each generation of the family.

Old Desai turned to the one man in the room to whom he felt close, his Partner Brother, still spry in spite of his years and his sorrows, a man whose sons had died before him. He alone could truly appreciate his dread of losing Mahadev.

Partner Brother's small eyes gleamed behind his heavy, horn-rimmed glasses. 'Well, where shall we start?' he asked.

Baroda Brother took off his pince-nez and polished them, to indicate that he was getting ready for action. Since Mahadev, fleeced by the dacoits, had not arrived at Delhi, he was, in his opinion, lying dead somewhere along the railway track. He kept his belief to himself, however, and suggested briskly, 'We could search either bank of the railway track for some miles on each side of the site of the robbery.'

'The police will have already done that,' said Partner Brother.

The thorough, ponderous mind of Mahadev's own brother had not been idle. 'Father,' he said, with a trace of excitement, 'if there were anything dead within a couple of miles of the railway track, vultures would have come in clouds and would have been clearly visible; the police would have gone immediately to see what was attracting them.'

The other men looked at him in surprise. There was a stunned silence, and then everyone spoke at once.

'He *must* be alive,' said old Desai, his voice trembling.

Baroda Brother-in-law put his pince-nez firmly back on to his nose, and added, 'He must, since his body was not on the train.'

Mahadev's brother gritted his teeth. Even when he showed intelligence, he fumed, nobody really noticed. Even his name was forgotten by most; he was simply Husband or Brother or Son – or, worst of all, Mahadev's Brother – a simpleton in the background of other people's lives, lost in the shadow of a more brilliant brother and bullied by a shrewish wife.

Yet, who supervised all the account books of his father's great concerns? he asked himself. Who checked the incoming interest and made the first moves against those who failed to pay? Who sat up late at night, to comb carefully through each agreement, so that not once had they lost a court case when some outraged landowner took them before a magistrate?

He hoped, in the forefront of his mind, that Mahadev was safe. But, deep inside, he wished savagely that he was lost for good. He chewed again his already closely bitten fingernails.

His father's voice cut through his rumination. 'We'll first inquire of every Desai Society along the route, up to a distance of fifty miles from here. There is no great town to comb, unless he is, say, a hostage, in Shahpur itself – only villages.'

He then began to organize them. 'Dress plainly,' he advised. 'You are moneylenders going about your normal business. On no account mention the jewels. Go by bicycle or by horse carriage.' He tapped his fingers on his little desk, and then went on, 'Take a servant or one of the others with you – if we find the task too great, we'll close the office and use the clerks.' He wagged his finger warningly. 'Be careful to be courteous to the Headman or the Panchyat, when you inquire. And stop at isolated huts – and don't forget the Untouchable quarters.'

All the men nodded agreement.

'Should we inform Dean Mehta now?' asked Partner Brother.

Old Desai considered this question carefully. He would have preferred to keep the matter secret, but the Mehtas might hear a rumour.

A fresh fear struck him. Such rumours might well reach the dacoits. If Mahadev had been left for dead, if he had seen the robbers' faces and they realized that he was still alive, would not they also start to hunt for him?

He winced, as he foresaw a quick knife thrust under Mahadev's well-covered ribs, the moment he showed himself. Impatiently he pushed the unwelcome thought out of his mind, and answered his brother's question. 'I'll go to his office to tell him – so that, for the moment, his family does not have to know.'

He remembered grimly his Baroda Sister's remark, when she had first been asked to act as go-between. She had said, 'The girl is not lucky – she has already lost one fiancé.' He had snubbed her thoroughly as being superstitious and old-fashioned.

The men got up and stretched, and he clapped his hands. When his Chief Clerk came running, he told him to bring in the morning mail, together with his notebook and pencil. While he was doing this, old Desai turned to his younger son and instructed him to stay and mind the business. After he had dealt with his letters, old Desai tottered into the long, dark room which was his general office. His half dozen more junior employees all rose to salute him obsequiously. He made this round of the office daily, pausing to poke into every small detail that caught his eye. Occasionally, he left some young man trembling and ashen-faced, after being upbraided. All his employees were in some way related to him, and it was unlikely that he would ever discharge one of them; but he held the purse-strings tightly in his rheumaticky hands, and it took devoted service and slavelike hours of work to loosen them.

After having left a trail of moral destruction in the office, he returned to his younger son in a more amiable frame of mind. He wanted to compliment him on his deduction that Mahadev was probably alive, and he considered giving him the emerald ring he always wore. He half slipped it off his finger; then his lifetime habit of parsimony re-asserted itself, and he slipped it on again. Words, however, cost nothing, and he left his son considerably cheered up, when he finally climbed into his carriage to drive himself to the University.

From the depths of his dusty cubicle, Dean Mehta's secretary informed him that the Dean was at the Marwari Gate temple and would be a little late that morning. He looked at his watch, and said, 'He should be back in about ten minutes.'

'I'll wait,' Desai decided, and he was shown into the Dean's office.

The secretary returned to his work and Desai could hear him shouting down the telephone. Desai fretted that he should have telephoned before he came. He had a telephone in his office on which he received incoming calls, but he could never bring himself to make a call. Lines could be crossed, he worried, and the contents of very private agreements be overheard by outsiders; skeletons might rattle in family closets; thieves might overhear. The telephone was, indeed, not something to be used lightly. In fact, most telephone calls received by the Desais resulted in one or the other partner driving over to see the caller.

The Dean came in slowly, his ascetic face mirroring clearly his sharp abstinence from food that day and his lack of sleep.

He bade Desai welcome and sent for tea for him. He then sat, amazed, listening to his story. In the back of his mind, he wondered if Mahadev had absconded. Though Desai had not mentioned it, he guessed that Mahadev had been carrying valuables, probably jewellery. A fortune in jewels would be a great temptation to a young man who would know how to dispose of them and who seemed to like living in the West.

They discussed whether to tell Anasuyabehn and decided that she had better know. A rumour would disturb her almost more than knowing the truth of the matter.

The Dean asked what assistance he could give. His brother, he said, had already arrived to help with the wedding and was supervising the delivery of supplies for it.

'If you hear anything that might bear on my son's disappearance, would you let me know?'

'Naturally, I will.'

The Dean forced himself to stand up and see Desai out to his carriage. As they walked along the corridor, quiet except for the occasional burst of a lecturer's voice as they passed a half-closed door, Desai said that, if Mahadev was all right, he wished to bring forward the date of the wedding. He wanted to send the boy and his new wife to Paris again for a little while.

The Dean foresaw cries of objection from his sisters and his sister-in-law; women were always so fussy about ceremonies – and the astrologer would be full of forebodings, no doubt, at a change of date. He was, however, a little uneasy. Since her first outburst, Anasuyabehn had said no more to him about breaking the betrothal. Aunt had assured him that the girl now seemed quite reconciled to it.

Yet, he felt, he would be thankful when it was over; his last family responsibility would have been fulfilled.

As they paused at the top of the front steps, he said, 'The preliminary invitations have been sent out, but I'll hold back the second ones and the special invitation letters, until I hear from you.'

Desai smiled and saluted him. 'A-jo,' he said, and got back into his shabby, little carriage.

24

'Where can a woman cry in peace?' Anasuyabehn asked herself miserably, as she went back home from the park. She felt that if she did not cry soon she would choke. Her last stronghold, her bedroom, was at present invaded by her two cousins. They would not leave until after her marriage – and, after that, she would cease to be a person in her own right and be an appendage of Mahadev's.

Apart from her grief at Tilak's behaviour and her approaching marriage, she was still haunted by memory of the fearsome monk. Her religion, with its ruthless rules for the purification of the jiva, the soul, during each rebirth, had re-asserted itself that morning in a most alarming way.

In betrothing her to Mahadev, her father had broken only a rule of caste, which had crept into the originally classless, casteless Jain belief. Jainism had, at first, been a movement of revolt against caste, she thought, and, to be honest, he was marrying her into a group which epitomized Jain life.

If she ran away with Tilak, she would commit the sin of filial disobedience and would, in addition, marry a man of another religion, a high-caste Hindu. Even to love a man so much was in conflict with the teachings of her religion, she moaned to herself. To become too attached to anything or anybody was a prelude to suffering, and, as tears welled up in her, she knew the teaching had meaning.

'When are the merchants bringing wedding saris to show you?' broke in one of her cousins excitedly. 'I'm longing to see them.'

'Ask Aunt,' replied Anasuyabehn shortly. 'She has it all arranged.'

They turned hopefully to the old lady, to ask about everything to do with the marriage. 'When shall we visit the Desais? Can we go to a potter's yard? We want to mark his wheel with red powder and buy some pots for the marriage booth? And Lord Ganesh must get an offering of rice from us and have his elephant head specially marked, mustn't he, Aunt? Respected Aunt, do tell us?'

Aunt laughed and answered them amiably, while the object of all the preparations trailed slowly behind her and began to regret bitterly her sharpness with Tilak. Perhaps, she argued, he had been held up by his work, so that he could not meet her. And there simply had to be a reasonable explanation of his attendance on Miss Armstrong, if she could only think of one.

The servant had put out string beds on the roof for the gentlemen and on the veranda for the ladies, each bed swathed in a mosquito net.

On arriving home, the Dean immediately excused himself and went to his study to perform his evening devotions, while his more worldly brother betook himself to the roof with a copy of *Gone with the Wind* and a flashlight by which to see to read it. The older ladies retired to one end of the veranda to say their prayers and sink thankfully into their beds. The younger ones sat, cross-legged, on their beds and loosened their long plaits of hair, while they continued to whisper across to Anasuyabehn for some time. She was taciturn in her replies, however, and eventually feeling a little deflated they curled up and slept.

Anasuyabehn could not rest. For greater comfort, she took off her blouse and wrapped her sari loosely round herself. Her throat ached with suppressed tears.

Finally, she slipped out of bed and went into the house. There was no light under the study door, so she assumed her father had gone up to bed on the roof. She made her way to her own room and switched on the light. The heat of the house was almost intolerable, but the need to cry was urgent. She paced up and down restlessly; the tears, so long repressed, would not come.

Undeniably, Tilak still had the intention of marrying her; otherwise, he would not have bothered to follow her to ask about the passport. She understood the importance of the question; a large deposit was needed in order to obtain one, and government procedure was extremely slow.

Well, she had a passport, obtained when she had accompanied her father to a conference in Sri Lanka. The problem was how to get this information to Tilak and how to ask his forgiveness for her rudeness.

Her cotton sari was soaked with perspiration. She went to the window, opened it and leaned her head against the iron bars. There was not a breath of wind. She stared aimlessly out at the rural scene lit by a moon partially shrouded in dust. She hoped that houses would never be built behind her father's bungalow.

Then she remembered that, unless Tilak moved quickly, she would soon leave this pleasant home for the cramped and ugly Desai Society, behind high walls in the inner city. She had not seen it, but she could well visualize its crumbling walls and worn steps, its wavery, tiled roofs, its lack of fresh air. Aunt had told her that not many people lived in its multitude of rooms, that the business took up a number of them. She thought of Mahadev's little girl wandering, solitary, through them. What was she like, after being pushed about by a spiteful aunt? Anasuyabehn felt suddenly cold at the thought of having to establish her seniority over her future sister-in-law – her aunt had warned her about this. And then there was the lonely, sad uncle whose wife and children were already dead. What was he like?

'I can't face it,' she cried softly. 'Tilak Sahib, how can I get a note to you?'

Her question was answered as if she had rubbed a magic lamp. From outside the window came an urgent whisper, 'Put the light out.'

Mouth half-open in surprise, she stood motionless, and then began to giggle almost hysterically.

'The light, Bahin.'

Still giggling, she went obediently and switched the light out.

'Come to the window,' pleaded Tilak.

She stood with her hand on the switch, trying to calm herself. She succeeded only in bursting into tears.

'Come, Rani.'

She ran to him, tears pouring down her face. Putting her arms through the bars, she clasped them round Tilak. A very delighted Tilak slipped his arms through the maddening bars to hold her as best he could. The bars bit into their flesh.

'My love, my dear love,' he murmured. Endearments and passionate kisses passed between them, and the passport was momentarily forgotten.

Suddenly, from the roof, Anasuyabehn's uncle shouted, 'Who's there?' Keener of hearing than his elder brother, he leaned over the parapet and swung his torch wildly about, the darting beam moving too fast to pick out any single detail.

Without a further word, Tilak slid away from the windowsill. Like a squirrel, he streaked along the backs of the bungalows, then cut across the field path into common land, where he lay panting in the dry grass, until the lights went out again in the Mehta home. Then he jogged back to his room, cursing under his breath.

25

The following day, Dean Mehta asked his brother to come into his study. 'I must tell you something,' he said.

His brother had just washed his mouth out after lunch, and a few drops of water still clung to his chin. As he followed his brother into the stifling room, he dabbed his dripping face on his sleeve.

Contrary to the best advice of his guru, the Dean had an electric fan. Though he could not bring himself to stop using it altogether, he turned it off during his fast days.

'A fan,' the guru had said, 'injures the souls in the air. Yours, being electric, can also kill insects.'

Today, the fan was back in its cardboard box, and the windows were shut to keep out the onslaught of the afternoon sun. The heavy Western desk and chairs, the crowded bookcases, added to the oppressiveness of the atmosphere. Because of the extra people in the house, the boy servant had not had time to attend to the chattyas, the heavy copra mats which covered the outside of the windows and usually dripped comfortingly with water to cool the room. There was nothing to mitigate the sweltering weather.

The Dean's brother wondered how he was going to endure the house for a whole month. He deposited himself on one of the stuffed chairs, which immediately caused him to perspire even more.

The Dean told him briefly of Mahadev's disappearance. He did not mention his own suspicions that Mahadev might have absconded. He ended by saying, 'I shall, of course, tell Anasuyabehn. She has a right to know.'

'Anasuyabehn isn't very lucky, is she?' his brother responded glumly. 'If Mahadev turns up, we'd better hold the marriage as soon as possible, before anything else happens.' And then I can go home to an air-conditioned house, he added to himself.

'It's odd that you should say that. Desai said the same thing this morning. They have some business in France they want to send Mahadev to attend to; they want his wife to go with him.'

The younger Mehta scratched miserably at the sweat rash on his stomach. 'Certainly we can manage it, if Sister is agreeable.' He examined the backs of his hands thoughtfully; the skin was already dry and cracking from Shahpur's desert climate. 'Anasuyabehn was not very keen on this match, was she?'

'Not at first,' replied the Dean. 'It came as a surprise to her. Her aunt assures me that she's quite happy about it, now she knows more about the family.'

'It was a pity we could not find her a scholarly man.'

'Well, those we considered were either without prospects – and I wanted her to do better than our poor sister – or they were personally unprepossessing. And young Desai is really keen on her. He sent her a superb diamond, you know.' He sighed, and then added a little defiantly, 'He's not ignorant either. He's a matriculate and has travelled a lot.'

The younger Mehta nodded. Then he suggested, 'Perhaps she should be a little more tightly chaperoned until her marriage – to avoid any hint of scandal.'

'Scandal?' The Dean looked shocked.

'Well, you know what people are,' his brother said defensively. 'She has a lot of freedom.'

'Well,' responded the Dean. 'We'll tell her aunts that she is not to go out of the house alone.'

Relieved that he had persuaded the Dean to have Anasuyabehn chaperoned, without having to mention to him vague suspicions aroused the previous night, he offered to send the girl in to see her father.

He found the ladies on the veranda. Each had a piece of needlework in her lap, but they, too, were wilting from the heat, and the needles were not being plied. When he came over to them, Anasuyabehn got up from the floor and her uncle could not help but observe the change in her from yesterday. The silence and the pinched look had gone from her. She was radiant, and when she spoke it was with the excitement of one in a fever.

He told her to go to her father and he watched her, as she vanished into the bungalow. He felt that she certainly had the strength of character to carry on an intrigue with a considerable amount of duplicity. Had he heard a man's voice last night or had he imagined it? he asked himself. Had she been saying her prayers, as she said she had? One did not pray in the dark, and, as he came down the stairs from the roof, he had distinctly heard a light being switched on. Her window had been shut, when his wife had gone into her room – he had asked particularly. Miss Anasuyabehn was up to something, he was sure, but he could not accuse her without proof.

He was worried about a scandal for another reason. Soon his daughters would face the same shortage of marriageable men as Anasuyabehn had. He did not want the problem made worse by a scandal in the family. Some castes were short of women and a girl could take her choice of eager young men, but amongst the Mehtas, at the moment, there seemed to be a real dearth of males. He must tell his wife to watch their girls, he decided.

Further down the veranda, Aunt was watching *him* out of the corner of her eye, wondering why the Dean had sent for his daughter. She, too, was giving thought to possible husbands for her nieces, and was going over in her mind all the young men who might be eligible. Unlike their father, she had taken into account that they were nearly a decade younger than Anasuyabehn – a different generation. 'Ah,' she exclaimed, satisfied, as she managed to thread her needle and at the same time recollect a possible sixteen-year-old boy.

26

'This man you've sent me to work for, this Tilak Sahib, is very strange,' remarked Tilak's new servant to his uncle, Ranjit.

'He's no stranger than most modern people. Be thankful for a job. Now you can eat well – and, with care, you can make a little money,' Ranjit scolded.

They were seated on John's back veranda, sharing what was left over of John's breakfast porridge. Having dispatched Tilak to his lectures, the nephew was on his way to the vegetable bazaar and had stopped for a minute or two to report to his uncle.

When he saw that Ranjit was cross with him, the boy immediately became obsequious. 'I'm grateful for the job, Uncle.'

'It isn't Tilak Sahib's fault that he has to cut up fish for a living,' Ranjit remarked. 'It's his father's fault for training him so.'

'Is he a fishmonger?' the boy asked, horror creeping into his voice. 'I thought you said he was a professor.'

'He is, he is,' replied Ranjit testily, as he collected up their dishes. 'He studies the insides of fish and frogs.'

The nephew's distaste, as he digested this information, was apparent on his ratlike face. Then he said uneasily, 'He went for a walk in the middle of the night – so late that the moon was beginning to set. What man in his senses would do that?'

Ranjit had the answer immediately. 'Perhaps he went to look at his experiment in the University.'

'What's an experiment?'

'I don't know,' said Ranjit truthfully, 'but I have heard from other University servants that, sometimes, professors go at night to check their experiments.'

'Oh,' said his nephew, and was satisfied.

Tilak was, however, news. Ranjit mentioned the late walk to another servant, joking that he might be hunting for another frog. This servant told the joke to someone else, and in due course it reached Miss Prasad's woman servant, who was one of Aunt's main sources of gossip, and Aunt learned that mad Dr Tilak went hunting frogs all through the night. She filed the information, with a lot of other more juicy titbits, for further use.

In the late afternoon, Ranjit went to town and ordered a tonga to come out to the house that evening, to take John to the home of Mr Lallubhai, one of the district's wealthier millowners.

Though Lallubhai was very rich, he was also a very conscientious man. His mills might hum with machinery forbidden by the Jain religion and turn out more cloth than any other works in India, but he combined in himself much that was good in a Jain gentleman. He provided housing for his workers which was the envy of other Shahpur citizens packed together in shocking slums. A small hospital, properly staffed, took care of the health of his workers, and a school for children up to the age of ten had recently been opened in his compounds. When building his house, he had installed outside his gates an extra water tap. This tap was considered miraculous because, no matter what the time of day, water ran out of it – and it ran fast, unlike the miserable trickle of the municipal supply. The tap was for public use, for all castes, and it was used with gratitude by Jain, Hindu and Muslim.

As John paid the tongawallah, and the chowkidar opened the gates for him, he watched the red-clad or white-clad women filling their water-pots. Amongst them stood Diana wiping her hands with her handker-chief. She smiled when she saw him, and the women all paused in their task, while they watched the couple.

She held out her hand to him, her discomposure at the end of their last meeting forgotten. 'My hands felt filthy from travelling on the bus, so I was washing them,' she explained.

John nodded, continuing to hold her hand and smile at her; she had four blue bracelets on her wrist, he noticed, and a hell of a lot of freckles.

A burst of giggles from the women, as they hoisted their water-pots on to their heads, made him drop her hand hastily. 'We should go in,' he said.

They turned and went through the heavy gates covered with beaten silver, and approached the huge, marble-trimmed bungalow. One broad picture window was lit up and they could see, on the inner wall of the room, a large copy of the famous painting of Gandhi and Nehru sitting together, a picture which graced many Indian homes. John grinned. The austerity of the great leader, clad only in his loin-cloth, seemed a bizarre comment on the ostentation of the house.

John's stick clicked across the terrazzo terrace. He could not think of anything to say to Diana and felt awkward in consequence. He thought she looked charming and he wondered that she had not been

410

approached by someone like Lallubhai to become either his mistress or his wife. Diana could have told him, had he asked, that she had become quite adept at turning down such offers.

He found himself indulging in thoughts suspiciously close to jealousy, when Lallubhai seated her on a settee next to him. Lallubhai's wife also noticed the seating arrangements. She was an extraordinarily beautiful Madrasi woman, her red sari draped round her shoulders to make a frame for a face marred only by an expression of cynical boredom. John bowed to her and sat down himself. She may be beautiful, he brooded sourly, as he accepted glasses of water and fruit juice from a bearer, but in this provincial backwater, Diana, with her red hair, is unique.

Lallubhai cracked a joke with Diana and made her laugh. Then he called the meeting to order. He might enjoy dallying with a pretty woman, but he was, first and foremost, a businessman with little time at his disposal.

Within half an hour, John found himself with enough mapmaking to last him through six months of spare time. A garrulous assistant from the City Engineer's Department, already overwhelmed at being amongst such wealthy people, was appointed to help John.

John was amused by the expressions on the faces of the remainder of the Committee, as Lallubhai apportioned to each of them a slum district to be visited, censused, as far as possible, and recommendations made regarding it. Since many of the slums were as horrifying as those of London in the eighteenth century, John was not altogether surprised at their sudden lack of enthusiasm. The police hardly ever visited such places and they were avoided by the health authorities, except at times of epidemics. The whole Committee quailed visibly and began to make excuses.

At last, a Christian missionary spoke up. He was a ghostlike, malaria-drained man from the American Middle West, white-haired, withdrawn. Though his voice was querulous, his white hairs demanded respectful attention.

'Gandhiji said that we *must* help ourselves,' he told them gently. 'If we can clean up and improve the city, we shall be acting on his behest. A healthier city benefits all of us – we shall have less to fear from disease, for one thing.' He paused, and put his hand on the back of John's chair for support.

John remembered when he had first come out to Shahpur, a brash, vulgar man with a text always on his lips. He had not had much success with his mission, but Shahpur had moulded him into a very fine person. Now, he put courage back into the Committee. He shamed them with Jain and Christian texts and his own eighteen years of work in the city.

As they rose, they promised, resignedly, to do as Lallubhai had asked them.

The old missionary sank down into his chair again, and John shifted himself round so that he could shake his hand. At the same time, he became aware of Lallubhai's rumbling bass voice, accompanied by Diana's protesting contralto.

'Miss Armstrong, you cannot go home alone at this time of night, even in a tonga. I won't hear of it. I have ordered a car for you; it will be at the front door in a few minutes. Unfortunately, I cannot accompany you . . .' He looked round, and at the same moment John turned back from the missionary. 'Ah, my dear Dr Bennett, I wonder if you would take care of Miss Armstrong. My chauffeur will drive you both to your respective homes.'

Diana's green eyes twinkled momentarily, though she resented John's obvious alarm.

'Why – why – of course.' John leaned heavily on his stick, as he got up from his chair. 'Delighted.'

Snugly ensconced in the back of Lallubhai's air-conditioned Cadillac, the uniformed back of the chauffeur comfortably anonymous in the darkness, Diana sat quietly by John, her hands folded in her lap. Nothing indicated the dejection within her. He had not really wanted to escort her – and why should he? She felt, suddenly, despairingly lonely.

'Do you think this survey will ever be carried out?' John asked her. Her sweet and heavy perfume was from Lucknow, he guessed.

'Yes, it will,' she replied. 'Lallubhai will see to that. He is so powerful – and he has a most vindictive tongue at times.'

So she didn't like Lallubhai all that much. In case the chauffeur understood English, he quickly changed the subject.

He said cautiously, 'I wonder if you would like to walk for a little while in the Riverside Gardens?'

She sparkled immediately and said she would.

John redirected the chauffeur, much to the man's disappointment. He had been wondering what an Englishman did when he was left alone with a gorgeous woman, and now he would probably never know. He clicked his tongue irritably and swung the car around.

A Cadillac stopping by the park gates caused a rush of beggars, each with his cry of woe. John had a busy moment or two while, with his stick, he kept them away from Diana. With good humour, he spoke to them in Gujerati, the homely language learned as a child from his beloved Ayah.

'Hey, Brothers,' he cried. 'Leave me enough so that I, too, may eat.'

They grinned at him, and whined, 'In the name of God, Sahib, you do not know the pain of an empty stomach.'

'I do know,' he said, and pushed pennies into sore-covered hands. The memory of his hunger in prison made him generous. 'Now, chelo,' he ordered them, and the chowkidar reinforced his order to them to go, by threatening them with his lathi.

Though she was not afraid, Diana kept close to him. So often, she had to face such people alone. Though their diseases, their starvation, their filth grieved her, one could get overwhelmed by sheer numbers.

They strolled into the nearly deserted park and John's stick thumped heavily on the asphalt path.

A man who had been leaning on the balustrade, his head buried in his hands, looked up suddenly. They were upon him before they realized he was there.

The light of a lamp fell full on Tilak's face, a face ravaged by weeping and lack of sleep, so filled with despair that it was hard to recognize the usually fretful, dogmatic man.

'Are you ill, old man?' John asked in concern, while Diana diplomatically stepped back a little.

'No, Bennett Sahib.' Tilak straightened up and made a great effort to appear calm. He rubbed his hands over his face. 'I may have a touch of fever, that's all. I thought it might be cooler down here. The servant you sent is very good – cooks quite well – and it hasn't dawned on him yet that the tradespeople pass our room by.' He rattled on, 'Ah, Miss Armstrong – it's pleasant down here, isn't it?'

Diana smiled shy acquiescence. Her nurse's eyes ran over the careworn face. Yes, probably fever – though, to her, he seemed terribly distressed mentally. Pity overcame her disappointment at not having John to herself.

John prepared to say goodbye and walk on with Diana, but Tilak was reluctant to let them go; it did not occur to him that there were times when John could do without him. When they moved, he moved with them, talking about odds and ends of campus news.

At first Diana left John to answer him. The serenity of the night enfolded her, a golden moon in its first quarter, a cloud of stars, the perfume of flowers ground to dust in the scorching daytime heat. Then, feeling that perhaps she should help John out, she interrupted the men to say brightly, 'Isn't the sky clear! No wonder poets praise the night.'

Tilak pounced on her remark and said, 'Poets create romantic illusions, Miss Armstrong. Romance has no place in India.'

His sharp response was unexpected, and she replied a little nervously, 'Come now, Dr Tilak. Indians are just as romantic as Westerners, and

413

the winds of change have made them more able to express it, nowadays.'

'There *are* some of us who try to assist the wind, Miss Armstrong,' he admitted. He shivered, though there was no breeze to chill him.

John had listened uneasily to the exchange, and now he said, 'You're shivering. Perhaps you've a touch of malaria. You should get into bed soon.'

Tilak shrugged, as if to indicate that it did not matter if he had.

They returned to the gate. John gave up hope of having Diana to himself that evening; it would have to await another opportunity. 'Let's take a tonga between us,' he suggested. 'We can take Diana home first.' Tilak agreed absently and left John to bargain with the tongawallahs. A bargain was struck with a Muslim as thin and brown as an old pipe cleaner, and they climbed into the awkward little carriage.

In the enforced proximity, knees touching, bodies swaying together, the two Europeans could feel Tilak continuing to shake. They both expressed their concern.

Tilak shook his head. 'It's – how do you say in English – a goose walking over my grave. I'll feel better later on. Don't worry.'

As they passed under a street lamp, however, Diana saw that his eyes were fever-bright. He's terribly overwrought, she thought anxiously. She ventured to advise him, 'As a nurse, I prescribe three aspirins and bed.'

He agreed to do as she had said. How could he explain to her, he thought, that the shivering was caused by a fearful apprehension? A primitive scenting of danger to himself.

He was overwhelmed by worry that he would not be able to whisk Anasuyabehn safely away, before she was married to Mahadev, and that it was almost impossible to communicate with her. His nerves were screwed to breaking point and he did not know which way to turn.

At Mrs Jha's house, John got down to see Diana safely to her door. He waited patiently while Mrs Jha could be heard fiddling with the great brass bolts on the other side. He looked down at Diana. She smiled at him, and very gently he bent down and kissed her on the cheek. At that moment Mrs Jha was checking on them through her peephole. She was greatly shocked. Her thin lips were even thinner, as she let her lodger in.

Diana herself was agreeably surprised and gave him another smile, as he said goodbye.

He climbed back into the carriage and said to Tilak, 'We can go first to your hostel and the tongawallah can drop me on his way back to town.'

Tilak had been wrapped in his own thoughts, but he said that he would prefer to get down at John's bungalow and walk over to the hostel.

'But you've got fever,' protested John.

'It's a fever of the mind,' Tilak snapped, his voice full of wretchedness.

'All right,' agreed John, and at his bungalow they had an amiable argument as to who should pay the tongawallah. John won, on the grounds that he would have taken a tonga, anyway. He was worried enough about his friend to offer him a drink before he went to the hostel, and this was accepted by Tilak with evident relief.

Tilak sipped cautiously at his whisky and water. It did not taste quite as foul as he expected; he would rather have died than admit that he had never tasted whisky before. Shahpur was a prohibition area, and John obtained a small ration of whisky each month, on the grounds that he had drunk it all his life and was, therefore, an addict. He was much teased about it.

Troubled by the ravages wrought on his friend in a few distressing days, he watched Tilak thoughtfully, as he sipped his own drink.

The unaccustomed alcohol loosened Tilak's tongue. He spoke first of the English Fellowship and then, more slowly, about his desire to take Anasuyabehn with him as his wife.

When he heard this, John sat up in his chair, pain in his legs forgotten.

'Look here,' he said. 'The only way in which you can marry Anasuya-behn is by formally asking her father, or getting your uncle to ask for you.'

'If she has a passport, she could be married to me in a civil ceremony in Bombay and we could go straight on to the ship. The problem is that the Fellowship does not commence until October, and she is scheduled to marry this Desai fellow next month.'

'That would, anyway, be tantamount to an abduction in the eyes of the law, here. Dr Mehta is my old and trusted friend; I could never be party to the abduction of his daughter.'

'I'm not asking you to be.'

'Well, there's another point. I wouldn't like you to face a charge like that in a local court. Apart from its being a very serious charge, you're a Maratha – and they'd have your blood.'

Tilak made a face. 'Gujeratis are not very fond of us, are they? We are also not very fond of them.' He sighed heavily. 'You know perfectly well that the Dean wouldn't even give me a hearing. Every time I meet him in the corridor I can see him trying not to throw up again – and some of his Arts colleagues are positively insulting.'

John sat taut and attentive. Unless he was stopped quickly, Tilak might ruin himself, and end up being thrown out of the world of scholars

– and out of his family, as well. He suggested gently, 'Look, Tilak. You've got this Fellowship. Take it. Go and work under Diamond – it's a chance in a thousand. Forget about Anasuyabehn. Mahadev is a decent man in his way, and her father, I believe, knows it.' He paused for breath, and then added persuasively, 'There are other women in the world, Tilak, women educated to your level. You'll find someone else in time.'

While John had been speaking, Tilak had left his chair and, with his hands clenched in his pockets, had been walking slowly up and down the room. Now, he went to the door and flung it violently open. He glared out at the inky shadows in the compound.

He was furious; he dared not speak. One word would have loosed an avalanche of anger on to John – and in his heart he knew that John was the only true friend he had in Shahpur.

He ran down the steps into the darkness. The compound gate slammed after him.

27

Mrs Jha shut the door on John, replaced the padlock, and then turned
to Diana. Beneath hooded lids, her black eyes were full of suspicion,
and her lips were tight with disapproval; it was not seemly for a young
woman to be seen home by a man. When previously Diana had been
to meetings at Lallubhai's house, she had always been driven home with
a number of guests, both ladies and gentlemen, in the car. Once she
had arrived home having been driven in solitary grandeur by Lallubhai's
chauffeur, which was bad enough; but after all a chauffeur was hardly
a man at all. Now Mrs Jha awaited an explanation, while Diana stood
in the hall in a half dream.

Mrs Jha rattled her keys, and Diana came out of her reverie. If she
did not wish to lose her room, some explanation of John's presence was
necessary.

'Mr Lallubhai asked Dr Bennett to bring me home,' she said. 'He's
a very learned man – some people say he is a sage – who lives near the
University. He writes history books about the Gujerati people.'

Mrs Jha's imagination was captured.

'Books about us?' she exclaimed.

'Yes,' replied Diana, with suitable gravity. 'He's made the Gujerat
famous in America and England, as a place of learned and pious people.'

'Ramji! Fancy, books about us. And he is a sage, you say?'

Diana smiled.

'Well, not quite,' she said, 'but he lives a bit like a monk.'

Mrs Jha's face fell. Although she had disapproved of Diana's being
accompanied home by a strange man, she was disappointed at being
robbed of a secondary interest in a romance. A sage, indeed!

She moved down the passage, hitching her sari as she went, while
Diana turned towards her room. Sages in ancient days were known to
fall from grace, the old lady ruminated hopefully, and this one had
certainly kissed the girl, which was quite shocking.

Diana took off her dress and wandered about her room in her cotton
petticoat. With a mind hopelessly overstimulated, she abandoned all

thoughts of going to bed for some time and decided that, in spite of the noise it would make, she would do her washing.

She got out the wooden paddle with which to beat the wet clothes on the veranda floor, a bucket of water made warm by the sun, a bar of common soap and the cardboard box of dirty clothes. Methodically, she sorted the clothes, taking each garment carefully out with her fingertips and shaking it well away from her, in case a scorpion or a snake should have taken up residence. Then she went through her skirt and blouse pockets to remove dirty handkerchiefs.

And there it was.

Fluttering silently to the floor from a handkerchief, a minute piece of paper with a blue line across its creamy whiteness. Diana watched it fall, her brows knitted in perplexity.

'Now where did that come from?' she muttered, and bent down to pick the scrap up.

The movement reminded her. Of course, she had picked it up on the way to Pandipura. She smiled at the thought of how she had amused herself by wondering how it came to be at the foot of a cactus in the bush.

Then the smile died, her eyes widened. She knew what it was.

The dead donkey! Her patient's fear! The missing noise in the village! It all fell into place.

Her first thought was to run to the police. But, no. These were not like British policemen – she might find herself in a dreadful mess with them. Then go to ask John's advice? That was hardly practical at eleven at night.

Her heart pounded and she ran her fingers feverishly through her red hair, as she sought for the best way of dealing with the unnerving revelation.

'Perhaps I should do nothing at all,' she dithered uncertainly. Then she remembered the Englishwoman lying dead in her First Class carriage in the robbed train, and indignation rose in her.

'It might have been me,' she thought.

Absent-mindedly, she picked up a garment, damped it and began to scrub soap into it. She rubbed and scrubbed and beat the washing in a spreading sea of soapsuds on the veranda floor. Then, as she rinsed her clothes in a bucket of fresh water, she decided that Dr Ferozeshah would be the best person to consult. He was intimately bound up in the life of the city and would understand all the factors involved.

'I'll ask him as soon as I go on duty,' she decided, and shook out a towel so forcefully that it made a sound like the crack of a bullet.

28

Unwilling to take a tonga, which would draw too much attention to them, and having long since exhausted the limited bus service, the uncles of Mahadev trudged from village to village. Where there were Desai Societies in a settlement, they commenced their inquiries at them. Failing that, they went to a member of the Panchyat, the Village Council. They did not neglect the miserable corners in which lived the Untouchables; the weavers, the tanners, the lavatory cleaners. Though they tried to make their inquiries casual, the news flew from mouth to mouth and, at times, a train of curious children and officious, advice-giving elders trailed along with them.

Occasionally, their queries about a Bania they were to meet and had somehow missed, as they put it, caused an electrifying attention, and they discovered that police, on bicycles, had already been through some of the villages seeking clues to the train robbery and a missing man.

After he heard this, Partner Uncle hired bicycles from a small shop. He and his servant wobbled along sandy lanes, cursing the heat and the dust and the smells, but progressing at least a little faster than they had done previously.

Partner Uncle was not a young man and, by late afternoon, he was trembling so much from exhaustion that he could no longer balance on his bicycle. When they reached a small well, he bade his servant dismount.

A young Hindu shepherd was drawing water for his sheep. The flock baaed and swirled around him, as he filled a trough for them from the waterskin. He paused, and politely offered water to the weary travellers. They thankfully squatted down, and he poured water from the skin into their hands. Trickles of the cool liquid ran down to their elbows and splashed pleasantly on to their sandalled feet.

With a grunt of relief, Partner Uncle wiped his dripping chin on his sleeve and sat down, cross-legged, under a nearby tree which gave a straggling bit of shade. His servant sat with him.

Both shepherd and sheep eyed them doubtfully. Then the shepherd settled his plum-coloured turban more firmly on his head and returned to watering his flock. As he guided the rope quickly over the well wheel, he shouted above the noise of the sheep, 'Have you come far, Brother?'

'We have,' replied Partner Uncle. Then he asked, 'The railway must run quite near here?'

'Yes,' agreed the young man and gestured towards the horizon. 'You can see the telephone poles that run along the top of the cutting.'

Uncle scrambled up to have a look.

'That's where the train robbery took place,' went on the shepherd.

'Were you here when it happened?' asked Partner Uncle, with sudden interest.

'No, sir.' He bent over the trough to empty the skin, still looking at the Banias out of the corner of his almond-shaped eyes. 'I took the sheep home, because I felt a dust storm was coming. It was time for supper, anyway.'

'Yes?' encouraged Partner Uncle, sensing that there was more to come. A blankness crept across the shepherd's handsome face, however, and he silently let down the waterskin into the well again. The wheel squeaked mockingly.

Frustrated, Partner Uncle tried again. 'Have you seen another Bania going this way? We were to meet him at the village back there, and we have somehow missed him.'

This innocent question caused the shepherd to blench. His hand shook so much that the rope nearly came off the wheel.

Used to the evasions of bad payers, Partner Uncle suddenly roared at him, 'You *have* seen him. Has he been hurt – or robbed?'

The boy cringed. 'No, sir. No.' His eyes were wide with stark fright. 'No – no one's passed this way, today – except for the milkmaids going to and from town – and the vegetable sellers very early this morning.'

The sheep scattered uneasily at the sharp voices. Uncle's voice came like a trumpet. 'Perhaps not today – but a day ot two back. He did, didn't he?'

'Sir, I don't know your friend,' came the fearful reply. 'I've no remembrance of a stranger doing business in our village.'

Uncle's voice dropped, and he wheedled, 'Come, lad, I mean no harm – but I do need information about such a man. I'm sure no traveller would be assaulted in your village. You can, therefore, safely tell me what it is that you have seen.' He palmed a couple of rupees and let them show out of the corner of his hand.

Grey-faced, but with his eyes on the money, the boy began to babble. 'Sir, we stole nothing. We took good care of the stranger – yet, it's best when dacoits are about to say nothing.'

'Quite, quite,' agreed Uncle, trying to be patient. He made himself smile as he looked down at his plain, respectable white shirt and homespun dhoti. 'It's obvious, at least, that I'm not a dacoit – only a business-man from Shahpur. You can speak safely to me. I'll tell no one else.'

'True, Bhai,' replied the shepherd, trying to stop quivering.

'Well, what happened?'

The shepherd gulped. 'Sir, it was like this. My eldest brother was returning from market in our ox-cart – on the day of the storm. He knew a storm was coming, too, so he took the new road along by the railway – it's easier for a cart to travel on, though it takes a little longer.'

'This was on Monday afternoon?'

The boy counted on his fingers. 'Ji, hun,' he agreed. 'It was already dark by the time he reached the cutting and the storm was howling round him. Being alone, he was afraid and he stopped to light the lantern for the cart. In the darkness and the wind, he couldn't find his matches, and then he heard horses nickering and thought they must be tied to trees nearby. Now, horses are not much used here, sir. And my brother wondered who would stop in such a lonely place in a storm – they would surely press on to seek shelter in our village. My brother became too afraid to advance up the road, so, as quietly as he could, he drew the ox-cart off the road and tethered it, hoping that the cacti would mask his presence.'

Partner Uncle could well visualize the nervous, superstitious peasant caught in the storm and fearing devils, robbers, angry gods.

'Yes, yes,' he said impatiently.

'My brother crept away from the cart and lay in a hollow. He saw flashlights flick on and off, but the dust was so thick and the night so dark, he couldn't see who was holding them. Then, through the earth, he heard the vibrations of the Delhi Mail approaching. There was a big explosion – and rifle fire – and the train stopped, instead of roaring onwards.'

The shepherd had now forgotten his fear and was absorbed by his story, embroidering in the details. 'He thought for a moment that the war with Pakistan had started – because we're only forty miles from the border, sir. Anyway, there were shrieks and cries – a woman screaming, and a rush of people, first down the cutting and then up again. Along the road and then across country the horses clattered, like devils sucked up into the sky.

'My brother lay perfectly still, quite safe, thanks to the storm – and, after a while, he heard the railwaymen shouting to each other, and the train started up.'

'The Bania?'

'I'm coming to that, sir. Did you say two rupees, sir?'

'Four, if you can tell me where he is now.'

'I don't know exactly where he is, sir.'

'Well, what *do* you know? Why are you telling me this long tale, which I can read in any newspaper, if you don't know?'

'Peace, Brother,' the shepherd's voice began to shake again. 'How will you understand if I don't tell you from beginning to end?'

Anger being a mortal sin, Partner Uncle did his best to swallow his. 'Well, what happened then?'

'My brother lay a long time in his hiding place. When nothing more happened, he crept back to the ox, listening intently. He got the cart back on to the road again and wrapped his turban round his face, because the sand was still blowing. He led the ox, for he still feared to show a lantern light, and continued slowly down the road. He had not gone very far, sir, when he heard a loud groan, right at his feet. Now, what would you have done, sir?'

With eyes closed, Partner Uncle stood up and stretched himself. 'I'd have fled,' he said sarcastically and then swore under his breath, mentally promising forty-eight minutes of penance to wash out the oath.

'Not my brother,' boasted the shepherd with pride. 'He looked about him, and, by the side of the road, saw a vague white bundle – like a fallen ghost.' He paused for effect. 'It moved a little. He advanced carefully, fearing it might be a wounded dacoit. It was a big, stout man weeping with pain – a townsman, he guessed.' The shepherd spread out his hands in a gesture of helplessness. 'My brother didn't know what to do. He went to the cart to get the lantern, however, and succeeded in lighting it.

'The man was a sorry sight, his face all covered with blood.'

Partner Uncle exclaimed in alarm.

The shepherd nodded, and went on, 'My brother wiped the blood from his nose and eyes. He tried to lift him up to put him on the cart and bring him home, but the man was too heavy for him and cried out in pain.'

Partner Uncle was, by this time, striding up and down in great apprehension. He stopped in front of the shepherd. 'Well, what next?'

'Brother took the blanket from round his own shoulders and covered the man with it – a good blanket, sir, now ruined by blood. He whispered to the man to try to keep quiet and he would bring help. He then tethered the ox again – because oxen are slow, sir – and ran home in the teeth of the storm.

'Five of us went out in that terrible storm, sir, and found the man and put him in the cart and brought him to my father's house. My mother washed away the blood and found he had two wounds, one on the top of his head and one in his shoulder. He was unconscious but mother said no bones had been broken. She bound him up – and all night we sat and wondered what to do. Ours is a very small village, sir, since the cholera killed so many, and my father is the eldest elder. The responsibility was his.' The shepherd paused for breath, and then asked, 'He must have been a passenger on the train? Would he be your friend?'

'I believe so,' replied Partner Uncle, and then, as the shepherd showed no sign of continuing the story, he queried, 'Well?'

The shepherd evaded Partner Uncle's anxious glare. 'Sir, the sun is going down. I must take the sheep home.'

Partner Uncle swelled with sudden rage; the veins on his forehead stood out. He swept his arms above his head and shook his fists, like an avenging god. 'What is this?' he shouted. 'What happened to my nephew?'

The countryman cringed, and responded uncertainly, 'Your nephew? Sir, you *must* speak to – to father.'

Partner Uncle screamed again in rage, his voice echoing round the empty countryside. Pointing a finger at the unfortunate shepherd, he advanced threateningly towards him, only to be brought up short by milling sheep. The boy stammered, 'Come home with me, sir. Father will explain to you.'

The frightened sheep eddied between them. Afraid that his furious master would have a fit, the servant caught him by the arm, and implored, 'Master, keep calm.'

Partner Uncle shook off the restraining hand, but he did thereafter try to control himself. 'Very well,' he snarled. He picked up the hired bicycle and motioned to the servant to pick up his. The sheep were called and herded to the path. In the blinding dust raised by ninety-six little feet, Partner Uncle followed the flock and its shepherd.

Partner Uncle found little solace in being half-choked by dust, but his anger cooled and his quick brain went to work. It did not take him long to realize why the boy had stopped his tale where he had. After cleansing the wounds, the old father would naturally look to see if his unexpected guest had been robbed, by checking his money belt; and if it was indeed Mahadev and his money belt was still round his waist, the old man would have been faced with the terrible temptation of a fantastic fortune having arrived in his poverty-stricken hut. How easy to add to Mahadev's wounds, take him back to the cutting during the night and bury the money belt under the floor until such time as it seemed

423

safe to remove himself, his family and the fortune to another part of India.

During the twenty minutes' uncomfortable walk, Partner Uncle felt it would be a miracle if Mahadev and the jewels were both safe.

Infinitely thin and wrinkled, Jivraj lay on his string bed. He struggled up to speak to Partner Uncle, however, and bade him sit beside him while he heard his business. Then with many a sly look over his shoulder, he confirmed his son's story of the robbery, and sent for his elder son, his nephews and his brothers, who all corroborated it. Though dreadfully afraid, not one of them said a word of how the robbers themselves had pounced on the village, uttering terrible threats and sweeping away all their donkeys with a promise of their safe return in a few days' time. In a matter of minutes in the dark night they had come and gone, leaving dismay and near panic behind them. And then, before the night was done, Jivraj had been faced with the problem of the wealthy, wounded stranger.

Now he must cope with this hard-faced Bania, just when it appeared that the train robbery was all but forgotten and all that remained was for the donkeys to be returned; he had no doubt that they would arrive home safely since their loss would cause comment all over the district, and the robbers would not wish to leave any indication of how they got out of the province.

'But where *is* my nephew?' demanded the frantic Uncle.

'Ah, Sahib, has no word come to you from the police?'

'No!'

Jivraj looked bewildered.

'But the doctor promised to find out who he was and inform the police, so that word might go out to his family.'

'Doctor?'

'Yes, Sahib. The morning after the robbery the stranger had high fever, and we feared he might die.' He looked helplessly at Partner Uncle, 'And then how would I explain away to the police a corpse with wounds?'

Another man pushed his way forward. 'I remembered that I had heard the white doctor was visiting a few villages away, so my son went for him.'

Partner Uncle took a large breath and relaxed a little. 'Did he come?' he asked.

'Oh, yes. He came with his big lorry. He said the Bania was very sick and had a bullet in his shoulder. He also needed medicine which the doctor didn't have with him. He asked what had happened, and we told him. Then he brought a cot from his lorry and we put the Bania on it and lifted him in. The doctor Sahib said he would take him to his hospital and inform the Shahpur police. We were deeply afraid of being implicated in the train robbery.' He stopped and looked uneasily round the group of anxious men who had gathered. 'The doctor said he would explain to the police for us – that he knew us to be honest men. He comes to the village occasionally.'

Partner Uncle stood up. 'Where's the hospital?'

The villagers looked at each other. Then one said, 'It's to the north – on the other side of Shahpur – ten or fifteen miles from here.'

'That side of Shahpur is desert. There couldn't be a hospital there.'

'That's where it is.'

A younger man bent down and whispered in Jivraj's ear, and Jivraj said to Partner Uncle, 'It's a God hospital – a Christ one.'

'Ah, a mission?'

Dusk was falling, and a woman of Jivraj's family came out of the hut with a lighted charcoal fire held in a pair of tongs. She put it down, put a covered bowl by it and began to slap rolls of dough between her hands to flatten them into rotis, preparatory to cooking them.

Jivraj looked at the exhausted old moneylender and was touched by the sadness in his face. 'Sir, if you can eat our food, one of my sons will serve you under the tree over there.'

Moneylenders are not popular in villages and Partner Uncle was surprised by the offer. He was glad to accept, however, and then he added, 'It's too late to find the hospital tonight. I'll return to Shahpur and set out again early in the morning.'

To his surprise, Jivraj said, 'To return to Shahpur from here is very simple. When they made the new road, they built a station for us at the nearby railway. In about an hour's time, a local train will come down the line. It's about a mile to the station.' He bridled with pride in the new facility.

So Partner Uncle found himself eating good millet bread and sag with a little yoghurt, under a tree in a strange village, and ruminating on the unexpected courtesy and kindness of country folk. Deep inside he felt a trifle ashamed of the many times he had, in years past, pounded money out of just such people.

'Ah, well, they owed it,' he thought, as he scraped the last bit of sag off the palm leaf on which it had been served.

'Not at 144 per cent interest,' said his conscience.

The young man who served him was the shepherd he had met at the well, and he put the promised four rupees into his hand; the boy took

425

them without protest, as his due. An older man then brought a lantern and led them, as they pushed their bicycles, over an almost invisible track down to the small railway station.

There are no words of thanks in the Gujerati language and Partner Uncle did not offer to pay for his meal, but the villagers knew and Uncle knew that a bond of hospitality had been forged between them. One day, when the opportunity arose, it would in some way be repaid.

Less than two hours later, Partner Uncle was reporting to old Desai, who himself had had a fruitless day.

'I know of the hospital,' said old Desai. 'It is called the Mission of Holiness. Once I met that doctor.' He picked his toes thoughtfully. 'I formed the opinion that he was not altogether trustworthy – you know how one senses it?'

Partner Uncle sighed, and nodded.

'Tomorrow, Baroda Brother and I will go to the hospital and inquire. You must rest.'

Partner Uncle agreed. It did not occur to either of them that the Mission of Holiness might be on the telephone – nor was it.

29

Tilak never remembered clearly how he got through the night and the following morning, after leaving John so precipitously. A veil seemed to be cast over his conscious mind and he was guided merely by habit.

Realizing that the Sahib was in some way ill, his servant made up his bed and suggested that he sleep. He helped Tilak off with his clothes and held back the mosquito net while his master silently clambered into bed. After a while, he slept.

Soon after daybreak, the servant brought him hot water for shaving and then a brass tray of breakfast. After he had laid out clean clothes, he sat down in a corner and wondered apprehensively what Uncle Ranjit would say if he ran away.

Tilak shaved mechanically, turning over his lecture notes as he did so. A plop of shaving soap fell on them and he wiped it carefully away with the towel. He continued to read while he ate wheaten porridge and drank some milk. Then he put the notes into his briefcase, dressed, gave the servant money for the day's food, and walked down to the University.

Though the sun was already well up, he shivered occasionally as though he were cold. It was not chill, however, but rather an inner perception that he faced a long, hard road to travel. He felt helpless, unable to accept the bitter facts regarding Anasuyabehn, which John had pointed out the previous evening.

When he arrived at the Arts and Science Building, some of his students were hanging about outside it. They looked sullen and turned away from him, but he was too absorbed in his own problems to notice them. Inside, other students were hurrying to lecture rooms. They stared at him as he strode unseeingly to his own lecture room. He opened the door and walked in.

The room was empty.

Surprised, he looked at his watch. He was punctual. He put down his briefcase and took a few uncertain steps towards the window. Then he wheeled around and went out to the corridor again.

While the last students scurried through doors, like rabbits down their burrows, the Vice-Chancellor's secretary hurried up to him.

Tilak asked, 'Do you happen to know if they changed the room for my lecture? Is the Dean in yet?'

The secretary blinked excitedly from behind thick spectacles. 'The room? I don't know. The Dean has just gone over to the English Department. Dr Prasad, however, wishes to see you now.'

'I can't possibly see him now. I have a lecture – only all my students seem to be late or are in the wrong room.'

The secretary replied portentously, 'They are not late, Sahib.'

'What do you mean?' A fuming irritation at the fool standing before him began to invade him. 'Well?' he snapped.

'They're on strike, Sahib.'

'Strike?'

'Yes, Sahib. That's why Dr Prasad wants to see you.'

Seated in front of the Vice-Chancellor, Tilak looked at him amazed. He had not heard Dr Prasad's opening words, except that he realized that his tone was sympathetic. Now Dr Prasad was saying, 'This is a situation which I had not foreseen. It will be the work of three or four hotheads. I have sent for Dean Mehta – he will know who are likely to be the miscreants, and I can assure you that disciplinary action will be taken.'

He waited for Tilak to say something, but Tilak was so taken aback that he was beyond words. All this because of a little dissecting? It was absurd. Yet, in his heart, he knew it was not absurd. He had struck at the roots of Jain belief.

'Would you like to take some leave while we deal with this?' asked Dr Prasad.

'Of course not,' Tilak assured him. Anger began to take the place of surprise and he felt like throwing something at the dolts who could not see that India, whether its inhabitants liked it or not, was a part of the twentieth century.

'I suggest leave, my dear Dr Tilak, because Dr Bennett mentioned to me, when I saw him recently, that you had had a brick thrown at you. It disturbed him because it happened on campus – and students are apt to be a little unstable.'

'Are you afraid of violence of some sort?'

Dr Prasad hesitated, and then said, 'I shall try to avoid it, of course.'

'Well, I'm not afraid of it – my mother and sister have gone back to Bombay, so I don't have to worry about them.' He laughed sardonically, and commented, 'It would be ironical if our Jain friends took to violence to defend non-violence!'

'It would, indeed,' agreed Dr Prasad sadly. 'But I hope it won't come to that. Meantime, I really think it best if you went on leave for two or three weeks.'

An hour later, the University's Head Peon was dispatched to town to make a reservation on the Bombay Express for that afternoon. Tilak's servant went scuttling down to the river, to rescue his master's shirts from the boiling vats of the washerman, and Tilak himself tried to deal with the chaos in his room.

Sheets, mosquito net, blankets, bedding roll, were spread all over the floor, as a result of his flustered servant's efforts at packing. Clucking with irritation, Tilak made up his own bedding roll and packed a trunk with his books and papers. As he worked, he considered how to let Anasuyabehn know of his impending absence. Dr Prasad had turned down the idea that he remain in the city, but not teach. 'It's better to be right out of it,' he had insisted. He felt physically weak and the sweat rolled down him, as he struggled with leather straps and recalcitrant buckles.

He began to weep helplessly and sat down suddenly on the bedding roll. Would it be better simply to walk out of Anasuyabehn's life? Go away to Bombay and never come back?

He gave a shuddering sigh. He couldn't do it; he must at least let her know what had happened. After a little consideration, he decided to ask John to deliver a note to her.

He scribbled a quick explanatory note to her, saying he hoped to return in two weeks, and enclosed it, unsealed, in another note to John. His servant could take it over to him.

Anasuyabehn, too, had spent a bad morning, wondering how to inform Tilak that Mahadev was missing, that there was a chance he had been killed, but that, if he were found, her wedding would take place sooner than expected.

She did not want to wish a man dead. This unexpected happening, however, made her hope that he would be missing long enough for the marriage to be deferred.

In the late afternoon, while the aunts and her cousins slept and Dean Mehta went back to the University, she sent the boy servant to the students' hostel, with a cryptic note giving some indication of her predicament.

'Go first with this,' she instructed him, as she handed him the chit, 'and, on the way back, buy some fresh pan leaves from the pan seller up the road. Give the note only to Dr Tilak. Nobody else. Do you understand?'

The little boy grinned slyly and slipped quietly out of the sweeper's door and up the field path. At the hostel, he found himself facing a padlocked door.

The wife of a student, baby on hip, was standing at the door of the next room, and she asked him what he wanted. He told her that he had brought a letter from Dean Mehta's daughter to Tilak Sahib.

'From Dean Mehta,' she corrected.

'No. Bahin wrote it herself.'

The woman looked thunderstruck. Then she said cunningly, 'Leave it with me, little Brother. I'll give it to him when he comes in.'

He held it behind his back and took a step or two away from her. 'No. It's for Tilak Sahib only. When will he be back?'

In a fury of curiosity, the woman answered him, 'He went away with all his luggage this afternoon. Perhaps he won't come back.' She started to advance towards him. The child turned, and ran helter-skelter down the stairs.

The middle-aged mother of another student opened her door further down the passage. 'What was that?' she asked the woman with the baby.

The woman told her, and so the story was sent on its way. Two days and several dozen gossips later, it was said on the campus that Dean Mehta's daughter was pregnant by Dr Tilak, who had fled to escape the consequences.

30

While Dr Ferozeshah was preparing to receive the morning rush of outpatients, Diana showed him the piece of paper she had found and told him of her deductions.

'Keep out of it,' Ferozeshah advised promptly.

'But the police might be able to trace the dacoits if they knew about this,' protested Diana. She was dressed in her white, nurse's uniform and was getting together the doctor's stethoscope, his thermometer, cotton wool and bottle of disinfectant and putting them ready on his desk.

In response to her protest, Ferozeshah said firmly, 'Never go near the police unless you have to.'

'I haven't done anything wrong!'

'Neither of us has. But once they are here, they'll hang around and expect to be fed – and if we really want anything done, they'll expect suitable baksheesh.' He finished buttoning up his white coat.

'Oh,' said Diana, immediately deflated.

'Cheer up. I'm sure you're right. But, at best, that piece of registered envelope you found is a clue; it's not concrete evidence against the dacoits. And, you know, the villagers will be punished – and the dacoits would still get away with it.'

That evening, after an early dinner, Diana went on the bus to see John and ask his opinion. Ranjit admitted her and managed a polite smile, a smile that faded immediately he returned to his back veranda; it was replaced by a look of great anxiety.

John agreed with Ferozeshah. 'I've heard that they have sent a good man down from Delhi to investigate, because of the murder of that Englishwoman. Let *him* get on with it.'

Diana sighed. 'I suppose you're right – I felt so clever working it all out. But how will those poor people in Pandipura cope?'

'I bet the donkeys are back in the village by now. The villagers haven't suffered much and they'll all be as quiet as mice – they don't want the dacoits to burn the place flat next time they come this way.'

'That's awful! It's bullying!'

'We live in an awful world,' responded John almost flippantly.

His acceptance of human wickedness surprised her. It savoured of a Hindu outlook.

He continued. 'They probably had a plan to get the proceeds of the robbery out of the province and, because of the storm, it went wrong, so they pounced on the nearest village – they needed transport that fitted into the landscape and could carry, say, builder's sand, with the loot buried in it. Donkeys would be perfect. Horses stick out like sore toes, here.'

'Why use horses at all?'

'Speed – to get away from the scene, in the first instance. They probably had a string of camels waiting, and missed them in the dark and the dust.'

'My patient was so frightened and worried that she nearly died.'

'That's too bad. Is she all right now?'

'Yes. She'll be OK.'

'Good. I say, can you stay to dinner?' he asked shyly.

Diana looked up at him and smiled. 'I'd love to,' she said, and hoped she could eat a second meal.

John took up his stick and went to consult Ranjit. The bearer agreed morosely that he could provide enough food. John turned to go back into his room.

'Sahib . . .'

'Yes?'

Ranjit, seated on the floor in front of his precious Primus stove, looked up. He looked as sour as a piece of dried tamarind. 'Nothing, Sahib,' and he leaned forward to pick up his paring knife.

Really, John thought, Ranjit was a queer old stick sometimes.

As he re-entered, John asked Diana, 'Do you happen to know Anasuyabehn Mehta?'

'No. Who is she?'

'Dean Mehta's daughter. Lives a few doors down. I just wondered.' He did not like to say that in his cash box lay the love letter for her, left by Tilak's servant earlier that day, which he wanted delivered to her. He had read it. It said simply that Tilak had to return to Bombay and was consulting his uncle. It would mean the world to Anasuyabehn, and, even if Dean Mehta saw it, there was nothing dishonourable in it.

Diana watched him cross the room, leaning on his stick. 'I don't think that you need to use that stick all the time,' she said abruptly.

Startled out of his thoughts of Anasuyabehn, John glanced down at the offending stick.

'Do you have any pain now?'

'Not often, unless I've hit myself on something.'

'I don't think Ferozeshah has examined you for a long time. He's been rushed off his feet.'

'Oh, I only ask him for a sedative. In England, they told me not much more could be done.'

She gazed at John standing uncertainly before her, his face slowly reddening with embarrassment.

'Forgive me,' she said gently, 'for being so personal – but I saw a fair amount of similar injury during the war and how it was treated. I believe you could learn to walk without a stick – and quite straight. It would mean that the rest of your body wouldn't ache so much from being out of position. I imagine it does ache?'

He nodded, and she got up and went to stand in front of him. 'Would you like to try?' she asked. 'I'll help you.'

She was not a tall person and seemed very diminutive to him. Her eyes crinkled up with humour, and she said, as if she had read his thoughts, 'I'm quite strong.'

'I wouldn't mind having a bash at it.'

'OK. I need first to see exactly how you put your feet down. Put your hands on my shoulders and I'll walk backwards, while I watch your feet.'

He laid his stick on the divan and shyly put his hands on her shoulders. It was so long since he had touched a woman that, at first, his thoughts were not about learning to walk. He stumbled, only to be steadied by a surprisingly strong arm round his waist.

Diana held him for a moment; then quickly let her arm drop, afraid that her instinctive movement might be misconstrued. John was thinking, 'She's too bloody innocent for words.'

'Let's try again,' she said in her bright, professional voice, and he glumly gave his attention to what she was saying.

He held on to her and advanced as she retreated.

Ranjit peeped through the half-open door and was horrified to see such abandoned behaviour. He went back to his cooking pots wagging his head in a hopeless fashion.

It was even worse when he went in to announce dinner. The copper and the dark heads were bent close together over the desk, while the Memsahib drew indecent pictures of men doing peculiar actions with their legs.

Ranjit hardly slept that night.

31

On a littered desk, lay Mahadev's money belt like a pallid, dead snake. Seated before it was a man leaning his head on his clenched fists. He had not moved for twenty minutes.

An increasing ruckus outside the window reminded him that patients were gathering there for morning surgery. He lifted his bald head wearily and rubbed his eyes with his knuckles, to look around his cluttered little office, where the few pieces of furniture were all piled high with dusty records. The corners of the room were festooned with cobwebs, and the uncurtained windows were opaque with dust, a myriad of smears and finger-marks. One window was open and, through it, he could see the dreary, flat, semi-desert landscape shimmering in remorseless heat.

The chatter outside the window increased; the Mission of Holiness was a very busy place, and the missionary himself felt tired to death.

He opened one fist.

On his soft, white palm glittered a beautifully cut ruby, its perfection undimmed by the gloom of the office.

It must be worth thousands, he thought, and glanced at the money belt in front of him. There must be a fortune in that!

The money belt was a plain strip of grubby white cotton, which had been folded and stitched down one side. Along the whole length of the belt, at about one and a half inch distance from each other, lines of stitching divided the belt into small compartments. Judging by the feel of it, each compartment held a stone at least as big as the ruby.

''Strewth, I wonder what it's all worth?' he muttered. 'I bet it'd buy a hundred new hospital beds, the salary of another doctor, two nurses and an operating room – and a stack of penicillin ceiling high. And bibles – dozens of them in Gujerati.'

He again looked at the ruby and smiled grimly.

'I could sell a gem like that in the jewellery market of Bombay or Delhi as easily as falling off a log – and who would know? I can simply say that he had no belt on him when he arrived here.'

As he ruminated, the waiting patients outside were being marshalled into a queue by a middle-aged Indian. The missionary had found him in a ditch, the sole survivor of a family of refugees from Pakistan who had died of starvation.

The whole queue would be suffering from malnutrition, thought the missionary despondently, apart from their heat boils, their venereal diseases, their tuberculosis and heaven only knew what else.

There was a knock on the door, and he hastily swept the belt into his desk drawer, and stood up.

It was only the woman sweeper coming to do the floor, and he walked up and down one side of the room while she swept the other side. The ruby was still clutched in his hand. What was he to do? And who was this man, anyway?

In the waist of his homespun dhoti had been knotted a return Interclass train ticket to Delhi. A small purse, pinned in the same place by a large safety-pin, had yielded twenty-three rupees and some change. His linen had, at one time or other, been marked with a D in Western script. Having found the money belt, the missionary could well understand why his patient had made such a frantic effort to escape from the train.

The sweeper opened the door to the passage and swept through it the dust she had collected. She began to sweep her way slowly and ineffectually towards the front door.

From beyond the door she faced, came the sound of loud, authoritative voices. A rifle butt was banged on the woodwork.

With lightning speed, the missionary shut the door of his office, snatched the money belt out of the drawer and bundled it and the ruby into the wall safe.

The sweeper opened the door and came flying into the room, at the same time trying to touch the feet of the police officers accompanying her. After them came the Mission's head nurse, protesting in Gujerati that the Doctor Sahib was very busy. It seemed suddenly that the room was filled with armed men, though, in fact, there were two police constables with rifles and one officer with a pistol in his holster.

Calmly and benignly, the missionary rose from his desk chair, one hand raised as if to bless. On the desk lay his bible, open as if he had been studying. 'Good morning, gentlemen. What can I do for you?'

The belligerent attitude of the police gave way to faint respect. The small man with the pistol stepped forward and answered him in good English. He said that they were looking for a missing Bania and that they had heard that he had recently had a Bania as patient. Before he could be answered, he turned to the constables and told them to wait outside.

The missionary answered calmly, 'Please sit down,' and motioned his unwelcome visitor to a chair. With his eyes on the doctor, he sat down with a rattle of accoutrement.

On his part, the missionary weighed up his visitor. A Bengali by the accent, supremely shrewd, a very senior police officer judging by the good cut of his khaki uniform. From a corner, the head nurse watched them both, and tried to stop his teeth chattering.

'We do have a man here, who by his dress appears to be a Gujerati Bania,' agreed the missionary.

'I believe he arrived here under unusual circumstances and that he had a bullet in him.'

'Yes. He has had high fever for three days, so we have no idea who he is. Had his temperature not gone down during the night, you would have heard from us today. He is now under sedation. He is obviously exhausted and needs to sleep.'

'I'd like to see him,' said the officer, still watching the missionary.

'He won't wake for at least two more hours. You could try waking him now, of course, but I doubt whether you would get any coherent response from him.'

'You should know that in circumstances such as these, the police should be informed immediately.'

'Ah, yes, of course, quite,' the missionary was at his vaguest, with a gentle smile. 'We have no telephone – and we are so busy – you have seen the queue outside. I could not spare anyone to go to town. I knew he would recover. It was not a question of murder.'

'It's a question of attempted murder,' replied the Bengali tartly. 'I'll leave a constable to sit by his bed, and I'll return in about two hours; I've other business in the neighbourhood.' He stood up, ready to leave. 'Exactly how did this man come to you?' He had already heard the story from the Mission's lorry driver, who had been roughly questioned a few minutes before, but he wanted to hear the American's version.

Now, he found that it tallied quite well with what he already knew.

'The Pandipura villagers saved his life, of that there is no doubt,' the missionary told him. 'They are to be commended.'

'It would seem so,' grunted the officer.

After the officer had gone, the American took out the money belt and carefully eased the ruby back into it. Then he went to see his patient.

Mahadev was sleeping quite relaxedly and his colour was good. By the bed, sat a police constable, his rifle across his hairy knees. He was already dozing.

'Are you ready, Doctor Sahib?' his nurse inquired. 'There's a long queue.' He had his hand on the door latch of the dispensary.

The American sighed and said he was ready. How much penicillin would a ruby buy, he wondered?

32

That morning, old Desai was so anxious that, for the first time in his life, he missed reading his morning mail. After drinking a glass of milk, he set out at daybreak for the Mission of Holiness. A servant drove the carriage, and Desai snarled at him unceasingly to hurry.

The old man had a brass box of lunch on his knee and a full water-jar on the seat beside him. Next to the water-jar, sat Baroda Brother. He was placidly polishing his spectacles on his shirt end; the morning was relatively cool, and he was enjoying the drive through the half-awakened city. By the driver sat his son, thrilled at the adventure.

The narrow city streets gave way to wide gravel boulevards, lined with trees shading the graceful houses and bungalows of the city's well-to-do millowners. These petered out to become a rough track; and the last mile was little more than lorry wheelmarks in the sand, through which the horse could hardly drag the carriage. Finally, the passengers got down and walked along beside the vehicle and made better progress.

Meanwhile, Mahadev lay in his hospital bed, under a mosquito net, and listened. His head ached so intolerably that he could not bear to open his eyes. When he tried to shift himself slightly, the pain in his back made his senses reel. One of his arms seemed to be tied to his chest. A short distance from him a number of voices made a steady hum – he wondered if it were the dacoits and lay very still, so as not to betray his presence.

Then he realized that he was in a bed of sorts, and made himself open his eyes for a second. He caught a glimpse of an old-fashioned English screen making a wall around him. Above the wall, he could see a shelf with glass containers sitting on it; over them a squirrel scampered.

He tried to think.

That was it! The trip to Delhi, to return the Maharaja's jewels. He had borrowed against them to set up a radio factory and now he wished to pay his debt.

The jewels!

With his unconfined hand, Mahadev felt round his waist. The belt was gone.

The shock was so alarming that he tried to sit up, only to fall back as rivets of pain went through him.

'Doctor Sahib,' called a voice beside him, and he forced himself to open his eyes again.

He did not know what he had expected, but the sight of a constable gaping down at him was a further shock. Apprehension about the loss of the stones gave way to fear for his personal safety. What had he done that he should be under arrest? In a split second, Mahadev saw himself flung into a filthy prison or, at best, reduced to utter poverty, a lender of single rupees.

In response to the call, a man came round the screen. An Englishman! The sense of lunatic nightmare increased.

'Ah, I see we are better,' the missionary said, his professional smile covering his own despair. 'I'm probably damned if I steal that belt,' his thoughts ran, 'and, if I don't, I'm condemned to this unmerciful round of watching patients suffer for the lack of simple drugs. Why, O Lord, why?'

He took the patient's wrist in pudgy, capable fingers, and added to himself, 'And if this guy pays his bill, I'll be lucky.'

'How's the head?'

Mahadev ignored the question. 'Where am I?' he asked.

'You're in the Mission of Holiness Hospital. I brought you in from Pandipura, near Ambawadi.'

'How badly am I hurt?'

'Bullet lodged in your shoulder – I've got it out, and a neat furrow across your skull where another one hit you – that was a near thing.' He turned and asked the constable to help him prop up Mahadev, while he looked at the head wound. The constable, who had never been in a hospital before, was fascinated, and did what the doctor ordered very carefully. Mahadev cried out with pain, however.

The doctor was undoing the bandages round his head. 'You'll be OK,' he assured the shattered moneylender, who was certain nothing would ever be OK again. The conversation was in Gujerati and the police constable watched and listened attentively. 'What happened? Do you know?' the doctor asked.

'The dacoits must've been short of men, because none of them caught hold of my carriage door, so I opened it and slipped down on to the track and ran for the embankment. A huge dust storm was raging – confusion – horses – screams. I started to climb further up the embankment where there were trees and bushes. They must have seen the movement.' He sighed and winced. 'When I came round, the train had gone.' He stopped; the effort of talking was too great. The missionary removed the dressing, and when the pain of it subsided, he went on, 'I

439

remember trying to crawl to the new main road – and a woman washing me.'

The constable spoke. 'It's better to stay in the train in a raid by dacoits. If you hand everything over quickly, you're usually all right. Not so with Muslims, of course.'

Mahadev looked at him sourly and nearly shrieked when the missionary muttered, 'Ah, healing nicely,' and clapped a new dressing on to his head. When he had replaced the bandages, he said, 'Well, sir, you've had a lucky escape. Later on today, you could try moving around a little. But, first, I want to look at your shoulder. And I want to know who you are, so that I can inform your family.'

Sulkily, Mahadev told him. He wanted to ask where his money belt was, but was frustrated by the presence of the constable. Never tell the police anything, had been drilled into him from childhood. Of course, he thought miserably, the police themselves might have the belt, in which case he would leave to his father the delicate negotiations to get it back.

'What day is it?' he asked, and was thoroughly perturbed to hear that it was Friday morning. The raid had taken place on Monday evening.

As the doctor worked, he chatted, partly to cover his own worries and partly to reassure his patient. 'A police bigwig will be here in about half an hour, to question you,' he informed his patient.

'A *Delhi* police chief,' interjected the constable reverently. He had parked his rifle against the bed, so that he could see better what the doctor was doing.

Mahadev closed his eyes and tried not to feel too bitter. A Jain gentleman was forgiving, patient under affliction. He did not feel like that – only cross and petulant and dreadfully weak.

He realized that the glass bottles ranged around the wall contained pickled specimens of foetuses, and his empty stomach began to heave. Fortunately, a woman in a white sari brought him some water to drink and distracted his attention. She was followed rapidly by the tramp of boots across the floor, heralding the return of the tiny police chief.

A little later, a triumphant and much relieved old Desai was shown into the dispensary. He stumped across the room, muttering that private initiative had been better than the perfidious police force. Had he not found his son himself?

He was much chagrined when, rounding the screen, he saw a very yellow and shrunken Mahadev lying on a bed and an obviously frustrated and fuming police chief sitting cross-legged on the chair beside him; Mahadev was not going to be much use as a witness.

The police chief looked up, as the old man entered, followed by his brother-in-law and nephew. He understood something of what was passing through old Desai's mind. The police had, in finding Mahadev first, scored over him. He immediately felt better and rose politely to salute him. 'Here is your son, sir. You may take him home as soon as you wish.'

Driving back from the Mission of Holiness in the early afternoon, old Desai was very quiet. It had been agreed that Mahadev should remain in the hospital for two more days. Baroda Brother-in-law asked him, 'Are you worrying about Mahadev?'

'No, the boy is obviously recovering. That English doctor knows what he is doing.' Old Desai could never remember that Americans were not English.

'It's what he was carrying?'

'Yes. We couldn't ask him with the police all round him.'

'Where do you think it is?'

'It's not with Mahadev. He touched his waist and made a tiny gesture to indicate that.'

'It'll be a frightful loss.'

'We shall have to pay. It's our reputation which is at stake. We've never failed to return securities lodged with us.'

'Do you think the train robbers took it?' asked Baroda Brother, thankful he did not have any share in Desai's business.

Desai replied slowly, 'I suspect that the English doctor has it.'

'What? He would've told us.'

'Not all English people are so honest.'

'It couldn't be. Anybody could've taken it when he was unconscious.'

Old Desai did not agree. He had not built up his enormous business without acquiring a profound knowledge of human nature. Like the Bengali detective, he sensed that the Mission doctor was hiding something. The man was disturbed in some way, and such a fortune would tempt the holiest of men.

'Have you told the Maharaja anything yet?'

'I sent a telegram saying that our representative would be with him in a few days' time.' He chewed his lower lip. 'I don't know yet *what* we send him, however.'

Their gate was opened by the chowkidar, who had been watching for them, and the whole family and staff swooped upon them.

Old Desai creaked slowly down from the carriage. He picked up his silent, wide-eyed, little granddaughter. 'Papa is coming home in two days' time,' he announced to her, 'and I think Aunt should get the tailor to stitch you a new dress for the occasion.'

The child smiled and relaxed, her head on his shoulder. Dear Grandpapa.

33

'I wish your father would make up his mind when the marriage is to take place. Everything is upset. The astrologer says he can't find a better day than was originally arranged. Now it's got to be changed, and the wedding invitations have the wrong date on them,' Aunt grumbled to Anasuyabehn.

Anasuyabehn hardly heard her. The boy servant had just returned from his visit to the hostel. She could see him through the window, cowering in a corner of the compound, apparently afraid to enter the house.

'Your father said that it was your future father-in-law who wanted the date brought forward,' chimed in the visiting aunt.

'I should imagine that the tailors will need at least another three weeks to finish the stitching,' interpolated the eldest cousin. She was stroking, with avaricious fingers, a gift of three silk saris still sitting amid its wrappings on the floor.

Aunt pursued the subject of the change of date. 'I don't quite know what the fuss is about,' she admitted. 'Mahadev has not yet returned from Delhi.' She wondered if there were any truth in the rumour she had heard that he had disappeared, but felt it wise to keep that to herself. She turned again to Anasuyabehn. 'Immediately after your marriage you are to go to a place called Paris in England – very strange to me – in my day, you would have remained at your father-in-law's house.'

'Ji, hun,' agreed Anasuyabehn. She went to the window. 'Bhai,' she called to the servant. 'Hurry up, now. Light the stove on the veranda for me, and put some water on for the lentils. I'll be out in a minute.'

'Let me help,' offered a younger cousin, who had taken a great liking to Anasuyabehn.

'No, no. The boy will do most of the work – I must just guide him.' She made an effort to smile at the golden-faced girl, and, after a little while, made her escape to the side veranda, where she could already hear the fire crackling in its little stove.

'Gone away?' she exclaimed to the boy, as he handed back her note.

'Yes.'

'Who told you?'

'A lady next door.'

'Did she see the letter?'

'No, Bahin.'

'Good boy.' Her whole body trembled with fear and, again, before her eyes danced the calm face of the monk, the all-seeing eyes ripping her secrets from her. Bad actions brought bad results. Had Tilak fled because she was already affianced? How cruel could men be? He had promised – and he had failed her.

She held on to an old water-pot stand for support, as the veranda whirled around her. She felt trapped, like a ground squirrel cornered by dogs. Until Tilak came striding into it, her life had seemed useless and empty. Now, he was gone like fluff on the wind, without a word to her. Spasms of pain shot through her and perspiration poured down her face.

Her cousin wandered through the door from the kitchen. 'Bahin!' she cried in alarm and ran to her. She put her arms round the swaying girl, while the servant squatting by the fire watched nervously.

'I'm all right,' murmured Anasuyabehn through clenched teeth, '. . . heat made me faint.'

'I'll get mother,' said the girl.

'No,' cried Anasuyabehn sharply. 'I'll sit down – it's only heat.'

Her cousin lowered her carefully to the floor and she leaned her head against the cool stone of the water-pot stand. Her cousin took the water-ladle from its hook and filled a brass jar with water. She then dipped her sari end into it and, kneeling down by her, she dabbed Anasuyabehn's face with it.

The cold water revived her and she surreptitiously slipped her note to Tilak into her waistband, under cover of her sari. Then she very gratefully put her arms round her cousin and leaned her head on her shoulder. Her cousin, mystified but sympathetic, held the trembling bride-to-be, and instructed the servant to get on with his work.

'Let me ask mother to come,' she begged Anasuyabehn, after a few minutes.

'Don't worry. I stayed too long in the sun this morning, talking to Savitri.' Her courage came slowly back to her and she again was able to put on her armour of patient amiability, so that her cousin was finally convinced that, indeed, nothing much was wrong.

34

A week later, Mahadev Desai, accompanied by several members of his family, came to the Dean's home for a little ceremony. Some fruit and a green stick were solemnly buried in a hole which was to hold one of the supporting poles of the wedding tent. The story of his adventures had preceded him and, with his arm in a sling, he was looked upon as something of a hero. He was unusually pale and moved about very carefully. He was allowed to see his bride-to-be at the ceremony, but did not get much chance to speak to her. After the visitors had had tea and departed, three carpenters took over the compound and proceeded to dig holes all over it for the remainder of the supporting poles.

Their activities impeded the delivery of sacks of grain, sugar and pulses and tins of vegetable oil, all of which the Dean had had to buy on the black market, because some were rationed and some were in very short supply. He and Aunt, therefore, went to the big storeroom to see the stuff weighed. They already had a house full of guests and, closer to the wedding day, would have to feed many more, including the Desai contingent. To accommodate everybody, a house down the road had been rented.

There was a lot of gossip amongst his current guests on the pros and cons of the marriage; such things were always picked over and examined in detail in families. But it was public gossip which was worrying Aunt, as she scolded the coolies for being clumsy.

That morning, the Vice-Chancellor's ayah had dropped in to pay her respects. The ayah always knew a lot about the doings on campus, so Aunt had edged her away from the visitors and back to the compound gate, while they talked. The ayah was simply breathless to confirm with her that what she had just heard was not true and that the wedding was, indeed, going forward. She felt it her duty to inform Aunt that there was a rumour that Anasuyabehn was expecting by Dr Tilak and that he would be forced to marry her. Aunt had been shocked to her very sandals, had scolded her and sent her packing with instructions to deny such a calumny everywhere.

Anasuyabehn was not with child, that, at least, Aunt was sure of. Only last week she had kept the three days of retirement from cooking and other household tasks, which she had kept ever since she was

445

fourteen. And Aunt had herself dispatched the bloody clouts to the Untouchable washerman. As for her virginity, that was another matter. And Aunt was very apprehensive about this.

Anasuyabehn had done obediently everything she was required to do in connection with the marriage. The whole family had, on Mahadev's return, been to dinner at his house and the girl had sat quietly with the women who would be her in-laws. Mahadev's little daughter had been brought to her during the meal, and she had persuaded the child to sit with her and had fed her with food from her own tali. According to the Dean, this had pleased old Desai greatly when he heard about it. Mahadev had put in a limited appearance because he was still quite weak, but he had smiled on his bride when she arrived. But would he, quaked Aunt, smile if he had been cheated?

She picked up a paper which was being blown about in the draught, her mind elsewhere. She could not read, so she handed it to the Dean. 'Is this a receipt we should keep?' she inquired.

The Dean, who was tired, unfolded it impatiently and glanced down at it. His expression changed and he closed his hand over it quickly. 'Come into the study,' he commanded Aunt. Puzzled, she followed him. 'What's up?' she asked.

The Dean closed the door after them. 'Where did you find this?'

Aunt shrugged. 'It was on the floor. What is it?'

'Beloved,' read the Dean, a break in his voice. 'Meet me at the far end of Riverside Park tonight. I will wait from 9 till 11.'

Aunt felt sick. On top of what she had heard that morning, this was too much to bear. What could she say? The hope of being regarded as the family's finest matchmaker suddenly vanished, with all the delights that such a reputation would bring. Instead, she heard the sniggers of the womenfolk and the dirty jokes of the young men. Somehow the Desai marriage had to be saved.

'Is it signed?' she asked, to give herself time to think.

'No. I know the handwriting, though. It's quite distinctive.'

'Whose is it?'

The Dean looked very grim. 'It's Professor Tilak's. He and Anasuyabehn – I would never have dreamed of it!'

I might have done, thought Aunt, if I'd thought about it. With an effort, she asked, 'Is it addressed to her?'

'No.'

'Then it may belong to one of her cousins.'

The Dean disagreed. 'I doubt if they've even met him.'

Suddenly he pounded his desk with his fist. 'The stupid girl!' he

446

shouted. 'Bring her to me *quietly* – before that mob outside realizes that anything is wrong.'

Aunt hurried to Anasuyabehn's room. Before opening the door, she slowed to her usual shuffle. Anasuyabehn was seated cross-legged on her bed with three cousins and Savitri. Curled up together, they were chattering amiably. Anasuyabehn was listening, her deepset eyes ringed with black, her mouth drooping.

How ill she looks, thought Aunt. Not at all like a girl about to be a bride. And all Aunt's misgivings returned.

As she approached the girls, she forced herself to smile. 'Your father wants you in his study, niece. Run along, now.'

Anasuyabehn slipped off the bed and hastily smoothed her hair and hitched up her sari. Since the safe return of Mahadev, she had steeled herself to face the fact that Tilak had deserted her and that she must marry the big, widowed moneylender.

The pain of Tilak's leaving her was almost more than she could bear. It ate into her like an acid, an unbelievable anguish. She felt removed from events around her; everything seemed distant and unreal. The slightly smutty jokes her cousins had been making seemed sickening to her; she could not laugh.

The only person who impinged upon her understanding was Mahadev himself. His first task upon his return had been to call upon her, despite the agony of being jolted along in his carriage. They had faced each other, not knowing what to say in front of their relations, she resentful, he longing. Through her misery, she had realized that within him lay a powerful personality; he was not to be trifled with.

When she had been to dinner at the Desai Society, he had found a moment in the bustle of departure to hold her hand. She had looked up in astonishment at the firm, warm touch, her first physical contact with him. He had laughed down at her and she had caught a glimpse of a man instead of a moneylender. She had been afraid.

As she entered her father's study, closely followed by Aunt, she inquired politely, 'Ji?'

She was shocked, when he shouted at her, 'What's the meaning of this?' and thrust a sheet of paper at her.

Bewildered, she took it from him. It was worn at the corners and must have been lying about for days. She bent her head and read it.

Her first reaction was one of overwhelming joy. So he had tried to communicate with her. A singing happiness made her giddy for a moment. She kept her eyes on the missive. The paper was much handled. When had it been written? Of course! He had been in the

447

Riverside Gardens with her. The joy faded, but she held on to the paper tightly – it was part of him.

'Well,' snapped her father.

The desire to protect Tilak was instantaneous, and with elaborate care she lifted her eyes to her father. She made her eyes twinkle and her lips curve in a smile. 'We seem to have stumbled on somebody's little romance – where did it come from?'

Aunt was watching her intently. She's clever, she thought, but not quite clever enough. That letter is hers, all right.

She continued to stare out of the corner in which she squatted, as the Dean, his burst of temper unexpectedly checked, asked, 'Well, isn't it yours?'

'I've never seen it before,' replied Anasuyabehn quite truthfully. 'It's very old. I wonder where it came from – it isn't even signed.'

'Oh, I know who wrote it – the writing is unmistakable.'

'Who?' asked Anasuyabehn, ignoring her father's angry frustration.

'That doesn't concern you, daughter, since you say it is not a letter to you. If it's not yours . . .' He glared at her. 'Then the wind must have blown it in.'

'We've had a great many visitors, including the Desai family,' Anasuyabehn pointed out. 'Any of the younger women could have dropped it.'

The Dean was stopped in his tracks. 'Of course,' he muttered. 'Of course.' He sat down in his chair and tapped his fingers on the desk, while Anasuyabehn waited politely. 'I'm glad that you have not done anything despicable.'

'What she says is very likely,' Aunt interjected, and Anasuyabehn was grateful for the unexpected support.

The distant buzz of talk from relations on the veranda suddenly ceased, as if it had been switched off. Aunt looked towards the door of the room, as if she would love to go to investigate.

Outside, an English voice asked for Dean Mehta.

'Dr Bennett!' exclaimed the Dean. Then he sighed. 'This note is not yours?'

'No, father.' Anasuyabehn hated to lie to her father, but could not find any other safe answer. She turned to go.

There was a knock on the study door. The servant showed John in. He was carrying a parcel and stood diffidently blocking the doorway, not realizing Anasuyabehn's frantic need to escape.

'I've . . . er . . . um,' he began, and looked down at Anasuyabehn. God, how ill the girl looked and almost as if she were going to cry. 'I've brought a little something for Anasuyabehn, if she may accept it. I –

er brought it myself, because I was afraid any other carrier might drop it.'

He did not add that he had in his pocket a letter which had far more import to her. Tilak was a damned pest to leave him such a job. He had racked his brains for days to find a way to get the letter to Anasuyabehn, but no opportunity had presented itself. If he had posted it, he knew that the Dean would automatically open it and read it himself, before giving it to his daughter.

Now, on his desk at home, lay his invitation to her wedding reception. And he did not know what else to do, other than buy her a present and watch her marry a man she did not want to marry. Poor kid. She would get over it, he supposed; Mahadev was no fool and presumably knew a bit about managing a woman. He hoped that when Tilak heard the news of the wedding being hastened, he would not blow out his brains.

Caught between loyalty to his old mentor, the Dean, and affection for Tilak, he now stood in the middle of the Dean's study, a box of fine English china in his arms, sensing that he had stumbled in on some kind of domestic crisis.

Dean Mehta was the first to regain his equilibrium. 'Come in, come in. You shouldn't put yourself out on our behalf.' He watched, with growing astonishment, as John walked slowly, but quite straightly, to his desk to put the parcel down. 'You're not using your stick,' he exclaimed.

John grinned with satisfaction. 'Trying to manage without it. I left it parked on the veranda.'

'Well, well. That's excellent. Anasuyabehn, bring a chair for Dr Bennett.'

Anasuyabehn pushed a chair up behind him, and John sat down rather suddenly.

He smiled up at the careworn girl. 'I've brought you an English tea service,' he told her. 'I know the family will shower you with all kinds of beautiful things, but I thought you might enjoy some china – something different.'

Anasuyabehn shyly thanked him.

'May I wish you much happiness,' he said gently.

As if in unbearable pain, her creamy eyelids half-closed, while she nodded a polite acquiescence. John cursed himself for being a clumsy clod; yet he knew that he could not tell her father. Either she or Tilak must speak up.

Anasuyabehn had turned back to her father, 'May I be excused, father? Savitri is waiting for me.'

Her father, his hands clasped on his desk, nodded absently. She said thank you in English to John and went quietly out of the room. Aunt

449

slid after her, making a polite namuste towards John as she passed him. He jumped, not having noticed her presence.

Savitri! Why hadn't he thought of her before? A thoroughly modern woman, who drove her own car and was liable to shock everybody by talking about trial marriages. He was certain she was tolerated in the Dean's house only because her father was a Professor Emeritus. She and Anasuyabehn were great friends – and she was smart.

Whether Anasuyabehn was actually married to Mahadev or whether she was not, she was, John argued, entitled to receive any correspondence addressed to her. Thin, bespectacled Savitri would enjoy being the messenger. Who knows? he reflected. Tilak just might be able to turn the tables, in an honourable and decent way.

And in Bombay, Tilak pleaded for Anasuyabehn before a sardonically amused uncle and a bewildered, affectionate mother. 'You could telephone the Dean at the University,' he begged.

35

The Desai business was too large to be totally neglected during the week before the wedding. Old Desai, Partner Uncle and Mahadev, therefore, stayed in the Desai Society, while the rest of the family moved over to the house rented by Dr Mehta for his guests.

Mahadev had had a trying time commuting between the Society and the Mehtas' home, to attend the various ceremonies preceding the actual wedding day. Though his head ached abominably and his left arm was still in a sling to protect the shoulder while it healed, his paternal aunt had insisted, at one of the ceremonies, that he must have the traditional iron ring tied into his hair. It seemed that every time he lay down, he lay on the ring. He wished passionately that the Mission doctor had shaved his head completely, when preparing to stitch up his wound; instead the doctor had considered that he might be a Hindu and had, therefore, kindly left one longish tuft, to which the ring had been appended.

His father and his Partner Uncle had spent weary hours with him discussing the expansion of the French business. They were all agreed that, in these uncertain times, they should have some money invested outside India.

In one of the earlier marriage ceremonies, he had sat in the flapping marriage tent, with a silent, veiled Anasuyabehn beside him, and had hardly glanced at Ganesh, the benign elephant-headed god, remover of hindrances, who was being worshipped. His mind had been filled with the legal difficulties of the French investment, so much so that he had jumped when a lucky woman, taking four pieces of wood and dipping them in oil, had touched his forehead with them. Then the ring had been tied into his hair.

Ceremonial gifts of rupees had been given to him and to Anasuyabehn. Other money gifts had also been presented by relatives, to be kept until after the ceremony, when they would be divided between his and Anasuyabehn's paternal aunts.

A company of elderly Jains had been specially invited for the later ceremonies; they would inspect the quality and the quantity of the wedding gifts.

Mahadev sighed frequently. Though the marriage festivities would be

451

briefer than those for his first marriage, they were time consuming. It was well that he had been able to get plane reservations for Paris for the second day after the vows had been completed.

Gradually, however, as the day of the actual wedding came closer and his health improved, his mind turned towards his bride and he began to think of the pleasures of again having a wife. He dearly wished to please her and to see her eventually installed in a modern house of her own, where his little daughter might thrive better and have brothers and sisters. He never doubted that Anasuyabehn would care for the child, and in this he was correct.

One morning, he had to compose convincing arguments to persuade the Government of India to allow an overseas investment, and when he finally put down his pen, it was with a feeling of relief that he had done it skilfully. He sat in his dreary office, feeling wells of hopeful anticipation rise in him. He collected up his papers and at the same time began to sing a morning raga. The clerks in the counting house lifted their heads in amazement, as the strains of this devotional hymn came rolling out of the private office.

With a fine disregard for his comfort, Mahadev's brother had been ordered to oversee the wedding party at Dean Mehta's rented house and to travel back and forth daily to supervise the counting house. Now, while Mahadev carolled away in his room, in another little office his younger brother was inquiring of his father, 'What are we going to do about the Maharaja's jewels? I sent a telegram saying we would send another messenger. But what are we to do now?' His plump face creased with anxiety.

His father leaned back on the sausage-shaped pillows of his divan. 'Humph. Didn't Partner Uncle tell you? We shall indeed dispatch another messenger. You're going to go – and take the stones with you.'

He watched in quiet amusement, as his son's weak mouth opened in surprise. There was also a gleam of fear in the younger man's eyes – he knew he was no hero, and he dreaded violence of any kind.

'You'll go by plane – in spite of the cost,' his father assured him.

'But we haven't got the jewels?'

'Oh, yes, we have,' the old man chuckled. 'I put them in the strong-room myself.'

Relief replaced anxiety. 'But . . . but . . .'

Old Desai wagged his finger at his son. 'Your brother's sagacity is something to emulate.'

The younger man appeared to shrink into himself. The small button eyes almost vanished amid the folds of fat. The chin sank down to the chest and the chubby fingers were clenched. So the almighty Mahadev had done something wonderful again.

'What did he do?' he inquired dully.

Old Desai clasped his hands over his stomach. 'Well, it was interesting. Your uncle and I were sitting by the bed at the Mission, wondering how to broach the subject of the missing money belt in front of a constable, who was still there. We didn't want to accuse anyone of taking it, and find we had a libel suit on our hands. Anyway, when Mahadev was dressed and ready to be discharged from the hospital, he sat on the edge of the bed, to rest himself before making the further effort of going to the carriage.' Desai ran his tongue round his few remaining teeth, while he looked at his dejected younger son.

'Well?'

'He was quite clever. When the Mission doctor entered the room, he looked at him and said, "I'm ready to put on my money belt now. Will you kindly fetch it for me?"'

The younger brother was intrigued. 'What happened?'

'The doctor replied, "Certainly." And then he went to get it.'

'How extraordinary!'

'Yes, it was. If he had not intended to keep it – if he could – the Mission doctor would surely have mentioned to Mahadev that his valuables were being kept in safety. With his simple request, Mahadev gave the impression that he remembered the belt being removed from him by the doctor.'

The brother sighed, and old Desai glanced again at him. In comparison with Mahadev, the boy was dull. He was, however, extremely useful; he dealt with all the irritating details of the business. Old Desai thought suddenly of the Maharaja and his brand new radio factory. The Maharaja might be willing to pay an experienced accountant very well, to come to him. And all over India new enterprises were springing up which needed more than an abacus-rattling clerk to keep their accounts; his younger son might easily plunge into a new life, away from his family.

Old Desai did not like these ideas; the boy was flesh of his flesh; he did not want to lose him.

He picked up a memo pad from the portable desk beside him on the divan, and unscrewed his fountain pen. As he addressed his son, he wrote down each point. 'Now that you have reached years of discretion,' he said, as if he had been patiently waiting for his younger offspring to grow up, 'I shall put more responsibilities on your shoulders. I can no longer travel, as I used to, and your uncle is also feeling the strain. This Delhi trip will be the first of many for you, for Mahadev has, in addition to his other responsibilities, to watch the Paris and Bombay businesses.'

He could almost feel the relief shooting through his son's veins. Just to get away from his wife, thought the old man grimly, would probably cheer him up. And to travel on a plane was definitely prestigious. Though it pained him to say it, he added, 'And you will need to draw more money in future.'

The plump figure ceased to slump. It expanded to its full girth. Dignity descended upon him like a new garment slipped over his head. As a trusted representative of the family, always bustling off to new places, he would at last be able to patronize his wife.

As expected, the Desais had not yet paid their hospital bill. The medical missionary, however, knelt by his bed and thanked the Lord for removing the temptation of the money belt. The muttered prayers ceased for a minute or two, while the sorely tried worshipper rested his head on his string bed. Then, in an almost businesslike voice, he again addressed his God, 'And now, Lord, about some funds. The need of your children is terrible. Must they suffer so?'

Perhaps God heard, for about that time some ladies in California met together and, for the sake of something to do to fill their spare time, decided to have a fund-raising drive to extend the Mission of Holiness near Shahpur in India.

36

Though Savitri and her parents, being Hindus, had not been asked to Anasuyabehn's wedding, they were, like John Bennett, invited to a reception to be held after it. Because she was a close friend, however, Savitri came and went freely in the house. Her thin scornful voice mocked the ancient ceremonies, until Anasuyabehn asked her wearily to cease.

Though Savitri's eyes were myopic, they missed little. She had guessed from Anasuyabehn's lack of enthusiasm that her friend was not very keen on the marriage. She had suggested that if Anasuyabehn was not happy she should refuse the offer. Anasuyabehn had said dryly that she had not been given much opportunity to do so; everything had been fixed before she was consulted. When Savitri mentioned this to her own parents, they had ordered her to hold her tongue; Dean Mehta knew what he was doing. Rather cowed by her parents' joint outrage at her attempted intervention, she had obeyed.

Her spirits crushed by Tilak's apparent desertion, Anasuyabehn wanted to curl up in some secret lair and never come out again. But she was being carried along by events and had no one to trust, except her father. She clung to the idea that the reward of filial obedience was a well-ordered and contented life. Clutching at this frail hope, she complied with all her aunt's requests. In any case, what use was there in fighting when there was no one for whom to fight?

She had spent one night seething with rage and frustration, asking herself madly why Tilak should so suddenly vanish. Involved in the preparations of the marriage within the two families, she had not heard the rumours as to the cause of his quick departure. It had naturally not occurred to her father or the Vice-Chancellor to tell her the exact reasons.

The white light of morning had brought a dawn of commonsense. Tilak was an honourable man. Perhaps he had left her because she was already affianced and, anyway, of another religion and caste. The furious temper was curbed, the burning desire held down. She bowed her head and told herself, without much hope, that true happiness was to be found in a loyal partnership with a man chosen by one's parents.

On her wedding morning, she submitted quietly to the ministrations of her cousins and aunts. They bathed her, washed and oiled her hair and plaited it with flowers. With great care, her eldest cousin knelt before her and painted her face with delicate flower designs. Another one stained the palms of her hands and the soles of her feet a soft orange. Finally, they wrapped her in a fine red silk sari embroidered with gold thread.

Before they pulled the sari end down over her face, they brought her a mirror, so that she could admire herself. She looked into its shiny depths and saw a stranger, a very glamorous one. She looked at the image expressionlessly; then she thought of Tilak seeing her when the veil would be lifted, and her lips curved in a gentle smile. The smile faded. Bitter tears welled up and coursed unrestrainedly down her cheeks, to spoil the paint and to trickle over the large, glittering nose-ring and fall like small diamonds into her lap.

The cousins laughed and mopped up the tears. They touched up the painted flowers and agreed that everybody cried when they had to leave their home.

'When you've got a little son in your arms, you'll be truly happy,' Aunt assured her.

Dressed in their best, the families were waiting in the compound. She had, therefore, to compose herself and join them in worship, her face mercifully veiled.

Fourteen young girls were merrily feasted. Armed with gifts of wheat, dates and coconuts, they then streamed down the lane, where a potter awaited them. He cheerfully supplied them with four water-pots.

The fun of a wedding overflowed the compound and spread around the neighbourhood. Little groups of servants, sweepers and village people on their way to town stood in the lane, to glimpse what they could of the fine clothes and jewellery. At the side of the house, the caterers built up their great charcoal fires again and again, and sweated and shouted and turned out innumerable sweetmeats and savouries.

In the storeroom, the Dean's younger brother, with a couple of nephews to assist him, doled out sugar, nuts, flour, spices, oil and vegetables, with a sure hand, seeing that nothing was wasted or stolen, and that yoghurt and water were kept cool and not spilled.

A small band of musicians drummed and squeaked in a corner, their well-practised efforts often lost under the babble of dozens of voices.

The Brahmin, who would officiate at the actual marriage rites after sunset, was fed and fussed over, his shaven head and gnarled hands gesturing a polite 'No', as his palm leaf plate was heaped higher and higher.

The Dean wished that his daughter's wedding should be a joyous occasion. He sailed amongst his guests, greeting them jovially, giving no hint of his inward worry about Anasuyabehn, with whom he had spent an uncomfortable half-hour the evening before. In response to his forecasts of a happy family life, she had responded sadly with a simple, 'Yes, father.' He hoped sincerely that Mahadev knew enough to make her happy.

Meanwhile, in the rented house, a slightly abashed Mahadev was submitting to other ceremonies. Still clucking about the mess his shorn head was in, his paternal aunt replaced the iron ring attached to his topknot with a silver one. With suggestive jokes, the barber washed and powdered one of his toes. A group of giggling young women swooped on him and fed him with sweets.

His friends then helped him mount a decorated horse. His shoulder objected strongly to the exercise, and he winced. As they rode to the temple to worship, they chaffed him that he was lucky the dacoits had left him able to consummate the marriage.

In a splendid procession of cars, horses and pedestrians, he was taken from the temple to Anasuyabehn's home. His heart beat furiously under his silk shirt, and he hoped the girl would like the jewellery he had bought her.

The sun was going down, as they went through the streets. Women and children lolled on the little verandas above the shop fronts, as they waited for the evening breeze to come rippling down the ovenlike, smelly streets. On the pavements, their menfolk squatted idly, smoking and gossiping after their evening meal.

The flickering lights of the procession brought everyone to their feet. At one corner, a beggar in the crowd stood and cursed. He shook his fist at the bridegroom. The bystanders laughed at him; they knew him well. He was harmlessly crazy. They knew he hated the Desais because they had foreclosed on his little shoe shop and forced him into beggary; but, then, none of them liked moneylenders.

As gold and silver trimmed saris, gold bracelets and jewelled necklaces glimmered in the beams of the car headlights, the watchers admired unrestrainedly. They sniffed appreciatively, as waves of flower perfume passed over them from the multitude of garlands carried in the procession. The men admired the horses and the shining cars. Except for that of the beggar, there was no animosity at the display of wealth; they enjoyed the spectacle and never thought of it in relation to their own pressing needs. The Desais, however, were not very trusting. The walking ladies were confined within heavy ropes carried on either side of the procession by their servants and younger male members of the family. Nobody was given the chance to snatch at so much as an earring.

In the centre of it, Mahadev, his pain soothed by aspirin, his spirits high, enjoyed the pomp of his wedding day. Unhaunted by thoughts of his first wife, for whom he had gone through the same performance, it was as if he went to his first marriage. This time, he told himself, he was marrying for love, and he knew a great content from the thought of it.

The compound had seemed quite full before the advent of the Desai party. Now it was jammed. Space was somehow made, however, for the bridegroom to make his way to the bungalow, where a crushed Anasuyabehn sat dully behind a curtain.

As required, she spat betel juice at him, while her maternal aunt, in lieu of her dead mother, marked him with auspicious marks and threw little balls of rice and ashes over him. The aunt then waved a vessel of water over his head, managing not to splash his magnificent, flower-bedecked, silk turban.

From behind the thin curtain and her shrouding red sari, Anasuya-behn watched him out of the corner of her eye. He looked very fine in his bridegroom's clothes, and there was nothing about him to which she could truthfully object, except that he was not Tilak.

Escorted by their relations, the couple were now taken through the stifling March heat, to the marriage tent. There, a committee of leading Jains awaited them in festive mood. Mahadev's friends brought forward his gifts to the bride and laid them before these gentlemen, who rapidly totted up their value, were greatly impressed by it and announced that the gifts were most generous. The gifts were then handed over to the bride's friends.

Mahadev and Anasuyabehn were seated side by side and shook hands with each other. Under the stare of so many witnesses, Mahadev did not dare give Anasuyabehn's hand a hearty squeeze; he had to content himself with a light shake. The end of her sari was then tied to his scarf.

One of his friends brought him a box, which he handed to Anasuya-behn. When she opened it, her aunts leaned forward eagerly to view its contents. Rings and bracelets of solid gold made them gasp enviously.

With his face aglow, Dean Mehta brought his offering for his beloved daughter. Iridescent saris, blouse lengths and petticoat lengths to match, a finely-wrought gold necklace, more gold bracelets. Anasuyabehn had never owned so much in all her life. Father has spent too much, she fretted, and wondered if he would have enough money to retire on; then she remembered that he would need no money. As a monk he would need nothing, not even her. She would have no one to turn to – except her husband. She sighed a little sobbing sigh. Hearing her,

Mahadev turned quickly towards her but could see nothing but the vague glimmer of her face behind the silk.

In the half-light of the oil lamps, old Desai seemed to float towards his son. Aided by an ancient cousin, he washed one of his son's hands; Anasuyabehn's maternal aunt did the same for her. She then placed Anasuyabehn's hand in that of the groom. Mahadev cheerfully held on firmly and, despite her depression, Anasuyabehn was forced to take cognisance of the fact that the man sitting by her was real, with needs to which she must give attention. She began to tremble and Mahadev, feeling it, massaged her palm gently with his fingers. He tugged her to her feet and they solemnly circumvented the flickering fire before which they had been sitting. Four times, left to right, they paced together, while lucky women pressed forward to receive sopari nuts from Mahadev; thus must husband and wife walk together equally, like oxen, pulling the wagon of life.

Sweets cooked by a Brahmin were offered to the couple and were formally refused.

They walked together into the house, where worship was offered to Anasuyabehn's gotrija, her kinsmen of lineal and collateral descent from a common ancestor.

The couple were, next, to go in procession to the rented house for a similar ceremony in honour of the bridegroom's ancestry. The day had been a long one and, before setting out, Anasuyabehn whispered rather frantically to her maternal aunt, and was given permission to go to the bathroom, escorted by her favourite young cousin.

The sweeper's door into the bathroom had been left open for ventilation and, when she went to close it, she saw to her astonishment Savitri standing hesitantly on the field path.

'Hey, Bahin,' cried Savitri, stumbling towards her along the rough path.

'Hurry up,' whispered her cousin, from the other side of the door which led into the house.

'Anasuyabehn,' panted Savitri, keeping her voice low. 'I've been trying for two days to get you alone – and now I don't know what to do – it's the letter.'

'What letter?' Anasuyabehn pushed her veil back from her eyes, so as to see her friend's troubled face more clearly.

'From you know whom – John Bennett gave it to me – he couldn't deliver it himself – though he said he called on you.'

Anasuyabehn remembered John bringing the box of china himself. By all the gods who ever reigned, he had had a letter to deliver! The trembling which had begun in the compound became a helpless shake.

'Give it me.'

'Come on,' urged her cousin and opened the other door.

Savitri ignored the young girl and took the letter from under her sari. It smelled faintly of her perfume and Dr Bennett's tobacco, and the envelope was quite dirty.

Ignoring her watching cousin, Anasuyabehn tore open the envelope, her fingers clumsy. The cousin pressed forward, but a glare from behind Savitri's heavy spectacles made her shrink back.

And so the screw was turned once more.

The gentle, courteous words and promises, so quickly penned, seemed to hit her under the heart. The pain was so intense that she cried out, before she fell fainting into Savitri's skinny arms.

The shocked little cousin rushed forward and together they half dragged, half lifted, Anasuyabehn into the passage. The younger girl opened her mouth to call her mother, but Savitri was made of sterner stuff, and whispered, 'Shut up. Wet your hankie under the lavatory tap – quick.'

The cousin obeyed.

The touch of the water on Anasuyabehn's face failed to bring her round. Her aunts could be heard calling to her to hurry. There was a shuffle of footsteps on the veranda. Savitri rose, and ran towards the footsteps, while the frightened cousin pillowed Anasuyabehn's head in her lap.

A bevy of ladies hurried into the passage, calling, 'Hurry up!' In the background, Mahadev inquired if anything was wrong.

Savitri composed herself and said quietly to the first lady, 'Anasuya-behn has fainted. It must have been the heat and the excitement.'

The little cousin discreetly slipped the note from under Anasuya-behn's trailing veil and stuffed it down her blouse. She had no idea what the letter was about, except that it must be most important to Anasuyabehn. With thumping heart, she gave way to Aunt and wrapped her sari loosely round herself, to hide the telltale bulge.

Between them, the ladies got Anasuyabehn on to her bed and crowded round her, chattering anxiously, while word spread in the compound that the bride had been taken ill. 'A bad omen,' muttered one old lady to another.

Dean Mehta, old Desai and Mahadev pushed their way into the crowded room. To give the patient air, the Dean ordered that the room be cleared, except for the three gentlemen, Aunt and Mahadev's aunt. This was done, though the little cousin continued to stand, unremarked, by the head of the bed. Savitri had considered it prudent to sidle quietly out of the house through the sweeper's door.

A lota of water was brought by the boy servant and Aunt sponged her face. After a few minutes, the eyelids fluttered under their smudged paint – and closed again, as she realized her predicament. She was now legally married to Mahadev – and, far away in Bombay, Tilak was trying to start negotiations to marry her; he had not deserted her, he had not run away. He loved her and she loved him. Waves of grief broke over her, as if someone had died, and she sobbed helplessly before her astonished relatives.

How many times do we die in our lives, she wondered, our spirits crushed and broken? And yet the body lives on.

The marriage garland round his neck withering in the heat, Mahadev could bear the sobs no longer. Regardless of convention, he pushed Aunt away. Kneeling by her bedside, he took her hand and himself massaged it gently to get the circulation going. At first Anasuyabehn neither knew nor cared whose hand held hers, whose fingers carefully rubbed her wrists. It was, nevertheless, comforting, as if someone, at least, realized her suffering. Eventually, the weeping ceased. She lay with eyes closed, while Aunt leaned over and gently wiped the wet cheeks.

Her eyelids felt heavy, too heavy to open, but Mahadev waited patiently, and, finally, she did open them, to come face to face with the anxiety and fear clearly mirrored in his usually cold, intelligent eyes. Dimly she knew that, of all the people gathered round her, Mahadev cared the most – and Mahadev was innocent – he had not done anything that contributed to her predicament; she had received nothing but kindnesses from him. 'I'm sorry,' she said, and closed her eyes again.

Old Desai and Dr Mehta were relieved to see her come round, and began in hurried whispers to debate what they should do. Aunt interposed to say that the wedding must go on, as soon as Anasuyabehn was a little recovered; it would be too unlucky otherwise.

Anasuyabehn felt so tired that all she wanted was to be left alone. But Mahadev was there, still rubbing her hands. With a great effort, she swallowed her tears, opened her eyes again, and said that, if she could have a very hot, strong cup of tea, she thought she could go on – the time taken to prepare it, she argued, would give her a few minutes of rest.

Mahadev laughed out loud with relief. He whispered that she could have the whole of Gujerat if she wanted it. She made her lips smile.

The tea was made, the guests reassured, and, by the light of the moon, they set out in procession for the house rented by Dean Mehta. Laden with sweets, dates, money and the kernels of four coconuts, the

461

Mehtas returned home exhausted, to go to bed for the remainder of the night.

The following evening, shaken but composed, Anasuyabehn sat quietly amongst her cousins, while the committee of eminent Jains inspected further gifts from her family. Then alms were distributed to an eager crowd of beggars and saddhus waiting at the compound gate.

Normally, the guests would have been feasted for several more days, but Mahadev had to go to Paris, so, to the sound of steady drum beats, Anasuyabehn dipped her hand in red powder and marked the house walls with the imprint of her palm. In the marriage tent, she impressed an auspicious mark on Mahadev's brother's forehead, making the gesture very respectful and leaving him beaming contentedly. Someone handed her yet another sari, and she wondered vaguely how many dozen she now owned. A coconut was put into her hand and, with Mahadev smiling down at her, she stepped into his carriage. Another coconut was put under the wheels of the carriage and the vehicle jolted over it to break it. The pieces were then offered to her, with four sweetmeats and two brass vessels.

The driver whipped up the horse. Cars and carriages slid out before and behind them. In procession, they made their way into the old part of the town to the Desai Society.

'This is it,' she thought numbly. 'In that old house they will have prepared a bed covered with rose petals and I will sit on it and Mahadev Desai and I will be alone for the first time.' She knew what to expect and she felt dull and lifeless. She could feel the warmth of her husband's thigh against hers, and she turned towards him instinctively. 'Don't be afraid,' he told her gently. 'Everything will be all right.'

At home, the Dean looked at the imprint of his daughter's hand and prayed for her. Then he went to say farewell to most of the guests, pressing some to stay a few days more. He did not yet want to be alone.

In the hopelessly untidy kitchen, deserted for the moment, Anasuyabehn's faithful little cousin surreptitiously read Tilak's letter. Through the crumpled paper, she saw Anasuyabehn's face, so colourless, so dead, her lips hardly moving as she forced herself to say, 'Burn it.' To the young girl it was as if something in the new bride had burned with a mighty flame and was now cold ashes, and the youngster trembled with fear of love not yet experienced.

She struck a match, lit the letter and held it in her hand until it was reduced to a tiny corner of paper attached to curling, black embers. Then she dropped it into the ashchoked charcoal brazier.

37

On the morning after Anasuyabehn's departure, Aunt stood on the veranda and surveyed the appalling muddle. Pieces of tissue paper, palm leaves, withered flowers and garlands, two pieces of cloth flapping loose from the marriage tent, a pair of chuppells abandoned on the steps; behind her, in the kitchen, a mass of teacups and glasses to be washed, and unsorted laundry to be dealt with, seven house guests still to be fed, and a reception for some thirty people to be arranged for that evening. The last item, thank goodness, would be dealt with by the caterers and her younger brother; she could already hear him talking to two of the cooks; and Dean Mehta, she supposed rather sourly, was probably at his devotions. Lucky for some people that they had so much time for prayer and meditation; she herself had to be content with hastily repeated mantras as she made the morning fire.

The postman, his khaki uniform already black with sweat, picked his way through the debris and handed her the morning's letters.

Although she could not read, she recognized amongst them the hand-writing of a great-uncle who had been invited to the wedding. What a mercy that old windbag was too old to travel, a walking gossip column, who would have smelled out the rumour about Anasuyabehn and would have retailed it on every veranda between Shahpur and Calcutta. She sighed, when she thought about this, and hoped that Anasuyabehn's first child would not arrive before ten months – in fact, twelve months would be better.

When she knocked at the study door and opened it, the Dean still had his rosary in his hand. She put the letters on his desk and retreated to the kitchen.

After he had put his rosary into its box, the Dean mechanically opened his letters. It was with considerable shock that he read Tilak's uncle's preliminary inquiry regarding a match between his nephew and Anasuyabehn.

It seemed to him, at first, that he must have misread, and he perused again the careful description of Tilak's assets, both physical and monetary. But there was no doubt that it was an offer for his daughter.

Here was proof that the girl had lied to him. His little daughter had lied. He was engulfed in wretchedness. What had she been doing?

463

As he stared at the letter, his fear and disappointment at his daughter gave way to anger against the hapless Tilak. He tore the letter up and flung it into his wastepaper basket.

If he heard so much as a breath of scandal about Tilak and his daughter, the man should go. If it were the last thing he did as Dean, Tilak should be made to rue the day he ever tampered with Anasuyabehn.

The letter from Bombay crossed with one from John to Tilak, in which he told of entrusting Tilak's letter to Savitri for delivery. He wrote also of the haste with which the marriage was being solemnized, and that he hoped that Tilak would find someone else and be happy with her.

When the servant brought John's letter to Tilak, he was sitting by his mother's couch while she had her morning tea. As he read the missive, a fearful numbness crept over him, and his mind refused to accept the news it contained. He continued to sit, the letter in his hand resting on his knee, while the numbness gave way to a ghastly emptiness.

It seemed to him that he had been stripped of his clothing and walked by himself through a vast empty space, a cold wind beating upon his bare flesh. It seemed that he walked for a long time, ignoring the wind, refusing to be afraid, and gradually his senses returned.

When he opened his eyes, he did it carefully and slowly, as if letting in the light would also let in something horrible; but it was only his mother's troubled eyes which met his.

She had put down her cup in her saucer, and she asked, 'What's the matter?'

Tilak was unable to speak. He handed the letter to her and she read it, her English being quite adequate to the task.

'Your friend in Shahpur – the Englishman?'

'Yes.' With that single word, all the emotion which he had tried to control since he left Shahpur suddenly erupted. He fell to his knees by the couch and buried his head in the Kashmir shawl draped over it. He hammered the couch with clenched fists. 'Why couldn't Uncle get through on the telephone?' he almost screamed.

His mother put down her cup and saucer with a clatter, and leaned forward to put her arms round her wilful, dreadfully hurt son. 'The lines to Shahpur were simply choked by calls, my dear child. Uncle couldn't help that – it'll be years before we get a proper service.'

38

Because both Tilak's uncle and his mother feared a nervous breakdown, they did their best to dissuade Tilak from returning to Shahpur.

'There's nothing you can do, my son.'

'I know that, mother. But I want to see the Vice-Chancellor and find out how things are in the University, and I would like to hear from John Bennett exactly what happened.'

Though he was obviously distraught, he was, they felt, trying to be rational, so they reluctantly agreed to the journey. The following morning, he and his servant arrived at Shahpur station. In the vast Victorian waiting-room there, he took a shower and changed his clothes. He was calm enough to eat a little breakfast in the empty first-class dining-room, while his servant ate in less sumptuous surroundings at a platform stall.

He had an overwhelming desire to see Anasuyabehn once again, just to look upon her face. He told himself sardonically that one is permitted to look on the face of one's dead. He did not wish to call on her; apart from it being too modern an idea for the Desais to accept, it would awaken again in her the despair she must have felt at having to go through with her marriage. But just to see her passing by was a gnawing need.

The servant came into the dining-room to inquire what he should do next, and Tilak instructed him to take his luggage to his rooms in the students' hostel.

The servant looked scared, and whispered that perhaps the Sahib should not show himself there for the present. Wouldn't a hotel be safer?'

Tilak told him roughly not to be a fool. The students were not going to hurt him. 'For myself, I may stay a night or two with Bennett Sahib. I have to see him.'

Satisfied, the servant went away to find a porter.

After giving up his ticket, Tilak went through the barrier. He hesitated on the steps outside, and a motorcycle rickshaw drew up quickly by him. 'Sahib?' the man queried hopefully, revving his engine.

'Do you know the Desai Society – the one in the city centre?'

'Ji, hun. Everybody knows it.'

'Right. Put me down fifty yards before you get to it.'

465

They drove through narrow alleyways thronged with people, then into an area where the alleys were little more than passages lined with the high boundary walls of various Societies. They came at last to a square which held the goldsmiths' bazaar, and there the rickshaw wallah stopped.

He pointed to an archway on the other side of the square. 'Through there, Sahib, is a vegetable bazaar. Opposite it, is the Desai Society's gate.'

Tilak paid the man without comment. He had a shrewd suspicion that he had been taken on a tour of the old city and that probably there was a much shorter route from the station, but he could not be bothered to bargain; his mind was on Anasuyabehn.

Uncertain what to do, he walked through the archway and found the compound gate without difficulty. A few women and children were standing near the gate, sweepers or the very poor, and one or two professional beggars squatted with their backs against the Desais' wall, their begging bowls in front of them. Tilak hastily crossed the tiny square and pretended to look through the vegetable bazaar.

'What are the people waiting for?' he asked a stallholder.

The stallholder told him of the great marriage just performed. Today, the rumour was that the bridegroom was going to take his bride on an aeroplane. He thought that the women were waiting, in case, at the time of departure, the Desais felt like giving a little more in charity.

As he was talking, a taxi came from the further side of the little square and drew up at the gate.

The compound gate was opened by a chowkidar, who immediately kicked one of the beggars to make him move out of the way. The grumbling beggar moved about six inches and then was forced to his feet by the rush of onlookers who closed in on the entrance. Tilak himself was propelled, not unwillingly, towards the gate by a couple of eager youths and three giggling country girls, and was soon hemmed in by a small crowd.

A servant put two suitcases into the taxi. Then a very old man in horn-rimmed spectacles was assisted in, while the crowd murmured in nervous awe; everyone knew of old Desai.

Surely, the bride would come now. The women pushed forward and Tilak, to his consternation, found himself to the front of the crowd with the beggar who had been so ignominiously kicked, and rows of women pushing behind.

A murmur of women's voices came from within the Society. Anasuyabehn, her face half obscured by her flowered silk sari, stepped on to the street, followed closely by a man in white khadi, who, Tilak presumed, was her husband. They were followed by several ladies and gentlemen who stood around the gateway. Anasuyabehn turned her head, as if to say goodbye to one of the ladies – and then she saw him.

For a moment she stood transfixed, the words of farewell unspoken. She lifted her sari further over her face to shield herself from the gaze of the jostling relations.

Oblivious of the reason for her momentary pause, Mahadev put his arm gently round her back to move her towards the taxi, and in the self-same second the beggar, knife in hand, lunged forward as if to stab her.

Tilak saw the knife flash as it was drawn and he leaped between them, taking the knife in his own back, as he and Anasuyabehn crashed to the ground.

She screamed as she fell and, in the rush of people towards her, the beggar turned and ran for his life.

A shocked Mahadev beheld a man with a knife in his back lying over his new bride. The crowd began to move hastily away, while the chowkidar lifted Tilak up slightly so that Mahadev could get at his wife. He pulled her free and lifted her to her feet. She was dust-covered and bruised, but was able to stand on her feet, one hand to her mouth, as Partner Uncle bent and very carefully withdrew the knife. He tore a light cotton shawl from round his neck and pressed it on the wound, while he shouted for someone to bring a string bed to carry the man into the compound.

From his more elevated position in the old-fashioned taxi, old Desai had watched with horror. Now he scrambled out and went to Mahadev. 'Is she hurt?' he asked anxiously.

Mahadev was gently wiping his wife's bruised cheek. 'No bones broken,' he said. 'The man seems to have taken most of the fall, somehow.'

Old Desai whipped round to look at his Partner Brother kneeling by Tilak. Partner Brother looked up and said, 'He's dead.'

Anasuyabehn turned her face into her husband's shoulder, while a Desai aunt tried to persuade her back into the compound. Mahadev, his face deadly pale, held the shuddering young woman. 'Wait a minute,' he urged the aunt.

Old Desai turned back to his son. 'Take your wife and go to the airport. Catch the plane. This is a police matter, and they'll keep you here for weeks as a material witness. Your wife can tend her bruises and change her sari in the airport.'

Mahadev stared at him, overwhelmed for the moment by the sight of murder.

467

'Go, boy, go,' his father urged. 'That knife was meant for *you*. Your wife nearly died instead of you, because just at the very second he struck, she moved in front of you. Seated in the taxi, I saw exactly what happened, and I fear there may be other dacoits nearby who will make a second attempt.' He paused for breath, an old man fearing the loss of his eldest son. He caught at Mahadev's sleeve. 'Wake up, boy, and get into the taxi, quickly.'

Mahadev forced himself to speak firmly, as he wrapped Anasuya-behn's sari end round her bruised arm. She was not weeping, only breathing heavily, her face almost colourless. He half-lifted her into the taxi and, when he followed her, she clung to him, burying her face in his shoulder. During the nights he had spent with her, he had been very gentle, making sure that she was pleasured. Last night, he thought with a sudden glow, she had turned willingly to him and had responded to his overtures.

Despite the shocked looks of two older ladies, who had scrambled into the taxi after him, he continued to hold her and to whisper to her not to be afraid; he would protect her.

Thankful to get away, the taxi driver hooted to persuade the stallholders, who had replaced the original crowd, to get out of his way while he turned in the small space.

At a point where the narrow street he was travelling debouched into a main thoroughfare, he was stopped by an armed policeman. The constable flung open all the doors, took a good look at the passengers, made sure no one was hiding under the seats, and then motioned them onwards.

Through his mirror, the driver saw a police jeep ease its way into the rabbit warren he had just left.

39

Immediately the police jeep was noticed coming down the lane, the stallholders shot back to their vegetables and began assiduously to rearrange them; the open-mouthed women pulled their plain white saris over their heads and became anonymous bundles hurrying through the far archway, following their menfolk. After them ran a bunch of little urchins afraid of being left behind.

The old American army jeep slid to a stop on its smooth tyres, and the Bengali police-chief leaped out. A constable dropped off the back of the vehicle and hammered on the door with his rifle butt. The iron bar across the inner side squeaked as it was turned, and the nervous chowkidar let in both the police chief and three constables.

Despite the melting away of possible witnesses, which he had observed as he came into the small bazaar, the Bengali was hopeful that he might now get a lead on the dacoits. In the back of his mind, he had rather expected that an attack might be made on Mahadev. The passengers in the held-up train would have seen only a vague collection of men with their faces covered; Mahadev had left his carriage and might easily have seen how they moved the loot.

Old Desai was amazed to see the police arrive so fast. He was in the process of going through Tilak's pocket book, so that he could identify him when he himself telephoned the police.

'I telephoned them as soon as I saw what had happened,' his younger son told him.

The Bengali, as he approached and heard his remark, smiled with approbation on the stout accountant. 'Very wise,' he told him. 'There are not many entrances to this area, and I sent men on bicycles to block them immediately.' He shrugged, as he approached Tilak's body, lying on a narrow bed in the shade of a loggia. 'Of course, if the man climbed a wall and went through one of the Societies, we might not be lucky.'

Chairs and glasses of water were brought and, while his men lounged on the other side of the compound, the Bengali got down to detail. The contents of Tilak's wallet had hardly yielded the letters about the Fellowship, which gave his name and Bombay address, before old Desai's office telephone rang. A nervous clerk came to say that the police chief was wanted on the line.

The Bengali listened intently and said, 'Charge him.' He slammed the receiver down and came crossly back to the waiting Desais. While they waited, he sat down and lit a cigarette. At last, he addressed old Desai.

'We've got the man. He ran into the arms of one of our men on his usual beat, struck the constable and was arrested for assaulting a police officer. He fits your description.'

Everybody present sighed with relief. The Bengali continued to stare at the body. Then he added, 'He's not a dacoit. He's known to the beat constable. He was a shoe merchant on whom you foreclosed, and he's been known to utter threats against you.'

'I didn't recognize him,' said old Desai.

'There's a lot of difference between a well-to-do merchant and a mad, starving beggar,' replied the Bengali and swung off his chair and on to his feet.

The group of men in front of him stiffened visibly, as they realized his contempt for them, in spite of their wealth.

The detective called his men over, and told them to bring a stretcher and remove the body.

He had seen a lot of death, had this small Bengali; yet it angered him that a man clever enough to obtain an English scholarship had died instead of one of these accursed moneylenders. His small, snakelike eyes regarded Desai. 'You were fortunate that such a brave man was near. Otherwise, you would undoubtedly have lost your son.'

'Yes,' said Desai, who by this time was feeling that he had had as much as he could endure, 'I am grateful to him – very grateful.'

Remorselessly, the Bengali then went on to upbraid him for allowing a material witness like Mahadev to depart from the country.

Old Desai was nearly sulky when he replied, 'I was afraid there might be other dacoits in the crowd; they might have struck again. How was I to know he was only a debtor of ours?'

After warning old Desai to hold himself in readiness to attend the inquest and the subsequent trial, the detective followed his men swiftly out of the compound, and left the demoralized Desais to their own consciences.

As the stretcher-bearers lifted the stretcher to put it into a small van which had drawn up behind the jeep, the Bengali stopped them. He lifted the cloth laid over Tilak's face and looked down at the beautiful, calm features. He was remembering a remark of one of the older ladies, when he asked if anyone knew the vicim. She had said, 'Our new daughter seemed to know him – she turned to look at him, before he was struck down.'

As he let the cloth drop, he muttered, 'I wonder why you were in this unlikely part of town this morning? Was there a connection between you and the new bride?'

The puzzled bearers pushed the stretcher into the vehicle and slammed and locked the doors.

The Bengali returned to his jeep and climbed in beside the driver. He wondered if he had stumbled on a love affair as well as a murder, and, with all a Bengali's understanding of the passions of human nature, he decided it was unnecessary to intercept the younger Desais at the airport; he could get a conviction without them. In his own mind he was certain that the victim had given his life for the sake of the girl – old Desai's exact description of the movements of his son and his wife and the beggar at the moment of the tragedy made that fairly clear.

As his driver took him slowly through the ancient streets, he thought about Mahadev Desai and his new wife, and then about the fine scholar whose life had been so summarily ended. There was a story there, he was sure of it.

He threw his cigarette end out of the window and it was immediately pounced upon by a beggar. Who am I to muddy the water further, he asked himself angrily. Tilak Sahib, rest in peace; I'm going to hang the bastard that killed you; but it's one of those cursed moneylenders who should be at the end of the rope – they drove him mad.

40

The news of Tilak's murder came too late for that day's newspapers, and the Bengali police chief, taking his address from the letters found on him, informed only his family in Bombay. Neither John nor the barber who had come to cut his hair that afternoon, were, therefore, aware of it. John, however, was not in the best of tempers; he felt indescribably petulant and he had been unable to concentrate on his writings. The arrival of the barber had been a relief, and he limped out on to the veranda and sat down in his basket chair.

The barber wrapped a clean towel round his neck.

'Have you got my comb and shaving brush?' asked John. 'I prefer them to yours.' And he looked with distaste at the grubby shopping bag of barbering necessities lying on the veranda floor.

The barber looked pained and his beautifully waxed moustache twitched with irritation, but he answered, with a slight bow, 'Of course, Sahib. Ranjit has brought everything, including hot water in your own lota.' He pointed to the little brass vessel sitting on the veranda rail.

'Good,' grunted John. 'Very well.'

The barber began to comb. Since all Englishmen have an unnatural interest in the weather, he talked about the weather. Diplomat, gossip, messenger, the barber studied all his customers, and, as he went from house to house and village to village, he retailed the news, views and scandal of the district, slanted according to the views he supposed his customer of the moment held.

'Getting a little thin just here,' he announced, planting an accusing finger on a non-existent bald patch amid the thick thatch on John's head. He put down his comb and rummaged in his shopping bag.

'To avoid losing one's hair it's important to oil it daily. Now I have here a new oil which many of my customers are finding most efficacious . . .' and he waved a bottle in front of John's nose.

John blinked as the bottle sailed dangerously near, but managed to read *Asoka Medicinal Hair Tonic* on a flower-decked label.

'What does it smell like?' he asked doubtfully.

The barber whipped out the cork and a tremendous perfume immediately enveloped them both.

'I'd rather be bald,' said John decisively.

The barber bit his lower lip and looked hurt, then he surveyed John's head from the front, cocking his own head first on one side and then on the other. 'Well, of course, it doesn't show in front,' he said at last, 'but it won't be long.'

'I couldn't stand it,' said John, all his sales resistance hastily marshalled. 'Perfumes – er – perfumes make me sneeze,' and he sneezed to demonstrate the fact.

The barber leaped out of range of any droplets, and said with a regretful sigh, 'Pure mustard oil might help, though I think it's really too far gone for that.'

Frown lines on John's forehead warned him that his customer was getting irate.

'Well, well, never mind,' he said. 'I expect you would like a shave, as usual, Sahib.'

'Yes,' John replied.

'Ears cleaned? They need it – you've got hairs growing in them.'

'Very well,' his customer agreed resignedly.

'Nice wedding Mehta Sahib had for his daughter,' said the barber as his scissors clipped merrily.

'I expect so,' said John. 'I didn't go to the wedding – only to the reception for friends the next day.'

'Oh, it was very fine indeed, though the number of guests was limited by the size of the compound. She has married a very fine gentleman – his toenails were clean and well clipped,' he added as a professional detail.

'Did you get the toe powdering job?'

'Yes, indeed. I did his brother, too, when he was married.'

'Decent tip?'

'Fair, fair.' The barber did a rapid run round John's left ear with the scissors. 'Of course, they're moneylenders – but so rich, Sahib, it is unbelievable. You should have seen the gifts.'

'I can imagine them.' John ducked as the scissors shot across his forehead.

'Keep still, please, Sahib.'

The barber stepped back in order to view his handiwork, and then said coyly to John, 'I hear you're considering marriage, too, Sahib.'

'What?' shouted John, sitting up in his chair so suddenly that he nearly lost an eye to the advancing scissors.

The barber jumped backwards, scissors held engarde, his professional aplomb severely shaken. 'I – I – er just heard a little word about it,' he said, eyeing John nervously.

John laughed at him and relaxed again into his basket chair.

'Wherever did you hear it?'

The barber took up his comb and combed furiously, while he considered his reply. He bent his head to look at the hairline he had trimmed. 'I think that'll do,' he muttered, and whipped a hand mirror out of his shopping bag.

John glanced at himself in the tiny mirror. 'OK,' he said. 'No oil. Where did you hear it and who is to be the bride?'

'Aren't you going to be married, Sahib? I must say I thought it unlikely, in spite of other rumours to the contrary.'

He looked down at John's spare body and the hurt legs.

John was irritated by the look. 'Well? I want to know who I'm to marry – Miss Prasad?'

The barber ventured a snigger at the mention of this prim, dedicated female. 'No, no, Sahib. The English lady with the copper-coloured hair, Sahib. She's often in the villages, working with Dr Ferozeshah. I don't know her name.'

'Oh, Miss Armstrong. Well, she's a friend of mine. I wonder why anyone should think I'm about to marry her, though.'

'It was your inquiry about the house which Dean Mehta rented temporarily for his daughter's marriage. It's to let again. A good house, Sahib, with its own well.'

Despite being smothered in shaving soap, John sat bolt upright in his chair.

'Look here,' he almost shouted, 'I haven't made any inquiries about that house.'

The barber tut-tutted and wiped soapsuds off John's eyebrows.

'The landlord himself told me, Sahib; I came straight from him to you. He said you had asked about repairs and rent, so naturally he assumed you were about to marry – the lady comes to see you regularly.' The barber waved his razor in the air rather hopelessly. 'It seemed quite natural, Sahib.'

John sniffed. 'I've made no inquiries and I don't intend to get married just to please my neighbours. The man must be out of his mind.'

'Just bend your head a little to the left, please, Sahib. That's better.' The fearsome razor swept gracefully round his neck. 'Your skin is not what it might be, Sahib. The sun is very hard on white skins. Now, I have here . . .'

'No,' snapped John resolutely. 'My old red hide is doing quite well, thank you. Married, indeed.'

'Well, Ranjit said it would be quite soon.'

'He did, did he? Hmm. I suppose it was he who actually saw the landlord?'

'Of course, Sahib.' The barber was by now completely bewildered, and silently tackled the cleaning of John's ears, while John sat and fumed.

The mirror was again produced and John looked at himself.

For the first time for years he really considered what he looked like. Heavens, his face was seamed and weatherbeaten, and was that really grey hair at his temples? Surely, at thirty-four he should not be grey?

The crushed barber saw his client's fingers stray up over the offending skin and hair and hastened to pay a compliment.

He smiled ingratiatingly and said, 'Most distinguished-looking, Sahib.'

'Humph,' said John, nonetheless slightly comforted. 'How much?'

The barber was paid, packed his shopping bag and retreated down the path to the compound gate, promising to come again in two weeks' time.

'Ranjit!' roared John, and, at the tone of voice, Ranjit appeared with the speed of a rabbit, hastily wiping his wet hands on his sweat cloth.

'Just what have you been doing? That lunatic of a barber said you were inquiring about the house for rent down the road.'

Ranjit swallowed, considered what he should say and only succeeded in looking very guilty.

'Well, Sahib, it . . . er.'

'The wretch suggested I was going to be married . . . now I'll be bothered by everybody asking me if I am, blast it, and every tradesman in the district will try to sell me things. What on earth have you been doing?'

'I happened to meet the landlord, Sahib, and I asked him – er, out of general interest, Sahib. You will remember that we were talking about the need for you to have a better house a little while ago?'

John took a large breath and reminded himself that Ranjit was his most devoted friend.

'And getting married?'

This question in Ranjit's opinion demanded a straight answer. It was obvious that his young master – John was permanently about eighteen in Ranjit's mind – did not know what he was doing. Otherwise he would not ask such a silly question.

'Sahib, even in England, if you favour a young woman with your interest and she eats with you and you sit close to her, doesn't that mean that you'll marry her?'

Despite his indignation, John's eyes began to twinkle. 'It depends on your intentions.'

'A man such as yourself could not possibly have any intentions, except marriage,' declared Ranjit stalwartly, but wondering suddenly if Englishmen were, perhaps, a little like Indians in some respects.

John's temper had cooled. He took out his pipe and lit it, putting the dead match carefully back into the box, before he answered.

'I've no intentions at all, Ranjit. You know that my legs are a mess. They don't work very well and they are scarred. I'm also no longer young. I wouldn't like to ask a woman to marry such an old crock.'

Seeing that the storm had passed, Ranjit ventured to sit down on the top step. He rubbed the grey stubble on his chin, as he considered John's last remark. He loved his master, as if he were his own son, and enjoyed serving a bachelor, but lately the Sahib had been fretful without reason. He had seen him watch the little Memsahib go down the path to the gate, and then turn back to his desk, to sit silently staring at the papers before him, unable to work.

It was the law of all Hindu families that parents should marry off their children. Men and women should enjoy their spouses and only in age turn to asceticism. The Sahib had never known the joys of marriage and this was not normal.

Few servants liked to serve a married couple – wives had a habit of poking their noses into every domestic detail – but Ranjit was prepared to do this, if it made his master content. He, therefore, cleared his throat, blew his nose, and went into battle.

'Women, Sahib,' he began, 'are peculiar creatures. When they care for us, it is frequently because of our deficiencies and stupidities.'

John blew a cloud of smoke, and laughed.

Ranjit looked indignant. 'You laugh, Sahib, because you have no experience. The little Memsahib . . .'

The laugh died in John's throat. 'Well, what about her?' he asked quite sharply.

Determinedly, Ranjit plunged on. 'The little Memsahib doesn't see that you are a little older than some. She does not *see* your sick legs, though she will help you to cure them. She sees only you, Sahib.'

John looked silently out over the shabby compound. Ranjit had the eyes of a vulture, missing nothing.

At last he said, 'Have you asked the lady for me, Ranjit?'

'There is no need, Sahib. It is in every look she gives you.'

'Do you like her, Ranjit?'

'Yes, Sahib.' He searched for words, pulling nervously at his little pigtail at the back of his head as if to stimulate the brains within. 'More than other English ladies I have served.'

'Ah, well, Ranjit. Cats can look at kings, and I suppose I can look at a pretty woman sometimes. Now I am going to think about this map

476

I am to draw for Shri Lallubhai. Go away and make me some dinner.'

'Ji, hun,' assented Ranjit, heaving himself to his feet and wondering if he had done any good at all with his attempt at matchmaking.

Dusk came while John was still working on the map. Lacking a large table, he had pinned big sheets of paper to the walls of his room. Propped up by the end of his table, he stood in front of these, pencil in one hand and ruler in the other, while he roughed in the districts that he knew. He hoped that his assistant from the City Engineer's Department would be able to add more details to his work.

He had turned to pick up a fresh pencil and to switch on another light, when he thought he heard the compound gate click. He paused, took up his stick and went towards his open front door.

It was much darker than he had realized, the stars already lay like brilliants on indigo velvet and the world was quiet with after-dinner hush.

She saw him before he saw her, his spare figure silhouetted against the light of the lamp, and she came towards him like a drifting ghost.

'Diana,' he exclaimed.

The sound of her first name made her pause, then she came swiftly up the steps, her arms full of rolls of paper, her face aglow.

He took the rolls from her and tossed them on to his couch, then took her arm and drew her into the softly lit room. He did not let go of her arm, but stood looking down at her.

'This is a pleasure,' he said.

'Ranjit said in the bazaar this morning that you wanted to show me the map, so I came as soon as I could and brought that stuff from the City Engineer.' She pointed to the pile of papers, and then realized that he was still holding her bare arm. She faltered, and looked up at him a little beseechingly.

'Ranjit is apt to be a trifle premature,' he said rather grimly, and continued to hold her arm and look at her, until her pulses quickened and she dropped her own gaze, lest he realize how disconcerted she was.

'Come and sit down,' he said, and led her to the couch. He moved the blueprints and sat down beside her. He had never done this before, and she looked at him out of the corner of her eye. He caught the look and she smiled at him. The tight, withdrawn expression on his face faded, but he continued to look at her as if he had never really seen her before. He knew suddenly that he wanted her like he had never wanted anything for years. Not only did he desperately want her in his bed, but he wanted her to be opposite him at breakfast, to listen to his hopes and fears – and even to his very bad jokes. He slowly let go of her arm. Dare he ask her?

His eyes moved over the short, red-gold hair to the little, freckled triangle of skin under her throat, burned red by the sun, and he realized that she had on a different dress, the neckline of which plunged and curved delicately over full, white breasts. It was a dress meant for dinner dates and moonlit evenings, not for hard work on maps. He chuckled, and grinned at her engagingly.

'Could you stay to dinner once more?' he asked hopefully. 'I don't have enough company these days.'

To his further amusement, she blushed furiously, scarlet running up to her hairline. She fingered her glass bangles nervously, before she answered.

'Ranjit said you would expect me to stay to dinner whenever I came. He said you always asked people because you didn't like eating by yourself.' She said it teasingly, as if to belie the telltale blush.

It will be a marvel if he hasn't asked her to stay to breakfast as well, he thought, but he answered without hesitation, 'Ranjit is quite right.'

'Then I shall be delighted to stay.'

John stood up and went to the window.

A well burnished moon was rising. The University gardens would be a pretty haven tonight, he thought, and he turned back into the room, his mind made up.

'Ranjit,' he roared. 'Make dinner for two. Armstrong Memsahib has come.'

Ranjit came through the door from the back veranda. He had shaved and had on a clean shirt. He grinned toothlessly, as he announced, 'Dinner is ready now, Sahib, and there is plenty for two.'

'Ranjit, you are a genius.'

And Ranjit viewed the rather self-conscious couple and replied contentedly, 'Yes, Sahib.'

Yes, Mama

To
Nora Walton (Sylvia Poole)
who was my friend when I most
needed one.

*'The prejudices remain within society,
within families and, above all, within the law.'*

Virgina Ironside and Jane Horwood,
*How can I explain to my daughter that
she isn't a little bastard?*
WOMAN magazine, November, 1986

1

I

Much to her mother's annoyance, Alicia Beatrix Mary decided to be born on May 12th, 1886, during a visit to Liverpool of the dear Queen to open the International Exhibition of Navigation, Travelling, Commerce and Manufactures. On the day of Alicia's slightly premature birth, the Queen was to drive down the Boulevard from Princes Park, on her way to St George's Hall. As a result of Alicia's arrival, her mother, Elizabeth Woodman, missed the chance of seeing her Sovereign.

Mrs Dorothea Evans, the wife of a Liverpool shipping magnate, had graciously invited Elizabeth to view the procession from her bedroom window, which faced the Boulevard. 'If you wore a veil and a large shawl and came in a carriage, no one would realize your – er – condition. You could watch in absolute privacy from behind the lace curtains.'

Elizabeth had been thrilled by an invitation from such an eminent lady, who was herself to be presented to the Queen. She had looked forward to extending her acquaintance with Mrs Evans. She guessed that it would please Humphrey exceedingly if she were to make a friend of the wife of such an influential man – and Elizabeth knew that in the months to come, she would have to do a lot to mollify an outraged Humphrey Woodman, her husband of twenty-two years.

Between the painful contractions, as her forty-year-old body strove to deliver the child, she was consumed by anxiety, an anxiety which had commenced when first she knew she was pregnant.

Had Humphrey realized that the child was not his?

It was always so difficult to be sure of anything with her husband, she worried fretfully. He was so wrapped up in his multifarious business activities and the woman in the town whom he kept, that he rarely talked to his wife, never mind slept with her. But, of late, his usual bouts of temper had been so violent that she felt he must suspect her. And yet he had never commented on her condition.

Could it be, she wondered, that her huge skirts and swathing shawls had been a sufficient disguise, and that he had never realized her condition? She had found it difficult to believe, but she had still clung to the idea, hoping that she might miscarry. Now she prayed that, faced with a living child, he might use his common sense and accept it.

Peevishly, between gasps of pain, she commanded that the heavy, green velvet curtains be drawn over the ones of Nottingham lace. 'The sunlight's hurting my eyes,' she complained to the midwife. Mrs Macdonald, a stout, middle-aged woman in an impeccably white apron and long, black skirt, sighed at her difficult patient and hauled the heavy draperies over the offending light. The huge, brass curtain rings rattled in protest.

'I'll need some more candles, Ma'am.'

'Well, ring for them,' panted Elizabeth.

'Yes, Ma'am.' Mrs Macdonald went to the side of the fireplace and tugged at the green velvet bell-rope.

Though the bell rang in the basement kitchen, the distant tinkle was answered immediately by Fanny, a skinny twelve-year-old skivvy, who had been posted outside the door by Rosie, the housemaid, with orders to bring any messages from her mistress to her while she snatched a hasty lunch in the basement kitchen.

The child opened the bedroom door an inch, and hissed, 'Yes, Missus?'

'Fanny, tell Rosie to bring us some more candles immediately and make up the fire,' ordered Mrs Macdonald. 'And bring another kettle of water – and a trivet to rest it on.'

'I'll do fire afore I go downstairs.' A hand with dirt-engrimed nails gestured through the narrow opening of the door, towards the brimming coal scuttle by the fireplace.

Mrs Macdonald was shocked. 'Good gracious me, no! A young one like you can't come in here. Send Rosie up to do it.'

'Ah, go on with yez. I 'elped me Auntie last time.'

'Don't be so forward, young woman,' snapped the midwife. 'Get down them stairs and tell Rosie.'

'She int goin' to like doin' my job. Fires is *my* job.' Fanny shrugged, her thin lips curved in a grimace as she turned to do the errand. She was stopped by the sound of a querulous voice from the bed. 'Mrs Macdonald, ask Fanny if Miss Florence has arrived yet – or Miss Webb. Or Mr Woodman?' The voice sounded flustered, as Elizabeth named her husband.

'Nobody coom to the front door, Ma'am, not since doctor coom an hour ago,' piped Fanny.

'Where is everybody?' muttered Elizabeth exasperatedly. She moaned, as another bout of pain surged up her back and round her waist.

Mrs Macdonald answered her soothingly. 'It's early hours, yet, Ma'am. There's no hurry. Just rest yourself between the pains.'

Elizabeth grunted, and clutched the bedclothes. The thud of Fanny's big feet on the long staircase seemed to shake her and added to her fretfulness. Would the girl never learn to walk lightly?

Mrs Macdonald picked up a clean sheet and leisurely began to wind it into a rope. She looped this over the mahogany headrail and laid the twisted ends beside Elizabeth's pillow, so that her patient could pull on it when the need to bear down became intense. On the bedside table by the candlestick lay a new, wooden rolling-pin; Mrs Macdonald knew from experience that mothers giving birth needed something to clutch when their pains really began.

'Dr Willis should have stayed; he knows I need him,' Elizabeth complained, as the surging misery in her stiff body subsided.

'He promised to look in again in a couple of hours, Ma'am. Would you like a cup of tea, Ma'am?'

'I'd rather have a glass of port.'

'I wouldn't advise it, Ma'am. It might make the baby sleepy.'

Elizabeth sighed. 'Very well. I'll have tea.'

'That's better. I'll make a good, strong brew.'

Mrs Macdonald moved through the shadowy room to the fireplace to put a small, black kettle on to the fire. On a side table, lay a tray with a flowered teapot, a tea caddy and cups and saucers. The midwife liked to have tea handy and not be dependent upon a far-away kitchen. Tea always diverted a patient, made them feel that something was being done for them.

A soft knock at the bedroom door announced the arrival of Rosie, the housemaid, bearing a kettle of water and a brass trivet. Several long white candles stuck out of her apron pocket. She had not yet finished her lunch, and was cursing her employer under her breath, as she waited for Mrs Macdonald to bid her come in.

As she entered, Rosie composed her face. She handed the kettle, trivet and candles to the midwife and then made up the fire. She made a polite bob towards the bed and turned to leave.

'Rosie,' called Elizabeth from the depths of her supporting pillows.

'Ma'am?'

'Tell Maisie to show Miss Webb straight up when she arrives. You will all take your instructions from her. I also want to see my daughter, Mrs Browning, when she comes. Tell Cook that both ladies will probably be here for dinner.' Elizabeth paused to take a big breath as a stab shot through her abdomen. Then she went on, 'And, Rosie, none of the servants is to leave the house without Cook's permission.' She twisted suddenly in the bed and arched her back. 'Ah!' she cried.

Waiting to be dismissed, Rosie stood woodenly facing her, while the spasm passed. 'Blow her,' she thought, 'just when I were thinkin' I could nip out a few minutes to see the Queen. And Miss Webb is a *single* lady – she won't want to come into a birthing room, any more'n she'd want to look into a midden full o' garbage.'

Mrs Macdonald wrung out a cloth in cool, scented water and began solicitously to wipe the patient's face. Elizabeth pushed her impatiently aside. 'Has Mrs Ford come?' she gasped to Rosie.

'Yes, Ma'am. She's bin waitin' in the kitchen this past three hours.'

'Send her up – I'll see her – while I still can,' Elizabeth ordered pessimistically.

II

Mrs Polly Ford was a widow, aged twenty-three. Six weeks before the Queen's visit, her husband, a docker, had fallen into the hold of a ship and had died, almost immediately, of his multiple injuries. Two nights later, in her parents' crowded cellar dwelling, his frantic widow had given birth to her first child.

Born on to a pile of rags in a windowless, waterless, heatless home, without even a clean sheet to be wrapped in, the baby boy had decided, three weeks later, that life was not worth living and had quit it. Polly wished passionately that she had been allowed to follow him. She was, however, a strong, healthy woman and, despite her despair, her milk surged in her.

Weeping helplessly, she had sat by a tiny fire lovingly built for her by her father, James Tyson. He had walked down to Seaforth sands to search for driftwood, in order to provide a little heat for her.

'We didn't know the babe was goin' to come so quick – or be born here – and we run out of coal and money,' he told her almost apologetically, his bearded face turned up towards her, as he knelt to feed the flames with chips from an old railway sleeper which he had found on the shore.

'I know, Dad,' she told him gently between her sobs. 'You shouldn't've took the wood from the sands – you could've been arrested for it.'

'Och, I know that. Devil take the bleeders!' He got up off his knees and stood leaning against the rough, brick chimney, the firelight catching the golden hairs of his beard and eyebrows. 'What you goin' to do now, duck?'

Her mother, Bridie Tyson, had been sitting beside Polly on the backless bench. Wrapped inside her shawl, to keep him warm in the foetid cellar of the court house, lay Billy, Polly's baby brother. His wide brown eyes glittered, as he peeked out of the enveloping shawl to watch the dancing flames of the fire. Now his mother sighed, and asked, 'Aye, what to do?'

'She can stay with us,' responded her husband immediately.

'Aye, Dad, you've got enough trouble without me,' Polly told him.

She looked helplessly round the tiny room, dimly lit from the open door leading to the steps up to the court itself. Down those steps, on wet days, trickled sewage from two overflowing earth lavatories which served the fourteen houses surrounding the court, to add to the overwhelming misery of the ten people living in her parents' windowless room below ground level. But her father was a casual labourer on the docks, and this, though he was as good a man as ever heard a Wesleyan sermon, was the best he could provide for his family from his irregular earnings. Also living with him was his widowed sister-in-law and her five children.

Polly's aunt had been sitting, almost unnoticed, on a three-legged stool tucked up by the fireplace. Under her black shawl, her stomach was swollen with pregnancy. She cackled suddenly, 'Youse wet with milk. You could mebbe wet-nurse.'

Polly's breasts ached with milk. She had let her little brother, Billy, suckle from her to ease the pain, but still the milk pressed within and damped her calico dress.

'Some fine lady'd pay good for that – and you'd be well fed to keep it up,' her aunt went on.

'Aye, you'd live the life o' Riley,' her mother agreed eagerly.

James Tyson looked down at his womenfolk and shrugged. This was woman talk, and, anyway, it was time to go down to the dock gate again, to stand in the rain and hope to be picked out for half a day's work. He patted Polly on the shoulder as he passed, and left them to it.

Through a grapevine of female cousins and aunts, inquiries went out to ask anyone in service whether their mistresses were expecting.

From Fanny, the little skivvy in the Woodmans' house, came the information via her aunt, that the Missus was expecting any day and was proper mad at it. In Fanny's considered opinion and judging from the gossip in the kitchen, she would be glad enough to be relieved of feeding the expected child and of looking after it; its nearest brother,

487

Master Charles, was ten years old and had gone away to boarding school. *His* nurse had long since been let go.

On her Sunday afternoon off, Fanny visited her aunt in her tiny house in Shaw's Alley and confided to her that a real blow-up about the child was expected daily, between her Master and Mistress. 'It int his kid,' Fanny told her. 'And he's got a temper like you'd nevaire believe. Always pickin' on her, he is – and yet *he* can't talk – he took up with a woman as keeps a tobacco and sweets, back o' Water Street, downtown.'

Fanny bent to wring out a rag in a pail of cold water and reapplied it to one of her aunt's eyes, which her husband had blackened the previous night. Her aunt was hardly listening to her niece; she was wondering dully if, after last night, she would be in the family way again, and she sighed at the very thought of it. It would be the fifteenth and, out of the whole bloody issue, only three of them full grown.

Wearily, she tried to give her attention to what Fanny was saying, and replied, with pity, 'Well, you talk to Rosie and Mrs Tibbs about Polly Ford. The poor gel is broken-'earted and 'er Mam is near out of 'er wits over it.'

.

III

While Elizabeth Woodman's affairs were discussed in one of Liverpool's worst slums, Elizabeth herself had wandered round her handsome Upper Canning Street house through the last days of her pregnancy, and viewed with dread the birth of her child.

She had done her best to get rid of the child. She had drunk bottle after bottle of gin and had sat for hours in hot baths, while Fanny stoked up the kitchen fire to heat the water in the tank behind it, so that Elizabeth could keep renewing the water in her fine mahogany-encased bath in the bathroom. To no purpose.

She had even contemplated throwing herself down the main staircase in order to dislodge the foetus, but when she had looked at the steepness of the flight her courage had failed her.

She watched with horror her expanding figure and worried at her husband's complete lack of comment about it. As the months went remorselessly by, his silence began to terrify her. They had not slept together for months. He must *know* it's not his, she agonized. Is he going to ignore the fact or will he throw me out at some point? And where shall I go? What shall I do?

Perhaps it will be born dead, she thought hopefully. Then he won't *have* to say anything.

But Alicia Beatrix Mary had no intention of being born dead; Elizabeth, Polly and Fanny would all have their lives totally altered by her existence.

2

I

Fanny consulted Rosie, the Woodmans' housemaid, about Polly. Rosie spoke to Mrs Martha Tibbs, the cook-housekeeper, an unmarried lady graced with the appellation of a wife because it was the custom.

In consideration of receiving Polly Ford's first month's wages, if she got the job, Mrs Tibbs graciously agreed to broach the subject of a wet-nurse with Elizabeth Woodman. Since nothing had been said to the domestic staff about the impending addition to the family, Mrs Tibbs went about the matter very delicately.

Bored to tears by three months' confinement during the more obvious period of her pregnancy, anxious to keep the child away from her husband as much as possible, assuming it were born alive, Elizabeth was almost grateful to Mrs Tibbs and agreed to look at Polly.

It took the efforts of all her extended family to make Polly look respectable for the interview. She had a black skirt in which she had been married. A black bodice was borrowed from a distant cousin down the street; she had had it given to her by the draper whose tiny shop she cleaned. It had been eaten by moths at the back, but with Polly's own black shawl over it, the holes would not show. A battered, black straw hat was acquired for a penny from a pedlar of secondhand clothes, after hard bargaining by Polly's married sister, Mary. Polly's mother washed and ironed her own apron to an unusual whiteness, so that Polly could wear it for the occasion. Polly had boots, though they were worn through at the bottom and were bursting round the little toes. 'I'll keep me feet under me skirt,' said Polly dully.

Through all these preparations, Polly wept steadily. At her mother's urging she suckled little Billy. 'It'll nourish 'im and it'll keep the milk comin', luv,' her mother consoled her.

It was comforting to hold the small boy to her. Though as grubby as a sweep, he was a merry child, who laughed and crowed and tried to talk to her.

Before Polly could aspire to a job as an indoor servant, she had, somehow, to acquire a reference from another lady. At first, Polly's mother had suggested that Mrs Tibbs' recommendation would be enough, but, through Fanny, Mrs Tibbs herself insisted that Polly must produce a written reference.

'Aye, she's right,' Polly agreed. Then, trying to make an effort for herself, she added, 'Now I've got a hat, I could go and see that ould Mrs Stanley, and ask 'er.'

Before her marriage, Polly had cleaned the doorsteps and the brass bells and letterboxes of a number of elegant houses in Mount Pleasant. For five years, she had donkey-stoned the front steps of a Mrs Stanley, an ancient crone who claimed that she had once danced with King George IV. Mrs Stanley lived with a white cat and an elderly married pair of servants.

With feelings akin to terror, Polly pulled the bell of the servants' entrance of Mrs Stanley's house. The same bent, bald manservant she remembered answered it. He did not recognize her, and asked, 'And what do you want?'

She told him.

'I'll ask the wife,' he told her, and shut the door in her face.

She was almost ready to give up and go home, when a little kitchen-maid opened it and said shyly, 'You're to coom in.'

She was led into a well-scrubbed kitchen where, on a bare, deal table, a meal was laid for four. Bending over to poke the roaring kitchen fire was an elderly woman-servant. A good smell of roasting meat permeated the room; it made Polly's mouth water.

The old woman straightened up. She wore a white, frilled cap tied under her chin and a grey uniform with a long, starched apron. Poker still in hand, she turned and said, ''Allo, Polly. What's to do? Didn't expect to see you again, after you was married.'

Polly explained her need for a reference. 'To say I'm honest, like.' She omitted to tell the woman that she had been widowed, because she thought she would start to cry again if she did so.

The older woman looked at her doubtfully. 'Well, I'll ask for yez,' she said slowly. 'I doubt she'll even know your face, though. Ye 'ardly ever saw 'er, did yer?'

'Not much,' agreed Polly humbly.

'I'll go up. Sit down there.' She pointed to a wooden chair set by the back entrance. Polly obediently sat on it.

A bell suddenly bounced on its spring in a corner of the ceiling and ting-a-linged impatiently. The manservant put on his jacket and went to answer it. The little kitchen-maid stirred the contents of an iron pot on the fire and carefully put the lid back on. A young woman in a pink-striped, housemaid's dress put her head round the door leading to the rest of the house, and shouted, 'Mary Jane, the Mistress wants her bath water. Hurry up.'

The kitchen-maid put her ladle down on to an old plate in the hearth. A somnolent kitchen cat slunk from the other end of the hearth and quietly licked it clean. The girl took a large ewer from a hook and swung it under the oven tap at the side of the huge kitchen fire. Boiling water belched into it. She grinned at Polly, as she waited for the water jug to fill.

Polly smiled faintly. Jaysus! Was she going to have to wait for the ould girl to bath and dress?

Two and a half hours later, by the clock hanging on the kitchen wall, Madam completed her toilet. The servants came at different times to eat their midday meal at the kitchen table. They ignored Polly as being so low that she was beneath their notice.

The morning-room bell tinkled. The manservant wiped his lips on the back of his hand, put on his black jacket and went upstairs. A few minutes later, he returned and said gruffly to Polly, 'Mistress'll see you.'

Her chest aching, her throat parched, her heart beating wildly from fright, Polly followed the old man along a dark passage and up two flights of stairs equally Stygian. 'You're lucky,' he piped. 'Mistress don't bother with the likes of you that often.'

Polly kept her head down and did not answer. Surreptitiously, under her shawl, she scratched a bug bite on her arm. She was so inured to vermin bites that they did not usually irritate. Her mother had, however, insisted that she wash herself all over in a bucket of cold water, scrubbing her yellowed skin with a rough piece of cloth. It had made her itch. After that, both of them had gone over the seams of her clothes to kill any lice or bugs that she might be carrying. 'You can't help your hair,' her mother had said. 'I haven't got no money to buy paraffin to kill the nits in it.'

The old servant pushed open a green baize door and suddenly she was in a blaze of sunlight coming through the stained glass of the hall window.

Blinking against the light, she tiptoed after the servant across the hall rug to a white-enamelled door.

The servant knocked gently, paused and then entered the room, while Polly, terrified, quivered on the red Turkey doormat.

'Come on in,' the old man breathed irritably. 'She's waitin'.' He shoved Polly forward and closed the door behind her.

Before she lowered her eyes, Polly caught a glimpse of an incredibly thin woman, her heavy white hair done up elaborately on the top of her head. She was waiting bolt upright in an armless chair and was staring out of the window at the garden. Nestling in the folds of her grey silk skirt was a huge white cat. Heavily ringed fingers tickled the cat's ears.

Polly stood silently looking at the richly patterned carpet, and waited to be noticed.

'Well?' the old lady barked.

Polly swallowed and then curtsied. She wanted to run away and cry, cry herself to death, if possible. 'I'm Polly, Ma'am,' she quavered, 'wot used to scrub your steps and do the brass . . .'

'I know who you are,' snapped the voice. 'What do you want?'

Polly glanced up at her erstwhile employer. The lady was still staring out of the window; the cat stared at Polly. 'Well, Ma'am, I – er . . .'

'For Heaven's sake, speak up, girl.'

'Yes, 'm, I'm wantin' to get a job as wet-nurse to a lady called Mrs Woodman in Upper Canning Street – and I was wonderin', Ma'am, if you would write a letter to her about me.'

'A reference?'

'Yes, Ma'am.'

'A wet-nurse, humph? Have you been in trouble? I don't believe in helping servants in trouble.'

'Oh, no, Ma'am.' Polly was shocked out of her fear. 'I were a married woman.' Her voice faltered, and for the first time, Mrs Stanley turned to look at her.

'Lost the child?'

'Yes, Ma'am. He was born a bit early – 'cos me 'oosband were killed – in the Albert Dock, Ma'am. It must've bin the shock.' She gulped back her tears, and then went on. ''E fell in an 'old, Ma'am.'

'How very careless of him.'

'Yes, 'm.' Tears coursed down the girl's cheeks.

Madam stared at her thoughtfully. Everybody lost children; she had lost all hers. Still, it was depressing. And doubtless Mrs Woodman, whom she had met once or twice at parties, would be glad of a wet-nurse. She understood that, nowadays, they were difficult to obtain.

'Have you been in service before?'

'Yes, Ma'am. I were a tweenie when I were ten, 'elping the 'ousemaid empty the slops, and like. The Missus died . . . and then I found I could earn more specializin' in doin' door-steps.'

'Humph.' Mrs Stanley's lips curled. The lower classes were remarkable in their ability to survive.

'And for how long did you – er – clean my doorsteps?'

'Five year, Ma'am.'

'Why don't you go back to it?'

Polly heaved a sigh. She was so tired that she thought her legs would give under her. 'Me Mam wants me to improve meself,' she burst out, with sudden inspiration.

'Very commendable. And do you go to Church, Polly?'

Polly had never been to Church in her life. And only once to an open air Wesleyan meeting with her father. She knew, however, what the answer must be. 'Oh, yes, Ma'am. I go to St Nick's – I mean, St Nicholas's.'

'Humph. Protestant, then?'

'Yes, Ma'am,' replied Polly promptly, wondering suddenly what she really was, since her mother was a Roman Catholic and her father a Wesleyan.

'Mrs Woodman is a Protestant, I believe.'

Polly did not care if Mrs Woodman worshipped golden idols, like the blackie seamen who walked the streets of Liverpool in silent, single files. All she wanted was three meals a day, to lessen the pain in her stomach, and a baby to suckle, to ease the pain in her chest; even the thought of suckling made her breasts fill and she could feel the milk trickling down to her waist.

Mrs Stanley smiled thinly. She did not care for Mrs Woodman, a fluttering widgeon of a woman with an upstart husband who dabbled in many commercial enterprises in Liverpool. Distinctly lower-class. She thought it might be amusing to send them a wet-nurse who was probably lice-ridden.

'Bring my desk from over there and put it on this table beside me.' Mrs Stanley gestured towards the far wall.

Polly did not know what a desk looked like and glanced, bewildered, towards the furniture indicated by the delicate white hand.

'*There*, you fool – that – er – sloping box.'

Polly carefully lifted a pair of crystal inkwells and a matching candle-stick off the desk and laid the desk on the table indicated. She then replaced the inkwells and candlestick.

Irritated, Mrs Stanley moved inkwells and candlestick to the back of the desk, so that she could open the lid and extract a sheet of paper, a goose-quill pen and a piece of sealing wax. In exquisite copperplate, she wrote To Whom It May Concern that Polly Ford was honest, indus-trious and had worked for her as a charwoman for five years. She was desirous of improving herself, and Mrs Stanley felt that she would give satisfaction.

She sanded the paper to dry the ink. She then took a phosphorus match from the candlestick, struck it and lit the candle. She held the stick of sealing wax to the flame and allowed a small drop to fall upon

494

the letter and seal it closed. Into the molten wax, she pressed a ring from her forefinger, to imprint her own seal.

'There.' She turned in her chair and handed the note to Polly. With a bit of luck, that would give the odious Woodmans a fair amount of trouble.

'Oh, thank you, Ma'am.' Polly's voice was full of genuine gratitude as she made a deep curtsey.

Mrs Stanley gave a stiff nod of acknowledgement, and then ordered, 'Put the desk back on to the far table.'

'Yes, 'm.' Polly did as she was bidden, being particularly careful not to spill the red and black inks from their crystal containers. She then backed to the door, bobbing little curtsies as she went.

'James will show you out. Pull the bell by the fireplace.'

The only thing by the fireplace which could be pulled was a long piece of embroidered canvas hanging from the ceiling. Polly hoped for the best and pulled it. Then she stood with hands neatly clasped in front of her and examined the pattern on the carpet. She was stupid, she told herself. She should have realized that she would have to be escorted out of the house in case she stole something. Not that I would, she told herself crossly.

The old manservant arrived with commendable promptness. 'Yes, Ma'am?'

'Show this woman out – by the servants' entrance.'

'Yes, Ma'am. Of course, Ma'am.' He twisted his toothless mouth into a tight knot. As if he would ever show a member of the lower classes out of the front door. After fifty years of service, Madam ought to know that, he thought irritably.

II

Sent upstairs by Rosie, Polly stood with head meekly bowed and examined the blue and white Chinese carpet in Elizabeth Woodman's room, while her new mistress looked her over for a second time.

The young woman seemed healthy enough; and with a reference from the high-and-mighty Mrs Stanley *and* a personal recommendation from her cook-housekeeper, Mrs Tibbs, she should be satisfactory. Yet, Elizabeth smelled a rat. Mrs Stanley was notorious for her perverted sense of humour. A leftover from the wilder days of King George IV and King William IV, the old devil was capable of all kinds of japes and capers.

As she peered in the candlelight at the humbly bent head, a much

495

sharper pain shot through her and she cried out. Mrs Macdonald came to the bedside immediately. She picked up the rolling-pin from the bedside table and handed it to the sufferer. 'There, there, Ma'am. Hold on to this.'

Elizabeth clutched at the pin and gritted her teeth, as she waited for the next pang. She felt tired already, worn out from worrying over the coming child's existence. She was petrified at the thought of the outburst which might occur from Humphrey when he actually saw the baby.

But if she employed this Polly Ford, the child could stay in the old nurseries on the top floor for months, and as far as Humphrey was concerned, out of sight might be out of mind. And she herself would be freed from the boredom of feeding the baby. She could go out and fulfil her social obligations, be free to spend afternoons with darling Andrew, as before, though they would have to be much more careful.

She let another spasm go over, managing not to cry out. Then she said to the midwife, 'Mrs Macdonald, tell Mrs Tibbs to see that this woman is bathed, her head rubbed with paraffin, and her present clothing wrapped up tightly and sent to her home. Mrs Tibbs should have her uniform ready by now.'

'Yes, Ma'am. I'll ring for Rosie.'

Polly kept her head down. This was much better than she had expected. Both she and her mother had been worried about getting her a uniform, fearing that the pedlar might not give them credit. Now the clothes were to be given to her. If she had dared, she would have sighed with relief.

Elizabeth knew from sad experience that vermin could come into a house in a servant's trunk. She took no chances and always provided uniforms.

Polly endured without comment the humiliating complaints of her fellow servants, as a tin bath was lugged up to the windowless box room which would be her bedroom. Loquacious Fanny hauled two ewers of hot water and one of cold up the endless stairs from the basement kitchen, together with a bottle of paraffin, a bar of laundry soap, a piece of flannel and a worn bath towel. 'Mind you don't make no splashes,' she warned Polly.

Polly had never had a bath in her life; she had simply rubbed herself cursorily with a bit of cloth wrung out in cold water. Now, Fanny laid an old copy of *The Times* on the floor and said, 'Take off all yer clothes and put 'em on this. Mrs Tibbs'll get next door's gardener's boy to walk down with 'em to yer ma's.'

Polly looked at the girl appalled. Take off *everything*?

As if she could read her mind, Fanny said, with a grin, 'Everythin', 'cept yer stockin's and boots – you're to keep them.'

'Well, you go away, Miss, while I does it,' snapped Polly defiantly. Even Patrick had never seen her completely naked.

At the thought of Patrick, tears welled. Fanny saw them, and said sympathetically, 'Don't take on so. They did this to me when I coom. Fussy, the Mistress is – wash all of you every day, she allus says.' She glanced up again at Polly, still standing uncertainly by the bath. 'These days, I fancy a bath meself now and then – takes the aches out of yez. I'll bet she'll make you scrub your dairies every day.' She nodded her head like a disapproving old woman. 'Proper finick, she is.'

While she waited for Fanny to leave the room, Polly sat down and unlaced her boots. One of the bootlaces broke and she looked at it ruefully, wondering where she would get a halfpenny from to buy a new one. 'What's the Master like?' she inquired carefully – her mother had warned her long ago, when she had been a ten-year-old tweenie in a big house, to keep out of the way of the men of the house.

'Himself? Och, you don't have to worry about him. He's got a fancy woman downtown. Maisie – she's the parlour-maid – says the woman keeps 'im exhausted!' Fanny chortled and looked wickedly at Polly. Then she said more soberly, 'They do say as once he got a maid in trouble and the Mistress sent her packing. Nowadays, he don't even notice you're there, though. He's got a lousy temper, though. Just keep out of his way of an evening when he's drunk.'

Polly digested this advice, and then, as Fanny picked up her empty ewer and moved towards the door, she asked, 'What part of town do you come from?'

Fanny laughed. 'I dunno, for sure. I got an auntie wot lives in Shaw's Alley, but I coom 'ere from the Workie. I were born in there – and bloody glad I was to get out of it. At least the Mistress don't beat you. It were me auntie that got on to you.'

'Is your Mam still in the Workhouse?'

'Not her. She died when I was only an itty-bitty kid. The Workie Gaffer hit her one day for something she said – and she lay down and I remember she were cold.'

Polly did not bother to ask her where her father was. In her experience, fathers often remained unknown. She sighed and said, 'It must've bin proper hard for yez.'

Fanny's eyes twinkled. 'I wouldn't give a dead farthin' to go through it again,' she replied forcefully. Swinging her empty ewer, she turned and plodded down the stairs to the basement.

Polly quickly stripped off her blouse, skirt and stockings. She put a

497

cautious toe into the steaming water and then stepped into it. It felt comfortable, so she carefully lowered herself into it and reached for the soap lying on the floor. She took the hairpins out of her plaits and loosened her hair. She found that holding the hot flannel to her breasts eased the ache in them and she was able to expel some of her milk. It would be a day or two, she realized, before the baby would be able to suck, and, in the meantime, she must keep the milk coming.

After she had dried herself, she kneeled down by the bath and uncorked the bottle of paraffin. Holding her breath because of its smell, she rubbed it liberally into her damp hair, until it dripped into the bath. Then, using a fine-toothed comb which her husband, Patrick, had given her as a present, she combed the long, damp locks until she reckoned she had all the lice out; the paraffin would kill the nits, so, if she were lucky, she would be free of them.

Two full-skirted, ankle-length, cotton dresses with petticoats to go under them had been provided. In Polly's eyes, the dresses were beautiful, far nicer than anything she had ever worn before; they had narrow, blue and white stripes. There were three large white aprons to wear over them and three white cotton bonnets to pin over her hair. To go out-of-doors, there was a navy-blue jacket, and a navy coif to go over the white caps.

She would have to find stockings and shoes for herself, and she wondered if her mother could prevail on the pedlar to let her have them on two months' credit. Her first month's wages would be appropriated by Mrs Tibbs, the cook-housekeeper, as her fee for getting her the job. As she thought about this, she replaited her hair and wound it into a neat bun at the back of her head.

When Fanny came back up the stairs, carrying a pair of slop pails in which to remove the bath water, she gaped at the newly created Nanny. 'Well, I never,' she exclaimed. 'You look proper pretty.'

Her spirits revived, Polly gave the girl a playful cuff about the head for her impudence. Then she asked, 'Wot time is servants' meals?'

'Breakfast at six-thirty, dinner 'alf-past eleven, tea at five. If Ma Tibbs is in a good mood, you get a bit o' somethin' afore bedtime – depends on wot's left from the Master's dinner. The Mistress isn't mean, but Ma Tibbs is. She takes food to her sister's house.'

'I'm awfully hungry,' admitted Polly, her voice trembling slightly.

'Oh, aye. *You* could get a mug o' milk or ale anytime you want – and I suppose I'll 'ave to bring it up.'

She plunged her slop pail into the scummy bath water.

'Bring me some milk and a piece of bread now,' wheedled Polly. 'There's a pet. I'm clemmed.'

Fanny glanced up at her. 'And the baby not even born yet?' she teased.

'Come on, Fanny. I'll share it with yez.'

'Well, seein' as I know yez, I'll ask for it.'

3

I

At half-past eleven that warm May night, Alicia Beatrix Mary yelled her first impatient complaint in this world.

Dr Willis declared her a healthy child and Mrs Macdonald gave her her first bath. To ensure a flat, well-healed navel, a flannel binder was wound tightly round her stomach.

On a dresser lay a pile of baby clothes originally prepared for a brother, who, eight years before, had died within a month of his birth. Mrs Macdonald picked up a cotton napkin and one of terry towelling and enclosed Alicia in these. Then the child's tiny arms were pushed into a flannel vest. A long cotton petticoat followed and then a flannel one, each tied at the front. Over all this went a fine white baby gown, frilled and embroidered and hemstitched in an Islington sweat shop. The long petticoats and gown were folded up over the protesting little feet, and she was finally wrapped in a warm, white shawl crocheted for her by her mother's spinster friend and lifelong confidante, Miss Sarah Webb.

Almost smothered by the amount of clothing, Alicia carried her complaints to Humphrey Woodman.

Humphrey had been called from his booklined study by Dr Willis to inspect the new addition to his household and was uncertain, at first, whether he should go up. He had been startled when Maisie, the parlour-maid, had told him that his wife had commenced her labour. He had hoped to the last that his wife would miscarry, so that he would not have to face directly the fact of her infidelity.

Maisie was waiting, politely holding the door open for him, so he slowly pushed himself away from his desk and got up. As he straightened his velvet smoking jacket and gravely marched upstairs, a slow anger burned in him. He did not care a damn what Elizabeth did as long as she was discreet; but having a child at the age of forty was, alone, enough to interest the gossips and raise speculation.

Since Dr Willis and Mrs Macdonald were present, he kissed his wife dutifully upon her white cheek, and, afterwards, went to inspect the minute bundle lying in the frilly, draped cot which had served all his children.

His breath began to come fast as he gazed at the crumpled red face, and he seethed inwardly; at that moment he would have liked to murder Elizabeth and her lawyer, Andrew Crossing, whom he was fairly sure was the child's father. Yet, in a sense, he also felt defeated. There was no question of his divorcing his wife; he must maintain his carefully built-up image of a well-respected city businessman with an impeccable home-life. To maintain society's rigid proprieties, he would have to accept the baby as his. He knew it and he guessed that his wife was counting upon it – the sanctimonious bitch!

At the back of his mind, too, was the need to protect the future of his daughter, Florence, who was standing by him, bending over the little cot and tenderly touching her newborn sister with a careful finger. Florence was herself seven months pregnant. She was the wife of the Reverend Clarence Browning, a gentleman with small private means bent on a career in the church. A divorce between her parents, or even a separation, might put an end to his hopes of obtaining a bishopric one day.

Humphrey loved Florence. She was the only person to whom he showed any real affection. Her marriage portion had been as handsome as he could make it. Though at this moment he itched to beat her mother to death, he knew he would never make a single move that might injure his little Flo. When Alicia's time came, however, he thought savagely, she would not get a penny out of him.

'Isn't she lovely, Papa?' cooed Florence.

Humphrey continued to gaze expressionlessly at the crabbed little face, as he said politely, 'Yes, my dear.'

While Dr Willis went to use the Woodmans' magnificent new water closet, Mrs Macdonald stood, hands folded over her apron, at the foot of the bed, waiting for the series of visitors to pass. She would stay to nurse Elizabeth for a couple of days, before handing her over to her friend, Sarah Webb, to be cared for during the rest of her ten days' lying-in.

As Humphrey turned to leave the room, he felt suddenly drained. His anger began to subside and he thought longingly of his Mrs Jakes. Most of his friends had a *little woman* tucked away somewhere in the town, and Mrs Jakes was his woman. Her well-patronized sweets and tobacco shop, on the corner of one of the crowded streets behind his office in Water Street, offered a fine excuse for visiting her. His need for tobacco for his pipe and the occasional gift of sweets for his children accounted easily for his going there. When the shop was empty of customers, he would slip behind the counter and through the door to her living-quarters. She would send her dull, thick-waisted daughter to tend the shop, lock the intervening door and draw the lace curtains over the window in it. They could be very cosy together behind the lace-draped door, sitting in front of her blazing coal fire; or they could go up the stairs which led to her bedroom above. It was a discreet, mutually agreeable arrangement. Why could not Elizabeth have been equally circumspect? he fumed.

Now, ignoring his wife, he said goodnight to Mrs Macdonald and told Florence to go to bed soon. Mrs Macdonald, much experienced in these matters, drew her own conclusions.

Downstairs, Humphrey waited in his study until the doctor should be shown in. Dr Willis, when he did come, accepted a glass of port and lifted it in a toast to the newborn. Humphrey bent his head slightly in acknowledgement, but he did not raise his glass. As Dr Willis drank from his glass, his eyebrows rose slightly – so his own wife's gossip about Elizabeth Woodman had a sound basis. Woodman was showing none of the jovial relief at a safe delivery that most men exhibited. He hastily finished his wine, put down his glass and said that he would call again the following morning, to check both mother and child.

II

Upstairs, Mrs Macdonald was deferentially solicitous and wondered privately who would pay her bill. She said, as she fussed round her patient, 'Miss Webb wondered if you would like a bite to eat, Ma'am?'

Sarah Webb, being a spinster, would not visit her friend until the morning; not having been married, she was supposed, officially, not to know how babies arrived. The following day seemed to her to be a polite time to come up. She had, meanwhile, taken over the housekeeping, and Mrs Tibbs had had a long, uncomfortable evening as Sarah began to cope with a kitchen unused to being visited by its mistress.

Florence reinforced the suggestion of food. She said, 'Yes, Mama, you should take something to eat. You have to keep up your strength.' Florence was deadly tired, her bundly body aching in every direction, but she spoke brightly to her mother.

'Very well, dear,' Elizabeth responded wearily. 'Tell Mrs Tibbs to make me a plain omelette and toast – and some Madeira to drink.'

Mrs Macdonald pulled at the bell rope.

Elizabeth continued to talk to her daughter. 'I have a wet-nurse for the child,' she told her with a wan smile. 'I don't propose to feed her myself. At my age . . .'

Florence nodded understandingly. She had not been informed of her mother's pregnancy until a week before the birth. Elizabeth had not felt able to tell a pregnant daughter that she was expecting an infant. At forty, it was indecent to be in such a situation; she herself had not expected it to happen.

As her mother's figure burgeoned under the flounces and heavy drapery of her elaborate dresses, the situation had been clear to Florence for some time. She was, however, much too well brought up to mention the subject until her mother cared to bring the matter up and she expressed suitable surprise when Elizabeth suddenly blurted out that she would be brought to bed within the month. She had been much alarmed that her mother would not survive and had prayed earnestly each night that she be safely delivered. Now, she thought, she must pray for herself.

As if the midwife divined her thoughts, she turned towards her and smiled faintly, 'You look very well, if I may say so, Ma'am. You'll soon know the joy of your own wee babe in your arms.' There was oily comfort in every word.

'Thank you, Mrs Macdonald,' responded Florence graciously, 'With your help, I'm sure I will.'

In answer to the bell, Maisie, the elderly parlour-maid, arrived and was instructed regarding a meal.

'Tell Mrs Ford she may now come to remove the baby,' Elizabeth told the maid. 'I trust a fire has been made in the nursery – and in baby's bedroom?'

'Oh, yes, Ma'am. Fanny's bin watching both fires ever since atternoon.'

Up in the nursery, Polly, lulled by the heat, had gone to sleep in an old easy chair set by the fireplace. In the glow of the coals, she looked softly pretty, tidier, more clean than she had ever been in her life.

When Fanny clumped in with yet another hod of coal, she woke up with a start.

'Coom on, now,' Fanny commanded her. 'The Missus wants you to take the baby.' She dumped the heavy coal hod into the fireplace, picked up a pair of tongs and lifted a couple of lumps of coal on to the blaze. 'Maisie and Rosie'll bring the cot up.' She yawned enormously, her stunted little body stretching as she did so. 'Aye, I'm that tired. Seems to me as if none of us is goin' to get to bed tonight. And I got to be up at five, 'cos ould Tibbs raises Cain if she don't have a hot oven by six o'clock, ready to put the bread in.'

Polly got up and stretched. Then she peeked into the mirror over the dresser, to check that her hair was still neat and her cap on straight. 'Fancy having a mirror,' she thought to herself gleefully. She picked up the candle from the table.

'Aye, don't leave me in the dark,' protested Fanny. She hastily tipped the rest of the coal into a brass coal scuttle at the side of the hearth. 'It's proper ghosty up here, what with Mr Charles and Mr Edward gone away and not usin' the rooms on the other side o' the passage.'

Polly waited for the little skivvy and then, carrying the candle, led her down the dark staircase, the coal hod clanking like chains behind her.

On the floor below lay Elizabeth's bedroom and beside it the dressing-room in which Humphrey had slept for the last year or so. Also on this floor, lay Florence's old bedroom, a guest room and the main drawing-room; the latter was shrouded in dust sheets, because Elizabeth could not entertain in the last months of her pregnancy; it was not the thing. At the back of the house, on this same floor, was Elizabeth Woodman's latest status symbol, a brand new water closet and a handsome adjoining bathroom with hot and cold water which belched from shining brass taps.

'You're not allowed to use the water closet,' Fanny warned Polly, as they passed it. 'You got to come down to the closet outside the back kitchen door – or you can use a chamber-pot and empty it yourself down there. I 'aven't got no time to be running up and down with a slop pail to clear it for yez. There's an old slop pail in the nursery cupboard if you want to use it.'

Polly reached Elizabeth's door at the same time as Maisie was about to enter, so she followed her in. They both stood just inside the door-way, hands folded, eyes down, waiting for orders.

Elizabeth was sitting up in bed, wrapped in a pink shawl, her hair plaited neatly over each shoulder. She was feeling better and, though her eyes were black-ringed, some of her normal high colour had returned to her cheeks; the birth had, in fact, been quite an easy one. She fully expected that, thanks to Mrs Macdonald's modern ideas of well-scrubbed hands, boiled aprons and sheets, she would be spared that plague of new mothers, childbed fever.

Replete with omelette and half a bottle of Madeira, her breasts bound tightly by Mrs Macdonald to prevent the flow of milk, all she wanted now was that the child be taken away, so that, as much as possible, she could forget it. She hoped, also, when trouble with her husband had blown over, that she could be reunited with Andrew Crossing, only in a more private place than on her drawing-room settee.

504

'Polly,' she snapped at the trim, black-haired wet-nurse. 'Take the baby upstairs. See that it is fed every three or four hours and has its napkin changed frequently to keep it dry.' She turned to Maisie. 'Take the tray away. That will be all for tonight.'

'Thank you, ma'am,' Maisie replied, took the tray and fled thankfully to her bed. Polly approached the cradle cautiously and picked up the tiny bundle which was Alicia Beatrix Mary. The infant opened its eyes and whimpered.

'Polly.'

'Yes, 'm?'

'There is a good supply of clothing in the chest of drawers in the nursery. Fanny will remove any washing including your own. She will also bring up your meals. The washerwoman will come twice a week. See that the dirty clothes and sheets are down in the wash cellar by six o'clock every Monday and Thursday morning.'

Polly bobbed a small curtsey to indicate agreement.

'I have instructed Mrs Tibbs to feed you well and let you have as much milk as you can drink.'

Having met Mrs Tibbs, Polly did not have any great hope of these instructions being followed properly. She whispered, however, a faint 'Thank you, ma'am.' She allowed herself a small shivering sigh – it had been a long and eventful day for her – and then asked, 'What's baby's name, ma'am?'

'Alicia Beatrix Mary,' replied Elizabeth, having decided that it was better to name the child herself, rather than ask Humphrey his opinion. Though she would not have liked to admit it, there was the thought in the back of her mind that, like its baby brother, it might die within the month, anyway; and that would solve a lot of her problems.

Andrew had assured her that since she and Humphrey lived together the child was legally his, unless he repudiated it. Nevertheless, she supposed she would have to go herself to register its birth, as soon as she felt well enough; Humphrey was hardly likely to do anything about putting *his* name on the birth certificate. She must also write a note to Andrew, she reminded herself, telling him of Alicia's birth; she could say that she wanted to alter her Will slightly to include a small legacy to the new baby. She sighed, and hoped he would come soon.

'You may go,' she told Polly, patiently standing in front of her with the baby in her arms.

505

III

Unaware of the inconvenience her arrival had caused, Alicia Beatrix Mary was carried up to the attic nurseries. To Polly, the child was sent by the Holy Mother herself to replace the little boy she had lost and to comfort her in her widowhood. For her part, Alicia learned to turn to Polly for mothering; it was Polly's voice she knew first and Polly's face that she first recognized.

4

I

Alicia had barely learned how to suck, when Elizabeth, after ten days'
of lying-in, descended one afternoon to the pleasant, sunny morning-
room on the ground floor. She was escorted solicitously down the stairs
by her friend, Sarah Webb, and was met by her elder daughter,
Florence, in the little sitting-room.

As her own confinement drew near, Florence looked white-faced and
drawn. She dreaded the birth of her baby, because she had no idea how
it would make its way into the world. There did not seem to be an
aperture big enough to give it access! She wondered if she would split
down the middle, like a pea pod giving up its peas, and the idea terrified
her. She was much too afraid of her stout, dogmatic husband, the Reverend Clarence Browning, to ask him. Having been taught nothing about
sex and having been horrified when Clarence took her on her honeymoon, she felt that life was vulgar enough, without giving him further
opportunity for lewd remarks and disgusting behaviour. She simply did
not believe frustrated Clarence's assurance that their sex life was
normal.

She was relieved to see her mother looking very elegant in a copper-
coloured gown with the hint of a train at the back and a velvet collar
edged with cream lace. It was comforting to realize that her mother had
always survived childbirth, despite whatever ordeals it presented.

With the aid of her friend and her elder daughter, Elizabeth was
gently eased into an armless easy chair near her work table in the
window. Florence had brought a bunch of fat, pink roses from her own
garden and had set them in a silver bowl on the table. She had also
thoughtfully placed her mother's workbasket by her chair. Her mother
still followed the old custom of making and embroidering her own petticoats and drawers, though Messrs George Henry Lee, a fashionable
shop in the town which made her dresses, cloaks and hats, would have
been happy to undertake the work for her.

Florence had already been up to the nursery to see Alicia, and now
she asked her mother if she had seen the child that day.

Elizabeth was silent for a moment. Then she said heavily, 'No. Polly will bring her down at teatime.'

'She *is* thriving, isn't she?'

'I believe so.'

Though Florence had herself been cared for by a nanny, she was worried about the little mite so summarily handed over to a wet-nurse. The baby seemed contented enough, but her mother showed no interest in it; and the nursery, when Flo had visited, appeared neither clean nor tidy. She had spoken sharply to Mrs Tibbs and to Polly about the need for cleanliness. Mrs Tibbs, all indignation, had promised to order the housemaid to turn the room out immediately.

Now, with Sarah Webb nodding agreement, she strove to awaken her mother's interest in Alicia. 'Polly needs supervision,' she told her.

Her mother merely sighed absently, unable to tell her daughter of the sweating fear within her. She asked Florence to serve each of them with a glass of port from the decanter on the sideboard and to hand round biscuits from the biscuit barrel; when her glass was given to her she drank the contents with unmannerly speed.

'It's a pity Papa won't keep a carriage, isn't it, Mama? Such a lovely afternoon. We could have gone for a drive round the park.'

Elizabeth replied acidly, 'You know that your father has money for everything – railways, roads, ships, are all he's interested in. Never thinks of my needs.'

Sarah Webb, anxious to cheer up her friend, broke in, 'Dear Elizabeth, if you don't mind being driven in a governess cart, I should be delighted to take you out. I stabled it in Crown Street during your confinement, so that I would have it close by. As you know, I can handle the reins quite well.'

The idea of being seen in her old friend's extremely shabby, humble vehicle, made Elizabeth shudder.

'No, no, Sarah, thank you. If I wished, I could, I suppose, hire a carriage from the stables. Thanks to my own dear Papa, I am not without funds for such things. And Andrew has managed my portion so well that it has increased.'

Elizabeth's dowry, legally tied up so that Humphrey could not touch it, provided her with a good wardrobe and sufficient pin money for small luxuries, like a hired carriage to take her shopping. But if Humphrey was so mean that he would not provide her with a fashionable vehicle, she preferred to put him in the wrong by being a martyr among her better-equipped friends. So, while Sarah and Florence sought to raise her spirits, she sighed and sulked, and looked forward with absolute dread to her husband's return from his office in the city.

She had not seen Humphrey since the night of Alicia's birth. As he had done for the past year, he had slept in the dressing-room next to their bedroom; in addition to the entrance to the bedroom, it had a door leading on to the landing, so he came and went without entering her room. Today, unless she feigned fatigue and returned to her bed, she would have to meet him at dinner. Later in the afternoon, Sarah and Florence would both go home and there would be no one present to make it necessary for him to control himself. The prospect made her feel sick, and she wondered what Andrew would do, if she ordered a carriage and fled to him.

As she drank her second glass of port and listened to Sarah and Florence talking about the joys of motherhood, she wanted to cry. Where was Andrew? He could have called or, at least, have sent some flowers from his wife and himself. He was her lawyer. He had every right to call on her. But in her heart she knew Andrew. He was in many ways weak; he would avoid a troublesome mistress as if she had the plague.

'Babies are such darlings,' gushed Sarah, none of whose nephews and nieces had ever been presented to her by their nannies, unless dry, fed and sleepy. She herself would not have known what to do with a sopping wet, hungry, howling infant, except to coo over it.

Florence was smart enough to realize this. She remembered her younger brother, Charles, with whom she had shared the nursery for a while; he had been anything but lovely. Clarence had told her flatly that they could not afford a nurse for their baby and that she must do the best she could with the aid of their cook-general and kitchen-maid. Because Charles was a boy, she had never seen him either bathed or changed. How did you change a small, wriggling creature like a baby? Or bathe it? Or put it to the breast? She hoped, rather frantically, that Mrs Macdonald, the midwife, would instruct her; she could not ask such vulgar questions of Mama. In some despair, she had made a point of arriving at her mother's house quite early, during the past ten days, having taken the horse-bus from home, so that she could go upstairs to watch Polly struggling with Alicia.

II

Polly was herself learning on the job, though she knew much more about birth and babies than poor Florence did. Before coming to the Woodman household, she had received some strict advice from her mother and from her Great-aunt Kitty, herself a midwife to the slum women around her. The result was that, much as she protested, Alicia was scoured twice daily from head to heel. To Fanny's irritation, the child was changed the moment she was damp; it was poor Fanny who had to carry the pails of dirty napkins, petticoats and gowns down to the cellar ready for the washerwoman.

'All for nought but a little bastard,' Fanny had muttered, as she heaved the heavy pails down the stairs.

To the Woodmans, Fanny was nothing but a quiet, little shadow responsible for all the coal fires in the house. As she went from room to room, she had become well aware of Andrew Crossing's interest in her mistress; raucous jokes at his expense had been a real source of entertainment on quiet evenings in the kitchen, as the maids sipped their fender ale.

Fanny had also seen something of the bitter fights between Elizabeth and Humphrey. When she went through the house to make up all the fires and they heard her knock, they would stop their shouting and upbraiding and would stand rigidly staring at each other while she poked up the fire and added more coal; as soon as she was out of the door, coal hod in hand, she would hear them renew the battle.

It was Fanny who danced out into the street to find a cab to take Florence home. She took her time because it was so lovely to be out in the afternoon sun, and, when she found one, Florence gave her twopence for her trouble.

Florence was thankful that her mother had insisted on giving her the money to pay for the cab; otherwise, she would have had to take the horse-bus again. Though Elizabeth had great faith that the Reverend Clarence Browning would make his way upwards in the Church and would, in due course, be able to afford a carriage, Florence was acutely aware that he was far too outspoken, far too direct, ever to be recommended for high office. Florence herself was content to preside over the little vicarage they occupied, thankful that a man so intent on the saving of souls had managed, in spite of church politics, to rise to a vicarage. She asked no more – except for a nanny.

In order to conserve her strength for the coming confrontation with Humphrey, Elizabeth tried to take a nap in the afternoon, but she was so filled with anxiety that she returned to the morning-room in time to take tea and to receive Polly and Alicia.

Alicia was hungry and was screaming. Elizabeth inquired of Polly if she had everything she needed for the child and then sent her thankfully back upstairs.

III

When Humphrey bowled swiftly into the dining-room for dinner, his white-faced wife was already seated, and Maisie, the parlourmaid, was hovering over the laden sideboard.

Humphrey ignored both of them. He indicated that he was ready to be served by simply shaking out his table napkin and spreading it across his stomach. In complete silence, Maisie served them both.

Never a man to waste anything, Humphrey ate his way stolidly through soup, roast beef and steamed pudding. He knew, as his wife had already sensed, that this was the evening to make clear his attitude towards Alicia, who, like his wife, he had hoped would either miscarry or be born dead.

Impotent rage surged through him. Hemmed in by the constrictions of social propriety, he was certain there was not a great deal he could do about the situation without coming to grief himself, and this knowledge added to his boiling anger. He helped himself to hot mustard and cursed under his breath when the condiment stuck to its spoon. He banged the tiny spoon on the side of his plate and in the tensely quiet room it sounded like a pistol going off.

Elizabeth kept her eyes down and picked uneasily at her food. Her mind leaped wildly between fear of Humphrey and heartbreak that she had not heard from Andrew.

She jumped when Humphrey asked for a second helping of pudding and more wine. Really, the man ate like a hog. The only thing he seemed to notice in the house was when Mrs Tibbs' cooking was not up to its usual standard.

Humphrey had, indeed, not noticed for months that his wife was pregnant. When he did, he had hastily checked his office diary. It told him with certainty that the child could not be his. Plump, comfortable Mrs Jakes kept him so exhausted that he had rarely slept with his wife. Elizabeth had not seemed to care about his neglect.

Elizabeth had been more than thankful to be relieved of her wifely duties. Her lifelong friend, Andrew Crossing, had been only too willing to meet her needs, since his wife was a useless invalid. As Maisie took away her untouched roast beef, she thought agonizedly of how she had rebelled against marrying Humphrey, how passionately she had loved her childhood playmate, Andrew. At nineteen, Andrew had had no money and had failed his first year at University; her father had been adamant that he was not suitable for her. In contrast, at twenty-five, Humphrey was already well-established with his father, in a brokerage business and, as the elder son, he was to inherit the entire enterprise.

What her father had not realized, Elizabeth fulminated, was that Humphrey was not only physically repellent to her, but also had the hoarding instincts of a jackdaw; his ambition was to accumulate capital to invest in shipping or railways. He lectured her regularly, from the days of their unhappy honeymoon onwards, on the fact that capital accumulated by personal savings was the only sure way to expand a business. Money made in a business should be ploughed back in. He had rationed her and, later, poor Flo, to two pairs of black woollen stockings and one pair of white silk every winter of her married life; any extra ones had had to be bought out of the money left her by her father. And he still went over Mrs Tibbs' account books with her each month and railed at her for waste.

It had taken twelve months of unmitigated pressure by her parents to make her marry him, twelve months during which no other young man had been allowed to get more than a single dance with her and she was never left alone.

It was Andrew himself who finally had broken her resolve.

At a banquet and ball given by the Mayor, Mr Gardner, to celebrate the marriage of the Prince of Wales to Princess Alexandra of Denmark, he had pushed his way through the throng, to find her sitting demurely beside her mother and her aunt, while her bearded father and his brother had gone to join their friends for a drink. He had formally asked for a waltz.

Her mother had answered frigidly for her. 'Elizabeth's programme is full, I am sorry.'

Elizabeth, faced with the handsome, blond, young man, had said desperately, as she handed him her tiny programme, 'I have one more dance to fill, Mama.' Two chaperones sitting near were watching the little exchange with interest, so, rather than cause a public fuss, her mother had said no more.

They had hardly taken a dozen steps, after Andrew came to claim her, when he blurted out, 'It's no good, Liz. I've tried to get the old man to persuade your father to allow an engagement, with no luck at all. He's furious with me for muffing my exams, and he's insisted that I begin all over again in law. Law's what I always wanted to do, anyway, but he was dead-set on my entering the church, so I had to do Divinity.'

'I can wait for you.' Elizabeth remembered her utter despair when she had realized that Andrew himself was backing out.

As they whirled amid the colourful throng of dancers, she had looked up at him and seen the tremulous uncertainty in his face; he had always been weak, she thought bitterly, as she contemplated her steamed pudding, and in her heart she knew without doubt that he had again deserted her. She wished that Mrs Macdonald had not been quite so skilful, and that she had died having Alicia.

Her reverie was broken by Humphrey's saying to Maisie, 'The Mistress will take her tea in the drawing-room.'

Elizabeth swallowed. Humphrey was choosing the field of combat, the upstairs room from which loud voices were least likely to be heard by the servants.

'Yes, Sir. I'll ask Fanny to make sure the fire is made up.'

While Humphrey ate his gorgonzola cheese and biscuits there was a flurry in the kitchen as a swearing Fanny fled upstairs with a shovel full of burning coals from the kitchen fire, to start a fire in the drawing-room. She had been so sure that the room would not be used that evening, there being no visitors, that she had not bothered to light the fire.

Elizabeth thought resignedly, 'So be it. What does it matter?' and went up to sit by the struggling blaze. Though it was May, the room was cold and clammy. Outside the tall, velvet-draped windows, a fine rain was falling. Elizabeth picked up a shawl and flung it around her shivering shoulders.

If Andrew had been anything but a family lawyer, she would have taken a chance and run to him now, told some suitable story to his fragile, rheumaticky Eleanor, and simply stayed with him, daring him to say a word. But in his profession, he dealt with the Estates of a number of widows, with Trusteeships like her own dowry. The slightest hint of scandal and he would lose a lot of business.

When she had told him of the coming child, he had immediately and fearfully repudiated any idea that he was the father. It had hurt her immeasurably.

'Humphrey will know it is not his,' she had replied dully.

'You're married to him, so the child will be born in wedlock.'

'Not if he denies it.'

They had been sitting, arms around each other on the big sofa facing her now, and he had drawn away from her. He had walked stiffly up and down the room, while she stared at him aghast. He had finally turned towards her and said through lips that quivered slightly, 'Come on, Liz. It can't be mine.'

'It can be and it is.'

'I simply don't believe it. I've never fathered a child before.' He came to sit down beside her, and added in a wheedling tone, 'Anyway, you can manage Humphrey, I'm sure.'

Tears sprang to her eyes. 'You don't know him. He's got a a murderous temper.'

She had wept and had implored him to take her away – to Italy, to

513

anywhere they could live together. But the irresolute boy had grown into a vacillating man, and gradually she had realized that, if she pressed him, he would abandon her entirely.

She had bravely dried her tears and said that, somehow, she would brazen it out with Humphrey. In an almost motherly fashion she had decided that he probably needed protection against a scandal more than she did.

'Don't worry, sweetheart,' she whispered, as he thankfully said his farewells. 'Just find a place where we can meet more safely than this. I love you, remember.'

He had replied, somewhat woodenly, that he loved her, too, and that he would find a trysting place.

His visits had grown rarer, however; he did not attempt to make love to her and she began to despair. Through the last months of her pregnancy, she had reassured herself again and again that he was merely being careful for the sake of the child, but, in more realistic moments, black hopelessness had almost overwhelmed her.

'Well, you slut. What have you to say?' Her husband had come into the room so quickly and so quietly that she had not heard him. Without warning, he clouted her across the back of her head.

Determined to feign innocence, she cried out indignantly, 'Humphrey, what did you do that for?'

'I suppose you think you're going to fob off Crossing's brat on me? Thought you'd get away with it?'

The blow had made her reel in her chair. Now she tried to rally herself. 'Humphrey, how could you say such a thing?' She angrily pushed some hairpins back into her bun. 'And to strike me, when I've only just got up from childbed. You must be drunk.'

He stood facing her, head thrust forward, his lips drawn back from tobacco-stained teeth. 'Don't try that on me. I know what's been going on – and now we've got a bastard in the house.' His hand shot forward and slapped her a stinging blow across the mouth, followed by another one with his left hand. 'And you, milady, are going to pay for it. This brat isn't mine and you know it.'

Shocked and terrified, she stared back at him, in too much pain to speak.

He pushed his face close to hers. 'You know, don't you?'

She edged to the side of her armless chair and slid out of it with what dignity she could muster. 'You must be mad!' she muttered, from between her swelling lips. 'You're my husband – it's normal to have babies.'

'I've not been with you for over a year – and you must know it. *And* I know about your happy afternoon hours with Crossing.'

Her eyes shot wider open, but she answered as steadily as she could, 'Andrew's my lawyer. He has to manage father's Trust for Clara and me, so, of course, he comes to consult me. Anyway, we've known him for years.' She held her hand to her mouth and closed her eyes with pain. Then she said, half-crying, 'If my brother were in England, you wouldn't dare to say such dreadful things – or hit me! And for no reason!'

'That jigger rabbit is three thousand miles away, in Ceylon. He'd be ashamed of you, anyway.' He advanced towards her and she hastily put the width of the chair between them and began to back towards the door. As she fumbled with the handle, he caught her by the shoulder and spun her back into the room, her full skirts splaying out round her. She stumbled and fell, face down.

He whipped his razor strop out of his pocket. Raising his arm, he brought it down across her shoulders with all the force he could muster. She screamed and covered her head with her arms as the wicked leather strap whistled down on her again. Four months of suppressed outrage were vented on her, as she sought to crawl away from him and reach the door.

'I've been waiting for this,' he yelled at her. 'I hope you enjoy it.' The strop came down again across the back of her head.

Her screams stopped. She lay immobile.

He paused, scarlet-faced, panting over her, the desire to rape her urgent in him. He heaved up her heavily gathered skirt, but she was tightly entangled in her three petticoats. He tore at his trousers and emptied himself over her.

'You damned Jezebel,' he snarled and kicked her in the stomach. She did not move.

'Go to hell,' he shrieked. 'Look at another man, and I'll make sure you do.'

He flung open the door, and ran down into the hall, buttoning up his trousers as he went. He seized his hat and stick from the rack and went out of the front door muttering like a madman. Five minutes later, he was sitting primly on the horse-bus on his way to visit Mrs Jakes.

515

5

I

Fanny found her when she came to rake the cinders out of the fireplace before going to bed.

With a frightened squeak, she dropped her coal hod and knelt down to turn her mistress over. When she saw the swollen lips and tear-stained cheeks, she knew what had happened; she had seen the same thing so often in her aunt's home.

'Oh, Missus! Can you sit up, Missus? Look, I'll turn yez on your back and give you a heave up.'

Elizabeth moaned as she managed to turn and raise herself sufficiently to lean her head against the little skivvy's shoulder. Fanny swallowed, and looked desperately around. 'Is anythin' broke, d'yer think?' she asked.

Elizabeth shuddered, then whispered, 'I don't think so.' She began to cry.

'Well, let's try and get you on that low chair there, and then I'll run and get Maisie to help you up to your bed.'

'Not Maisie,' Elizabeth murmured. 'Or the others.' She paused, her breath coming slowly and heavily. 'Ask Polly – she'll mind her own business.'

She cried out in pain as Fanny slowly sat her upright while she brought the small chair closer, and moaned again as she was eased up on to it.

'There, Ma'am. Lean your head against the high back, and I'll be back with Polly in half a mo'.'

As she flew to the door, Elizabeth halted her by saying hoarsely, 'Not a word of this – from either Polly or you – to the other servants.'

Fanny had been thrilled at the idea of telling everyone about the drama on which she had stumbled. But, as Elizabeth spoke, she realized that to her mistress it was a terrible humiliation. She warmed with pity and said reassuringly, as she went out, 'Of course, Missus. Don't worry, Missus.'

Once Elizabeth had been laid gently on her bed, Polly sent Fanny back to the kitchen, where Mrs Tibbs promptly scolded her for being so long in doing her raking out, and sent her off to bed.

Elizabeth said stiffly, 'I shall be all right now, Polly.' She lay on her side, legs curled up, arms crossed over her injured face.

'I'll help you undress, Ma'am. Fanny said she thought your back was hurt. Let me have a look, Ma'am. If you've got any arnica, I could paint it on the bruises. First, will I get some brandy from the Master's study?'

'No!'

'Don't worry, Ma'am. He's out. He won't miss a small glass, Ma'am.'

With one hand, Elizabeth gestured to indicate reluctant agreement.

In the hope that it would ease her mistress's pain, Polly brought a generous glass of Humphrey's brandy, and, after Elizabeth had swallowed it, she allowed Polly to unbutton her dress.

'Jaysus!' Polly exclaimed, when she saw Elizabeth's back. Weals ran across it from the hairline to just below the waist. Where her corset had softened some of the blows, the marks were scarlet; above that, they were purple. 'It's a miracle if nothin's broken, Ma'am. We should get the doctor.'

'We can't, Polly.' She looked up at the other woman, tears beginning to course again down her ravaged face. She had given no explanation of her situation, because it was obvious that both Polly and Fanny had guessed what had happened; wife-beating was common enough amongst the lower classes, though it might have surprised them how often it occurred amongst their so-called betters.

'No, Ma'am. I do understand, Ma'am. I'll get the arnica from your medicine chest and maybe that'll do the trick.'

While she carefully sponged the bruised back with cold water and then applied the arnica, she was thinking fast. 'Would it be best, Ma'am, if you went to stay with someone? 'ave you got a sister or anybody? Till things blow over, like?'

Her mistress winced, as Polly dabbed on the tincture, and replied frankly, 'Last time he beat me, I went to my sister in West Kirby. She told me it was my fault and I shouldn't provoke him. She's unmarried and doesn't understand,' she finished brokenly.

Polly sighed. 'What about Miss Florence's?'

'She has a difficult life herself – and her baby is due any moment.' Elizabeth's voice strengthened. 'I don't want *anyone* to know, Polly. The disgrace would be more than I can bear. That's why I sent for you instead of Rosie or Maisie. You seem to keep to yourself.'

'Aye, you was right. I'll keep me mouth shut.' She eased her mistress's nightgown over her head, and then she blurted out, 'It were that Maisie wot is the root of the trouble. She told 'im every time, accordin' to Rosie.'

Elizabeth's eyes opened slowly. 'Told him what?'

'Told 'im when Mr Crossing called – and 'ow long 'e stayed.'

'Good Heavens!'

'He give 'er a shillin' every time.'

'Ach!' Elizabeth was sickened. 'Are you sure, Polly?'

'I wouldn't put it past her.'

Never in her life before had Elizabeth spoken so frankly to a servant. But never before had she needed an understanding friend more. Now she said grimly, 'I'll dismiss her. And I'll make sure she's gone before Humphrey finds out.'

'Yes, Ma'am.' Polly was putting her mistress's clothes away. Now she examined the back of the gown Elizabeth had been wearing. 'I think your dress is ruined, Ma'am.' She held it up for Elizabeth to see and lifted the candle closer to it.

Elizabeth heaved, and Polly hastily dropped the dress and picked up the bowl holding the water she had used to bathe the bruises. 'Take a big breath, Ma'am,' she ordered the sickened woman.

The nausea subsided, only to rise again each time she remembered what Humphrey had done. 'Oh, Polly,' she moaned, 'how could he?'

'Better outside than inside, Ma'am,' replied Polly with a quick quirk of humour. 'You can do without another baby.' Elizabeth heaved and brought up the brandy and what little dinner she had eaten. Afterwards, she said, 'Wrap up the dress and put it in the midden – bury it under some of the rubbish.'

'Oh, aye, Ma'am. Don't you worry about it.'

Polly put it about that Elizabeth had tripped over her gown and had fallen, hitting her face on the doorknob of her room. 'Made a couple o' rotten bruises on her cheeks and mouth,' she told Mrs Tibbs.

Mrs Tibbs had heard similar excuses several times before and simply shrugged slightly and went on with her cooking.

While Humphrey went on with his life as if nothing had happened, Elizabeth stayed in bed for three days. When she was ready to descend, she put on a black silk dress with a high neck edged with white frilling and dressed her hair low on her neck, to disguise the terrible bruise now yellowing there. A heavy dusting of rice flour helped the marks on her face. She sat silently in her favourite chair in the morning-room, her sewing untouched on her lap, and hoped Florence would not call for a few days more.

At dinner, she sat at her usual place at the foot of the table. She never raised her eyes, except to order Maisie to serve or to clear the table. Humphrey smiled at her – it was not a pleasant smile and it filled her with dread; in the months that followed she rarely spoke to him.

For several months, she cancelled her At Homes and invited no one to dinner, neither did she accept any invitations; she gave as the reason that Alicia's birth had been difficult. As time went by and Andrew Crossing did not communicate with her, she felt physically and mentally ill.

She waited patiently until Humphrey went to Manchester to stay with his brother, Harold, for a few days. Then she gave Maisie a week's pay in lieu of notice and told her to pack her bags. When Maisie protested, Elizabeth told her that they had decided to reduce staff.

'I want to speak to the Master,' retorted Maisie mutinously.

'Don't be insolent,' ordered Elizabeth coldly. 'I decide who works in this house. And it is I who will write references for you. Do you want to be turned off without a reference?'

At this deadly threat, Maisie caved in. Rosie was promoted to wait at table. When Humphrey noticed that Maisie was missing, he was forced to ask his wife where she was. She told him frigidly, between clenched teeth, that she was not going to be spied upon by a servant and that Rosie was quite satisfactory as parlourmaid. To get even with her, Humphrey told her that she would have to manage without a replacement girl.

Rosie came into the room, bringing another bottle of wine for which Humphrey had sent her, so Elizabeth sat stonily eating her dessert and did not reply.

Rosie and Fanny had to carry the work of a housemaid between them, and Rosie remarked thankfully that she would be married to the milkman by the end of the year. Fanny, who to her joy had had her wages quietly raised by a shilling a week, said nothing. She was learning to be a housemaid and that was real promotion for her.

II

'When is Alicia to be christened, Mama?' inquired Florence, when finally her mother ordered a carriage from the stable and went out to visit her.

'Well, I thought dear Clarence might do it in your church. It would be so nice to keep it in the family, wouldn't it? I'll get Mrs Tibbs to make a christening cake.' She paused and took a nervous sip of the Reverend Clarence's atrocious sherry from the glass in her hand. Then she babbled, 'Charles went straight from school this year to stay for a few days with one of his friends – I thought as soon as he came home – a nice little family party?' Her voice trailed off. She knew she could not face having the christening in her own church, St Margaret's in Princes Road. It was almost certain that Humphrey would not attend it – and that would cause enormous speculation, a fresh flurry of unwanted interest.

Florence felt that her mother was being unreasonable in getting her to have the party; it could be quite a large one, she thought wearily, if all her father's relations came and her mother's friends, not to speak of Aunt Clara from West Kirby, who was such a professional invalid that she would rearrange the whole Browning house to suit her convenience. 'I hope that I'm not taken to bed at the wrong moment, Mama,' she said anxiously.

'Well, then we'll make it a joyful double christening,' responded Elizabeth unfeelingly.

III

Elizabeth had been thankful that her younger son, Charles, had been away in boarding school during the more obvious period of her pregnancy and during her lying-in; she had certainly not wanted the cold, dark blue eyes of a ten-year-old examining her during this confinement.

When confiding to Sarah Webb, her oldest friend, the secret of her unwelcome breeding, she had wept on Sarah's shoulder, afraid of Humphrey, afraid of the hazard of giving birth at forty years of age. Speaking of Charles, she had added, 'Children always sense when something is wrong. And Charles always wants such precise answers to a question.'

Sarah sighed, and stroked her friend's dark hair. She had not only known Charles all his short life, but had been friends with Elizabeth and with Andrew Crossing since they first attended the same children's Christmas parties together. She had watched with pity, as her beautiful young friend had been bullied by her parents into marriage with Humphrey.

But Elizabeth had loved languid, charming Andrew, fair as some Icelandic god, a boy who appeared slow and lazy to her parents. His charm had, however, served him well in his subsequent career as a family lawyer, Sarah ruminated; even she herself, plain and studious, had worshipped from afar. She had been present at a ball, a few years back, at which Elizabeth had met and danced with him again; up till then, his old senior partner had always dealt with the affairs of Elizabeth's father's estate, so they had rarely seen each other. That winter, Andrew's senior partner died and the care of Elizabeth's affairs came into the hands of Andrew. Sarah had been greatly worried when Elizabeth promptly asked him to her next At Home.

'Is it wise, my dear?' she had asked, as she arranged her furs in front of Elizabeth's mirror before going home. She was the last guest to leave and Elizabeth herself was prinking before the mirror.

'I don't care,' Elizabeth had hissed savagely.

'Well, ask his wife as well,' suggested Sarah.

'I did – but you know and I know she can't stir out of the house – she's stiff as a board with rheumatism and she has to be carried everywhere. And, anyway,' she went on defiantly, '*anybody* may call on At Home days.'

Sarah sighed glumly. 'It's foolish, my dear – very foolish.'

Elizabeth bridled, and twirled in front of the mirror to show her fine, plump figure.

Over coffee in Elizabeth's morning-room the following day, Sarah had argued again.

'I can't help it, Sarah.' Elizabeth's wide dark blue eyes, so like those of her son, Charles, had a hint of tears in them. 'I must see him,' she said, 'I simply have to. Humphrey has his fancy woman – surely Andrew and I can be friends.'

Sarah bit her lips and said no more.

IV

When young Charles finally came home at the end of June, Elizabeth met him at Lime Street station.

Charles had spent his Easter holidays with his Uncle Harold and his cousins in Manchester, so he had not seen his mother since the previous Christmas. She looked suddenly much older than he remembered, but when he inquired about her health as the hackney carriage traversed Lime Street, she told him brightly that she was quite well. She added that he now had a baby sister called Alicia – and, of course new babies were notorious for being rather tiring little people.

'Well, that's nice,' he responded politely, 'having a little sister, I mean.' He was not really very interested. Babies came in all the households that he visited; they often died. He vaguely remembered having a baby brother who had died very young, though, when he thought about it, it was the memory of his elder brother, Edward, being upset about it that had stayed with him. Death had always upset Edward; funny that he should have become a soldier.

Reminded that Edward was now a fixture in the 11th Foot, he also recalled a conversation he had once overheard between his father and Edward. His father had been furious when Edward had refused to join his brokerage firm and had asked permission to join the army instead. He recalled his father shouting that it cost money to maintain a son as an officer in the army, and Edward replying nervously that it might not cost as much as sending him to university to study Divinity, so that he could enter the Church.

Charles guessed that the main thing Edward wanted to do after finishing boarding school was to leave home. He had been awfully stubborn and finally his father had given way.

Their father had, later, talked to Charles about the advantages of joining the family firm. Though Charles thought that buying and selling stocks and shares would be a dreadfully dull way of earning a living, he had not dared to say any such thing to his father; he had merely smiled what he hoped was a nice little-boy smile, and said nothing. His maths teacher, old Fancy Moppit, wanted him to take more chemistry and maths and think about going to university. He wondered, now, if his father would pay for university.

'Have you heard from Edward lately?' he asked Elizabeth. 'I got a card from him at Easter, but I haven't heard since.'

'Not *got a card,* Charles – *received* a card.'

Charles grimaced, and said, 'Yes, Mama.'

'I heard from Edward quite recently. He is in Burma – and he's a full Lieutenant, now.'

'Oh, cheers!'

Charles was glad to be home for the remainder of the summer. Though nothing very interesting ever happened there, Mrs Tibbs produced all his favourite dishes and his mother didn't mind how much he read. Probably the family would go, as usual, for two weeks' seaside holiday in North Wales, and he would be able to add to his extensive collection of shells; he already had a glass case full of them, each neatly tagged with its Latin name.

After he had been down to the kitchen to see Mrs Tibbs, he climbed the five flights of stairs from the basement to the top floor, to see his new sister, Alicia. 'Her nurse's name is Polly. Be polite to her,' his mother had instructed.

Rosie and Fanny were left to toil up the stairs with his trunks.

'Holy God! Wot's he got in 'em?' puffed Fanny, as they paused for rest on the second landing.

'Books,' opined Rosie. 'Proper little bookworm, he is.'

Polly was glad to have a young boy sleeping in the back room across the landing. As Fanny had said, it could feel ghosty away at the top of the house; Rosie and Fanny shared a basement room and Mrs Tibbs had her own private bed-sitting room off the kitchen.

In case Charles came into the nursery while she was feeding Alicia, Polly took to wearing a shawl over her shoulders so that she could cover her breasts. She had been instructed by Elizabeth to keep Charles out of the day nursery at such moments, but, as Fanny said, 'If he don't learn now how a baby's fed, he may not know never.' So Charles learned a few interesting facts of life that summer. He also watched her being bathed, one day, and observed that she did not have a penis; this confirmed what other boys had told him, that girls did not have such appendages. He found it very peculiar.

The day after his return, he went out to visit Florence in the company of his mother and Miss Sarah Webb, and attended Alicia's christening. He noted uneasily that Florence was uncommonly stout, but he dared not comment on it.

To Florence's mystification, Humphrey and Uncle Harold and his wife, Vera, did not attend the christening; they had urgent business to attend to in London that day. Elizabeth bought the customary silver christening mug and had it engraved, *To Alicia Beatrix Mary, from her loving parents, July 1886*.

Elizabeth had written to Andrew and his wife, inviting them to the christening. She received no reply and, after the christening tea, she had retired to Florence's privy and wept at the snub. She wondered if Mrs Crossing had even been shown the invitation.

As the long summer holiday progressed, Charles began to feel bored. He inquired of his mother when they would be taking their holiday in Wales. He was taken aback when Elizabeth snapped at him sharply that Papa was far too busy this year to think about holidays.

Feeling contrite about her peevishness, Elizabeth asked him if he would like to spend a few days with his Aunt Clara at West Kirby.

'Not really, Mama,' he replied. Though Aunt Clara lived by the sea, her many ailments did not make her appealing to him.

He began to accompany Polly when she wheeled Alicia in her pram through Princes Park. He liked Polly; she had never seen either shells or seaweed or even sand and had shown a most respectful interest when he had explained what they were.

In the park, she always paused for a little chat with a young gardener weeding the flower beds; he regularly managed to be working somewhere along the usual route of their walk, and Charles teased Polly about him.

In the course of one of their walks, Charles discovered that Polly could not read. He stopped in the middle of the sandy carriageway, and stared up at the handsome young woman. 'Really?'

She smiled down at him mischievously. 'Aye. I don't know nothin', 'cept lookin' after Miss Alicia and a few things like that.'

He began walking again, kicking a stone along in front of him. 'I'd have thought you would be able to read easily. Servants always know so much.'

'I suppose they do – folks like Mrs Tibbs. But me? I only scrubbed doorsteps and cleaned brasses and helped me Mam sell fents in the market sometimes, afore I were married.'

'What are fents?'

'Bits of old or damaged cloth – for dusters, like.'

'I see. I didn't know you were married.'

'I'm not no more . . .' Her voice faltered. In the weeks since she had been with the Woodmans, she had wept fairly constantly, alone in her windowless garret. Her only comfort had been the delicious sensation of Alicia's contented sucking at her breast. 'Me oosband,' she picked up again, 'he were killed in the docks.'

'How dreadful!' Charles was genuinely shocked. He understood that to be a widow was very hard; even the Bible said that you had to look after the widowed and the fatherless.

'It were proper awful,' Polly confided to him. 'And me baby died – so I come to look after Miss Alicia.' She smiled sadly down at the sleeping child in the old basketware pram in which Charles himself had been wheeled as an infant.

'Well, I'm glad you did come. These hols are boring enough. Say, would you like to learn to read? It's easy, once you know how. I've still got my first books up in my bedroom – and I bet there are some girls' books in Flo's old bedroom. I could teach you in the evenings.'

So that summer Polly learned to read and discovered a wonderful dream world.

She also learned to sew better than she had previously done. Elizabeth sent up to the nursery loads of sheets and other household linens, demanding that they be neatly darned or patched; servants should be kept busy, according to Elizabeth.

At first, Polly had been appalled at the huge pile of mending, but Elizabeth had told Rosie to instruct her, particularly on how to patch and how to turn a sheet *sides to middle*, and they both spent long evening hours by Polly's single candle carefully weaving their needles in and out of the heavy linen cloth.

When Alicia had acquired a pattern of sleep and it was fairly certain that she would continue to sleep for an hour or two, Polly took a piece of sewing down to the big basement kitchen and sat for a little while with Rosie and Mrs Tibbs round the roaring fire in the kitchen range. 'I'll go crackers if I don't have a bit of a jangle with somebody,' she told Mrs Tibbs, and Mrs Tibbs had agreed that a little gossip was necessary to one's sanity. Except for minor squabbles, they got along together fairly well and they would talk about the neighbours and their servants, about the Woodman family and their own families, while Fanny toiled through the washing-up and the scouring of the big, soot-covered iron saucepans.

From these agreeable sessions, Polly began to learn how such a fine house was run, how you could acquire a few perks to take home, like a half-used tablet of soap, nearly finished bottles of wine or perfume, odds and ends like buttons, discarded in the wastepaper basket. In addition Mr Bittle, the gardener, according to Fanny, would sometimes provide a few windfall apples or pears or even a seedling geranium in a pot. 'Me auntie were made up when I bring 'er a little geranium,' she confided to Polly, as she sat down on a nursery chair to rest, after bringing up a hod of coal. 'Mrs Tibbs makes quite a bit on the side, Rosie says. She'll take a slice or two off a joint or a little bitty butter or cheese – not much, but it adds up to a meal or two by the time 'er day off come around. She takes it to 'er sister.'

Another time, she remarked, 'Ould Woodie is a mingy master, a proper pinchpenny, so he's askin' for theft. I suppose the Missus is used to 'im being mean and pokin' his nose into the housekeepin' book. And him payin' out for his fancy woman; the poor Missus must lose out because of her,' she giggled knowingly.

Polly laughed. Then she said more soberly, 'It's hard when you've no man interested in yez.'

As Polly's grief over Patrick diminished, she had begun to look for someone to replace him; she was young and strong and could not imagine life without a man in it. But she lived in a world of women domestics, and the valet of the Colonel who lived next door was, she soon found, not interested in females. 'And he a fine lookin' man,' she tut-tutted to Fanny. Fanny's reply was ribald in the extreme.

Every time Polly went home to see her parents, however, she was reminded how lucky she was. The stench of sewage and the lack of even a decent cup of tea had not bothered her in earlier days – she had taken hardship for granted; but not any longer.

The overcrowding had been lessened by the removal of her paternal aunt and her five children to another cellar, but she was grieved to see her struggling mother grow progressively wearier and her unemployed father more despairing. She gave them most of the two shillings a week

525

she earned, and, after her few hours of freedom, she would return thankfully to the nursery, to have only the smell of the baby round her and to know that tea might not be a very large meal but it would certainly arrive.

Though not given to pondering on what the future held, she began to consider how she could continue working for the Woodmans after Alicia was weaned. As a possible alternative, she dreamed occasionally of the gardener in Princes Park. He had never asked her out but he always seemed glad to see her. If he were promoted, he might be given a tied cottage in the park; they were sometimes provided for more senior gardeners. There he might be able to keep a pig and grow some vegetables – and keep a wife.

Unlike Rosie, she did not meet the tradesmen who came to the house and lingered round the back door until they were sent packing by Mrs Tibbs or, in the case of the grocer, invited into her private bed-sitting room to discuss the week's groceries.

In the darkness of the early morning, Rosie, the house-parlourmaid, used to scurry down the path in the back garden, to get a kiss and a quick fondle from the milkman, who was courting her. Then, trembling with desire, she would rush back into the house and tear upstairs to wash out the great bath with its mahogany surround, before Humphrey Woodman got up. She would lay out his cut-throat razor, his moustache scissors and his shaving cup on the bathroom dressing-table and wipe down his leather razor strop which hung on the wall beside the sink.

'He used to tan 'is sons' hides with his razor strop,' Rosie told Polly. 'I remember Master Edward gettin' it so hard once, he fainted. And even then he never lifted a finger against 'is Pa. Loovely young man, Master Edward is; always says "thank you".'

Rocking the baby in her arms as she paused at the doorway of the bathroom she was not allowed to use, Polly remembered the dreadful state of Elizabeth's back after she had been beaten and she wondered if he had used the strop on her. No one, she thought passionately, should use a strop on such a pretty lady, no matter what she had done. Since that day, she had more than once found her Mistress with tears on her face. She wondered what else he had done to her, and she shivered.

6

I

Elizabeth had no idea whether her husband had expressed any feelings in public about the new arrival in the family, but she suspected that Maisie had done so and that the news of Alicia's doubtful origins had reached some of her acquaintances. Certainly, the number of invitations she usually received had dropped off, and one or two ladies appeared not to have seen her when she met them while out walking.

Her conscience told her that, as Andrew and she moved through their usual group before the birth, mutual friends must have sensed the attachment between them – and her pregnancy, at so late an age, must have caused speculation behind delicately waving ball fans.

She decided that she did not care; she would brazen it out. And Humphrey could take himself to hell, as long as he kept her. Once she had recovered from the beating, she had done some urgent arithmetic, and had decided that she could not possibly live on her marriage settlement from her father; it provided pin money, but that was all.

In her despair, she had considered writing to her brother in Ceylon and asking if she could make a home with him; but he had always been a poor correspondent and lived up country on his tea plantation, sharing a house with his partner. Two bachelors together, she thought wryly, would not want to be saddled with a woman. And it was said that men sometimes, well, sometimes did intimate things together – and she could not face the possibility of that.

So she decided to use Humphrey to her own advantage. If he threatened to beat her again, she would say sharply that she would show the bruises to the wives of his business associates. Stiff-necked Presbyterians, most of them, they might feel she deserved it, but faced with it, they would freeze out Humphrey. They'd be a pack of Pontius Pilates, she thought maliciously.

The armed truce prevailed, with occasional tiresome arguments which never resolved anything.

Though Elizabeth's friends might snub her, Humphrey found, to his embarrassment, that when he met business acquaintances accompanied by their wives, several of the ladies inquired after Elizabeth's health and whether the baby had been a boy or a girl.

The same thing happened when he attended social events alone. Where was dear Elizabeth and how was the new baby?

He knew he must, to save unwanted conjecture, persuade Elizabeth to accompany him occasionally, and he must learn to reply civilly to polite inquiries. He could not ignore both mother and daughter indefinitely. His Manchester brother, Harold, and his wife, Vera, had been offended at not being asked to the christening, and he had told them that it had been very quiet because Elizabeth was still weak and Florence was in the family way herself. Though his brother accepted this, Vera felt that it confirmed her own suspicions.

At St Margaret's Church, Humphrey and Elizabeth stood side by side each Sunday morning in frigid silence. He hoped that she had been privately Churched, attended a traditional service of thanksgiving; otherwise, the minister would ask awkward questions.

Elizabeth had, indeed, been Churched. One morning, she had kneeled alone before the priest, while he intoned over her Psalm 127, with its uncomfortable references to men with quivers full of arrows, and she wept quietly for Andrew Crossing, the darling of her youth, who had deserted her. In a worldly way, she knew he had been wise to slip quietly out of her life, by the simple process of handing over her legal work to one of his partners. She knew he should have done it long before. But it hurt.

It was common enough for women to cry after giving birth, so the priest ignored the tears stealing down Elizabeth's cheeks. He was, however, kind enough to invite her into the vicarage, where he handed her over to his sister, who kept house for him. She was a fussy, plain woman who produced a strong cup of tea and ten minutes' bracing conversation on the joys of having children. It gave Elizabeth time to blow her nose, before walking home.

III

Alicia's first Boxing Day was a Sunday. Harold and Vera Woodman, accompanied by their three sons, came to spend the day with Elizabeth and Humphrey. At tea time, Alicia was brought down by Polly and laid in her mother's arms; she behaved admirably and gurgled and smiled at the company.

Aunt Vera stroked the fine down of ash-blonde hair on the child's head. 'She's as fair as a lily – and with such light grey eyes,' she remarked, watching Elizabeth's face.

Elizabeth bent her own dark head over the baby and kissed it. 'My brother is quite fair,' she lied; at least *he* was not likely to come home for years; with luck, his black hair would have turned white before he returned to England.

Humphrey chewed his moustache and turned to look out of the lace-draped window. His brother and nephews joined him – babies were not very interesting, particularly when they were girls.

Vera pursed her lips and made no further comment. She brought out from her reticule an ivory ring with two silver bells attached to it. 'Here, Alicia,' she said. 'Here is a pretty present from Father Christmas for you.'

Alicia clutched at the ring, and Elizabeth sighed with relief.

When, the following year, the Queen's Jubilee was being celebrated in Liverpool, Elizabeth's sister, Clara, came to stay and to join in the festivities. She was older than Elizabeth and lived in a small house left her by their father, in the village of West Kirby on the Wirral Peninsula. She had been ill with bronchitis at the time of Alicia's birth and this had left her with a painful cough, making travelling too arduous for her. Thanks to the patient ministrations of her companion-help, she was now feeling better, and had come to see her new niece.

She was a spinster and sometimes quite lonely. When she saw the little girl in Polly's arms, she said impulsively to Elizabeth, 'You must bring her to stay with me. The sea air will put some colour into those pale, little cheeks.'

When Elizabeth demurred that the presence of a young child might put too much strain on her delicate health, the older woman replied, 'Let Polly come as well.'

So Alicia's early childhood was enlivened by visits to the seaside, occasionally accompanied by Elizabeth, more often by Polly. Though frail and slow-moving, Aunt Clara taught her niece how to build sandcastles and took her to collect shells and to paddle in the shallow pools left by the tide.

Polly had never seen the sea before and was, at first, terrified of its bouncing waves. She soon discovered with Alicia the joys of paddling and she, too, looked forward to these little holidays.

Humphrey had invested money in a railway line to link West Kirby with Liverpool. Because it failed to draw enough passengers and part of it had to run in a tunnel under the Mersey, which was more expensive than expected, he suffered a resounding financial loss. When, finally, it did go through, it was a joyous occasion for Alicia, because dear delicate Aunt Clara could then so easily visit the house in Upper Canning Street. Humphrey was consoled by the fact that a piece of land that he had, years before, bought in West Kirby suddenly became immensely valuable because it lay close to the new station. He sold it for housing development, at a handsome profit.

IV

'Wot you goin' to do when our Allie goes to school?' Fanny asked Polly, as, one night, she snatched a moment in the nursery to rest her aching feet. She had asked a similar question when, at eighteen months of age, Alicia had finally been weaned.

At that time, Polly had been very troubled. The under-gardener in the park, of whom she had had hopes, had failed to appear during two successive walks. According to a surly park-keeper, he had been dismissed for impudence. Polly's dream of presiding over a tied cottage with a small pigsty vanished with him. A brief encounter with a regular soldier, also met in the park, had come to an abrupt end when his regiment was sent to India. Statistics were against Polly's ever marrying again; the district had far more women than it had men.

The longer Polly continued to live in the comfort of the nursery attic, the less she wanted to return to the teeming slum in which she had been raised. A high standard of living, she found, was very easy to get used to. She had been thankful when Elizabeth had used her, in part, to replace Maisie.

Fanny was now a small, pinched seventeen-year-old and had replaced Rosie as a housemaid. Rosie had married the milkman as soon as he was satisfied that she was pregnant; a working man had to be certain that his wife could have children to maintain him in his old age.

A tweenie was no longer employed to care for fires, empty slops and carry water. Instead, Humphrey ordered Elizabeth to employ a charwoman, who came early in the morning to clean out the fireplaces and remake the fires. She also filled all the coal scuttles. To cut down on the carrying of water, more use was made of the bathroom taps, though the servants were still not allowed to wash themselves or use the lavatory in the bathroom. Elizabeth ended a custom of centuries, abandoned the chamber-pot under her bed and trailed along to the bathroom; she felt it was a real hardship.

Safe in the nursery with Polly, for many years Alicia understood little of the bitterness which lay between her mother and Humphrey Woodman. She learned early, however, from Polly that Papa was to be feared and that she should keep out of his way. As soon as the child could talk Polly taught her that the pretty lady who lived downstairs was to be obeyed without question, no matter how unhappy her decisions made little girls and nannies. Nannies said, 'Yes, Ma'am, of course, Ma'am.' Little girls said, 'Yes, Mama,' she instructed.

Alicia's first day at Miss Schreiber's Preparatory School approached and Polly was again worried.

'I suppose I'll have to look for another place,' she sighed to Fanny. 'It'll fairly kill me to leave little Allie – she's my baby more'n anybody else's.' She glanced across to where Alicia was kneeling on a chair at the table. She was quarrelling with Florence's elder son, Frank. They were playing Snakes and Ladders and she was protesting to the boy that he must slide down every snake on which his counter landed. He retorted that if he wanted to he could slide down only every other one. A fight threatened, and Polly got up to settle the squabble.

'Now, you play nicely, Master Frank, or I'll send you home.'

Frank looked at her mutinously, picked up the board and tipped the counters off it, then slid down from his chair to go to the rocking-horse. Still watching Polly, he climbed on to it and began to rock as hard as he could. 'Cheat!' shouted Alicia, and, aggrieved, went to sit on Polly's lap.

'You could wait at table.' Fanny grinned wryly at Polly. 'The Missus says I'm even worse'n Rosie was.'

'I don't know how neither.'

'Ask the Missus to train you. You and her is as thick as thieves – she'll jump at the idea. Now the Master is wantin' to have more dinner parties, she'll need a proper parlourmaid.'

''Ow d'you know he wants more people in?'

Fanny looked wise, 'I 'ear it all.'

When Master Charles came home for the summer holidays, soon after Alicia's fifth birthday, he found his old friend, Polly, waiting at table. For the first time, Alicia was allowed to have lunch with him and with his mother in the dining-room. He noticed, uneasily, that Elizabeth was most impatient with the little girl, as the child floundered over the various knives and forks. He teased her gently that she would soon be a grown-up young lady and the threatening tears turned to a shy giggle.

'I'm going to school soon,' she confided proudly, and wondered if she dare ask for another spoonful of strawberry jelly. She looked up at Polly, hovering over her mother, water-jug in hand, and decided not to. She had long since joined the silent conspiracy of servants in the kitchen; she knew that after the meal she could go down to the basement to ask Mrs Tibbs for a bit more and would be given it gladly.

After this first venture at lunch in the dining-room, she asked Polly, 'Why are you dressed up differently in the dining-room?'

' 'Cos as well as lookin' after you, you cheeky little bugger, I got to be the parlourmaid in a parlourmaid's uniform.'

Miss Schreiber, at the preparatory school, was horrified when, one morning in September, Alicia called a teasing boy a cheeky little bugger. For the first time in her life, the child received a sound slap. She learned quickly that there was more than one English language.

Alicia tended to be secretive and very quiet when in her mother's company. Miss Schreiber's complaint forced Elizabeth to pay more attention to her daughter's language, and this made Alicia more than usually tongue-tied. Only in the kitchen, where she was treated with easy affection, was she able to express herself freely.

She also tended to be struck dumb in her sister's home, where she was taken by her mother to play with her nephew, Frank. Frank now had a small brother and a baby sister.

'They're no good to play with yet,' he told her, in reference to his siblings. 'He wets his trousers and she only sleeps – do you know, she hasn't got any teeth?'

The latter interesting fact stirred Alicia out of her usual wordlessness. 'Perhaps she's lost them,' she suggested. 'Aunt Clara lost hers once – we found them in her dressing-table drawer.'

For months after that, Frank checked his teeth from time to time, to make sure that they were still firmly fixed in his mouth.

Alicia was always thankful, after these visits, to be returned to the safety of the kitchen in Upper Canning Street; Frank tended to push her about and she did not enjoy it.

7

I

Several times in her life Alicia was visited in her nursery by a man so tall that it seemed to her that his head would touch the ceiling. He was very thin and stood awkwardly in the open doorway of the nursery, until he was invited in by Polly, who curtsied to him.

He was dressed in tweeds which smelled of tobacco smoke and his black hair was cropped close to his head. He always went to stand with his back to the fire and then he would survey the room and say, in a deep friendly voice, 'This is the only place in the world which never changes – and old Toby is still there!' He would move over to pat the head of the rocking-horse, which Alicia loved to ride.

At first, Alicia tended to shrink behind Polly's skirts; her knowledge of men was limited to Humphrey, who had never been known to enter the nursery, and the Reverend Clarence, who never spoke to her. Polly hauled her out, however, and said, 'Come on, now. You know your big brother, Master Edward. He's come all the way from India to see yez. Come and say how-do-you-do.'

With the offer of an ivory elephant, just the right size to hold in her hand, she was beguiled on to his knee while he talked to Polly. Polly made up a story about her *furrie* elephant; it was some time before Alicia realized that she meant a fairy elephant and not a fur-clad mammoth such as she had seen in a picture in one of Charles's old books.

Perhaps because the room was Edward's childhood nursery and Polly was not unlike the nanny he had known long ago, his military stiffness left him. While Alicia dozed in the warmth of the fire, her head on his shoulder, he talked easily to buxom, blue-eyed Polly.

Polly watched the yellowed, strained face and fell helplessly in love with every line of it. On other nights, while Alicia slept in the next room, she listened avidly, with her sewing needle poised above her mending, to his stories of the jungles of Burma filled with small, brown men who wore only loincloths. Glad to have a genuinely interested audience, he described the wild beauty of the Himalayas and a particularly dangerous spot called the Khyber Pass, where wicked men in turbans hid amongst the rocks and fired at British soldiers. Normally, he was a quiet, dull man, who, as a boy, had tried to live up to his father's expectations and had failed. To escape, he had joined the army – a nondescript foot regiment – and he knew he would never be a particularly outstanding soldier either. To Polly he seemed a wonderful person, and she treated him as such.

'Aye, he's a lovely man,' she said wistfully one day to Fanny, who, quick of eye, had noticed the blush which rose to Polly's cheeks when Master Edward's name was mentioned in the kitchen and had later teased her about it.

'Does 'e coom to your room?' inquired Fanny with great interest, as she quickly dusted the hallway of the top storey.

Polly was changing into her afternoon uniform, ready to open the front door to Elizabeth's callers, and she paused in tying her apron.

'Aye,' she whispered, 'but don't tell no one, Fan. He's a really good man and I wouldn't want 'is Mam to find out.'

'Watch out you don't get in the family way,' Fanny warned, as she commenced to dust down the bare wooden stairs that led up to the nurseries. After a moment, she looked up again. 'Be careful. *He* could tell someone. Some of 'em is real organ-grinders. When did it start?'

Polly adjusted her frilly cap and prepared to come down the stairs. 'He'll never tell nobody,' she replied firmly. Then, in answer to Fanny's question, she went on, 'It all coom about, the year 'e coom down with malaria. Remember, 'e coom home and the mistress and me 'ad to nurse 'im? He were home a long time, till 'e got over it.' She sighed. 'It were then – when he were better and not yet called back to 'is Regiment.' As she sidled past Fanny on the stairs, she giggled suddenly. 'He couldn't do it, first time – he were too weak!'

'Do 'e give you anythin' for it?'

'No. I don't want nothin'. I love 'im.' The dark head with its frilled cap was raised proudly, as she paused, hand on banister, to look back at her fellow servant.

Fanny opened the staircase window and leaned out to shake her duster. She laughed. 'Aye, you've got it bad, you 'ave.'

Polly sighed again. 'Aye. I wish he didn't 'ave to go to them furrin parts. The Missis told the Master as he's goin' back to India soon – he's bin in Aldershot so long, I begun to think he'd be there always. It makes me sick to me stomach to think about them blackies in their turbans, with their guns.'

When Edward did return to India, this time to the Punjab, Alicia began to get regular letters from her brother. He would invariably end them by sending his love to her and asking her to remember him kindly to Polly, who, he trusted, was well. In neat script, seven-year-old Alicia would equally invariably reply that Polly was well and sent her best respects.

II

In an effort to re-establish herself, Elizabeth had, about a year after Alicia's birth, plunged into the fashionable world of charitable undertakings. The ladies of St Margaret's Church found her so useful, when planning church bazaars, that they began to ignore the occasional innuendo which reached their ears about their fellow parishioner.

With one or two other ladies from the church, she became a fundraiser for the new Royal Infirmary and for the Sheltering Home for Destitute Children in Myrtle Street. She was occasionally snubbed, but a number of the ladies appreciated her hard work and, with them, she was sometimes asked to receptions given for the many important visitors who passed through Liverpool. Humphrey soon discovered that she was acquainted with the wives of men he would like to know, and he suppressed his smouldering anger with her sufficiently to be able to address her and encourage her to ask these people to dinner.

A handsome, well-dressed woman in her forties, forced to deny her natural sensuality, she became, as the years went on, extremely peevish with those who served her.

'Forever pickin' on yez,' Fanny complained to Polly, while they prepared the dining-room for a formal dinner in September, 1896. She pushed a mahogany chair more exactly in position at the glittering table. Quick and impatient, she could be nearly as irritable as Elizabeth was.

'Aye,' agreed Polly, 'and I'll get it if I don't hurry. Got to collect Allie from Miss Schreiber's.'

'She's risin' eleven now. She's old enough to take 'erself to school and back.'

'The ould fella says as she's to be escorted. I heard 'im. Gettin' at her, he was, pickin' on her for nothin'. Tryin' to make things awkward for her. *She* said as Allie were old enough.'

'Don't want 'er to stray like her Mam,' opined Fanny, positioning finger bowls round the table with mathematical precision. 'It's herself what needs escorting. She's still fine lookin'.'

'Fanny!'

'Well, she's forever trailin' her petticoats afore one man or another. You watch her tonight.'

'Nothin' comes of it,' Polly responded forcefully. 'It's just her way –

and she must be all of fifty by now – an old woman. You shouldn't say such things – and about a good Mistress an' all.'

'Aye, she's quite good,' agreed Fanny reluctantly. She turned to poke up the fire. 'How do we know what comes of it? Anyway, who's comin' tonight?'

'A professor and his missus and two other couples. They're all at that big meeting in St George's Hall. A real famous doctor come to talk to 'em. Read it in the paper. Name of Lister.' Polly surveyed the table, set with Elizabeth's best china and Bohemian cut glass. 'Well, that's done, anyways.'

'Better snatch a cup o' tea while we can,' suggested Fanny, putting down the poker on its rest in the hearth.

'Not me. I must run to get Allie.'

III

After school, Alicia sat by the kitchen fire, watching a harassed Mrs Tibbs baste a huge joint of beef, while Fanny stirred a cauldron of soup. Polly thrust a glass of milk into the child's hand and told her that after she had drunk it she should go into the garden and do some skipping in the fresh air.

'Do I have to?'

'Aye, coom on, luv. I'll come with yez and count your peppers for a mo'. Then I got to help Cook.'

She put her arm round Alicia and together they went out of the back door, which led into a brick-lined area, and then up well-washed stone steps to the long, narrow walled garden. A straight, paved path ran from the area to a wooden door in the high, back wall. The wind was whirling the first autumn leaves along the path and over the lawn, and the single aspen tree at the far end shivered, as if it already felt the cold of winter. Opposite the tree, on the other lawn, stood an octagonal summerhouse, where Alicia occasionally played house with a little girl called Ethel, who also attended Miss Schreiber's school. Nearer the house, an apple tree bore a crop of cooking apples almost ready for picking.

At Polly's urging, Alicia did a fast pepper, her skipping rope thwacking the path quicker and quicker. Polly counted, and they both laughed when Alicia finally tripped over the rope.

'Seventy-two,' shouted Polly.

The latch on the back gate rattled suddenly, as it was lifted. A grubby face, topped by wildly tousled hair, peered cautiously round the door.

A very thin boy, about eleven years old, entered like a cat on alien ground. His breeches were in the last stages of disintegration and were topped by a ragged jacket too large for him. He wore a red kerchief round his neck and was bare-legged and barefooted. Alicia smiled at him; he was Polly's brother who came sometimes, when he was unemployed, to beg a piece of bread from her. Though he smelled like a wet dog, Alicia accepted him as part of her small world, as she did the coalman, the milkman and the postman.

This visit was obviously different. The boy was blubbering like a brook in spate, and when he saw Polly he ran into her arms.

'Why, Billy! What's to do?' She hugged him to her white, starched apron.

'It's Mam,' he told her. 'She's took bad – real bad. Mary's with her and Ma Fox from upstairs. Dad says to come quick.'

Unaware that his sister had suckled both of them and was equally loved by Alicia, he ignored the girl and clutched at Polly.

'Jaysus! What happened?'

'She's bin sick of the fever for nearly a week and she don't know none of us any more.'

Fever was a scary threat, and Alicia interjected impulsively, 'Polly, you must go. I'll do my homework while you're away.'

'I'll have to ask your Mam. We got a dinner party.' She looked down at the mop of hair on her shoulder and gently pushed the boy away from her. 'Don't grieve, luv. I'll come, somehow.'

Billy stepped back and wiped his eyes with the backs of his hands. This left a dirty smear on either cheek.

For the first time, he seemed to realize that Alicia was there watching him, her skipping rope dangling from one hand. He stared at her for a second and then, obviously trying to re-establish his manliness after such a bout of tears, he carefully winked at her. While she giggled, he turned on his heel and trotted back down the path. The garden door banged behind him, and, as he ran, they could hear his bare feet thudding along the back alley.

With Alicia hurrying behind her, Polly fled back to the kitchen. She was met by an anxious Fanny.

'The Missus is in, and in a proper temper, askin' why you wasn't there to open the door for her. I told her as you was in the garden with Allie, but she's real put out and sez you've not put the claret glasses on the table.'

'Bugger her.' Polly stripped off her kitchen apron, snatched up her frilly parlour one and whipped it round herself. The ribbons of her cap streamed behind her, as she shot upstairs, leaving a surprised Fanny facing Alicia and asking, 'And what's to do with her?'

IV

The dining-room door was ajar. Elizabeth, still in her osprey-trimmed hat, was standing in the doorway, tapping her foot fretfully.

The moment the green baize door to the back stairs opened to reveal a breathless Polly, Elizabeth turned on her. 'Polly, claret glasses, girl, claret glasses – and couldn't you find a more interesting way to fold the table napkins?'

Polly's panic over her mother immediately gave way to her mistress's wrath, and she responded humbly, 'I thought it was your favourite way of havin' the napkins, Ma'am.'

'It is not. And the claret glasses?'

Polly bobbed a little curtsey. 'I'll get 'em immediately, Ma'am. I wasn't sure which wine you was having.'

Aware that she was not being quite fair to a woman she respected, Elizabeth tried to control her irritability, and turned to pass through the hall and climb the red-carpeted staircase to her bedroom. Polly followed her anxiously to the foot of the stairs. 'Ma'am, may I speak to you, Ma'am?'

Her plump white hand on the carved newel post, Elizabeth turned to look down at her. 'Yes?'

'Ma'am, I just had word that me Mam is very ill and is callin' for me. Can I go to her?'

'Really, Polly!' Elizabeth burst out. 'What has come over you? First the dinner table, and then this! How can you go anywhere when Professor Morrison is coming to dinner? Who is going to wait at table?'

'I thought, perhaps, Fanny could do it, for once. Mam's real ill – she wouldn't send otherwise.'

'Fanny is too clumsy – and I am sure other members of your family can care for your mother for a few hours.' Elizabeth was shaking with anger. 'If you *must* go home, you may go immediately after you have brought in the tea and coffee trays. Fanny can clear up afterwards. But make sure you are back in time to take Miss Alicia to school in the morning.'

Polly kept her eyes down, so that Elizabeth should not see the bitter anger seething in her. I'll get another job, I will, she raged inwardly. Friend? She's no friend. Aloud, she said, 'Yes,'m. Thank you, Ma'am.'

538

As she got the claret glasses out of the glass cupboard, she cried unrestrainedly for fear of what might have happened to her mother.

When she went down to the basement kitchen, it was in turmoil. Mrs Tibbs missed not having a kitchen-maid and she still tended to lean on Fanny for help. Fanny worked hard. During the day, she still had to carry hods of coal to all the fireplaces in the house, in addition to her cleaning duties as housemaid. Though she resented the totality of her work, she was, like Polly, thankful to be reasonably fed and warm under a mistress who did not usually penetrate to the kitchen. Polly, also, found herself hard-pressed to keep up with the work of parlourmaid and take care of Alicia, as well as do the extensive mending required and the careful pressing of Elizabeth's elaborate dresses, while Humphrey strove to keep the costs of his household down.

Today, his housekeeper-cook, Mrs Tibbs, usually fairly calm, was in full spate in the steaming kitchen. She shouted to a reluctant Fanny to fill up the hot water tank by the blazing fire and then to peel the potatoes. The light of the fire danced on her sweating face, as she tasted the mock turtle soup and added a quick shake of pepper to it.

Polly was weeping as she came through the door, and Mrs Tibbs, Fanny and Alicia all looked up. They listened in shocked silence as Polly told them what Elizabeth had said about her going to her mother. Polly turned to Fanny. 'Could you manage the clearing up, Fan?'

''Course I can, duck. Mrs Tibbs and me – we'll manage, won't we, Mrs Tibbs?'

'I'm sure I don't know how – but we will,' sighed Mrs Tibbs. She picked up a ladle and opened the big, iron oven at the side of the fireplace to baste the joint of beef in it. Then she carefully closed the door on it again. She turned to Polly, who was wiping her eyes with a corner of her apron. 'Now, Polly, make yourself tidy again, and then you could beat the cream for the trifle – and give Miss Alicia her tea.'

Alicia had come forward to watch Mrs Tibbs deal with the meat. The cook asked her, 'Would you like a bit of our Shepherd's Pie, luv?'

'Yes, please, Mrs Tibbs. Can't I help you – or do some of the dishes for Fanny?'

Mrs Tibbs smiled at her. 'No, luv. It wouldn't be proper. Your Mam wouldn't like it.'

So Polly carried a tray containing Shepherd's Pie and trifle up to the nursery – Mrs Tibbs had made the dessert in a little glass dish specially for Alicia.

As Polly put the tray down in front of her, Alicia asked, 'Why doesn't Mama let me come down to dinner, now? All the girls at school have dinner with their parents. I'm nearly grown up – and it would save you such a lot of running up and down, Polly.' She shook out her table napkin and put it on her lap. 'I could even eat my meals in the kitchen with you and the others. And, you know, I could have helped Mrs Tibbs today, so as to free Fanny to wait at table.'

'Bless your lovin' heart.' Polly bent and gave her a quick kiss on the top of her flaxen head. Then she hastily rewound the plaits of her own hair more tightly and settled a clean cap on top of them, while she considered how to answer the girl.

'It's not proper for you to eat with the servants, luv. And your Papa gets cross very quickly, as you well know. So your Mam probably wants him to have his dinner quiet, like.'

'I don't think it's because of that, because I can be as quiet as a mouse. I think they don't like me, not even Mama. There must be something wrong with me.'

'Och, no! Parents always like their kids,' Polly lied.

'Well, I don't understand why I can't be with them.'

No you don't, thanks be, thought Polly. I'd hate you to find out. She was anxious to get back to her work, but Alicia was following her own line of thought, so she lingered for a moment, as the child asked her, 'Do you think Mama would be grumpy, if I asked Mrs Tibbs to teach me to cook? Some of the girls at school are learning from their Mamas. You see, I could then help Mrs Tibbs.' She looked earnestly up from her dinner.

'Well, you could ask your Mam. But don't say nothin' about helpin' – she might not like that.'

'Surely I can help a *friend*?'

Polly did not respond. She merely said she must get back to the kitchen and fled before she had to explain the limit of friends allowed to little girls.

Alicia licked both sides of her trifle spoon and sadly scraped the empty dish. She put the dish back on to the tray. As she slowly folded up her napkin and pushed it into the ivory ring which Edward had sent her from India, she thought there was no explaining the idiosyncrasies of parents. She leaned back in her chair and her lips began to tremble – she wanted to cry. It was so strange that the other girls at school had parties at Christmas and birthdays and went on holidays with their mothers and fathers, and no such things ever happened to her – she was not even taken shopping by her mother – Polly took her to Miss Bloom, the dressmaker, to have her dresses and coats fitted, or to Granby Street to buy the few Christmas gifts she did not make herself. Polly even took her to All Saints Church most Sunday mornings.

She got out her spelling book to do her homework for the following day. But the letters seemed to jump erratically, as she realized suddenly that not only had she never given a party; she had never been invited to any other girls' parties, either.

8

I

James Tyson did not take much notice of his wife, Bridie's, complaints of fatigue and of pain in her legs; women always complained of their feet and that they were tired. He himself suffered chronic pain in his back, a relic of his work as a docker; it made it impossible, now, for him to find work, except occasionally as a nightwatchman. It was Bridie selling her rags and old buttons in the market who kept them from starvation. When one morning she failed to get up in time for the opening of the market, it was suddenly brought home to him that her complaints were not the usual ones.

'Me head,' she nearly screamed to him. 'It's me head!'

She was hot with fever, so a worried James suggested that she should go to the public Dispensary to ask for medicine.

'I couldn't walk it,' she gasped. 'I'll be better later on.'

James woke Billy and sent him off to work; he had a job cleaning up after the horses in a stable belonging to a warehouse. On the way, James said, he was to call in on his sister, Mary, and ask her to come to her mother. Mary arrived at Bridie's bedside half an hour later, her newest baby tucked inside her shawl. She was followed by her daughter, Theresa, a fourteen-year-old who plied the streets at night. They both stared down at Bridie tossing on her truckle bed; neither knew what to do.

Finally, Mary sent James upstairs to the tap in the court, to get some water to bathe Bridie's face with. 'Looks as if she's got the flu,' she suggested, as she handed her baby to Theresa to hold.

Nobody else attempted to put a name to the fever; there were all kinds of fevers, and people either got better from them or they died. And pain such as Bridie's was something you put up with.

The news went round the court that Billy Tyson's Mam had the flu. Nobody wanted to catch it, so they stayed away. James went to peddle Bridie's fents in the market.

Word that Bridie had the flu very badly reached her Great-aunt Kitty, who lived in the next court. She hobbled down the stairs from the attic in which she lived and, slowly and painfully, dragged her arthritic limbs into the Tysons' cellar room. She was panting with the effort as James, returned from the market, made her welcome; few people knew as much about sickness as Great-aunt Kitty did. She pushed her black shawl back from her bald head and bent over to talk to the patient.

''Ow you feelin', Bridie?' she croaked.

Her eyes wide and unblinking, Bridie tossed and muttered unceasingly.

'Lemme closer,' the old lady commanded Mary. 'And give me the candle so I can see proper.'

As was the custom, Bridie still had her clothes on; clothes kept you warm at night as well as in the daytime. Only her boots had been removed, to show black woollen stockings with holes in the heels and toes.

As she shuffled closer to the bed, the old lady muttered, 'Well, it int cholera, praise be, or she'd be dead by now. Is 'er stummick running?'

'No. She ain't even pissed.'

Aunt Kitty paused and looked up at Mary. 'She truly 'asn't?'

'No. Not a drop. I bin 'ere all day.'

'That's bad.' Aunt Kitty bent still lower, the candle dripping wax on Bridie's blouse, while she lifted the sufferer's chin and held it firmly in order to take a good look at her face. 'Lord presairve us!' she exclaimed. She touched a dark encrustation at the corners of Bridie's mouth, and then drew back thoughtfully.

She turned to Billy and James and ordered, 'You turn your backs. I'm goin' to take a real look at 'er all over.'

Filled with apprehension, Billy followed his father's example.

Great-aunt Kitty gestured towards Mary with the candle. 'Lift up her skirts. I want to see her stummick.'

Mary hesitated, her brown eyes wide with fear of what her great-aunt might deduce.

'Come on, girl.'

Kitty was said to be a witch, so rather than be cursed, Mary did as she was bidden, though she felt it wicked to expose her mother so.

Underneath the black woollen skirt were the ragged remains of a black and white striped petticoat. Mary lifted this and her mother's stomach was exposed; she wore nothing else, other than her stockings.

Holding the candle so that it did not drip on Bridie's bare flesh, Kitty ran her fingers over the sick woman's stomach. She bent down to peer very carefully at it. Beneath the grime, she was able to see dark red blotches. Her lips tightened over her toothless mouth.

She felt down the rigid legs and her sly old face, for once, showed only a terrible sadness. Very gently she took the petticoat and skirt hems from Mary's fingers and laid them back over Bridie. 'You can look now,' she told the male members of the family.

While she made her examination, James had retreated to the back of the tiny room. Now she turned to him.

''Ad any rats 'ere lately?'

'There's always rats, you know that,' growled James.

'Hm.'

Billy interjected, 'Mam found a near-dead one in the court a while back. Proper huge it were – like a cat. She threw it in the midden with the rubbish.'

'I knew it,' muttered Great-aunt Kitty. 'I seen it before. She's got gaol fever, God help us all.'

A hissing sigh of fear went through the other members of the family.

'Typhus?' James whispered.

'Aye. Haven't seen it for a while. But I seen lots of it in me time.'

'What'll we do?'

'Doctor from Dispensary might come.'

'They'll be shut by now.'

'Well, first light tomorrer, you go after 'em. Aye, this'll cause a pile of trouble.'

'What?'

'They'll burn everythin' you got, to stop it spreadin'.' She pointed to Bridie, still staring at the blackened rafters above her head and chattering incoherently. 'They'll take 'er to the Infirmary no doubt – keep 'er away by herself.'

'To die by herself?' James was aghast.

'That's wot 'ospitals is for, int it? To die in.' She gave a dry, sardonic laugh. 'They daren't leave 'er here, 'cos everybody in the court could get it from her.'

'Christ!' He rubbed his face with his hands. 'Are you certain sure?'

'Aye, I'm sure.' She hesitated, and then said, 'Well – almost.' She looked round the little room, lit only by the candle in her hand, at its dirty brick walls, its earthen floor, its empty firegrate. 'And you take care o' yourself and our Bill,' she warned. 'Take all your clothes off and wash 'em, and kill every bloody louse and flea you can find. The cleaner you are, the better you'll be.' She turned to Mary, and asked, 'Anybody else bin in here?'

'Our Theresa and the baby was here. I sent 'em home just now.' Mary began to cry.

'Well, you got a copper in your house. You go home and put all your clothes in it – and Theresa's and the baby's and our Billy's and your Dad's stuff. And boil the lot real hard.' She looked disparagingly at the fat, rather stupid girl in front of her. 'And if it's wool and it can't be boiled, borrow an iron and iron it well. Go over all the seams – with a good, hot iron, mind you.'

She turned back to Bridie, who periodically was letting out short shrieks. She put her hand on her niece's forehead again, and then turned to James. 'See if you can get a bit of milk from somewhere and feed it to her.' She swung back to Mary and snarled at her, 'Stop wingeing.'

Mary sniffed and wiped her face with the end of her shawl. She cast a glance of pure hatred at the humped back bent once more over Bridie; witches ought to be burned, in her opinion. Aloud she said, 'I'll go and get the fire lit under the copper. Tell our Billy to come straight over to our 'ouse – I'll do 'im first. While the water's gettin' hot, I'll run back with a bit of conny-onny for Mam.'

Kitty straightened up and sighed. She felt around in her skirt pocket and brought out a penny. 'Get a pennorth o' fresh milk, as you go by Mike's dairy. Conny-onny int goin' to do her much good.'

With a pout, Mary took the proffered coin, said goodbye to her father and clumped up the steps to the court.

'I'll stay for a while,' the old woman told James, who had moved closer to look anxiously at his tossing wife. 'Gi' me a chair, Jamie boy.'

James hastily moved a small stool closer to the bed and she slowly lowered herself on to it. ''Ave you got any firing? I could use a cup o' tea.'

'Aye, I got some driftwood.' He took the water bucket up to the court to draw water for tea from the common tap.

Crouched against a wall, Billy had listened dumbly to Great-aunt Kitty's diagnosis. His mother was his world. Sharp-tongued and quick to slap, nevertheless, she kept the family together. Without her, there was only darkness. Now he crept forward, to ask, 'Is she goin' to die, Aunty?'

His great-aunt looked up at him from her stool, her bloodshot eyes glittering in their black hollows. 'Coom 'ere, duck.'

The lad moved closer to her, and she put a long bony arm round him. 'She might,' she said. 'She 'asn't got no strength.'

Billy began to blubber like a small boy, while his mother raved on her bed. 'Na, then, luv.' Great-aunt Kitty's arm tightened round him. 'There's a time when all of us has to go. You must pray nobody else gets it.' She sighed. 'Your Pa should've asked the Dispensary for 'elp before.'

'Mam didn't want 'im to. She's afraid of us all endin' up in the Workie.'

545

The very word 'Workhouse' was enough to make anybody panic, thought Great-aunt Kitty, so she nodded understandingly.

'Well she *is* real ill now, lad, and the Dispensary is the only one what might save her.'

II

Wrapped in a black woollen shawl, her straw hat skewered by two huge hatpins to the top of her plaited hair, Polly ran through the ill-lit city. Though she was by no means young she was nervous in the Woodmans' neighbourhood of being cornered by half-drunk, smartly dressed men out for an evening's entertainment; further into the city itself, prostitutes paraded followed closely by their pimps, all of them anxious to defend their own particular territory. As she cut through side streets to reach her home near the junction of Scotland Road and Cazneau Street, homeless men dozing in doorways called to her, and an occasional group of seamen on shore leave shouted after her. She gave them all wide berth.

The narrow street off which the court led was almost dead dark, and she feared she might not find the entrance. As she passed, she let her fingertips brush along the rough brick wall, watching that she did not trip over front steps which occasionally protruded on to the pavement.

A slight difference in the light and nothing under her fingertips told her that she had found the narrow archway.

As she entered, the smell hit her, the appalling reek of the midden full of a month's rubbish and the overflowing earth lavatories. Very faintly, from the steps leading down to the cellar, came the glow of a candle. She walked lightly towards it, afraid of slipping on the cobblestones, greasy from half a century of filth. Then she ran down the narrow outside staircase and into the room.

Though there were only three of them, the cellar seemed full of women, wrapped in their black, crocheted shawls, all watching tearfully, as her mother on her straw mattress muttered softly. The light of the solitary candle barely reached her father, who was pacing up and down a narrow space by the fireplace. He was beating his breast with one clenched fist, in time to the movement of his feet. Crouched on another palliasse laid on the floor, his head against the wall, Billy dozed, his tousled hair shadowing his face.

Polly's quick footsteps on the stairs woke the boy, and all heads turned towards her.

Polly had eyes only for her mother, and the women edged back as she ran to the narrow bed and flung herself on her knees by it. 'Holy Mary!' she breathed, as she saw the black-encrusted mouth and the frightening staring eyes. She laid her arm round her mother's head and whispered, 'Mam.'

Bridie ignored her, and continued to toss and mutter with an occasional near shout.

Polly looked round wildly. 'Aunty! Aunty Kitty, what's to do with her? Can't you do somethin'?'

Perched on her stool like a roosting crow, her great-aunt said heavily, 'I think it's gaol fever.'

Polly drew back from the bed in horror. 'Has anybody bin to the Dispensary to ask the doctor?'

'Billy'll go as soon as it's light – mebbe somebody'll be there.' She looked down at the terrified girl. 'You come away from 'er, duck. You can't do nothin', and you might catch it.'

Mary let out a sudden wail, 'Aye, we'll all die unless we're lucky – and our Billy wouldn't come over and 'ave hisself washed and 'is clothes boiled.'

'Now, Mary, don't take on so. Time enough for that later.' This from Mrs Fox, Bridie's distant kinswoman and the family's landlady, who, to her credit, had come down from her ground floor room to see if she could help.

But Bridie was beyond help. She died before midnight in the arms of her old aunt, her half-nourished body unable to withstand the ravages of the terrible disease.

In the first light of morning, as they listened to the unearthly sound of keening coming from the Tysons' cellar, her Catholic neighbours formed an uneasy knot on the far side of the court; occasionally, one or the other of them would cross themselves.

They whispered questions to each other, and, finally, a woman ran across to the iron railing guarding the cellar steps. She leaned over. Great-aunt Kitty was sitting exhausted on the bottom step, and she asked her, 'What's to do?'

The old woman looked up and replied, without hesitation, 'Typhus, I reckon. It's our Bridie, dead from typhus.'

The woman flung her hands across her chest, as if to protect herself, her face a picture of horror. 'Jaysus, save us!' she screamed.

At her shriek, panic went from face to face. People not yet up leapt from their palliasses to the windows and flung them up, as the woman turned and spread the news. Nobody came near the cellar, tending instead to bunch themselves in the far corners of the foetid yard and draw comfort from excited talk with each other.

James wept unrestrainedly, not only because he had lost his wife, but also because she would have to be given a pauper's funeral, the last great humiliation.

''Aven't even got a sheet to wind her in,' he sobbed bitterly. 'Will they 'ave to strip 'er?'

'Aye, for their own safety, they'll have to take everything of ours off 'er and burn it,' Great-aunt Kitty told him. 'They'll bring a shroud, though.'

III

Though his neighbours did not come near him, it seemed to James that that day, the rest of the population of the city tramped through his miserable dwelling.

Money being a terrible necessity, Billy was sent, weeping, off to work. On his way, he ran to the Dispensary to put a note, written by Great-aunt Kitty, through the letter-box. An anxious doctor arrived within the hour. He confirmed Great-aunt Kitty's diagnosis.

He said he would inform the Medical Officer of Health immediately, so that the court could be fumigated and cleansed in an effort to contain the disease.

As he was going out of the court, he was stopped by a middle-aged man who wanted to know if the disease was typhus. The doctor said it was and that the authorities would assuredly do their best to stop others getting it. He explained about fumigation to get rid of fleas and other vermin.

When this information was passed to the other inhabitants of the court, they were very upset, and they blamed Mrs Fox, James's landlady, for harbouring Catholic Bridie's Protestant husband, a man who was known to have attended Methodist revival meetings.

'It's the wrath of God, it is, strikin' at us for havin' a heretic here,' one old biddy raged.

Fear of catching the disease by touching anyone who had been near the corpse, however, forestalled the donnybrook which might otherwise have ensued. They contented themselves by shouting obscenities at James and Billy whenever they emerged. Father and son, wrapped in their own grief, hardly heard them.

Billy longed for Polly to comfort him, but after her mother died, Great-aunt Kitty persuaded Polly that, for her own sake, she should return to the Woodmans' house. 'Good jobs is hard to find,' she told her practically, as she held the younger woman to her. 'Your Dad and

Mary and me, we'll manage. Away you go, now. And change your clothes and wash them.'

Weeping all the way, Polly obeyed.

IV

Knowing that the undertaker would not touch the corpse unless it was washed, Great-aunt Kitty, assisted by a frightened, sobbing Mary, took off the dead woman's clothes and gently sponged her down; her jaw was bound with strips torn from her petticoat and two pennies, provided by Great-aunt Kitty, were placed on her eyelids after Kitty had closed them. They had nothing better to cover her with, so they spread her thick black skirt over her. With her arms crossed over her breast, Bridie looked, in her nakedness, a dreadful travesty of the woman she might have been.

The undertaker and his assistant were by no means as inhumane as James had feared. They wrapped his wife's remains in a coarse shroud and laid her carefully in a rough coffin. Mary had shamed her husband, Mike, into coming to help to carry her coffin, and he did help James and Billy to lift it out of the court and to lay it in the undertaker's horse-drawn van.

Alerted by Mrs Fox, the landlady, a local Roman Catholic priest arrived, just as the van was about to move off. He scolded James for not calling him earlier, so that Bridie could have received Extreme Unction before her death. James simply stared at him unseeingly. He made no objection, however, when the priest undertook to read the service for the committal of the dead; and the four men trudged through the uncaring streets, following the slow clip-clop of the horse's hooves.

V

Early the following morning, an extremely perturbed sanitary inspector arrived at the court; he knew only too well how major diseases could sweep through parts of Liverpool. He had not yet gone through all the houses, when he was followed by the midden men to empty the rubbish from the midden and a rat catcher to check for rodents; it all caused no little stir amongst the fuming, fearful inhabitants.

The house in which James lived would have to be fumigated, the inspector announced, which meant all the twenty-one inhabitants would be homeless for a day while the smelly job was done. The same people

549

would all have to be examined by a physician. Mrs Fox felt free to have a strong attack of hysterics and allow herself to be comforted with sips of rum provided by her sympathetic neighbours.

Though in one way the neighbours were angry with James for his heresy and the upset which they believed it had caused, they also enjoyed the excitement of being the centre of so much attention; it gave them something new to talk about and they felt suddenly important. They were sorely disappointed, however, to hear that there there would be no Wake.

The rent collector representing the absentee landlord, having heard from the sanitary inspector in extremely strong language about the state of the property, felt the need to look as if he were doing something about it, and sent Mrs Fox once more into hysterics. He not only demanded that James be kicked out of his cellar, which, several years back, had been condemned by the sanitary authorities and boarded up, but gave Mrs Fox and her numerous tenants notice to quit.

Stout and ferocious, the landlady took her fight with the rent collector outside, where she screamed, 'I never miss me rent, you stinking bugger – and do you think I'm goin' to let me own flesh and blood sleep in the streets when I got a cellar wot only needed the boards takin' down?'

The rent collector backed, only to find himself hemmed in by a delighted crowd. Arms outflung, Mrs Fox appealed to them, stressing her own kindness and humanity. She threw herself down at the rent collector's feet, as he tried to protest that the house was overcrowded. Enjoying herself thoroughly, Mrs Fox turned on her back, to kick her heels like a child in a tantrum and reveal legs like the pillars of St George's Hall.

The subtenants began to gather closer round the beleaguered man. 'Want to swallow a fist full o' knuckles?' inquired a bony youth, thrusting a leathery clenched hand into his face. Another man laughed. 'Throw 'im in the midden,' he suggested, while Mrs Fox screamed louder and a dazed James watched from the top of his cellar steps.

The rent collector turned, pushed his way through the jubilant crowd and fled.

Mrs Fox turned off her screams immediately. Triumphant, she rose from the cobbles and shook out her skirt. She simpered at the younger men, and said sorrowfully, 'Charity it was, to let the cellar to our Bridie, seeing as how 'er 'ubby int what he might be.' She sniffed slowly and dramatically, 'Out of love of God and love of 'er, I did it, pore dear.'

'Well, put him out,' snarled a wizened hunchback.

Mrs Fox looked down at him. 'I'll think about it,' she responded loftily, and went back into her house.'

VI

The Roman Catholic priest mentioned to the minister of the Wesleyan chapel in Scotland Road that there had been a case of typhus in the parish; they were well-acquainted with each other and often cooperated in schemes to improve the lives of the teeming parish. James was not a member of his chapel but the minister had met him at a Revivalist meeting once and had visited him a few times over the years. Now, without hesitation, he struggled into his shabby jacket and walked down to the court dwelling.

It always took him all his courage to enter closed courts; if the attitude of the Roman Catholic inhabitants should turn ugly, there was only the single narrow exit. When he arrived, however, the only people in the court appeared to be two housewives, buckets in hand, gossiping by the water tap, their children playing in the dirt at their feet, and two labourers shovelling out the midden.

To avoid others getting the disease, Bridie's burial had been necessarily fast and Billy had gone straight from her funeral to work, because the need for money was desperate. When the minister knocked on the cellar door, Mary with her suckling baby at her breast, answered it. James, nearly out of his mind with pain in his back, was seated, teeth clenched, on a bench. In the light of a guttering candle, the room looked even barer than usual, because both the straw palliasses had been taken away to be burned.

Pushing her straggling black hair back from a tearstained face, Mary invited the minister to enter, and James rose slowly from his bench. 'Come in, Sir. Sit down, Sir.' He pointed to a stool opposite him.

James was sober, observed the minister with relief; temperance vows sometimes got forgotten, and the homes he visited would be packed with drunken, wailing relations, not to speak of the corpse propped up in a corner so that it could view the proceedings.

He found that talking to James was rather like addressing a corpse. The man sat as if deaf, hearing nothing of the minister's homily on accepting the Will of God or the subsequent prayers delivered by him. Only when he was leaving did James bestir himself.

As he dumbly followed the minister to the foot of the steps, he suddenly broached his worries about Billy. He said, 'Our Billy is only a young 'un yet; me daughters is all right – one married and one in service.' He cleared his throat, and the minister paused to listen. 'He's a good lad. If aught should 'appen to me, would you look out for 'im? Mary here 'as her own to care for – and more to come, no doubt.

There's nobody to look for our Billy.' He laid his hand on the minister's arm, and implored, 'Don't let 'em put 'im in the Workhouse, ever.'

The minister nodded, 'I'll do my best. You know, Billy should come to chapel and then we can keep an eye on him.'

'We don't have no money to give – and no half-decent clothes to wear – and Billy's Mam raised 'im more of a Catholic, like.'

'Well, you'll probably live a long time yet,' replied the minister briskly, 'and you'll see the boy safely started yourself.'

'Oh, aye. Maybe.' He let his hand drop from the minister's arm, and half turned away.

The minister felt a stirring of guilt; James was the type of person John Wesley had first tried to succour. He hesitated, and then said, 'I'll ask one of our lay preachers to make a point of visiting you.'

'That's proper kind of you.'

Mary had said nothing during the visit, but when the visitor had left, she buttoned up her black blouse, hitched the shawl more tightly round the sleeping baby, and said, 'I'll go 'ome to make a bit to eat. You and Billy come over and share with us. I'm goin' to wash Billy's clothes, anyways, tonight, and you stay over with us, till you find somewhere else to live.'

'Ta, luv,' James responded dully, as she ran up the steps.

He closed the door and then stood in the middle of the room and looked round him. Without Bridie and her piles of fents, the place was desolate. Beside the stool, the stripped truckle bed gave not even a remembrance of her. A few dishes and two saucepans, with the gutted candle in a bottle, cluttered the deal table, the water bucket underneath it. From nails in the walls hung James's docker's hook, unused for a year, the rope he used to tie wood from the river into bundles, and his ragged jacket. A mouse ran across the floor.

He was shaking with hunger and pain, but there was no food. He continued to stand uncertainly for a minute. Then he moved the stool to a more central position.

He took down the rope from its nail, made a noose in it and tied it firmly to a meathook in the rafters. He climbed on to the stool, put the noose round his neck, kicked the stool from under him and, not very quietly, hanged himself.

The fumigators found him the following day.

9

I

Sick at heart, Billy went straight from work to his sister's house, so he was spared the shock of finding his father dead.

For fear of bringing more trouble to the court, no one there was prepared to talk to Health Officials. Faced with a wall of silent dislike, the medical officer did not manage to trace any of the Tyson family and, in consequence, was unable to quarantine them. Looking like an offended empress, Mrs Fox swore that she had never been near Bridie. 'I got more sense,' she told the harassed, overworked doctor.

Defeated, the authorities sent in an additional rat catcher and had the court itself thoroughly sluiced down with water and carbolic, after Mrs Fox's house had, over her protestations, been fumigated.

By the time Mary's husband, Mike, returned home from his job as stableman in a dairy, Billy, sniffing miserably, had had the first bath of his life, in Mary's wooden washtub. While he rubbed himself dry in front of the kitchen fire, Mary heated a borrowed iron on the fire and pressed his jacket and breeches, to kill the lice and fleas. He wore nothing else, except a red handkerchief round his neck, so she did not have to heat up her clay and brick wash boiler.

Mike greeted the boy surlily; he was mortally afraid of contracting typhus himself. He and Mary had had a tremendous row, when she had insisted that they must give a temporary roof to her father and her brother. Though he had struck her several times in the course of the quarrel, she had persisted stubbornly that it was the least they could do. To save face, he had shouted that Billy must pay his wages to him, and if her father did not like it he could get out. She sullenly agreed.

When she had to tell Billy of their father's death and that he would be buried in a suicide's grave, the boy clung to her, unable to cope with the destruction of his small world. Her children played in the street, unaware of the tragedy; only her eldest daughter, Theresa, watched with sly, knowing eyes. Mrs Fox, who had brought the news, sat in Mike's chair by the fire and wiped her eyes, said it was proper awful and had a most enjoyable cry.

II

Since officially there were no Tysons available to deal with poor James's funeral, Mrs Fox undertook to cope with the city authorities. This did not stop Polly asking Elizabeth Woodman for a half-day off, so that she could follow her father's coffin to the cemetery. Permission was reluctantly given, and she, Mary and Billy waited a few yards away from the undertaker's van until the coffin was brought out of the court. They then quietly followed it, and only their prayers consigned his remains to the earth.

Because of Polly's absence, Alicia was allowed for the first time to go to school by herself. Elizabeth Woodman had put on weight and climbing stairs or hills made her pant, so she did not consider taking the child herself.

'I simply cannot spare Fanny to go with you,' she fretted to Alicia. 'It's At Home Day, and I cannot think how we're going to manage without Polly. Go straight to school and come straight home again. And don't speak to any strangers.'

'Lots of girls go to school alone,' Alicia assured her. 'I'll walk part of the way back with Ethel – she lives in Falkner Square.'

'Is that the child who came to play with you once or twice?'

'Yes. I've asked her several times since, but she's so busy.' Alicia sighed. 'She swots a lot.'

'Swot is slang, Alicia,' Elizabeth responded mechanically. Blast them, she thought. The girl's parents must have found out that Alicia was illegitimate; Ethel would certainly not be allowed to associate with Alicia in future. Aloud, she said, 'Never mind, dear.'

Alicia confirmed her mother's suspicions by saying pensively, 'Ethel says that her mother chooses her friends for her – and she doesn't like it much.'

'Some mothers are unreasonably fussy.'

Alicia was sitting on a small stool facing her mother, her hands neatly folded in her lap. 'When will Polly come home?'

'She had better be home tonight or I shall be very cross with her. I can't endure these constant absences.'

Alicia gazed doubtfully at Elizabeth. 'She cries a lot,' she said. 'I suppose parents' funerals are important?' She was genuinely curious. With a father and a mother whom she rarely saw and with few friends, she wondered about the relationship between parents and children.

Elizabeth was shocked by the question. She thought, for a moment, that Alicia was being sarcastic. The child's face with its light grey eyes was so innocent, however, that she stifled her sharp reply and sat staring at her daughter. She carefully put down her after-lunch cup of coffee on the table beside her, before she replied, and then she said, 'Parents care a great deal about their children; children should therefore grieve very much if their parents die. As the Bible says, parents are to be honoured.'

A little bewildered, Alicia said, 'Poor Polly! I don't know what to say to comfort her.'

'Oh, servants don't feel as we do. Polly will soon get over it. She shouldn't cry in front of you. I'll speak to her about it.'

Alicia opened her mouth to disagree with Elizabeth, and then thought better of it. If you wanted to avoid being spanked, you agreed with everything Mama said. Polly always said that Mama knew best. So she muttered, 'Yes, Mama,' and wished that she had not mentioned Polly's grief. She stood up, preparatory to going back to school for the afternoon and waited for her mother to dismiss her. She rubbed her black-stockinged leg with the toe of her house shoe.

Rather put out by the whole conversation, Elizabeth told her irritably to stop fidgeting.

Alicia immediately stood straight, like a small soldier. She said, 'I'm sorry, Mama.' Then, since her mother still did not dismiss her, she said politely, 'Of course, Mama, I would be sad if I had to go to *your* funeral.'

Jolted, Elizabeth looked up from contemplation of her wedding and engagement rings. Her daughter was smiling gently. 'Would you?' Elizabeth asked her.

'Of course, Mama.'

'Ah, well, I hope you won't have to for a long time. Run along now.'

III

In a new black alpaca dress, Elizabeth sat calmly and charmingly through her At Home. She dispensed China tea from her best silver teapot, while Fanny proffered small iced cakes from a silver cake-basket. She wished Florence was with her, to help to keep the conversation spritely. But Florence had six children now and had little time for social occasions.

All the usual ladies called, to sip tea and exchange gossip. Some brought daughters who had just Come Out. One had brought her newly married daughter, shyly pretty in a fine tweed costume and one of the new big hats.

Viewing them from behind her teapot, Elizabeth felt sadly that none of them were ladies of substance, except for her lifelong spinster friend, Sarah Webb, who was the daughter of a baronet; she was sitting quietly in a corner as a single gentlewoman should. All the women present, though prosperous, were of a lower social class than herself; the wives of Liverpool's truly important men had dropped her, now that she felt too tired and depressed to continue her charitable efforts.

As she watched the painted rose at the bottom of each teacup slowly drown in the tea she poured, she fretted about Alicia. What was she going to do when the girl grew older? She could not live forever in the attic nurseries with Polly. Even now, if she had been an ordinary daughter, like Florence, it would have been expected that, after school, she would join her mother in the drawing-room, to be made a fuss of by her friends and be encouraged, perhaps, to recite a piece of poetry.

Fortunately, some of the ladies present were barely aware that she had a younger daughter and those that knew would not wish to face the fact, because they would feel that they had to drop Elizabeth if they did so – and Elizabeth was their social superior and worth cultivating from that point of view. It was certain, however, that if Elizabeth began to introduce the girl, the old rumours would come up again and both mother and daughter would be snubbed. Elizabeth, passing the sugar bowl with a smile as sweet as its contents, thought bitterly that, with this mob, out of sight was out of mind.

Behind her bright chatter, her anguish grew. Alicia was becoming more like Andrew every day, a constant reminder of her lover's defection. The more apparent the likeness became, the less she wanted mutual friends to observe it; Andrew was, after all, a well-known family solicitor who moved in good circles in the city; some people would have actually met him in the Woodmans' house when, before Humphrey realized what was happening, she had asked him to parties. If in a few years' time she Brought Out Alicia, even amongst her despised guests the connection would be made, and, without a very large dowry, Alicia would not stand a chance of marriage.

But Alicia was growing up and was beginning to ask questions – childish ones, but nevertheless very disconcerting to her Mama.

After her second *petit four*, Sarah Webb delicately dabbed her three chins with a lace-edged napkin, and inquired, 'How is dear Florence these days? And little Alicia? I don't think I've seen Alicia since last Christmas. She seems to have been at school whenever I called.'

Sarah was assured that dear Florence was well, though still a little delicate after her last baby. And, according to Miss Schreiber, Alicia was doing very well at school. Elizabeth wished crossly that Sarah had enough sense to keep her mouth shut. But Sarah loved her godchild and did not agree with Elizabeth's keeping her in such seclusion.

Bent on suggesting a different future for Alicia, Sarah said cheerfully, 'Perhaps Alicia will follow Charles into university – I hear he's doing well at Cambridge.' She looked coyly at the other ladies, and studiously evaded Elizabeth's warning eye. 'Perhaps she'll become a New Woman!' she speculated, and accepted yet another *petit four* from the silver basket.

The suggestion of university for a girl set off a heated argument; even if she were accepted, what use would such an education be? They all agreed that men did not like to marry educated women.

'I wish I could have gone to university,' responded Sarah wistfully. 'I would love to have studied botany.'

The ladies felt that botany might be a suitable study for a woman – it was quite *nice*. 'But what would you have done with your learning, Miss Webb?' inquired one of the younger ladies quite earnestly.

Sarah looked bewildered. Then her chins wobbled, as she laughed and confessed, 'I really don't know. But it would have been so good to understand the theories behind it all. And, you know, some young women *are* continuing their education, nowadays.'

An elderly widow, her black veil flung back from a wizened face, retorted, 'It is not nice for women to be exposed to vulgarity, when sitting at lectures with a host of young men to whom they have not been introduced!'

Two or three other guests nodded their heads in agreement. Sarah Webb was a fool who had not succeeded in getting married.

A very blonde lady in a fashionable hat loaded with white veiling, giggled and suggested, 'University won't teach you how to manage men!'

The guests laughed, and agreed.

The conversation and Sarah Webb's remarks about university remained with Elizabeth long after the guests had departed. She dined with her husband, and the meal was as usual practically silent.

After dinner, Humphrey normally retired to his library to drink brandy and coffee while he read the evening newspaper; Elizabeth took tea in the morning-room, where she continued her endless embroidery of underwear or made beautiful hand-stitched clothes for Florence's children. This night, however, after the cheese and fruit had been brought in, she took her courage in both hands, dismissed Fanny to the kitchen, and said to an unsuspecting Humphrey, 'I have to speak to you about Alicia.'

Humphrey always did his best to ignore the plain, shy child he met from time to time on the stairs or in the hall. On the rare occasions when the family was gathered together, such as at Christmas, he tolerated her presence rather than face awkward questions from Florence or her children, but he avoided speaking to her. Florence's husband, the Reverend Clarence Browning, appeared to understand the situation because he also ignored the child. It was Humphrey's brother, Harold, who, when visiting from Manchester, pitied Alicia and brought her little tins of chocolate drops; he persisted in this, even when his wife, Vera, protested that the little girl was 'not quite the thing'. 'What nonsense,' he would reply. 'She's only a child.'

Alicia had once said wistfully to Polly that she wished she could have a birthday party where her father would be present. 'Ethel's father actually played Blind Man's Buff with them last time,' she said.

'Your Papa is a very busy man, luv,' Polly had told her. 'And you had a nice birthday last time, remember? Miss Webb took you on the ferry boat to New Brighton, and Mrs Tibbs made you a birthday cake for when you come 'ome.'

Alicia's eyelids had drooped and she had bitten her lower lip, and agreed. Polly had cut the cake in the nursery, and Alicia had taken a piece down to the morning-room for her mother.

Elizabeth had thanked her and looked as if she were going to cry. She had fumbled amid the muddle of her sewing and brought out a tissue-paper parcel which she handed to Alicia.

It contained a coral necklace which she said she used to wear when she was a little girl, and Alicia had been so delighted that she had kissed her mother on her cheek. Her mother did not respond.

Now a very nervous but determined Elizabeth surveyed her husband's red face at the other end of the dining-table, his scarlet neck oozing over his stiff white collar, his stubby fingers wielding the cheese knife. As he transferred a piece of gorganzola to his plate, he said icily, 'Alicia is your business. I don't want anything to do with her.'

Elizabeth's hand trembled so much that she was unable to peel the grape on her plate. Under the table, her feet were tensed against the floor, so that if Humphrey threatened her, she could jump from her chair and make for the door.

'I'm fully aware of that,' she managed to reply. 'However, since she lives here, she's officially your child.' She abandoned the grape and clenched her hands in her lap. 'That means that you have to go through the motions expected of a parent. She's ten years old now and a clever little girl.'

Humphrey took out his ivory toothpick and asked, 'And what particular paternal duty did you have in mind?'

Elizabeth ignored his sarcasm. 'I want to send her to Blackburne House School. Miss Schreiber says she's clever and recommends that we do so.'

'Why don't you send her to boarding school? That would get her out of the way until she's eighteen.'

'Would you pay the fees?'

'No, I would not!' Humphrey shook his toothpick at her. His face was rapidly turning purple.

Though she was deadly afraid, Elizabeth's temper began to rise. 'Precisely. Blackburne House would be much cheaper.'

'If you think I'm going to pay for your bastard to go anywhere, you're mistaken.' He pushed back his chair and slapped his linen table napkin down on the table. 'She doesn't need an education – she can marry.'

'It's doubtful if she can ever marry – unless you dower her – she might stand a chance then.'

'Me? Dower her? Don't be absurd. And don't expect me to provide for her after my death.'

'Really, Humphrey, you've carried on this vendetta too long. It's not the child's fault.'

'No, it isn't her fault, is it? Ask yourself whose fault it is – and don't expect me to bear the burden of it.'

Elizabeth swallowed her rage; anger only ended in her being struck, and the older she became the less she was able to endure it.

Her husband glided from the room, his house shoes making no noise on the Turkey carpet. The door clicked shut.

Alone, she bowed her head and thought bitterly that, apart from the running sore which was Alicia, her husband blamed her that their eldest son, Edward, was stupid, incapable of adding two and two when it came to arithmetic, and was still dependent upon an allowance from his father to augment his army pay. He also despised Charles, a thin, bent bookworm taking Chemistry as a major in university. 'Who is going to carry on the business?' he would shout at Elizabeth in his frustration.

Sitting defeated at the table, she longed to rest her head on the shoulder of a gentle, sympathetic man; she did not go so far as to admit that she would like to slip into bed with one; she fought her sexual desires as if they were an importuning dragon to be slain.

She leaned forward and rang the bell for Polly.

She had her elbows on the table and was resting her head in her hands, when Polly arrived carrying her big clearing tray.

''Ave you got an 'eadache, Ma'am?' Polly inquired solicitously.

'Yes, I have, Polly. I think I'll lie down for a little while. You may clear the table.' In a slow dignified fashion, she rose from the table and made her way out of the room.

'She's bin cryin' again,' Polly reported to Fanny, in the great cavern of a kitchen. 'His Nibs must've bin at her.'

'Take her up some tea to her bed,' advised Fanny. 'She always likes that.' She looked compassionately at Polly, whose face was pinched, her mouth tight with unexpressed grief. 'And 'ave a good strong cup yerself, luv. Funerals is 'ard to bear.'

10

I

After taking a tray of tea and ratafia biscuits up to a tear-sodden Elizabeth, Polly fled up the remainder of the stairs to the day nursery. She flung herself into the old easy chair and wept unrestrainedly.

She ignored Alicia sitting at the centre table, struggling with her Saturday task of history homework. Shocked at her nanny's distress, Alicia slipped from her chair and ran to her. She put her arms round Polly's shaking shoulders. 'Please don't cry, Polly,' she pleaded. She fumbled for her handkerchief neatly tucked into her waistband, and handed it to the distraught woman.

Polly took the embroidered scrap of cambric and held it to her mouth, while she tried to control herself.

'Is it about your Papa, Polly? Has anything else happened?'

Polly leaned her head on her little charge's shoulder, and sobbed. 'It's me poor Dad. He 'ung himself – so this afternoon they put 'im in a suicide's grave – and there wasn't no priest. It were awful.'

Alicia stiffened. Outside the covers of novels, she had not heard of a suicide. Did people *really* take their own lives? The idea was awesome, and she whispered in horror, 'Oh, Polly!'

Polly lifted her head and blew her nose on Alicia's handkerchief. She looked at the white, anxious little face before her, and said hoarsely, 'He couldn't make do, without me Mam.' She began to cry again.

'I assumed he'd died of fever like your Mama,' Alicia said, her voice puzzled. She had never seen Polly's home or her parents, and she asked with wonder, 'Did he love her so much?' She felt as if she had stumbled on a true romance.

'Aye, I think he did. His back were so bad, he could 'ardly work, and she took care of him.'

In Alicia's mind, the humble labourer joined other star-crossed lovers, like Romeo and Juliet. She began to cry, too.

Polly lifted her on to her lap and held her close. They wept together as if they were mother and daughter joined by a common sorrow.

Polly knew then that no matter how irritating Elizabeth Woodman became, she could never leave Alicia.

II

The next morning, dressed in her morning uniform of pink-striped dress and well-starched apron, she carried Elizabeth's breakfast up to her bedroom. Elizabeth was awake and was sitting up in bed; she looked as weary and hollow-eyed as Polly did.

As Polly laid the tray on her bedside table, she inquired, 'The funeral? Is everything settled in your family, now?'

Polly fought back her tears. 'Yes,'m.' She went to the window to draw back the velvet curtains.

'Good.' Elizabeth began to pour herself a cup of tea. 'Next term, Polly, I shall enrol Miss Alicia at Blackburne House. I think she will be able to walk there quite safely by herself, except in winter when it will be dark and you'll have to take her.'

Elizabeth had as yet only a glimmer of an idea of how she was going to pay Alicia's school fees, but she felt that by telling Polly it might be more certain to come about; it would strengthen her resolve to have Alicia educated sufficiently for her to be a governess.

'Yes,'m. Of course, I'll take her.' Polly was not sure what Blackburne House was exactly nor did she know where it lay. 'Is that everything, Ma'am?'

'No, Polly. In future, I want you to see that Miss Alicia is dressed for dinner. Unless there are visitors, she will take her meal with us.'

'Yes, Ma'am. Shall I tell her, Ma'am?'

'No. I will tell her.' Elizabeth's mouth trembled. Humphrey was going to be furious at having to eat his dinner with Alicia and even crosser if she managed the fees for Blackburne House.

As Polly prepared to leave the bedroom, Elizabeth asked casually, 'What did your mother die of, Polly? I trust she was not in pain?'

Polly paused, her hand on the doorknob. After a second's thought, she said carefully, 'She had a fever, Ma'am. She weren't that strong – she couldn't stand up to it.' She closed her eyes and saw, for a second, her tortured mother tossing on her palliasse. She dared not say that it had been typhus; she might lose her job, as a frightened mistress tried to distance herself from such a virulent infection. 'Doctor didn't put a name to it.'

'I see.' She already knew from Polly that James Tyson had committed suicide. She disapproved strongly of this – suicide was a sin. She picked up her silver spoon and began to crack her boiled egg.

Outside the door, Polly began to cry silently.

Later on, she mentioned to Mrs Tibbs that Alicia would be coming down to dinner in future.

'Oh, my! Maybe the Master's got used to her bein' around and got to like her,' Mrs Tibbs suggested.

This opened up a new point of view to Polly, and she replied quite enthusiastically, 'Oh, aye, I hope you're right, poor lamb.'

While Elizabeth ate her breakfast egg, she also considered Alicia. Sarah Webb's idle remarks at the At Home had reminded her sharply that Alicia was past the usual age for confinement to the nursery. If the girl did not soon join the rest of the family for the main meal of the day, acquaintances would hear from the servant grapevine that Alicia was not being treated as the daughters of others were. It would confirm the rumour of her illegitimacy, and no doubt the story of Andrew Crossing and herself would be dug up again. She felt, with a sense of panic, that Andrew's name must never suffer more besmirchment than had already been the case.

Then she asked herself why she should care about him – he had hurt her dreadfully. The answer came readily, 'Simply because I love him – and always will.' She leaned her head back against her pillows and closed her eyes in an agony of remembrance.

School fees were a different problem. She herself had managed to pay Miss Schreiber's fees out of the allowance sent her each month by Andrew's partner, who now administered her father's Estate. She had not been consulted about the transfer and, when she inquired, young Mr Simpkins had explained that the firm was the Trustee, so any partner could attend to the administration. No doubt, Mr Crossing would explain to her the internal reorganization of the office on the death of their most senior partner. Mr Crossing never had explained, thought Elizabeth fretfully; the stupid idiot had never been near her since Alicia's birth.

During the night, it had occurred to her that Sarah Webb might help with the Blackburne House fees, since she was Alicia's godmother. Or Elizabeth's elder sister, Clara, in West Kirby, might do it simply to spite Humphrey whom she detested. But Sarah at least knew the true story of Alicia, and she loved the child.

As Elizabeth nibbled her last piece of toast, she felt a guilty pang that she did not love Alicia. She was honest enough to admit that she resented her very existence. And to look at her was to see a small mirror of Andrew, which was of no use to a woman who longed passionately to feel his hands upon her, hear him whisper to her as he assuaged the mad sexual urge within her. If Alicia had not been conceived, they might have continued lovers indefinitely; she might have been expecting him that very afternoon. She put down her toast and began to cry.

Later on, she pulled herself together and, when Alicia came home for lunch, she sent for her in the morning-room and told her that Polly would dress her that evening and she should come down to dinner.

Alicia was thrilled. She said, 'Oh, thank you, Mama,' dipped a little curtsey and, without waiting to be dismissed ran out of the room and down the back stairs to tell Polly.

III

Humphrey Woodman sometimes thought that, to a large degree, he lost effective control of Elizabeth on the day that Alicia first came down for dinner.

Before banging the dinner gong in the hall, Polly carefully seated her little charge in the mahogany dining-chair which had been occupied by Edward whenever he was home. Alicia's hair had been combed rigidly back from her face and plaited down her back. She wore a white cotton dress trimmed with lace and had a narrow blue ribbon tied round her waist. On her feet were her best white slippers; they pinched slightly because she was growing fast and they were becoming too small for her. Her hands were clasped tightly in her lap and her eager expression bespoke her excitement.

'Now, you mind your manners,' Polly instructed her, as she plaited her hair. 'You don't open your mouth till you're spoke to, remember. Hold your knife and fork proper, like your Mama does.'

Bubbling with excitement, Alicia promised to be perfect.

Now, as Polly spoke down the blower to Mrs Tibbs in the basement and ordered the soup to be sent up in the dumb-waiter, Elizabeth entered. She cast a quick glance over Alicia and the table settings, and then sat down.

'Remember, Alicia, to be quiet,' she told the girl. 'Mr Woodman dislikes chatterboxes.' She wondered nervously what exactly Humphrey's reaction would be to the girl's presence.

Alicia smiled up at her mother and responded, 'Yes, Mama.' Then she added shyly, 'You do look pretty in your dinner dress, Mama.'

While Polly leaned over to pick up the serviette by Alicia's plate and spread it over the girl's knees, Elizabeth acknowledged the compliment with a slight smile.

Despite a feeling of fatigue which nowadays sometimes bothered him in the evening, Humphrey bowled into the room with the same small, purposeful step that at other times propelled him rapidly along Castle Street to the Exchange Flags, where, amid eddying groups of top-hatted businessmen, he searched for the right contacts, the right pieces of inside information, to promote his considerable investments.

On meeting the nervous, pale eyes of Alicia, he paused, disconcerted, and glanced at his wife. She clenched her teeth and stared coldly back at him. Through her teeth, she said firmly, 'Alicia will have her evening meal with us, in future. She's a big girl now; she has to learn how to behave as a grown-up should.'

At the sideboard, her back to the room, Polly stood, for a second, soup ladle poised over a dish, waiting for the outburst.

Faced with the anxious stare of a little girl he hardly knew and with a servant in the room, probably dying with curiosity and ready to run into the kitchen to relay anything he said, he was for once nonplussed. He sniffed, and with great dignity pulled out his chair and sat down. He shook out his huge linen table napkin as if it were a flag and placed it neatly across his knee. While he considered the situation, he bowed his head and muttered, 'For what we are about to receive may the Lord make us truly thankful, Amen. Where's the soup?'

'Amen,' responded Elizabeth and Alicia in quiet chorus, while Polly hastily slipped a bowl of soup in front of Elizabeth and another in front of Humphrey. She then brought a small helping for Alicia.

Painfully aware of the tension between her parents which she did not understand, Alicia carefully drank her tomato soup with a huge tablespoon. 'God, don't let me spill anything on the tablecloth or on my white frock,' she prayed earnestly.

If Humphrey did not initiate a conversation, Elizabeth rarely did, except when visitors were present. Their verbal exchanges were usually limited to complaints by Humphrey or reports of household needs by Elizabeth. On that day, Humphrey never said a word, while, out of the corner of his eye, he watched the quiet child negotiate her way through the meal.

Dead spit of Crossing, he brooded, and was surprised to find that, though on the surface of his mind, he was irritated at Elizabeth's temerity in bringing Alicia to the dining-room and the fact that she cost him money to maintain, his fury of earlier times had gone; he realized that he simply did not care; his life, his real life, had been transferred out of this house. He was content amid the swarm of businessmen on Exchange Flags, behind the Town Hall, or in the clubs and restaurants of the city.

He found physical comfort curled up in Mrs Jakes' feather bed; he never felt a twinge of desire for Elizabeth – let her and her damned daughter rot, he thought savagely.

Occasionally, he glanced up from his plate to look at Alicia, and he noted that the girl would sometimes lift her eyes towards Polly, as if to inquire if she were doing everything properly, and the parlourmaid would give her the faintest smile of approbation.

He did not normally notice who was waiting on him, because he was so used to a pair of hands putting food in front of him; they were simply a necessary part of the furniture. Now, he idly examined Polly, as she deftly went about her work. She was quite old, at least thirty, he surmised, a trim-looking woman with a good waist, though beginning to show the heaviness of middle age. He recollected that he paid her three pounds a year plus uniform and keep, and she obviously got along well with Elizabeth. For a moment, he toyed maliciously with the idea of dismissing her, simply to annoy Elizabeth, and then decided it was not worth the rumpus which would probably ensue.

Although Alicia was used to being alone a lot, resigned to being quiet, she was not without pluck. The silence of the dining-room, however, was almost unbearable and her disappointment very great. Promotion to the world of grown-ups had suggested something exciting. Instead, she had become acutely conscious of the animosity between Humphrey and Elizabeth. By the time Polly served the caramel pudding, she was so unnerved that she could hardly eat it and was grateful when Polly whipped her dish away.

At bedtime, soon afterwards, as Polly unbuttoned her dress for her and slipped it over her head, she asked tremulously, 'Do I have to go down every day, Polly? I'd much rather be as before – or I could have my dinner in the kitchen with Mrs Tibbs, if it would save you trouble?'

Kneeling in front of her, the dress in her arms, Polly smiled at her, 'Your Mam wants you to learn nice manners – to be a young lady, luv. That's why she wants you down. Perhaps she'll begin to take you out with her a bit, now you're a big girl. That would be a bit of all right, wouldn't it, now? You might get to know some other girls.'

'I suppose it would be nice.' She sounded so forlorn that Polly put her arms round the skinny child and hugged her to her.

But the remorseless dinner hour came round every day; Alicia found herself unable to eat much and Polly began to worry that she was losing weight. The maid wondered if she should point this out to Elizabeth. She talked it over with Mrs Tibbs and Fanny. They decided unanimously that they should not intrude on the delicate balance between husband and wife. Instead, Mrs Tibbs made a little bedtime supper for the girl and invited her to come down to the kitchen and sit by the fire to eat it. This hour in the warmth of the kitchen became the highlight of Alicia's day and she gained weight and joined gaily in the spirited repartee between the three servants.

Very lonely herself, Elizabeth began to call the child to the morning-room for half an hour or so after dinner. Though still handsome, Elizabeth had lost her vivacity and Alicia found these sessions boring. Her mother did not take her out with her, because she rarely went out herself; to entertain or to be entertained seemed increasingly tiring, and tradesmen were only too happy to send their errand boys with an assortment of goods on approval, from which she could choose; there was no need to go shopping.

The presence of Alicia in the morning-room provided a little undemanding company. She was also useful. She helped to wind knitting wool and sorted out Elizabeth's cottons and embroidery silks. And, increasingly, when the Reverend Clarence Browning and Florence called, she minded any offspring which Florence might have decided to bring with her.

Her hair hanging in untidy wisps round her face, her hands reddened in a most unladylike way, Florence had for years been much too harassed by her unruly family and the calls made on her as a Vicar's wife, to pay much attention to her half-sister, about whose birth Clarence had told her a most shocking story.

When Alicia had been small, she had been sometimes sent to stay with Florence for a few days; but Alicia had dreaded the visits. Her eldest nephew, Frank, was a big, heavily-built boy who, as he grew older, bullied his siblings ruthlessly. He had once pinned a terrified Alicia in a corner of the garden wall and demanded that she lift up her petticoats and dress, so that he could see what she was like underneath. She had instinctively fought him off, and the encounter had been mercifully interrupted by one of his younger brothers in pursuit of a ball. After that, though he stalked her from time to time, she had made sure she always stayed close to his sisters. Fortunately for Alicia, as time went on, it became increasingly expensive for Elizabeth to hire a carriage to take her to the Vicarage, so she had not been to her sister's house for at least a year before Edward came on a leave long delayed by tribal uprisings near the Khyber Pass.

IV

On the day after her first essay into the dining-room, Polly told her on the way to school, 'Your Mama says Mr Edward's comin' home on leave tomorrer. Let's ask him to take you down town, to see the Punch and Judy show on the Quadrant.'

Alicia looked up, and asked in sudden hope, 'Do you think he would?'

'Oh, aye, he will. Don't ask 'im the first day, 'cos he'll be tired after the voyage.' I'll make sure he does take you, me darlin', she promised herself.

Edward did not dock in time to have dinner with his family the following evening. He did, however, come up to the nursery before Alicia went to bed, to see his little sister and Polly.

Despite his tanned face, he looked ill. Periodic bouts of malaria had taken their toll, and his sideburns were flecked with grey. His face lit up, however, when he entered the nursery. He swung Alicia up into his arms and told her that, in the three years since he had seen her, she had become a young lady. While Polly watched gravely, she put her arms round his neck and giggled delightedly. He looked over Alicia's head at her nanny, and Polly knew, with joy, that her time would come. She was so lucky, she thought, that Fanny and Mrs Tibbs slept in the basement. Only when young Master Charles was sleeping in his room on the nursery floor, did she and Edward have to be really careful.

Edward produced an ivory goddess from his pocket for Alicia and it was carefully installed on the mantelpiece, next to a paperweight which Charles had given her the previous Christmas.

Polly looked down at her little charge, as the child chatted animatedly with Edward, and was glad of the affection between the two. Alicia was not nearly so close to Charles – Master Charles had always struck Polly as someone who tolerated his family, but did not really *belong* to it, perhaps because he had been sent to boarding school so young. But Edward was grateful for love.

In response to a request whispered to him by Polly in the small hours of the morning, Edward declared his intention of going downtown to see the Punch and Judy Show and invited Alicia to accompany him, and to have ice cream and lemonade in Fuller's Tea Rooms, afterwards. A thrilled Alicia acceptd the invitation.

The ladies taking afternoon tea in Fuller's glanced surreptitiously at the straight-backed, rather distinguished-looking dark man in civilian clothes that were too loose-fitting to be smart, and at the ash-blonde little girl in a plain white linen dress and untrimmed straw hat. 'A singular combination of colouring for a father and daughter,' murmured one elegant woman to her friend.

Edward and Alicia were blithely unaware of the watching eyes; they were both enjoying themselves, two shy, diffident people who could relate to each other.

As he watched Alicia mop up her strawberry ice, Edward thought about Polly. He could barely understand why he had felt so happy to slide, once more, into Polly's narrow bed. She was, after all, only a maid and no longer very good-looking. But she was totally unlike the girls of the Herring Fleet, as they were called, who came out to India each winter in the hope of finding a husband. Each year he looked at these young, hopeful products of ladies' seminaries, and swore that he could not afford to marry. But he knew that the real reason was Polly. Polly gave everything and asked nothing and, had she been of the same class, he knew that he would have married her long ago, and somehow juggled successfully with his finances. But even in a modest Foot Regiment, she would be ostracized by the other officers' wives because she was not a gentlewoman; marriage was out of the question.

Troubled about what might happen to her, he had, the previous night, fished around in his net purse and had given her a sovereign.

She had flushed, and had handed the gold coin back to him. 'You don't need to pay me,' she told him as she quivered against him and nuzzled into his neck, before kissing him goodbye behind her bedroom door.

He embraced her tightly and refused to take the money back. 'It's not a payment, my dear. It's a keepsake for a rainy day, because I dare not bring you a present; if Mother spotted anything unusual in your room, she'd dismiss you – and then what would we do?' He smiled down at her, the candlelight catching the harsh outlines of his face. 'You can put this away safely somewhere, because it's small. Servants – I mean, people – normally have savings for their old age.' He stroked her black hair tumbling down her back. 'I'm going to add to it – and you never know, you might be glad of it.'

So she accepted the gift and hid it in an old black and white cardboard pill-box at the back of the ancient chest of drawers in her bedroom.

Edward remained in England for a year, teaching modern tactics at Aldershot Military Camp. He had frequent leave, and Alicia became actively aware of a close relationship between her brother and her nanny, which she did not understand. She had taken their friendship for granted; after all, they both loved her – it was, to her, natural that they should be friends. It seemed to her, however, to be one of those many things which nobody ever mentioned, so she never brought the matter up. Throughout her life, there had been a close conspiracy between her and Polly against 'Them, downstairs'; she added the sound of soft footfalls, voices and a creaking bed next door, to her list of secrets, though, as she grew older, she wondered sometimes why Edward visited Polly only at night.

To Polly, it was a wonderful year. She lived in a mixed state of joy at having her lover so often with her and fear of having a child. As a defence against pregnancy, she used a wad of cottonwool, soaked in vinegar, tucked inside her, something she had learned from Great-aunt Kitty.

The single sovereign grew into a small pile, as Edward sought to give her a nest egg.

11

I

On the evening on which Edward had returned from India, Alicia had taken her skipping rope into the garden. She was surprised to find Billy, Polly's brother, kneeling by Mr Bittle, the gardener, helping to weed a flowerbed. She had always regarded herself as Mr Bittle's assistant, and she approached the two bent figures with a sudden feeling of jealousy.

Billy scrambled to his feet and touched his forelock respectfully. Mr Bittle half turned to look up at her.

'Evenin', Miss Alicia,' he greeted her, his toothless mouth spread in a grin.

'Good evening, Mr Bittle. Good evening, Billy,' Alicia replied, a little frostily. 'What are you doing here, Billy?'

Billy swallowed. How to tell this pretty little girl that he was keeping out of the way of his drunken brother-in-law? Billy cleared his throat and responded uneasily to Alicia's question, 'I coom to see our Polly, only she's busy, like. So I asked Mr Bittle if I could help 'im – to fill in the time, like. I hope your Dad won't mind?'

'I see.' Alicia swung her skipping rope and continued down the path.

Though Billy dutifully handed his week's earnings over to his brother-in-law, Mike, his life with Mary and her husband was, within a week of his father's suicide, almost intolerable. Mike's iron fists and vindictive temper became a menace to him, so he had found temporary refuge in the Woodmans' garden.

On the second evening, Alicia paused to talk to him, as she passed him sitting on the steps. He was munching a large slice of bread which Polly had given him. He stood up immediately and took his cap off. She asked if he were going to help Mr Bittle weed that evening; Mr Bittle liked to get every scrap of weed out of the garden before the winter set in.

'Yes, Miss. He said 'e'd be glad of help.' He grinned shyly.

'Well, I might as well get my sackcloth apron and help, too.'

Amused at having two volunteers, old Mr Bittle thankfully left them to kneel and weed, while he pruned.

II

Eight days after James's suicide, his granddaughter, Theresa, Mary and Mike's eldest daughter, gave birth to an illegitimate daughter, father unknown. As she lay on a straw mattress and shrieked with the pain of childbirth, her cries were, most of the day, almost drowned by the sounds of singing and raucous laughter in the court. A seaman had returned home with three months' pay and his friends, including Mike, were busy drinking it away for him. A barrel of beer had been purchased and had been set up in a corner, and the stone flags of the court resounded to dancing boots.

As Mary worked with her daughter to speed the coming of the after-birth, and the new baby squawked on its child-mother's breast, the beer barrel became empty and the party began to break up. Mike's unsteady tread could be heard in the downstairs room.

'What the hell's to do?' he shouted up the stairs, as he heard the baby's thin cry.

'Our Theresa's baby coom,' his wife shouted back, as she eased a fresh wad of newspaper under her daughter's buttocks.

'Christ!' Mike swung unsteadily into the tiny windowless bedroom. The smell of blood made him want to heave, as the afterbirth came clear. Behind him, Billy tried to peer round Mike's back to see what was happening. He had never seen a human birth, though he had watched the horses foal in the warehouse stables.

'Another bloody mouth to feed,' Mike growled, anger against his daughter rising in him. 'Haven't you taught her enough to make her keep clear o' the boys?'

'Now, Mike, you know how she got the kid,' Mary said in as soothing a voice as she could manage. 'She can't help it, with what she's havin' to do – and Father Gallagher frightened her so much, she wouldn't swaller wot Auntie Kitty offered her to get rid of it.'

Bubbling with frustrated rage, unable to accept that his daughter walked the streets, he turned about and bumped into Billy.

'Hm! Maybe she got it from nearer home,' he snarled down at the boy. He seized Billy by the shoulder and shook him. 'Eh?'

Billy cringed. 'Me? I never touched 'er. I never bin with a woman yet.' He tried to back down the narrow staircase. Mike gave him a push, and he turned and half tumbled, half stumbled, down the stairs. Mike came down after him.

'If this one isn't yours, the next one likely will be,' he shouted suddenly, and clouted the staggering boy across the face.

Billy squealed.

Mary deserted Theresa and rushed down the stairs.

'You leave our Billy alone, Mike. The lad's only just past eleven! Don't be daft.'

Billy tried to move towards the door. Mike lurched forward and caught him a stinging blow across the head. 'You keep out o' this,' he yelled at his wife. 'Months ago I seen him making eyes at her. He'll get her again, for sure.' Billy was caught in a corner of the room and whimpered helplessly, as he was struck again.

'Mike!' Mary caught his upraised arm and clung on to it. 'You know how she got this kid. It weren't Billy. I don't know how we'd go on without her money.'

'You sayin' I don't provide?' The question was full of drunken outrage.

'No, Mike!' Mary dropped his arm and backed away from him. 'But without wot she brings in, we'd not eat, many a time.'

In his furious frustration at their need for his daughter's earnings, Mike forgot about Billy, and the boy slid noiselessly out of the open door into the court, where he stood panting against the blackened wall.

He heard Mary shriek, 'No, Mike! No!' and the thwack, as Mike hit her.

'She's no bloody good to anyone,' Mike yelled back. 'I'll larn her to bring a brat to disgrace us – and I'll larn you, too, you lazy bitch.'

As Mary began to scream steadily under Mike's beating, Billy burst into tears. He felt his way through the now deserted court to the street and began to run.

III

He ran down into Great Homer Street and trotted aimlessly along it. Where could he go? What could he do? It was almost certain that Mary would not dare to take him in again. He had given his last week's wages to Mike. He would have to work for nearly a week before he got any further wages, and he was already hungry. Tears made grubby lines down his face, as his feet thudded along the empty pavement and a fine rain began to soak through his clothes. His face throbbed and his teeth ached from the blows he had received. He was used to being trounced by the men with whom he worked, but nobody struck as hard as Mike did.

As darkness closed in, the public houses shut their doors and drunken groups began to roll slowly and unsteadily along the pavement. Billy became nervous for his immediate safety – drunks were not fussy if they found a boy, instead of a woman.

He hid himself in the dark doorway of a warehouse, huddled down and snivelled miserably. He longed despairingly for his mother.

Dare he go to Polly? What would her mistress say, if she heard him knocking on the back door in the middle of the night, even supposing the garden door leading to the alley were unlocked?

He wiped his nose on his sleeve. He decided that it did not matter how caustic Polly's mistress turned out to be, Polly was the only person he could ask for help with any hope of getting it. He heaved himself to his feet and set out through the drizzling rain on the long hike to Upper Canning Street.

He was much too afraid to go to the front door of the house; nobody of his low origins ever set foot on a front doorstep. He tried the gate, which was the tradesmen's entrance and opened on to a set of steps leading down to the front basement kitchen door. The cast-iron gate was locked and the spiked railings guarding the twelve-foot drop from the street did not encourage him to climb over.

He walked again down the street to the entrance to the back alleyway. Beyond the flickering gaslight at the entry, the darkness was so intense that, at first, his courage failed him. How was he going to find, in the dark, the correct, unnumbered, wooden back door?

Frustrated, he leaned his forehead against the unfriendly brick wall and cried again. He would have to wait until morning.

Behind him, on the pavement, he suddenly heard the measured tramp of heavy boots. The scuffer on the beat, he guessed. Fears of being arrested as a vagrant or for loitering with intent shot through his mind. As lightly as he could, he fled straight across the road and dived round a corner.

He found himself in a street of small shops and he crouched down in the darkest doorway he could find. The rain did not reach him there, and he dozed uncomfortably.

He was roused by the clip-clop of horses' hooves and the rattle of drays, as milkmen and coalmen began their rounds. The rain had passed and the street shone in the early morning sun. He had little idea of time, except that it was early, so he remained where he was, cramped and aching, until he heard a window being flung open and a woman's voice from the shopkeeper's flat above him.

Unsure of exactly where he was, he got up and stretched and then joined a growing number of people hurrying to work. Caught up in the crowd, he was soon lost.

In a desperate need to relieve himself, he turned into a back alley and thankfully paid a call against the wall. Then he went slowly back to the street he had left, to glance rather hopelessly up and down it. Finally, he stopped another youth, dressed as poorly as he was, to ask where Upper Canning Street was.

'Oh, aye. You're best off to come along o' me. I work in Falkner Square garden.'

In their clumsy boots, they walked along together, and the gardener's boy pointed out the side entry which led to the house's back alley.

'Ta, ever so,' Billy said gratefully.

When he tried the door, it was bolted on the inside. He looked up at the ten-foot high brick wall guarding the garden; to deter thieves and vandals, it had great shards of glass embedded in the top.

'Oh, Jaysus!' he wailed.

He stared at the door's unyielding woodwork and was just about to turn away, to see if the tradesmen's entrance at the front was yet unlocked, when there was the sound of a woman's quick step on the other side and the bolt was drawn back.

The door was opened, as if the woman were about to glance into the alley. Instead, she was faced with a small, but strong-looking youth.

'Oh!' she shrieked, and slammed the door in his face. He heard the bolt grating shut again.

He shouted, 'Don't be afraid, Missus. You know me. I'm Polly's brother – Polly Tyson.'

'Whoja say?'

'Billy Tyson. I'm looking for me sister, Polly.'

The bolt once more squeaked open. Fanny put her head cautiously round the door, to take a good look at him. Then she opened the door wide. 'Give me a proper fright, you did, standin' there. I were lookin' for the midden men.' She surveyed his dusty rags of clothing, which looked even worse than usual after being soaked and then slept in in a doorway. 'Coom in. You can sit on back step, like always. She's up and layin' breakfast for the Master. I'll get 'er for you, though.'

Billy followed her up the garden path, past the pretty summer house and well-laid out flower beds, one or two roses still in bloom. To him, the garden always looked fit for the old Queen herself to sit in.

As they descended the steps into the brick-lined area surrounding the back door, Fanny said, 'I'll tell Mrs Tibbs you're here and I'll get Polly; but you'll have to wait.'

Billy nodded and sat down on the steps still wet from rain. He shivered with the damp.

When Fanny opened the kitchen door, a delicious smell of frying pigs' ears was emitted, and Billy could have cried again, this time with hunger.

Polly came hurrying out of the kitchen door, her face wrinkled with anxiety. 'What's to do?' she asked.

He told her, and then went on, 'I can't go back, Pol. Mary'll get it again, if I do – I'm sure of it.' He looked at her imploringly.

Polly sighed. 'I don't know what to do for yez, luv. I really don't. Nor for poor Mary neither.' She clasped her arms across her breast, and looked round her in perplexity. Then she said, 'See here. I got to serve the Master and take up the Mistress's breakfast, and give Miss Alicia hers and get her ready for church – and I got to take her to church.' She looked round, seeking somewhere dry for him to sit. 'You sit on the loo here and wait for me.' She opened the door of the servants' lavatory, as she looked at her brother's bruised face and bloodshot eyes. 'You bin out *all* night?'

'Aye.'

''Ve you got any money at all?'

'No.' He snuffled miserably.

'Well, you stick here, and I'll ask old Tibbs if she can spare a bit o' porridge for yez.'

Used to Polly's begging a little food for Mr Bittle's helper, Mrs Tibbs splashed a ladle of thick porridge into an old soup bowl and pushed a tin spoon into it. She shoved it across the kitchen table to Polly. 'I don't know what the Master's goin' to say, if he ever finds out what I give that kid,' she grumbled.

'Ah, he won't find out if you don't tell 'im,' Polly assured her. 'Ta, Mrs Tibbs.' She took the bowl out to her brother and then flitted silently back upstairs to the dining-room in time to hear Humphrey Woodman's quick steps coming downstairs. 'Send up porridge, quick,' she panted down the blower to Mrs Tibbs. ''Is Nibs is comin'.'

While Mrs Tibbs prepared Elizabeth Woodman's boiled egg and thin bread and butter and tea, Polly came out to the area carrying her own bowl of porridge. Billy opened the lavatory door as she put the dish on the step. She ran back into the kitchen, to return with two big mugs of tea drawn from the enamelled teapot on the back of the kitchen range. 'There's lots of sugar and milk in it,' she told her brother with a smile, as she handed him one. A small grin relaxed his pinched face, before he eagerly gulped down the hot drink.

Polly leaned against the door jamb of the lavatory, as she began to shovel porridge hastily into her mouth. She said, 'I bin thinkin' what to do, and what I think is that you should go to Great-aunt Kitty. She's only got one little room, but she'd never deny you a corner to sleep –

and she might be glad to have a strong lad with her at her age. You can give her your wages for your keep. It'll keep you out of the workhouse or an 'ome.'

It was an idea that had not occurred to Billy, but he looked uneasily at Polly, as he replied, 'She's a witch.'

Polly laughed. 'Not her. She's an old, old woman wot knows a lot, that's all. She's not even off 'er chump, like some old biddies. Remember how gentle she was with Mam?'

Billy reluctantly nodded agreement; she'd been gentle with him, too.

'She might be able to think up somethin' better for you. I don't know what – but she might. She knows everybody.'

The tea and porridge restored Billy's spirits a little. And Polly's suggestion at least gave him hope of avoiding the workhouse – God and his Angels preserve him from *that*. Nevertheless, Great-aunt Kitty was uncanny – she seemed to know what you were going to do, even before you thought of it yourself!

'Think she'll do it?'

'Sure she will. What else, anyway? And mind you go to work come Monday.'

He laughed suddenly, and gave her a playful nudge. 'You sound just like Mam.'

Then, at the memory of his tart, capable mother, his face fell and he looked down at his boots. There was a silence between them.

Polly gave a tremulous sigh. 'Poor Mam,' she said.

She rummaged in her skirt pocket and brought out a sixpence, which she handed to Billy. 'Here's a tanner to help you out, duck,' she added more briskly. 'I got to get back to me work – there's Mrs Tibbs callin' me.' She picked up the mugs and porridge plates from the steps. 'Away, now. Give me love to Auntie, and tell 'er as I told you to come to 'er.'

IV

Though Great-aunt Kitty was surprised she was not displeased to see Billy at her door. He told her that Polly had sent him. She grasped his elbow with long, bony fingers and drew him into her tiny, foetid room.

'Coom in, and tell me what's to do,' she invited, in her high-pitched, cracked voice. 'Like a cuppa tea?'

Without waiting for a reply, she pushed him towards a wooden settle and then picked up a pair of bellows from the hearth and inserted them at the base of a few embers in her fireplace. She blew the embers into tiny flame, then added a few small pieces of coal to them and plunked a sooty kettle on top. She pushed an indolent black cat off a rocking chair and sat down herself. The cat stalked over to Billy and sniffed at him.

Billy shuddered and recoiled slightly from it, movements noted with amusement by his great-aunt. 'Tea won't be long,' she assured him. 'It's not that old.'

The cat sat down opposite Billy and yawned. It seemed to Billy that it was looking through him with its great green eyes; a real witch's cat.

He jumped when Kitty got up suddenly and went to a wall cupboard. She opened it, to reveal a surprisingly large store of food for one so poor and elderly. She took down a loaf and a piece of cheese and put them on the table, together with a bottle of whisky. With a knife which looked like a dagger to a nervous Billy, she cut a big slice of bread and then a slice of cheese to put on top of it. ' 'Ere you are, duck,' she said, as she handed it to him.

With his mouth full, Billy began to relax and he told her about Theresa's child and her father's rage.

'Aye, I saw Theresa when I were with your Mam; I know'd the kid were about due. And I know Theresa's on the game. She should've done wot I told her; then she wouldn't have had to 'ave it.' She paused to reflect, while Billy watched her over his slice of bread and cheese. Then she said, 'Anyways, Mary should've called me to help with the lyin'-in. Mike wouldn't 've touched either of 'em, if I'd bin there.'

Billy swallowed his current mouthful of bread with a gulp, as he again shivered. He had no doubt that Great-aunt Kitty, with her unearthly powers, could stop Mike dead, if she wanted to.

The old lady took the kettle off the fire and poured the reboiled tea into two tin mugs, one of which she handed to Billy; the other she laid on the hob to keep warm for herself. She slopped some milk from a milkcan into both mugs and followed it with generous spoonfuls of sugar from a tin. Then she offered the boy another slice of bread which, despite his timorousness, he accepted eagerly.

He wondered how she managed to have such a handsomely full food cupboard, though the rest of her room looked as skint as that of a family the day before payday, when everything pawnable would have been pawned.

Great-aunt Kitty was, in fact, a busy woman. Like many elderly women, she was in demand to help to deliver infants or nurse the sick or lay out the dead, for which she was paid a little either in cash or in food. Her main income came, however, from moneylending, illegal lending to hard-pressed housewives in nearby streets. She would lend them sixpence on a Monday, provided they paid her back eightpence on the following Saturday, when most of them got their housekeeping money from their husbands. The women were enormously grateful to her. She enjoyed their goodwill until they fell behind with their payments and she arrived like an angry raven on their doorsteps to collect. Knowing the borrowers' ignorance of the law she frightened them with threats of Court proceedings, or, more practically, with the wrath of their husbands if she told tales of the wives' borrowing. If they failed to pay her, even after being solemnly cursed with gruesome maledictions, she still made a tremendous profit from those who did meet their obligations.

When she had heard Billy through to the end, she leaned forward and shovelled a small pile of damp, slack coal over the little fire, to keep it burning slowly without having to use larger lumps. Then she sat back in her wooden rocking-chair and thoughtfully stroked her chin, which was as thickly covered with white hairs as that of an old man.

After a minute or two, during which Billy watched her nervously, she suddenly asked, 'You a Methody or a Catholic? I were never sure.'

Billy was nonplussed. He had never been to any kind of church. Caught between a harried Roman Catholic mother and a father who was an oddity who went to open air Wesleyan meetings, and living in a court not very often visited by clerics of any persuasion, he had no idea what he was. His mother had once taught him how to say a rosary; his father had been firm that one must pray directly to God, though, mostly, he had assured Billy, prayers were not answered. For himself, as a toddler in the court, Billy had learned that it was essential for survival to join the solidly Roman Catholic male population in ambushing and beating up Protestants on Orange Day – and to duck participation in Roman Catholic Processions on Saints' Days if he did not want a pummelling from Protestant lads.

Nonplussed by Kitty's query regarding his religious affiliations, he muttered, 'I dunno.' He did not dare to take a chance on settling upon one or the other religion, in case it turned out to be the wrong answer to give a witch.

'Well, if you was a Methody, now, that Holy Joe wot come to see your Dad, he might help you.' Her toothless mouth spread in a wry grin. She considered herself a Roman Catholic, but she knew that if she asked a local priest to help Billy, the boy would probably end up in the Kirkdale Industrial Home or some similar institution, which in her opinion would be like condemning him to hell everlasting. She said aloud, 'And I don't want you to end up in the Workie either.'

The mention of the Workhouse was enough to make Billy begin to blench. 'Oh, no, Auntie! Can't I stay with you?'

She looked at him not unkindly. 'It's whether I can stay with *you*, duck. I 'aven't got that long.' She was silent while she considered the increasing swelling of her stomach, the fierce ache in her back, her sticklike thinness, and the opium she bought from Vietnamese sailors to ease her pain. No, she had not long. But she, too, was determined to stay out of the Workhouse by never going near the Dispensary, never mind a Workhouse doctor. She would die in this very room, she was determined of that, and in her mattress lay enough silver coins to pay for a decent funeral.

Billy stared at her. His heart raced with a fear of the ruthless discipline of charitable Homes and the semi-starvation in the Workhouse, of the beatings, the confinement, the bullying and misuse of him by other inmates, the toil of grinding bones or breaking stones. Holy God, preserve him from such places! He had heard that in the Workie you were kept so hungry that it was a relief to eat the rotting marrow out of the bones before you crushed them for fertilizer.

Like everyone else, he was terrified of crossing the path of a Workhouse Master. Better to go to gaol, any day – at least there, you eventually came to the end of your sentence and were let out.

'Let me stay, Auntie,' he pleaded. 'If you want to move to another room, I could help you. I'm strong.'

'You can't help me where I'm goin',' she replied drily. She sucked her toothless gums and poured herself another cup of black, stewed tea. Then, with shaking fingers, she managed to pull the cork out of the whisky bottle and splashed some of the contents into her cup.

She rammed the cork back into the bottle, and said to Billy, ''Ere, put this back into cupboard for me, before a neighbour comes in and spots it.' A decent display of abject poverty was, she had always felt, necessary to her personal safety.

As Billy obeyed, she continued the line of conversation. 'If I were to send you to live with anybody we knows, the same thing would happen as 'as happened at Mary's – the man wouldn't want you around – particularly as you grows bigger. You could work your heart out and give 'em everything you earned, without keeping a meg for yourself – but soon they'd get fed up with yez – and out you'd go. And you'd have no place – and that could mean the Workie.' She sipped her laced tea thoughtfully, as Billy's heart sank ever lower.

She noted his expression, and grinned at him. 'It int that bad, duck. The more I think about it the more I think you'd better be a Methody

– after all, your Dad was – and I think we'll do it. Tomorrer we'll go down to the chapel and see the Holy Joe wot came after your Mam died. He might have some new idea – and we can always say No, if we don't like it.'

12

On the last day of September 1896, as the rays of the evening sun gleamed softly over the smoking chimney pots, Billy Tyson eased open the Woodmans' alley door and crept quietly down the path towards the kitchen.

'What do you want?' inquired a disembodied female voice.

Billy whirled round. He could see no one. He glanced nervously up at the house windows above him; they were empty of people.

There was a chuckle from high in the apple tree to his left. He turned and looked up. A pair of long, black-stockinged legs topped by divided drawers swung suddenly down to a lower branch. Then Alicia jumped in a flurry of spreading calico pinafore and pleated serge skirt. He caught an embarrassing glimpse of the prettiest little white bottom, as she landed on all fours, bringing with her a shower of small green apples and loose leaves. She picked herself up and rubbed her hands free of bits of damp grass.

Though Alicia had accepted him with almost the same ease that she did Mr Bittle, Billy was aware of the big social gap between them. He whipped off his cap and waited cautiously for her to speak.

'How are you, Billy?' she asked cordially.

'I'm all right, thank you, Miss.' Then, unable to contain his excitement, he burst out, 'I got some good news for our Polly.'

'She's clearing up dinner, but I can get her for you, if you like.'

He blushed and glanced uneasily away from her, and then answered, 'If you would, Miss – for a minute, like.'

She noticed his change of colour under the heavy grime, and she smiled. She flitted across the grass and down the steps to the kitchen door, her silver-fair hair, for once unplaited, flowing softly behind her. He watched her, fascinated, as she lifted the latch and went indoors; she was so white, unlike the young girls in the courts.

When Alicia entered the kitchen she found Polly unloading the dirty dishes from the dumb-waiter. On hearing that Billy wanted to speak to her, she left her work and hurried anxiously into the brick area and up the stone steps towards him.

When Billy saw her worried face, he laughed and shouted to her, 'I'm going to Canada, Pol. Day after tomorrow – to work on a farm.' He ignored Alicia, who had followed behind her.

Polly paused at the top of the steps. Her mouth fell open. Then she gasped, 'To Canada? Holy Mother save us! How come, luv?'

He persuaded her to sit down on one of the steps, while he explained to her about Great-aunt Kitty's and his visit to the Methodist minister.

'I'm going proper quick 'cos I'm taking the place of a boy what died last week; the Methody is fixin' it. Ordinary, like, they don't send kids out at this time – they send 'em at the beginning of summer. But they got so many that they're sending this lot special through the Kirkdale Home.'

Polly was appalled. For her brother to be delivered to the untender mercies of the Kirkdale Industrial School, even for a few days, was shocking enough to her; to be sent to Canada was like being tipped over the edge of the earth.

Billy was babbling on about the Methodist minister. 'He says I'll get a farm of me own one day, if I work. A farm, Pol!'

'You'll never come back, our kid,' Polly wailed. 'People go there – and that's the last you ever hear of them.'

'I'll come back,' he promised earnestly. 'I'll come and fetch you when I got a farm.'

Polly's eyes glistened with tears and she twisted the ends of her apron with agitated hands. Alicia had crouched at her nanny's feet while she listened. Now she put her hand on Polly's knee, and said, 'Don't cry, Polly, dear. Billy'll write to you, won't you, Billy?'

''Course, I will, Miss. I'm not that good at me letters, but I know enough to write – don't you fret, our Polly,' he reassured his sister. 'Anyways, when I work on a farm, the farmer has to send me to school. The Methody promised.'

Alicia looked up at Polly. 'There, you see. You don't have to worry.'

Polly nodded her head hopelessly. 'But it snows all the time there – and there's the Red Indians and the Frogs – I mean the French – it int safe.' All the novels that Polly had read about the American West came to the fore of her mind.

'I'm goin' to get warm clothes given me,' Billy assured her. 'And I'm not going where the French are.'

'Where are you going, Billy?' Alicia asked.

'I don't know exactly, Miss. It depends where the farmer is who wants me. I have to write home and say where I am, soon as I get settled.' He turned to Polly. 'Cheer up, Pol. There's lots of us going – all orphans, like me.'

'It's dangerous, chook. It's too dangerous.' She wiped her damp face with her apron.

'It's not – they wouldn't send us if it was. I'll save me wages and I'll buy a farm.' He sighed blissfully. 'What a chance, Polly! Dad would've jumped at it.' He leaped up and spread out his arms to encompass the pretty garden. 'When I got a farm, you can come and make a garden like this for yourself.'

Polly threw her apron over her head and began to keen. 'It'll take ages. How will I go on without you? There'll only be Mary and me.'

'And me,' interjected Alicia softly, suddenly shaken by the idea that Polly could leave her.

Though Billy was still young, he had all the common sense of his mother. But for the moment he was far away, dreaming wildly of a little house on land as big as Sefton Park, a house with apple trees around it. Flitting in his mind's eye was a little creature living there with him, a creature with long fair hair and a wicked chuckle who liked climbing apple trees. After the destruction of his way of life that sad September, he had suddenly been handed a little hope and it was almost too much for him to cope with.

13

I

The winter came to Liverpool with gales howling in from the Atlantic. Rain pelted on the burgeoning city, swirled in the filthy courts, flooding the latrines and spreading stomach ailments amongst the sodden inhabitants. Hardly strong enough to creep across the yard to the privy, Great-aunt Kitty took to her bed, swallowed a large dose of a drug bought some time back from a Thai stoker, and died alone.

It was two days before the tenant of the house noticed her absence, and it was only when Polly went to visit her three weeks later, on one of her afternoons off, that the family learned of her death. By then, the room was occupied by someone else, and the landlord said that all the old lady's possessions had been thrown in the midden in case she had died of something catching.

Through her tears, Polly upbraided the man for not sending for Mary or Mrs Fox. 'You knew where to find them, you lousy bugger,' she shouted at him. But in her heart she knew that the room had been picked clean by him and he had then reported the death to the Medical Officer as being that of a destitute old woman. Like her niece, Bridie Tyson, Great-aunt Kitty had had a pauper's funeral.

Polly had seen it happen before. Boiling with anger but unable to prove any misdoing, she went away to see Mary and to grieve with her for the death of a wise old woman. She did not mention her loss to Alicia.

II

One day in January, as Alicia sat at the nursery table carefully sketching into her botany exercise book the root system of a piece of Shepherd's Purse, Polly looked up from her mending, and said, 'You know, I'm that raddled with worry about our Billy. Three months and no word from him.'

'You could go to see the Reverend Whoever-he-is at the Methodist Chapel, and ask if he's any news.'

'I already done it on me Sunday off. He were proper nice and he said the children reached the Home in Toronto safely. He says, though, that each kid is supposed to write home to say his exact address, 'cos they get sent all over.'

'I suppose he can write, Polly?'

'Aye, he can a bit. Me Mam sent 'im to dame school, same as me. 'Course, I never learned me letters proper – it were Master Charles wot really taught me.' She bit her cotton off with her teeth, and then said, 'But he's smart enough to get someone to help 'im, if he needed to.'

Alicia leaned back from her drawing and put her pencil down on the table. 'Perhaps Canadian stamps are too expensive for him,' she suggested.

'Well, I dunno. Surely wherever he's workin', they'd give 'im one stamp, so as he could write home?'

III

Alicia was right. Everything is too expensive to those who have nothing. Even if Billy had been free to go to the Metis village some twenty miles from the tiny sod hut in which he found himself, he had no money to buy a piece of paper, a pencil or a stamp.

To a street arab like Billy, though used to the discipline of work, the Canadian Children's Home which was his first destination felt like a prison. With the sixty other children who had travelled with him, he endured it for a week, while he was supplied with warm clothing, new boots and a Bible to put in the almost empty tin trunk given to him by the Kirkie. He then said a cheerful goodbye to the other children and was put on an immigrant train travelling westward, in the care of the conductor.

For twenty-four hours, the train chugged its way through what appeared to be endless forest and gradually his spirits fell. The immigrant families in the train spoke other languages and ignored him. He ate the two slices of bread given to him by the Home.

In the chilly, early morning hours, the train stopped at a wayside halt, and the conductor let him down on to the tiny wooden platform. There was no sign of any building or people and he could not see anything which indicated the name of the place.

As the conductor helped the boy lift his small trunk down from the train, he said cheerfully, 'I've no doubt somebody'll be along to collect you as soon as it's light.'

As he blew his whistle for the train to proceed, he looked down at the thin, small figure in its shabby secondhand overcoat and cloth cap standing forlornly by the tin trunk, and he thought with compassion, 'Another poor little bastard, God help him.'

As the train vanished into the forest, Billy looked around him and absolute terror began to grip him. Beyond the end of the tiny platform huge pine trees, black in the dawn light, pressed in upon him. The eery silence was broken only by the soughing of the wind through the wall of evergreens.

Where was he?

He wanted to scream in terror, and run – run anywhere. He looked along the shiny track of the railway lines over which he had travelled. It had been like this – just trees – all day yesterday, with only tiny settlements in clearings by halts like this or a solitary Indian watching the train pass.

He sat down on his trunk and clasped his arms round his knees and tucked his head down. His breath came in quick gasps, making a small cloud in the cool air.

'Holy Jaysus, send somebody,' he prayed. 'Anybody!'

There was a rustle in the undergrowth and stories of bears rushed into his head. He screamed, and clutched himself tighter.

'You William?' a voice inquired.

At first the question did not penetrate his paralysed mind, but when it was repeated, he slowly looked up.

What he saw was not reassuring. A strangely garmented man with a dark face framed by black plaits down either side loomed in the half light.

The boy took a moment to find his voice. Then he quavered, 'Yes. I'm Billy Tyson.' He got slowly to his feet.

'Come.'

Billy looked uncertainly down at his trunk. The man bent down to take hold of the handle at one end and gestured to Billy to take the other end. Watching the stranger all the time, Billy did as he was bidden. The man smelled strongly of wood smoke, and his coarse, woollen coat was heavily stained at the front. His trousers, tucked into knee-high laced boots, seemed to be made of skin and were equally dirty.

Without a further word, the man led him down a narrow, slatted slope at one end of the wooden platform and along an almost invisible track through the trees.

The path led into a cleared circle in the centre of which were huddled several log cabins. Smoke curled from stone chimneys. A dog barked at their approach and was joined by a chorus of yapping from numerous other tethered canines, all with big fluffy tails and heavy coats.

As they came towards the cabins, the wind brought another odour besides that of burning wood, an odour all too familiar to Billy from his work in dockside warehouses, the sickening smell of untanned or partially tanned hides.

They put down the trunk at the threshold of one of the cabins. The man opened the door and preceded him inside.

As Billy hesitated on the doorstep, it seemed to him, in the poor light of an oil lamp and an open fire, that he saw nothing but eyes. They peered out at him from rough bunks against the walls; they stared up at him from the floor and from round a wooden table.

Gradually the eyes had faces added to them and then untidy bodies. A woman was squatting by the fire, cooking something on a heated stone. She wore a long, brightly printed cotton skirt with what looked like a black, woollen bodice. As the man sat himself down at the table, she glanced up at Billy and said to him in a strong Scottish accent, 'Come to the fire. You must be cold.'

As Billy nervously advanced towards the blaze, she rose and gingerly picked up some of the hot bannock she had been cooking and put it in front of the man at the table. She spoke to him in a strange language, as she took down a mug from a shelf and poured out coffee for him from a pot which had been standing in the hearth.

The dark brown children – for most of the eyes belonged to children – slowly began to gather round Billy. They touched his long overcoat and giggled, black eyes reflecting the dancing flames of the fire. He felt suddenly safer and grinned back at them.

Their mother was going to a tumbled bed at the further end of the big, stone fireplace. She carried a mug of coffee with her, and a thin, wrinkled hand took it from her. A white head was turned. For a second, Billy was the recipient of a glance so piercing that it seemed to the boy that in that moment a total inventory of him had been taken. Then the eyes were politely averted.

Billy timidly extended his hands to the fire and rubbed them. If the weather was as cold as this in October, he wondered what it would be like in January; he wished he had some gloves.

He looked surreptitiously round the hut. The interior was not unlike the cellar dwelling in which he had grown up, except that the smell was different and the fire seemed enormous.

The woman put a warm piece of bannock into his hand and then distributed pieces to the children. He stood near the fire with the other youngsters and wolfed down the food gratefully, while the woman explained to him in good English that he was to wait with them until full daylight and then a man would come for him.

She turned to her husband and spoke to him in their own language. He nodded, and grunted agreement. 'Macdonald,' he said directly to Billy.

The woman poured coffee for herself, and Billy watched her shyly. Then he ventured a question. 'Are you farmers?'

She took a sip from her coffee, and then answered, 'No. We trap.'

The blank look on Billy's face made an older girl begin to giggle, and her mother, realizing that he did not understand, explained, 'We trap animals – beaver and foxes mostly – for their fur. Soon it'll be time for my husband to set his trapline.'

At this interesting reply, a whole mass of questions tumbled into Billy's head, but the parents were obviously taciturn, so he ventured one more only; he felt he had to know the answer. 'Are you Red Indians?' he inquired, with breathless interest.

The woman smiled, and glanced at her silent husband placidly stirring his coffee. Billy realized suddenly that, unlike the rest of the family, her eyes were blue like his mother's. 'No,' she responded slowly. 'We're Metis people.'

Billy was very disappointed; he had looked forward to meeting a Red Indian, complete with feathered headdress and tomahawk, as described to him by Polly. He wondered what a Metis was.

The mother turned to the children and said something in the second language. A small boy opened the door. The morning sun was flooding the clearing with light, and the children wandered out into the warming sunshine, except for two babies crawling about on the floor. The biggest youngster, a girl with a long black plait, pulled at Billy's sleeve and indicated that he should go out with her. He glanced back at the woman and the quiet brown man drinking his coffee. She nodded agreement, so he followed the girl outside, at the same time struggling out of his coat. He laid coat and cap on top of his trunk. Without them, he hoped that other people would not stare at him; his jacket, breeches, long socks and black boots would, perhaps, look similar to the garments of his Metis host.

The girl indicated to him to wait, while she went to pick up a couple of buckets from beside the corner of the cabin. The tiny settlement was gradually coming to life. A man in a tall, widebrimmed hat brought out a horse, mounted it and rode away into the forest. An old woman crouched over a smoky fire with fish drying over it. Innumerable children ran about and then came to stare at him. The girl turned to shout at them in the strange tongue, which everybody except himself seemed to understand.

As the girl returned with a clanking pail in each hand, he asked, 'Can you speak English?'

The girl was the same height as he was. Her almond eyes twinkled at the question. 'Yes. Why?'

'Well, nobody else seems to, except your Mam.'

'A lot of us can speak it – if we feel like it! Even Dad knows it, though he speaks Algonquin mostly. Mother's father was from Scotland. He came out here to buy furs and then he married Grandma and stayed, to trap himself.'

While Billy digested this information, she led him along a path from behind the cabin to a little river, where two women were filling buckets with water.

Steadying herself by holding on to an overhanging tree branch, she reached down and filled the buckets from the swiftly flowing water.

Billy insisted on carrying one of the filled buckets back for her and in tipping its contents into a barrel by the cabin door. It took three trips to the river to fill the barrel, and Billy's aid to the girl brought forth some good-humoured jeering from a couple of youths lounging in the doorway of one of the homes.

Billy did not understand the words, but realized they were disparaging, and he asked, 'What did they say?'

She hesitated, and then said, with a grin, 'They said you were doing women's work and you must be like a woman.'

Billy scowled. 'Dirty bastards,' he snarled, but decided that it was not worth a fight, particularly when the opponents were taller.

They had just put away the buckets, when a heavily-built white man clumped past them and, without knocking, entered the cabin.

He came out again almost immediately. Billy stared apprehensively at him. 'Come on, you,' he ordered the boy testily. He bent and pushed Billy's overcoat and cap into the dust, to pick up the trunk and swing it on to his back.

Billy picked up his coat and cap and then glanced back at the girl. Her face was expressionless. His earlier fears returned to him, but he said to her, 'Thank your Mam for me.' Then he ran after Macdonald.

His new master crossed the railway line. On the other side was a lane where a horse and cart stood waiting. The man slung the trunk into the back of the cart and indicated that Billy should climb in after it.

He scrambled up beside a heavy sack of flour and stood uncertainly for a moment, not sure what to do.

'Sit down, you stupid bugger,' Macdonald snarled.

Billy hastily squatted down, his back against the side of the cart. Some of the children from the settlement had followed them and were standing on the higher ground of the railway embankment. He waved to them and they waved back. He felt better.

Macdonald mounted the driver's seat, cracked his whip and the horse started forward. The sudden upward jerk of the two-wheeled cart sent both Billy and his trunk skidding backwards to the tail. Macdonald laughed.

Ruefully rubbing a banged elbow, Billy crawled to the front of the cart and sat with his back to the driver. His fears returned.

The lady at the Toronto Home had explained to him that he would be bound to this white man until he was eighteen – and that would be nearly seven years. He was to work for him and, in return, he would be fed and clothed and sent to church and to school. At sixteen, he would be entitled to wages – two or three dollars a month. But in the streets and warehouses of Liverpool, Billy had seen types like Macdonald before and he was filled with dread.

Peeping over the side of the cart, he watched with despair the everlasting ranks of trees on either side of the track. Where was he? The train conductor must have known the name of the halt, but Billy had been expecting a proper station with a name on it, so it had not occurred to him to ask the man. He peered once more at the crumpled label tied to the buttonhole at the neck of his coat; it had a confusing series of numbers and Macdonald's name; how could he have known that the numbers were a surveyor's description of a particular quarter-section of land in an area of forest just opened up to settlers?

14

I

The cart bumped its way slowly along a narrow lane thickly carpeted with pine needles. Once or twice, between breaks in the trees, Billy caught a glimpse of a twist of smoke against the intensely blue sky, a suggestion of human habitation. There seemed, however, to be no sound left in the world, except for the squeak of the cart's wheels and the muffled clop of the horse's hooves. To Billy, used to the hurly-burly of the docks and the city, to a boy who had never even seen the English countryside, it was extremely frightening. But most of all, he feared the man who was driving. At one point, he got up enough courage to kneel up behind him and ask him, 'Where are we? What's the name of the place we're goin' to?'

The response was curt. 'Sit down, and mind your own business.'

Billy sat down. He longed for something to eat and for a horse blanket like the one Macdonald had across his knees, to wrap round himself to keep out the chill invading him.

They turned off the track they had been following on to an even bumpier one, and then several more turns, each time on to a narrower path. The pine trees closed in more tightly than ever, brushing their fronds against the cart and shutting out the sunlight. Billy felt as if a gaoler had closed the door on him.

In the afternoon, when it seemed as if they would never get out of the forest, the track debouched into an area where raw tree stumps indicated a fresh clearing. There was a large vegetable patch partially harvested; and newly washed clothes had been laid out to dry over a few bushes which had already lost their leaves to autumn. From a rise in the ground, came an unexpected plume of smoke. A baby wailed in steady, demanding notes, and from a nearby tree, a tethered goat complained loudly. Billy looked at the goat in bewilderment and decided it must be some kind of sheep.

The driver shouted at the horse and the cart stopped at the rise in the ground. Billy kneeled up to see over the side of the cart. To his astonishment, he was in front of a cabin half-buried in the ground. The roof was covered with turf.

Nearby, a rough enclosure had been made of logs and looked as if it were in process of being roofed with timber.

A woman holding a tiny baby wrapped in fur came up out of the cabin. She had on a black skirt and shawl, such as Billy's mother had worn; her long, narrow face was red, as if she had been in the sun too long; her hair was scraped back from it and tied in a knot on top of her head. As Macdonald climbed down from the cart, she said in a strong Scottish accent and without preamble, 'I want some water.'

Billy climbed carefully over the back of the cart and dropped to the ground. He was stiff with cold and the long hours of sitting in an awkward position. 'Give 'im the bucket,' Macdonald growled.

To Billy he said, 'Put that fancy overcoat down and get 'er some water.' He pointed to a narrow path leading into the trees on the other side of the clearing.

Bewildered and scared, Billy was slow in finding a place to lay his coat down. The man came to where he stood glancing anxiously about him, and shouted into his face, 'Get a move on. When I tell you something, you *run* and do it. Understand?' Bloodshot eyes glared at him from a bristled face.

Billy hastily bundled up the coat and laid it near the logs which formed the visible part of the cabin. Mrs Macdonald picked up a galvanized bucket and handed it to him. He snatched it from her and ran towards the path which had been indicated. The pines' long fingers seemed to lock over his head, but after a couple of hundred yards the pencil-thin path sloped down to a narrow swift-flowing river with more close-packed forest louring at him from the further bank.

For a moment, he could not think how to dip the bucket into sufficiently deep water to fill it without getting his boots soaked. In a semi-panic, he scouted up the river a few yards, following another little path. At the end of it he found a point where the river swirled in and out of a slight curve in the bank. He lay on his stomach and dipped the bucket in.

When he first tried to lift the vessel out, it was so heavy that he splashed half the contents over its sides. He tried filling it again and, when hauling it out, he rested it, half way, on a jutting stone. He scrambled to his feet and managed to get it up on to the bank. He carried it slowly and carefully back to the cabin.

'You took your time,' the woman snarled at him, and snatched the pail from him so clumsily that she splashed herself. 'Careful!' she shrieked at him, as he looked helplessly at her, his throat constricted with dread of the whole place and its inhabitants.

He spent until nightfall helping Macdonald roof the unfinished building he had noticed on his arrival. He was sick with hunger.

For the most part, the time was spent in silence, but he did learn that Macdonald was clearing his first quarter-section. This alerted Billy to the fact that an immigrant could, indeed, own land, and he ventured a cautious question or two as to how the quarter-section had been acquired.

Macdonald told him that when he first came out from Dundee, he had worked on the farm of an established settler. Later on, when he had obtained the land, he had commenced to clear it during quiet months on his employer's farm. The family had lived in a lean-to tent while he built the cabin. He had hoped to get a crop in that summer, but had managed only a large vegetable patch.

'If we get through this winter,' he told Billy gloomily, 'it'll be a bleedin' miracle. The other boy they sent me was no help.'

More fear clutched at Billy's throat; he knew how, even in Liverpool, a bad winter could pick people off.

As the sun went down, Billy was ordered to put away the saws and axes, while Macdonald milked the goat.

Macdonald had actually driven down to the Metis village the day before and had continued on to a farmer who owned a small mill. There, he had bought a sack of flour for the winter and had picked up Billy at the railway halt on his return journey. Together, they now heaved the sack into the cabin.

Mrs Macdonald complained that she did not know where to store it. Macdonald told her sharply to shut up; she was lucky to have it.

The interior of the cabin seemed to Billy's weary eyes infinitely cosy. A good wood fire blazed in a stone hearth. The floor was earthen, but that was no different from the floor of the cellar in which he had lived with his parents. The walls were made of logs chinked with clay. Near the top of one wall a pair of shutters opened to the fresh air. At one side a sacking curtain was drawn across the little room and on another side was a closed door, which Billy later discovered led to a storeroom. A couple of benches and a table, obviously homemade, and a bunk against a wall, appeared to be the only furnishings. On the walls were hung tools, basins, a tin bath and some articles which Billy did not know the use of.

A pannikin of water lay on the table and Macdonald rinsed his hands and face in it and dried himself on a piece of rag. He indicated to Billy that he could do likewise and should then take the pannikin outside and empty it on the vegetable garden. Billy did as he was told. When he seized the handle of the shallow pan, he slopped the water on the floor, and Mrs Macdonald's tight lips exploded with an angry 'Tush! Look what you're doing.'

He came back into the cabin to find a modest dish of rabbit stew and potatoes waiting for him. He thankfully ate this whilst standing at the table. The Macdonalds sat down on a bench side by side, the baby sleeping in its mother's lap, and ate much larger helpings.

As soon as Billy put down his empty plate on to the table, Macdonald told him, 'Go out and split some logs from the woodpile and bring them in for the Missus.'

'Lay them at the side of the chimney here, to dry,' Mrs Macdonald chimed in, as she rose from the table, holding her baby against her shoulder.

Billy looked longingly at the remains of the stew in an iron saucepan on the table, but the hint was not taken. He turned, and trailed slowly up the wooden steps to the door.

Billy had expected that outside it would be dead dark, but once his eyes got used to it, he found he could see fairly well in the starlight. He went, first, down to the privy, a hole in the ground inside a shack as yet unroofed.

As he split the logs, he remembered when he had helped his father do the same thing. They would go at night to the shore to steal driftwood, bits of wrecks, wooden boxes, even trees, swept on to the river shore by the tide, and the next day they would reduce them to firing easy for his mother to handle. Swaying with fatigue and lack of sufficient food, he let the tears fall. 'Aye, Mam,' he cried to the uncaring pines.

He stumbled back and forth to the stove with the firewood, until Mrs Macdonald said it was enough and that he could go to bed in the bunk by the storeroom door. He took off his boots and, after opening them out to dry, he fell into the coffinlike bed and spread over himself the coarse blanket he found there. Without even a straw mattress or pillow, the bed was hard, but he was so exhausted that he slept immediately. He awoke, feeling very cold, when Macdonald shouted to him from behind the sacking curtain to make up the fire.

Except for a few embers on the hearth, the cabin was dark, and Billy could not at first think where he was. Then memory reasserted itself, and he stumbled out of the bunk to do as he was bidden.

It was still dark outside, when Mrs Macdonald shook him and told him it was time to get up. The baby was sobbing heartily and, from behind the sackcloth curtain, Macdonald shouted to her, 'Can't you shut the brat up?'

She did not answer him. Working by the light of the fire, she was stirring something in a saucepan; the baby, to Billy's complete astonishment, was hanging in what appeared to be a bag hung on the wall beside the fireplace. He dared not remark on it. Agonizedly stiff and cold, he staggered towards the warmth of the fire, and was immediately handed a plate of porridge. 'Eat up,' Mrs Macdonald commanded, 'there's coffee in the pot on the hearth there. Then get your boots on and get the goat out of the barn. See if you can find a tree to tether it to where the grass is clear of snow.'

So that was what the animal was. A goat!

'Will it let me?' asked Billy, as he knelt by the hearth to fill a mug of coffee. He sipped the bitter brew cautiously; he had never tasted coffee before. 'I've never seen no goat before.'

The woman laughed, as she put porridge out for her husband. 'Where've you kids been all your lives? You're the second boy we've had and neither of you've seen a goat!'

Macdonald pulled back the sackcloth curtain and emerged, tightening his belt buckle as he came to eat his breakfast. He laughed with his wife. 'Take the little pail off the nail there – try milking her when you've tied her up.'

Billy learned to hate that goat. He hated it even more than he had hated the subnormal boy who had bullied him as a child in the court.

Shivering in the cold of the October morning, he forcibly dragged the reluctant goat out of the relative comfort of the barn, found a tree with less snow under it than most, and tethered the animal to it. Then he put the pail under the suspicious animal, squatted down by it and attempted to milk it as he had seen the cows milked in the dairy where Mike worked. The goat edged away, turned and butted him crossly. Billy unbalanced and toppled sideways. The goat backed away from him to the furthest extent of its rope, put its hard little head down and prepared to charge. Billy scrambled out of reach, his hands freezing in the snow.

From the doorway, Macdonald guffawed with laughter. He came forward, picked up the pail and motioned Billy to watch him. He went up to the angry animal, spoke surprisingly softly to her, squatted on his heels and put his head against her side and she let him milk her, while she took occasional bored nips at tufts of grass poking through the snow. Occasionally, she raised a resentful, malevolent eye towards Billy.

The goat did not produce much milk, and Macdonald said she was nearly ready for mating again, but the nearest billygoat was almost fifteen miles away; it was a long way to take her.

'Is that the nearest farm?' asked Billy, thoughts of escape to the forefront of his mind.

'Yes. And there's only a narrow trail to it; I can't get the cart through from this side.'

He handed the pail to Billy and told him to take it to Mrs Macdonald.

'Anybody else live round here?' asked Billy, trying to sound casual, as they walked towards the cabin.

'There's the Metis village that you saw, but that's nearly twenty miles from here. They trap, and there's one or two more as come from further away; they've got traplines along the river.' He pointed to the water barrel. 'Fill it up for her. Then we'll finish roofing the barn. The horse's got to have cover for winter.'

The following day, Macdonald took the horse to the field he was clearing for ploughing in the spring; there were, apparently, numerous tree roots that he had either pulled loose or dynamited out and he needed to clear them away, if they had not already frozen to the ground.

Billy was left to help Mrs Macdonald. He hauled more buckets of water from the river than he cared to remember, to fill the water-barrel and a tin bath for doing the washing. By the time he was finished, he was sopping wet down one side of his breeches and his boots squished as he moved around. The water was bitterly cold, and he was thankful when Mrs Macdonald called him indoors to build up the fire for her, while she kneaded bread dough, using a piece of old dough as a raising agent. His boots were hardly steaming in the hearth, when she took him outside again to show him, quickly, how to fire a clay oven which her husband had built for her near the door. She said she would bake the bread and a rabbit pie in it.

The baby yelled, and he was told to stay out of the cabin while she gave the child her breast. Later, while the baby, swaddled in its rabbit skins, slept in its parents' wooden bed behind the sackcloth curtain and the bread was left to rise on the hearth, she and Billy pulled out the last of the carrots from the vegetable patch; not having time to harvest them earlier, she had hastily heaped earth and leaves over them in the hope they would not freeze. In these temporary clamps, they appeared to have survived, so they buried them in wooden boxes of river sand which Mrs Macdonald had dried at the side of the fireplace.

Finding that Billy was interested in what she was doing, she began to talk a little. She told him that the barrel in the corner of the cabin was filled with sauerkraut. He did not know what that was, so she explained that it was shredded, salted cabbage being allowed to ferment in its own juice. 'A German showed me how to do it,' she volunteered.

She asked if he could fish, because she had learned from the Indians how to dry fish, though there was not much time before the really intense cold set in. 'We've done well this year to have such a mild autumn,' she told him.

'I never learned to fish,' Billy said, in response to her question. 'There isn't many fishes in the Mersey now. Me Dad told me that when he were a boy he went fishin' with his Dad, and they always ate fish of a Friday. Now you got to go out to sea to get it – into the Bay, like.'

'There's a lake near here full of them,' Mrs Macdonald informed him. 'But Angus hasn't got the time; he must get the land cleared.' She sighed. 'If I'd got some money, I could buy any amount of fish from the Metis. Somehow, I'll get Angus to teach you how to ice fish – that would help feed us in the winter.'

In the late afternoon, Macdonald returned. The horse was dragging a spruce which had been roughly cleared of most of its branches.

Billy's immature muscles already ached as if he had been beaten, but after a piece of bread and a cup of coffee, Macdonald ordered him to take the other end of the saw and help him reduce the spruce to logs. When Billy did not pull or push hard enough, Macdonald cursed his ineptitude.

From the general tenor of the tirade, Billy learned that the same threat that beset Mrs Macdonald with her store of carrots, onions and sauerkraut, also bedevilled her husband. The winter.

The wood pile must be built up and up. Every scrap of food they could raise or barter for must be stored before the winter fell on them. Hay and oats and anything that could be culled from the forest or begged from the settlers he used to work for – the neighbour with the goat – must be collected to keep the horse and the goat alive.

When Macdonald paused to wipe the sweat off his face, Billy said, 'The Missus says as you'll teach me to fish.'

'Aye, I will. And to trap rabbits.'

The pain in Billy's back when he was roused the next morning made him cry out. Mrs Macdonald laughed at him and said he'd get used to it and to go and get her some more wood.

Outside, it was freezing and a powder of fresh snow lay on the ground. His damp boots were soon icy, as he hefted the split logs into the cabin.

At the end of a month he was still as hungry as he had ever been in Liverpool, and he was struck or kicked far more by both husband and wife than he had ever been in the great port.

No matter how he phrased the question, neither husband nor wife would tell him where he was. That information, they reckoned with a sly grin to each other, would give Billy a basis on which to work out how to run away, like the previous orphan had.

Remembering that the Macdonalds were supposed to supply him with clothes, he asked Mrs Macdonald if she could give him a pair of gloves. 'Me hands is so cold they froze to the bucket handle this morning,' he told her, fear of what the cold might do to his hands making him desperate.

She looked at him as if he had asked something absurd. Then she went to a wooden trunk in the storeroom and rummaged through odds and ends of clothing. She fretfully flung him a pair of her husband's old socks with large holes in their heels.

As he caught the socks, hatred of her seethed in him. Young and terribly disappointed, he gave no thought to her despair. He was, however, thankful to slip his hands into the heavy, smelly socks.

The water-barrel had been moved inside the cabin. Now she told him to refill it, as usual. 'Remember to keep breaking the river ice, to keep it open round where you get the water. Soon you'll have to cut steps through it to get at the water.'

Billy nodded. He had already been breaking the ice for some time, with the aid of a dead branch. When he contemplated Mrs Macdonald's forecast, he began to shake with fear. Would he freeze, too?

Could he follow the railway lines back to Toronto? he wondered frantically. How far did a train travel in a day and a night?

A few days back, he had tried to retrace his way to the Metis village, because he could not even follow the railway track until he found its shining lines. He had hoped that the Metis family he had met on his arrival might listen to him and help him. But within twenty minutes, mistaking an animal track for one of the turnings he had originally taken, he became lost. Fortunately, in his subsequent panic, he walked in a circle, and in the forest's uncanny silence he had heard Mrs Macdonald's voice shouting angrily for him. He had stumbled back to her through the bush and got a sound cuffing for his pains. She also told him that, earlier in the year, her husband had shot a cougar trying to get at the goat, and that it was capable of eating a boy.

'What's a cougar?' he had asked, as he thankfully swept the floor of the cabin for her and got warm again.

'It's like a lion.'

After hearing that, Billy never left the clearing alone, except to go for water, and sometimes in the evening, if he had to walk the trail to the river, a rustling in the undergrowth would cause him to break out in a cold sweat.

One night, in the cabin, when he was whittling dowels for his master, he thought about the Metis children at the railway halt. He wondered if they went to school. This reminded him that he was supposed to be sent both to church and to school.

School seemed suddenly like a rest cure, five or six hours of perfect peace after the intolerable load of work he was doing. He did not care about church, but attendance would ensure a comfortable sitdown, a happy change from working seven days a week from long before dawn to after dark. He paused in his whittling, penknife idle, while it struck him that he did not even know what day it was.

Sunday had been a day when both his father and mother had been at home; frequently it had been a day on which they went down to the shore to pick amongst the rubbish thrown up by the tide for anything that might be useful, a day when Polly sometimes came, bringing her wages and interesting gossip. An agony of loneliness went through him.

Macdonald looked up from the horse-collar he was repairing, and Billy hastily resumed his careful whittling.

The prim lady at the Home in Toronto had promised that someone would visit him at the farm where he settled, to check that he was happy and behaving well. Not realizing the complexity of arranging such a visit, or that it might cost money, he had waited as patiently as he could for the visitor to arrive, so that he could ask to be moved. But, like many other such children, he was in a place so isolated that no local worthy could be recruited to visit – not that it would necessarily have done much good; children were usually interviewed in the presence of their employers and were too afraid to complain.

Since his arrival at the cabin, Billy had seen no other person than his employers, and he wondered, suddenly, if other settlers disliked the Macdonalds as much as he did.

With a small burst of bravery, he broke the silence of the cabin, by asking Macdonald, 'When will I be able to go to school? And church? Like the lady at the 'Ome promised?'

Startled out of his usual moroseness, Macdonald stared at the boy, his needle poised over the collar's leather. Mrs Macdonald laughed almost hysterically.

'Where'd you go? The nearest school is thirty miles off. And church the same. Have to wait for months, sometimes, for a priest to come through to marry you – or christen you.' He gestured with his needle towards the child sleeping on its mother's lap. 'He'll be on his feet before he's christened.' He resumed his stitching, and then went on, 'Anyway, you're too big to be wasting your time in school; I can't spare you.'

Having got the man to talk, Billy asked once more, 'Well, what's the name of this place and the name of the place where the school is.' He tried to sound casual and went gravely on with his whittling, as he waited for a reply.

Macdonald growled, 'None of them's got names yet.'

Billy picked up another piece of wood and began carefully to pare it into rough shape. He wondered if the boy Mrs Macdonald had mentioned before had run away. 'What happened to the boy you had before me?'

'Drowned. He tried to cross the river on the ice and it gave under him. That's what comes of running away.'

Billy was shocked at Macdonald's laconic response.

'That was proper awful!'

'Bloody fool. Should've known better.'

II

Was it always going to be like this? Billy wondered. His ears hurt as they warmed up again, after going for the day's water. He stood inside the cabin at the foot of the steps, brushing the last of the snow still on his boots with a besom Mrs Macdonald had made. One boot had a small hole in the bottom and he had stuffed some straw from the barn into it to stop his foot freezing; he feared having to ask Macdonald for leather and tools to mend it.

Before he could take his overcoat off, Mrs Macdonald turned from feeding the baby cuddled under her shawl, to say, 'Go and open up the oven and get the bread out for me; it'll be more than done.' The baby lost her breast and whimpered. 'Take the basket off the shelf to carry it in.'

With a sigh, he swung the basket down, while she grumbled, 'After this lot we'll be down to bannock. It'll be too snowy out there to use the oven.'

'Oh, aye,' he agreed indifferently. If you had any sense you said as little as possible to the Macdonalds. Then you could not be clouted for impudence.

'Have you got the peel?'

He hastily unhooked, from a wooden peg by the door, a long-handled wooden shovel with which to get the bread out of the hot oven.

He had never been given this job before, but he had noticed that Mrs Macdonald was slowly pushing many of her household chores on to him – he had done a bath full of washing for her only a few days earlier, spreading the garments out on the bushes to dry. At first they had frozen; yet, to his astonishment, they had eventually proved to be almost dry.

He approached the oven with respect. He reckoned it must be very hot, but when he put his hand on the outside it was merely comfortably warm. Very cautiously, he opened the wooden door which was lined with metal. As the interior heat hit the cold air outside, a burst of steam blew into his face. The odour of the bread made his saliva run.

With great care, he first took out a covered stewpot and stood it in the shallow basket. Then, one by one, he shovelled out the round loaves and laid them in the basket, round the pot. When he had finished, he stood in the warmth still emitted by the oven and looked down at the bread. Hunger was a constant pain with him, and he suddenly pulled the sock off his hand, bent down and snatched up a loaf. Despite the bitter air, it was still extremely hot, but he broke it open and shoved a cob into his mouth. Though it burned the top of his mouth, it was good beyond words, and he tore another piece off and crammed it into his mouth.

Absorbed in the rapture of eating, he did not hear the quiet plod of the horse's hooves or the squeaking wheels. The whistle of Macdonald's buggy whip, as he bent from the seat of the cart and swung it across the boy's back, was the first indication Billy had of Macdonald's return from his field with a load of stones he intended to use to hold down the edges of the barn roof.

Billy nearly choked on the bread, as he cried out and swung round to face his attacker.

Red with fury, Macdonald leaped from the cart and caught him by the shoulder, forcing him to turn his back. 'I'll teach you to steal,' he roared. He raised his whip again and hit the boy across the back with the handle. The end of the lash snaked viciously round Billy and cut his lower lip.

Billy struggled to escape the remorseless grip as the blows rained down on him. 'I were that hungry,' he appealed frantically. He put his hand to his bleeding lip.

Macdonald hurled him face down on the oven's curved side and, holding him by the back of the neck, beat him unmercifully.

Twelve-year-old Billy was strong, but he was no hero. He howled so loudly that Mrs Macdonald came flying out, the baby crying in her arms. 'What's he done?' she cried. She stopped, to look bewilderedly at her loaves scattered in the snow and the stewpot, half-tipped over. Then she saw that Billy was bleeding at the mouth, and she yelled, 'That's enough, Angus! You'll kill him!'

Macdonald let go and threw Billy to the ground. Weeping and bleeding, he crawled through the snow to seek sanctuary behind Mrs Macdonald.

Ignoring him, Mrs Macdonald bent down to rescue the loaves and straighten the stewpot before it lost all its contents. The baby objected to being jostled about and cried all the harder. The half-eaten loaf told its own story.

'You greedy bugger,' she fulminated at Billy struggling to his feet, and sped back indoors out of the cold.

Macdonald strode back to the horse, to lead it to the barn. He turned and barked at Billy, 'You get over to the barn and get the ladder out, and you lay these stones along the edge of the roof till I tell you to stop, you damned thief.'

Unable to straighten his back properly, Billy dragged himself towards the barn. Sobbing, he looked down at his long, clumsy overcoat. Added to its dirtiness, it now had bloodstains from his swelling lip.

The stones would be frozen, he thought hopelessly; Macdonald must have had to use a pickaxe to loosen them from the pile by the field. Fear of further beating, however, drove him painfully towards the barn, to wait sullenly by the ladder while Macdonald unharnessed the horse and tipped the cart to let the stones roll off it.

As Macdonald led the horse into the barn to join the goat bleating in a corner, Billy stood staring at the stones; a skiff of snow was already powdering them over. Rage took over from pain.

'I'll kill him,' he promised himself savagely. 'One day I'll kill him. And then I'll run away. I'll die in the forest before I stay here.' He slowly lifted the home-made ladder and set it against the barn wall; the stones were heavy and awkward to carry up a ladder which rapidly became slippery and every journey hurt his battered back.

It was Mrs Macdonald who came through the early darkness, a lantern in her hand, to tell him to come in. He had not put many stones in place but in the dark his poor efforts went unremarked.

'Come on,' was all she said.

They passed a silent Macdonald going to the barn to check the horse and put a blanket over it before he went to bed.

In the candlelit cabin, Mrs Macdonald told him to wash his face, while she put some stew out for him. Afterwards, he went to the fire and stood warming his frozen hands and feet. 'Get to bed before he comes back,' she urged, so he took his plate and spoon into his bunk with him. He was beyond talking, but his hunger was such that he managed to eat his supper despite his hurt lip.

'Holy Mother, hear my prayer,' he whispered to himself, rage gone from him leaving him cowed and exhausted. 'Holy Mary, Mother of God, send the lady from Toronto – send her soon.'

III

November and December slipped away in unremitted work. He fed the animals, cleaned tools, went for water, shovelled snow away from the door and kept a path open to the frozen privy, cut kindling and did the washing. He also helped Mrs Macdonald make a pair of knee-high mocassins for each of them out of roughly tanned skins. As the sun curved through the sky closer and closer to the horizon, he waited and hoped.

In their despair, the Macdonalds did not keep Christmas, and Billy spent Christmas Day chipping steps into the ice in order to reach water in the river. Macdonald taught him how to snare small animals, skin them, scrape their skins clean and prepare them for eating. Together, they walked through the bush to a small lake, frozen like everything else. There they built a rough shelter with spruce boughs, bored a hole through the ice and Billy learned to fish. If Macdonald had been a more kindly man, Billy would have enjoyed learning these new skills, but his employer was, at best, irascible, at worst a bully to be feared.

In January, the cold became a dreadful nightmare and carrying water from the river, in clothing suitable for an English winter, became a battle which Billy began to feel he would lose. He begged another pair of socks and an old woollen shawl from Mrs Macdonald. The shawl he wrapped round his head and neck over his cap, to save his ears and cheeks from frostbite.

One night, the cabin became lined with ice and the baby froze to death. For once, Billy was sorry for Mrs Macdonald. She did not cry, but sat silently by the fire, her hands in her aproned lap, her domestic tasks undone. Macdonald tried to rouse her, without success. It was Billy who took whatever game he and Macdonald had been able to find and made stews out of it and tried to persuade the woman to eat. It was Macdonald himself who had to take the tiny bundle which had been his son outside and cover it with some of the stones from his field so that it could not be eaten by predators, until Spring should come and he could bury it. Both of them began to fear that Mrs Macdonald had lost her reason.

In the latter part of the winter, when rabbits became hard to find, they lived on oatmeal and on the odd fish, caught on days when the weather eased a little. Macdonald tried to cheer up his wife by saying that with the first money they got from next year's crop he would buy a rifle, so that he could hunt moose to fill their winter larder. To Billy, he worried that the horse and goat might not survive; it was a simpler matter to replace a baby than it was to replace a draught animal.

Billy crept on from day to day, numbed by the gruelling cold and, alternatively, the confinement to the tiny cabin.

One March day, when it seemed that the weather was indeed a little warmer, despite its being overcast, they took the horse out and felled another tree. By the time it had been dragged home, however, snow was beginning to fall and Macdonald said uneasily that he thought they were in for a storm. They stabled the horse and put its blankets over it and fed it. Macdonald had built an inner enclosure for the goat and laid spruce branches thickly on the floor of it and the animal was surviving, though it had chewed all the bark off the logs forming its pen.

The snow came down heavily and a wind whipped it into deep drifts, so that Billy was glad that Macdonald had earlier connected the cabin entrance to the privy by a rope; he knew that as long as he held on to the rope, he could find his way back to the cabin after relieving himself, no matter how thickly it was snowing.

It was this rope which led a trapper, caught in the white wilderness of the storm, from the edge of the clearing to their door. In his thankfulness at finding a warm refuge, he did not know that Billy was convinced that he had been sent by the Holy Mother herself.

IV

To Polly and Alicia in crowded England, it seemed impossible that Billy could have been in a place so isolated that it did not even have a proper name, only numbers from a survey map, a place where there were no shops or even another person, except his employers, until in a storm, a half-French, half-Red Indian man had sought shelter with them. Yet, there it was, all set out vividly in stumbling print over both sides of three pages torn from an account book.

Polly looked at the letter dumbfounded and then handed it to Alicia. 'It shouldn't happen to a dog!' she exclaimed. 'He were lucky that man told him the route down to the railway line; a simple way, even if it were longer – so he didn't get lost. Eight hours' walkin'. It's terrible!'

Alicia, too, was horrified by Billy's story. 'Poor boy! Thank goodness, he had enough sense to wait until the Spring came before he set out.'

'Aye.' Polly heaved a sigh. 'He never should've gone to Canada. I knew something awful would happen.'

'Well, it sounds as if he's all right now,' Alicia comforted her. 'The old pedlar who picked him up near the Metis village seems a decent sort. I'm sure he'll find it much easier helping him to sell buttons and cotton and things than working on a farm.'

Polly agreed, and then asked, 'But where's Winnipeg? That's where I got to write back.'

'It's in Manitoba on the Red River. I'll get the atlas and show you.'

Polly and Alicia had been tidying the linen closet opposite her mother's bedroom when the postman had brought the afternoon mail. Now she ran up the stairs from the second floor landing to the nursery and, more slowly, brought down her school atlas. While she looked for the page containing Canada, Polly said, 'He says that next Spring, they'll leave Winnipeg and go west.'

'Hm.' Alicia found Winnipeg and, leaning the atlas against the wall, so that Polly could see better where she was pointing, she said slowly, 'You know, Pol, there's an awful lot of Canada west of Winnipeg. I wonder where his pedlar's taking him?'

'Maybe when Master Edward comes home on leave – he's due soon – we could ask him if he knows the likely places.'

Alicia smiled. 'Of course we could.'

'I'd like to write back to Billy tonight. Would you help me, Allie? I'm not that good at writin' letters.'

'I'd love to.'

After dinner, Alicia sat for a short while with her mother and told her about Billy's adventures. Elizabeth did not appear very interested and Alicia was finally reduced to silence. Then her mother said, 'I want to talk to you about school.'

Sarah Webb had willingly agreed to share the cost of sending Alicia to Blackburne House School, so Elizabeth spent a few minutes explaining the advantages of the new school to Alicia. 'You will start in September,' she said.

'Yes, Mama.' She knew that the school was considered a good one, but she felt nervous about leaving Miss Schreiber and the girls with whom she was familiar. September was, however, a long way off, and in the meantime she had promised to help Polly with her letter, so she said no more and sat waiting for her mother to say she could go.

A little nonplussed at the absence of enthusiasm from Alicia at being sent to such an excellent school, Elizabeth dismissed her.

To help Polly, Alicia took her mother's tea tray down to the kitchen. Rosie, who had married her milkman at Christmastime, had not been replaced and Fanny and Polly were having to carry her work between them. They grumbled a great deal about the extra load and, recently, in bed at night, Alicia had felt sick with dread that they might hand in their notice and leave her faced with strange, new servants to take care of her.

15

I

In November 1899, Alicia lost an old friend.

After getting wet through on her day off, Mrs Tibbs caught pneumonia; she took to her bed with a temperature and a hacking cough, and Fanny and Polly grumbled at the extra work they had to undertake. It was assumed, however, that she would be up again in a couple of days.

Elizabeth endured several days of complaint from Humphrey about Polly's cooking before she descended to her cook-housekeeper's basement bedroom to inquire when she expected to be better.

Mrs Tibbs was obviously in pain and she did not recognize her mistress.

A frightened Elizabeth sent for the doctor, who on seeing the patient had her immediately transferred to the Infirmary. There, overnight, she died.

Elizabeth told Humphrey that she would try to find a good, new cook.

He glanced up from his desk in the library and replied, 'Teach Polly how to cook – we can't afford a full-time cook, anyway,' a remark which was far from true.

Elizabeth protested. Out of pure malice, Humphrey refused to budge. 'It wouldn't hurt you to do some of the cooking yourself,' he bellowed at her. 'Get off your fat bottom and do something, for a change.'

Shocked that he should mention any part of her anatomy, Elizabeth flounced out of the room.

In the hall, she bumped into Alicia on her way back to school after lunch. Her face flushed with rage, she paused and said angrily, 'I really don't know why Mrs Tibbs had to die so inconveniently. Polly will have to learn to cook from her cookery books!'

'Why, Mama?' Alicia had moved towards the front door and had her hand on the big, iron key, ready to turn it.

'Mr Woodman won't let me replace Mrs Tibbs.'

'He didn't let you get anyone instead of Rose when she got married.'

Fuming, Elizabeth ignored her daughter's remark, and said crossly,

'Fanny and Polly will simply have to split the work between them. Perhaps I can get a charwoman from the Workhouse to help in the mornings.'

'Yes, Mama.' As she opened the front door, her heart beat faster with apprehension. 'I hope Polly and Fanny don't feel the work is too much – and leave us, Mama?'

'I'll raise their wages,' promised Elizabeth, 'no matter what Mr Woodman says. I can't do it from my own money – with Charles to help – and then there are the Blackburne House fees . . . ,' she trailed off. Then she said impatiently to Alicia, 'Run along now – you'll be late.'

'Yes, Mama.'

Her mother swept across the hall to the dining-room where Polly was brushing up the crumbs from the linen tablecloth with a tiny crumb-tray and brush.

Alicia turned the key in the lock, swung open the heavy, oak front door and went slowly down the steps. She was deeply puzzled about Elizabeth's remark regarding school fees. She had always imagined that fathers paid for their children's education – and she knew from an overheard complaint of Humphrey's that he paid Charles's university fees – and, yet, if she had understood correctly, her *mother* was paying for her to attend Blackburne House. It seemed very strange and again suggested to her that there was something that made her different from other daughters.

II

Both Polly and Fanny were, at first, very resentful of the imposition of yet more work. Polly ventured to protest to Elizabeth that they already ran the house with two less staff than when she had first come to serve her. 'There's Maisie *and* Rosie gone,' she pointed out aggrievedly.

At the threatened loss of his remaining domestics, Humphrey grumpily gave in, and Elizabeth raised Polly's wages by thirty shillings a year and Fanny's by a pound – it was still much cheaper than replacing Mrs Tibbs. The two servants promised to think her offer over, and retired to the kitchen to boil up an extremely strong pot of tea and drink it with double helpings of sugar, while they angrily discussed their position.

Alicia came home from school while they were still talking. She ran to Polly and flung her arms round her. 'Guess what, Polly? I got full marks for my essay on Canada. Isn't it great? I'm sure it's because of writing to Billy and finding the places he goes to, on the map.' She turned excitedly to Fanny, 'I didn't even have a spelling error – first time it's happened.'

Fanny looked at Polly and began to laugh. Alicia looked at the two maids. She dropped her arms, and said crossly, 'Well, I don't think it's anything to laugh at.'

They hastened to comfort her and assure her that they were not laughing at her, but at themselves; they were both delighted at her success.

'I couldn't leave 'er, not if I tried,' Polly said to Fanny, when Alicia insisted on carrying her mother's tea tray up to her, to save Polly's legs.

'I knowed it – that's wot made me laugh,' replied Fanny, with one of her wide grins. 'And I don't know no other place. We'll manage somehow, we will.'

Polly made a list of the work to be done and submitted it to Elizabeth for approval. Elizabeth reluctantly agreed to it. It entailed doing house-cleaning at times other than the weekday mornings, ''Cos Fanny'll never get through it, now she's got to wait at table while I cook – and most times she'll have to answer the bell,' Polly said.

It particularly irritated Elizabeth that the morning-room, which she regarded as her own private sitting-room, was not cleaned before she rose in the morning. Sometimes, the work was done on a Saturday morning, and Alicia never forgot the problem of routing her mother out, once she was settled in her chair.

She would put her arms under her mother's armpits and say, 'Let me help you up, Mama.' Then she would heave her forward from the depths of the chair. It seemed as if, every month, her mother grew heavier, and that she did not smell quite as nicely as she used to. Her favourite, grey morning dress always seemed to be a little spotted with tea and in need of sponging and pressing. Her magnificent hair was bundled care-lessly into a snood at the back of her neck. As Alicia eased her carefully up the stairs to the big formal drawing-room to sit and have her coffee while the morning-room was cleaned, she would complain steadily, and Alicia would do her utmost to quell her own girlish impatience and respond non-committally by simply saying, 'Yes, Mama. I do under-stand how difficult it is for you.'

III

One by one, Elizabeth had given up her charitable endeavours; they had always been tedious to her and she found them increasingly tiring. Because they failed to attract the type of woman she would have liked to mix with, she ceased, also, to hold her weekly At Homes.

Added to the innuendo that followed Alicia's birth, ladies said behind their fans that she flirted too much at the dinners and dances which her husband insisted she attend with him. Her dresses were just a little too loud, her wit a little too sharp, and Elizabeth knew she was asked because she was Humphrey's wife, not from friendship towards her.

The ultimate humiliation had occurred at a private New Year Reception. She had heard a budding young medical specialist from the School of Tropical Medicine make a vulgar joke at her expense, and it had punctured her self-respect beyond repair – because it was so close to the truth. Afterwards, she began to lose her hold on life and to give way to her inward despair.

When she heard that Andrew Crossing's wife had died, she had enjoyed a few months of wild hope that he would seek her out, demand that she should divorce Humphrey and marry him. But after six months, he married his secretary.

Moving towards womanhood with all the dreams of a young girl, Alicia found it more and more difficult to endure her mother's moods; yet Polly assured her that it was her duty to do so. 'She's your Mam,' she reminded the girl sharply. 'You be patient with her; daughters have to bear with their Mams.'

On the rare occasions when Alicia went to church, the preachers would point up the need for young people to honour their parents. She also knew of older single women in the district who cared for ageing parents. She decided that Polly must be right. It irritated her, however, when Florence on one of her brief visits would take it for granted that it was Alicia, and not herself, who was going to do the honouring. 'Does marriage let you off?' Alicia wondered crossly.

IV

If it had not been for Polly and Fanny, Alicia would never have seen anything of the excitement of the special New Year which ushered the world into the twentieth century.

While her parents drove in a hired carriage to the home of one of Humphrey's friends for a New Year dinner, Alicia had eaten her own dinner at the kitchen table, rather than have Polly bring a tray up to the loneliness of the day nursery.

On her way down to the basement, she had been unnerved by the sound of quarrelling coming from her parents' bedroom. She knew that Humphrey sometimes hit her mother and the idea of anyone being struck sickened her, though Polly had often slapped her when she had done something wrong.

Elizabeth had failed to get up on the last day of the century. Humphrey had insisted that they *must* attend the dinner to which they had been invited. Finally, he had rung the bell furiously, and Polly had shot upstairs to answer it.

'Help your mistress get washed and dressed,' Humphrey had ordered her. His face purple, his white moustache quivering with rage, he had gone back into the dressing-room to change into his dinner clothes. 'The carriage will be here in an hour,' he had shouted to the women, as he slammed the door after himself.

Elizabeth was not ill. She simply did not want to make the effort, yet again, to be civil to women who obviously did not really want to know her. Since Polly was there, politely waiting, she did reluctantly rise from her bed, and within the hour Polly managed to have her washed, dressed and her hair well brushed and neatly braided round her head, though the style was most unfashionable. As she handed her mistress her long, white satin gloves and an ivory brisé fan, she felt some pity for her. 'You look very fine, Ma'am, in that plum colour,' she whispered encouragingly.

'Thank you, Polly. I had better put on my heavy cloak, though it doesn't match this gown.'

Polly got out the black velvet cloak and wrapped it round Elizabeth. Then she helped her down the stairs.

Humphrey was already waiting in the hall, his cloak over his shoulders. He carried a top hat and was impatiently drumming his fingers on its hard top. 'Hurry,' he called to his wife. 'We mustn't keep the horse waiting.'

He'd keep me waiting for hours, Elizabeth thought savagely, whenever he felt like it, but not a horse – not a horse.

The minute the front door had been shut after the Master and Mistress, the atmosphere of the house changed. Alicia had gone to wash her hands after her meal, and when she returned to the kitchen, she found the two maids sitting before the fire with their feet on the steel fender, a fender which badly needed polishing. On the floor between them was a jug of porter. They each held a mug in their hands.

'Coom on, luv,' invited Fanny, shifting her kitchen chair to make room for the girl. 'It's a proper shame they never thought of you havin' a bit of fun tonight.'

Alicia was so used to having to fill her evenings and holidays herself that this point had not occurred to her. Left to herself, she would have done her piano practice and then read until bedtime.

'Pull up a chair, duck,' Polly encouraged her, her plump face and blue eyes gentle to this child who was almost a woman.

As Alicia turned to get herself a chair, Fanny said, 'Polly and I was thinkin' we'd go up to the crossroads – you know, at Smithdown Road and Lodge Lane – afore midnight. Do you want to come?'

Alicia smiled. 'Why would you want to go up there?'

'Don't you know? Thousands a people goes every New Year. We have a great time. Everybody joins hands and the circle goes in and out of all the streets that meet there. And we sing and we have a good laugh. Then the men go first-footing, 'specially the dark ones 'cos they bring good luck.'

'What's first-footing?' Alicia asked, as she plunked herself down on the edge of her chair.

Fanny looked at her in amazement. 'Hasn't Polly never told you about it? You *have* bin missin' out. That's where they goes knockin' on all the doors, to come into the house – to be the first visitor, like. They has a bit o' bread in one hand and a bit o' coal in the other. And they get a drink for it.'

'It brings good luck to the house,' Polly interjected. She took a sip of porter and wiped her mouth with the back of her hand.

'Does anybody first-foot our house?'

'Well, when you was a little girl, when your Mam used to give a party, the Reverend, Miss Florence's husband, used to come, 'cos he's as dark as can be.' Polly took another sip, and sighed. 'But not no more. Do you remember, luv, at all?'

'Not really. They were grown-ups' parties. I used to hear them, sometimes, when I was lying in bed.' She paused, and reverted to Fanny's suggestion that they should go up to the crossroads. 'I don't think Mama would like me to go out in the dark.'

'Och, you'd be safe enough with the two of us, wouldn't she, Pol?'

'For sure you would. And if you don't tell your Mam, she won't know nothin'.'

Alicia did not reply. She felt that she could not forbid the maids to go; she guessed that, for years, those girls not likely to be missed by her mother had gone cheerfully off to this gathering. Tucked up in the attic nursery bedroom, she could often have been left alone in the house, if her parents were out, and she would not have realized it.

Now she was nearly grown up, Polly did not fuss so much about bedtime; and here she was, sitting with her two best friends, and, outside, the magic of this special New Year beckoned. What would the twentieth century be like, she wondered, lurking out there in the darkness, a mysterious unknown. And passionately she wished that it would be fun, that she might have a bicycle and go spinning out to the countryside on it – or even learn to play tennis, like Charles.

She looked up and smiled at Polly. 'What should I put on?' she asked.

'Wrap up warm,' Polly told her, as she got up from her chair and took her empty beer mug to the sink. 'And put your grey shawl up round your head and shoulders – then you'll look like everyone else up there and nobody'll know you.' She was suddenly uneasy that someone might recognize the girl; but then not many people knew her that well, she reassured herself.

They set out about half-past eleven, skipping along together. They passed out of the quiet streets and squares which formed their own salubrious neighbourhood, into a district of older small houses and shops. They soon joined a stream of humanity, the majority young working men. The whole concourse was extremely merry, and, with two mugs of porter inside each of them, both Polly and Fanny were very talkative. The excitement of the crowd was infectious and Alicia tripped along gaily between the two maids.

They joined a huge ring of people holding hands. Alicia's shawl fell back from her white-gold hair and her plait swung behind her, as she laughed up at Fanny.

A burly man in blackened labourer's clothing pushed between the young girl and Fanny. 'Allo, la, Fan. The ole girl let you out tonight, aye?' He grasped Alicia's hand, without looking at her, so as to keep the continuity of the ring.

Fanny laughed at him, and shouted back, 'I coom, anyways.'

'Must've known I'd be here.'

'Don't flatter yourself.'

Alicia clung on to Polly, on the other side of her. The crowd lifted their clasped hands and danced forward, converging on the point where all the streets met. Then they retreated backwards down each individual street as far as they could, without loosing hands, until, in the narrowness of the roadway they were face to face with part of the human chain on the other side of the street. Alicia found herself almost nose to nose with three well-dressed young men about seventeen years of age. They were all staggering and were largely held on their uncertain feet by the force of the people on either side of them.

'Alicia Woodman!' hiccuped one of them, as he recognized the daughter of a neighbour much talked-about by his parents. Loose-mouthed, he grinned at her before he was nearly thrown off his feet by the movement of the crowd as it reversed. He was hauled up by his friends and a moment later they staggered forward again towards a frightened Alicia.

One of the other youngsters shouted, 'Who is she?' and the original speaker replied, 'She's a neighbour. The Woodmans' kid.'

'What's she doing here? A lady?'

They were so close to her now that Alicia could smell the alcohol on their breath, and she was sickened.

They stared at her with an unpleasant intentness. She gave no hint that she knew who they were and dropped her eyes behind her gold-rimmed glasses.

As the dancers parted again, there came one of those tiny silences that occasionally occur in the biggest crowds, and she clearly heard the first speaker snigger and say, 'Like mother, like daughter; they say she's a bastard.'

The words were filled with scorn and Alicia's heart leaped with apprehension. A bastard? What did that mean? Clearly something not very nice. She glanced up at Polly; she urgently wanted to go home to the safety of the nursery. But Polly was singing at the top of her voice, as they swayed back down a narrow street with the rest of the dancers; she did not look down at her charge.

Bent on flight, Alicia became aware of the huge hand clasping her on the other side. She knew the face of the man, though it was not as black as usual; it was the coalman. When she looked up at him, he grinned down at her in a friendly way, and she felt a little comforted. But what was a bastard?

'Enjoyin' yerself, me duck?' he asked.

'Oh, yes,' she replied politely.

As if ordered, the crowd stopped moving and stood very quietly.

Through the cold, mist-laden air, hooters blared from the ships in the river and then church bells began to ring.

There was a great united shout. 'Happy New Year! Happy New Century!' It was followed immediately by hundreds and hundreds of voices singing 'Auld Lang Syne'.

At the end of the song, arms were raised in a kind of last farewell to the old year, and the ring broke up. The coalman caught Fanny round the waist and gave her a smacking kiss. Still holding her, he turned to Alicia. 'A happy New Year to yez, Miss,' he said.

Struggling to stay near to the couple in the surging crowd, she replied, 'Thank you, and a very happy one to you, too.' Then she jumped in

614

fright, as from behind her two arms encircled her waist. She half turned in the unexpected embrace and one of the hands was shifted to fondle her small young breasts beneath her shawl. 'Happy New Year,' her youthful neighbour breathed.

Alicia was aware of Fanny's shocked face half behind the coalman. The coalman took one look at the youth, and said to Alicia, 'You'd better go home, luv.' Then to the boy he growled, 'You, mister, you leave go of her.'

Alicia panicked and began to struggle. 'Let go,' she whispered.

The grip tightened and the fondling began to make her feel very odd indeed.

A large dirty fist was interposed between the back of her neck and the nuzzling nose of the youth. 'See this,' roared the coalman. 'You bugger off or I'll smash your bleedin' face in.'

For a second, the hold on her loosened and Alicia broke free. She ran into Fanny's arms. She was trembling all over and cried, 'Take me home, Fanny. Where's Polly?'

'In a minute, luv. We'll have to let the crowd go a bit.' She eased the girl and herself behind the comforting bulk of the coalman.

The young man had raised his fists and squared off, ready to fight. His friends, seizing the opportunity of a small break in the press around them, tried to haul him backwards. This unsteadied him and he sat down suddenly on the cobbled street, to the amusement of a circle which had begun to form around the adversaries.

Alerted to trouble, Polly struggled back to Fanny and Alicia. She heard the stream of abuse hurled at the coalman by the fallen youngster and instead of stepping over his straddled legs, she deliberately trod on his ankle, as she passed. The abuse ceased in a shriek of pain.

A couple of women wrapped in black shawls nodded approval, and one cackled at the youth, 'Serves yer right, yer cheeky bastard.'

Alicia, held tightly by Fanny, heard her and decided that if it were a term of abuse, a bastard must be a dreadful thing. Her trembling was renewed.

'Get outta here, quick,' the coalman ordered the maids and Alicia. Still facing the seated boy, who was now being tended by his anxious friends, he backed away a little. Then he hitched up his trousers, bent slightly and with a horrible grimace, he snarled, 'Get back to your Mam afore I marmalize you.' He turned and with deliberate slowness lounged after the scared maids.

The deflated little group was swept down Upper Parliament Street by the homeward-bound revellers, Polly muttering bracingly to Alicia, 'Soon be home, luv. Time for bed.'

In the comparative quiet of Grove Street, they paused to say good-night to the coalman. 'You shouldn't've took her,' he scolded Polly and Fanny. 'It's not fit.'

Both women were very sober now and Polly was crestfallen as she answered him, 'We wasn't to know we'd bump into a little runt like that. He should've bin in bed – in his cradle.'

The quick walk had calmed Alicia, and now she said earnestly to the coalman, 'It's very kind of you to bring us home. I'm all right now, and I'm most grateful to you.'

The coalman looked down at the white, worried face glimmering in the gaslight from the street lamps. 'Aye, it were nothin', Miss.' With the grey shawl over her head, she looked oddly like his little sister. He smiled, teeth flashing red and yellow against the coaldust ingrained in his skin. 'You'll be safe with our Fanny and Polly now.' He turned away with a muttered, 'Tara, well,' to the maids and strode up the almost deserted street.

While they drank their bedtime cocoa, seated round the dying embers of the kitchen fire, Alicia did not contribute much to the conversation, except to say that the coalman was a very nice person. Within her lay a cold snake of fear. What was a bastard? Before she got into bed, she took down her school dictionary from the nursery shelf to look up the offending word. It was not in it.

V

Charles was spending his Christmas and New Year's holidays with friends in London. Even if he had been at home, thought Alicia wistfully, he would have been out most of the time; she suspected that he avoided his family as much as possible because Papa shouted at him so much. Papa thought that university was wasted time. She sighed, as, on the last January day of her school holidays, she strolled alone through Princes Park under trees dripping with sea mist, the grass seared, the silence absolute. If Charles had been at home, she could have asked him, perhaps, what 'bastard' meant. 'Could it be a slang word?' she wondered. 'Even if it were, what did it mean?' She wished Edward would come home from the war; he knew so much.

After her walk, she took her mother's four o'clock tea tray up to the morning-room.

'Where's Polly?' asked her mother, looking up from the rose she was embroidering on a party dress for Florence's eldest daughter.

Alicia explained that Polly was very busy preparing dinner.

Elizabeth nodded, and accepted a cup of tea from her daughter. Really, there was no reason why Alicia should not make herself useful in the house, she thought suddenly.

Alicia was often at a loss for conversational gambits when with Elizabeth. Today, however, she remembered that Elizabeth had been to a New Year Party, so she inquired if she had enjoyed it.

Elizabeth roused herself sufficiently to describe the menu and the guests. Alicia listened politely. She found sitting with her mother much more tedious than sitting with dear old Sarah Webb, her godmother, who was always delighted to discuss the news or ideas about education or religion or anything else that Alicia might be interested in.

She wondered if she dare ask Elizabeth what 'bastard' meant. She did not want to ask Polly, because if the word had a bad meaning, Polly would be sure to ask where she had heard it and she would have to own up that it had been thrown at her when they were out together; it might make Polly feel badly.

On consideration, she concluded that her mother might be the best person to ask. On another matter, Polly had said quite forcibly that it was a mother's duty to explain things. A thoroughly scared Alicia had gone to Polly to say that she was bleeding – underneath. Had she caught consumption or something?

Polly had hugged her and told her calmly that all women bled every month and this simply meant that Alicia was now a young woman.

Alicia had gaped at her.

'It's true, duck. I'll boil some rags and show you how to keep it off your petties. Don't be frightened, now. It don't mean nothin' more. I'll tell your Ma.' She stroked the girl's hair and kissed her. 'If you get a pain, you tell me.'

Alicia did not get a pain. She learned, however, that mothers had at least one duty – to tell their children things – what things, she was not quite sure. She poured her mother another cup of tea, and asked, as she handed it to her, 'Mama, what's a bastard?'

Elizabeth blenched. At first she thought she must have misheard. Then, as she realized that Alicia had indeed asked such a diabolical question, she exclaimed in horror, 'Alicia! Where did you hear such a dreadful word? It is most vulgar – never used by a lady under any circumstance.' Her breath began to come in short gasps, as she tried to control her sense of panic.

'I'm so sorry, Mama. I didn't know that. I – I – er just thought it was another word I should learn how to spell. Are you all right, Mama?'

'I feel faint. Get my smelling salts – they're on the table here –

somewhere.' She leaned back in her chair and closed her eyes, unable to grapple with the inference of Alicia's question.

Alicia jumped from the straight chair on which she had been sitting and scrabbled anxiously amid bits of satin and hanks of embroidery silk until she found the tiny blue glass bottle. She whipped off its top and her eyes blinked as the ammonia fumes hit them.

'Here you are, Mama.' She held the open bottle under her mother's nose.

'Thank you,' Elizabeth gasped as she inhaled. She took the bottle from Alicia and held it under each nostril in turn. Alicia watched her apprehensively; she had not expected such an extreme reaction to her query.

After a few moments, with eyes still closed, Elizabeth asked, 'Where did you hear such a dreadful word? You are not to mix with people who use such language.'

Nonplussed that one word could make a person feel faint, Alicia did not know how to reply. Finally she said, 'An old woman in a crowd called a boy it, and I heard her.'

'I see,' Elizabeth swallowed. 'You really must be careful about words you pick up from the lower classes. Fortunately, Polly speaks fairly well now – but even with her you should be careful about new words.'

Alicia agreed in a very subdued voice, 'Yes, Mama.' What could a bastard be? She glanced up at Elizabeth whose complexion was slowly returning to a reasonable pink. 'Do you feel better now, Mama? Would you like me to get you some fresh tea?' she asked, anxious to make amends.

'No, thank you. I'll rest in my chair for a little while.'

'Then I'll take the tray back to Polly.' She looked contritely at her mother. 'I'm truly sorry, Mama, to distress you.'

Her mother did not answer; her mind was in a tumult. She had never before faced honestly the fact that, despite the restricted life Alicia led, sooner or later, she was likely to learn of the scandal her birth had caused. The neglected child was now a young woman, and Elizabeth prayed that she never asked Humphrey what a bastard was.

VI

A very puzzled Alicia took the teacups off the tray and put them into the kitchen sink. Then she turned to Polly making pastry at the big square table in the middle of the kitchen.

'Polly, what's a bastard?'

The rolling-pin stopped dead. Polly raised startled eyes to Alicia's solemn little face. She had not heard the young man's remark on New Year's Eve, so she did not know what had sparked the question. She looked down at the pastry and carefully gave it a long slow roll. Then she said honestly, 'It's a kid wot don't have no real papa.'

Alicia's eyes widened in surprise. She approached the table and gazed up at Polly's averted face. 'But, Polly, when we were out on New Year's Eve, that drunk young man called *me* a bastard – and I've got a papa.' Her lips trembled, as Polly continued to roll the pastry. 'And he made it sound wicked – and he was rude about Mama. He frightened me, Pol.' The last words were entreating as she begged for reassurance.

Polly turned to the girl, forcing herself to smile, as she inwardly cursed Elizabeth for not, in some way, preparing Alicia to face her illegitimacy. She said cheerfully, 'Anybody as called you that is only tenpence to a shillin'. You poor kid – don't you worry your head about it. The Master 'as you in this house, so he's your papa all right – all proper and legal.'

Alicia clicked her tongue fretfully, and then fumed, 'Well, I don't understand why he should be so rude about Mama and me. Is it really wicked to be one? And how can anybody *not* have a proper papa?'

'It's not wicked to be one,' replied Polly firmly. 'Kids can't help being born. What happens is sometimes people fall in love and maybe they can't get married – no money or somethin' – but a baby comes. And that baby is called a bastard. It's proper sad and it's real hard on the kid's Mam. But the baby isn't wicked – the nice name for him is a love child – somebody special, like.'

Poor Polly hoped she had laid the matter to rest and she lifted her pastry carefully into a piedish. But worse was to come.

'I didn't know you could have a baby without being married!' exclaimed Alicia, her high, white forehead wrinkled by her complete confusion. 'I don't even know how babies come, except I'm sure they don't come in the doctor's bag – they'd smother in it.'

'You don't have to be married,' Polly floundered. 'Hasn't your Mam ever spoken to you about it?'

'No.' Alicia heaved a sigh. 'Should she? She nearly fainted when I asked her what a bastard was. She didn't tell me.'

I bet she didn't, thought Polly sourly. Aloud, she said, 'Well, it int a word that ladies use.'

'How do babies come, Polly? Ethel at school says she saw a cat have kittens once – and she really believes that babies come the same way. She said it was awfully messy. She said that Fluffy opened up between her legs and the kittens squeezed out – and there was blood and things.'

Her voice faltered, and she looked appealingly at Polly as if she hoped Polly would deny it.

Better she knows, thought Polly. She had heard Elizabeth talking to Humphrey about the necessity of Alicia going to Blackburne House School, so that she was educated enough to be a governess, if she did not marry. And in Polly's opinion, governesses needed to know as much as housemaids did, since they were just as vulnerable to unwanted advances. Why hasn't the bloody woman said something to her about men? Polly cursed. Now she had the job. That Ethel should've kept her mouth shut.

'She's right,' she blurted out. 'Oh, aye, she's right.'

Alicia was so startled by this revelation that she knocked the recipe book off the table.

'You mean women – we open like that?'

Polly piled apple slices into the tart she was making. She looked up with a small grin. 'Yes, chook. Don't be scared. It's as natural as anything.'

'But doesn't it hurt? Babies are quite big.'

Polly rested her floured knuckles on the deal table. 'It does a bit – not much,' she admitted. 'And you forget about it when the kid's in your arms.'

Alicia recovered herself slightly and bent to rescue the cookery book from the floor. She laughed nervously, as she straightened up. 'You're teasing me, Polly, and in a vulgar way. How could a baby get inside its mother, in the first place?' she asked, as she sat down on a stool.

Holy Mother, save me! I'm lost, thought Polly anxiously. Aloud, she insisted, 'I'm not teasing, luv. It's God's truth.'

Alicia still doubted her and was angry; Polly should not tell such stories when she had asked a serious question. 'Well, how do we get there?' she demanded.

Polly sighed and lifted more pastry on to the wooden pastry board, ready for rolling. At least they had got away from the direct subject of bastards. 'I think you should ask your Mam,' she advised.

'Oh, Polly!' Alicia exclaimed crossly. 'You know she never talks to me about anything much.'

Polly swallowed and then nodded. Here I go, she fretted. 'And I hope I don't lose me job if the Missus finds out.' She paused in her rolling and was quiet for a moment, and then she began, 'Well, you know as I was married once and had a little baby? And he died?'

'Yes.' Alicia was tremblingly alert now. 'I'm sorry he died.'

'Well, I loved our Pat, me hubbie, somethin' terrible.' She heaved a sigh at the memory of him, though, with no photograph to help her, she could not always remember his face clearly. She leaned on her rolling-pin and cleared her throat. 'When you love a person like that you don't mind what they do to you – you don't mind 'em touching you anywhere.'

Demonstrating with her floured hands, she explained very simply, and Alicia listened, wide-eyed and nervous, yet not frightened. This was what all the mystery was about, this simple action. And when she thought about the world around her, it was a logical explanation.

'It feels lovely,' Polly finished up, 'and you and your hubby are happy afterwards.'

Alicia sat shyly examining her fingernails, and then she asked, 'Do you and Edward feel happy like that?'

Polly had picked up a piece of pastry to cover her apple tart. Paralysed by the question, she stood staring at Alicia, while the pastry drooped and stretched. A slow red flush went up over her forehead and down her neck.

'Now, our Allie!' she protested, giving Alicia her baby name.

Alicia grinned mischievously. 'I'm sorry. I shouldn't ask personal questions. But I thought you must be feeling awful with his being in the war in South Africa – if you do love him.'

Polly gulped and closed her eyes, so that Alicia should not see her agony of mind. Then it burst from her. 'Oh, I do, luv. I worry all the time.'

Alicia slipped from her stool and impulsively wound her arms round the back of her nanny, leaning her head on the maid's bent back. 'Oh, Polly, I'm so sad for you. I love him, too. It makes me feel sick to think of Africa.' She sighed. 'Being a soldier is a dreadful life, isn't it? When you think about it – having to kill other men before they kill you. It must be terrible for Mama.'

Polly turned round and, despite her floury hands, she clung to Alicia.

So rarely did Elizabeth say much to either of them that neither realized that she did not know that her son was in South Africa. Edward wrote to her about once a quarter and never to his father; no mention was made in his letters of where he was, in case the missives fell into enemy hands. He also sent little notes to Polly, care of her sister, Mary, who now had a decent house provided by the City Council, where the postman delivered daily. He signed his notes only with his first initial. Polly treasured them, and it was she who had told Alicia that she was fairly certain Edward had been moved to South Africa – last time he was home they had agreed on a code word by which he could tell her approximately where he was.

The apple pie which Polly had been making was not a great success, because Polly forgot to put in the cloves and cinnamon. Alicia forgot that Polly had not exactly explained how she came to be called a bastard, though a small, nagging apprehension remained with her.

Was she really Alicia Beatrix Mary Woodman? If she was not, who was she? She surreptitiously combed the dictionary in the library; it told her no more than Polly had. And Polly had been quite firm that she was legally Papa's child.

Reading novels with a new alertness, she found there were many in which the heroine was 'betrayed' and often seemed to die in the Workhouse while having a baby with no husband to love and take care of it. Was that how a bastard was born? It was all very vague, except that the baby's life was invariably very difficult.

She never thought of asking Fanny, who could have enlightened her in a few seconds, having been born one herself and having watched the progress of Elizabeth's love affair. Though Fanny was a dear friend, she was not, in Alicia's opinion, very knowledgeable and Alicia had a tendency to lecture her, which sometimes made Fanny laugh.

16

As Elizabeth grew older and her mind dulled, she rarely read more than the headlines in the newspaper. Polly and Alicia, however, read them quite thoroughly after Humphrey had put them into his waste-paper basket, both anxiously watching the news from South Africa.

At dinnertime, when such news might reasonably have been discussed, Alicia never spoke for fear of having Humphrey snarl at her to hold her tongue. She listened to her parents' conversation, and hearing their quarrelsome arguments made her question Fanny's and Polly's assertions that marriage was a highly desirable state. She herself was always thankful to escape from them to the nursery or the kitchen. She did, occasionally, share afternoon tea with her mother, and, one day, she remarked, without thinking, that it was worrisome to have dear Edward involved in South Africa.

'He's in *India*,' responded Elizabeth lazily. 'Mr Woodman remarked that the Bank was still sending his allowance there – he said that since he was a soldier, he *ought* to be in South Africa.' Elizabeth had, for years, not given much thought to her stodgy elder son, of whom she had few real memories and occasionally forgot completely.

Alicia swallowed, realizing her slip, and hastily agreed that he was probably still in Amritsar. Poor Polly! She had inadvertently nearly betrayed her. She would not have known what to say, if her mother had asked why she imagined Edward was in Africa. How could she tell her that Edward wrote letters to her maidservant? Polly would be dismissed without notice simply for receiving such a missive.

II

One morning late in March, when Mr Bittle's daffodils were blowing cheerfully in the back garden, Humphrey was handed his letters by Fanny, who was waiting on him at the breakfast table. He looked through the envelopes and then quickly extracted one from the War Office. Apprehensively, he slit it open.

Good God! Edward! Dead of the typhoid? He was as shocked as if Edward had been his most beloved son, instead of a constant irritation to him. And he'd died at Ladysmith?

A searing pain went up his chest and neck; he could not breathe properly. And the boy had not even managed to be killed in action, dying for King and Country! That hurt. The pain leapt through him, and he had a flash of memory of a little boy bowling an iron hoop and bumping into him and his being very sharp with him for such careless behaviour. As he fought for breath, a muddled sense of guilt went through him.

Fanny was tidying the sideboard and had her back to him. Now she heard him gasp, 'Brandy!'

She whirled round.

Her master was clutching his chest, obviously in great pain.

She whipped open the sideboard cupboard, snatched up a glass and the crystal decanter and ran to him. She slopped a little brandy into the glass, putting her arm round his shoulders to steady him. He managed to swallow a sip as he leaned against her starched apron. The pain receded slightly, and he muttered, 'Help me – library couch. Call the Mistress.' His speech was slurred.

She was a tiny woman and thought he would collapse on to the hall floor, but she did manage to ease him into the book-lined room and he tumbled on to the couch. He struggled to breathe, as she shook out a crocheted shawl lying at the end of the couch and put it over him. 'I won't be a mo', sir.'

She ran out of the room, hitching up her calico skirts as she took the stairs two at a time.

She hardly stopped to knock, as she flew into Elizabeth's bedroom. 'Oh, Ma'am, please come quick. The Master's took sick.'

Elizabeth put down her teacup carefully on to her breakfast tray. 'Really? Where is he?'

'On the couch in the library. Please hurry, Ma'am.'

Elizabeth slowly reached for her dressing-gown hanging on the bed-knob, pushed back the bedcovers and extended one fat leg. Fanny took her hand and helped her out. As Elizabeth carefully tied the cord, Fanny wanted to yell at her, 'Hurry up, for Christ's sake!'

Her mistress stood unsteadily by the bed. Her head ached abominably. 'What happened?'

'He can't breathe, Ma'am, not proper, that is. He were holding 'is chest.'

Herded by a distraught Fanny, Elizabeth staggered to the door and stumped downstairs. When she entered the library, she found Humphrey lying slumped against the raised curve of the end of the couch. His eyes were closed; his breath was coming in irregular gasps.

His wife stood over him, trying to gather her wits together despite her throbbing head. 'What's the matter, Humphrey?'

'Get Willis – heart attack.'

'Are you sure?'

'Yes. Quickly.' His voice faded and he moaned.

Fanny was fluttering nervously in the background. She turned to the mahogany desk, picked out a piece of notepaper from the stand and laid it on the blotting pad. 'Here you are, Ma'am,' she said to Elizabeth.

Like a sleepwalker, Elizabeth went to the desk. Fanny dipped a pen into the silver inkwell and handed it to her. Obediently, Elizabeth wrote. She recollected that she had not had to call Dr Willis since Mrs Tibbs had been taken ill. Mrs Tibbs had died, she thought dully.

'I'll run with it, Ma'am.' She hesitated, and then inquired, 'Shall I ask Polly to come up – to be with you, like?'

Elizabeth looked indifferently at the suffering man. She felt far away from the proceedings, as if she were watching a boring play. In answer to Fanny's question, she said mechanically, 'Yes. Ask her to bring up a glass of brandy – two glasses.'

Polly arrived very speedily with the brandy and suggested that she should watch her Master, who seemed more comfortable after the restorative, while Elizabeth got dressed for the doctor's visit.

Elizabeth tossed down her glass of brandy at a gulp. Then, feeling a little stronger herself, she agreed to go and dress.

Polly did not dare to sit down in front of the Master of the house, so she stood at the foot of the couch, hands clasped tightly in front of her, alternately glancing at the sick man and then through the lace curtains, to see if the doctor's carriage was coming.

She was surprised when, in a whisper, Humphrey addressed her, his eyes still closed. 'Polly.'

'Sir? Are you feelin' better, sir?'

'A little. Polly, I have to break it to your Mistress that Master Edward died at Ladysmith. I want you to be here, in case she faints – that is, if Dr Willis hasn't arrived by the time she comes down again.'

Polly swayed on her feet, as if he had struck her. Strength seemed to run out of her and she thought *she* would faint. Edward, dearest Edward. She clutched at the edge of the desk behind her.

Unaware of the distress he had caused, Humphrey lay perfectly still and tried to breathe normally, as the pain threatened again. The only sound in the room was that of a fly buzzing on the windowpane.

Polly did not answer Humphrey. She could not. She simply stood, trembling from head to foot, trying not to scream or sob, for fear the stricken man before her noticed.

Fanny knocked on the door. When she received no reply, she opened it cautiously. She was still panting from her fast run to Dr Willis's. 'Aye, Polly, I thought the Mistress would be here. Doctor's comin' now.' Then as she saw Polly's evident anguish, she asked in alarm, 'What's up?'

Polly fought to keep her senses. 'Fanny, watch the Master till the Missus comes back. I got to go upstairs.' She pushed past the little maid to the hall. Holding hard to the banister, she went quickly up the two flights of stairs to her narrow bedroom next to the day nursery. She flung herself on to the bed and let blackness roll over her.

Humphrey was vaguely aware of the verbal exchange between the maids, but his need to rest was paramount. As long as someone was there to deal with the hysterics he expected from his wife, he did not care.

III

Dr Willis consigned Humphrey to bed indefinitely. He promised a bottle of medicine and ordered a light diet. 'And no cigars.'

At the latter instruction, Humphrey's eyes shot open. 'Surely, Willis, I can smoke?'

'I have found that my patients' bouts of pain are much reduced, if they don't smoke,' the doctor declared firmly. 'You may have whisky and an occasional glass of wine. I shall, of course, come in each morning.'

Elizabeth had left the room, while the doctor conducted a physical examination of his patient. Now Dr Willis rose from his chair by the couch and announced that he would go to explain to her what Humphrey could eat. From under heavy grey eyebrows, he looked down at the exhausted man on the couch. 'Have you a manservant to help you to bed?' he inquired.

'No. I'll send for my son-in-law.' It was an effort to speak. 'Probably my brother – Harold – come from Manchester.' He paused to get his breath. 'I can stay here for a couple of days, if necessary.' The pain threatened again and he winced.

Dr Willis took some cushions from an easy chair and gently propped the patient into a more upright position. 'Carefully, Sir,' he warned. He turned to drop his stethoscope into his Gladstone bag.

'Willis, I need your help.' The request was barely a whisper.

'Of coure, sir. What can I do for you?'

'Tell Mrs Woodman that our son, Edward, died at Ladysmith. Letter – under the shawl here.'

'My dear fellow! I'm dreadfully sorry! Of course, I'll tell her. And we were all so thankful last month to hear that the town had been relieved. How very sad for you.' He again looked keenly at Humphrey. 'Was that the cause of the chest pain?'

'I believe so.'

'My deepest condolences. Would you like *me* to send for the Reverend Browning and your daughter? I have an errand boy who could go on his bicycle.'

'Please, do.'

'May I see the letter – so that I can be more precise when talking to your poor lady?'

Humphrey nodded, too exhausted to find the letter for him.

Dr Willis felt round under the shawl and found the crumpled missive. As he read it, he moved slowly towards the bell-pull to call Fanny. 'Rest quietly, sir. I'll deal with this. Indeed, the Lord giveth and the Lord taketh away,' he added piously.

When Fanny showed him into the morning-room, Elizabeth was seated in her favourite chair by the window. Fanny brought him a straight chair and set it close to Elizabeth. He was a tall, elderly man, a product of Edinburgh Medical School, and when Elizabeth turned inquiringly towards him, he surveyed her puffy, overly red cheeks and bloodshot eyes with professional assessment. She smelled of port wine.

Fanny turned to leave the room but the doctor indicated, with a discreet gesture, that she should stay. If Mrs Woodman fainted or went into hysterics, he felt he might need help. He put down his bag and sat down.

Elizabeth's beringed hand was resting on the padded arm of her chair, and the doctor took it in his. 'I'm pleased to tell you, dear Mrs Woodman,' he began, 'that Mr Woodman will recover quite well, if he takes care now. He must stay in bed. And when he is well enough to go outside again, he must never go in cold or blustery weather.' He smiled. 'I'll send in a bottle of medicine later. See that he takes it whenever the pain threatens.'

Elizabeth inclined her head and thanked him. A glass of brandy followed by two of port had created a comfortable euphoria. The doctor sighed. 'I have, however, some very sad news to impart.'

Since she had just been assured that Humphrey would recover, Elizabeth could not think what news the doctor might consider sad, so she smiled slightly. Fanny, however, standing quietly behind her chair, stiffened. With insight and compassion, she again saw Polly's stricken face. Master Edward! It had to be.

Dr Willis told Elizabeth as gently as he could about her son.

Elizabeth did not faint. She sat suddenly very upright. 'Why did not Mr Woodman tell me himself?'

'The news was the cause of his heart pain, I believe.'

'I see.' She was breathing rather heavily and took a moment to let it subside. Then she said, 'To die of typhoid in a foreign land is dying for one's country, is it not, Doctor?'

'Indeed it is, Mrs Woodman, and you may be proud of your son. Disease causes more deaths in the army than actual fighting does – and our men know, when they go forth, that they have to face both enemies, both deadly.'

The doctor continued to sit and pat her hand, expecting tears to burst forth any minute. But they did not. Finally, he told her of the arrangement with her husband that his delivery boy would take a message to Florence and her husband. Then he added, 'My daughter attends Blackburne House and I seem to remember her telling me that your daughter's there. Would you like me to send for her, as well? I'm sure that you'll wish your maids to remain with you, and not go on messages.'

She looked around her rather helplessly. 'Yes – um – yes, I would, if your boy would take a note to her Head Mistress. Fanny, where are you, Fanny?'

'Here, Ma'am.' Fanny came swiftly from behind her.

'Bring my writing case.'

The doctor rose. 'I'll just look in on Mr Woodman again. Someone should sit with him for the next few hours.'

Elizabeth nodded agreement, and she scribbled a note to Alicia's Head Mistress and then folded it up. 'Where's Polly?' she asked Fanny.

'She were took poorly, Ma'am. I think it were her stummick.'

'Dear me!' exclaimed Dr Willis, as he picked up his bag. 'Would you like me to see her?'

'No, thank you,' responded Elizabeth stiffly. 'See Dr Willis out, Fanny, after he has looked at the Master again.' She held out her hand to the doctor and he shook it.

'I'll send in a draught which you yourself might be glad to take at bedtime,' he promised her. She was much too quiet, he thought; she should be shrieking like a steam locomotive. But, then, perhaps she was too drunk to realize completely what had happened. 'I will come again tomorrow morning,' he assured her. 'In the meantime, if there is a recurrence of the pain, please do not hesitate to send for me.'

When Fanny had closed the front door after the kindly doctor, she hesitated as to whether she should go back to her mistress or go to Polly.

She sprinted silently up the stairs to the top floor.

Polly was curled up on her narrow, iron bed, a bundle of sobbing misery. Fanny flew to the bedside and knelt down by her. 'Aye, I'm sorry, luv,' she said as she gathered the weeping woman into her arms. 'There, Pol. There, there,' she crooned.

After rocking her backwards and forwards for a minute, as if she were a child, Fanny urged her to get up and wash her face. 'The Mistress'll want us both, and she mustn't know, luv. She mustn't never know what was up between you and Master Edward.'

'I don't care if she does.'

'You got to care, Pol. Or you'll be out on the street without a reference.'

'I don't care. I want to die.'

'Come on with yez. Think of our little Allie. What's she goin' to do without you? You're her Mam, really; it's you who loves her. And she'll be home in twenty minutes or so – Doctor's sendin' a note for her – maybe he thinks the Master won't live.'

At this, Polly slowly sat up and wiped her eyes with the back of her hands. 'She loved Eddy,' she said brokenly. 'He was forever sendin' her little presents. Aye, he were a lovely man.' The tears burst forth again.

Fanny got up off the floor and went to the washstand. She poured some water from the flowered pitcher into the bowl, took up a flannel and wetted it. 'Wipe your face, luv. You got to go down.'

Still crying, Polly obediently took the flannel and washed her face. Fanny handed her the towel.

After drying herself, she staggered up off the bed and went to a small mirror on the wall. She hastily pulled out her hairpins and redid her hair.

'Where's your cap?' Fanny asked, hunting round the pillow for it.

'Get me a clean one out of the cupboard.' Polly was struggling, now, to quell the storm of grief within her.

When Fanny returned to the morning-room, Elizabeth asked irritably where she had been. 'I've been ringing the bell for ages,' she complained.

Lying glibly, Fanny told her that she had had to attend to the butcher's delivery boy at the back door and that Polly was now making a sponge cake and dare not leave it in the middle. 'Would you like to lie down a bit, Ma'am? Polly or me'll watch the Master. I'm proper sorry about the young Master, Ma'am.'

'Thank you, Fanny. Ask Polly to make some coffee and bring it to the library. And make up the library fire.'

'Yes,'m.' Fanny helped to heave her out of her chair and, teetering slightly, she went into the hall and through to the library. There, she peered down at her husband. He appeared to be sleeping, but his cheeks, drained of their usual ruddiness, were wet and a tear had got caught in his moustache.

'I should be crying, too,' thought Elizabeth vaguely. 'But I can't. I've seen so little of him – and he was always so dull, not a bit like Charles.' She sat down by the embers of the fire, and thought of the three miscarriages which had followed Edward's birth; they had left her weak and depressed. She decided fretfully that probably Edward had been happier with his nanny than with her.

Down in the untidy kitchen, Polly mechanically set a tray, including a cup for Humphrey.

'Make a good strong cup for yourself as well,' Fanny instructed her. She had been to the coal cellar and had a full coal scuttle in one hand. Her sackcloth apron and her hands were black with coal dust. 'Put a drop of the cooking rum in it,' she advised Polly, as she crossed the kitchen. 'Keep yer goin', it will.'

Still sobbing, Polly nodded agreement.

17

I

'Polly! Polly!' Alicia sped down the area steps and pushed open the heavy back door. 'Polly! What's happened? Why am I sent for?' She slammed the door behind her to keep out the chill March wind, and slung her satchel on to the floor. She pulled off her hat. Her face was more than usually pale and was wet from the rain through which she had run.

Polly put down the kettle which she was filling at the sink and quickly skirted the big deal table. She took Alicia by the elbow and ushered her towards the kitchen range. 'Come by the fire, duck, and get warm, and I'll tell you.'

In the heat of the fire, Alicia struggled out of her damp coat and looked at Polly.

'Polly, you've been crying. Something awful's happened. 'what is it?'

Polly sank down on to a wooden chair, her starched apron poofing out in front of her. She put an arm round Alicia's waist. 'It's Master Edward, luv. He died at Ladysmith – caught the typhoid during the siege.'

'Oh, Polly!' Alicia gasped in consternation. 'Oh, Polly, Polly!' She put her arms round her nanny's neck and buried her face in her shoulder. 'And we'll never see him again?'

'No, duck. Try not to grieve, luvvie. He were a soldier, and he were brave; so we have to be brave like him.' Her voice quavered and broke; she wept unrestrainedly.

Alicia cried with her. 'He wasn't just my brother, he was my very best friend,' she moaned. 'And he's gone.'

Ever since their conversation over the apple pie on the subject of bastards, Alicia had understood the relationship between Polly and her brother, and, after her first burst of tears, she tried to comfort her nanny. She patted Polly's bent back, and whispered, 'Dearest Polly, I'm so sorry for you. It must be terrible.'

The young girl's understanding made Polly jump. She pushed Alicia gently a little back from her and looked into the concerned light grey eyes. 'God bless the poor little lamb,' she thought, and hugged her close again, as she sniffed back her tears. 'Aye, Allie, dear, I could wish myself dead.'

'Oh, no, Polly. What would I do without you? And we have to help Mama – just think what she must be feeling! I'd better go up to her.' She took her handkerchief out of her blouse pocket and wiped the tears from Polly's lined face. Polly looks so old, she thought with a pang, and she feared suddenly that she might lose her, too.

As Polly slowly got up from her wooden chair, Alicia turned away and blew her nose. 'Has anybody told Papa? And Florence and Charles?' she inquired.

Polly sniffed and swallowed. 'Aye, and that's another thing,' she said, and told Alicia about Humphrey's heart attack and that Dr Willis was sending a message to Florence.

Alicia looked at her as if she had seen a ghost. 'And Mama?' she stammered.

'She's all right. She's sittin' with your Papa. I don't think she's cryin' or anythin'.'

'She's probably tipsy,' Alicia thought unhesitatingly, and she glanced despairingly around her; she felt hemmed in.

She heaved a great sigh and said courageously, 'Look, Polly, dear. Everybody's going to need to eat, so you make lunch – you'll feel better if you're busy, I think. Make enough for Florence and Clarence. And I'll go to see Mama and Papa.' She wiped her nose again and it shone red in the firelight.

Polly nodded. 'You're right, me little duck; you're a good little girl. You go to your Mam.'

'What's Fanny doing?'

'She's bin makin' up all the fires, because the wind's cold today, and now she's changin' the sheets on the Mistress's bed and puttin' in hot water bottles to warm it. When the Reverend and Miss Florence come, we'll get the Master up to bed – he's in the library at present. And Fanny'll make up the bed in the dressing-room for your Mam so she'll be close by.'

As she picked up her damp hat and coat, Alicia felt reluctant to leave the safety of the warm kitchen, but she said quite firmly to Polly, 'I'll go up and see them.' She could not imagine her bad-tempered, taciturn father lying sick. He never spoke to her, except to reprimand, and she wondered what to say to him, what to do.

As she hesitated before climbing the stairs, Polly turned from poking up the fire, and called, 'Off you go now. They need you.'

The idea that her parents might need her was a new one to Alicia, and again she had the uncanny feeling of events closing in on her.

Mechanically she hung her coat and hat in the big hall cloakroom and changed into house slippers. Inside her was a hard lump of misery and she whimpered to herself, 'Edward, Edward, I always thought – hoped – you would come home for good one day and be with Polly and me.'

At the door of the library, she stifled her sobs and rubbed the tears from her eyes. She knocked and entered.

Humphrey looked pitifully small under the eiderdown Fanny had brought to cover him, an object of fear, now deflated like a burst balloon. Her mother looked slovenly, with untidy wisps of hair hanging round her flushed face. Alicia went cautiously towards her and gave her a light kiss on her cheek. 'I'm so sad for you, Mama,' she said. 'Polly told me.'

Elizabeth nodded, and said thickly, 'What a waste – to die of typhoid.'

'Yes, indeed, Mama.'

Her mother relapsed into silence, and Alicia turned timidly towards the man on the couch. 'How are you feeling now, Papa?'

He had been watching her since she entered the room. He did not answer, but contented himself with a slight movement of his head, which seemed to Alicia to indicate that he was not feeling very good.

'I'm so sad about Edward,' she faltered, the tears threatening to brim over again.

With eyes closed, he nodded again.

She stood uncertainly between the couple, the silence clawing at her. What should she do? She stole a glance at her mother whose head had fallen forward as if she had suddenly fallen asleep. The reek of alcohol from her was sufficient for Alicia to realize that she would get no help from her. She yearned for Florence to come, though Florence never seemed to know what to do in any circumstances; she was a flurry of muddle and uncertainties, but at least she spoke to one, and she, too, might care about Edward.

'He's my brother,' she thought desperately, 'and Mama doesn't seem to realize that it hurts – it hurts most dreadfully – that he's dead.' In a flash of anger, she wanted to strike both parents. Her teeth began to chatter, and through it she stammered to Elizabeth, 'I'll see if Fanny's done the bedroom properly for Papa.' And she fled from the room.

She met Fanny coming out of the master bedroom, a pile of tumbled sheets in her arms. 'Oh, Fanny,' she wailed in relief.

Fanny dropped the bedclothes and put skinny arms around the frightened girl. 'It's all right, Allie, dear. Everything'll be all right in a wee bittie.'

Alicia hugged Fanny's small frame and kissed her on the cheek. Then she let her go. 'Mama doesn't seem to be very well, Fanny, so you make sure that everything is clean and neat up here, ready for Father – water in the carafe – and soap and towels – before the Reverend Browning gets here. He's so picky.'

Fanny knew perfectly well that Alicia meant that her mother was drunk again, so she said, 'Don't worry, pet. Polly and us'll manage together, won't we? We'll get your Dad better.'

Alicia nodded. She watched the tiny maid collect up the sheets from the floor, and she asked, 'Fanny, will they bury Edward in Africa – in Ladysmith?'

Fanny looked up, a little confused, 'They must've done it already,' she replied slowly, as she straightened up.

'But he'll be so lonely.' Alicia looked up beseechingly at Fanny. 'Can't he be brought home?'

Fanny hesitated, anxious to comfort, but not sure how to do it. Then she said, 'He might like to lie with his friends, luv. A lot of men died at Ladysmith.'

'Perhaps he would.' Alicia managed a tremulous smile. Then her expression changed as she remembered Charles. 'I don't think anyone has thought about telling Charles,' she said. 'I must ask the Reverend Browning to send him a telegram.'

II

Alicia never went back to Blackburne House. Forced by circumstances, as her mother became daily more incompetent, she grew up very fast. She took over the management of the house and, under the guidance of Dr Willis, the care of Humphrey. When she wailed to Polly that everything was too much for her and that she did not know how to cope, Polly would say, 'It's your duty, duck, to look after your Ma and Pa. It's a daughter's job. Me and Fanny'll help you.'

Yes, thought Alicia, but you don't really have to face Papa.

Humphrey had no intention of remaining an invalid for the rest of his life. Because he refused to have a nurse in the house, for several weeks he had to accept the help of Alicia. It was either Polly or Alicia who emptied his bedpans, and Alicia, who had never in her life seen a naked male, who washed him. A curious, close relationship grew up between them, like that between prisoner and gaoler. There was no love between the thin wisp of a girl and the stout, frustrated man, but there began to be a reciprocal respect. In the end, Humphrey found it satisfyingly ironical that it should be Crossing's bastard who served him so faithfully.

Numbed by hatred of him, there was no sympathy from Elizabeth. Yet she feared that if he died, there would be only absent-minded, self-centred Charles to protect her. She rarely went into her husband's bedroom and spent most of her time slumped in her easy chair or, as the summer drew on, in a chair in the garden. Polly and Fanny bore as best they could her continuous complaints about slowness in answering her bell and lateness of meals; it was as if the reality of caring for an invalid, or the fact that she should be helping, had not impinged on her brain at all.

Following Humphrey's heart attack, Florence came to stay for a couple of days. When told about Edward, she sat and wept copiously and the next day went into black. After that, she returned to her impatient, fussy husband, who had brought her to the house and who had stayed long enough to help Humphrey to his bed, before he went back home to supervise those members of his rowdy family not yet in boarding school.

Alicia hid the key to the wine cellar long enough to get Elizabeth into one of her good, black dresses and keep her sober while she attended a Memorial Service for Edward arranged by her son-in-law. After the service, Elizabeth, clutching a black-edged handkerchief, received a stream of visitors who called formally to present their condolences; one or two went up to visit Humphrey as well, but he was very weak and could not stand long visits.

Humphrey's brother, Harold, and his wife, Vera, came from Manchester for the service, and Alicia soberly sat with them through lunch in the dining-room. 'Mama is lying down– naturally, she is rather indisposed,' Alicia explained. She did not say that her mother had a racking headache and was raging in her room, because she could not find the key to the wine cellar, nor could she find a single bottle of anything to drink in the rest of the house.

When, later, the couple went upstairs for a short visit to her, she was propped up in bed drinking tea and was barely civil to them.

In the next room, they conveyed their condolences to a recumbent Humphrey, and Harold promised to come to visit him again the following week.

Charles came down from University and wandered round the house, looking helpless. He had grown a beard and had trimmed it in imitation of the dashing Prince of Wales, so that Alicia barely recognized him.

Charles had few memories of Edward and could not grieve at his death any more than if he had been a casual friend who had died. He did, however, sit with his father and refrained from any hot answer when Humphrey grumbled that he needed him at home now, to help him in the office.

Despite the gloom in the house, Charles joked with Alicia and told her she was managing everything wonderfully. A few days later he went thankfully back to Cambridge and his research.

At the end of two weeks, Elizabeth's cash box being empty, Alicia gathered up her courage and asked Humphrey for some housekeeping money.

'Mama doesn't seem to have any; and I must pay Fanny and Polly and the grocer and the butcher.'

He turned his head on his pillow and looked at her in astonishment, a thin slip of a fourteen-year-old – Andrew Crossing's bastard. Then he laughed. It was not a pleasant laugh and it frightened Alicia. But she stood her ground and waited.

'What's your mother doing? *She* should have come to me for her housekeeping.'

Alicia gulped. She did not want to say that her mother was often dazedly drunk or lay in her bed with racking headaches. Finally, she told him, 'Well, Mama is so upset about Edward – and about you – that she is not well herself; so I've been doing things.'

'I see. Get the housekeeping book from your mother and bring it to me – I check it each month. If she is well enough, ask her to come in to see me. Last time I saw it, the entries did not match the tradesmen's bills.' He looked suddenly exhausted, and Alicia felt a quick jolt of apprehension. Supposing he died, what would happen to her and to Mama – and Polly and Fanny?

'And may I have some money, Papa?'

'I must first speak to your mother.'

'Of course, it would be impolite for me to look after the housekeeping without first asking her,' responded Alicia soberly, as if she had not been battling with it for the previous two weeks.

Politeness was not what Humphrey had in mind. Now a little recovered, he wanted to know what his wife had actually been doing while he was ill. Was she so drunk that she could not run the house?

He rested for a moment while Alicia stood apprehensively by his bed. Then he took a large breath and made a further effort. 'You remember Mr Bowring, my clerk, who came to see me after the Memorial Service?' he asked.

'Yes, Papa.'

'Write him a letter to ask him to call on me tomorrow afternoon – at three o'clock. And get the maids to bring up the side table from the library – and a chair – and put them in the window, here, so that he has a place to work.'

'Yes, Papa.'

Outside the room, she stood in the upper hall and cried quietly to herself. How long was it going to be like this, she wondered. When would she be able to go back to school?

18

I

On January 22nd, 1901, the old Queen died after a very brief illness. Few of her subjects had ever known another monarch, and they felt bereft when they discovered that she was not immortal. Theatres closed and church bells tolled mournfully; they went on and on, until even the most devoted mourners had to grit their teeth to endure even one more slow dong-dong.

All the dressmakers in the city, including George Henry Lee's who usually provided Elizabeth's better dresses, were inundated by orders for funeral mourning.

On February 2nd, Humphrey and Elizabeth were bidden to the Cathedral Church of St Peter to attend a memorial service for the Queen.

When Humphrey found the invitation in his morning mail at the breakfast table, he felt that they should attend. Though not as strong as he had been, he was fairly recovered from his heart attack and had taken up again most of his usual pursuits.

He met his wife emerging from the master bedroom, after having her breakfast in bed – he had long since returned to his single bed in the dressing-room; once his heart pains had retreated, he had announced that he preferred its more masculine atmosphere. This morning, Elizabeth was still wrapped in her grubby, blue woollen dressing-gown, her grey hair tumbling round her shoulders. She had assumed that Humphrey was already on his way to his office and she was now in search of a drop of brandy.

He informed her of the cathedral service, and she responded sulkily that she had no decent black dress to wear.

'Nonsense,' he replied shortly, 'you must have an enormous wardrobe.'

'Nothing fits.' Elizabeth sounded as if she did not care very much.

'Well, for God's sake, get a new dress or costume.'

'I still owe Lee's for the last one – and I know that Mrs Blossom has so much work that she can't promise a dress in less than a month.'

'Can't you even manage to pay your bills?'

'If you'd give more to Charles for his university expenses, he wouldn't be such a drain on *my* resources.'

'Charles should be in the office with me; I wonder if he'll ever learn that he must earn a living.'

Elizabeth ignored this old complaint, but went on unwisely, 'Alicia should have a black costume, also.'

Humphrey's little eyes nearly vanished in the folds of flesh around them, as he turned towards the bathroom door. 'Alicia's personal needs are your concern, not mine. She's lucky that I feed her and give her a bed.' He pushed the door open and then looked back over his shoulder. 'And don't forget, Madam, that I give *you* a roof – many men wouldn't. I shall order the carriage for 10.30 on Friday morning. See that you are ready. And make sure the servants have black arm bands sewn on their outdoor clothes.'

He stalked into the bathroom and closed the door.

Elizabeth shivered and wondered, for the hundredth time, whether her brother in Ceylon would give her a home on his tea estate, if she suddenly arrived there. Then she envisioned again dealing with the partner with whom he lived and with a totally strange country, and she discarded the idea; she rarely considered what would happen to Alicia if she left her husband; she did not enjoy thinking about the girl at all.

She went downstairs into the dining-room; the brandy bottle in the sideboard was empty. She pulled a chair away from the table and sat down on it. When Polly came up to clear Humphrey's breakfast dishes, she found her mistress weeping quietly, her hands screwing up her wet handkerchief in her lap. Tray in hand, Polly asked kindly if she could help her. Elizabeth made no attempt to hide her tears. She mumbled, 'Yes, Polly. Find me a glass of port and my smelling salts.'

II

The fine black broadcloth costume, lined with silk and trimmed discreetly with black silk velvet binding was a miracle produced by two elderly ladies from George Henry Lee's who sewed nearly all night for several nights, first the calico fitting and then the dress material cut from the calico pattern. Though a seamstress was sent up to the house for the first two fittings, Lee's was so busy that Elizabeth had to go down to the shop for the final one.

When Elizabeth had said she would hire a closed carriage for this journey, Humphrey said she could hire anything as long as *she* paid for it. Otherwise, she could use the electric tram, as he did. This led to one of their tremendous quarrels, from which the whole household reverberated for the next twenty-four hours.

When Sarah Webb called and was told by Elizabeth about Humphrey's meanness, she promptly offered to take her angry friend down to Lee's in her governess cart; she herself always wore black as being the most economical colour. Elizabeth reluctantly accepted this modest form of door-to-door transport, and had the dress billed to Humphrey.

A new hat being too much expense, an old one was taken out and retrimmed with swirls of black velvet, taken from an evening gown with a twenty-two inch waist which Elizabeth could no longer get into. There was enough material in the skirt to furnish a dress for Alicia; this was made up for her by a new dressmaker who had recently set up in Crown Street; it neither fitted nor suited Alicia, who complained bitterly to Polly about it.

'It's the best your Mam could do; be thankful for it,' replied Polly unsympathetically.

Alicia thought uneasily about this apparent need for economy and then put on the hated garment.

Alicia herself bound four white handkerchiefs with black edging, two for Humphrey and one each for her mother and herself, not that Alicia wept much for the old Queen; she had a feeling that Edward VII might be more fun.

While her parents were at the service and the subsequent luncheon, Alicia thankfully took off her ugly mourning dress and put on an old summer frock, in order to help Fanny give the morning-room and the library a much needed cleaning.

The house was far too big for two maids to cope with, and Alicia had realized that parts of it were gradually becoming very neglected. Elizabeth took little interest in it. No parties had been given in it for some time. Few ladies called on a woman who did not have an At Home any more. Only Sarah Webb panted her way up the front steps at least once a week to sit with her old friend and visit her godchild.

Shabby curtains and rugs which might normally have been renewed went unnoticed by their depressed owners. When Alicia pointed out that moths had got into the dining-room curtains and suggested new ones, her mother retorted impatiently that it was too much trouble and, anyway, Humphrey would never agree to the expense. In this latter remark, she was probably right; Humphrey was finding his old friend, Mrs Jakes and her tobacco shop, quite expensive, at a time when he had suffered a number of financial losses, including money invested in a mad scheme to build a railway tunnel under the Mersey; the railway had been built, but had been a consistent money loser.

'Shall we take up the carpet, Allie?' This from Fanny in the morning-room. 'It needs beating badly.'

'There isn't time, Fan. They'll be back from Church before we're finished, if we take it up. Scatter tea leaves over it and give it a thorough brush with a stiff broom. We'll take the curtains down, though, and give them a good brush and shake in the garden; I don't think the velvet ones have been down for years.'

'You should leave me to do it, Allie. You should go out for a bit. Haven't you got a school friend you could visit? That Miss Ethel you used to walk home with sometimes?'

At the top of the stepladder, Alicia carefully lowered one end of the heavy brass curtain rail into Fanny's hands. Dust flew from the curtains as they slid to the end of the rail and Fanny pulled them off. Alicia sneezed, and this gave her time to consider her reply. She had learned to accept the fact that when she offered friendship to a girl, there always seemed to be an obstacle to its flourishing. She did not really understand why, and usually blamed herself for being uninteresting or not well-dressed enough to please the parents concerned.

Now, she wondered sometimes if there were another, darker reason. She had come to understand, after sly questioning of Polly, that illegitimacy was a dreadful burden for a child to bear; but, again and again, she came back to the fact that Papa was very much a presence in the house. He was terrifyingly bad-tempered and he rarely spoke to her, except to scold or swear at her. Nevertheless, he existed, so that when she had been called a bastard, it had seemed untrue. That her mother's long-held reputation for flirtatiousness, on top of the rumours of Alicia being the daughter of Andrew Crossing, made anxious mothers feel that their daughters should not be exposed to such an influence, did not occur to bewildered Alicia.

Fanny's suggestion that she should go to see Ethel disturbed her and she did not know how to answer. Finally, as she slipped another curtain off its rod, she replied, 'You know, Fan, I often feel a long way away from other girls, as if I were much older than them.' She climbed slowly down the stepladder. 'I met Ethel in the chemist's one day. She said she was swotting to go to university, which is something I would have liked to do; but which university is going to accept a lady?'

'I dunno anything about that. But it int natural for a young girl to have no friends,' responded Fanny firmly. 'Your Mam ought to do something about it. Who's going to come to your Coming Out Dance, if you don't know nobody?'

Alicia bent over to bundle up the curtains, to take them into the garden to shake. 'Mama hasn't said anything about my Coming Out yet – I'm really not quite old enough, am I?'

'Suppose you talk to Miss Florence about it?' Fanny suggested, as together they staggered out under their loads of drapery.

'Perhaps I will – one day,' Alicia replied doubtfully.

III

Except for a necklace of seed pearls from her godmother, Sarah Webb, and a book of children's poetry which arrived by post from Florence, Alicia's sixteenth birthday on May 12th , 1902, went unremarked outside the kitchen.

Polly baked a birthday cake and presented her with a pair of hand-knitted gloves; Fanny gave her two bars of highly scented soap. In addition to the cake, they had strawberry jelly for tea.

When Sarah called, Elizabeth was so deeply asleep that Alicia was unable to waken her to greet her old friend. Sarah kept her concern at this to herself and had a cup of tea and a piece of birthday cake with Alicia in the morning-room.

Alicia was enchanted at having a real pearl necklace and flung her arms round Sarah gleefully.

She did not tell her godmother that, as usual, her mother had forgotten her birthday and that Papa and Charles never seemed to remember anybody's birthday. She wondered sadly if there were other girls whose birthdays went unremarked; most of the girls at school, she remembered, had had not only presents but parties to celebrate the day, parties to which she was never invited. This persistent overlooking of her meant, she was by now convinced, that there was something seriously wrong with her own character, so that she failed to please – or that she was, indeed, by some odd quirk, illegitimate and, therefore, outside the social pale. These fears about herself tended to make her withdrawn, though not when with her quiet, charming, old godmother.

While she plied Sarah with tea, down in the basement kitchen Fanny voiced her usual complaints about the neglect of Alicia's birthday.

'Lady Mucks of Muck Hall round here, they are. Anywhere else, they'd've forgotten years ago wot 'er Mam did – and you'd think the Master would've guv up on it by now. But, no! The poor little bugger has to go on being put in 'er place, like she were born in the Workhouse, like me.'

'Her Mam's not well enough to see to her,' Polly defended her mistress.

Fanny replied tartly, 'There's nothin' wrong with her Mam, 'cept she drinks and totters round like a hen with the staggers. She's just gone to bits, she has.' Fanny wrung out the dishcloth, as if she were wringing Elizabeth's neck. 'If she'd a scrap of sense, she could've helped the kid get some friends, so they could've come to a do on her birthday.' And she added, as she emptied the washing-up water down the sink, 'There's no excuse for not givin' her a present.'

Polly had heard it all before and agreed with her friend, but she warned, 'Hush, Fan. It int our business.'

IV

On a warm, late September day, Florence and three of her children dropped in for afternoon tea. After enduring the children while Alicia served tea, Elizabeth suggested wearily that they should take the youngsters for a run in the garden, so Alicia and Florence took them outside.

Alicia pointed out with jubilation that, today, she had her hair up for the first time, and she turned her head so that Florence could admire the neat bun at the back of her neck.

Florence said absently that it was very nice, and turned to chide three of her children who were romping through a bed of delphiniums, the pride of Mr Bittle, the gardener. Her scolding was ineffectual and she felt wearily that she had not the strength to heave them bodily out of the flowerbed, so she turned a fretful face back to Alicia.

Alicia was saying, 'Flo, do you think I'm old enough to have a Coming Out Party?'

Away in her parsonage ever since Alicia was born, Florence had little idea of the day-to-day isolation of her half-sister, and she replied casually, 'I imagine you could have your friends in. The drawing-room is big enough for a little dance.'

'It needs a good clean,' replied Alicia ruefully. 'You had a dance, didn't you? And that's how you met Clarence?'

'Yes. Mama asked the sons of friends of hers, and he was one of them. The idea is to meet possible husbands.'

'Are you happy with him, Flo?'

The sudden question disconcerted the older woman. Under the brim of her straw hat, her eyes were troubled. 'Well, of course. Clarence is very good and the children are a great consolation. What else can one expect?'

'Were you in love with Clarence, I mean truly, romantically in love?'

'Really, Alicia, I think that is a rather impertinent question. Naturally one loves one's husband – it's the duty of a wife.' They sat down together on the garden seat and Alicia stretched her arms above her and then clasped her hands behind her head. 'I'd like to be in love,' she declared, 'really and truly in love.'

'Alicia! Don't stretch yourself in public; it's most unladylike. In love? Well, I hope it happens.' She thought how nice it would be to be sixteen and not know anything about the nastiness of love and the pain and exhaustion of child-bearing – and how totally unreasonable husbands could be. She pushed back errant wisps of hair from her face; she looked terribly tired and old, and Alicia pitied her.

'You know, Flo, if I get married, I'm not going to have a lot of children.'

Florence smiled sadly. 'You don't have any choice. They simply come.'

'Even if you don't get married?'

Florence hesitated. 'Well, you know that old maids don't have them. But you don't want to be an old maid, do you?'

'Aunt Sarah seems to be quite happy in her little house and with her pony and trap.'

'Ah, yes, but Miss Webster was left quite a competence by her father.'

'Well, won't Papa leave you and me something? I thought all fathers did.'

Florence did not know how to answer the question. Though Humphrey tolerated Alicia in his house, Clarence had not hesitated to state that Alicia was illegitimate and that her mother's morals had been a source of gossip for years. He had, at the same time, pointed out that a Vicar's wife must always be above suspicion.

Under Alicia's steady gaze, Florence squirmed uneasily. Though her father sent her generous monetary gifts for her birthday and at Christmas, she knew that he never gave anything to Alicia; he seemed to ignore the girl as far as possible. And Clarence was in part correct; her mother had been in times past rather a flirt and her clothes had tended to be extremely fashionable and too bright in colour for a place like Liverpool. Alicia was, however, waiting for an answer, so she said hesitantly, 'Well, I'm not sure. I suspect that he is not quite as well off as he used to be, so I can't say.'

The cheerfulness engendered by her mother's permission to put her hair up went out of Alicia, as she looked at her obviously embarrassed, prevaricating sister. Papa was certainly being quite careful about money; yet she felt that Florence was trying to evade replying to her question. As it had done many times lately, a sense of dread invaded her and made her stomach muscles clench. Without Papa, what would happen to Mama and to herself? If they could not pay Polly, she, too, would have difficulties and would have to find another job. Alicia wondered how she could live without Polly. She licked her lips, and tried to be practical, as she suggested, 'Perhaps I should forget about Coming Out; the girls at school used to say that it wasn't the party you gave yourself that was so much fun, but the parties of the other families to which you were invited. And who is going to ask me? I never see another girl these days – I mean, nice girls – when I go shopping; they are all in school.' She stopped, her expression pensive. Then she added heavily, 'I must be the most boring person on earth.'

Florence did not deny her last remark; Alicia was rarely spritely. She did feel, however, a sense of guilt. If her mother was not well enough to bring Alicia out, she should herself help the girl a little – though what Clarence would say if she suggested giving parties for Alicia would probably be unprintable.

Yet, Coming Out launched you on the marriage market, gave you a chance to meet eligible young men. Even plain girls like Alicia had to marry – what else were they to do? The few girls who earned their living in offices or stores were lower class. There was, of course, nursing, thanks to the efforts of Florence Nightingale; but if Alicia became a nurse she would have to live in the hospital amongst a lot of ignorant, Roman Catholic Irish girls, and Florence shuddered at the thought of the amount of floor-scrubbing and cleaning of bedpans she would have to do before she received her nurse's cap.

The very thought of giving even a Tea for Alicia made Florence feel tired to death, but she said reluctantly, 'I'll mention it to Mama, if you like.'

'Would you, Flo?' She looked wistfully at her sister. 'I would so love a party with a special dress – not made by old Miss Blossom!' She smiled at her own reference to the elderly dressmaker whose clothes always seemed behind the times.

'I'm sure you would.' Inwardly, Florence sighed. The hint that the girl was a bastard, added to that almost white, wispy hair, the light grey eyes with their pale lashes behind glasses, the quietness of the girl. There was nothing to recommend her to a well-placed youth unless she had a good dowry. She's pleasant and she's capable and that's all, thought Florence.

The recollection of Alicia's ability to organize her mother's house reminded Florence of her own need for additional help at home.

'You know, Alicia,' she said slowly, 'if Papa was not able to leave either of us any money, the Reverend Browning would give you a home; Clarence is a little stern, but he would never let you starve.'

Alicia's lips looked almost grim because at this remark she clamped them together so tightly. No, she screamed inwardly. Heaven preserve me from becoming an unpaid help in a brother-in-law's house, penniless, and without a moment's privacy or peace. Better to be a paid governess in the house of a stranger. She said aloud, 'That would be very kind of you both, Flo. Thank you.'

V

Florence broached the subject to her mother on one of Elizabeth's rare visits to the Vicarage.

Because Humphrey had had a new lock put on the wine cellar, Elizabeth was unusually sober. Seated in Florence's pokey little sitting-room, a glass of the Reverend Browning's poor quality Madeira in her hand, she was doing her best to sip the wine genteelly while she longed to gulp it down and ask for another glass. Her hands trembled and her mind had a tendency to wander.

Sarah Webb who had driven her out to the Vicarage noted her friend's predicament and thought that, later, she would warn Florence not to offer her mother alcohol. Poor Elizabeth would kill herself with drink, if she were not watched.

Elizabeth was caught off balance by Florence's request for a Coming Out for Alicia. She blurted in reply, 'Your father would never allow it.'

'But, Mama, I had one.'

'It – er – would be so expensive, nowadays.'

Florence tried again. 'It would not need a great deal, Mama. I'm sure we could cater it ourselves – and get flowers from the garden. I could play the piano for dancing. And that leaves only wine – which Papa probably already has in his cellar.'

Cornered, Elizabeth cast a frantic glance at Sarah.

Sarah knew all too well that a Coming Out Party would cause another round of malicious gossip and would probably not result in Alicia getting a husband. Elizabeth had already told her of Humphrey's angry remark that he would leave nothing to Alicia, and, of course, Elizabeth's capital left her by her father could not be touched; she could use only the interest, so, presumably, Alicia had no dowry.

Watching Alicia slowly take over the housekeeping, Sarah sensed that, in any case, Elizabeth simply did not want to alter the current situation; for once, Elizabeth and Humphrey were in silent agreement; it was convenient to have a trustworthy, unpaid housekeeper.

Anxious not to hurt Alicia, Sarah took a careful sip from her teacup, and said to Florence, 'Your Mama and Papa are far from well, dear – and the passing of Edward . . . the wear and tear of a party could be too much for them.' She turned to Elizabeth, and asked, 'Would Clara in West Kirby give a little party for her and invite the local young people?' That, she argued, might introduce the girl to a new group, give her a little chance.

'Clara is totally bed-ridden now; her companion-help has to do everything for her. She could not even come to Edward's Memorial Service. She's been very kind in asking Alicia to visit her to get the sea air . . . but I haven't been able to spare her lately . . .' Elizabeth could hardly hold her teacup steady and leaned forward to put it down on the side table, before she dropped it.

All this time, Alicia had been kneeling in front of the windowseat on which she and Florence's youngest daughter had spread a jigsaw puzzle. As she half-listened to the debate on her Coming Out, she felt a painful sadness; her mother's remark about her aunt's invitations, however, was comforting; dear Aunt Clara had not forgotten her, as she had often assumed. Now it struck her that arthritic hands and sheer age had probably made it difficult for her to write many letters and, naturally, she would write, when she could, to Elizabeth. Mama, being often drunk, had probably forgotten to pass on the gentle, kindly messages.

As her little niece triumphantly placed a corner piece in the puzzle, Alicia felt again that walls were closing round her – and the walls had no doors or windows. Though she had never had a social life, she had always hoped that as she grew up she would get a chance of making a circle of cheerful, intelligent friends.

Elizabeth was woodenly declaring that dear Alicia did not need to Come Out; her place was with her mother.

Alicia wanted to cry; the walls loomed even bigger and more menacing.

She had wept and raged one night recently, while helping Polly plough through the household mending. 'Why can't I be like other girls and go back to school? At least I was learning something there.'

Pitying her and anxious not to add to the girl's burdens, Polly had tried to rationalize the situation for her. She had said, 'Well, luvvy, your Ma and Pa need your help very badly at home; any girl would do the same as you and look after them. It's a single daughter's duty – you see it all the time.' She had put down her sewing on the table and had leaned over to touch Alicia's hand. 'You've got enough book-learnin', already, to last you a lifetime, duck.'

Alicia had hung her head, so that Polly should not see the rebellion in her expression, and had continued to cross-stitch round a patch in a flannel sheet.

Polly changed the subject to divert her, and asked, 'When I done this hem, will you help me write to Billy? Come on. Here's a hankie to dry your eyes.'

Resignedly, Alicia wiped her face, blew her nose and agreed to help. Billy did not write that often, but at least three or four times a year, a long, printed epistle would arrive, and his adventures in Canada were sometimes very funny, as he described them to the sister for whom he hoped to make a home.

Now, in Florence's dowdy sitting-room, young Beatrice carefully put the last piece into the puzzle and smiled up at Alicia in triumph. She scrambled down from the windowseat and went to ask Florence for a piece of cake.

Alicia got up off her knees and quietly took a seat by the completed puzzle.

As the debate on a party for her petered out, she felt defeated. She knew she had duties towards her parents, duties defined by the Church which she no longer had the time to attend and by a society which did not hesitate to keep a daughter at home and single, if it were convenient to her parents.

Doesn't anyone have duties towards me? she wondered forlornly.

VI

In an effort to alleviate the disappointment her godchild must be feeling, Sarah Webb changed the subject of conversation, by asking Alicia, 'Did you see the Indian troops pass through on the electric tram, dear? They're here for the Coronation.'

'Yes, I did,' replied Alicia a trifle defiantly, as she glanced at her surprised mother. 'Polly and I walked down to Sefton Park to see them.'

Her mother blinked. She was quite shocked. 'Alicia! You should ask before you leave the house. To go out with the common herd to gape at foreign troops!'

'You were asleep, Mama. I did not wish to wake you.' She did not add that her mother had been sleeping off a bottle of port which Elizabeth had ordered Fanny to go out and buy for her. 'I wanted to see the kind of men that Edward commanded.' Her nose went into the air in a movement like that of her mother in earlier days, and she added, 'They looked very fine – very handsome. I was safe there with Polly – and really a lot of most respectable-looking people had turned out for them.'

Elizabeth responded sharply, 'Well, it's not to happen again. You are not to leave the house without my permission.'

An outraged Alicia opened her mouth to protest, but Sarah took one of the girl's hands and pressed it urgently. Alicia swallowed her anger, and answered sullenly, 'Yes, Mama.'

19

Though Alicia never knew it, the idea of her being Brought Out was finally killed by the Reverend Clarence Browning. With his eyes on promotion in the Church, he forbade Florence to have anything to do with it. 'I cannot forbid you to see your *half*-sister,' he had fulminated, 'but the less attention drawn to her – and to her mother – the better it will be for us.'

Florence protested at the slur cast upon Elizabeth, but the biting sarcasms thrown at her sent her weeping to her bedroom. Alicia would have to fight for herself, Florence decided in desperation. And as for her mother, Florence had an uneasy feeling that she was losing her wits; she seemed so stupid at times.

Alicia would not have seen anything of the festivities for the Coronation of King Edward VII on August 9th, 1902, had not Sarah, pitying her confinement, persuaded Elizabeth that an old woman needed someone with her if she were to mingle with the crowds in the city.

'I know you don't want to go,' she said, 'so I want to borrow dear Alicia just for a couple of hours.'

'I can't imagine why *you* want to go – the city will be packed – full of vulgar curiosity seekers,' responded Elizabeth fretfully.

'I always did love crowds,' Sarah replied sweetly, so Elizabeth reluctantly gave her consent.

There was so much traffic on the roads to the city centre that the two ladies decided to go by electric tram; and it was a pleasure to Sarah to see Alicia's face light up when she saw the gay buntings and streamers strung from the lamp-posts and the delightfully decorated trams, one of which had been specially illuminated in honour of Alexandra, the pretty new Queen.

When Sarah's legs began to fail, they went into a small café much frequented by lady shoppers. Sarah ordered an assortment of iced cakes, lemonade, ice cream and tea and watched with pleasure as Alicia enjoyed them. The child can be quite vivacious, she ruminated, given a chance – but she does look dreadfully frumpy amongst the other young women in here.

On the way home, Alicia thanked her godmother profusely for the outing. 'I must be very frivolous,' she confessed, 'but I do love going out.'

'Nonsense, child. I wish I could take you more often.'

At sixty, Sarah was feeling her age and, though she hated to admit it, she could no longer afford such expeditions; like many others, her income inherited from her father now bought considerably less than it had twenty years before. She was preparing to give up her governess cart because she could no longer afford the stabling fees and she had already dispensed with her live-in maid; she now managed with the aid of a grey, silent charlady from the Workhouse, who came in every morning.

Despite her growing infirmities, however, she arranged another little outing for Alicia, one that did not cost anything. She insisted that she and Alicia should go to see the opening of the new Toxteth Branch Library. Elizabeth complained capriciously that she could not spare Alicia, to which Sarah had roundly replied, 'Rubbish, my dear. You should come along yourself; it is an important local event which we should be a part of. The library will make a lot of difference to this district.'

'I couldn't possibly come,' Elizabeth replied. 'Standing amid the rabble would be too tiring.'

'Well, then I promise not to keep Alicia more than two hours. Where is the child?' And she insisted that, there and then, Alicia be sent for, so that she could be invited personally. She wanted to make sure that her godchild actually received the invitation; Elizabeth was most forgetful.

Polly was surprised when, the next morning, Elizabeth asked where Alicia was.

'Miss Webb came for her about an hour ago, Ma'am, to go and see the new library.'

Elizabeth looked a little bewildered and then answered, 'Yes, of course she did.'

As Sarah Webb and Alicia walked down to the new little brick building, Sarah's double chins wobbled excitedly as she told Alicia, 'Mr Andrew Carnegie himself has condescended to come to open it – you know, he has provided the money for it. It's a real chance to see a great man.'

Thankful to be out in the fresh air on a brisk October morning with leaves whirling in the gutters, Alicia cheerfully agreed.

'Once you join the library, you'll be able to borrow books ad lib – anybody can.'

'Could Polly? She loves to read.'

'Indeed, yes. She will be made welcome. It is meant to bring books within the purview of the poorest.'

'Mama says it's vulgar to belong to a free library, that one might catch diseases from the books.'

'Well, I'm not vulgar,' puffed the older woman firmly. 'I shall be happy to borrow books from this library; it'll save me having to go to town to get them from Lee's private library.'

They found a good position across the road from the new building and watched a constable keeping people back from the entrance. The wind was quite cold, and barefoot children ran in and out amongst the adults, to keep themselves warm.

One little tike with sores on his head thrust his hand out in front of Alicia, and asked hopefully, 'Gi' us a penny, Miss.'

Alicia looked down at the wizened, worldly-wise face and replied truthfully, 'I don't have any money with me.' She flushed slightly, feeling humiliated in front of Sarah, who produced a coin from her old-fashioned, black velvet bag.

It was some time since she had had any spending money of her own. From childhood, her mother had each Saturday given her a silver threepenny piece. Lately, she had not done so, and Alicia was worried that, from the current month's housekeeping, she had had to spend twopence on hairpins and then enter it in the account book; she feared greatly what Humphrey would say about it. As he had done with Mrs Tibbs, he queried almost every item.

'Naughty little thing,' Sarah said, with a chuckle, as the child slipped away.

After the ceremony, they strolled back to Sarah's house, where they were to have a cup of tea before Alicia went home. Sarah said gaily, 'You'll be able to tell your friends that you saw Andrew Carnegie, and even tell your grandchildren.'

Remembering that she had friends in Polly and Fanny, she was able to agree with Sarah, though some of her pleasure in the pleasant morning went at the thought that it would be a miracle if she ever had children, never mind grandchildren. There did not seem to be much future, beyond dancing attendance on her parents.

Once the library was running, she and Polly often sat up late in the nursery, sharing a candle – Humphrey was fussy about the number of candles consumed in the house – in order to read a stream of novels Polly borrowed.

Both of them dreamed of a great aristocrat who would ride into their lives and whisk them off to a gorgeous manor house. It was a delicious indulgence, but both of them knew that dreams were ephemeral.

The hard work which had been Polly's lot had taken her earlier prettiness. She was quite heavily lined and, when she was tired, her pale lips drooped and her eyes had a look of sad disillusionment.

Despite her love of Edward, she had in earlier years sometimes picked up a likely young man lounging round the waterfront, hoping to make a marriage which would release her from the bonds of domestic service. There was, however, in Liverpool South, a great shortage of men of her own age group, and, as she often said to Fanny, 'With no work, a wife's a luxury to a man – they can't afford to marry.'

She was thankful for the small store of golden sovereigns given to her by Edward and for the silver shillings from her wages which she had added to them; they would cushion her old age.

During the same month that Alexander Carnegie visited Liverpool, Sir Wilfred Laurier, the Premier of Canada, came to open the new Produce Exchange. When Polly read about it in the newspaper, her face lit up, and she ran up to the nursery, where Alicia was sponging and pressing her mother's winter dresses. 'Would he have news of our Billy?' she asked breathlessly.

Alicia laid her iron on a trivet and pushed it over the fire to heat again. Though she wanted to smile, she replied gravely, 'I don't think so, Polly. He comes from Ottawa in Ontario – and Billy's in a provincial district – Alberta – and it's a long way off – thousands of miles.'

Polly's face fell. 'Aye, I suppose you're right.' She sighed, and turned to go downstairs again. 'I wish he were 'ere,' she said wistfully. 'Our Mary and me, we miss 'im. He were such a good lad.'

II

Used to being part of a tight family unit, Billy did not forget his sisters and often wished they were with him as he scratched for a living in an alien world.

When a ragged tomtit of a boy had crept out of the bush at the side of the trail leading down to the railway halt by the Metis village and had begged Ben Reilly, an elderly pedlar, to show him the way to Toronto, Ben had picked him up and put the exhausted boy on the back of one of his horses. As they proceeded along the trail, the boy had wept and told him what had happened to him on the Macdonalds' farm.

Ben Reilly had seen such children many times in his travels, and as he plodded through melting snow, chewing on a plug of tobacco and listening to the tale of woe, he felt that Billy might help to solve his own problems. He, therefore, set up camp for the night at a distance from the Metis village, and he and Billy shared a sparse dinner of bannock and bacon, while they got to know each other. The boy was eager to help him and obviously knew how to handle horses.

Though Reilly came from southern Ontario, he was to Billy a bit like any Irishman on the Liverpool docks, and the man's language was similar; he certainly had the same flow of swear words, as he built a smoky fire with damp, dead wood. 'In a month or two, it'll be so dry, we'll have to watch we don't start a forest fire,' he asssured Billy, and Billy didn't miss the inference that they would still be together. He wondered suddenly if the man would expect to sleep with him and he watched him warily, as Reilly took a bottle from a saddlebag and settled down by the fire to drink. He motioned to Billy to sit near him. Billy carefully left a foot between them. The bent hobgoblin of a man laughed and spat his tobacco into the fire. 'I'm not goin' to touch you, lad.'

Billy smiled sheepishly, but kept his distance. 'Do you know *where* Toronto is?' he asked after a small silence.

'Aye, I do. But there's no way you can get there 'cept by ridin' the train. It's hundreds a miles away.' He chewed the end of his heavy, white moustache thoughtfully. 'Best I can do for you is to miss calling at the next village, 'cos they may remember you there, if Macdonald comes lookin'. We can go to the farms I usually do after that – they won't know your face. You could get work on the farms, but I tell you it wouldn't be any better than what you gone through already.'

Expert salesman, Ben Reilly had a merry, elfin quality about him, and Billy gradually relaxed.

According to Ben, the pickings for a travelling packman like himself were getting thinner in Ontario, as settlements grew, roads were built and shops were established. What he wanted to do, before he got too old, was to go further west. Had Billy ever heard of Calgary – or Edmonton?

Billy had not.

'You can get land for nuthin' out there – or next to it.'

Billy looked at him pop-eyed, his fatigue forgotten. Land for nothing? As the night wore on and the old pedlar, glad of company, began to talk out his ideas, Billy's almost forgotten dream of a farm of his own began to revive.

It was dead dark and the forest was full of night noises by the time Ben Reilly had worked his way round to asking Billy if he would like to go west with him and work as his assistant. 'All I can do is feed you, till we get started. You look an honest boy. You play fair with me and I'll play fair with you.'

Billy agreed, and for two months they travelled Ben's usual round. Under his tutelage, Billy extended his knowledge of how to bargain with both buyers and sellers, how to wheedle small animal skins out of isolated settlers in return for sewing cotton, needles, nails, nuts and bolts, screws and good knives. Fur traders in the cities were always interested in decent pelts, he told Billy.

When the warm weather came, they stowed away on a train bound for Calgary. They were kicked off it at Winnipeg.

Unperturbed, Ben took the opportunity to buy a number of small tins of simple remedies, like zinc ointment, which he assured Billy would sell very well in isolated places at twice the price. They then caught another train.

Though they did their best to lose themselves in a large group of Ukrainian immigrants, an angry conductor picked them out and threatened them with delivery to the North-west Mounted Police, if they did not pay up. While Billy tried to make himself invisible behind Ben Reilly, the pedlar resignedly slit the lining of his coat and produced the fare for both of them, swearing that they had joined the train at Regina.

The conductor had heard the same story a hundred times before; nevertheless, he decided to accept their protestations, rather than waste more time arguing that they had got on earlier.

With a contented grin at Billy, old Ben put his head down on his pack and slept. Billy sat squashed on a wooden seat beside two restive children in fur waistcoats.

In Calgary, they found shelter in the straw-filled loft of a rooming house, which they shared with three young men, also new immigrants. Ben and the other men all smoked, and Billy spent a week of most uneasy nights, fearing that one or the other of them would set the straw on fire. He survived, however, and set out for the countryside with Ben, refurbished packs, and a horse of most uncertain temperament.

Ben Reilly never spent a penny, if he could help it, and Billy learned from him to do likewise, to cadge and beguile meals and a place to sleep. Sometimes, they ate off the land, snaring rabbits, catching fish, and adding wild plants to the subsequent stew.

After a while, they moved their base to Edmonton where the competition was less. Reilly began to feel his age as the years went by, so when Billy was seventeen he sent him north to St Albert and Lac Ste. Anne, to branch off wherever he found a settlement. Billy met housewives using many different languages and he took the trouble to learn the names of the objects in his pack in Russian, Norwegian, Dutch and Icelandic. His efforts brought friendly smiles to the faces of many lonely women.

Though he was strictly honest with Ben Reilly, he found ways of earning a few extra dollars on the side. A housewife whose husband had a closely guarded flock of sheep – the coyotes picked them off, if they were not careful, the woman said – used to spin and knit garments for her family. He offered to sell for her on commission any extra ones she had time to make. She persuaded an Icelandic neighbour to knit as well, and Billy had no difficulty in getting rid of the warm woollens in lumber and mining camps, where he sold tobacco. Well-established settlers sometimes had feathers to spare; Billy suggested to one lady that she put hers into bags made of a gay print which he provided, and he sold them as cushions, again on commission. Ben Reilly began to pay him a better commission himself. Cents became dollars, and Billy stitched them into his jacket. He grew into a short, amiable man, who kept out of the taverns and out of trouble, as best he could in a rough frontier world.

He did not drink or smoke, because in his opinion the cost was too great, and he had his eyes set on applying for a quarter-section of land. Though the land cost little, he knew he would need a horse and plough, seed and axes, if he was to get a good start; his wife, if he ever got one, was not going to pull the plough, as he had seen Ukrainian women do when their husbands were breaking land.

Because he was sometimes lonely, his letters to Polly became longer and more interesting as he ruefully described his adventures on the road. In the spring, when everybody was bogged down by mud, he helped the man who owned the stable where he had first lodged in Edmonton and made a lifelong friend of him. He told of going during the winter into logging camps where no women were, to sell tobacco, cigarette papers, boots, socks and pipes. He mentioned Chinese, some of them his competitors, who had worked on the railway and had never gone home because they did not have enough money. Some of them had opened tiny cafés and he found he liked the food they served. He was used to oriental faces on the docks where he had worked as a boy, and, unlike many of their customers, he would talk with them if they knew enough English; so now he had one or two Chinese friends.

'Chinese food!' exclaimed Polly incredulously. 'He must be starvin' to eat that.'

Alicia laughed – she had a pretty, tinkling laugh like her mother's. 'I read somewhere that the Chinese are the world's best cooks.'

'It's a good thing Mrs Tibbs int here to hear you,' replied Polly. 'Pack o' heathens. Seen 'em walkin' round down town – come off the boats, they had. Aye, poor Billy. What he must be goin' through!'

But Billy was happy. He felt he was on his way to better things. Very slowly, but steadily, the dollars sewn into his jacket increased.

20

I

'Aye, 'e's dead,' Fanny assured Alicia lugubriously, her voice muffled. She was cleaning the flues of the kitchen range and puffs of soot flew round her, as she pulled out the long wire brush from the oven flue. 'Colonel Milfort's valet, next door, told me.' She turned away to sneeze, and then glanced at Alicia sitting by the white-scrubbed table. The young woman was wrapped in a dressing-gown long since discarded by her mother; her nose and eyes were red from a heavy cold and she was shivering in the unheated kitchen.

Alicia had come downstairs early, in hope of a cup of tea to ease her aching head, but the kitchen range had, the previous day, not been drawing properly, so the fire was not yet lit because of Fanny's cleaning efforts. Until she had finished, there would be no means of boiling a kettle and no hot water flowing from the bathroom taps – which would make Papa furious.

She leaned one elbow on the table and rested her head on her hand. It was nearly six o'clock, and outside the high, barred window overlooking the stone area, the February wind was howling, as it had done for the last twenty-four hours. In the kitchen, a single gaslight hanging from the high ceiling cast cold rays on grubby walls and grey stone floor.

Dear old Mr Bittle dead? He'd been the gardener since before she was born – and next May she would be twenty. A lump rose in her throat and she wanted to cry. She took out a much-used handkerchief and blew her stuffed-up nose. In her mind's eye, she saw the gardener's heavy, work-hardened fingers delicately splitting a seed so that she could observe its interior under her magnifying glass. She remembered how, as a little girl, he had recruited her to help him clear cluttered corners of the garden which might harbour wicked slugs and snails, how he had scattered lime round his precious seedlings and had encouraged starlings and toads, to reduce voracious pests. 'Natural things'll help you in a garden, if you let them,' he would say.

Fanny put away her long flue brush and picked up the poker to rake out the previous day's ashes. She said, of Mr Bittle, 'Colonel Milfort's man said he were found lyin' in the street in the middle of the storm yesterday. Proper awful, poor man. The wind must've bin too much for him, after he left here.'

Alicia winced. Dear humble man, out there in the cold. And nobody left in his little cottage off Crown Street to know or care that he had not returned.

She had felt depressed throughout the winter and this news added to it. A woman who did her duty was supposed to be content, knowing that she had done it; but, increasingly, Alicia felt she wanted to run out of the front door and dance and laugh and be free, swept along by the wild wind outside, into some madcap new world. Yet, she knew, from Polly and Fanny's stories, how cruel that outside world could be and the thought of facing it alone and penniless kept her rooted in Humphrey's house; at least Papa was a known devil.

After putting a new lock on his wine cellar door to protect his stock, Humphrey had told Alicia and the servants that, on no account, were they to provide Elizabeth with alcohol. Elizabeth vented her misery on Alicia.

Fanny, however, had had in some ways a very close affinity with Elizabeth, ever since she had found her badly beaten so many years ago. Armed with money from Elizabeth's allowance, she would sneak out to buy the occasional bottle of port or brandy for her desperate mistress. Such occasions were the only times when Alicia had a peaceful day, as Elizabeth slept it off. With her head spinning, Alicia dreaded today; since the weather was so bad, she would not even be able to persuade her mother to take a little walk in the fresh air.

Not that walking out with Elizabeth was exactly exciting. Accompanied occasionally by Sarah Webb, the most adventurous walk would be as far as Princes Park at the pace of elderly ladies. Alicia would dawdle along, watching enviously as working-class couples strolled past them, arm-in-arm, or cuddled close to each other on the park benches. She watched families picnicking or playing impromptu games of cricket on fine Sunday afternoons; and girls, not much younger than herself, enjoying equally impromptu games of rounders or shuttlecock and battledore. She had herself almost forgotten what it was like to play anything. In any case, her mother referred to the happy players as very vulgar. Was everything that was fun vulgar? Was she always to be an onlooker of life, never a participant? she wondered bitterly.

Yesterday had been a rotten day, she thought mournfully, as Fanny swept up the hearth after her cleaning. Papa had, when doing the household accounts with her, seized upon the butcher's bill and complained that it was far too high. She should, he said, scold Polly for extravagance.

'The price of beef went up recently,' Alicia had told him sullenly.

'Don't be pert, girl. Do as I say.' He had slapped the next month's housekeeping down in front of her, and she had picked up the precious gold coins, and whispered frightenedly, 'Yes, Papa.'

She ran from the room, forgetting to shut the door and had fled upstairs to the almost unused day nursery, not heeding Humphrey's angry bellow, as he got up to shut the door. She had sat down on Polly's chair and wept passionately, for the empty ache inside her and for her isolation.

Now, on this miserable February morning, Polly came whirling down the servants' stair, tying her morning apron as she came.

When she saw the empty fireplace and Fanny all covered with soot, she stopped. 'Aye, Fan!' she cried. 'Hurry up, luv. The Master will be wantin' his shavin' water and his brekkie.'

Fanny turned her smudged face towards Polly and shrugged helplessly. Alicia said savagely, 'Let him wait. It won't hurt him.'

Polly picked up a wooden tray and put it on the table. 'Now, Allie, luv, none o' that. Your Dad's a busy man.' She took a traycloth out of a drawer and laid it on the tray. Then she turned to the dresser to get the breakfast crockery.

'He should buy us a gas stove, Polly. I've asked him several times. But, no. Coal was good enough for Mrs Tibbs, so it's good enough for us.'

'Well, it would save us a lot of work,' agreed Polly, with a sigh. 'But mostly we can manage. Couldn't you do the flues at night, Fan?'

'Often the range is too hot, still,' Fanny replied, as she put a match to screwed-up newspaper she had laid in the grate. The wood on top of it began to crackle and she carefully added small pieces of coal.

'Ah, well, I'll give 'im scrambled eggs – they're quick. Tell 'im the pork butcher didn't 'ave no pigs' ears. Butcher says they're gettin' harder to get, anyways.' She picked up a tiny saucepan and went to the sink to fill it, and then gave it to Fanny. ''Ere you are, Fan. Put this on for 'is Nibs' shavin' water.'

'I can't do much until the fire gets going, so I'll go up and dress,' Alicia said wearily to Polly.

As the green baize door at the top of the stairs flipped closed behind her, Polly remarked worriedly, 'Our Allie is proper low these days.'

Fanny shrugged, and took off her sackcloth apron and hung it on a hook. 'Who wouldn't be? She don't have no fun, no friends, no nothin'. That old bastard keeps her kennelled like a dog, and her Mam's never lifts a finger to help her.' Fanny ran her tongue round her mouth and spat soot into the fire. Then she put the little saucepan over the flames.

'What that girl needs is a young man to walk out with, strong enough not to be afraid of her ould man. Pack of bloody nuns we are, in this 'ouse.'

Polly looked worried. 'God forbid she gets mixed up with a man,' she exclaimed. 'I don't want her in trouble.'

Fanny took a soot-blackened kettle, filled it at the tap and then hung it over the fire by a hook in the chimney. 'Never did *us* any 'arm,' she replied drily. 'A bit of playin' put and take would do us all good.'

Polly had to smile. 'You not doin' so well with the new coalie, as you did with ould Jack?' she inquired.

Fanny made a vulgar gesture, and then sighed, 'Jack were a good fella. I always fancied 'im. Kept 'is Missus goin' and me, sometimes.'

'No one better this side of Wigan,' agreed Polly, though she herself had not succumbed to Jack's charms. 'It were the dust from the coal that put 'im in the Infirmary – definite.'

Fanny nodded agreement. 'It'll be a bloody miracle if he ever gets out, with a cough like he's got.' She glanced round the kitchen, as she whipped the little saucepan off the fire. 'Where's old fishface's shaving mug?'

'Blast! I forgot to bring it down. It's in the bathroom. Run up and fill it for me, duck, while I finish the brekkie trays. Then you could light the fire under the copper. There's the tablecloths still to wash; I didn't have time Monday.'

'Oh, Jaysus!' moaned Fanny, and trotted upstairs, hot saucepan in hand.

She met Alicia coming out of the bathroom. The girl was shivering, having washed herself in cold water, as she usually did.

'Aye, duck, you should wait till the kitchen fire heats the hot water. Fire's blazin'. It won't be long.'

'You know Papa always lectured Charles and me on the benefits of washing in cold water,' Alicia replied morosely. 'Washing in warm water is waste of fuel, he says.'

'He uses hot himself; he'll raise Cain this mornin' 'cos the tap won't run that hot yet.' She took the lid off the little saucepan and poured the steaming water into a rose-wreathed shaving-mug on the bathroom table. She was about to say something more when Humphrey suddenly emerged from his bedroom. He was wrapped in a heavy, camel hair dressing-gown and his fur-lined slippers could be heard brushing along the hall carpet.

'Beat it,' urged Fanny in a whisper to Alicia, and Alicia fled upstairs. The instinct to keep out of Humphrey's way was still very strong.

Later, Alicia ate a bowl of porridge with the maids and then again went upstairs to make her bed and clean her room.

'The kid's gettin' desperate,' declared Fanny, as she cleared the dishes and put them into the sandstone sink. 'Do you think you could talk to Miss Webb about her? Proper nice, the old girl is. Get her to talk to the Missus, now she's a bit more sober.'

Polly looked tired and troubled. The baker had just delivered the day's bread and she was putting it into the bread bin. She closed the heavy, metal lid slowly. 'I'll try again. She don't get any pocket money these days – and the Missus always gave her some.'

'It's Allie who pays us, so she's got money.'

'That's housekeepin' only. And it's time you and me got a raise. We haven't had one for years.'

Fanny made a wry mouth. 'Wages isn't goin' up much anywhere.'

II

Polly was still wondering how to broach the subject of Alicia's loneliness to Miss Webb when, the next day help came from an unexpected quarter. She answered a prolonged ring at the doorbell to find Charles, looking very cheerful, standing impatiently on the top step and stamping his feet to keep them warm in the bitter wind. His loose, tweed overcoat flapped around his legs and the ends of his long woollen scarf danced in the wind. On his head, he wore a greasy-looking deerstalker hat. One gloved hand clutched a Gladstone bag and the other a meerschaum pipe.

'Lost my key,' he explained, as Polly hastily shut the door before the house was totally chilled. 'How are you, Polly, my old love?'

She smiled and replied, 'I'm very well, thank you, sir.' She took his bag and put it on the floor, while he pulled off his scarf and overcoat. He handed the garments to Polly and took off his hat and put it on her head. 'Where's mother?' he asked.

Seated in the morning-room with Sarah Webb, Elizabeth had already heard her son's voice, and she got up from her chair unusually quickly and went into the hall. 'Why, Charles, this is splendid,' she cried, as he bent to kiss her. 'How long are you here for?'

'For a week this time.'

'You should have written.' She turned to Polly and ordered in her old, firm voice, 'Ask Fanny to open up the blue bedroom – put a fire in it and get it aired. And bring me another teacup.'

Charles shook Sarah's hand, and it was she who ushered him closer to the fireplace, so that he could thankfully rub his hands before its warmth.

As he exchanged pleasantries with both women, he felt that the room looked more depressing every time he returned home. The curtains were grey with dust and carelessly half drawn back, the chintz covers on the chairs were so worn that the pattern on them was barely visible. On every surface there was a clutter of books, sewing and old newspapers, something that he had not observed before. In her day, his mother had been such a methodical woman and he felt a sad pang when she sat down near him. She still had a fine, white skin, but a double chin and layers of fat had taken their toll. Her hair was bunched into an untidy bun covered with a snood at the back of her head.

After he had inquired politely about his father and Alicia, who was at the grocer's, and a cup of tea and some biscuits had been pressed into his hand, his mother asked him if he had just come to see her or whether something special had occurred.

With a mouthful of biscuit, he murmured, 'Of course, I've come to see you. But I've also got an interview at the University College. They're establishing a Chair of Bio-Chemistry.'

His mother's face brightened. At last the backing she had given her son in his studies was going to have some result of which Humphrey might approve, which would be a pleasant change.

Charles saw the change in her expression, and he laughed. 'No, Mama, I'm not yet qualified enough to hold a Chair. Where there is a Chair, however, there is usually a need for Readers and Lecturers – and laboratory staff – so I wrote a general, exploratory letter, and I received a very kind letter back from the man who will hold the Chair. He's asked me to come to see him.'

'That sounds very nice.' She was a little disappointed.

'It would mean, dear Mama, that I would not have to take any further financial help from you. You have been so good to me.'

At these personal disclosures, Miss Webb rose and said that she should go home.

'Oh, dear Aunt Sarah, don't stand on ceremony. She mustn't, must she, Mama? She knows all about us.'

But Sarah Webb, who did know all about them, nevertheless felt that it was only ladylike to leave, so Polly was rung for to show her out, and Charles accompanied her to the front door, to save his mother getting up again.

At the door, Sarah Webb took his hand in her tiny gloved one, and he bent to kiss her. She smiled and looked up at him. Then she said very earnestly, 'It would do your family a world of good, Charles, if you do come home. Your mother – and little Alicia, particularly – need you.'

While Polly stood in the background, politely deaf, blind and dumb, and inwardly rejoiced, Charles was suddenly very sober, not being clear in his mind as to her meaning. 'They do,' Miss Webb assured him. 'Goodbye, dear boy.'

Polly helped Sarah on with her cloak and handed her her umbrella. After Sarah's departure, Polly locked the door and Charles said to her uneasily, 'Polly, what's up? Really up, I mean?'

Polly licked her lips and lowered her eyelids. She clasped her hands primly over her apron, while she sought for words. 'I – er – I couldn't tell you all in one go, sir,' she whispered, with a pointed glance at the open morning-room door.

'Is mother ill?' Charles whispered back.

'In a manner of speaking, she is, sir. Could I talk to you later, sir?'

'Is she going to die, Polly?'

'Oh, no, sir. It's not consumption or anythin'. It's her and Miss Alicia's spirits mostly.'

'I see. Mother may herself confide in me.'

Polly looked relieved. 'Yes, mebbe she will, sir.'

'When will the Master be in?'

'He usually comes about seven o'clock – for dinner.'

'Thank you, Polly.'

She was dismissed. Feeling dispirited, she went slowly down to the basement kitchen.

Very thoughtfully, hands in trouser pockets, Charles spun slowly round on his heels, gazing at the hall's fine ceiling, now hanging with spiders' webs. Alerted by Sarah, he was considering the state of his home with the same care that he would have used when looking at the results of one of his experiments. His eyes followed the worn carpet up the stairs. In the old days his mother would not have tolerated such a tattered stair rug, and he wondered if his father had lost money. The place reeked of neglect.

III

'Charles,' yelled Alicia in a most unladylike way, as she ran into the morning-room to greet him. He caught her in his arms and swung her round.

'My goodness!' he exclaimed. 'You've grown up.'

She tossed her head when he put her down. 'I'm nineteen. I've been grown up for a long time – only you've never noticed it, you wretch.'

He grimaced sheepishly. It was true. When he came north, he would pay a short duty visit to his family and then go to visit the livelier homes of his old friends, now married and scattered round Merseyside.

As they sat around the fire, they discussed the reason for his visit.

'You'll live here, of course?' Alicia asked hopefully.

'Well, at first I would,' he hedged. He was determined not to be subject to his father any longer than he had to. If he got a post at the College, he would build a small house for himself and get a housekeeper.

Humphrey received Charles's news with more equanimity than his son had expected and promised to talk to him about it after dinner. He then went up stairs to wash.

As the brass tap in the bathroom trickled hot water into the huge porcelain basin, he peered at himself in the mirror which was slowly steaming up. He felt immensely tired, drained of his usual vigour. 'Damn her,' he muttered, to himself, 'damn her!'

IV

Humphrey had spent the previous two hours with Mrs Jakes. They had proved unexpectedly stormy. Instead of cosying up with him in her feather bed, she had first suggested a drink and had sat him down by her living-room fire. A little surprised, he had accepted a tankard of porter, while she took a glass of port.

After a few moments of silence, she had said, 'It's me daughter, our Stella May. You know she's not really the marrying kind – and she were twenty-five come last Christmas – and that puts her on the shelf, if you know what I mean.'

She took a sip of wine and then went on to suggest that Stella May would stand a better chance if she had a dowry, and Mrs Jakes hoped that dearest Humphrey would provide it.

Dearest Humphrey had huffily refused; this was not the first request that his mistress had made for additional money. 'She's not *my* daughter,' he said frostily. 'In any case, she'll inherit your shop. Wouldn't that be enough to tempt a promising young man?'

'Well, you know her,' replied Mrs Jakes, sipping daintly at her port, while she controlled her anger. 'She's all right behind the counter, but she don't know nothin' about tobacco or how to blend it – nor about accounts – and she don't seem able to learn.' She bridled, and went on, 'And in any case, I expect to live for many years myself, so I need the shop – it really don't keep more'n one comfortable.'

Humphrey considered the cloddish, amiable face of the young woman in question, and saw no reason why he should provide for her. 'Whatever Stella May needs is your business,' he told his paramour bleakly.

Mrs Jakes pressed and argued until Humphrey's irritation gave way to anger. He was sick of the whining bitch, he decided suddenly. He put down his tankard, rose from his chair and gathered up his top hat and gloves.

Suppressing her fury, Mrs Jakes smiled up at him sweetly. 'Don't go yet,' she urged. 'If you don't have the money, you could ask Mrs Woodman – make some excuse. I hear as she's a well-off lady.'

'My wife is no concern of yours.' Humphrey rammed his hat on to his head. He was outraged at the calm suggestion.

'Oh, but I always felt concerned for the pore dear. Bein' an invalid, like.'

Humphrey was perfectly aware of the implied threat behind the sweetness of the voice. It was the oldest of warnings from women like her: 'I'll tell your wife what you've been up to.'

Mrs Jakes looked reflectively at her empty glass, as she continued, 'If it isn't convenient, like, to get it from her, I did hear as you're likely to do very well out of the underground railway, when you've finished makin' it electric. You don't have to help our Stella May now, but, say, in six months' time. What about then?' she wheedled.

He was still standing stiffly on the hearth rug, as if ready to leave, and she hastily put down her glass in the hearth and began to fiddle with the buttons of her high lace collar. 'You think about it, dearie, and, meantime, let's have a bit of a roll.'

Slyly, she undid the buttons until the cleft between her heavy breasts was visible, and she smiled up at him knowingly.

Despite his fatigue, he felt a jump of desire; she would do anything for him in bed. But he was for the first time afraid of her, afraid of blackmail. It was one thing that most people, including your wife, knew that you kept a mistress – most well-to-do men did. But it was unpardonable if the mistress surfaced with loud complaints. He knew he must frighten her.

He snatched up his overcoat and moved quickly to the lace-draped door of the shop. With his hand on the knob, he said firmly, 'It seems that our friendship has come to an end. Good afternoon, Ma'am.'

Followed by an outraged cry of 'Humphrey!' he closed the glass-panelled door and marched through the tiny shop, with its rich odour of molasses. He ignored Stella May's simpering, 'Evenin', sir,' and slammed the outer door after himself, so that the little bell screwed to it tinkled angrily.

He stepped into the street. A small, nagging pain throbbed in his chest. The wind was freezingly cold and he struggled hastily into his greatcoat.

He did not know why he was so glad to see Charles in the hallway, when Polly let him in. He had certainly never been fond of him, a boring bookworm, if ever there was one. But today, lurching in from the inclement weather, and being faced with a fairly sturdy young man, wreathed in friendly smiles, had been a relief. A son was a son, after all, especially when you felt old as well as furious.

Now, he washed his trembling hands with carbolic soap and splashed his face with water. Charles had reminded him suddenly of Edward, buried in the African veldt, and the memory hurt him. He went slowly downstairs, to rest in the library until Polly should bang the dinner gong.

After dinner, he sat with Charles by the library fire, a decanter of whisky on a small table between them, and Charles listened patiently to his worries about the poor state of the cotton market; the loss in the Mersey River, the previous month, of a schooner in which Humphrey had had a share; the uncertainty that the Mersey Underground Railway would make money even after electrification; the need to raise capital.

The old man was almost garrulous, thought Charles, and, with a sagacity that his family rarely gave him credit for, he concluded that something had rattled him severely. He was used to his father losing his temper, blowing up like some great Icelandic geyser, but not to his fretting so loquaciously about the ordinary ups and downs of business. Polly's remarks had already made him uneasy. He had always taken his family for granted, assumed that they would be there, in the fine house on Upper Canning Street, ready to greet him whenever it pleased him to come home. Now, he wondered if his mother was more severely ill than Polly had indicated and whether this was upsetting his father.

Humphrey did finally turn to the subject of a post at the University and discussed the pros and cons of it for a few minutes. Then he dismissed the boy on the grounds that he had work to do, and Charles left him hunched over his littered desk, his white hair bunched over his stiff collar and scarlet neck like the feathers of a chilled magpie.

V

In search of Polly, Charles went up to the day nursery. When he opened the door he found a lighted candle on the old candle table by the easy chair and the embers of a fire still lingering in the grate, but no one was there.

He stood uneasily in the doorway and then crossed the room to stroke the nose of the rocking-horse. He looked round the shadowed room. Like everywhere else in the house, it seemed cluttered and neglected. On a table by the window stood a dead maidenhair fern, and on the floor by the chair there was an untidy pile of linen and an open sewing box. The only sound in the room was the steady tick of the clock on the mantelpiece. He smiled at it, almost expecting it to smile back because they knew each other so well. In the bookcase lay the volumes that he and Edward had read as children, and across the top of them had been laid further books. He picked one up. It was a school text on botany and he flicked through it; he was surprised at the careful detail of the notes that Alicia had added on every margin.

He snapped the book shut and rang the bell at the side of the fireplace. If Fanny answered, he would simply ask her to make up the fire.

Polly realized who was probably ringing the nursery bell, and she came hurrying up the stairs. The last flight seemed longer than usual; her knees hurt and she was panting, as she entered the nursery.

Charles was waiting with his back to the warmth of the dying fire.

'Come in, Polly, and sit down. I wanted to ask you quietly a bit more about Mother. She insisted that she was quite well, when I asked her.'

Polly took the chair indicated. She straightened her long, black skirt and her short, afternoon apron, put her feet neatly together, folded her hands in her lap, and looked up at him inquiringly.

'Alicia says mother has been drinking heavily for a long time and that, when she gets the chance, she still does. Why would she do that, Polly?'

Polly responded with prim virtue, 'It int my business to inquire, sir.'

'Come off it, Polly. You're part of the family.'

Polly's eyes twinkled almost girlishly. She relaxed and said, 'Well, sir, I dunno for sure. She's bin goin' slowly downhill ever since I bin here – ever since Miss Alicia were born. Fanny says she used to be really light-hearted and happy when *she* first come. People visitin' her and her goin' to parties and the theatre – and buyin' pretty dresses.'

'Yes, I remember her like that,' Charles answered soberly.

'I can remember when I first come, she were always busy with her charities – and then she had her At Homes. And sometimes they'd give a dinner. Fact is, she were too busy to even take much note of Miss Alicia when she was a baby. But then, after a while, she seemed to lose heart and some days she wouldn't even get up.'

'Has she seen a doctor?'

'Not for years, that I know of. And another thing, sir. She's gettin' so forgetful. At first, I thought it were the drink, but now she's not getting that much. And she *still* forgets. The Master gets awfully cross with her sometimes.'

'Hm. My parents never did see eye to eye.'

'No, sir.'

Servants knew everything, he thought irritably. Feeling rather frustrated, he said, 'Well, thank you, Polly. I didn't want to bother Father.' He did not say that he knew that his father had never taken much interest in his mother, except to make sure she did not overspend.

Polly got up to leave him, and he asked, 'Where's Miss Alicia?'

'In the kitchen, sir. She's bakin' a cake.'

'Cooking? What for?'

'She does quite a lot, sir. Your father – that is to say, the Master – likes a good table – so she helps me a lot.'

'So you're actually the cook now?'

'Yes, sir.'

'And the parlourmaid?'

'Yes, Sir.' As she watched him, she wondered where his eyes had been all these years that he had not noticed how the staff had been cut.

'Who looks after Mother and Miss Alicia?'

'Miss Alicia looks after herself – she runs the house now – and we all do our best for the Mistress.'

'Fanny's still here. I saw her. What does she do?'

'She works real hard, sir. She's got all the cleaning, and the fires to tend and slops to empty and beds and washing – and this is a big house, sir, and real old-fashioned.'

'Poor Fanny,' commented Charles glumly, and then as Polly prepared to leave him, he reverted to the question of Elizabeth. 'I don't think there's anything to worry about over Mother,' he said. 'She's getting on a bit – and I imagine it's natural that she tends to forget things.'

Polly agreed with him, and after she had answered polite inquiries about her own health, she went slowly back down the stairs.

Charles stood staring at the old rocking-horse. He felt suddenly that he could not live in the house; it depressed him. He wondered how Alicia endured it – but then girls were different. If he got a post in the University he would definitely seek lodgings in the town.

VI

The gale finally blew itself out. In the Woodmans' garden the snowdrops flowered late amongst a flood of yellow and purple crocuses. The weeds also flourished and, since there was no one else to do it, Alicia cleaned the intruders out. That evening, she mentioned to her father that they should start a new gardener soon, before the garden ran wild.

Humphrey never used the garden himself. He had paid Mr Bittle to keep it tidy, so that it was in line with those of his neighbours. He said he would think about it, see if he could find a suitable man.

A few weeks later, she reminded him again. In the meantime, she had continued to weed and had given the small lawn its first mowing. 'I can't afford a man,' he had snapped. 'You seem to be doing it quite well yourself – it'll improve your health to spend more time out there.'

Worried that money seemed so short, she had left him and continued to weed and to cut the lawn; in desperation, she left the vegetable patch untouched. She felt she could not face another argument with Humphrey; only two weeks earlier, she had persuaded him that if he wanted to keep his two maids, he must improve their wages, and she had squeezed out of him another shilling a week for each of them. She had concluded that business in the city must currently be in a very bad state, to make her father so mean.

Charles was successful in his application and it was arranged that he should join the University College staff the following October. Meantime, he had to return to Cambridge.

He was thankful to escape from his father's house, and was firm in his intention not to live there; it was so dreary. Even Alicia seemed awfully dull, sitting there with his mother, holding her knitting wool or untangling her embroidery silks and saying little beyond, 'Yes, Mama,' to their mother's fretful utterances. One night he had offered to take both mother and sister to a concert, only to be told coldly by Elizabeth that they did not care to go out at night. When he had opened his mouth to protest that they should do so, Alicia had signalled him frantically to keep quiet. Later, as they were sitting down to dinner, she had whispered an apology to him and explained that, 'If she is crossed, Mama gets nearly as angry as Papa these days.'

'You should go out yourself sometimes,' he had whispered back, as they waited for their parents to come to table.

'I haven't any money,' replied Alicia dejectedly.

'None? No pin money?'

'No.'

'You should ask Father.'

She was quiet for a moment, wondering how to explain her dread of incurring Humphrey's displeasure, the hunch, that over the years had become a conviction, that she was not his daughter and that, if he felt like it, he could throw her out into the street.

In answer to Charles's advice, she said, 'I'm afraid to ask him. He gets absolutely furious if you mention money and it's not good for his heart.'

'I'll ask him for you. He'd never help me at University beyond the bare fees, but he can find a bob or two for you – all daughters get pin money. Have you asked Mother?'

'Yes, several times. But she forgets – and I rather think that Mr Simpkins, her lawyer, is keeping a tighter hold on her income – perhaps Father warned him about her drunkenness.'

'I see.' He began to whistle under his breath; the whistling stopped abruptly, as his father entered the dining-room.

The next time Alicia presented her household accounts to Humphrey, he closed the book with a snap after examining it, and said, 'You may in future take a shilling a week for your own pocket.'

Though Humphrey's lips were clamped together as if he had just swallowed castor oil, surprise and delight shot across Alicia's face. 'Really, Papa? Thank you – thank you very much.' She picked up the housekeeping money that Humphrey had set out on his desk, crept from the room in her usual subdued way, and then ran down to the kitchen to break the good news to Polly.

Polly was grating cheese and she looked up from her work, and said, 'About time, too, luv!' To herself she grumbled, 'The old skinflint!'

VII

During his visit, Charles had gone out to the Vicarage to pay a duty call on Florence and Clarence, and had mentioned idly to Florence that Alicia seemed to have a very dull existence. 'Couldn't you take her with you to a play or a concert or something, occasionally?' he asked uneasily.

Florence had replied defensively that except for visits to her parents and her in-laws, they did not go out much themselves. 'I have Sunday School and Church visitors and the Flower List and the Women's Embroidery Guild – the Guild is making new hassocks for the church at present and it's a lot of work. I hardly know how to manage myself. Clarence is also very busy – he is writing a book, on top of everything else.'

'God! I don't know how you stick it.'

'Charles!'

'Beg your pardon, Flo.' He chewed his thumb fretfully and decided that Alicia was a lost cause. What boring lives women lived.

21

I

Florence usually visited her mother accompanied by her younger children, but while her boys were home from boarding school at Easter she decided that it was time dear Mama and Papa saw their whole flock of grandchildren. She wrote a note to her mother saying that she and Clarence would bring them for dinner on Easter Saturday, since Clarence would be busy with Easter Services on the Sunday.

Elizabeth was delighted and ordered two dozen eggs to be hard-boiled and then dyed, so that the children could play at egg-rolling in the garden.

'But, Mama,' Alicia protested, 'aren't the children rather old for that? Frank, Tom and Freddie are all young men.'

Elizabeth looked bewildered. 'Are they really?'

'Yes, Mama. I think only Beatrice and Teddy might still enjoy it.'

'Well – er – do what you think fit.' Her mother smiled sweetly at her. Then her smile faded and she looked puzzled.

Alicia told Humphrey of the impending invasion and he grunted acknowledgement. Though he loved Florence and always looked forward to seeing her, he did not enjoy her unruly offspring or the pompous scholar she had married.

Alicia and Polly spent the whole of Good Friday preparing for the visit. To save time, though it cost more, Alicia got the poultryman to bring the roasting chickens already feathered and drawn. She did not dare to buy the Easter Cake, however, and stayed up till midnight in order to bake, ice and decorate one. She had done the same thing at Christmastime, when the whole family had descended on them, and she thought what a relief it would have been if Florence had invited their parents to the Vicarage instead. The older Alicia's male nephews grew the less she liked them. The eldest, Frank, treated her with less respect than a kitchen-maid could normally have expected, and she thought sadly that his pontificating father was not much better. She could not say what it was that bothered her, except that they were patronizing, as if she were her mother's companion-help, instead of her daughter.

The young people did not dare to misbehave when Humphrey was

673

present, so the dinner went off quite well. Afterwards, the three older boys and their father went away to the library to have a glass of port with their grandfather, and five-year-old Teddy and his sisters joined Elizabeth, Florence and Alicia in the morning-room for tea.

The little boy began to whine and be awkward.

Alicia finally suggested that he come with her to the old nursery and have a ride on the rocking-horse.

He accepted with alacrity and was soon restored to good temper. They chose a good jigsaw puzzle for him to take down to the morning-room, and Alicia opened the nursery door to go down again to the family. Lounging outside it was Frank, smoking a cigarette.

He nodded curtly to his little brother, 'Your mother wants you. Hurry up.'

The child clattered obediently down the stairs, while Alicia looked uncertainly at Frank.

He came into the room and shut the door behind him. Suddenly nervous, Alicia edged away from him, so that the centre table was between them. He laughed, and threw his cigarette end into the fireplace.

She said in a light, bantering tone, 'I don't think your father would wish you to smoke, Frank.'

'What Father doesn't know about won't bother him. Come over here and sit on the sofa. We'll have a bit of fun together.'

She was shocked, but she managed to say calmly, 'No, Frank. You know that wouldn't be right – besides, I have to go downstairs to help with the children.'

Her coolness annoyed him. He whipped round the table, caught her by the shoulder and turned her to face him. She tried to pull herself away, but she was pressed against the table and he was a big, heavy youth. He shook her like a dog shakes a rabbit it has caught. 'Come on,' he ordered her roughly. 'Give us a kiss – you Queen of the Midden – if you don't want to get hurt. For a bastard, you're too proud by far.'

He let go of her shoulder, put his arm round her waist and held her chin while he tried to press his mouth against hers. Terrified, she turned her face away, but not before she had seen the savage glint in his eyes.

To stop herself falling backwards on the table, she grasped frantically at the table's edge. Her fingers came in contact with a thin textbook she had left on it. She picked it up, and, as she was pushed backwards, she became for a second sufficiently separated from him to swing it hard against his face.

The swipe was so painful, as the corner of the cardboard cover caught his eye, that he let go of her and staggered back, his hand to his stinging cheek and outraged eye.

In a second, she was round the table and had the door open. 'You bitch,' he shrieked at her, tears running down his face from the injury.

'I'll tell Father,' she snarled back at him, as she ran through the door.

As she closed the door, she heard him yell derisively, 'Tell Crossing? That'll be funny!'

She feared he would come after her, and she tore down the familiar staircase and across the hall to the green baize door leading to the kitchen stairs. She swung it open, and nearly sent Polly backwards down the staircase. The teacups rattled on the tray and the teapot sent an angry burst of tea from its spout, 'Carefully, duck!' Polly cried. Then she saw her charge's frightened face, and she asked anxiously, 'What's up, luv?'

'It's Frank. He tried to kiss me – it was horrid.'

'Tryin' it on, is he? Run downstairs to Fanny and stay with her. I'll be down in a mo'.'

As the door swung closed behind Alicia, Polly paused for a moment to rearrange her tray. She heard heavy feet coming quickly down the upper stairs, a door opening and then a bathroom tap running.

'Blast him!' she muttered, and hastened to deliver the tea tray to Elizabeth. 'The dirty warehouse rat!'

When, later, the visitors said their farewells, Frank's sore eye – he had got something in it, he said – drew people's attention. But in the general confusion of departure, no one noticed that Alicia was not present.

II

A shaken Alicia dried the dishes for a loquacious Fanny; she told her nothing about Frank. Then, when the noise of departure had ceased, she went up to escort her mother to her bedroom; she had had to do this recently, because Elizabeth seemed occasionally to lose her sense of the time of day. This evening, however, Elizabeth was already napping in her chair and allowed herself to be helped upstairs to bed without argument.

Though she had defended herself, Alicia had been terribly frightened by Frank's attack on her. What would he do the next time he came? And he might easily visit more often, since he had now finished school and was, in May, to start work with a Liverpool wine merchant. And young Tom and Freddie might be equally aggressive.

675

Though she did not know the word 'rape' she began to fear some such attack. And what did he mean by 'Tell Crossing?'

It was only when she was drying the dishes that his last words really impinged on her mind. What *did* he mean? Who was Crossing? She wanted to ask Polly if she should tell Humphrey. Would Humphrey laugh at her for refusing to be kissed? Would he say that Frank was her nephew and it was quite natural to kiss his aunt occasionally? But not the way Frank had tried it, she felt sickeningly; he had tried to put his tongue in her mouth.

Trying not to cry with the sense of humiliation that she felt, she ran back downstairs to the kitchen and was relieved to find the two maids, feet on fender before a blazing fire, the earthenware kitchen teapot steaming on the hob.

As she advanced towards them, it seemed that Polly had already told Fanny that Alicia was in some kind of trouble with Frank. Fanny, not usually so demonstrative, put out a tiny, swollen, red hand towards her, and said, 'Come on, luv. Sit down and have a cuppa and tell us all about it.'

Alicia smiled down at her and joined them to tell them exactly what had happened.

'That little twerp!' exclaimed Fanny. ''E aint fit to practise on! But don't you let 'im put you off. There's plenty of nice young men as you'll want to kiss one day.'

'I don't feel like it at the moment, Fanny,' Alicia replied with a shaky chuckle.

'That's better,' Polly said, as she heard the hint of laughter. 'It's somethin' to laugh at! And thank God nothin' worse happened.'

'I'm afraid of next time he comes – because I hurt him – I didn't mean to do more than make him let go, but I think I hurt his eye.'

'Well, luv, whenever he's in the house, you be sure you're with somebody. Stick with your Mam – and with your Pa, if necessary.'

'Shall I tell Father? It's no good telling Mama – she'd forget half the story before I'd finished telling it.'

The maids looked at each other doubtfully. Then Polly cleared her throat and said, 'Mebbe not this time. If he touches you again, you better had.' She thought uneasily that Humphrey might not care if Alicia was mauled a little by the boys; but even he would surely object to rape in his own house. With sudden apprehension, she hoped that he would not make such goings-on an excuse to throw Alicia out. Better he knew nothing, if possible.

They continued to discuss the occurrence, and, also, times when they had themselves been caught in awkward corners by importuning men, until the teapot was empty and the fire had fallen in. Then Fanny went to her little room in the basement. She liked sleeping down there alone; she could occasionally smuggle a man in on a cold winter's night.

Polly and Alicia made their way up to the attic. At the door of her bedroom, Alicia kissed her nanny. Then she said, 'Polly, could I come into your room and talk to you some more?'

She rarely went in to either maid's room, but felt tonight that for some obscure reason Polly's was safer than hers for a secret conversation.

Polly was ready to drop from fatigue, but she unhesitatingly opened the door and let the girl into the chilly room with its black, iron single bed covered with a plain white bedspread. 'What is it, pettie?'

Realizing that something was still bothering the girl, she sat down on the bed and drew Alicia down beside her. 'That Frank didn't do no more'n try to kiss you, did he, luv?'

Alicia replied absently, 'No. I hit him before he could.' She looked down at her hands in her lap, and then raised her eyes to Polly, who was unpinning her cap. 'It was what he said, Polly, that I wanted to ask you. It's something that's been in the back of my mind for years.' She swallowed nervously, 'You see, I said I would tell Father of him, and he laughed in a really nasty way, and shouted, "Tell Crossing?" What did he mean, Polly?'

Polly put her frilled cap carefully on to the bed beside her. She gazed dumbly at the empty wall opposite her and wondered how to answer. Should she deny any knowledge of the reason for Frank's remark and leave the girl guessing?

'Polly?'

She made a great effort to get the story straight and to be cautious. She put her arm round Alicia's waist, and said, 'Well, what I know was told me after I coom here. I haven't never seen Mr Crossing, though Maisie – you won't remember her – she were the parlourmaid when I first come here – she said as he were a very handsome gentleman, your Mam's solicitor, and he visited her often.' She paused and sighed. 'Maisie and Fanny told me that your Mam fell head over heels in love with him – and when you were born, your Pa – that is, Mr Woodman, said you couldn't possibly be his child – and there was an awful row and Maisie were fired for tattling to the Master about the goings-on.'

Alicia was watching her face with amazement, as all kinds of odd happenings in her young life fell into place.

'For a while it looked as if your Mam would be thrown out the door and you as well – but it would have been a terrible scandal and your Pa's, the Master's, business might well have suffered. It did cause a scandal – a sort of underground one, 'cos Maisie talked up and down

677

the street, and people remarked that, after you was born, Mr Crossing was never at your Mam's dinners – and maybe through the solicitors' clerks it went round that Mr Simpkins had been made her solicitor instead, because of this. Some maids gossip somethin' awful – and their mistresses find out things from *them*.'

'Poor Mama.'

'Aye. When I first coom here, she were a lovely lady to look at – she were the kind people would gossip about, anyways. Your Pa wouldn't have nothin' much to do with her after that; he put up with her in the house and made her keep house, and I had orders to keep you upstairs out of the way.'

She stopped, and Alicia asked, 'Is Mr Crossing my Papa?'

Polly laughed a little cynically. 'Well, it's a clever child what knows its own father,' she replied. 'But Fanny says as you are the dead spit of 'im, with your nearly white hair and light eyes.'

'And does that make me a bastard, Polly, like that boy said when we went to that New Year's gathering?'

'Not legally, love. Officially the Master is your father, because he never publicly objected to you – and you live in 'is house. But it do leave a kind of shadow on you – it's a kind of excuse for people to feel better'n you, like. And a lot of women was jealous of your Mam's looks, I think, and she were careless of people, sometimes. I've heard her crack jokes about people that were very funny – but kind of cruel to the person they were about. And people don't like that.'

'Yes. She can be quite cutting at times.' Small quivers of fear went through Alicia, as she asked, 'Could Papa throw me out even now?'

Polly smiled. 'I doubt he would. It would cause too much comment – and you're too useful in the house.'

'I wish I could see my real father.'

'Nay, love. Never think on it. He's a married man – that's why he couldn't marry your Mam, even if she could get a divorce. Fanny says his wife were an invalid.'

'I suppose this explains why, when I was small, Papa would shout and rage at me and tell me to get back to the nursery. He still gets very cross with me, if I'm a ha'penny wrong in the housekeeping.'

'Aye,' agreed Polly, her lined face grave.

'And Mama doesn't really care about me, does she? She's never taken me out with her – and I've never had parties like other girls – and the idea of bringing me out just died.' Alicia's tone was bitter, as the resentment of years began to surface.

'I wouldn't say she doesn't care for you, luv. Seems to me it were all too much for her – and you know she hasn't been herself for years now.

She sent you to school proper – and I heard her fighting the Master about sending you to Blackburne House.'

'Did she? Mama really does believe in education, I know – she helped Charlie for years. But it wouldn't have hurt her to take me out sometimes, would it?'

'I know, luv, and when I think on it I could spit blood.' Polly tightened her grasp around Alicia's waist. 'But . . .' She paused, and looked at Alicia squarely, 'You know, he's beaten her something cruel more'n a few times and I 'spect she's had as much as she can take.'

'Papa! Beat Mama?'

'For sure. You must've heard her cry out sometimes.'

'I've heard them shouting at each other. I didn't know that men like Papa hit their wives! I thought only working . . .' She stopped, realizing that she might offend Polly.

'That only working men did it?'

'Yes.'

'Ha! Don't you believe it. You just thank God if you get a husband wot don't beat you.'

'I'll never get a husband – I don't go anywhere to meet anybody. And I doubt if Papa would give me a dowry, to help me, if I'm not his daughter.'

Polly agreed cautiously. 'You shouldn't count on it, luv.'

Alicia turned to Polly and put her arms around her. 'You know, Polly, I think you – and Fanny – are the only people who love me. Don't ever leave, Polly,' she implored.

'Nay, luv. I'll never leave you. You're my baby.'

'I wish I was,' replied Alicia, as tears began to run down her face.

'Nay. You take care of your Mama, duck. She needs you. She's had enough.'

'I suppose I must. But, oh, Polly, it's so terrible to feel that there is something the matter with you which is not your fault – it really is.' And she wept.

III

Alicia began to observe Elizabeth and Humphrey with new, informed eyes. Like others with very narrow experience, she had assumed that her family was a typical one, that, despite all the love stories saying otherwise, married couples lived dull, parallel lives, communicating only with spiteful remarks. Now, she wondered if her family were exceptional.

She felt a growing bitterness against her mother for not having made an effort to guard her from the results of her indiscretions, to give her lover's daughter a better chance in life. She thought passionately that if she had had a baby by a man she loved, she would have treasured it as being part of him; instead, she had hardly seen her mother during her childhood; it was Polly who had mothered her.

She realized suddenly that she owed a tremendous debt to Polly and to her godmother, Sarah Webb. Without them, life would have been insupportable.

Why didn't Mama run away? she wondered.

The answer came readily; for the same reason that her daughter could not; the lack of money and the lack of decent occupations in which to earn it.

She might have gone to her sister, Aunt Clara, in West Kirby, ruminated Alicia; she would probably have sheltered her. But Aunt Clara's competence from their father was not very large either, and being so delicate she might not be able to tolerate a baby in the house.

When considering Humphrey, Alicia could believe quite easily that he had beaten her mother; she had suffered many painful clouts from him herself when she was younger and had strayed downstairs.

One Spring evening, when Humphrey had been particularly rude because the dinner was not to his taste, Alicia had flown down to her usual refuge, the kitchen, and said forcibly to Polly, 'The only way out of this is to run away. You heard him, Polly, when you were serving. He's impossible!'

A very concerned Polly spent an hour warning her about the fate of young women who had neither home nor work. 'You could try for a governess's job,' she said, 'but it lays you open to a lot of nasty things – a governess isn't family and she isn't a servant – she don't belong nowhere – and the men of the family can take advantage of her, though you'd be safer if you was a good deal older. And another thing, once you leave here, the Master might not let you return.'

With patience, she talked the angry girl into a better frame of mind, though when she said soothingly, 'One day some nice young man'll want to marry yez and you'll have a home of your own,' Alicia smiled grimly. Her mirror too often showed her a nondescript girl in gold-framed glasses and frumpy clothes – and dowerless.

'I doubt if Papa would even pay for my wedding,' she said sarcastically to her long-suffering nanny.

IV

When Florence arrived with Teddy on one of her periodic visits to her mother, Alicia felt suddenly sickened by her. If Frank knew the secret of her birth, he must have learned it, directly or indirectly, from something his parents had said, and she wondered what her flustered sister really thought of her.

Both sisters' attention was, however, diverted to Teddy. As they entered the morning-room, the little boy ran ahead towards his grandmother's chair. Elizabeth, startled, looked up from the photograph album she was leafing through and asked blankly, 'And who are you?'

At first, Florence thought that her mother was teasing the child, but she was looking earnestly at him, obviously awaiting a reply.

Teddy stopped, put his finger in his mouth and, after regarding her steadily for a moment, said, 'I'm Teddy, 'course.'

His grandmother's face broke into a gentle smile. 'Oh, yes, of course. How are you, Teddy?'

Florence viewed the tiny exchange with alarm. She went forward to kiss her mother and sit down beside her, while Alicia, more used to her mother's mental slips, went to make some coffee for them.

How could Mama forget a grandchild? She was only sixty – too young to be senile. Yet, now Florence considered it, Alicia was constantly reminding her mother of small items, like the impending visit of Miss Bloom, the dressmaker, or that it was time to go for a little walk up and down the road, or even that, perhaps, she should go to the bathroom. Inwardly, she became quite agitated, as she considered the implications of Elizabeth's memory loss. She flinched at the very thought of ever having to cope with someone senile, in addition to her husband and children. And, sick or well, Clarence was not likely to tolerate Elizabeth in his house very willingly.

Alicia returned bearing cups of coffee and, as Florence looked up at her and took the proffered cup, she felt a sense of relief. There was Alicia, who, with a bit of luck, would always be there to nurse her mother. A plain, dull young woman with a shadow over her origins was not likely to be married. It would not hurt her to have only a mother to look after – single women had such easy lives.

V

Humphrey hardly bothered to address Elizabeth at all; he barely saw her, except at dinnertime. He dealt with Alicia regarding domestic matters; she had the dual advantages that he did not pay her a salary and, unlike the usual run of housekeepers and cooks, she did not steal.

One autumn evening, as he sat in front of his desk in the library, hands clasped across his stomach, he reviewed his household with the same care that he had just gone over his financial affairs. He felt a little surprised to realize that he no longer felt the wild rage of jealousy which the very mention of Alicia used to produce; it had all happened so long ago, and the fat, untidy woman sitting opposite him at dinner bore no resemblance to the woman who had been seduced by Andrew Crossing. He did, however, feel a lingering sense of defeat; he had originally been very proud to marry Elizabeth, a handsome, fashionable woman highly suited to his station in life. He had been so sure of himself that it had not occurred to him at the time that she did not want to marry him and that they would spend their lives sullenly hating each other.

And now he had dismissed Mrs Jakes. She, he thought, had humiliated him beyond pardon and he had been furious; yet there was a certain relief in being free of her.

VI

A few days after Mrs Jakes' request for help for Stella May and the angry spate between them, physical desire had again driven Humphrey along the familiar street to the small tobacconist's shop.

He had been agreeably surprised to be welcomed as usual, though in the ensuing weeks Mrs Jakes continued to make sly mention of Stella May's needs. She said nothing to Humphrey about the root of the problem which was that she wished to remarry. However, her suitor, a retired plumber, disliked Stella May intensely and wanted her out of the house, seeing visions of himself presiding over Mrs Jakes' lucrative little business. The only way out of this predicament, as far as Mrs Jakes could see, was to marry Stella May off.

In spite of the façade of goodwill, Humphrey ceased to enjoy his encounters with her, and the day inevitably came when, curled up in Mrs Jakes' bed, he failed to perform.

Mrs Jakes was not without skill, but she could not ease the dull ache in his chest nor the feeling of breathlessness which activity caused him. In any case, what was once spontaneous was now mechanical. Though unaware of the ministrations of the sturdy plumber, Humphrey sensed shrewdly that she was no longer really thinking about him, and he resented it.

Mrs Jakes complained irritably that she had been left unsatisfied. He flung himself crossly on to his back, his round paunch humping up the bedclothes, and told her that it was *her* duty to satisfy.

She turned on him angrily. She looked slightly ridiculous, as she sat up beside him, tousled hair, grey at the roots, drooping breasts hanging over the sheet she was clutching round the rest of her body. 'Well, if you don't like what yer getting, yer don't have to coom, do you? I can find others, I can tell yer, as'll be glad of me.'

Too late, she realized that any hope of money for Stella May had gone, killed by a few angry words. As he flung back the blankets, heaved himself out of bed and stalked, naked, to the chair where he had laid his clothes, with his bowler hat set neatly on top of his folded-up woollen combinations, she panted with sudden fury. 'Nice story this'll make when it goes the rounds,' she hissed, and then added spitefully, 'Sufferin' Christ! Wot I've put up with from you, you mingy-arsed bastard.'

He did not answer her. He heaved himself into his underwear and then sat on a corner of the bed to put on his winter socks, while she kept on raving at him. He was shocked at such a tirade. Outraged, he hurried into his suit and shoes.

Without even looking at her, he clapped his bowler hat on his head, took up his walking-stick and overcoat, and opened the bedroom door, to clump steadily down the narrow wooden stair into the living-room. Here, he paused for a moment to get his breath and to look numbly round the tiny room. Three stuffed pheasants sitting on a mantelpiece draped with green velvet stared at him without malice. In that easy chair by the fire, he had sat with this woman on his knee, regarding her as a humble friend. He had shared her fender ale and her bed, and each month had playfully dropped a couple of sovereigns into the blue glass bowl in the centre of the table. And all that had gone in a trice!

He was glad. In future, he would occasionally find himself a whore. All he wanted now was to go home, shut himself in the library, take a large shot of brandy and sit down by the excellent fire he knew Fanny would have made, until his chest felt comfortable again. And he hoped that Polly had made a roast of beef – she did it very well.

22

I

That evening, Fanny banged the gong in the hall, as usual, to indicate that dinner was ready. As its final vibrations sank away, she stretched her tiny frame and then smoothed down her apron. She was bored and wished she was going out that night with the warehouseman she had met during her last afternoon off, a chance encounter which had delighted her. She had earlier said to Polly that at the advanced age of thirty-one she was on the shelf; the advent of the warehouseman suggested that her time had been extended.

Neither Polly nor Fanny gave much thought to their future. Though poorly paid, they considered themselves well fed and each had a bedroom of her own, a rare luxury when in domestic service. The big Upper Canning Street house was home to both of them.

Though Billy still wrote to her, Polly had given up any thought of his fulfilling his promise to bring her to Canada, and Fanny thought that the very idea of emigration was terrifying, even if one could raise the cost of the passage.

Elizabeth came slowly into the dining-room. For once, her hair was tidy and she had changed into a plain grey silk dress with a high, boned-lace collar; Miss Bloom had made it for her out of a long-abandoned crinoline dress taken from a trunk in the attic. In the light of the gas chandelier over the table, she looked, Fanny thought, a real lady. She pulled out Elizabeth's chair for her.

Alicia came hurrying through the door to the kitchen stairs, tucking wisps of hair into her bun as she entered the dining-room; her plain black dress with a white frill round its high neck made her look older than she was. As she sat down, she smiled at her mother, who smiled brilliantly back at her.

With her hands tidily behind her back, Fanny stood ready to serve the neat row of sardines set out on chopped lettuce.

'Do you think the Master heard the gong, Fanny?'

'He should've done, Miss; he's in the library.'

'Where's Charles?' asked Elizabeth.

'He's in Cambridge, Mama. He doesn't live with us any more,' Alicia answered her patiently.

'Oh, yes.' Again the bright smile. Elizabeth took her table napkin out of its silver ring and spread it across her lap.

'Give the Master a knock, Fanny,' Alicia requested. 'He may have gone to sleep in his chair.'

Alicia heard Fanny knock on the library door and then cautiously turn the door handle.

She shrieked, 'Oh, Allie! Come here!'

Alicia leapt from her chair and flew out of the room and across the black and white tiled hall. Fanny stood in the library doorway, her hand to her mouth. She turned in dismay to Alicia.

Alicia pushed past her.

On the Turkey rug in front of the fireplace, Humphrey lay face down. He looked as if he were asleep. His laboured breath was like a snore.

Alicia swooped towards him and fell on her knees beside him. She shook him gently by the shoulder. 'Papa, are you much hurt?'

He did not respond, so she tried to turn him on to his back, while little Fanny fluttered uncertainly beside her. He was too heavy to move, so she said to the maid, 'Get Polly – quick – and then run for Dr Willis. Tell him Father has had a fall – or it could be a stroke. Run, Fan.'

Fanny edged round Elizabeth who was approaching across the hall. 'What's happened?' she asked, but Fanny skidded past her, muttering, 'Everything'll be all right, Ma'am,' and sped down the kitchen stairs, while Alicia anxiously felt along Humphrey's arms and legs for broken bones. She looked up, as her mystified mother entered, and told her, 'Papa has had a fall, Mama, and I don't know how much hurt he is – there doesn't seem to be anything broken. Could you help me turn him on to his back, so that I can prop him up with cushions; he might be able to breathe more easily. It doesn't seem to be a faint – his face is very red, still.'

Elizabeth obediently lowered herself on to the rug beside Alicia and, showing surprising strength, helped to heave him on to his back. 'There,' said Elizabeth brightly.

They managed to ease some of the sofa cushions under Humphrey's head and shoulders and then tucked a shawl round him, to protect him against the draught along the floor. Alicia sat back on her heels and surveyed the unconscious man, doing her best to stay calm. 'I'll get him a glass of brandy out of his desk,' she said to her mother kneeling on the other side of him.

Polly's calm voice came from behind her. 'Nay, luv, don't give 'im nuthin' till doctor's seen 'im – he could choke on it.' She bent to help

Elizabeth to her feet. 'You sit 'ere, on the sofa, Ma'am, while I undo 'is collar.'

Alicia was already trying, with trembling hands, to get Humphrey's stiffly starched collar undone. Polly pushed her gently away and then skilfully pressed the hinge of his gold stud and pulled the collar loose.

As the maid opened up his collar band and undid his fitted waistcoat, Alicia mouthed silently to Polly, 'What is it, Pol?'

'Stroke, almost certain.'

Elizabeth was saying in a haughty voice, reminiscent of her earlier days, that her husband should have a glass of brandy – and she should, too, to calm her nerves.

'It might kill 'im, Ma'am,' Polly replied shortly, and as she listened to Humphrey's stentorian breathing, she thought it would be better that he died than be paralysed. He could live, she thought, a hopeless log of a man for years and years – and it was poor little Allie who would bear the brunt of nursing him – as if her life were not already circumscribed enough.

Alicia got to her feet. 'Hurry, hurry, Dr Willis,' she prayed. Polly looked up at her and advised, 'You take your Mam and go have your dinner. It's all ready in the dumb-waiter.'

'I don't want anything.'

'Look, take your Mam and go.' She jerked her head towards Elizabeth, who had got up from the settee and was trying to open Humphrey's locked desk. 'You'll be up all night, Allie, one way and another. You must eat.' She twisted herself round and said formally to Elizabeth, 'Dinner is served, Ma'am.'

'Oh, yes, of course.' Elizabeth began immediately to move towards the dining-room, completely ignoring her suffering husband. 'Come along, Alicia. You'll be late,' she said over her shoulder to her daughter.

Alicia grimaced ruefully at Polly, and then followed her mother.

As she hurriedly served Elizabeth with lukewarm lamb chops, potatoes and peas, her mother asked fretfully, 'Why doesn't Fanny serve? Where is she?'

Alicia tried to sound cheerful, as she replied, 'She's gone a message for Papa, Mama. She'll be back just now.'

'And where's Humphrey?'

'He asked us to start. He'll be with us soon.' Alicia had long since learned that detailed explanations were lost on Elizabeth.

Elizabeth shrugged and picked up her knife and fork and began to eat.

Alicia quickly served herself and was nearly through her main course when Fanny returned. She came straight to Alicia. 'He's coomin',' she panted.

Facing Elizabeth's uncomprehending stare, she quietly slipped her shawl off her shoulders and held it behind her.

'Who's coming?'

'Dr Willis, Ma'am.'

'To dinner?'

Fanny swallowed, and looked to Alicia for help.

'He's coming to see Father, Mama. You know he does sometimes.'

'I see. You may serve dessert, Fanny.'

Dr Willis was at the front door before Alicia had managed to swallow her sago pudding and jam. Rising hastily, as she wiped her lips on her linen table napkin, she said to her mother, 'Excuse me, Mama. I have to see when Father wants his dinner.' She wanted to wring her hands at the uselessness of explaining anything to her.

As the doctor divested himself of his coat and jacket, Alicia poured into his ears the news of Humphrey's fall.

In the library, he took one glance at the recumbent man and exclaimed to Alicia, 'My dear young lady, I am glad you called me.' He quickly put his Gladstone bag down beside Humphrey and then knelt to examine him.

Alicia watched him, white-faced, inwardly terrified. She disliked Humphrey to the point of hatred; but she was dependent upon him – and so was Polly.

Polly had risen from the floor at the entry of the doctor and had silently bobbed a curtsey to him. She also caught Alicia's eye and tried to smile reassuringly at the girl.

As he hastily took out his stethoscope, Dr Willis asked, 'Have you any hot water bottles?'

'Yes, a number of them,' Alicia assured him.

'Kindly have them all filled and put into Mr Woodman's bed. And a good fire in his room – we must apply as much warmth as we can.'

Alicia gestured to Polly and the maid hurried out of the room. The doctor went on, 'I thought that this was what had happened, so I brought a stretcher and my errand lad, John. He and my groom can carry Mr Woodman up to his bed – I remembered that last time I was called to him you had no one to lift him.'

'Thank you,' Alicia answered warmly, grateful for his forethought and his presence.

Having alerted Fanny to the need for hot water bottles and a good fire, Polly was returning to the library. She was caught in the hall by an extremely irate Elizabeth demanding to know where her tea tray was. They both appeared in the doorway and Alicia went quickly to her complaining mother and told her that tea would be a little late. Dear Papa was poorly and Dr Willis had ordered him to bed. Elizabeth calmed down and greeted the doctor graciously; she still ignored poor Humphrey.

Dr Willis stared at her in surprise. Then he asked Polly to tell his groom and errand boy to bring in the stretcher. He would deal with Mrs Woodman afterwards.

With a quick apology to the doctor for leaving him, Alicia persuaded her mother to go into the morning-room and promised that one of them would bring her tea very shortly. She lit the morning-room gas lamps and sat her mother in her easy chair and put a half-finished jigsaw puzzle on a tray close to her. Elizabeth's attention was immediately diverted, and Alicia fled back to Dr Willis. She met the doctor's men coming in with the stretcher, and was surprised how easily they managed to roll Humphrey on to it.

As they led the men up the stairs, Alicia said to Dr Willis, 'I'm sorry about Mama. She simply doesn't remember anything from one minute to the next.'

'Indeed? Poor lady. Perhaps we can talk about her difficulties later on.'

As Polly had foretold, Alicia was up for most of the night. Between a mother who kept inquiring what the matter was, regardless of how often it was explained to her, and a doctor who seemed to need everything in the house, Alicia thought her mind would split.

She was not allowed in Humphrey's room, while the doctor gave him an enema and drew water from him. Noting Polly's wedding ring, the doctor asked if she could help him, and she did.

When, at last, Humphrey was tucked up in bed, still breathing like a half-stranded whale, Alicia took Elizabeth in to see him. Though Elizabeth had kept forgetting what the turmoil in the house was all about, she did observe it and was restless and uneasy. Now, seeing her husband sound asleep, she realized that it was her own bedtime and that the house was quiet, and she allowed Alicia to put her to bed.

Alicia afterwards went to see the doctor. He was seated by Humphrey's bedside, his fingers on his patient's pulse. He smiled kindly as, after knocking, the young woman came in.

When she looked down at Humphrey's face surrounded by supporting white pillows, she was shocked. His whole face seemed to have fallen to one side and he was drooling from one corner of his mouth.

Dr Willis rose and drew her quietly out of the bedroom. As he rolled down his shirt sleeves, he said that he felt that her dear father would recover, though not perhaps completely. 'You will need a night nurse and a day nurse,' he advised her. 'I can recommend two reliable women.'

Alicia opened her mouth to protest, but the doctor silenced her with a gesture. 'There are many unpleasant duties in connection with a case like this,' he told her, 'and a single young lady like yourself cannot perform them – and Mrs Woodman herself seems too delicate to undertake them. It would probably be better if the day nurse lived in, if you can accommodate her.'

Alicia wanted to burst into tears. Another room to clean, another mouth to feed out of her limited housekeeping, and then the endless running up and down to serve both nurse and invalid. How was it to be done?

She took a big breath. 'Two things, Doctor. Is it really a stroke? And will he be ill for a long time?'

The doctor hesitated. 'It's a stroke,' he said. 'I think he will get better – but he'll never be the man he was.' He paused and then said more optimistically, 'Good nursing and proper exercise will certainly help him.'

'Of course, he must have whatever you say, Doctor . . .' She thought for a moment and then plunged in. 'Could you advise me, Doctor, how I can arrange for money to pay everybody? Will Papa be able to sign cheques and orders – and things?'

'Not for some time, Miss Alicia. Could Mrs Woodman arrange it?'

'Well, Mama has her own small income. But Papa pays everything and gives me money for housekeeping.'

'Ah, I understand. Your brother – I recollect that you have one – or perhaps an uncle – will have to apply for Power-of-Attorney. Meanwhile, perhaps Mrs Woodman can draw on her funds for a short time.'

'I suppose she could,' Alicia replied doubtfully. 'She does sign cheques.' She sighed, and thanked him.

Dr Willis said he felt that he had done all he could and that he would go home. He would come again in the morning, and, meanwhile, someone should sit with Humphrey. Alicia agreed and led him down to the library, where he put on his jacket again. She asked, 'Did you have time to dine, Doctor? Polly could make something for you.'

He smiled at her, and replied, 'No. But Cook will have saved a meal for me.'

'A glass of wine, then? Do sit down for a minute to rest before you leave; you've been on your feet for hours.'

'Thank you.' He seated himself on a straight chair, while Alicia took her housekeeping keys from her pocket and unlocked a cupboard at the side of Humphrey's desk. She took out a bottle of port, a glass and a tin of biscuits. She poured out a glassful of wine and opened the tin, and put both by the weary physician. No time – at half-past one in the morning – to stand on ceremony, Alicia thought, as she sat down herself on the edge of the sofa.

The doctor thankfully took a sip of wine, and then said, 'Mrs Woodman has not consulted me for years and I always assumed that she was in good health. Has she seen a physician lately?'

'No. She is rarely indisposed.'

'But she forgets things?'

'Yes.'

'Has she been like this for long?'

'It's crept upon her gradually over several years. Recently, I've given up explaining much to her, because she doesn't take it in. Can anything be done about it?'

'No, Miss Woodman, there is nothing. She is ageing – it's God's will.'

Alicia gave a little shivering sigh. 'I presume it will get worse, then?'

'It is probable, unfortunately. She may need a companion – someone to be with her all the time – later on.'

It seemed to Alicia that as she heard these words a portcullis slammed in the distance. Who but she would take care of her mother? Certainly not Florence, if she could get out of it, she thought grimly. And it seemed that Papa would end up a semi-invalid and the responsibility for his care would be hers – and yet he was not truly her papa: he was a man who ruled her life like a despot, knowing that she had no real means of escape from him.

The doctor saw her face whiten. 'Take care of yourself, Miss Woodman. Please feel free to call on me for help.' He rose, and mechanically Alicia went to pull the bell, to call Polly to show him out. Polly, asleep before the dead fire in the kitchen, awoke with a jump and ran upstairs.

In the hall, as Polly handed the doctor his coat, Dr Willis turned to Alicia. 'Would you like me to send telegrams to any of your family for you? I would be happy to do so.'

Alicia heaved a sigh of relief. 'I would be so grateful.'

'Give me the addresses, then.'

She ran back into the study and scribbled the addresses of Florence, Charles, and Uncle Harold in Manchester. When the doctor read the list, he said, 'It would be quicker to send my errand boy to Mrs Browning. I'll arrange it.'

As Polly opened the front door, he hesitated, and then said, 'I have presumed that you would not wish Mr Woodman to go into the Royal Infirmary?'

Alicia stared at him, shocked. 'Of course not,' she responded sharply. 'Hospitals are for the poor.'

The doctor smiled. 'Well, not so much nowadays. You might like to consult your family about a nursing home, though.'

As she bowed her flaxen head on to her clasped hands, she muttered, 'Yes.' She listened dumbly to the clip-clop of the horse's hooves, as the groom, who had been patiently walking the animal, saw the light streaming from the front door and brought the carriage back. The little errand boy had been told to run home and get into bed.

'I'll return in a few hours,' Dr Willis promised, as he ran down the steps. Poor girl, he thought. She'll spend most of her life tending invalids.

Alicia began to cry quietly. Polly quickly closed and locked the front door. 'There, pettie. There, there. We'll manage somehow,' she murmured, as she turned to hold the girl in her arms.

II

Polly made a cup of cocoa for each of them and then insisted that Alicia go to bed. 'I told Fanny to go up, because she has to be up at five to do the fireplaces and make the fires. You go and get rested while you can; tomorrer, this house'll be like Lime Street station, with all the comings and goings. I'll sit with your Pa and see he's warm an' all. I can nap a bit in a chair by 'im, and find an hour to have a sleep sometime tomorrer.'

Alicia saw the wisdom of this, since Polly could not deal with the arrival of the family the next day. She told her about the nurses who would also be arriving.

Over her cocoa cup, Polly made a face. ' 'Strewth!' she exclaimed. 'Nurses is the end in a house. Constant trouble, they are. Worse'n havin' cockroaches or rats.' She put down her cup and got up to light the bedroom candles and then handed one to Alicia. 'It'll be better for you, though. There's a lot of heavy liftin' and it's a messy job lookin' after somebody paralysed. I seen it before in the court when I were young.'

Alicia went up to bed and lay crying into her pillow for some time. When she finally knelt down to say her prayers, she asked for strength to do her duty – and then for God to lift the duties from her, if he could, which was almost heresy; women were supposed to bow their heads and accept, she thought hopelessly.

With a cheerful grin, Fanny called her at seven the next morning. 'Brought you a cuppa, to get you goin', like,' she said kindly. 'I've remade your Pa's fire, and Polly's kept puttin' fresh hotties round 'im all night. And she keeps wettin' his tongue and his lips. He's still breathin'.'

Filled with anxiety, her thoughts tumbling between what might happen to them all if Humphrey died and fear of the intolerable load of nursing if he lived, Alicia gulped down the tea gratefully. 'Fanny, dear, could you make up Edward's bedroom for the use of a nurse – there'll be two of them, one night, one day, but only the day nurse will be likely to sleep here.'

'Oh, aye, that's what our Polly was tellin' me,' Fanny replied philosophically, as she prepared to go downstairs again.

Alicia scrambled out of bed. 'To be honest, Fan, I haven't the foggiest notion how we're going to manage. Florence, Charles, Uncle Harold – they're all likely to turn up.'

Fanny laughed, and responded sarcastically, 'Oh, aye. And all expectin' four-course meals, as usual.' Then she added mischievously, 'You could send Miss Florence down to the kitchen to cook.'

This made Alicia giggle, as she poured water from the pitcher on her washstand. 'Fan, you are naughty! She's always been too busy to learn to cook, as you know.'

'Do 'er good to learn,' replied Fanny downrightly, and hurried out, before Alicia could scold her.

A few minutes later, after she had washed, Alicia arrived at Humphrey's bedside, to find Polly dozing. Her cap was askew and her face was grey with fatigue. Though she jumped when Alicia laid her hand gently on her shoulder, she got up from the chair slowly, acutely aware that she was no longer young. The night had seemed endless, as she had conscientiously boiled kettles on the fire and refilled the hot water bottles round her patient and kept his mouth and lips moist by sponging them with a wet flannel.

'How is he?' Alicia asked.

'Well, he hasn't changed much, 'cept I think he can move just a wee bittie – 'is right hand fingers.' Her voice was doubtful. Then she said, 'I couldn't change 'is sheet by meself, so I waited for you to come. He's in a bit of a mess. He needs washin'.' She yawned and stretched.

'Well, we washed him when he had his heart attack. Is the kettle hot? We can use the bowl on the washstand.'

'We'll need a couple of buckets with cold water to put the sheets in – and all the old sheets we've got.'

'I'll get them, Pol. And afterwards, you should go downstairs and get some breakfast and then go to bed.'

When they had everything assembled, they used the sheet the helpless man was lying on, to pull him over to the unsoaked side of the double bed and then tucked his hot water bottles round him again under the blankets, while they dealt with the soiled side.

They laid an oilcloth tablecloth culled from the kitchen over the damp patch on the mattress and covered it with several layers of old sheets. Their most difficult task, after washing and changing him, was to get him back to the original side of the bed; he was very heavy and they were both panting by the time they had inched him on to the layer of old sheets. Alicia began to realize why nurses, trained in such matters, had been recommended by Dr Willis.

'You'll have to get a real macintosh sheet to protect the bed, Allie,' Polly said.

'The nurses are sure to want all kinds of things. I do hope Uncle Harold comes soon – he'll be able to arrange the funds.' The two women spoke over the head of Humphrey, completely ignoring the fact that he might, to a degree, be able to understand them and be distressed at being left out of the conversation.

They washed him as best they could, and Alicia wiped the distorted face. Then, taking a clean handkerchief, she dabbed cool water round his lips and over the lolling tongue. As she did it, she spoke gently to him, but he made no response.

They had barely finished when Fanny brought a tall, thin woman up to the bedroom. She wore a navy blue uniform and heavy black shoes. A woven basket trunk was carried up for her by a small street urchin, who stared round the bedroom landing with little bright eyes like a cock robin. She dismissed him at the bedroom door with a penny tip and Fanny took him back downstairs. She turned to Polly and Alicia and announced herself as Nurse Trill. As she divested herself of her jacket, she made it clear that she would do no cooking, laundering or tending of fires. She was entitled to three meals a day plus a tea tray and she had not yet had her breakfast.

Polly took one look at her and cast her eyes heavenward, as if asking for Divine help. War, to the last teaspoon, was instantly declared.

Alicia took her quickly away to Edward's bedroom, which she slowly surveyed. It was apparent to Alicia that it did not please her, but neither said anything, and Nurse Trill took off her bonnet and laid it carefully on top of the tallboy. She then opened her straw trunk and took out an elaborately pleated, starched white confection, which she pinned on top of her head and then tied its strings in a huge bow under her chin. She put on an apron so starched that it crackled when she moved, and then turned to Alicia and, with a queenly nod, indicated that they should return to the sickroom. As they crossed the passageway, she said to Alicia, 'See that my breakfast tray is brought up immediately.'

Inwardly quailing, Alicia promised that she would attend to it as soon as nurse had seen the patient.

Nurse Trill looked at Humphrey with jaundiced eyes. She screwed up her mouth in a grimace which clearly said that, in her opinion, he did not stand much chance. Then she said, 'Dr Willis felt he might be able to take a little water or milk this morning. Please let me have these.'

She was surprised to learn that Humphrey had already been washed and changed, and she looked Polly and Alicia up and down. Polly put her nose in the air and said primly, 'I'm a widow, and I done it for 'im before, when he had an 'eart attack.'

Nurse Trill grunted.

Alicia glanced at Humphrey and was astonished to see him watching them with one eye. The lid of the other eye still drooped.

She went to him and spoke softly to him, explaining that Nurse Trill had come to look after him. She was not sure that he understood. He closed his eye again.

That day, it seemed to Alicia that she and the two maids never stopped running up and down stairs. Fanny answered the door, hauled coal and water, and carried trays to the sick room, in between keeping Elizabeth to her usual routine, as far as possible. Alicia helped her mother wash and dress and took her down to the morning-room, where she took up her embroidery quite happily, having obviously forgotten the events of the previous evening.

About eleven o'clock, Polly was preparing lunch for them all and for the expected invasion of anxious relations, when she suddenly swayed and had to sit down. She called out to Alicia, who was in the cellar stirring the dirty bed linen in the copper. Alicia put down her wooden paddle and ran upstairs. Seeing her nanny lying back in old Mrs Tibbs' easy chair, she ran to her.

'Get me some water, luv. I feel faint.'

Alicia got the water for her and upbraided herself angrily. 'I should have sent you to bed long since. Away you go this minute. I'll watch the lunch.'

Polly temporized and then agreed to go up for a nap. Alicia insisted on escorting her up the long flights of stairs.

III

Dr Willis had earlier been to inspect his patient and confer with Nurse Trill. He was very pleased to see definite movement of the right eyelid and some suggestion of movement down the whole of Humphrey's right side. He spent a considerable time massaging Humphrey, to show the nurse how to do it. She told him indignantly that she knew very well what was required.

Afterwards, he went with Alicia to pay his respects to Elizabeth, who had forgotten who he was but received him most graciously. As he left her, he sighed helplessly.

IV

Alerted by a telegram from Dr Willis, Charles arrived from Cambridge, having been able to pick up a fast train for Liverpool at Birmingham. He ate a hearty lunch, sat with his father for ten minutes, spent about the same time with his mother, who was most surprised to see him, and then left again to visit his friends in Liverpool University.

Florence did not come and Alicia began to feel aggrieved; surely she *should* come – her father loved her.

'Send her a telegram,' advised Polly, when she woke up from her nap, about four o'clock in the afternoon.

'It seems that one of us has to go down to the telegraph office. And I must talk to Uncle Harold if he comes – and you *must* do the dinner – and Fanny's nearly crazy answering the nurse's bell all the time.'

'Well, if she don't come by tomorrer mornin' and we're still stuck, you could run next door and ask Colonel Milfort, if his valet could go down to the Telegraph for yez. Proper nice, they are.'

'Father doesn't think they're nice at all. He won't even bow to either the Colonel or his friend who lives with him – nor will Mama.'

Polly grinned knowingly. 'It takes all kinds to make a world, luv. You take my word for it, you'll be safer goin' into that house than any house I know. Remember to give the valet a bit for himself for goin' for yez.'

'Would you go, Polly? I feel shy.'

'Nay. You'll get more respect than me.'

Early the next morning, Colonel Milfort found the faded young daughter from next door sitting nervously on the edge of one of his leather easy chairs in the front room. An ex-hussar with a pronounced limp from an old wound, he still looked to Alicia a very handsome elderly man.

'Good morning, madam,' he addressed her politely, as he limped slowly across the room towards her. 'What can I do for you?'

Alicia blushed and jumped up from her chair. She apologized for troubling him so early and then explained the need to send a telegram to Florence to tell her that her father had been taken seriously ill.

'Of course, I'll send my man immediately,' he promised. Then he inquired how Humphrey was progressing and wished him an early recovery.

As a gentleman, he could not sit down until she did and his leg was aching intolerably, so he pushed a straight chair under her and begged her to be seated. She complied, and he thankfully sank into a chair himself.

From her small clasp purse, she took a slip of paper with the message for Florence scribbled on it, and handed it to him with a half-crown. 'The change will be a little thank you for your man,' she told him shyly.

The Colonel was amused and pressed the silver coin back into her gloved hand. 'It's my pleasure,' he assured her, as he looked at Florence's address. 'In fact, if you will permit me, it would be much quicker to send Francis to your sister's house on his bicycle.'

The tired young face before him lit up. 'Would you?' she asked eagerly. 'I'd be so grateful. You see, Mama is also not herself – and I badly need Flo's help.'

He nodded understandingly and rose from his chair, to indicate dismissal; he was afraid she might stay half the morning, telling him her woes. They shook hands and he himself saw her out of the front door. He watched her until she was safely inside her own house; then he slowly closed the door. It was the first visit he had had from a neighbour since the local widows had realized that neither he nor the quiet friend who lived with him were interested in women. Behind hands and fans, the word had gone round the district that the two army officers in the house with brown curtains were you-know-whats. Not nice at all.

Alicia told Polly that the Colonel had been an absolute dear.

Florence arrived on her own bicycle in just over an hour. In her haste, she had lost half her hairpins en route and had got bicycle oil on the hem of her grey tweed skirt. She burst into the kitchen, raging. 'When I told Clarence about the Colonel's message, he produced a note from Dr Willis which he had been carrying around in his pocket and had forgotten to give me. He had not opened it because it was addressed only to me, the stupid man.' She pulled the hatpins quickly out of her felt hat. 'How is Father?' Without waiting for an answer, she went on,

'The Reverend Browning does not like eating alone, but I told him he simply must manage, at least for lunch.' With an exasperated air, she flung her hat on a chair and followed it with her jacket. 'I'll go up.'

'Yes, Ma'am,' Polly replied, without looking up from the potatoes she was peeling, and when she had heard the green baize door swing softly shut, she muttered disparagingly, 'Listen to her with the gob! A fat lot of help she'll be.'

V

Florence wept for an hour by her father's bed, while Nurse Trill sat unperturbed by the fire, knitting a grey scarf.

Alicia had hoped that Florence would stay for a few days, but she was bent on returning to her overbearing husband as soon as possible. 'Dear Clarence gets so upset,' she confided to Alicia, as she pushed hatpins into her hat. 'And I've the Women's Bible Study group this evening. I'm sorry that I have to go; I'll come again soon.'

Afterwards, Polly comforted Alicia by reminding her that the night nurse would be coming, and if they all got a proper night's rest, they could manage.

The night nurse proved to be an Irish woman in early middle-age and Polly took to her immediately. In order to save Fanny carrying up a tray, she cheerfully ate her late supper at the kitchen table before going on duty. Then she ran upstairs to relieve Nurse Trill, who was standing in the middle of the bedroom, her knitting neatly bundled up under her arm, waiting, watch in hand, to retire to Edward's bedroom.

Uncle Harold had arrived that same afternoon, very concerned about his acerbic brother's illness. He conferred with Dr Willis, when the doctor made his evening call. Afterwards, he sat down with Elizabeth and Alicia to discuss the situation.

He soon found that Elizabeth could not recall remarks he had made a couple of minutes before, and he was horrified. Humphrey had, during visits to Manchester, complained that his wife was very forgetful, but it was now clear to Harold that the poor woman's mind was fading completely. He looked at Alicia and she gave a tiny shrug, so he said he would like to rest and took his leave of Elizabeth.

Five minutes later, he and Alicia had a heart-warming conversation in the library and his first question was whether she could manage, with the aid of the nurses, to care for his brother. Dr Willis had suggested a nursing home or even the Royal Infirmary, but was certain that Humphrey would be much more likely to get better if he were in his accustomed surroundings. Alicia had drawn her ideas of hospitals from Polly's lurid tales of certain death if you ever found yourself in one, so she agreed, without hesitation, that he should be nursed at home. 'I'd never be able to face my own conscience, if he died in hospital,' she said honestly.

Uncle Harold was very relieved at her decision and he undertook to see Mr Bowring, Humphrey's clerk, on the following day and to discuss a Power-of-Attorney with Humphrey's lawyer. 'Meanwhile, I'll open a small banking account for you from my own funds, so that you can pay the nurses and the staff,' he told her.

In the days that followed, Alicia discovered that Harold Woodman's idea of a small banking account was quite generous, and, when she wrote her first cheque under the careful direction of a rotund, solicitous Bank Manager, she felt a new pride in being trusted with so much money.

Harold had been quite shocked to learn from Mr Bowring that Humphrey's main bank was the Manchester and Liverpool District Bank.

'A radical bank!' he had exclaimed.

'Yes, sir. Very good bank, if I may say so.'

'I always thought my brother was a Tory.'

'Oh, he is, sir, he is. But the Manchester and Liverpool is very forward-looking. Backed many of Mr Humphrey's investments in times past. And, of course, now Mr Humphrey is doing so well, he is a very prized customer.'

Harold was surprised to hear that Humphrey was doing well. Not too long back, his brother had complained that nothing that he touched seemed to be coming to fruition, and Alicia had said that her father was very hard up.

Mr Bowring begged Mr Harold to be discreet and then brought out Humphrey's account books, which confirmed that Humphrey was reaping quite a fortune.

VI

Once it was apparent to him that his father was not likely to die from his stroke, Charles was thankful to leave everything to Uncle Harold and Alicia. He was busy paying his addresses to a Miss Veronica Anderton, the daughter of a Cambridge don. Since his application for a post at Liverpool University had been successful, he felt, now, that it would be wise to marry the lady before she realized that she might be called upon to help to nurse his two invalid parents. As long as Alicia lived, of course, he comforted himself, he did not have to worry. Still, life could be very uncertain, so he took the first possible train back to Cambridge.

VII

Her mind freed of financial worry, Alicia was able to establish a routine and even keep Nurse Trill reasonably satisfied.

Polly and Fanny thankfully took their usual weekly afternoon off, and Polly suggested that Alicia should do the same, even if it were only to attend church on Sunday evening.

'You don't never get round the shops, neither, never mind church,' Polly said. 'You go while you've got the chance, duck.' She was ironing heavy linen sheets as if her life depended upon it and she slammed the iron back on to the fire as if to emphasize her words. 'It worries me no end, the way you bin kept in these last few years.'

Alicia slowly digested the fact that neither of her parents was in a position to be aware of her absence. 'What would Uncle Harold say, if he arrived and I wasn't here?' she asked doubtfully.

'Och, him? He's a real gentleman – remember how he allus brought you bits of chocolates when you was a kid? He'd have a fit, if he knew how you've bin treated since you left school. I don't mind tellin' 'im what a time you've had, if you like.'

Alicia was so used to being confined, her biggest expedition being an occasional visit to the grocer, that it was strange to her that the cage door was suddenly open.

Polly watched her out of the corner of her eye, as she spat on a fresh iron to make sure it was hot enough. She was relieved when Alicia said suddenly, 'I'd love to walk down to see Aunt Sarah Webb – she's too frail now to come over to see us.'

A few days later, she delighted Sarah Webb with a visit, and she poured out her news of Humphrey and Elizabeth to the old lady. Elizabeth's steady decline distressed Sarah greatly. She said sadly, 'I've seen it coming for some years – but we have simply to be patient with her. It happens to all of us, sooner or later.'

After this first plunge, Alicia took her shilling pocket money each Friday and, sometimes, spent most of it on tram fares, happy to sit on a slatted wooden seat and watch the great city go by.

VIII

One Friday afternoon, a letter came for Polly from Billy, and she read it while leaning against the back door jamb to get a little fresh air while she waited for the kettle to boil for Elizabeth's and Nurse Trill's tea trays.

Billy wrote fairly regularly three or four times a year, but no letter had puzzled her as much as this one did, so she showed it to Alicia as soon as the girl returned, glowing, from a brisk walk in Princes Park.

'He's got 'imself a new job,' Polly explained. 'Workin' with 'orses in a stable – he always did love 'orses when he were in the warehouse. Says the pedlar chap's gone 'ome to Montreal – but he does a bit o' peddling 'imself, still, when things is slack at the stables.'

As Alicia began to read the badly printed letters and was amused, as usual, by the total lack of punctuation, Polly went on darkly, 'What's worryin' me is he's all mixed with them Chinamen again – he's forever talkin' about this man, Huang. Says he's gone into partnership with him and put some of his savin's into making Huang's Café look nicer, so as to draw a family trade – and feed weddin's and parties – says he built shelves and tables for him. Throwin' his money down the drain workin' with 'eathens! Needs his head examining,' she fulminated.

Alicia laughed, as she turned over the page and read on. 'Well, you never know. Perhaps there is no nice restaurant there – it could be a good idea. I see that he says his main aim is still to get a farm. He wants to run horses on it. ' She looked up at Polly. 'Horses should be a pretty safe thing – people always need them.'

Polly made a face. 'He's proper daft,' she said, and returned to her ironing. 'I hope he gets enough to eat.'

'I expect he can always get a meal in the café.'

'At the rate he's goin', he should stick with his stable, silly bugger. Savings is savings,' and she thought of her sovereigns still sitting in their pillbox at the back of her dresser drawer. A lump rose in her throat at the sudden memory of Edward.

Alicia smiled impishly at Polly's rank disapproval and took off her hat and coat. Despite the constant worry of two sick people, she had begun to feel much better since being able to go out. She now said cheerfully, 'I'll take mother's tea up, if Fanny is busy.'

As she went upstairs with her mother's tray, she wished she could convince Elizabeth to visit her old friend, Sarah Webb. She had tried on a number of occasions and had once got Elizabeth partly down the road towards Sarah's house, only to have her suddenly baulk and almost panic. No amount of reminding her of her dear friend had persuaded her to go a step further. Alicia had had to bring her home.

Despite her mother's persistent refusals to go out, she had twice been found wandering down the street in her house slippers. Now, the front door was kept locked and the key was removed, for fear she strayed and became lost. Sometimes, she would find her way downstairs to the back garden and would meander amid its increasing wildness. Polly locked the door to the alleyway.

When she entered the morning-room with the tea tray, she found her mother standing by the window, staring pensively out of it.

She turned a bright face to Alicia, and inquired, 'Have you a stamp? I must write to Andrew.'

Alicia put the tray carefully down on to the table beside Elizabeth's favourite chair. 'Andrew, Mama?'

'Yes, dear, Andrew Crossing.' Then seeing the surprise on Alicia's face, she added a trifle impatiently, 'My lawyer. He always makes me save some of my allowance and I want to ask him to let me draw a little more from the Bank – you're not getting enough pocket money and I want to increase it now you're fifteen.'

Alicia swallowed hard, and answered carefully, 'It's very sweet of you to think of me, Mama – but Mr Simpkins is your lawyer. Of course, he hasn't been to see you for ages, so I'm not surprised you've forgotten.'

The smile faded from Elizabeth's face and, to Alicia's distress, tears welled up in her mother's eyes and rolled slowly down the fat cheeks.

'Oh, Mama, don't cry.' Alicia eased herself round the intervening furniture, and went to put her arms round her mother. She took out her handkerchief and wiped away the tears. 'Come and sit down, Mama, and have your tea. You'll feel better, and if you wish we'll send for Mr Simpkins. Who is Andrew Crossing, Mama?'

But the curtain fell once more over Elizabeth's mind and Alicia did not get any pocket money from her mother; the lawyers continued disinterestedly to transfer the same sum each month from the Trust established by her grandfather to her mother's banking account, and it began to be difficult to persuade Elizabeth to write cheques to pay Miss Blossom, the old dressmaker, or for cash for her other small needs.

701

23

I

Though it took months, Humphrey did make a partial recovery and managed to get around the house with the aid of a stick. He tried hard to deal with his affairs again and his clerk, Mr Bowring, became such a frequent visitor to the house that Alicia had a table put in the library for him to work at.

Humphrey's temper, never good, became worse. His irascibility sometimes reduced Polly and Alicia to tears; Fanny kept as far away from him as possible. He was frequently unpardonably rude to Elizabeth, but she would simply look at him in a bewildered fashion and it was clear that within a few minutes of his biting attacks, she had forgotten what he had said.

His patient clerk, Mr Bowring, mindful that he was getting to the end of his own working life and that he would in old age be largely dependent upon whatever small sum Humphrey settled on him, kept very quiet and did his best to care for Humphrey's interests and to guide him where necessary.

When Humphrey first saw the housekeeping book, he flew into a temper at Uncle Harold's generosity; but when his brother came from Manchester he finally accepted his explanation that there had been many unexpected expenses in connection with his illness. With some temerity, Harold pointed out to Humphrey that, in addition to the expenses entered in the book so meticulously by Alicia, Alicia herself needed both clothing and pocket money.

'You owe your life to that girl's patience with you,' he said. 'With Elizabeth sick herself, nobody in this world is going to look after you the way she does. She attains her majority this coming year and could very well leave you if she is not happy. My wife pointed out years ago that she hadn't a decent garment to bless herself with and she's dreadfully shabby now.'

Harold was aware of Alicia's likely origins, but had, in an absent-minded way, always treated her as his niece. Now he said, 'I realize why you dislike her so, but you could regard her as a valued employee. If she left, you would have to pay heavily for someone else.'

Humphrey saw the sense of the argument. Mr Bowring was instructed to pay Alicia a wage of eight shillings a week. Mr Bowring opened his mouth like a landed goldfish at the order, and then said quietly, 'Yes, sir.' Poor young lady, he ruminated; he had grown fond of Alicia.

When he paid her, he did not humiliate her by calling the money a wage. He said kindly that her father had instructed him to see that she got some pin money each week, and she flushed with pleasure.

Without asking permission, she continued to take Friday afternoon off and Humphrey found himself facing a frigidly polite Polly whenever he wanted something on that afternoon. Usually, he wanted to be read to, because he could not hold a book or newspaper steady and got too tired when he laid them on his desk to read. He was very angry on the first day he discovered Alicia's absence, but Polly told him coolly, 'I can read to you, sir.'

He was surprised, and asked, 'You went to school, then?'

'No, sir. Mr Charles taught me when I first come here and he were a little boy.'

'Well, I'm damned. Bring in the newspaper.'

So while Fanny kept an eye on Elizabeth, Polly sat primly in the library reading aloud.

Alicia found that there were less expensive ways of dressing oneself than going to George Henry Lee's or to Miss Blossom. She discovered the world of Lewis's, a department store, where for a few shillings she could buy decent blouses, hats, shoes and a thousand oddments; her newfound wealth stretched much further than she had imagined it would. She was very thankful for this, because her father had had a number of visitors during his illness and a few of these gentlemen came regularly to see him. She had had to receive them, since, as she explained, her mother was indisposed. In her shabby skirts and home-made blouses, broken shoes and general air of dishevelment, it was obvious that they had thought her to be some kind of companion-help, and their surprise at finding that she was a daughter of the house had been apparent from their expressions. She had felt hurt.

At first, her father's speech had been so slurred as to be unintelligible to anyone but Alicia, who was with him so much that she was able to follow what he was trying to say. Dr Willis, however, sent a middle-aged lady to see him, and, for what Humphrey regarded as a monstrous fee, she taught him how to improve his articulation. In his frustration, he used to get very angry with her, but she persisted until there was a kind of rueful friendship between them.

On her own initiative, Alicia ordered a carriage one sunny November afternoon to drive him and her mother through the park. While Humphrey was eased into his outside clothes, he shouted at her that it was needless extravagance. Fanny helped Elizabeth into her fur coat and she wandered about the hall saying it was bedtime and too late to go out. Once out, however, they both seemed to enjoy the trip.

Colonel Milfort watched their departure from his drawing-room window. He observed the difficulty with which Alicia managed to persuade her mother into the carriage and then hoist her stiffened father into it. He was also sorry for the girl, whose history he had heard from his batman, who had got it from Fanny.

He limped to his desk and wrote her a note offering the loan of his carriage one afternoon a week, so that her parents might take the air in the park. His batman would be pleased to assist her father in and out of the carriage and to drive it.

Harassed and fatigued, Alicia burst into tears when she read the stiff little letter. She accepted the offer with alacrity, though she expected that her father would raise every objection he could think of, once he knew who had sent it. He had, however, enjoyed the outing that Alicia had arranged; it had given him a sense of assurance that he was indeed recovering his health, so he accepted Colonel Milfort's offer quite gracefully and instructed Mr Bowring to write him a note of thanks. The Colonel was surprised to receive the following Christmas from a grateful Alicia a hand-embroidered desk blotter, which she had worked during long hours of watching her mother.

'Well, damn me!' exclaimed the Colonel, running his fingers over the elaborate workmanship which held the blotting paper in place. He shook it free of its enveloping tissue paper and stumped slowly upstairs to show it to his friend, Major Ferguson, who was lying comfortably on a sofa in the drawing-room window.

The house on the other side of Humphrey's residence was put up for sale on instructions from the heir to the owner; according to Fanny, the heir lived in Jamaica and had no intentions of living in Liverpool. It was bought by a well-to-do carriagemaker, a tradesman called Hunter.

'Proper nice old girl, that Mrs Hunter next door is,' opined Polly, as she heaved a steak and kidney pudding out of a steaming pan of water. 'She'd be good for your Mam.'

'Mama and Papa wouldn't wish to know them, Pol. They're in trade, not commerce.'

''Strewth!' exclaimed Polly in disgust, but said no more.

One day in January, however, when the sun was gleaming softly between the forests of smoking chimney-stacks and when Alicia was about to pass Mrs Hunter's front steps, the lady had just descended from her truly magnificent pale green carriage. Beaming, she left her groom and rolled gently towards the younger woman, to inquire anxiously how her dear father was. They had, she said, seen Dr Willis's brougham regularly at the Woodmans' door.

Alicia was surprised to find that this exuberant lady knew a great deal about her parents and herself, forgetting that Fanny and Polly would indubitably gossip with the maids next door. Made nervous by this sudden revelation, Alicia retreated as gracefully as she could.

Not only did Mrs Hunter wish to ingratiate herself with the ladies in her new neighbourhood, she was also very kind. Armed with a large bunch of grapes for the invalid, she ventured to call on Alicia.

Not sure what to do with her, Polly took her upstairs to the cold, dusty drawing-room, and called Alicia. Alicia explained that her mother was indisposed and unable to receive visitors. She asked Polly to bring tea.

Mrs Hunter stayed half an hour during which time Elizabeth wandered in to join them. Seeing a lady dressed in hat and gloves for visiting, Elizabeth automatically dropped into the role of hostess; it was obvious, however, that she could not keep track of the conversation. Alicia was embarrassed, but Mrs Hunter gave no hint that she realized that all was not well with Elizabeth.

She told her amused husband afterwards, 'I've never seen such a dismal house. Hasn't bin painted in years. And it was that cold – no fire in the drawing-room! Can you believe it? And her poor mother's out of her mind – *non compos mentis*. Between her Ma and her Pa, I don't know how that girl stands it.'

Mr Hunter turned a page of his newspaper. 'So you saw Mrs Woodman? And Woodman?'

'No. According to his daughter, he's up and about, though. I saw him once, driving in the park.'

'Well, I'm glad I was wrong when I said you'd be snubbed,' he responded.

After her visit, Mrs Hunter always stopped to chat when she saw Alicia, and one day asked her to come in for tea. Alicia refused, but explained that it was not because she did not want to; she was simply so busy. She began to enjoy these small encounters with her neighbours, and was quite vivacious with Colonel Milfort and his friend, Major Ferguson, when they paused in their afternoon perambulations, to inquire after Mr Woodman.

For the first Christmas after Humphrey's stroke, Florence brought her maturing brood for Christmas tea rather than to midday dinner. 'It will save you having to cook so much,' she told Alicia. The visit was, however, quite hectic, and Frank was unsubtly spiteful to Alicia. Clarence spent half an hour with a barely coherent Humphrey, talking about the need for new choir-stalls for his church – woodworm had badly damaged the present ones.

Blithely indifferent to who cooked it or what the menu was, Charles shared a roast capon with Alicia and their mother at midday dinner and stayed on for tea. Alicia cut up some of the meat very small and fed Humphrey in his bedroom. He was propped up in an easy chair beside the bed.

Immediately after tea, Charles left to catch the train for London where he would stay with friends. It was he, however, who suggested that the library was large enough to be adapted as a bedroom for Humphrey, to save running up and down stairs.

Dr Willis saw the convenience of this suggestion and Humphrey liked the idea of being amongst his books and papers again, so a vast amount of furniture-shifting was done by Polly, Fanny and Alicia, including a commode and washstand which were concealed behind a folding screen near to the bed.

Being on the ground floor of the house undoubtedly encouraged Humphrey in his efforts to walk again. Fires in the morning-room and the dining-room, added to the blaze in the library, kept the whole area fairly warm, and he began to set goals for himself, to reach the chair by the door, then the chair in the hall, then to cross the hall. Once or twice, he fell and bruised himself, but after Dr Willis had warned him that he might break a bone, he would ring furiously for Polly or Alicia to help him to move about.

One night, after he had been put to bed, Alicia flopped on to a kitchen chair and sighed to Polly, 'I'm so tired of it all, Pol.'

'Aye, luv. We all are. But what else can we do?'

And there was no answer.

Sometimes, late at night, Polly would wake up to hear the nursery piano being played and she would lie fretting for Alicia – her baby.

II

In May 1907, on one of his rare visits to his family, Charles confided the news of his courtship to Alicia.

Alicia was thrilled and demanded every detail of Veronica Anderton's looks, likes and dislikes. Charles was so besotted by his prospective wife that he was unable to answer some of Alicia's questions and could not even recall for her, with certainty, whether her eyes were grey or pale blue.

Alicia was inwardly wretched. It was her Twenty-First Birthday, and when her brother came rushing into the house she thought it was to greet her on the day of her majority. Instead, he had come to discuss Veronica with her and had obviously forgotten about the birthday.

The day had also gone unremarked by both Humphrey and Elizabeth; Alicia thought sadly that her mother was becoming increasingly unable to remember anything.

The postman had brought a card and a little silver dish in need of polishing from her godmother, Sarah Webb. Her aunt Clara in West Kirby, immersed in her own invalidism, had also apparently forgotten, and Uncle Harold and his wife, Vera, had never marked her birthdays.

She had been touched by the gift of a violently pink shawl from Polly and Fanny, who must have spent hours late at night to produce it without her knowledge.

Now, as a sudden storm of rain beat against the windowpanes, she tried to keep her attention on Charles's problems. And he certainly did have a difficulty, because a prospective daughter-in-law might be reluctant to enter a family where she could have to care for sick parents.

'Not that she'll have to worry while you're here,' Charles was continuing, cheerfully taking it for granted that, while Alicia lived, it was her duty to care for their parents.

Alicia bit her lower lip and reluctantly agreed.

'What shall I do, Allie?'

'You'd better let Father know of your intentions, before you pop the question formally, don't you think?'

Charles sighed. 'Yes, I must.' He stroked his golden brown moustache thoughtfully. 'I wonder how much he'll give me, to start us off?'

Alicia made a face and carefully turned rightside out the sock she had been darning. 'You had better ask him.'

'Can he stand a visit, do you think?'

'He'll have to. He's reading. Mr Bowring's gone home.'

Charles rose and sighed again. He was surprised to hear Alicia chuckle, as she looked up at him and said, 'Don't expect too much!' He realized suddenly that Alicia appeared more self-assured than she used to. In the old days, he thought neither of them would have dared to make even the smallest joke about Humphrey.

At the sight of his son, a bored Humphrey thankfully closed the volume on the sloping book rest in front of his chair; he had difficulty in retaining what he read and even in turning the pages himself.

Charles did his best to smile, despite the smell of urine and excrement pervading the room from the commode behind the screen. What a mess the fine library looked, with a bed set in the middle of it, he thought depressedly.

Humphrey received his son's news with interest and asked some details of Professor Anderton and what dowry Charles expected Veronica to bring. His speech was very slurred and Charles had to concentrate hard to understand him. He seemed, however, to find Charles's replies to his questions acceptable and promised to dictate a letter to his clerk for Professor Anderton. 'I don't suppose your mother will write,' he added.

'She can't, Father. She simply doesn't remember what I tell her.'

'Hm. Turn down the light for me. My head aches and it's bothering my eyes. And get a whisky out of my cupboard – have one yourself.'

Charles stood up and adjusted the central gas-lights.

'Not that far,' his father told him testily, and Charles hastily turned the four lamps of the chandelier up again. He then got two glasses and a bottle of whisky out of his father's side cupboard and poured out two modest shots. He handed one to his father.

'God's teeth! Can't you even pour a decent sized whisky?'

Charles quickly added more to his father's glass, and then sat down in a chair opposite to him and slowly crossed his own legs. Would the old man come up trumps and provide a decent sum towards his marriage expenses?

Humphrey conveyed his glass to his mouth with some difficulty, while he laboriously meditated on how little he could get away with without losing standing with the Andertons. It always hurt to part with money, and the thought of it raised his blood pressure.

The silence began to depress Charles, and he said, 'Veronica is an only child, as I mentioned. She wants Alicia to be her bridesmaid and Florence her Maid of Honour. Her best friend would be another bridesmaid.'

Humphrey's head began to throb. 'Alicia?' He turned his gaze slowly upon his son. 'Alicia will not attend the wedding.'

'Father! She's my sister. Why not? Veronica's very keen about it.' He uncrossed his legs and leaned towards Humphrey, his face shocked. 'I understand that you and mother may not be able to come – but girls love weddings.'

'Alicia has to attend your mother and me.'

'Oh, surely, Father, Fanny and Polly could do that for one day.'

'They don't do things properly,' Humphrey retorted grumpily.

'But . . . just for a day, Father. It would do Allie a world of good – might introduce her to some decent fellows – it's time she got married.'

'Nonsense! She's not the marrying kind.' His voice rose. 'We should, in any case, not be left to the care of servants.' As he spat out the last words, saliva dribbled down his chin. His face went slowly purple and he trembled visibly.

Charles did his best to control his own anger and bewilderment. He said persuasively, 'I do understand your personal difficulties, Father, but surely it could be managed. Poor Allie will be frightfully disappointed – and so would Veronica – she . . .'

'Stop arguing with me. I will decide . . .' The empty glass fell from his hand and shattered on the brass fender.

For a second, the noise deflected Charles's attention, but then he snarled furiously, 'I won't stop arguing. Allie *must* come.'

'You say *must* to me? How dare you? Get out of this room. When you can be polite, come back again.' It seemed to Charles that his father's face swelled up and that his eyes suddenly protruded like glass marbles.

'Father!'

'Get out!'

Charles jumped angrily to his feet. He strode out of the room, slamming the door behind him, while Humphrey shouted something incomprehensible after him.

He stood quivering in the hall, and then went across it to the morning-room, to find Alicia.

During his absence, Elizabeth had come downstairs and, as he entered, Alicia was holding her arm and was trying to persuade her to go upstairs again. Elizabeth was resisting vigorously.

At the sound of the opening door, Alicia looked round. She said in an embarrassed fashion, 'Could you leave us for just a minute, Charley?'

'Of course.' Charles carefully shut the door again and wondered what womanly business meant that he had to leave them. 'Christ!' he muttered savagely.

The door was quietly opened behind him and he turned quickly. His mother smiled charmingly, 'Charles, dear. How nice.'

'Come along, mother,' Alicia said sharply. 'We have to go upstairs.'

'Why?'

Alicia blushed unaccountably and looked uneasily at her brother. 'Mama, I explained to you.'

'But Charles is here.'

'We'll be down again in a minute. Charles, dear, do go into the morning-room. We shan't be long.'

Mystified, Charles did as he was bidden and stood leaning against the mantelpiece. What the hell was the matter with the family this afternoon? He heard Alicia and his mother arguing, as they ascended the stairs.

It was about five minutes before they returned and, as his mother slowly lowered herself into her chair, Charles raised a querying eyebrow towards Alicia.

'Had to take her to the loo,' mouthed Alicia over her mother's head. Her face went scarlet. 'She wets herself otherwise,' she said baldly.

'O Lord!' muttered Charles.

Oblivious of any embarrassment, Elizabeth began to ask Charles how he was doing at school. He replied absently that he was doing all right – poor Mother seemed to be falling apart. He turned to Alicia and told her that he had had a row with their father over Alicia being a bridesmaid.

Alicia was not altogether surprised at the news. As she pulled out a chair and sat down near her mother, she asked, 'Was he *very* cross?'

Charles hesitated before answering and watched his mother trying to find the right colour of embroidery silk in her basket. Then he said, 'He was simply furious.'

'Oh, goodness! He would hate his routine to be upset.' She rose, and said a little anxiously, 'Perhaps I had better see if he is all right.'

'Why?'

'Well, you know we're not supposed to upset him – it might cause another stroke.' She moved towards the door.

'Oh, come on, Allie. He's all right. Fancy getting all het up about Veronica's bridesmaids!'

She nodded to him. 'Talk to Mother for a bit. I'll just take a peep at him.'

He heard her quick footsteps on the tiles in the hall and the opening of the library door. She was back in a second, her face white.

'Charley, come quick! I think he's dead.'

From Elizabeth came a startled cry. Her comprehension was fleeting. Then her face went vacant again.

24

I

In his Will Humphrey left Florence ten thousand pounds and Alicia a shilling for candles.

Polly and Fanny were sitting modestly at the back of the big upstairs drawing-room, which had been hastily cleaned for the gathering of the family; they had each been left one hundred pounds and felt they had been meanly dealt with. 'What's a shilling for candles?' Fanny whispered to Polly, as Mr Derby, Humphrey's solicitor, droned on.

'Dunno.'

'Will the Mistress be all right?'

'Aye, I think so. She'll get the use of the ould fella's money and when she dies Master Charles'll get it.' Aunt Vera, Uncle Harold's wife, turned and hushed Polly, and the two maids immediately became models of demure quietness. They watched, however, a sudden stir on the other side of the room, as Alicia got up from her seat beside her mother, the insulting sentence ringing in her ears. Mr Derby paused in his reading and the remainder of the group stared at her as she edged round the room to get to the door.

As the door clicked behind her, Mr Derby cleared his throat and continued, and the family turned back to hear that Humphrey had bequeathed his gold hunter watch, his seals and other personal jewellery to his brother, Harold Woodman.

Alicia had not expected that Humphrey would leave her anything; she was, she told herself, probably not his daughter. She had been shocked, however, to be humiliated before the family, when his Will was read, and, indeed, Mr Derby regretted it; he did not know who Alicia Beatrix Mary Woodman was and had unwisely assumed that she was probably a younger sister of Humphrey's who had displeased the family; he had certainly not expected a quiet, sensitive-faced young woman to be seated in front of him.

Alicia ran down to the kitchen and stood in front of the great, old-fashioned range, her arms clasped across her chest as if she had been wounded. The warmth of the fire was comforting, but, yet again, she felt herself hemmed in by circumstances not of her own making.

'How could Papa be so cruel?' she asked herself. Her nephew, Frank, sitting there with his parents and siblings, must be sniggering. Did they all know about her? She shrank from having to meet them again. And Uncle Harold's tall, dignified sons and their wives, to whose weddings she had not been asked? Did they know? Their mother, Aunt Vera, must know – probably knew more than Alicia herself did.

She heard the green baize door in the hall open and then Florence's voice, calling in a hoarse whisper. Reluctantly, she went to the foot of the stairs, 'What's the matter?' she inquired listlessly.

'Mother's soaked her dress and the chair,' Florence whispered again in great agitation. 'What shall we do?'

'Take everybody into the dining-room for cakes and wine – it's all ready. Send Polly down here to make the tea, and tell Fanny to serve. I'll take care of Mama,' Alicia responded practically. In the background, she could hear Elizabeth inquiring in a piercingly clear voice where Humphrey was.

After she had cleaned up her mother, Alicia did not again mingle with the funeral guests. Florence, as the eldest daughter, could do the honours. When the guests left, nobody thought to come to say goodbye to Alicia.

After Uncle Harold had seen his wife and family off to catch the train to Manchester, he returned, and Polly, as she took his hat and coat from him, was glad to see him. 'Are you staying overnight, sir?'

'Yes, Polly. As the Executor, I have to spend some time with Mr Derby. Where is Miss Alicia?'

Polly directed him to the morning-room, where he found Alicia entertaining her mother by going through an old photograph album of Charles's. He contented himself with taking Alicia's hand and telling her warmly that she was not to worry. 'We'll have a good talk in the morning,' he said, with an uncertain glance at Elizabeth who appeared to be regarding him as an intrusive stranger. He said to her, as he loosed Alicia's hand, 'I'm your brother-in-law, Harold.' He leaned over her chair and kissed her, and she gave him one of her brilliant, almost arch, smiles.

II

Uncle Harold proved to be very helpful. The house now belonged to Charles and he would have liked to live in it after he was married. He felt, however, that he could not turn his mother out and he was determined that his new wife should not be made responsible for his mother's care, which she would be if they moved in – even if Alicia stayed with them and became her mother's personal attendant. It would be better to rent another house for the first years of Veronica's and his marriage.

Thankful not to have to move, Alicia discussed with Uncle Harold her mother's growing incapacity, the doctor's assurance that it would grow worse and the problems of managing such an inconveniently large house.

With Alicia, Uncle Harold toured the place from cellar to attic nurseries, and then he conferred with Charles. Charles told him irritably to arrange any alterations he felt necessary, the cost to come out of his father's Estate.

The old basement kitchens were closed off, and after much trailing in and out by muddy-booted workmen, all grumbling that it could not be done, the butler's pantry on the ground floor was made into a modern kitchenette with a gas-stove. Gas-fires were installed in all the rooms still in use and the nursery floor simply had its doors closed and was left to gather dust.

'I know it saves steps,' Polly confided to Fanny, 'but when I locked me old bedroom door, I cried. Master Edward and me was so happy in it – and when I put a dust-cover over the rocking-horse in the nursery, it were like losing an old friend – Master Edward loved that horse.'

Fanny nodded glumly. With a fine, new bedroom on the first floor, she would not in future be able to ask a man to spend the night with her, as she had been able to when alone in her basement bedroom. But you can't have everything, she told herself, and never having to carry another hod of coal, never having to face the dust and soot of open fires again, was an overwhelming relief. 'All you has to do is strike a match and the fire's there,' she thought incredulously.

'Will your maids stay with you?' asked Uncle Harold of Alicia.

She looked at him in surprise. How could anyone imagine Polly and Fanny leaving her? 'Of course,' she assured him. Then she asked slowly, 'Do you think we could pay them a bit more? They are shockingly badly paid.'

'I imagine so,' Uncle Harold had replied cautiously. 'I'll ask your Aunt Vera what the usual wage is at present.' They were seated at the dining-room table, a mass of papers between them, and he looked at the pale, earnest face before him, and then went on, 'I can justify a salary for a companion-help for your mother, since she is far from well, and I would like, my dear, if you are not offended, to pay you this salary.'

He saw the startled surprise on Alicia's face, and added, 'It's the only way I can think of to provide for you.'

713

Alicia flushed, and then nodded sadly, 'A shilling for candles,' she said ruefully.

'Yes. I don't know what made your father cut you out of his Will,' he lied. 'But we have to live with it. So I hope you will accept the salary.'

'Thank you, Uncle Harold. Yes, I will.'

'I think your mother's affairs also need attention, don't they?'

'Yes, they do. She is no longer able to sign cheques for her clothing – and she used to buy books.' Alicia swallowed at the recollection of her mother's pitiful decay, but she sighed with relief when a few weeks later he was able to arrange for her signature to be acceptable on her mother's account, subject to Elizabeth's lawyers overseeing the Bank's Statements. He also opened a Housekeeping account for her and she was astonished at the generosity of the amount he felt she needed. With Charles's and his permission, she had the hall repainted and a new stair carpet laid.

No amount of money would halt the ruthless march of Elizabeth's illness, so it was decided to continue the use of the library as a bedroom and this, too, was redecorated before putting Elizabeth's bedroom furniture into it, so that it looked familiar to her.

As she became more and more irrational, Elizabeth acquired a stubborn fixation which made it almost impossible to persuade her to do something quite normal, like taking a bath. She became terrified of her own reflection in a mirror and, to avoid this happening, some mirrors were removed while the others were draped over.

Dr Willis insisted that, no matter how difficult Elizabeth was, Alicia must continue to go out at least once a week and leave her mother with the maids. 'You must maintain your own health,' he warned her. 'Where would Mrs Woodman be without you?'

Though in earlier days Elizabeth had had a friendly relationship with Polly, she seemed now to tolerate Fanny better, perhaps because the younger maid made less fuss over her and retained the formal status of servant with her, something to which Elizabeth had been accustomed all her life. Fanny never argued with Elizabeth, but simply used the standard phrases of a servant, however inappropriate, to beguile her to the bathroom or to eat.

Supported by Uncle Harold's interest and her spirits raised by the improvements to the house, Alicia was able to cope better with Elizabeth. The three women took it in turns to watch the benighted invalid, so that no one was herself nearly driven mad by Elizabeth's insane questions and illogical behaviour. And there was always the freedom of Friday afternoon to look forward to.

714

In the back of Alicia's mind, however, lurked fear of the future. What would happen to Polly and herself when her mother died? The best she could hope for would be that either Charles or Florence and Clarence would give her a home; an extra pair of female hands was always welcome in either kitchen or nursery, particularly when there was no obligation to pay their owner anything. One of them might also give Polly and Fanny jobs, since they were well-trained servants.

As she considered such a gloomy outlook, a slow, burning revolt against her own probable fate grew in her. It would be better to try for a post as governess or lady's companion, where at least she would be paid, and she began quietly to prepare for this and to save all that she could from the salary so kindly contrived for her from Humphrey's Estate. Polly was getting old, she worried, and she hoped that she might be able to help her financially, if necessary.

Late at night, she would sometimes leave her sleeping mother and run upstairs to practise on the grand piano in the huge, unused drawing-room. So that she could teach music, she put together a series of children's pieces and made notes on how she would introduce a child to it. She also spent time during her mother's afternoon naps studying from her old school text-books and putting together short lessons on a variety of subjects. When engaged in replying to Elizabeth's aimless and persistently repeated questions, she did some pieces of fine needlework to show a prospective employer or did pencil sketches, which she could show at the same time, to indicate that she could teach these ladies' accomplishments.

One Friday afternoon, she went to the Windsor Street library and borrowed two travel books and one on the care of pets, with an eye to having background knowledge for a post as Companion. Later on, she read a number of books on etiquette, for the same purpose. She became known to the librarians and began to regard them as her friends.

Christmas brought several letters. Charles wrote that, because of his family's being in mourning, he and Veronica had decided to be married quietly in Cambridge during the Christmas holidays. He realized, he said, that Alicia must look after Mama and would not be able to attend. Alicia presumed that Florence or Clarence had explained to him why she had been cut out of his father's Will and she smiled sardonically. Veronica's parents did not send her a formal invitation, so she blinked back her tears of disappointment and threw his letter into the fire.

There was a joyful letter from Billy to say that he had taken up a quarter-section of land in Alberta, a whole one hundred and sixty acres, he exulted, and he was clearing it while he worked part-time at the stable; he did not mention the excruciating, back-breaking work this entailed, but instead said that the land was the beginning of a real hope that he could bring Polly to Canada and have a place for her to live. It might take a few years yet, but he would do it.

Such a pang went through Alicia as she read this that she felt it difficult to say, with conviction, to Polly that it would be wonderful for her to go. How could she endure being separated from Polly? She would be totally alone.

As Polly read the letter again, she pursed her lips and said, 'Why don't he get married?' The idea that Billy might actually fulfil his long-ago promise made her suddenly nervous; she was not sure she wanted to meet a collection of Chinese, Red Indians and Frenchies.

'Perhaps he isn't the marrying kind,' Alicia responded lightly, as she remembered the short, inarticulate boy who had helped to weed the now totally neglected garden.

'He wrote once as there was more men than women in Alberta – maybe that's why,' Polly suggested, on consideration.

Alicia agreed. The talk of marriage reminded her of the other ceremonies in her Book of Common Prayer, and she asked idly, 'Was I ever christened, Polly?' She looked up from the tray of rice she had been cleaning, while her mother napped. They were in the new kitchenette and Polly had put down her letter, while she got out her new cookery book, *How to Cook with Gas*, to check the heat setting for a rice pudding. At Alicia's question, she turned round and smiled. 'Of course, you was, duck. The Reverend Clarence done it. Your Mam and Miss Webb stood for you – god-mothers, like. Now what put that idea into your head, all of a sudden?'

Alicia shrugged. 'Well, I wonder why I was never confirmed?'

'Confirmed?'

'Yes. You know – made a full member of the Church.'

Polly was gingerly lighting the gas oven and her reply was a little muffled, as she leaned into it. 'Probably nobody remembered to have you done.' She got up from her squatting position and closed the oven door. 'Now, Master Charles, he were done at school – I remember because your Mam gave me a parcel with a present to post to him.'

Alicia shook the cleaned rice into a basin in order to wash it. As the last grains plopped in, she said slowly, 'You know, Polly, it seems to me that nobody ever thought about me, except you.'

Polly smiled. 'Well, you always was my baby, luv.' Then, as she shook sugar for a rice pudding on to the small, brass scales in front of her, she added, 'Master Edward loved you like anything – remember?'

'Yes, he did – and I loved him so much. How I wish he'd lived, Polly. Both our lives might've been different.'

'Aye, they might've bin,' Polly sighed. Then she reminded Alicia, 'Your Mam cared enough to see you went to school, though. I remember she had a real set-to with the Master over it.'

'Surely school is every girl's right?'

Polly sniffed. 'Nobody never sent me to a proper school, except to Dame School to learn me letters. Even so, if Master Charles hadn't taught me, I wouldn't be able to read nor write now.'

'Nowadays, you'd have been sent to the Board School.' Alicia ran water from the tap over the rice and drained it. Polly concentrated on her recipe and did not reply to Alicia's comment.

'Polly, do you remember long ago, when we went out on New Year's Eve to the top of Upper Parliament Street, and that horrible Ralph Fielding from down the road called me a bastard?'

Polly glanced warily at her out of the corner of her eye, as she turned to get flour and lard out of the small pantry behind her. 'Yes?'

'When I finally found out what the word meant, it made me feel sick, Polly, and lots of things I'd never understood fell into place. I knew why the girls at school weren't allowed to be friends with me. It seemed so terribly unfair, Polly, because it wasn't my fault,' she said dejectedly, as mechanically she assembled the rice pudding. 'And then when I understood the absolute repudiation that *a shilling for candles* meant, I felt totally publicly humiliated. It confirmed my worst fears about Papa's feelings for me.'

'Well, I told you before, love, that he were your Papa as far as the law were concerned.'

'But not as far as his feelings were concerned. He often made my life a misery; he was quite different with Florence. Do you suppose that Charles's in-laws or his Veronica know the story about me?'

'Seeing as you wasn't asked to their wedding and Miss Florence and the Reverend was, not to speak of Mr Harold and all his kids, they must've got wind of it – people would talk about the Will and ask questions – and a proper nice piece of gossip it would be. I'm sorry, pettie.'

Alicia half-closed her eyes. She felt despised and rejected, and she wondered if the feeling would be with her all her life. Aloud, she said to Polly, 'I've tried so hard, Pol, to be a good daughter.'

Polly smiled wryly at her. 'You've bin more than good, chook.'

III

In the Spring of 1908, Charles and Veronica rented a newly-built house not far from Seacombe Ferry, on the other side of the River Mersey from Liverpool, from which Charles could commute easily to the University every day. Upper Canning Street, also, was not very far from the University and Charles dropped in occasionally to see his mother, though Veronica declared that was too far for her to visit. Charles's visits were short because Elizabeth no longer knew him with any certainty and he did not seem to have much to say to Alicia. Her absence from his wedding was never mentioned.

Florence also called from time to time. In an absent-minded way, she was gushily polite to Alicia but, as with her brother, any sense of ease there had been between them was gone. She, also, did not stay long.

'I bet Clarence has told her to have as little to do with me as possible,' Alicia thought shrewdly, well aware of her brother-in-law's ambitions. Her manner towards Florence became stiff and cold.

Viewing her small savings nestling in an old tea caddy, there were days when Alicia felt like taking flight; the money would last her for a little while. Yet, now she knew about Andrew Crossing, she felt an enormous pity for her mother who had, in some way, become locked into a marriage which did not suit her. Pity, a sense of duty and a fear of censure, if she left, kept her by her mother's bedside. She could almost hear the acidulous voices if she deserted a sick parent, 'You can expect wicked, outrageous behaviour from a bastard – nothing good in them.'

It became impossible to leave Elizabeth alone for a second, even if she were sleeping – she might wake up. She would wander all over the house, absently turning on all the gas lights without lighting them or aimlessly tearing up books and papers when she came across them. She occasionally smashed crockery by throwing it on to the floor and there was always the fear that she would fall downstairs or, as she once did, get into the bath and turn the taps on until she was soaked and the bath flooded. She was still physically quite strong and it was easier to follow her round the house than to try to persuade her back into her room.

'She's like a clock without a pendulum,' Polly once remarked in despair, as she sorted a pile of stinking bedding and clothing, the result of Elizabeth's incontinence. 'And yet she looks that well you'd never believe it.'

IV

Next door, Colonel Milfort quietly died of cancer and his heart-broken friend sold the house to a well-to-do grocer with a large family, who referred to Elizabeth as *that madwoman next door*. He forbade his wife to have anything to do with a family with the stigma of lunacy about them. This did not stop his children, when they met Alicia in the street, pointing at her and sniggering and, sometimes, calling 'Loony, loony,' after her. She passed them each time with slow, grave dignity and finally they gave up.

'District's goin' to pot,' said Fanny, in disgust, when she heard the racket the children made in the next-door garden.

The irrepressible Mrs Hunter, the Woodmans' other neighbour, continued to be extremely kind to Alicia and the young woman often had tea with her in her opulent, overstuffed drawing-room. Alicia found it comforting to be told that she was doing a wonderful job in caring so well for her poor Mam and to be presented with vases of flowers or bunches of grapes for the invalid. She became very fond of the stout lady.

Quite frequently, on her day off, Alicia would go down to tree-lined Rosebery Street to see her godmother, Sarah Webb, who was housebound by acute arthritis. 'It's just old age, my dear,' she would tell Alicia, as the girl put into her tortured hands bunches of roses or daffodils culled from the Woodmans' wild garden.

Alicia wept bitterly when, in January 1911, the old lady caught influenza and slipped out of life, a wise, erudite woman who had taught Alicia far more than the girl realized.

Alicia felt that her own life was slipping away without any of the normal consolations that made human existence worthwhile. Sarah Webb had done her best to contribute a lot of small happinesses to her goddaughter's lot and, without her, Alicia felt a terrible mental loneliness which even Polly could not fill.

Uncle Harold came periodically to check her accounts and discuss house repairs and any other small needs. It was he who first suggested a professional nurse to help Alicia with her mother. Remembering Nurse Trill, Alicia felt that such a person might only drive her mother to even greater perversity and stubbornness, so she replied uneasily that she did not think that the time had yet come for such help. 'Fanny is better with her than any nurse would be,' she added. 'Between the three of us we are managing – and Dr Willis is very helpful.'

V

Not too long after Sarah Webb died, when Spring bulbs were beginning to flower in the Woodmans' garden, Alicia helped Polly to peg out newly-washed sheets on the clothes-line. Both women were suddenly petrified by a great roar just above their heads. As Polly told Fanny, 'We dropped a sheet on the lawn and ran like 'ell into the house. There were an aeroplane right over our heads – could've nearly touched it. We'd never seen anything like it before – scared stiff we was.'

Upstairs, a terrified Fanny had held a panic-stricken Elizabeth firmly in her chair. 'Thought it were an earthquake,' she responded to Polly.

'Bloody madman! Ought to be put in Bedlam,' fumed Fanny, when, the next day they saw pictures of the plane in the newspaper. 'Ought to make a law about them.'

'Really, Fanny dear. There's no need for bad language. Aeroplanes are a fad – young men are always trying dangerous things,' Alicia rebuked her.

As if to belie her words about a passing fad, the selfsame young man, Mr Henry G. Melly, flew his plane safely to Manchester and back, the following day.

'He'll fall out one of these days,' prophesied Fanny, shaking out dried towels as if she were shaking the young man for his foolhardiness.

In a port, the loss of men and ships at sea was common news, but, as Alicia said, 'Nobody has to risk his neck in a noisy thing like a plane while we've ships and trains.'

'Nor drive them motor cars,' interjected Fanny huffily. 'Going around as if they owned the street. I were nearly run over the other day – and the horses is frightened to death by them – rear up, they do, as soon as they hear one comin'.'

'Upper Canning Street is getting quite busy, and I'm always afraid of Mama, somehow, wandering out and being killed,' Alicia replied, giving voice to an anxiety which had been with her for some time.

'Na, I bin keepin' the door locked – and I always keep the key in me apron pocket – never put it down anywhere; so I can answer the door quick enough and yet make sure your Mam can't pick it up,' Fanny assured her briskly.

VI

It was Fanny who returned from her afternoon off, one August day, looking like a sparrow that had been mauled by a cat.

Her best black straw hat was a tattered wreck and her greying hair hung like rat-tails down her back. She sobbed to Polly that she had been caught up in a fracas outside the *Legs o' Man* public house in Lime Street. Some railwaymen hanging round the station had begun to bait the constables on duty there. The police were nervous because there had been riots in the city as a result of a railway strike.

'Them buggers waded in with their truncheons and I got it. Me back hurts like hell, it does.' Polly had never seen her friend so upset. Fanny's face was drawn with pain, as she went on aggrievedly, 'And I were only talkin' to ever such a nice fella as was down there to see what was happening.'

'Come on up to your bedroom,' Polly suggested, 'and take your frock off so I can have a look.' But when, upstairs, she quickly commenced to unhook Fanny's print summer dress, the woman cried out in pain.

Polly stopped immediately. 'Maybe you should go to the Dispensary,' she suggested uneasily.

'Not me! They might send me to the 'ospital.'

'Well, look. You sit down here and I'll go and tell Allie. She's with her Mam. I think you've broken somethin'.'

Very concerned about her old friend, Alicia sent Polly for Dr Willis. She dared not leave her mother unattended, so Fanny sat alone in her bedroom, weeping with pain.

Dr Willis was annoyed at being asked to come to a servant at nine o'clock at night and sent his young partner, Dr Bell.

Though glad to see him, Fanny was horrified when he calmly took out a pair of scissors and cut her out of her best summer frock. She gaped at him and yelped, 'Wot you done?'

'You're more important than the dress, Miss Barnett,' he comforted her, as he peeled the dress back to expose purple bruises on Fanny's back.

As his delicate fingers probed round the wounds, Fanny sniffed back her tears. Nobody had ever called her Miss Barnett before.

He turned to Polly. 'I don't think anything is broken. Have you any arnica in the house?'

'Aye. Miss Alicia's bound to have some.'

'Bathe Miss Barnett's back with it, and I will give you a little laudanum to help her sleep tonight and tomorrow night.' He took a tiny bottle from his bag and dripped a little liquid into it from a bigger bottle. He corked it down firmly and handed it to Fanny.

'Thank you, sir.'

'Take care of yourself, Miss Barnett, and don't get caught in any more riots. You'll feel discomfort for some days, but the bruises and cuts will heal.'

Fanny looked up at him with wonderment, her pain forgotten. What a lovely man! *Miss Barnett!*

The encounter sparked a devotion which was to last her into old age. Many, many years later, she was to become his housekeeper.

On his way out, the young doctor met Alicia standing anxiously at the door of her mother's bedroom. Polly introduced them and Alicia shook his hand.

He looked at her with little interest, as the full glare of the evening sun struck her through the landing window. It showed him a very tidy, slim woman of almost no colouring, a firm mouth clamped too tightly, as if she, too, might be in pain. After he had answered her anxious inquiries about Fanny, he mentioned that Dr Willis had asked him to find out how her mother was, since he had not seen her for several weeks.

Alicia sighed. 'She is, as usual, totally forgetful. We never leave her alone, except when she has had her usual dose to make her sleep at night.'

She watched him descend the stairs with Polly and then went back to pick up her mother's sewing, books and jigsaw puzzles with which she had tried to amuse her.

Her mother's coordination was becoming worse, she thought sadly. She would put a few stitches into a petticoat that had lain in the sewing basket for months, and then drop it irritably because she could not place the stitches as she wanted. She could still occasionally manage a simple jigsaw puzzle, when someone sat by her and encouraged her to try, but her only true enjoyment, as far as Alicia could see, was to listen to her playing light classical pieces on the drawing-room piano. So every afternoon, of late, she had seated Elizabeth in an easy chair while she herself played. Somewhere in the recesses of her mother's damaged brain there seemed to linger a memory, not much more than an instinct, that the piano represented much happier times, when Elizabeth had played at parties she had given. Perhaps, thought Alicia, Andrew Crossing had stood by her to turn the pages for her. Nothing, however, would persuade Elizabeth to try to play once more, and as the music swirled around her, tears would run slowly down her mottled cheeks.

Alicia allowed her mind to stray from her tidying up and her sleeping mother, while she considered Dr Bell. She could not remember ever speaking to such a young professional man and she wondered if he were married. Then she told herself savagely not to be such a fool. She was not free to marry while her mother lived. Furthermore, she was now twenty-five years old, too old for marriage.

25

I

One February morning in 1913, Alicia received a registered letter from a West Kirby lawyer, informing her of the death of her Aunt Clara. He enclosed a freshwater pearl necklace left to her by her Aunt. She had died, he wrote, from a severe bout of influenza and he regretted having to send her such bad tidings. As the Executor of her Will, he needed to know the names and addresses of any other relations who should be informed.

Alicia berated herself for not going to see her Aunt on her afternoons off; but she had flinched at spending her precious few hours of freedom sitting beside yet another invalid, and she had kept deferring a visit. Now it was too late. She had, however, written to her at Christmas and Easter, ever since she had been a small girl, which was how the lawyer must have found her address. The fact that he needed the addresses of other members of the family indicated that Aunt Clara had not received letters from either Florence or Charles.

With tears in her eyes, she wrote to the lawyer and gave the addresses of Florence, Charles, Uncle Harold and, finally, of Uncle Henry in Ceylon, who she believed was the final inheritor of her maternal grandfather's estate. Uncle Henry, she remembered with wry amusement, had never been known to write to anybody and she had no recollection of his visiting her mother – he must have come home at one point or another, she ruminated, but she could not remember his doing so. She wondered if he had managed to live until now – long enough to collect a part of the Reversionary Interest from his father's Estate now available to him.

Alicia also wrote immediately to Charles, who went to West Kirby to check that his aunt had received proper burial and a suitable monument. The lawyer had seen to both matters, as instructed by Aunt Clara in her Will. 'Do this, so that I am no trouble to my young relations,' she had told the lawyer.

On his return, Charles came straight to see his mother and Alicia.

'Have you told Mother?' he asked Alicia.

'No. I didn't think I could make her understand.'

In some dim way, Elizabeth always seemed to recognize her son, and, when he told her gently about her sister, Clara's, death, she seemed to understand, because she exclaimed quite clearly, 'Oh, no!' She did not cry, however, and was soon talking in a fuddled way to herself.

'What about Florence?' Charles inquired.

'I thought I'd let the lawyer do it. I felt I could not stand Florence gushing all over Mother, who might be frightened and yet not understand what had happened. Flo always flounders so – perhaps because she's so tired.'

'She's not really tired,' he replied with a grin. 'She used to be worn out with the children. But since they left home, she is become pretty spry. She still runs all the church's women's groups. She just takes to her couch when Clarence is at home.'

'What on earth for?' Alicia was startled by this peculiar behaviour.

'Well, you *know*. Our Clarence always wants to leap into bed, even at his age. And Flo isn't the type.'

'Charles, I think you are being very vulgar.'

'No, I'm not. It's a reality of life – and it's great fun, if you haven't had absurd, old-fashioned ideas put into your head by a lot of school ma'ams – and so many women have.'

'Charles, you're talking to a single woman who knows nothing about the secrets of marriage.'

'Sorry.' He grinned down at her, and she felt suddenly left out, deprived of the knowledge of what fun was.

What was fun? Though Polly had explained matters of sex quite baldly to her, she had not suggested that there was particular *fun* in it. What was she missing?

She looked back on the dragging years of her adult life, spent trying to care for her parents. Now she had given up even trying to entertain her mother, which, at one time, when she had got a response from Elizabeth, had been an entertainment for herself. Now life was a steady, deadening routine, enlivened only by her afternoon off.

To try to keep Alicia from going out of her mind herself, Polly increasingly encouraged her to do all the shopping and go for walks in the park. When Mrs Hunter invited her to tea next door, she would say firmly, 'Don't worry about your Mam. Fanny's very good with her. You go for an hour.' Polly herself rarely went out, except to visit her sister, Mary, on her day off or perhaps to go with her to a music hall.

With the same upright carriage as her mother, Alicia would walk through Princes Park, even onwards to Sefton Park, a nondescript, middle-aged-looking woman, plainly dressed in a long grey skirt and a matching three-quarter length coat nipped in at the waist. Her fair hair was covered by out-of-date hats, trimmed and retrimmed with bits of satin culled from the boundless odds and ends of her mother's old clothes stacked in trunks in the attic. Two large hatpins anchored the hats to her head and were regarded by her, as by most women, as a useful weapon if attacked. But none of the young bucks who strolled through the park at the weekends would make a pass at such a prim-looking lady, and, anyway, the park keepers were always in evidence to keep order in their domain.

Other residents of Upper Canning Street had become accustomed to seeing her in the street and nearby shops. They would bow politely and pass on, though many of them had never heard the scandal of her origins. They had, however, heard of her mad mother. As one sharp-tongued inhabitant put it, 'It's a most peculiar household, I hear. A crazy old woman and a couple of servants who don't know their place and live as if they were part of the family; the craziness must run *in* the family. And then Colonel Milfort used to live next door to them – and we *all* know about him. Now there are the Bottomleys there – a very loud, vulgar family – not nice at all; I don't allow my children to mix with theirs. The whole of that end of the street seems to have gone down dreadfully.'

So nobody spoke to Alicia.

Fanny visited the other maids up and down the street and often talked to the Bottomleys' skivvy, as they both scoured their respective front steps. Fanny called the neighbours a lot of jangling old biddies, and she would throw her scrubbing brush into the bucket of dirty water at the bottom of the steps, and say viciously sometimes, 'I'd like to scupper 'em. Our Missus and Miss Alicia is the very salt.'

In the hope of getting some help and, perhaps, a little social life for Alicia, Uncle Harold went out to visit Florence, without result.

'They are simply too busy to take on anything else,' Alicia told him gently, when he mentioned his visit and his reason for it.

'They're simply too selfish,' he replied downrightly. He had tried without success to persuade his wife to invite Alicia for a little visit, to give her a holiday. His wife had loftily refused, saying, 'She is not a member of the family. Why should I be bothered with such a bore?'

For the sake of peace in his household, he had not pressed the point. He had said soberly to Alicia, 'You're carrying a very heavy load for the family. And anything I can do to lighten it, I will do.'

She had kissed the old man impulsively, and he had gone red in the face with embarrassment.

II

One evening, as her mother continued her eternal pacing up and down the room and Alicia watched her as she sewed herself a blouse, her mother began to mumble and tears to course down her face.

It was not the first time in her slow decline that Alicia had seen her weep, but it grieved her, and she jumped quickly from her chair and ran to Elizabeth to put her arms around her.

Elizabeth recoiled as if she had been attacked and pushed Alicia away. Then she backed away from her daughter, like a frightened cat. Shocked at her obvious alarm, Alicia stood staring uncertainly at her.

After a few seconds, Elizabeth resumed her unsteady pacing, and coming back across the room, she finally faced Alicia head on. Not knowing what to do, Alicia tensely held her ground.

Elizabeth, seeing her full face, said brokenly, through her tears, 'Alicia, dear.'

'Mama,' Alicia responded tentatively, and moved slowly towards her mother. They embraced warmly. Alicia was crying. Her mother had never held her like this before.

'I must have scared her when I ran to her,' she chided herself.

'When is Andrew coming?' Elizabeth asked, as she slowly loosed her hold on Alicia. She spoke much more clearly than she had done for a long time.

Perplexed, Alicia answered her, 'I don't know, Mama.' She slowly took out her handkerchief and wiped her mother's wet cheeks.

Andrew? Andrew Crossing, of course.

Deadly curious, she asked, 'Do you miss him, Mama?'

But Elizabeth's tattered brain had closed off. She smiled her usual charming smile and turned to walk some more.

Thereafter, Alicia always moved very carefully in her mother's presence and instructed Fanny and Polly to do the same.

It was, however, the last time that Elizabeth recognized her daughter, and, as Alicia steadied her mother when she walked, fed her, washed her, dressed her and dealt with her total incontinence, she would weep herself and cry, 'How long, O Lord, how long?'

III

Alicia and Polly were great newspaper readers; the arrival of the morning paper was often the only interesting event of their day. Fanny, however, had never learned to read and she got *her* news from the seamen and dockers she picked up around the Pier Head on her days off. The seamen sailed in rusty freighters to Hamburg and Trieste, to Istanbul, Odessa and Murmansk, to Madras and Vladivostock, and every port in between. Though they did not see a great deal of the places in which they docked, they picked up gossip in the bars and streets. When they returned home and had exhausted their complaints about women, and the food in the ships of their various great companies, they enlarged upon what they had seen and heard abroad. So it was Fanny who first said that the constant quarrels between the Balkan States would lead to a very big war. Alicia and Polly pooh-poohed the idea; the only place to be afraid of was Germany, and the Kaiser would never actually make war on his English royal relations.

On June 28th, 1914, Francis Ferdinand, heir to the throne of Austria –Hungary, and his wife, Sophia, were assassinated by Bosnian students while on a visit to Sarajevo, a lovely, almost oriental town, which few people in Britain had ever heard of.

Absorbed in their daily struggle to cope with Elizabeth, Polly, Fanny and Alicia were unaware that the death of this dogmatic prince would turn their lives upside down. They spent the last fragile days of the world they knew encouraging and half-carrying Elizabeth downstairs to the garden, to get the sun. The weather was perfect, the half-wild roses ran riot up the brick walls of the garden and Alicia wished, as always, that she had time to keep the garden tidy.

After they had set Elizabeth down in a chair on the overgrown path, she seemed to enjoy the warmth and colour and forgot her earlier intransigence. She leaned back and watched small, fat clouds drift across the sky. Alicia cut a rose, removed its thorns and gave it to her to hold.

Polly sat down on the back steps and began to turn the pages of the evening newspaper, and as she perused the headlines, she said uneasily, 'Aye, I'm that glad our Billy's away in Canada. I wouldn't want 'im in a war – though he's no kitten by this time. Same age as you, add a year – too old to fight.'

Since her mother seemed at peace, Alicia knelt down and began to weed round a clump of delphiniums. 'Billy seems to have done awfully well in Alberta, doesn't he?'

'Aye, he's a bright lad is our Billy, and he always did love horses. Now he's got land to breed them on, he'll not look back.'

Alicia smiled. 'He'll be sending for you at last, Pol.'

'Not he. He's forgotten wot he promised; and anyways I wouldn't leave you, luv.'

IV

It was in January 1915, that Fanny dropped a bombshell.

After Elizabeth had been put to bed, the three of them were seated round the gas-fire in the morning-room. Between the two maids, on the floor, sat a jug of ale which Fanny had fetched from the nearest public house; it was a custom which Alicia had never queried because the maids had nearly always enjoyed an evening pint together.

Fanny cleared her throat and, without preamble, announced, 'I'm goin' into munitions next week.'

Alicia's heart missed a beat and the little colour in her cheeks fled. Polly put down her glass and asked belligerently, 'Wot you mean?'

'I'm goin' to fill shells with – well, with whatever they fill shells with.'

'You're going to *leave* us, Fan?' Alicia was incredulous.

Fanny shuffled her feet uneasily and her ale slopped into the hearth. She cursed under her breath. Then she replied steadily, though averting her eyes from Alicia, 'Yes, Miss Allie. They pay like a ship's crew on leave – you wouldn't believe how much. And I haven't got nothing saved for me old age, except what your Pa left me.'

'You're crazy,' Polly told her sourly. She took a sip from her glass, and then said, 'It'll cost you more 'n you earn to live.'

'No, it won't. I bin talking it over with some of the other maids what has left – they've got good clothes and all from it.'

Alicia was suddenly terrified. Suppose Polly left as well! What would she do? She glanced nervously at the older woman and, as if she had read her mind, Polly turned to her. 'Don't take on, luv. Your old Polly's got more sense.'

Though her lips were trembling, Alicia smiled at her. But Fanny, also, was a most important part of her life and she was very fond of her. She gave a quivering sigh and said, 'I'm really sad, Fan. I know we don't pay you an awful lot. But you can be sure of it every week – and you've got a good bed and food – and uniform.'

Fanny shifted uneasily in her chair and put out a hand to touch Alicia's knee, as she replied, 'I know, Miss, and don't think I'm not grateful. But this is a chance for me to put something by – and I don't never want to see the inside of a workhouse again – I seen enough when I were a kid.'

Alicia tried to still the frightened beat of her heart and could not. The war was suddenly in her own home, and she did not know what to do.

'Think it over, Fan, before you make up your mind,' she urged through dry lips.

'I thunk about it, Miss. I thunk about it a long time. Mebbe Mr Harold can get you some help.' She took a sip of ale, and then went on a little defiantly, 'And somebody's got to fill shells.'

Reluctantly, Alicia agreed.

This idea of helping in the war had already begun to percolate into kitchens and drawing-rooms. Women rolled bandages and knitted bala- clavas and gloves for soldiers. A few brave women had volunteered to drive ambulances in France; and the newspapers had reported that women, dragging their long skirts behind them in the mud, had helped with the winter ploughing, because so many farm labourers had simply left the fields to volunteer.

Alicia got up from her easy chair and began to pace up and down the room. 'I'll miss you terribly, Fan,' she said suddenly, and burst into tears. Fanny whipped out of her chair and put her arms round her, and they cried together, while Polly stared into her ale glass. She was so tired already. How would they manage?

'I'll come to see you both,' Fanny was promising.

A fat lot of help that would be, Polly thought sourly.

26

I

With Fanny gone, the dining-room was left to gather dust. Cooking was reduced to the simplest recipes.

In fact, shopping for food began to take up more time than the cooking of it. The shops were short of many items, and of staff, too, as more men and women went into factories; people were not yet reduced to queuing, but they had to wait longer to be served and often had to carry their parcels home, because errand boys tended to serve behind the counter, instead of doing deliveries.

Elizabeth's physical health deteriorated, but she could still heave herself out of bed and walk, and had, therefore, to be watched all day. Time off for both Alicia and Polly became a distant memory. Nevertheless, Alicia decided that to improve their diet, she would try to dig a part of the garden and put in some lettuces and tomatoes. One day in early March 1915, she put on a pair of boots and her shortest skirt and began to clear an old flower bed, while Polly ironed linen sheets in the library, now her mistress's bedroom, so that she could keep an eye on the stricken woman and get some work done at the same time.

Alicia had just driven a spade into the heavy earth, when a shocked, male voice with a strong Liverpool accent stopped her. 'Miss! You shouldn't be doin' that!'

Frightened, she turned. A soldier in an infantry private's uniform stood behind her, cap in hand. She pushed back the old straw hat she was wearing and surveyed him coldly. 'Who are you and what are you doing in my garden?' she snapped as strongly as she could.

The man's face, already reddened by exposure, turned an even richer colour. 'Sorry, Ma'am. I come through the garden door. I come to see Polly. I'm her brother.'

'Billy!' She let the spade drop, rubbed her dirty hands together and then held out one to be shaken. 'How nice to see you. Polly will be thrilled. We both look forward to your letters so much. What are you doing here?'

'I come over to join the Army, Miss. Didn't write 'cos I reckoned I'd be here almost as soon as a letter.' He shook her hand shyly.

'Polly's ironing in Mama's room,' she told him. 'We have to watch Mama all the time, so we take work into her bedroom and do it there.' She smiled at him. 'Come in.'

She led him into the house, stepping calmly out of her muddy boots and putting on her slippers, as she entered, something no lady would do in front of a gentleman. Billy carefully wiped his boots on the tattered doormat. As she took him through the old kitchen, which smelled of damp and mould, and up the back stairs, she asked him, 'Have you joined the British Army – or are you with a Canadian contingent?'

'I come over with some horses for the British Army, Miss, about six months ago, and joined the South Lancs. What a voyage, Miss! Never again – lost 'alf the horses, with broken legs.'

She stopped in the hall, and told him almost coquettishly, 'Billy! You fibbed. It doesn't take six months for a letter to come from Alberta. You should have let us know you were here.'

'Well, Miss, I thought Polly'd be all upset if she knew I were in the Army – thought it better to show meself when I were settled in, like. She's goin' to be as cross as two sticks, anyway,' he said sheepishly.

'I doubt it.' The frank, light eyes surveyed him and his clumsy uniform. 'I think she's going to be very proud.' She opened the door of the library, and said to Polly, 'Come out a moment, Polly. I've a surprise for you.'

Polly glanced at Elizabeth, for the moment sitting quietly in a chair by the window. She put down her iron and came to the door. Billy could barely restrain his sense of shock when he saw the pale, gaunt, grey-haired woman. Polly?

But it *was* Polly and she had clasped him in her arms and was weeping on his shoulder. 'Billy, luv. Billy.'

'Take him into the morning-room, Polly. Make some tea,' Alicia urged her, as she took off the sackcloth apron she had been wearing. 'I'll stay with Mama.' She felt suddenly left out and wished that she cared for Charles like that.

With his arm round Polly's waist, Billy turned to her and said, 'If you'll excuse me for sayin' so, Miss, don't you do no more diggin'. I'll come over tomorrer in civvies, and I'll do it for you in a trice. I got three days' leave and me sister, Mary, isn't goin' to want me round the house all the time.'

'That's very kind of you,' she responded warmly, with the same grace her mother had had.

'Yes, you let 'im do it, Allie. Keep 'im out of mischief.'

Billy's dark eyebrows went up in surprised query. No *Miss Alicia*? Just Allie?

Alicia smiled, and went quietly into her mother's room and shut the door. Elizabeth, disturbed, turned and burst into angry incoherent speech.

In the shabby morning-room, Billy put his peaked cap down on to the sideboard. 'Is the Missus still ill?' he asked.

'Sit down, luv. You don't know the half of it.' Polly gestured to an easy chair. His question opened a dam, and Polly poured out the story of Elizabeth and of Alicia's bleak life looking after her and after Humphrey. Though she did not complain about her own harsh life, it was half an hour before she remembered to get up and make some tea.

Early the following morning, while Alicia was quickly putting Elizabeth's breakfast tray together, before the invalid woke up from her drugged sleep, she pushed back the lace curtain and peeped through the kitchenette window. Outside, there was a light mist which made the garden look soft and vague. Through it, however, she could see Billy digging with an even, methodical rhythm which she envied. She smiled.

'Will he have had breakfast?' she asked Polly, who was stirring a pan of porridge on the gas-stove.

'I doubt it,' replied Polly glumly. 'Our Mary don't have that much, what with the rent of her new Corpy house and her hubby drunk half the time.'

'Well, ask him in to breakfast – there's lots of porridge – and make some toast.'

Later on, when Alicia came back to the kitchenette, to eat her breakfast at its little table while Polly watched Elizabeth, he was still sitting, elbows on the table, lingering over a cup of tea. As Alicia entered, he hastily stood up.

'Sit down. Be comfortable, Billy,' she told him, an unusual cheerfulness in her voice, as she helped herself to porridge from the pan on the stove. It was exciting to have a visitor, other than Dr Bell or Uncle Harold.

As she sat down at the table, she glanced at him. This morning, he wore a pair of breeches with boots and leather gaiters. Knotted round his neck was a red and white cotton handkerchief. His eyes were brown, she noted, narrowed like a sailor's, as if used to seeing great distances in a bright light. The mouth was wide, quirked up at the corners to suggest much laughter. The sleeves of his union shirt were rolled up to reveal hairy forearms tanned by strong sunlight. As she began to eat, he hastily rolled down his shirt sleeves and reached for a heavy, plaid jacket with leather patches on the elbows. When he moved, a collar stud flashed below a strong, red neck. On a drain-board by the sink lay his dark, flat cap. He smelled palpably of the stable, and she

733

remembered that he had come across the Atlantic with a herd of horses.

Feeling suddenly a little shy in such silent male company, she urged him to have another cup of tea. She filled his cup and poured one for herself.

Except that she had filled out and become a woman, she was very like the child he remembered, he thought as he considered her out of the corner of his eye. Her hands were red from work, but the rest of her skin was still incredibly white; there was none of the leathery look of Prairie women. There were a few lines on her face; yet her mouth, pink as a white kitten's nose, was as innocent-looking as that of the child he recalled so vividly.

He suddenly became aware that she was staring at him over the rim of her cup, alert grey eyes making him feel uneasy and tongue-tied. She had overcome her nervousness and was thanking him earnestly for digging the garden. She did not offer to pay him and he was grateful for her not doing so; it confirmed to him in a subtle way his status as an up-and-coming young man.

Her next words, innocently spoken, put him back in his slums, and he was secretly angry. She said, 'Do you remember when you used to come here as a boy and Polly squeezed some breakfast out of Mrs Tibbs for you?'

'Yes, Ma'am,' he replied stiffly. She passed the sugar bowl to him and he took some and then stirred his tea quickly. And I've come a long way since then, Queen, he told himself crossly. And no matter what she may be thinking, I'm sitting here with her as if I were an old friend. And she int much different from Edmonton women I know – she's not the usual stiff madam as lives round here. I remember her like I remember nobody else except me Mam, jumping down from a tree and showing the longest legs and the prettiest little ass I ever saw in a pair of divided pantaloons.

'Are you still working at the stables – I mean when you're not in the army?'

He looked surprised and, with a spoon halfway to her mouth, she chuckled. 'You must forgive me, but I always saw your letters – in fact, I often wrote part of the replies, until Polly got good at writing.'

'Did you really, Miss?'

'Yes. It was like having a pen-friend.'

He was nonplussed at this revelation and was not sure how to reply. Finally, he said carefully, 'Well, I hope we are friends, Miss.'

Alicia smiled at him, as if amused at his embarrassment. 'Of course we're friends. You're Polly's brother and Polly's been like a mother to me.'

He slowly put down his cup, proffered a hand scarred from old blisters and she took it and they solemnly shook hands.

They grinned at each other like two small boys making a blood oath. 'Now we're really friends,' said Alicia, and then she reminded him of her question about the stable.

'Yes, Miss. Me job's there for when I go home. It's not a great job, but it brings in ready cash for setting up on the quarter-section, and it's kept me, meanwhile. I got a hay crop last year and some grain. And if you'll forgive me mentioning such a thing, I can't keep me mares in foal fast enough to meet the demand.'

'Do you live there?'

'No. I live over the stable. I got a Metis family livin' in a one-room cabin out there, lookin' after it while I'm away, and Ernie, me friend wot owns the stable, has promised to go out and check on 'im, an' all.'

A little later, he went away to spend some time with his other sister, Mary, while her husband was at work. He returned in the evening, however, and screwed some cup hooks into a shelf for Polly, while she prepared dinner; without asking Alicia, she made enough for four.

'What happened to that Chink you lent money to?' she asked idly.

'Huang? I didn't lend him the money 'cos he wasn't sure he could pay back. I bought a half share in 'is café when he were fairly on the rocks – it were only a little hole in the wall, but not a few bachelors used to eat there. So I took a chance on him. You should see it now – quite respectable, it is – fourteen tables and a coffee bar – built 'em all meself. 'Is wife and son and daughter help 'im, and sometimes of a Saturday night I give 'im a hand in the kitchen. Full, most nights, he is. Pays me me share every three months on the dot. We don't make a lot – but, you see, one day we will.'

'Strewth! Why on earth did you enlist – you got more'n plenty to do?'

'Well, you can get a white feather handed to you in Edmonton, same as you can in Liverpool, if you look young enough and aren't in uniform – and I didn't want no bloody feathers. So I talked it over with Ernie and with Huang and then, when there was a herd of horses goin' on the train to Winnipeg, I come over for nothin' for takin' care of 'em. I wanted to be in a Liverpool Regiment – and they was recruitin' for the South Lancs when I got here – and I thought that'd do.'

'Blow the feathers! You was plain stupid, our Billy. You should've stayed out of it and sold them horses and made money out of 'em. You could get yourself killed.'

'Well, this little lot's not going to last long. Finished by Christmas, they reckon. Then I'll take you back with me. You'll like it there. You'd be married quick as a wink, if you want to – lots of fellas there, not so many girls.'

'Don't be daft. Anyways, how can I leave our Allie before her Mam dies? The old girl could live a few years yet and Allie can't manage by herself.' She lifted the lid from a pan of potatoes and tested their readiness with a fork. Then she went on, 'It's so unfair on Allie, 'cos her Mam never really cared a damn about her – it were me that brought her up.'

He was silent for a moment, as he watched her drain the potatoes over the sink. Then he said slowly, 'I'd like to take Miss Allie as well, if she'd have me.'

'What?' Polly whirled round to look at him, steaming pan in hand. 'Now I know you're daft, lad. You don't know 'er – and she's a lady.'

'Not too much of a lady,' replied Billy shrewdly. 'She's got more'n a bit of you in 'er. And things is different in Alberta. The way I'm goin', I could use a wife what can hold her head up amongst the best. And it int true I don't know her; we used to work in the garden together with that ould gardener fella. I thought she were a princess – and I still do.'

Dumbfounded, Polly stared at him, her steaming potatoes forgotten. 'You serious?'

''Course, I am. I always wanted to do it. Only I thought she'd sure enough be married before I could give 'er the kind of home I want to give 'er. Even now, I can't give her anythin' grand – but I'm gettin' there, and I'm still not so old.'

'Well, she int married.' Polly plunked the saucepan she was holding on to the draining board and picked up a fork to mash the potatoes. 'She's never had a dog's chance of gettin' married; her parents saw to that – she's been too useful to 'em.' Then she said carefully, 'You'd better wait till you've finished winning the war, before you ask 'er.'

He stretched himself, and said, 'Oh, aye. I don't want to leave 'er a widow.'

Polly shook her fork at him. 'Now, remember, I don't know what she'll say – because she'll think first of her Mam – she knows where her duty lies. So don't take it too personal, like, if she says No.'

II

Billy's sister, Mary, prevailed upon him to stay with her on the last day of his leave, so he did not come again to see Polly and Alicia. A couple of days later, however, they received a letter from him saying that he was to be trained as a sniper, 'Seeing as I'm used to handling a hunting rifle.'

'I thought only rich people went huntin',' Polly remarked, as she put the letter down on the kitchen table.

'Well, he told me when he was here that he and his old pedlar often fed themselves by hunting or trapping.' Alicia picked up Elizabeth's breakfast tray to carry it into her room.

'Hm, Canada must be a proper queer place. Don't they have no butchers nor fishmongers?'

Billy never went for his training. With a number of other ill-trained men, he was rushed across the Channel and found himself with Haig's 1st Army, ready to attack a place called Neuve Chapelle. At first it seemed that the proposed breakthrough across the German lines would succeed; and a sickened, terrified Billy was thankful to a long-forgotten God for his survival. But his little unit ran out of ammunition, and the curtain of artillery fire which, on the third day, was supposed to soften up the enemy line, faltered for the same reason. Pinned down in a shell hole by the weight of German fire, Billy lay beside a weeping wounded man. With his field dressing, he did his best to staunch the blood from a ghastly rip in the man's back, to no purpose. He died, and Billy lay by him while machine-gun bullets rattled overhead. He himself screamed, when a swordlike piece of flack smashed into his left shoulder.

Desperate for help, he managed to inch himself out of the hole and then fainted. After dark, he was found by a Canadian medical orderly crawling round, looking for the wounded amongst the dead.

He languished for some months in a London military hospital, while they tried to save his arm. As his next of kin, Mary received a postcard saying where he was. Whey-faced, she hurried over to see Polly. Because her husband tended to beat her if she left home, she rarely visited Polly and the very presence of her, hammering on the back door, indicated disaster.

Once he was able to move about, Billy wandered round the over-crowded ward and helped the nurses to dish out food to their patients. From other outraged wounded, he learned that the shortage of ammunition had been caused by strikes and slowdowns ordered by trade unions seeking to oust unskilled people, like Fanny, from the factories.

'Ought to put the bloody skunks in the Front Line and see how they like it with no ammo,' he raged as his useless left arm reminded him of a life full of special problems to a man with only one working arm. He was suddenly glad that he would be going back to Canada. 'Who needs mates who'd betray yez like that?' he asked himself bitterly.

A worried Polly asked Alicia if she could possibly manage Elizabeth alone for one whole day while she went to London to see Billy. She had decided that this was a time when one of her long-hoarded sovereigns had to be spent.

Alicia agreed immediately, and Polly set out with a little basket of precious butter and sugar and some apples from the garden, to augment Billy's spartan hospital diet.

III

It was an extremely difficult day for Alicia. The moment she left the invalid to prepare a meal or go to the bathroom, Elizabeth would begin an unsteady perambulation through the house. The weather was cold and if Alicia turned off the gas-fires, Elizabeth became chilled; if she left them on, she feared that her mother might brush against them and set her skirts aflame; Elizabeth was, in any case, capable of turning them on and leaving them unlit.

At one point, Alicia guided her mother into the kitchenette and sat her down on a chair, so that she could prepare dinner and watch the older woman at the same time. Elizabeth objected violently to the strange, little room and the unaccustomed chair, and she had to be taken back to her library-bedroom. In despair, Alicia tied her into a small easy chair, with the aid of a couple of long scarves, and left her there; she shrieked steadily until Alicia returned with a tray of hastily assembled cold food.

She gave her protesting mother her bedtime sedative a little early and thought frantically that, if anything ever happened to Polly, she would have to find a nurse to help her. 'But where would I get a nurse in wartime?' she wondered hopelessly. 'They'll all be nursing the wounded.'

It was nearly midnight before she heard a key in the front lock. She ran to the door, to meet an equally exhausted Polly.

She helped Polly off with her coat and hat and took her into the morning-room. Then she brought her a tray of tea and sandwiches, which she had made ready as soon as Elizabeth had gone to sleep.

As Polly thankfully drank her tea, she described a white wraith of a man, still recovering from losing a great deal of blood and still in bandages. Her eyes filled with tears. 'They'll discharge 'im in Liverpool 'cos he volunteered here. He's finished for the Army.'

Alicia had picked up the sock she was knitting for one of Mrs Hunter's many warwork projects, but now she laid it in her lap. 'Poor man!' she exclaimed. It hurt her to think of the sturdy, self-confident digger of her garden being crippled. 'Life is too hard,' she meditated wretchedly. 'Even without a war.' Then, trying to be practical, she asked, 'Just how badly wounded is he?'

'It don't look as if 'is left arm is going to be much use to 'im. The doctor were talkin' of takin' it off, at first. But he wasn't havin' r ne of that. He hurts somethin' crool.'

'Will they send him to a Convalescent Home?'

'They might. Otherwise, he could go to Mary's while they fix up 'is pension. He says he's got to find his own way to Canada 'cos he enlisted here.' Polly leaned back in her chair to rest her tired head and a tear trickled down her cheek. 'I'm afraid of Mary's hubbie, Mike, kickin' up a fine to-do, if he stays long with them. It were bad enough when he spent his leave there. Mike's got a filthy temper.'

Alicia leaned over to clasp Polly's hand, 'Now, don't take on so, Polly dear. We'll think of something.'

While the older woman sniffed back her tears and poured herself another cup of tea, Alicia looked out of the window at the darkened garden and remembered contented afternoons helping Billy and Mr Bittle do the weeding. She turned back to Polly, and asked slowly, 'I wonder if Billy would like to stay with us while he's convalescing?'

Polly's head jerked upwards in surprise, and Alicia went on, 'We've got oceans of room, Pol. I imagine he wouldn't need much actual nursing. Do you think his wound would need dressing?'

'I doubt they'll let him out of 'ospital till it's fairly healed.' Polly paused while she considered the suggestion. 'He'd need to be helped, washin' and dressin', till he learned to manage himself, poor kid. But Mr Harold would have a fit, wouldn't he?'

'I think he'd agree if we wanted it very badly; he's tremendously kind and he's never refused any reasonable request I've made. It's Charles who might try throwing his weight about – not that he can really say much; neither he nor Veronica has ever given us an iota of help. Of course, this is really Charles's house – but I think Uncle Harold could deal with him.'

'And Miss Florence and the Reverend?'

'To hell with both of them,' replied Alicia trenchantly. 'Poor Billy's worth ten of them.'

'Now, our Allie,' reproved Polly. 'She's your sister.'

'Fat lot she cares about me. It's you who've borne with me all these years. Without you, my life would have been impossible. And it's *your* brother who needs help now – and probably very little, at that. Rest and quiet and good food – and we can provide that. We're stuck in this house, anyway, with Mama.'

There was quiet, except for the popping of the gas-fire. Then Polly smiled and said, 'Aye, Allie, I'd be so grateful – and I'm sure our Billy will be, too.'

'Well, ask him if he'd like to come,' Alicia replied, with quiet determination; for once in her life, she thought savagely, she was going to do what she wanted to do.

To forestall any snubbing of Billy, Alicia wrote to Charles, telling him of Billy's wounding and discharge and saying that he would stay in the house with them until he could get a passage to Canada. She said firmly that it was the least they could do for a man who had come six thousand miles to help them win the war.

Charles was, at first, shocked that a servant's brother should stay in his house, but when he read Alicia's letter to a very stout and petulant Veronica, he was surprised that she replied calmly, 'Polly's brother? Well, I expect he'll behave like a servant and not step out of line or steal anything. And what can you say? A wounded man?' So Charles made no objection.

Drained, and haunted by the horror of what he had seen in France, a sad and disillusioned Billy came thankfully to them.

At first, he was very quiet and spent a good deal of his time either propped up with cushions in an easy chair in the dining-room window, where he was not disturbed by the rest of the household, or sitting in the little kitchen, talking to whichever woman happened to be there.

He accepted humbly Polly's aid to wash and dress and managed to make a joke with Alicia over her having to cut up his meat for him. With every other task, he struggled with his one good hand. When he first arrived, he was too shaky to walk far, but one dry winter day he went carefully down the front steps and walked along beside the railings of the houses until he had encircled the block. Several men spoke to him and a number of women smiled at him gently, paying their respects, in effect, to his hospital-blue uniform. Their kindness cheered him up, and the next morning Alicia found him clumsily pulling up the empty stalks of her Brussels sprout crop, his bad hand tucked into his jacket pocket.

On two occasions, Polly walked with him to the Royal Infirmary, for examination, and the doctors there encouraged him to try to use both arm and hand, without much success. He went before several military Boards for consideration for a pension. The officers on the Boards tended to bully, regarding him as a possible malcontent who would malinger in an effort to get a pension.

Finally, he stood up and told them to stuff their goddamned pension – he could manage without it. As soon as the doctors felt they had done all they could, he wanted his discharge, so that he could go back to a decent country. Leaving the Board unified in rage, he stalked out.

He had written to Ernie, who owned the Edmonton stable, and asked him to send him his fare back to Canada from the monies he was managing for him. Alicia slit the envelope of Ernie's reply for him, and he read the letter with obvious satisfaction. 'Says business is roaring along and to hurry home,' he told Alicia with a grin. 'Soon as I cash this Draft, I can pay something for me board,' he said.

'What rubbish,' Alicia responded roundly. 'Father's Estate is quite large, according to Uncle Harold; it can certainly feed a wounded soldier for a while. I am sure Uncle Harold would be most upset if I took a penny from you.'

They argued for a few minutes, but she could not be shifted, so he went out and, after cashing the Draft, bought her a huge bunch of flowers.

She looked at them in wonderment, when he handed them shyly to her. No one had ever bought her flowers before. 'Why, Billy! Thank you.' Impulsively, she leaned over the bouquet and kissed him on the cheek, and went away to find a vase, leaving him a little pink, and surprised that so little could make a woman happy.

He had found it hard to come to terms with the fact of having only one good arm, but, as his general health improved, he began to think constructively again and his natural optimism asserted itself. Polly was thankful to hear him whistling one morning after he had, for the first time, managed to shave himself, no easy task with a cut-throat razor.

Alicia noticed his effort, offered some iodine for one or two cuts and congratulated him on being able to do it. Now that he had the money for his return home, she meditated sadly, it was only a matter of time before he found a passage, and she realized she was going to miss him intensely. Never before had she enjoyed the company of someone her own age; she had always silently endured her noisy nephews and nieces. But Billy was fun, always ready to make a joke at his own predicament or to help her where he could, even to sitting with her rambling mother so that both Polly and she could enjoy one of Fanny's visits together.

Fanny was far from well. Her skin had turned an unhealthy yellow. 'It's the stuff we put in the shells,' she explained. 'But the money's good,' she added defensively.

'You look dreadfully tired,' Alicia told her, surprised that someone used to working very hard indeed could actually appear exhausted.

'I'm all right,' she replied heavily, and got up from her chair. 'I'll go in to see your Mama for a minute.'

IV

Another day, while Alicia fled to the grocer's and the butcher's, Billy asked if he could sit with Polly in Elizabeth's room.

'Oh, aye,' said Polly. 'She don't know anythin' and she's all washed and tidied. Come and 'ave a bit of a jangle.'

So Billy sat with her and watched her trim Brussels sprouts. He felt restless, anxious to go home and pick up his life again. But he was not yet legally discharged from the army, and he was having difficulty in booking a passage home; both problems would not be solved for some weeks.

'I heard Miss Allie playin' the pianner in the big front room upstairs,' he said idly.

'Oh, aye. She loves 'er pianner and 'er weeds; takes 'er mind off things.'

'Weeds?'

'Aye, she tries to study a bit after her Mam goes to bed 'cos when her Mam dies she'll have to earn her living as a governess, she says. She's determined she's not goin' to live with Mr Charles or Miss Florence – unpaid servant she'd be for the rest of her natural.' She carefully divested a sprout of its collar of yellow leaves, and then asked, 'Unless you want to take her to Canada, like you said?'

Billy did not answer, at first. Finally, he muttered reluctantly, 'I love her, Pol, and I want her, but I'm a proper nobody compared to her. And now, well, who'd want me?' Then he said, more cheerfully, 'But you should come back with me, Pol. You owe it to yourself to enjoy life a bit.'

'I couldn't leave the girl to look after this alone,' Polly responded, gesturing towards Elizabeth babbling in her chair by the window.

Billy did not reply. As his strength returned, he had begun to desire Alicia in a very active way. Yet, when he examined the cobbled scars all over his shoulder in the dressing-table mirror, and when he massaged his practically useless hand, he flinched at the idea of showing such a horrid sight to any woman, never mind a gentlewoman. And thinking of his small ranch, he wondered how he would ever manage horses with one arm.

Polly was fretting, 'I don't know what'll become of her once her Mam dies. Being a governess is worse'n bein' a maid, sometimes.'

'She could emigrate to Canada herself – and teach school,' Billy said suddenly. He gestured towards the woman in the window. 'You're always sayin' her Mam never did a thing for her and now she don't even know her. Any decent woman could look after Mrs Woodman; the girl's daft to stay with her, give her whole life to her – let her sister have a go for a change.' He leaned forward and tapped Polly's arm, 'Believe me, we're that short of women in some parts of Alberta, she could come out and teach school for a term – and I promise you she'll be nicely married before the next term begins. And you must come, too; there's many a settler as would be glad of a woman as smart as you.'

Polly laughed, 'Go on with with yez!'

'I'm tellin' you God's truth. And neither of you'd be lonely, 'cos there's lots of men as have wives wot play the pianner and know how to behave like her. You could live like a lady yourself, given a bit of luck.'

'You're kiddin'?'

'No, I'm not. The minute her Mam's laid to rest, you both emigrate. I'll help both of yez get settled.' Though he sounded light-hearted, he wanted to yell at the unfairness of life; the thought of watching Alicia walk up the aisle of McDougall Church with some smug lawyer or doctor made him burn with jealousy – but it was better than thinking of her being a governess in England. He got up from his chair and began to walk up and down, clasping his useless arm across his waist with his good arm.

V

Late that evening, as they prepared Elizabeth for her bath, Polly told her of Billy's suggestion. They were all together in the huge bathroom, and Elizabeth was protesting strongly, as Polly undressed her, while Alicia tested the heat of the bathwater by dipping her elbow in it. Though Elizabeth had grown very thin because they could not persuade her to eat very much, she was still surprisingly strong, and it took their combined efforts to lift her into the bath without dropping her. Polly's remark had, however, sent Alicia's spirits soaring and she wondered why she had not herself thought of emigration.

Once in the soothing water, Elizabeth settled down and, panting, Alicia handed her a sponge to hold. Polly said, 'I'll wash her. You go out in the passage for a minute and get your breath back.'

Alicia thankfully accepted Polly's offer and went out of the bathroom, closing the door behind her. The passage was dark, except for the faint

743

penetration of the hall lights downstairs. She leaned thankfully against the wall and closed her eyes. Canada? Where no one would care about her illegitimacy, even if they found out, or would know about her poor, mad mother; a place where she could begin again.

'God damn it! Jaysus help me!' The door of the old guest room opened, and an enraged Billy shot out, a shirt clutched over his naked chest. He spun round to the head of the staircase, and, not noticing Alicia, he leaned over the hall banister, and called, 'Polly! Pol! Could you come up for a sec?'

There was no response and, fulminating to himself, he came slowly back towards his room.

He was embarrassed to see Alicia in the passageway. 'Can I help you?' she asked. 'Polly's bathing Mama.'

He modestly whipped his shirt in front of his chest. 'I'm sorry, Miss Allie. I didn't see you. Could you ask Polly to come in, when she's done with your Mam? I damped me vest when I were washing me face, and I can't get into a clean one. I tore the old one when I were getting it off of me,' he finished with a rueful laugh.

She moved towards him instinctively, used to helping invalids day in and day out. She said, 'I can do it for you, if you'll let me. I dressed Papa often enough.'

He looked at her warily, and swallowed.

'Where is your vest?'

'On the bed, Miss.'

'Come on, then. I'll get it on in a second for you.'

He wondered if she realized what she was about. He was not her Papa – and at that moment, seeing her slender form in the half light, he did not feel the least like a father.

He said carefully, 'Thank you, Miss,' and led her into his room.

The winter sunshine streamed through the lace curtains and showed the botched-up shoulder in painful detail. It also showed an otherwise well-knit man garbed only in hospital-blue trousers.

Alicia was jolted by the sight of him; she lowered her eyelids and picked up the recalcitrant vest, stretched it and then threaded the helpless arm carefully through one sleeve. She came close to him while he bent his head so that she could get the neck of the vest over it. She felt a tumultuous madness in her, but she gritted her teeth as he lined up his right arm and wriggled himself into the garment. Her hands touched his bare flesh, as she pulled the garment straight down over him.

Billy took one look at the wide, imploring eyes suddenly looking into his own brown ones. 'Oh, God!' he muttered, and pulled her to him with his good arm. As he kissed her, he felt her slender body nestle to

744

him. She put her arms round his neck and held him tightly. Blood racing, he turned her so that her back was against the door, which clicked shut behind her. Then he kissed her properly, his tongue exploring her mouth.

She hardly knew what she was doing or where it would lead to, but she realized, at last, as Billy caressed her, what had driven her mother into the arms of her father, Andrew Crossing.

'Allie, luv! I'm ready to get her out!' called Polly from the bathroom.

He let her go immediately and she stood leaning against the door looking at him bewilderedly, but behind the confusion the : was a hint of laughter in her face. She bit her lip and then smiled at him beguilingly. He leaned against her again and said, 'I love you, our Allie.'

The smile was wiped off her face. 'I love you,' she replied thickly. 'But I can't marry anyone because of Mama – you know that.'

He kissed her neck above the stiff, white frill of her dress and felt her tremble. Then he told himself desperately that he must keep his head. He moved away from her slowly, to pick up his shirt. 'You'd better go to Polly,' he said dully.

She let out a long, sobbing sigh and turned and opened the door.

27

I

'Billy, you dumb street mutt! What did you do to her? She were lit up like a street lamp last night.' This from Polly the following morning, as she dumped Billy's breakfast porridge in front of him.

'I kissed her,' replied Billy, a little sulkily.

'Holy Mother! Is that all? I'd like to see what she'd be like when you really got goin'.'

Billy slapped his good hand down on the table. 'Happy she'd be, that's what. I'd see to that.'

Polly sniffed, and peered out of the window at the blackness of a winter morning, eased only by the faint glow of a gaslight in the street and the flood of light from her own kitchen. She turned back to her brother.

'Well, you'd better marry her, then. You can't play around with her like she was some kid from back of Boundary Street. Not with folks like she's got. And if you marry her, you'd better watch your step, boy, or you could end up quarrelling like a pair o' cats – just 'cos you mayn't understand wot's the custom with folk like her.'

'I want to marry her and I think she'd marry me, even though I'm stuck with a useless arm,' Billy replied irritably. 'If Ernie at the stable can make a full-blooded Cree, complete with feathers, happy, I can do the same for her. And *you* brought 'er up, not her Mam. You must've taught her plenty. It's her Mam wot's the problem – she's ripe for the loony bin, she is.'

'Now, our Billy! Would you've let our Mam go into Bedlam?''

'Na, 'course not.'

'Well, she's the same about her Mam.' Polly sighed, and then said, 'If Mr Harold could get me some help, I could stay with her Mam and you take *her* to Canada.'

'Oh, no,' Billy replied firmly, 'I'm goin' to get you off this bloody treadmill an' all.' He picked up his spoon and began slowly to eat his porridge. 'I'll think of somethin'.'

'Maybe we should talk to Dr Bell and ask him. And then get hold of Mr Harold, her uncle. He's proper kind.' Desperate with sudden desire to be free herself, she said, 'Truth is, we've both gone on from day to day, and neither of us – nor her brother – ever really sat down and thought about what to do. Allie were here, so everythin' was all right and they left her to it.'

She picked up her porridge bowl and quickly put it in the sink, and warned him, 'Now, Allie'll be down in a minute to get her breakfast. You be careful what you do.'

'I'm not goin' to rape her,' he replied crossly. 'Anyways, I'll be most of the day up at the Royal Infirmary while they try to make me arm work.'

A few minutes later, when Alicia entered the kitchen, she was bitterly disappointed that he was not there. Polly, about to go to Elizabeth, explained that he had gone to get ready to walk over to the hospital.

The glow had gone out of Alicia. 'It's too far for him to walk,' she said. 'I feel angry every time he has to do it.'

'Let 'im try, luv. He's got to get strong again.'

With a leap of pure passion, Alicia remembered the strong embrace of the previous evening. She swallowed, and agreed. She had not kissed him out of pity or to comfort him; the kiss had been a spontaneous outpouring of a terrible longing which had grown in the months of his quiet stay with them. He was a lively, intelligent man, and the very thought of his return to Canada had been crushing.

She had agonized through the weeks of being with him; she was sure that to give any inkling of the love she felt would have encouraged a man when she could not marry; that he might have responded by simply becoming her lover never occurred to her. Though her mother had had a lover, she knew that nice girls got married and were faithful; Polly said so.

Reluctantly at first, though increasingly as the day progressed, she began to think, like Billy, of how her mother could be cared for by someone else. Not by Polly, she was determined on that; Polly had done enough.

By late afternoon, she was telling herself to stop worrying; she was basing her desires on one kiss. It was ridiculous.

Could Billy, perhaps, stay in England? In this house?

She was combing her mother's long, white tresses, as the idea occurred to her. She paused, comb poised, and considered what the situation would be.

There would not be much work for him in England, other than labouring, she thought sadly. These days, an uneducated man was fixed firmly at the bottom of the ladder. Would Charles or the Reverend Clarence help him to get started in some small business?

'Don't be funny,' she told herself, as she gently combed. 'They don't even help *you*.' And she shuddered, when she considered how her brother and her brother-in-law would treat Billy if they met him, no matter how well-dressed he was or how good his manners were. To them, class was class.

She did not see Billy when he came home and ate his warmed-up dinner in the kitchen with Polly. He was tired, depressed and in pain, so Polly got him a hot water-bottle and sent him up to bed.

II

Late that evening, Fanny rang the front door bell, and Polly answered the door.

'Didn't want to come up the back track,' Fanny excused herself, as she slipped inside. 'It's that dark.'

Polly replied, with a friendly grin, 'Och, nobody cares which door you coom through; there's only us here. How's yerself?'

Fanny sighed, as she took off her coat and hat and laid them carefully on a hall chair, smoothing the hat's tremendous satin bow. 'Well, I'm not too clever,' she said. 'I bin off sick a while. Goin' back tomorrer. We don't none of us keep too well in that place.'

'Well, coom in. It's nice to see yez.' She ushered the little woman into the old morning-room, and while she took a box of matches and knelt to light the gas-fire, she urged her to sit down. After she had slowly got up off her knees and had lit the gaslight, she glanced at Fanny's face and exclaimed, 'Holy Mary! You look like a Chink!'

Fanny promptly put a finger to each eye, to pull them into a slant. 'Chinky, Chinky Chinaman, chop, chop, chop,' she said with a wry laugh. 'Foreman says its the TNT wot does it.' She looked around the shabby room. 'Where's our Allie?'

'She's in with her Mam, changing her napkins.'

'Aye, poor soul! And her such a fussy lady,' Fanny exclaimed. 'She always took such good care of her looks – till the Master broke her spirit. God, he were a son of a bitch.'

'He were. He int much missed,' responded Polly drily. 'She's proper daft now. Don't know nobody nor nothin' much.' She went towards the door. 'I'll get a bevvie. Be back in a min!'

Over a glass of light ale, Fanny began to describe the various men from the factory that she had been out with and their sexual abilities. Then she triumphantly listed the hats and dresses she had been able to buy. At the end of the inventory, her voice trailed off and an uneasy silence fell between them until Fanny picked up the conversation again. 'It's proper scary, workin' there – you never know the minute when you'll be blown to glory.'

Polly got up from her chair. 'I'd not take the risk,' she said with a grimace. 'What about coming into the other room to see our Allie and the Missus? Allie'll be glad to see you.'

Elizabeth was sitting up in bed, her delicate, lined face almost saintly in its new-found thinness, giving no hint of the violent behaviour of which she was capable. Alicia was struggling to heave open the big sash-window to get rid of the odour in the room. Fanny went across to her, pushed her out of the way and lifted the window easily. She grinned at Alicia, and said, 'It's a knack. How are you, duck?' She ignored the woman in the bed.

Alicia put her arms round her and kissed her, while she exclaimed at her sickly complexion. Elizabeth gave a frightened murmur, a quavery questioning.

Fanny turned to her without hesitation, curtsied and said, 'I'm Fanny, Ma'am. Come to make the fire up.'

As if she understood, Elizabeth smiled slightly, and Fanny winked at Alicia. The maid moved towards the gas-fire and inquired, regardless of the lateness of the hour, 'And how are yer, this morning, Ma'am?'

Alicia watched fascinated. Though her mother did not reply, she inclined her head as if acknowledging the inquiry.

Fanny muttered to Alicia out of the corner of her mouth, 'Take her right back far enough and she often understands. Never had much difficulty with her, even when she got real uppity and lashed out at me. I could always settle her.' She turned to the bed and made a little curtsey to Elizabeth again. 'Has she had her evening cocoa yet?' she inquired of Alicia.

'Not yet. It's an awful job getting it down her.'

'Let me try giving it her.'

Polly, anxious to see what would happen, broke in and urged Alicia to let Fanny try.

Ten minutes later, Elizabeth was sipping cocoa quite contentedly from her invalid cup. Fanny held it for her and gossiped to her about small happenings of years back. It took longer to persuade her to swallow her sleeping draught, but Fanny did finally succeed.

Still playing her part as a young maid, Fanny put the cup back on its little tray, curtsied and quietly left the room. Polly followed her.

Outside the door, they looked at each other and giggled helplessly. 'Really, Fan, you are a one!' Polly exclaimed admiringly. 'And, you know, Dr Bell always says to get out photo albums of when she was a

749

girl. And it's true – she'll often sit quiet and let you show her old pictures, as if she remembers.'

After Fanny had gone, Polly made some more cocoa and gave Alicia a cup to take up to bed. 'You go and get a good night's sleep, duck.' She leaned towards the girl and kissed her. 'And you don't worry about nuttin'.'

'Little do you realize,' thought Alicia miserably.

III

Polly took another cup of cocoa and slowly climbed the stairs to Billy's room. The candle she was carrying dripped grease on to the stair carpet. She paused and looked down at the offending spot for a second, and then continued up. Who cared about the carpet? It was Allie she was bothered about.

The flicker of candlelight on his face roused Billy from sleep. He turned and groaned, as the movement pained his shoulder.

'I brought you some cocoa and a bickie, chooks. How you feelin'?'

'I'd hate to tell yer.' Billy heaved himself up clumsily, and she quickly put the cup down on a side table, and pushed a couple of pillows behind him. Then she handed the cup to him carefully, so that he could grasp the handle.

While he drank the scalding brew, she pulled up a straight chair and sat down by the bed. She folded her hands in her lap and watched him quietly. Then she asked, without preamble, 'You sure you want to marry our Allie?'

'Don't talk daft. You know I do.'

'Well, does she want to marry you?'

The answer was slower in coming. 'I dunno for sure, now I'm a one-armed Jack,' he said. 'And there's her Mam holdin' her back in every way. I can't solve that one either; if she don't want a disabled man, she could use her Mam as a polite excuse, come to that.'

He looked down at the muddy contents of his cup, his face so filled with despair that Polly wanted to hold him to her as if he were a small boy.

'I'm afraid to ask her – formal like, in case she turns me down. A kiss is one thing; marrying is another.' He looked up at his sister, and added, 'I couldn't bear to be turned down. I've had enough. All me life I've dreamed and worked for her, in a manner of speaking. And here I am, stuck with this bloody arm.'

Polly wanted to cry; in the world she had come from a man with the use of only one arm was a dead loss – how could he labour?

'That's no way to think,' she told him sternly, and she asked, 'Could you earn enough to keep her, do yer think?'

'Oh, aye. I bin lyin' here thinkin' for hours. There's timber on my quarter-section – I already built a cabin wot Simon Yellowknee, the Metis who's carin' for me horses, lives in. With him to help, and maybe one or two of me neighbours, I reckon I could put up a better cabin for her. And I always intended to run more horses.' He sighed heavily, while Polly waited for him to continue. 'I'm always goin' to have to pay help, 'cos I doubt if I can plough or carry sacks, but it can be done. And there's steady money coming in from the café – not a lot, but the way things are going, it'll grow; it were a lucky strike that I bought into that and didn't just lend 'im the money – it could end up being the best thing I ever did. A real friend, Huang is.'

'What about the stable?'

'I'll have to talk that one over with Ernie. When I think of it, by the time I left, I weren't actually handling horses that much – we'd a couple of stable lads, and it could be that I can manage more'n I think . . .' His voice trailed off. 'It could be I'll have enough without workin' for him.'

'Well, it don't look as if either of you would starve.' Her voice was forcedly brisk and cheerful. 'And you haven't allowed as she might help you a lot – she's a smart young woman when she's given half a chance. I bet she could learn how to breed horses and care for 'em.'

'A lady?' exclaimed Billy, scandalized.

'Aye, some great ladies with titles is very knowledgeable about 'orses.' She got up and took his cup from him, and then began to rearrange his pillows. 'Now, you listen to me. Tomorrer, you ask her proper – and you tell her what the odds are – don't hold nothin' back. And see what she says.'

'And what about her Mam?' He sounded bitter.

'Well, chook, you're not the only one as has bin thinkin' – and I might be able to solve that one.' She made a wry face at him and then laughed at his surprise. 'I got to get help from a lot of people – and Christ only knows if I can swing it – but first you got to ask her.'

IV

When Alicia entered the little kitchen the next morning, after giving her mother her breakfast, she blushed scarlet and muttered, 'Good morning, Billy.' She did not look at him, as she scraped the saucepan clean of porridge and dumped the sticky mass into a dish.

Billy emerged from the protection of the morning newspaper, and said, 'Hi.' He carefully folded up the paper as best he could with one hand and put it down beside his teacup.

She sat down opposite him and sprinkled sugar thinly on to her porridge. I behaved like a street woman, she chided herself silently. What will he think of me?

She nearly choked on a mouthful of her breakfast, when he asked suddenly, 'Allie, will you marry me?'

She put her spoon down slowly, and swallowed, while she picked up her table napkin to wipe her mouth. Tears welled up, and she exclaimed, 'Billy, darling, you know I can't.'

He licked his lips. 'Why not?'

'Well, you know I can't leave Mama.' In her distress, she sounded irritable.

'Is that the only reason?'

'Well, of course, it is. Why else should I say No?' Tears were running down her face. 'I love you, I love you.' The words burst from her.

In an instant, he was on his feet and by her chair, his good arm round her shoulders. 'Don't cry, luvvie. I can't bear it.' He held her against him. 'Come on, chook, cheer up. I didn't know ladies cried when men popped the question!'

She picked up her table napkin and wiped her eyes and giggled suddenly. But then she said, snuggling her face into him, 'I don't know what to do.' He felt her heave a great shuddering sigh. 'Oh, Billy, dear. You're the sweetest thing that ever happened to me.'

'And you don't mind the mess I'm in?'

'Your shoulder? For goodness' sake, Billy! I'd still love you if you were in a bathchair!'

Billy stroked her back, and said slowly, 'That's the best thing that anyone ever said to me.' He bent and kissed her upturned face.

Her porridge went cold while the kiss lasted, and then he drew back reluctantly, and told her, 'Our Polly says as she thinks she knows how to get your Mam cared for – proper,' he added the last word quickly, as mixed doubt and fear showed on her face. 'Not in a madhouse.'

'How?'

'She wouldn't tell me, but she's goin' to talk to you today.'

'She's not taking on the job herself?'

'No – that is, I don't think so. I think she wants to emigrate.'

Alicia made a wry face, and sighed. 'What a lovely dream, Billy.'

'Well, supposin' for a minute she can do it?'

'Yes?'

He hesitated. 'I don't have any fancy manners,' he said a little shyly. 'And, honest, I don't know how you'll put up with me at times. But there's some nice women around Edmonton who like to play pianners and speak nice – you'd have friends. Would you really come to Canada with me – serious?'

'With you, Bill? Of course. I'd go anywhere with you.' She clasped him more tightly.

'Well, Polly says I'm to tell you as best I can what we'll do there. And I can't promise you the earth, mind, and it'll be hard work.' He loosened her arms gently from round his hips, and turned to sit down again on his chair. 'Now, you come here and sit on me knee and I'll tell yez.'

'Billy, I couldn't sit on your knee!'

'Yes, you can, you silly judy. Come here.'

28

A little later on, Alicia carried to her mother's room a bundle of brooms, dusters and tins of polish, in order to clean it. She moved mechanically, as if in a trance. She wanted to drop her brooms and run back to the kitchen and cuddle again with Billy. How on earth could she let him go back to Alberta without her? The idea was unbearable.

As she opened the old library door, Polly glanced up from easing Elizabeth into a clean, white blouse. 'So he asked you?' she inquired knowingly.

Alicia leaned the brooms against a wall, and smiled dreamily back. 'Yes.' She pushed a few wisps of hair back into her bun, and then said, 'But I don't know what to do – he said you had some ideas.'

Polly quickly buttoned Elizabeth into her blouse and led her slowly to a couch in the window. Then she went over to Alicia and hugged her. 'I don't want to raise your hopes too much, luv, 'cos we got to get a lot of people to help. But the most important one is Fanny.'

'Fanny?' Alicia came out of her dreamy state immediately.

'Yes. You know she's gettin' sicker and sicker in them munitions. If it weren't for the money, she'd give it up, I'm sure. And for all she's a proper little man chaser, she don't like bein' 'arassed by men as she is being.'

'In the factory?'

'Oh, aye, she is.'

'How horrid!'

'Oh, aye, it is. So my line of thinkin' is, let's ask her to come to look after your Mam. Offer her a real housekeeper's job with a good housekeeper's wages.'

'Polly! It's a marvellous idea – but she couldn't manage alone – she's so small, for one thing. And to get nurses would be impossible – they're all going to the army.'

'Your Mam don't need professional nurses – only very kind and patient women. Now, at present there's many a soldier's wife with kids who can't make ends meet and yet can't leave the children for long; I bet that in the smaller streets round here, we could find half a dozen as would take turn and turn about for a few hours a day and be thankful for it. Mr Harold would have to pay 'em well, but Fanny could teach them and keep them in line – she knows what's to be done; and she's methodical, too.' She paused for breath, and then went on earnestly, 'Doctor did suggest a nursing home a while back. But you couldn't get her into one now, even if you wanted to, with all the wounded crowding in.'

Alicia agreed to her last remark. Then she said slowly, 'With your idea, she would be in her own home. Do you think such women would mind the washing and the cleaning up? It's a disgusting job, sometimes.'

'Women as has had three kids close together is used to such things. And a lot of them will've nursed, or seen nursed, old folks in their own homes – they'll know.'

Alicia nodded agreement. She slowly put down the brooms and dusters she had been carrying. As Polly watched her, she went over to the *chaise longue* in the window where Elizabeth reclined, fretfully kicking off the shawl over her feet. She looked thoughtfully down at her. Though at the moment her mother seemed comparatively quiet, Alicia knew she could get up at any moment, to rant and tear off her clothes and defecate on the polished, oak floor.

Elizabeth ignored her daughter's approach and Alicia slowly raised her eyes to stare out at the busy street. What Polly offered meant a new life to her, perhaps a hard life, but one with a person beside her who loved her. It was made possible, she thought, only because Elizabeth now recognized nobody. She felt a sense of desolation at the emptiness of her mother's life and at the terrible price she, her daughter, had had to pay for it. She had given her youth, as she did her duty in nursing Mama – and Papa, who had, so unwillingly, given her a home. She had paid a frightful toll, and it had been taken for granted by most of those around her, she thought bitterly.

She glanced down again at Elizabeth. She found it difficult to believe that this benighted woman was her mother who had once loved a tall, blond man with the same passion that Alicia felt for Billy – and the result had been an unwanted, neglected child who had become a servant – and only Uncle Harold had really tried to make the servitude bearable.

'If Mama had cared at all for me, she could have had my devoted love – instead of pity and duty,' she ruminated and felt again her childhood sense of being shut out by Elizabeth.

She turned slowly back to Polly, and said acidly, 'Dear Florence and dear Charles are going to have a fit.'

'Do them good. No reason why Mr Charles and his Missus shouldn't live in this house, if they're worried about your Mam; then they could supervise Fanny.'

'You're right.' Alicia's voice was suddenly brisk. 'I think we'd better start by talking to Dr Bell.'

Dr Bell felt that Polly's suggestion was workable. 'I remember Miss Barnett well,' he said with a smile. 'And, of course, she's been with Mrs Woodman nearly all her life.'

While Billy fretted impatiently, Alicia wrote to Charles and to Florence. They both arrived with their spouses the following day, Charles and Veronica first.

'Get married?' exclaimed Charles disparagingly. 'Who to?'

'A rancher from Canada called William Tyson.' Alicia sat calmly in front of him in the morning-room, her chin set defiantly in the air.

'What an incredible idea,' Veronica exclaimed, fear clutching at her heart. She sat down suddenly in Elizabeth's old chair by the window.

The surname of Alicia's proposed husband sounded vaguely familiar to Charles but he could not place him.

'Where did you meet Mr Tyson?' he inquired, watching his apprehensive wife out of the corner of his eye.

'I wrote to you about him nearly twelve months ago. He's Polly's brother.'

'What?' This from Charles.

'You couldn't marry a servant!' expostulated Veronica.

'I resent your remark!' Alicia flared. 'He can keep me and he's a very decent man. I see no reason why I can't marry him.'

According to them, there were a thousand reasons, and also according to the Reverend Clarence and Florence, who panted in about half an hour later, the most compelling one being the unspoken one that none of them wanted to care for Elizabeth.

The family row, through which Alicia fought her way stoically, was vicious. Apart from anything else, they said Alicia was betraying her class.

White with rage at the insult to Billy, Alicia announced that she would make arrangements for the care of Elizabeth with Uncle Harold, since he was their father's executor.

'But I'm her son,' shouted Charles indignantly.

'Then you look after her,' Alicia snapped back. 'Behave like a son.'

She swept from the room, beside herself with anger which she had never expressed before.

29

I

Alicia fled to the morning-room and shut herself in. She was trembling from the aftermath of the quarrel and sat down on her mother's old chair by the window, her hands clenched in her lap. The winter afternoon had closed in and it was almost dark. The gasfire was unlit and the room was cold. She put her head down on her knees and began to cry with great, hard sobs.

She barely heard Charles slam the front door after him when the family left. She was terrified that they would find some way to *make* her stay with her mother, make her break her engagement. Clarence had, after all, the awesome authority of the Church behind him and Charles was a brilliant scholar. She felt that beside them she was a nobody, simply a woman who should obey.

Would kind Uncle Harold feel that Billy was beneath her? Or that she should not leave her mother to a servant, however good?

Polly had been sitting mending in Elizabeth's room, while she watched her mistress. She heard in the distance the sound of angry voices and made a wry face, but she dared not leave Elizabeth who was restless and fretful. Poor little Allie. She wished that Billy was at home, but he had gone to visit his sister, Mary and his nephews and nieces.

A few minutes after the family's stormy exit, he came running up the front steps, whistling cheerfully. He let himself in and, after struggling out of his blue overcoat, went in search of Alicia. He found her still in the darkened morning-room, quiet now, except for an occasional dry sob.

He was beside her in a flash, his good hand on her bent shoulder. 'Luvvie! What's to do? What's up?'

She raised her head and turned to look up at him. Then she wailed, 'They all came and shouted at me. They said I was deserting Mama. All kinds of dreadful things.' She put her arms round him and laid her face against his rough, serge trousers, and began to cry again. 'Four of them, all going at me at once.'

'Aye, luv,' he soothed. 'They're not worth givin' away with a pound o' tea. Don't you fret. I'm goin' to marry you, come hell or high water. Then they'll have to do somethin' about your Mam.'

'But I can't simply leave her!'

'Na, of course not. You get a hold of your Uncle Harold. You always said as you got along with him, and he's the man what looks after your Papa's money, isn't he? He can fix to pay Fanny good wages and maybe talk some sense into your brother and sister.'

Alicia took out her handkerchief and wiped her eyes. 'I hoped a little bit that they might be pleased I was going to be married – and one of them might volunteer to look after Mama,' she said unhappily.

He pulled her up from her chair and held her to him. 'What does it matter whether they're pleased or not? We're goin' to be six thousand miles away, and I can tell you that there's people there as'll like you and be your friends. They'll be more like family to you than your brother and sister ever will.'

That night, Alicia wrote to Uncle Harold. He arrived at his late brother's house the following afternoon, perturbed and tired after an argument with his wife, Vera, about the suitability of Alicia's proposed marriage.

To Alicia, he looked very frail and she realized, for the first time, what an old man he was. She offered him a glass of brandy from the last bottle in Humphrey's cellar. He accepted it gratefully and leaned against the back of the settee on which he was sitting. Polly had brought up the brandy and, at a gesture from Alicia, she stayed in the room, hovering in the background while Alicia explained to him the details of the plan suggested by her.

He listened quietly, nodding his head from time to time, until she had finished. Then he cleared his throat, and said, 'I think I should meet Mr Tyson, first, if he's at home.'

Agreeably surprised, Polly went to find Billy, helped him into his hospital blue jacket and watched while he hastily combed his hair.

With some trepidation, he marched into the morning-room and stood respectfully in front of the old man, his left hand tucked into his buttoned-up jacket.

Uncle Harold looked the young man up and down and then held out his hand to him. 'Sit down, Tyson.' Billy shook hands and then perched on the edge of a straight chair.

Harold Woodman asked which Regiment he had served in and how he had been wounded, to which Billy replied briefly. Then he asked what Billy proposed to do when he was discharged, and, with some enthusiasm, Billy told him about his quarter-section and how he hoped to continue to raise horses. Hesitantly, he spoke of his share in Huang's cafe and how they were building it up; he was not sure what Uncle Harold would think of such a business venture. Uncle Harold, being a very shrewd businessman himself, thought it could be a remarkably good investment, and he said so. Then he held out his hand to Billy, and said, 'I've neglected to congratulate you; you're a lucky man.'

'I know it, Sir.'

'When is the wedding to be?'

Billy glanced at Alicia, who smiled at him. 'Soon as we can fix up Mrs Woodman,' he said firmly.

'And then you'll take Miss Alicia to Canada?'

'Yes, Sir. And me sister, Polly, here, so Miss Alicia won't feel lonely, Sir.'

'Can you pay the fares?'

Alicia interrupted here, to say, 'Between the three of us, we can, Uncle. I've saved from the salary you've been paying me and Polly has some savings, too.'

Polly thought it wise to bob a curtsey, and add, 'Yes, Sir. Between the three of us we've plenty enough.'

Alicia could do far worse with an Englishman returning wounded from the War, Harold Woodman ruminated, as he weighed up Billy. Unlike Charles, he remembered his own father's humble beginnings and how he had laid the foundations for the prosperity of his sons, Humphrey and Harold.

He chatted amiably for a few minutes with both Polly and Billy and then said that he was rather tired and would be glad to rest for a little while, so they left him with Alicia. Billy felt he had found an ally.

Alone with Alicia, Harold Woodman relaxed. 'Nice fellow, you've got there,' he remarked, as he took a sip from his glass.

Alicia was delighted by his approbation. She smiled.

'Mind you, my girl, you have to realize that he has been brought up differently from you. Are you prepared for that?'

'Do you mean that he's a working man?' Alicia bristled slightly. 'He's made his own way since he was twelve – and that's good enough for me.'

Uncle Harold laughed. '*My* father began life as a shoemaker,' he told her. 'But you have been fairly protected in your life.'

'To all intents and purposes, I was brought up by two maidservants, one from the workhouse and one from the slums,' she responded sharply.

He was hurt by the bitterness of her tone but he knew she was right.

759

II

That afternoon, Billy took a note from Alicia to Fanny's lodgings asking her to come over in the evening.

While Polly patiently sat with Elizabeth, a mystified and slightly flurried Fanny was installed in the morning-room with Billy and Alicia, a large glass of Humphrey's port in front of her.

'What's up?' she asked suspiciously.

When they told her of their engagement, she jumped up and embraced them both in turn, with whoops of pleasure that would have done credit to an Indian on the warpath. 'I knowed it!' she shouted. 'I seen 'im lookin' at yez.'

Laughing, Alicia disentangled herself from her and restored her to her chair. She then went carefully through Polly's plan with her. She finished up by saying, 'I hope you can come, Fan. I hope you can.'

Fanny had listened soberly and was thrilled. She was careful, however, not to express too much enthusiasm. She would be employed by Old Fishface's family and if they were anything like him where money was concerned, she felt she should play hard to get.

She drank her port, while they waited. She saw herself as companion-help to an invalid lady, a person of dignity, garbed in good black bombazine with a jet necklace and earrings – and a black silk apron to indicate her status. And best of all, savings locked up in a proper tin cash box in her bedroom.

'I wouldn't consider it for less'n the wages I'm gettin' now,' she told them. 'And I would need help 'cos I got to have me days off. And somebody'd have to help me lift her.'

Though Billy understood Fanny's ploy, Alicia did not and her face fell at Fanny's lack of enthusiasm.

Fanny saw her disappointment and felt that she had been too hard on her. She relented a little and said smilingly, 'I always loved your Mam, and I'm sure I could manage her as well as you could. I bin with her nearly all me life – and coming back would be like comin' home. Only I'm determined to improve meself.' She folded her hands primly in her lap to indicate her firmness about this.

Uncle Harold will never agree to wages equivalent to those of a munition worker, though Alicia despairingly. Aloud, she promised to talk to him.

III

That afternoon, after taking a short nap, Harold Woodman spent a few minutes lying contemplating the ceiling of his late brother's bedroom while he considered the best way of coercing either Charles or Florence into caring for their mother.

Then as a strategy occurred to him, his wrinkled face broke into a smile. He knew all the combatants fairly well and he earnestly wished for his sister-in-law to have the best possible care. He told Alicia that he would take the electric tram out to see the Reverend Clarence Browning and that he would probably be late in returning.

He accepted a quick lunch and left to get his tram without further explanation, leaving a very doubtful Alicia. Billy kissed her and told her, 'Cheer up, luv. I'm goin' to put the pressure on by booking passages to Canada – and we'll get the banns read.'

'How can you, Billy, without first settling about Mama?'

'We can and we will,' he replied grimly.

Equally grimly, Uncle Harold sought the help of the Reverend Browning.

After pleasantries had been exchanged and it was explained that Florence was giving a bible class in the church hall, Uncle Harold expressed the opinion that she was not strong enough to take over the care of her mother, if Alicia got married.

The Reverend Browning was very surprised at this; he had rather expected to be pressed into taking in his mother-in-law, after seeing how adamant Alicia was about going to Canada. His relief that this was not likely to be so was very great and he willingly undertook to go with Uncle Harold to see Charles.

Pleased that he had succeeded in his first manoeuvre, Uncle Harold surveyed the enemy over a cup of tea brought in by Clarence's elderly maid. Florence was, in his opinion, a disorganized fool. It would be far better to pin the responsibility on to Charles and his wife. Charles could move into what was, after all, his own house, close to the University. And Charles' wife, he knew, ran her home and children in an orderly manner. Cutting out Florence on grounds of ill-health would stop the brother and sister trying to push the burden on to each other. And getting the Reverend Browning on his side would, thought Harold, bring the weight of church opinion onto a reluctant Veronica.

After writing a quick note of explanation to be given to Florence on her return from her class, they set out by tram and ferry to Seacombe.

The family delegation was received by Charles and Veronica with little enthusiasm. They were expecting guests for dinner and were about to go upstairs to change into their dinner clothes.

'How sweet of you to call,' gushed Veronica, half her mind on her dinner party, despite apprehension about the reason for the unexpected visit.

The Reverend Browning beamed on her, his clerical collar shining in the gaslight, while Charles shook hands and offered them a drink.

Uncle Harold sat down in the most comfortable chair and took a glass of Madeira as if he expected to be there for some time. Charles's heart sank, as he handed the smiling Clarence a glass of port.

Harold Woodman wasted no time. He went straight to the point, outlining Alicia's plan to marry and the need for Elizabeth to have suitable care. 'You are legally responsible for her,' he told his nephew, and the Reverend Browning nodded agreement in a most annoying way. 'She's actually living in a house that you own close to the University. It would be easy to move your family into it.'

Veronica looked at him, appalled. Charles was about to reply, but before he could, Harold outlined the plan to employ Fanny to nurse Elizabeth. 'I am the administrator of your father's Estate and she can be paid out of it, as can any extra help she may need.' He handed his glass back to Charles to be refilled.

'What about Flo?' Veronica managed to interject. 'She's her daughter.'

Clarence broke in smartly. 'She's far from well, almost prostrate after the row she had with Alicia the other day. I fear for her mental stability if she had more responsibility laid upon her.'

Charles raised an eyebrow. 'She seemed all right when we saw her.'

Clarence gave him a look reserved for those who failed to pay their tithes to the Church, and Charles quailed.

'How can we move?' Veronica wailed. 'The children would have to change schools and that house needs renovating from top to bottom.'

'Good schools in Liverpool,' Uncle Harold replied inflexibly. 'Renovate the house when you're in it.' After two Madeiras, he was beginning to feel that nothing could stop him. 'You'd move quickly enough if poor Elizabeth were dead.'

'Uncle!'

'Well you would, and you know it. Move now.'

'Could we put mother in a nursing home?'

'Find me one not full of wounded.'

'Your dear mother, alas, may be called to her Eternal Rest in the not too distant future,' suggested Clarence. 'In my experience, such cases, once bedridden like your mother is, do not last very long.'

Charles longed to choke the man, and the argument continued until a very young maid knocked at the door and, on being told to enter, announced that the first dinner guests had arrived and that she had put them in the upstairs drawing-room.

Veronica looked at her in despair. 'Tell them I'll be with them in a few minutes. Serve them sherry.'

The maid withdrew and Charles said to Harold Woodman, 'Veronica and I will have to discuss this. Our entire life will be upset, if we move.'

'You'll enjoy it,' his uncle assured him. 'It's a fine house – only needs painting and some new rugs. Might do Elizabeth good to see you and get to know her grandsons – seems to me they've never been near her.'

Regardless of the fact that his own children had not visited Elizabeth for years, the Reverend Clarence turned a shocked face upon Veronica. 'Really?' he inquired in a tone which suggested that immediate damnation awaited her.

The accusation was true. If it were known to their acquaintances, she would be shamed. She bit her lips and bent her head in the face of clerical disapproval. Then she rose and said flatly, 'We have dinner guests. I must go to them.' She did not ask the visitors to eat with them.

Charles was standing uneasily with his back to the fire. His uncle again reminded him flintily of his legal obligations. 'You haven't much time,' he warned him. 'And Veronica should see Fanny Barnett – I'm sure she'll find her very capable.'

Foreseeing a long and bitter fight with his wife, which he knew he must win, Charles nodded, and then saw both gentlemen to the door.

Uncle Harold took the Reverend Browning to the Adelphi for dinner.

IV

Despite her uncle's assurances that all would be well, Alicia doubted it and wept when she went with Billy to arrange to have their Banns read in All Saints Church. She was surprised to hear that Billy also ranked as being of the Church's parish, since he had stayed so long in Humphrey's old house.

She cheered up considerably, however, when a stony-faced Veronica and Charles arrived a couple of days later. They looked over the house and decided which furniture should be discarded and where they would put their own belongings. Then they went in to see the invalid.

Charles hardly recognized the shrunken, restless figure in the bed and Veronica, who was not totally unkind, felt some pity for the mother-in-law she had never seen before. Alicia agreed stiffly to arrange for Fanny to go to Seacombe for an interview. Uncle Harold had already arranged a suitable salary with her, Alicia told Veronica. She should get into touch with him in Manchester about any more help she required.

Billy kept out of the way and concerned himself with hunting down a passage to Canada. Polly began to sort and pack her belongings and encouraged Alicia to do likewise.

Mr and Mrs Hunter, next door, heard from their servants that Alicia was engaged, and they offered the use of their carriage to the bride and groom on their wedding day. The good lady, when she found there was no one else to do it, also insisted that she and her daughters would have a little reception for them after the ceremony. Then she took Alicia shopping to buy a suitable dress. 'We have to bear in mind that almost everyone is in mourning, dear,' she said sadly, as they window-shopped. Alicia agreed and they settled on a pretty grey material and a matching hat. Miss Bloom's successor made the dress.

Alicia and Billy would have sworn that they had few friends in Liverpool, but it was surprising how many people Mrs Hunter suggested should be invited. There was Mary and Mike and Billy's nephews and nieces, Uncle Harold and his wife, his sons and their wives, and, of course, Florence and Charles and their spouses and children. Alicia rather dreaded the attendance of her nephews and nieces, particularly Frank, but since Mrs Hunter was the hostess she trusted that the party would go off well, despite them.

Fanny simply did not turn up for the shift at the munitions factory which followed her interview with Veronica. She moved into the house and began to take over the care of Elizabeth. Veronica had been agreeably surprised to be faced with an obviously well-trained servant at a time when they were at a premium; Fanny had looked her new mistress over shrewdly and decided she was manageable. A deal was struck.

Alicia was happy to have her friend back and the whole tenor of the household began to be more cheerful. With Fanny helping, Billy and Alicia took long walks in the park together like the lovers whom Alicia had so envied years before.

Billy received his formal discharge from the army and bought himself a civilian suit. Seeing him so neatly dressed seemed to Alicia to symbolise a break from the past for him as well as for herself. She thought, 'I don't care who comes or who does not come to the wedding. I've got Billy and Polly and a new start – and I'll have children in a new country, legitimate ones. I couldn't ask for anything better.'

She smiled at Billy, shy in his new apparel, and said, 'You can walk me down to the dressmaker. I'm going to try on my wedding dress.'